NEVADA
PRINTING
HISTORY

NEVADA PRINTING HISTORY

*A Bibliography of Imprints &
Publications, 1858-1880*

ROBERT D. ARMSTRONG

UNIVERSITY OF NEVADA PRESS

RENO, NEVADA

1981

PHOTO CREDITS:
The Bancroft Library, University of California, Berkeley, 515; The Beinecke Rare Book and Manuscript Library, Yale University, 488, 506; California Historical Society, 841; Department of Rare Books and Special Collections, Princeton University Library, 660; The Houghton Library, Harvard University, 60; The Huntington Library, 553, 587; National Archives and Records Service, 423; Nevada Historical Society, 162, 942; Nevada State Museum, 4, 160; Special Collections Department, University of Nevada, Reno, Library, 188, 634, 953.

UNIVERSITY OF NEVADA PRESS, RENO, NEVADA 89557 USA
© ROBERT D. ARMSTRONG 1981. ALL RIGHTS RESERVED
PRINTED IN THE UNITED STATES OF AMERICA
DESIGNED BY DAVE COMSTOCK

Library of Congress Cataloging in Publication Data

Armstrong, Robert D., 1931-
   Nevada printing history.

   Includes indexes.
   1. Nevada—Imprints—Bibliography. 2. Nevada—Imprints—Bibliography—Union lists. I. Title.
Z1223.5.N49A74   015.793   81-7422
ISBN 0-87417-063-X   AACR2

CONTENTS

INTRODUCTION

The first permanent settlement in what is now Nevada came in 1850, but it was not until 1858 that a printing press was hauled over the Sierra Nevada to publish the *Territorial Enterprise* in Genoa, then still a part of Utah Territory. In the following year the Comstock Lode was discovered a few miles away, and by 1860 people had begun to move into the area in great numbers to search for silver ore. As the population grew, so did agitation for separation from the distant government in Salt Lake City, and early in 1861 Nevada Territory was formed from the western portion of Utah. Nevada became a state on October 31, 1864, after serving a three-and-a-half-year territorial apprenticeship. The first session of the state Legislature, which convened later that same year, set for itself the task of converting the still barely workable territorial government into one that could serve the needs of its small, widely scattered citizenry. Because of the universal need of governments to inform themselves and others of their actions, the fledgling Legislature early in 1865 created the office of State Printer and chose a Virginia City newspaperman as its first incumbent. He was not paid a salary, but was expected to earn his living through the difference between what it cost him to have materials printed and what the law allowed him to be paid for printing them. Through 1878, five other men held the same post. For most of that period there seems to have been only occasional concern over the public printing, some of it serious but most having to do only with the slowness of getting executive reports printed and before the Legislature during its sessions. But the Legislature of 1877 approved a bill that would abolish the office, beginning with the 1879-1880 biennium. The sponsor, Assembly-man Henry R. Mighels, anticipating the protests of local printers, wrote a long apologia in his newspaper, the Carson City *Appeal,* on the day following the bill's introduction and passage in the lower house. After fulminating at some length about the "monstrous" and "exorbitant" prices charged by Nevada printers, he reached his most telling point. "If it shall be pleaded, as we think it probable that it will, in opposition to this bill, that it provides the letting of contracts for doing the larger part of the work in California, we have the ready answer that every State Printer this State has ever had has had all his book work and nearly all his Reports done in San Francisco.''[1]

Title page claims of Carson City printing for this period have perhaps discouraged intensive research into such matters, but Mighels was not idly repeating capitol rumor. He was himself a former State Printer who, by his own admission, had ''had his share of the plundering of the Treasury which is invited and justified by the old law,'' and it was, he said, ''scarcely less than just and right that he should so far make amends for his legalized robberies by doing what lies in his power to stop the leak.''[2] The burden of his argument was that the law as it then stood allowed the State Printer a fancy profit by authorizing rates much in excess of actual costs even in Nevada, where prices were indeed monstrous, and that even larger ''legalized robberies'' could be made by subcontracting the work to California printers who charged much lower rates. A fine profit could be made even after paying sizable transportation charges to and from San Francisco. And the windfall was not even the result of graft or venality, since the law sanctioned it and economic conditions demanded it. Moreover, until the mid-eighties there was no printing establishment in the capital or anywhere else in the state that was large enough or well enough equipped to satisfy the requirements of the Legislature or the many other state offices that submitted printing orders, with the exceptions of such small pieces as forms, letterheads, proclamations, and legislative bills. Neither was it considered a wise investment for the state to fund one, since the constitutionally brief legislative sessions would have left an expensive printing office idle most of the time. The State Printers, Mighels included, had acted only as intermediaries, negotiating lucrative private contracts with outside printers who were directly accountable neither to the state's publicly elected officials nor to the citizens who put them in office. These California establishments obligingly bowed to their Nevada benefactors and included in their imprints the name of the current State Printer and the ostensible printing site, Carson City, with no mention of their own part in the subterfuge, while the State Printers, who were for the most part practical printers, converted themselves during their terms of office into publishers.

Shortly after the effective date of the Mighels act, however, the Legislature convened again and undid what it had accomplished two years earlier. As the biennium progressed the already slumping economy had become worse, so local printers undertook a bipartite

1. Carson City *Appeal*, February 17, 1877.
2. Ibid.

campaign to restore their damaged pride and to take the public printing away from California contractors. The Legislature succumbed to the intense pressure and, early in the 1879 session, rescinded its earlier action by creating the office of Superintendent of State Printing and appropriating funds to build a state-owned printing establishment. The law took effect in 1881; equipment and material were purchased in anticipation of the next meeting of the Legislature, but completion of a building was delayed until 1886 and a full assemblage of equipment could not be provided until then. Newspaper accounts and the published reports of the Superintendent indicate, however, that all printing except the decisions of the state Supreme Court, which had always been contracted openly to California firms, was executed in Carson City from 1881 onward. Thus, although printing had regularly been authorized by territorial and state governments since 1859, the history of public printing of major pieces *in* Nevada did not really begin until twenty-two years later. The period covered by this bibliography coincides with the California experiment, when a great deal of Nevada printing was sent for execution to foreign publishers.

Little is known of the identities of the foreign printing houses that performed the work for Nevadans. None of the sub rosa contracts with the State Printers has come to light and the few extant records of the State Board of Printing Commissioners are so coyly worded as to be almost impenetrably opaque, leading one to the conclusion that the Commissioners were willing partners to the deception.[3] Perhaps, though, it is not unwarranted to speculate that the printing houses that were frequently used for above-board contracts may have been used as well when Nevadans were playing tricks with their title pages. In several cases (see, for instance, No. 764) this procedure is known to have been used. But the records of two of the houses that executed a large volume of printing with legitimate imprints—A. L. Bancroft & Company of San Francisco and H. S. Crocker & Company of Sacramento and San Francisco—were destroyed in fires in the mid-eighties, and those of Frank Eastman, also of San Francisco, appear to have been lost. Any records that may have been kept in the State Printing Office in Carson City were probably burned during a

3. "After careful measurement, extension and footing the said bills, one dated Feb 8th 1869 and marked, A, and the other dated March 8th 1869 and marked, B, were audited and allowed respectively for the sums of ($3683.84) three thousand six hundred and eighty three dollars and eighty four cents and for ($3770.60) three thousand seven hundred and seventy dollars and sixty cents." Record of the Proceedings of the Board of Printing Commissioners of the State of Nevada, meeting of March 10, 1869: Controller's records at the Nevada State Archives. Nowhere in the records is there an indication of what pieces of printing were under consideration.

fire there in 1897. There are a few clues, although most of them are inconclusive. For instance, an index to 1877 Controller's warrants contains hints to suggest that Crocker may have done at least a part of the state printing for that year.[4] And newspaper editors who were opposed to Mighels's bill noted with scorn that both Bancroft and Crocker had been seen in the legislative halls during the debate and implied that both gentlemen were lobbying for its passage to give them a chance at the state's commerce in 1879 and 1880; perhaps they were there because they had already enjoyed Nevada's largess and wanted it continued or renewed on an official basis (see, for example, No. 700). [5] Indeed, Bancroft was awarded the state's printing contract for the following biennium. Only the records of San Francisco's Towne & Bacon (later Bacon & Company) among the more frequently used printers have survived, at Stanford University's Jackson Library of Business.[6] And they show in splendid detail that in 1867 the firm was the de facto public printer for the state of Nevada. Of the seventeen pieces recorded here that bear the imprint of J. E. Eckley as State Printer for 1867, details for the printing of thirteen of them appear in Towne & Bacon's records. The records also reveal that the firm did similar work for public printers in Arizona and Idaho territories, and inspection of those pieces shows that no title page or other indication is given that would in any way connect the San Francisco firm with the printing. The implications for bibliographers of regional printing are large.

Nor were public printers the only recreants. Numerous private printing orders were also sent out of the state and even some of these were returned with Nevada "imprints." Churches and fraternal organizations also sought out the lowest bidders to publish proceedings of their meetings, and during the period it was seldom a Nevada printer who won their contracts. In addition to using California job offices they occasionally sent their printing orders as far afield as Chicago or Springfield, Illinois. The Nevada State Agricultural, Mining and Mechanical Society found it prudent to have its 1875

4. The index, in the Nevada State Archives, shows payments to John J. Hill, State Printer; D. A. Bender, freight agent at Carson City for the Virginia & Truckee Railroad; and Crocker, for printing state reports. The volume to which the index refers has not been located.

5. Carson City *Tribune,* February 17, 1877: "When doctors differ patients sometimes die, and when old office-holders recommend the abolition of offices, it is pretty good proof that there is something in the back ground; some interested motive, some ulterior benefit likely to accrue to the reformer. We dont [*sic*] pretend to say that the Speaker of the House [Mighels] had any personal motive in introducing the bill in question, but when such men as Crocker and Bancroft find it to their advantage to remain around the legislative lobby for weeks, there must be something in the wind."

6. I am indebted to James de T. Abajian, Calif. Hist. Soc.; George L. Harding, San Francisco; and Bruce L. Johnson, Univ. of Calif., Berkeley, for bringing these records to my attention.

report printed in San Francisco, an action that was protested, ironically, by Mighels on the ground that the work should have been given to printers at home. About the only organization that consistently had its work done in Nevada was the Washoe Typographical Union, which had a clear self-interest in supporting the local trade.

The reasons for the large amount of printing sent outside of Nevada were largely economic and were affected greatly by geographic factors. Nevada's population centers were nearly three thousand miles from the East Coast, the nation's primary center of the printing supply industry, and were separated by the rugged Sierra Nevada from their natural western supplier, California. Even after completion of the transcontinental railroad in 1869, prices were kept artificially high by the cupidity of the men in control of the Central Pacific Railroad, who decreed that shipments bound for Nevada from the East should be charged at a higher rate than those continuing on to San Francisco. Lack of competition left their edict without effective appeal. The sheer physical size of the state, its small, transient population, its underdeveloped transportation systems, and the short-lived status of many of its hundreds of mining towns and the resulting frequent movement of presses added as well to the cost of printing. In addition, one of Nevada's earliest and strongest labor organizations, the Washoe Typographical Union, maintained printers' wages at rates significantly higher than in California. Cheap materials and cheap labor were thus denied to those who required printing in Nevada, and it was less expensive in many instances to send their orders outside of the area, even with the added costs of drayage taken into account.

★　　★　　★　　★　　★

Regional printing bibliography is most often confined to an examination of products of the local press, with pieces that were printed outside the area rigorously excluded, even though they were designed primarily for use within it. The practice is for the most part a sound and sensible one. When the local industry is well established, an individual or an organization can order a piece of printing and expect with confidence to have it done inexpensively and with dispatch—and in the local printer's own shop. But when the press is located in a remote region the economics of isolation can have profound effects on the way the trade operates there.

Though geographically one of the nation's largest states, Nevada is demographically one of the smallest. Distances between settled areas are immense, almost incomprehensibly so to the resident of more densely populated states. Transportation—of people, of goods, and of presses, material, and the finished products of the press—has always been hard, not only because of the vast distances but also because of the difficult terrain and the underdeveloped means of getting across it. The factor of transportation alone would have caused printing costs to be high, but discovery of the Comstock Lode in 1859 brought to the area an economy that was based largely on hardrock mining; miners demanded and got wages that were unprecedentedly high in return for their eight- to ten-hour shifts in searing heat and scarcely breathable air. And if miners' wages were to be high, there were of course merchants and landlords and fleecers who would charge them huge prices for the needs and the niceties of life. Nevada's economy soon became one of the highest-based in the West, and it stayed that way even when the inevitable slumps came. But just across the Sierra Nevada range was California, with its comparatively lower prices for nearly everything. So those Nevadans who needed to have printing done often ignored political boundaries and ordered it from Sacramento or San Francisco. And, as has been shown, these orders were frequently returned from California with imprints indicating that they had been executed in Nevada.

The student of Nevada printing history must obviously know about this practice if he is to understand how printing needs were satisfied. He must also know as much as he can about which pieces were printed in Nevada and which were printed elsewhere. And why. So in this book I have included many pieces that would be banned from a conventional imprint bibliography. First, there are those books, pamphlets, and broadsides that bear the imprints of Nevada printers, even when it is known that they were printed outside of Nevada. When evidence of foreign printing has been found, it is included in annotations to individual pieces; unfortunately, it has less often been possible to indicate which ones bear honest Nevada imprints. Second, I have included a great many of those items that bedevil every historian of local or regional printing history, the ones that lack any indication of where they were printed or by whom. Many scholars have assumed local printing if the subject matter and presumed audience were local and if no contrary evidence had been found. I have no quarrel with such assumptions, but for Nevada they are not necessarily safe ones. And third, I have chosen to include a class of printing that will perhaps give pause to some. It encompasses those pieces that, while clearly displaying the imprints of foreign, usually California, printers, seem to me to be a part of Nevada's printing history.

6

Although few imprint bibliographers have seen the need to find space to describe such mavericks, their inclusion is not without precedent. The American Imprints Survey for Nevada,[7] published in 1939, recorded two hundred and forty-six items from the beginning of non-newspaper printing in 1859 (since moved back to 1858) through 1880. In an appendix, however, an additional seventy-seven "Nevada Publications Printed in California or Elsewhere" were recorded for the same period. Most of these latter items were publications of the state government during the time when Nevada experimented with letting state contracts to the lowest bidder. They are clearly not Nevada imprints, and several seem out of place even in this special category,[8] yet there seems to have been a recognition on the part of the survey's compilers that these out-of-state imprints somehow belonged with the Nevada printing record, even though it is doubtful that the reasons were fully understood at the time.[9] I agree, and have followed their practice of referring to these items as publications. I have defined publications here to include those pieces of Nevada origin, addressed to a Nevada audience, that under other, more or less ideal conditions one would expect to have been printed in Nevada. For example, in the case of territorial printing, the U.S. Treasury Department, which paid the bills, insisted that official work be executed at home; for the larger works, however, it was not, simply because adequate presses were unavailable in Nevada Territory. And one might reasonably expect a sovereign state to provide facilities for printing the many documents generated by its government; again, except for the smaller pieces, Nevada did not.

---

7. Historical Records Survey. *A Check List of Nevada Imprints, 1859-1890.* American Imprints Inventory, No. 7; Works Progress Administration, Division of Women's and Professional Projects (Chicago: Historical Records Survey, 1939). There appears to have been no reason to continue the coverage to 1890 except to maintain consistency with the WPA imprint bibliographies for seven other western states that went that far.

8. There is, for instance, a playbill printed in San Francisco that left spaces to be filled in to show the time and place of the performance by a traveling troupe. The recorded copy shows that a program was to be presented in Dayton, Nevada Territory, on June 26, 1862, but the same printing was surely used for performances elsewhere.

9. There are, however, some tantalizing statements in Douglas C. McMurtrie's Preface to *A Check List* and in the draft for it that was prepared by Dr. Lester Condit (in McMurtrie Papers at Michigan State University). In writing of the printing sites of the titles recorded in the book McMurtrie says (p. v): "Of these, 335 were printed *or published* [emphasis added] at Carson City. . . ." The comment is borrowed from Condit. McMurtrie omitted, though, another sentence from Condit's draft: "Perhaps state printers before 1879 had excellent reasons for not disclosing on their title pages the actual place of printing and the actual date of publication" (p.5, Condit draft). Condit had been writing of the State Printers' predilection for half titles in place of title pages and it may be that he was referring only to that aspect of their work. McMurtrie, however, eliminated two full pages of Condit's draft immediately following the sentence quoted above—two pages that were apparently discarded when McMurtrie decided not to use them. It is therefore tempting to speculate on what might have been written there and to wonder if it might have cleared up the question.

Beyond the public printing, there are items such as playbills, party invitations, political ephemera, petitions, newspaper extras and supplements, and many other similar kinds of things that one would expect to be printed locally. Then there are larger pieces such as proceedings of fraternal organizations and churches, by-laws of fire departments and mining districts, and briefs prepared for local courts. And there are still larger items, those that go beyond the pamphlet category, such as town directories. All of these, it would seem, "should have been" printed at home—or at least where their imprints say they were printed.[10] But Nevada, with its peculiar combination of topographical, political, and most particularly economic conditions, is not one to do the expected. Certainly in the first twenty-three years of its printing history Nevada did things rather differently than most other regions of the country.

Another reason for including publications here is that a book such as this has more than one audience. Besides specialists in local printing history, there is a body of historians of state and local government, churches, fraternal organizations, and other entities, that looks to these bibliographies for the location and understanding of basic printed sources for their studies. To deny these users a full record of their sources, on the ground that parts of the record were printed outside the area of study, would be a disservice.

The Nevada experience, it seems to me, argues strongly for a pragmatic approach to regional printing history. It was probably necessary to impose a rigid nationwide methodology on the essentially untrained workers of the American Imprints Inventory who in the late nineteen-thirties gathered the raw materials for the series of imprint checklists edited by Douglas C. McMurtrie. But it should be apparent from what has been said here that a method that works well in many places may not work at all in others.

★   ★   ★   ★   ★

Nevada's boundaries underwent several changes between March 1861, when Congress separated it from Utah Territory, and January 1867, when they reached their present limits. This bibliography is confined to imprints that were produced in the area that is now Nevada and to publications that were designed primarily for use there, regardless of the political body that governed it. Books, pam-

10. Composition for this book was executed in Reno and Sparks, Nevada, and in San Mateo, California. Printing was done in Dexter, Michigan, and binding in Grand Rapids, Michigan. Publication was in Reno, Nevada. Thus, although the book bears a Nevada imprint, it is also very much a Nevada publication.

phlets, broadsides, and folders are included. In general I have excluded letterheads, billheads, tickets of admission, invitations to private occasions such as weddings, menus, music, maps, lithographs, slip decisions of the state Supreme Court, newspaper supplements, and periodicals. Occasional exceptions are made for items of particular historical or typographical interest. I have also excluded Governor's appointment forms after statehood, and all other forms after the Utah territorial period.

Several other kinds of publications have been omitted as well. It will perhaps seem incongruous that most of them are related to what was throughout the period Nevada's principal industry, silver mining. But while the mines were physically in Nevada, the companies that controlled them usually were not. Most were chartered or incorporated in other states or territories, their stockholders were often Californians, and the profits accruing from them fled Nevada as quickly as their owners after brief and infrequent inspection trips. Thus the semiannual and annual reports of the companies were directed not so much to Nevadans as to their neighbors across the Sierra Nevada. Only those reports with Nevada imprints, most consistently those of the Yellow Jacket Silver Mining Company, are included here. But even some of these were printed in California (see No. L456).

As mining ground on the Comstock Lode became scarce, the search for silver ore spread to the east, north, and south. By 1863 mining camps had sprung up over much of Nevada Territory and its reputation as an area where fortunes could be made with little investment of time and trouble was well, if incorrectly, established. In a way that is reminiscent of today's land swindlers, groups of Boston and New York and Philadelphia entrepreneurs began to distribute alluring inducements to unwitting easterners. Some of the pamphlets produced by these charlatans were quite imaginative; most contained colorful maps and reports by mining "experts" who professed to see riches where there was naught but desert.[11] Any Nevada collection worthy of the name has at least a few of these come-ons, but they are not Nevada publications and they are not included here.

Another category that has been omitted is represented by *History of the Big Bonanza* (Hartford: American Publishing Company, 1876) by William Wright, better known as Dan De Quille, and *The Sazerac Lying Club* (San Francisco: Henry Keller, 1878) by Fred H. Hart. Both books are indeed about Nevada and both authors surely ex-

11. An example is *A Statement by the President and Board of Trustees of the Silver Series Mining Company, at Geneva, Smoky Valley, Lander Co., State of Nevada.* New York: Raymond & Caulon, 1866.

pected some sales there, but the primary audience that the two men sought was national rather than local. And although there are a few pieces in this bibliography that were issued by Adolph Sutro or his Sutro Tunnel Company, the bulk of his publications are not described here because they were designed to abet his efforts to obtain a subsidy for the tunnel project from the U.S. Congress and other sources.

The 1939 WPA survey described a great many territorial and state documents separately, even when no separate issues had been located, noting in most instances that they were parts of larger volumes. It was less careful in other cases, and the result was that several items were described as separate issues that, so far as can be determined, were not.[12] The practice led to extremely inflated item counts for some institutions. The present bibliography describes as separates only those items that have been seen by the compiler in original bindings or wrappers, or for which adequate newspaper or archival evidence of separate issue has been found.[13]

In 1969 I was able to visit the Library of the U.S. Department of Health, Education and Welfare in Washington, D.C. Several territorial and state school laws were located by *Check List* at the Office of Education Library, which had been absorbed by HEW. I was told that the laws had been transferred earlier that year to the Library of Congress and that they should be available to me there. Inquiry at LC brought the response that if they had been transferred they must still be awaiting cataloging, so I reluctantly returned home without seeing them. A year later I wrote to· HEW and to LC, and after an exchange of letters it developed that the laws, several of which were listed in *Check List* as unique copies, had indeed been transferred— and then consigned to the shredder. The Librarian of Congress wrote to me that his institution was overburdened with work and could not possibly evaluate every item that came into its Exchange and Gifts Division. He further excused the inexcusable by saying that the loss was not as great as I had claimed, since the *texts* of the laws appear in

12. The following serial numbers from *A Check List* are not included here because they were not separately issued: 47, 50, 51, 58, 59, 61, 67, 78, 128, 137, 156, 158, 161, 162, 163, 164, 167, 204, 208, 211, 213, 222, 225, 231, 241, 440, 504, and 510. Numbers 66 and 87 were not issued separately and there is some question whether they were issued at all. Numbers 73, 93, 114, 116, and 131 were not issued separately in the form described in *A Check List*. Numbers 110 and 447 were not issued; numbers 90, 145a, 437, 449, 472, 474, and 481 were not for Nevada distribution; and number 171 is a periodical.

13. There can of course be no guarantee that pieces once seen can be found again, at least in the same institution. I know of several items that have migrated from one collection to another, and in one case when I returned to reexamine an imprint the repository had undergone remodeling and the piece could no longer be found. And in more than a few cases items that I had intended to use as illustrations here could not be located for the photographer.

other places. The argument that librarians are among the greatest enemies of books gained at least one adherent because of this unconscionable act.

It is not, unfortunately, our national library alone that desecrates books and causes problems for the bibliographer. In innumerable libraries I found that librarians, desiring to have in one handy volume a full run of, say, the inaugural addresses of the Governors, had emasculated copies of the biennial cumulations of administrative and legislative reports to obtain them. Moreover, I suspect but have been unable to prove that separate issues have also been added to these runs by removal of their wrappers before binding. I do know that some institutions represent obvious disbinds from these cumulations as separate issues. In their well-intentioned wish to bring information to users these librarians have destroyed pieces of printing history, and in so doing have denied information to bibliographers and others. But perhaps I am especially sensitive to such practices because of the fifteen years I spent as an academic librarian.

★ ★ ★ ★ ★

Research for this book was conducted by checking a list of known Nevada imprints and publications against holdings of the institutions I visited and, whenever possible, discussing the project with the librarian or curator or archivist there who was most knowledgeable in the field. Through these discussions I was frequently able to learn of titles that did not appear in card catalogs or other finding aids. But the research consumed several years, and the list at the end of that time was considerably longer than at the beginning. Indeed, previously unrecorded titles were being discovered even while this book was going through the publication process—and will no doubt continue to be found long after publication, by me and by others. Ideally, the full list would have been rechecked in each of the repositories in order to provide complete holdings information for each title, both for items I missed earlier and for those that were newly acquired. Unfortunately, such a task was impossible and I offer my apologies to the institutions whose ownership of certain items is unrecorded here.

Titles are arranged first by year and then, wherever possible, alphabetically by Library of Congress entry. In some cases, such as when the Library has not established the form of an entry, I have followed my bibliothecal instincts and have provided one that seems to fit Library of Congress practice. For titles entered under Nevada I have relied on Helen J. Poulton's *Nevada State Agencies: From Territory Through Statehood* (Reno: University of Nevada Press, 1964). When the name of an official entity such as a legislative committee does not appear in Poulton, I have consulted the legislative journals to determine the form preferred there.

At the beginning of each year I have provided a summary of events bearing on the printing industry during the year, such as changes in printers' wages and the reasons therefor, and the number, locations, and migration of presses, since, it must be supposed, most if not all newspaper offices had at least some capability for job work.[14] There are also discussions of the laws relating to the public printing and of the controversies surrounding the office of Territorial Printer and State Printer. In notes to the titles themselves I have given information regarding their printing histories whenever it has been available, although too few records have survived to allow full recording of such data, and some of those that have escaped loss or destruction are not very helpful. But there are excellent records covering most of the territorial period in the National Archives, and occasionally revealing ones for later periods in the Nevada State Archives and elsewhere. To supplement these resources I have consulted the aforementioned Towne & Bacon records, the reports of legislative printing committees, and printing orders in the legislative journals. I have also used the state laws concerning printing, which describe in some considerable detail the methods to be used and the prices to be paid for printing; for the territorial period a circular issued by the First Comptroller of the U.S. Treasury Department was useful.[15] Official contracts between the state Supreme Court and California printing houses for the publication of the tribunal's reports have also been used. The most consistently useful tools for determining the approximate time of printing have been contemporary newspapers, which frequently acknowledged receipt of "comp" copies of legislative and executive documents. Newspapers were also helpful concerning privately issued pieces, but their most significant contribution to this book lies in the remarkable, sometimes outrageous comments by editorialists when a politician or rival editor or other natural enemy aroused their interest or their ire. Another useful source, at the University of Nevada, Reno, has been the diaries of Alfred Doten, whose career in Nevada journalism began in 1863 and is recorded in

14. Much of this information is taken from *The Newspapers of Nevada, 1858-1958: A History and Bibliography* (San Francisco: John Howell—Books, 1964) by Richard E. Lingenfelter. A revision of this valuable work is to be published by the University of Nevada Press.

15. See Appendix A for the text of the circular.

almost daily entries. Doten worked first in Como, later for several newspapers in Virginia City, and in 1867 became local editor of the Gold Hill *News,* one of the spicier papers on the Comstock. In 1872 he bought the *News* and remained connected with the paper until 1881.

In describing imprints and publications I have recorded lineation and ornamentation in the face of a body of scholarship that contends such detail in a bibliography of nineteenth-century regional printing is a needless frippery. At the beginning of this study I held a similar view, but I began to question it as work progressed and, as an experiment, I reworked a number of my descriptions. I was dismayed to find that the inattention to detail brought about by my early practice had not only caused errors in transcription, but in one or two instances had even caused the invention of punctuation. As I redid the descriptions I found a variant issue through differences in line division, and then another through altered placement of printers' devices. In one of these cases I found that the variants were printed nine years apart, a discovery that might not have occurred except through noting full bibliographical detail. It soon became apparent that accuracy was inimical to an early publication date for this book, but that accuracy was more highly to be prized. So each piece was inspected again and I believe the bibliography is a better one for it.

Again, I have been perhaps more detailed than some would think necessary in recording leaders, the dots or dashes used by printers to lead one's eyes across a page. Because in some of the pieces described here, as in legal forms, this device is used in place of a rule to provide a line to write on and not to lead anywhere, I have substituted "dotted rule" or "broken rule" as a more accurate description. In other areas, however, I have been less precise. Many bibliographers record measurements of the largest located copy to the nearest millimeter. If one could be certain that this largest copy was typical and not the result of an errant guillotine, the practice could easily be justified. But if in an issue of five hundred copies half a dozen were 24.4 centimeters tall and the rest were 23.6 centimeters and only a few of each have survived, one could easily be misled if the taller measurement were recorded. In the case of one title I was able to compare, side by side, over thirty copies, each varying slightly in size from every other and with the largest and smallest having widely different dimensions. To say which was typical or ideal or even usual would have been clearly impossible, so I adopted a compromise solution and recorded its measurements, and those of every other item in this book, to the nearest full centimeter.

Another approach that might be found wanting is the neglect of collation by signatures. In only a few instances that I know of would signature collation have contributed information significant to the history of printing in and for Nevada. In those few cases my notes address the problems involved. Neither have I indicated the color of cover stock on pamphlets with wrappers because of the widespread practice in job offices of using any bits of colored paper that might be found lying about the shop. Although all wrappers so far located are printed, I have noted that fact in each instance to accommodate the possible discovery later of pamphlets with unprinted wrappers.

Two types of imprints and publications are entered in short form, following the example of George N. Belknap in *Oregon Imprints, 1845-1870* (Eugene: University of Oregon Books, 1968). They are court briefs and legislative bills, and the reason is the same for both categories: there are simply too many of each to allow full-dress treatment. The census of Supreme Court briefs is swollen by an 1879 rule of the Court requiring that all briefs submitted to it must be printed. And runs of territorial bills that were required to be sent to Washington by the Treasury Department, now held by the National Archives, are augmented by an even larger group, apparently preserved by a member of the 1864 Legislative Assembly, at the Nevada Historical Society. Curiously, only two bills have been recorded for the period after statehood. There are horror stories of twentieth-century officials feeding bonfires in Carson City with state documents that were choking them out of their offices. The rumors, if true, would help to explain both this paucity and the lack of any bills at all in the Nevada State Archives; they might also provide clues to the disappearance of some other documents for which records of printing have survived. Unlike Belknap, I have recorded Army general orders with full detail because only one general order has been located for Nevada.

Nearly one quarter of the entries in this bibliography are for pieces that have not been physically located. I have included in my notes to these titles the evidence for their having been printed, usually from newspapers but in some cases from vouchers in the National Archives and from other printers' records. The serial numbers of items in this category are preceded by an "L"; as they are found the prefix can be dropped and a full transcription substituted for the descriptions now recorded. In some cases I have provided transcriptions, particularly for state documents, when it is known that unlocated separate issues were printed from the same type as their counterparts in located larger works. I have also followed Belknap's example in recording photostats and microfilm copies for institutions in Nevada only, unless photocopies of unique items exist only in institutions outside the state.

Among the microfilm copies recorded here are several that are the result of a happy circumstance. When the cornerstone of the Capitol in Carson City was opened in the summer of 1978 during renovation of the building the temptation to peek at its contents, even though they might not be available for inspection again for another hundred years or so, was too strong to resist. And when nine previously unrecorded titles were found, along with other pieces for which only a copy or two were known, the urge to include them was equally as seductive. So arrangements were made to have them filmed before reinterment. A fascinating sidelight to the cornerstone's contents is that of the nearly three dozen printed pieces in it, only two (Nos. 478 and 568a), except for issues of newspapers, appear to have been printed in Nevada. All others openly bear foreign imprints or were products of the State Printers when those officers regularly sent their work to California to be executed.

In the Preface to *Check List* there are elaborate tables showing the kinds and amounts of printing done for each year of the survey; there is also information regarding numbers of items in some of the libraries with the largest Nevada holdings. Although I have drawn together similar material for my own use, I have resisted the urge to inflict upon the user of this bibliography a series of not very useful charts. The library with the highest item count is of utterly no value to the potential patron if it does not have the piece he needs. Moreover, one can easily be deceived by such figures. For example, the three institutions with the greatest numbers of Nevada imprints and publications are the University of Nevada at Reno, the Nevada Historical Society, and the Nevada State Archives. But many of the University's holdings are on microfilm and are useful only to the scholar who does not need to examine the original item. The Historical Society's count is inflated by a large number of bills from the 1864 session of the territorial Legislative Assembly, and that of the State Archives by many dozens of court briefs. I do not intend to demean the importance of these materials—or of these repositories. I do suggest, however, that their presence can give misleading weight to the figures for an institution.

It is said that a people's artifacts and leavings are accurate reflections of their civilization. In the case of Nevada the comment would appear not be wholly accurate. Early Nevadans were a well-read lot. The Miners' Union Library in Virginia City was at one time one of the largest and most eclectic in the West, and the few remnants of the

Library show evidence of frequent use. Yet an analysis of the imprints and publications in this book indicates that only two pieces can be called literary, and orations and addresses number only twenty-three. Plays, operas, and other entertainments were popular forms of recreation, particularly on the Comstock but in smaller communities as well. Contemporary newspapers contained advertisements for them almost daily. But only sixty-three playbills are recorded here.[16] They were not of course intended to last beyond the performances they announced, but it is nonetheless surprising to find so few. There are other surprises. In a mining-oriented society one might reasonably expect that a large proportion of the surviving products of the press would relate somehow to the mines. There are, however, only 16 mining district laws and 23 legal forms used for recording claims. Further analysis shows the following counts in various other categories: fraternal organizations, 100; newspapers (prospectuses, extras, carriers' addresses, and occasional supplements), 79; political tickets, 63; invitations, 34; commercial, 30; politics other than tickets, 23; fairs, 21; religion, 12; unions, 10; directories, 9; legislative biographies, 9; education, 8; petitions, 8; ceremonies, 7; medical, 4; non-fraternal organizations, 3; and miscellaneous, 27. Government documents include 224 pieces produced for Utah and Nevada territories, 406 for the state of Nevada, and 51 for the United States, California, and local Nevada governments.

Sixteen Nevada printing sites are represented, with two other probables: Aurora and Sutro. Carson City has by far the largest number of imprints because of its position as the seat of government, but it must be remembered that the bulk of the documentary printing was actually done in California. Next in volume of production is Virginia City, followed in descending order by Gold Hill, Reno, Austin, Eureka, Winnemucca, Como, Elko, Unionville, Belmont, Hamilton, Silver City, Dayton, Genoa, and Washoe City. For a sparsely populated area to show products of the press from sixteen or more localities might seem a good representation until one considers that nothing has been found that can with certainty be identified with presses in eighteen other communities that had them for at least a part of the period: Battle Mountain, Belleville, Candelaria, Cherry

16. After one of the disastrous fires that destroyed much of Eureka, proprietors of that town's newspaper, the *Sentinel*, began the practice of pasting on the walls of the print shop the various products of the job office, including playbills. Unfortunately for the printing historian, when the available space was filled new pieces were pasted over the first layer, obscuring those on the bottom. The top layers contain broadsides that fall after the period covered in this book. The Eureka County Historical Society has plans to renovate the *Sentinel* office, including removal and display of items on the walls, but until sufficient money can be found to finance the project one can only imagine what might be there.

Creek, Columbus, Empire City (there is some doubt that a press actually existed there), Grantsville, Ione, Paradise, Pine Grove, Pioche, Ruby Hill, Schellbourne, Shermantown, Treasure City, Tuscarora, Tybo, and Ward. However, nearly one quarter of the titles recorded here lack imprints altogether, and some of them may have been produced in these towns. Of the nine out-of-state printing sites, San Francisco was the most active, followed by Sacramento, San Jose, and Monitor, California; Salem, Oregon; Chicago and Springfield, Illinois; Boston, Massachusetts; and Washington, D.C., with Oakland, California, as a possibility.

As illustrations I have chosen some of the more interesting broadsides, wrapper titles, and title pages that have not been reproduced elsewhere.

★   ★   ★   ★   ★

The holdings of sixty-eight institutions and four private collections in the United States were listed in *Check List* (one foreign library, the British Museum, was also included). The private collections have now all been dispersed or have gone in toto to libraries. Several of the *Check List* libraries no longer exist or have been absorbed by others, but I have visited as many as was practicable, thirty in all, in the quest for Nevada imprints and publications. I have visited an additional ninety-five libraries, historical societies, museums, and archives. Not all of them could be or needed to be searched as thoroughly as others, of course—one does not expect to find as much in a small county museum in Nevada as at the Bancroft Library—but an effort was made in each institution to be as comprehensive as possible. In some, however, there was nothing to be found. Selected manuscript and archival collections were examined for imprints as well as for supporting materials. An unsuccessful search was made for the copyright register that the federal district court was required to keep. I have been allowed to examine several items in private collections that could not otherwise have been included.

To get into and out of so many repositories with speed and ease one must of course have help, and I have had it in abundance. I have also had the assistance of many correspondents, before, after, and in place of institutional visits. I am indebted for favors to James Abajian, California Historical Society; Carolyn A. Allen, American Antiquarian Society; Susan Anderl, University of Nevada, Las Vegas, Library; Frederick Anderson, Mark Twain Papers, Bancroft Library; Mr. and Mrs. Adolphus Andrews, Jr., Brockway, California; Keith Arrington, Iowa Masonic Library; Inge Baum, Scottish Rite Supreme Council Library; Oscar C. Burdick, Pacific School of Religion; Alfred L. Bush, Princeton University Library; Glen Dawson, Dawson's Book Shop, Los Angeles, California; Mark G. Eckhoff and Clarence F. Lyons, Jr., National Archives and Records Service; Alan Fox and I. Albert Matkov, Massachusetts State Library; Robyn D. Gottfried, Federal Archives and Records Center, San Bruno, California; Robert Greenwood, Georgetown, California; Archibald Hanna and Joan Hofman, Beinecke Library; George L. Harding, San Francisco, California; Danielle L. Hopkins, Oregon Historical Society; T. Harold Jacobsen, Utah State Archives; Bruce L. Johnson, University of California School of Library and Information Studies; Tillie Krieger, University of Illinois Library; Harry V. Leonard, Jr., Las Vegas, Nevada; Richard E. Lingenfelter, University of California at Los Angeles; Russell W. McDonald, Reno, Nevada; Arthur H. Miller, Jr., Newberry Library; John H. Ness, Jr., and Evelyn Sutton, Commission on Archives and History, United Methodist Church; Dr. Peter D. Olch, National Library of Medicine; John A. Peters, Wisconsin Historical Society; Guy Louis Rocha, Nevada Historical Society; Jeanne Rogers, Grand Lodge of Nevada, F. & A.M.; Silas E. Ross, Reno, Nevada; Kenneth E. Row, Drew University Library; Robert E. Runser, Michigan State University Library; Virginia Rust, Huntington Library; Estelle Saralegui, Lander County Recorder, Austin, Nevada; Natalie Schatz, Harvard University Library; Cynthia A. Shepherd, Library of Congress; Wilbur J. Smith, University of California at Los Angeles Research Library; David L. Snyder, California State Archives; and Donald R. Tuohy, Nevada State Museum.

My especial thanks are due to Nicholas M. Cady, University of Nevada Press; Edwin H. Carpenter, Huntington Library; Pamela Crowell, Nevada State Museum; Mr. and Mrs. Edward Enger, Maplewood, New Jersey; Frederick C. Gale, Nevada State Archives; Suzanne H. Gallup, Bancroft Library; Ellen Guerricagoitia and Harold G. Morehouse, University of Nevada, Reno, Library; Anne L. Gurley, Graduate School of Library Science, Drexel Institute of Technology; Roberta Hankamer, Massachusetts Grand Lodge, F. & A.M.; L. James Higgins, Jr., Nevada Historical Society; and Saundra Taylor, University of California at Los Angeles Research Library.

For the first year of this study I was joined in the research by Jack I. Gardner, then of the Nevada State Library; his work in locating public documents made my job much easier. J. R. K. Kantor of the

Bancroft Library contributed both valuable editorial commentary to drafts of a part of this book and a cheerful willingness to perform long-distance sleuthery on my behalf.

A long, pleasant, and productive correspondence with George N. Belknap, University of Oregon, contributed much that is good here and prevented much that would have been less than good. Although we have argued about many things and still are arguing and will perhaps never agree on a number of matters, I thank him for the grace and good humor that make his letters both instructive and a joy to read. He has my lasting gratitude.

To my wife, Margaret, who counseled and who cared, go my special thanks.

I am also pleased to acknowledge my debt to the institutions that allowed use of photographs for the facsimiles following page 314.

The research for this book could not have been completed without two travel grants made available to me by the University of Nevada, Reno, Research Advisory Board, nor without a sabbatical leave from that institution in 1973-1974. I am grateful.

Readers who are unfamiliar with some of the terms used in this book may wish to consult one of the dictionaries of printing that were issued in the eighteen hundreds; several of them have been reprinted in this century and are available in many academic libraries.

I invite correspondence from those who find errors in my descriptions or who locate titles not recorded here that fall within the guidelines described on pages 8-10.

REFERENCES

THREE categories of references make up the following list. One is the very brief bibliography regarding early Nevada printing. Another consists of books and articles that are cited frequently, and the third includes manuscript and archival collections that were consulted during research for this book.

Alta California Bookstore. Catalogue 18: "Nevada." Berkeley, California, 1963. Cited: Alta California 18, followed by item number.

Angel, Myron, ed. *History of Nevada.* Oakland, California: Thompson & West, 1881. 680 p. Cited: Angel.

Armstrong, Robert D. "Early Printing in Carson City, Nevada: The Record Corrected." *Nevada Historical Society Quarterly,* XXI (1978), p. 152-156.

———. "Frank Eastman and the Nevada Masons: A Note for Printing Historians." *Nevada Historical Society Quarterly,* XIV (1971), p. 39-41.

———. "The Only Alternative Course: An Incident in Nevada Printing History." *Nevada Historical Society Quarterly,* XV (1972), p. 31-39.

Beebe, Lucius. *Comstock Commotion: The Story of the "Territorial Enterprise" and "Virginia City News."* Stanford, California: Stanford University Press, 1954. 129 p. Cited: Beebe.

Clemens, Samuel Langhorne. *Roughing It,* by Mark Twain. Hartford, Connecticut: American Publishing Company, 1872. 592 p. Cited: Twain.

Dawson's Book Shop. Catalogue 208: "West and Pacific." Los Angeles, 1947. Cited: Dawson 208, followed by item number.

Doten, Alfred. Diaries. Manuscript diaries at the University of Nevada Library, Reno, which supply information that was edited out of the published *Journals* (see next item). 79 vols., 1849-1903. Cited: Doten Diaries.

———. *The Journals of Alfred Doten, 1849-1903.* Edited by Walter Van Tilburg Clark. Reno: University of Nevada Press, 1973. 3 vols. Cited: Doten *Journals.*

Eberstadt, Edward, & Sons. *The Annotated Eberstadt Catalogs of*

Americana. New York: Argosy-Antiquarian Ltd., 1965. 4 vols., 1935-1956. Cited: Eberstadt, followed by catalogue and item number.

Greenwood, Robert. *California Imprints, 1833-1862: A Bibliography.* Los Gatos, California: Talisman Press, 1961. 527 p. Cited: Greenwood, followed by item number.

Historical Records Survey. *A Check List of Nevada Imprints, 1859-1890.* (American Imprints Inventory, No. 7: Works Progress Administration, Division of Women's and Professional Projects.) Chicago: Historical Records Survey, 1939. xv, 127 p. Cited: *Check List,* followed by item number.

Johnson, Bruce L. "Nevada Imprints Produced in San Francisco: The Role of Towne & Bacon." *Kemble Occasional*, 19 (1978), p. 1-6.

Katz, W. A. "Tracing Western Territorial Imprints Through the National Archives." *Papers of the Bibliographical Society of America,* LIX (1965), p. 1-11.

Lingenfelter, Richard E. *The Newspapers of Nevada, 1858-1958: A History and Bibliography.* San Francisco: John Howell—Books, 1964. xxiii, 228 p.

Mack, Effie Mona. "Nevada's First Newspapers." *Nevada Magazine,* I (1945), p. 4-8.

Nevada. Laws, statutes, etc. *Statutes of the State of Nevada.* Carson City: State Printer, 1865-1879. Cited: SSN, followed by year of legislative session.

————. Legislature. *Appendix to Journals of Senate and Assembly.* Carson City: State Printer, 1875-1879. Cited: AJSA, followed by year of legislative session.

————. ————. Assembly. *Appendix to Journal of Assembly.* Carson City: State Printer, 1866-1873. Cited: AJA, followed by year of legislative session.

————. ————. ————. *Journal of the Assembly.* Carson City: State Printer, 1865-1879. Cited: JA, followed by year of legislative session.

————. ————. Senate. *Appendix to Journal of Senate.* Carson City: State Printer, 1865-1873. Cited: AJS, followed by year of legislative session.

————. ————. ————. *Journal of the Senate.* Carson City: State Printer, 1865-1879. Cited: JS, followed by year of legislative session.

————. Secretary of State. Contracts of State of Nevada, Vol. I, 1865-1878. Manuscript records at Nevada State Archives. Cited: Nevada Contracts.

———. State Printing Commissioners. Proceedings. Names of entity and title vary. Manuscript records at Nevada State Archives; 1879 at Nevada Historical Society. Cited: PSPC, followed by year.

Nevada Territory. Laws, statutes, etc. *Laws of the Territory of Nevada.* San Francisco: Valentine & Company; Virginia City: J. T. Goodman & Co., John Church & Co., 1862-1864. Cited: LTN, followed by year of legislative session.

———. Legislative Assembly. Council. *Journal of the Council.* San Francisco: Valentine & Company, 1862. 295 p. Journals of the second and third legislative sessions exist only in manuscript form at the Nevada State Archives and on microfilm. Cited: JC, followed by year of legislative session.

———. ———. House of Representatives. *Journal of the House of Representatives.* San Francisco: Valentine & Company, 1862. 422 p. Journals of the second and third legislative sessions exist only in manuscript form at the Nevada State Archives and on microfilm. Cited: JHR, followed by year of legislative session.

———. Secretary. Letterbook. Manuscript volume of outgoing correspondence, 1861-1864, at the Nevada State Archives and on microfilm. Cited: Letterbook.

Norris, Thomas Wayne, *A Descriptive & Priced Catalogue of Books, Pamphlets, and Maps Relating Directly or Indirectly to the History, Literature, and Printing of California & The Far West, Formerly the Collection of Thomas Wayne Norris, Livermore, Calif.* Oakland, California: Holmes Book Company, 1948. 217 p. Cited: Norris, followed by item number.

Parke-Bernet Galleries, Inc. *The Celebrated Collection of Americana Formed by the Late Thomas Winthrop Streeter.* Vol. IV (p. 1475-1854). New York: Parke-Bernet, 1968. Cited: Streeter IV, followed by item number.

Sacconaghi, Charles David. *A Checklist of California Imprints for the Years 1865 and 1868, With a Historical Introduction.* Washington, D.C.: Catholic University of America, 1963. 219 p. M.S. thesis. Cited: Sacconaghi, followed by item number.

Simpson, Claude M., Jr. "Captain Jim and the Third House." *Western Folklore,* XV (1950), p. 101-110.

Talisman Press. Catalog 3: "California and Nevada," and Catalog 13: "Nevada." Georgetown, California, 1963, 1978. Cited: Talisman 3 or 13, followed by item number.

Towne & Bacon. Records. Manuscript records at Jackson Library of Business, Stanford University. Cited: Towne & Bacon.

U.S. Department of State. Records. Record Group 59 at the National Archives and Records Service. Cited: RG59.

————. General Accounting Office. Records. Record Group 217 at the National Archives and Records Service. Cited: RG217.

————. Library of Congress. *The National Union Catalogue: Pre- 1956 Imprints.* Vol. 412. London: Mansell, 1975. Cited: NUC 412.

————. Treasury Department. Comptroller's Office. *Circular.* Washington, D.C., October 10, 1855. 1 p. Cited: Circular.

Wegelin, Oscar. "An Early Nevada Imprint." *Quarterly Bulletin of the New York Historical Society,* XXIV (1940), p. 124-125.

LOCATION SYMBOLS

Az	Arizona State Department of Library and Archives. Phoenix, Arizona.
C	California State Library. Sacramento, California.
CBPac	Pacific School of Religion. Berkeley, California.
CBriM	Mono County Museum. Bridgeport, California.
CHi	California Historical Society. San Francisco, California.
CLU	University of California. Los Angeles, California.
COMus	Oakland Museum. Oakland, California.
CSbrFRC	Federal Records Center. San Bruno, California.
CSfCP	Society of California Pioneers. San Francisco, California.
CSfWF-H	Wells Fargo Bank History Room. San Francisco, California.
CSmH	Henry E. Huntington Library. San Marino, California.
CSt	Stanford University. Stanford, California.
CU	University of California. Berkeley, California.
CU-A	————. Davis, California.
CU-B	————. Bancroft Library. Berkeley, California.
CU-B(MT)	————. ————. Mark Twain Papers. Berkeley, California.
CoD	Denver Public Library. Denver, Colorado.
CtY	Yale University. New Haven, Connecticut.
CtY-L	————. Law School Library. New Haven, Connecticut.
DBRE	Bureau of Railway Economics Library of the Association of American Railroads. Washington, D.C.
DHEW	U.S. Department of Health, Education and Welfare. Washington, D.C.
DLC	U.S. Library of Congress. Washington, D.C.
DNA	U.S. National Archives and Records Service. Washington, D.C.
DNLM	U.S. National Library of Medicine. Bethesda, Maryland.
DSC	Scottish Rite Supreme Council. Washington, D.C.
ICN	Newberry Library. Chicago, Illinois.
ICSR	Scottish Rite Library. Chicago, Illinois.
ICU	University of Chicago. Chicago, Illinois.
IU	University of Illinois. Urbana, Illinois.
Ia-HA	Iowa State Department of History and Archives. Des Moines, Iowa.
IaCrM	Iowa Masonic Library. Cedar Rapids, Iowa.
In	Indiana State Library. Indianapolis, Indiana.
In-SC	Indiana State Supreme Court Law Library. Indianapolis, Indiana.

M	Massachusetts State Library. Boston, Massachusetts.
MB	Boston Public Library. Boston, Massachusetts.
MBC	American Congregational Association. Boston, Massachusetts.
MBFM	Massachusetts Grand Lodge, F.&A.M. Boston, Massachusetts.
MBS	Social Law Library. Boston, Massachusetts.
MH	Harvard University. Cambridge, Massachusetts.
MH-BA	———. Graduate School of Business Administration Library. Boston, Massachusetts.
MH-L	———. Law School Library. Cambridge, Massachusetts.
MH-Z	———. Museum of Comparative Zoology Library. Cambridge, Massachusetts.
MWA	American Antiquarian Society. Worcester, Massachusetts.
NHi	New York Historical Society. New York, New York.
NIC	Cornell University. Ithaca, New York.
NN	New York Public Library. New York, New York.
NNFM	Grand Lodge of New York, F.&A.M. Library and Museum. New York, New York.
NNLI	New York Law Institute. New York, New York.
NNNAM	New York Academy of Medicine. New York, New York.
NPV	Vassar College. Poughkeepsie, New York.
NcLjUM	United Methodist Church. Commission on Archives and History. Lake Junaluska, North Carolina.
NjMD	Drew University. Madison, New Jersey.
NjP	Princeton University. Princeton, New Jersey.
Nv	Nevada State Library. Carson City, Nevada.
Nv-Ar	Nevada State Archives. Carson City, Nevada.
NvALR	Lander County Recorder. Austin, Nevada.
NvC	Carson City-Ormsby County Library. Carson City, Nevada.
NvCR	Carson City Recorder. Carson City, Nevada.
NVEC	Elko County Clerk. Elko, Nevada.
NvEHi	Northeastern Nevada Historical Society. Elko, Nevada.
NvEuC	Eureka County Clerk. Eureka, Nevada.
NvGM	Mormon Station State Park. Genoa, Nevada.
NvGoEC	Esmeralda County Clerk. Goldfield, Nevada.
NvHi	Nevada Historical Society. Reno, Nevada.
NvLC	Clark County Library District. Las Vegas, Nevada.
NvLN	University of Nevada. Las Vegas, Nevada.
NvMiD	Douglas County Public Library. Minden, Nevada.
NvMus	Nevada State Museum. Carson City, Nevada.
NvPLC	Lincoln County Clerk. Pioche, Nevada.
NvPLR	Lincoln County Recorder. Pioche, Nevada.
NvRFM	Grand Lodge of Nevada, F.&A.M. Reno, Nevada.

LOCATION SYMBOLS

NvRH   Harrah's Automobile Collection. Pony Express Museum. Reno, Nevada.

NvRNC   National Judicial College. Reno, Nevada.

NvRW   Washoe County Library. Reno, Nevada.

NvRWL   Washoe County Law Library. Reno, Nevada.

NvSC   Nevada Supreme Court Library. Carson City, Nevada.

NvU   University of Nevada. Reno, Nevada.

NvU(NvMus)   ————. ————: indefinite loan from NvMus.

NvVSC   Storey County Clerk. Virginia City, Nevada.

NvVSR   Storey County Recorder. Virginia City, Nevada.

NvYLR   Lyon County Recorder. Yerington, Nevada.

OrHi   Oregon Historical Society. Portland, Oregon.

OrU-L   University of Oregon. Law Library. Eugene, Oregon.

PHi   Historical Society of Pennsylvania. Philadelphia, Pennsylvania.

PP   Free Library of Philadelphia. Philadelphia, Pennsylvania.

PPL   Library Company of Philadelphia. Philadelphia, Pennsylvania.

PU   University of Pennsylvania. Philadelphia, Pennsylvania.

PU-L   ————. Biddle Law Library. Philadelphia, Pennsylvania.

Pvt   Private collection.

RPL   Rhode Island Law Library. Providence, Rhode Island.

U-L   Utah State Law Library. Salt Lake City, Utah.

UPB   Brigham Young University. Provo, Utah.

UU   University of Utah. Salt Lake City, Utah.

UU-L   ————. Law Library. Salt Lake City, Utah.

ViU   University of Virginia. Charlottesville, Virginia.

ViU-L   ————. Law Library. Charlottesville, Virginia.

WHi   State Historical Society of Wisconsin. Madison, Wisconsin.

WyU   University of Wyoming. Laramie, Wyoming.

A BIBLIOGRAPHY OF IMPRINTS
AND PUBLICATIONS, 1858-1880

❧1858❧

The fur traders of the 1820s and 1830s knew well the area that is now Nevada and it was familiar country to most of the men and women who traveled overland to California in later decades, but it was not until 1850—the year that California became a state and Utah a territory—that it had its first permanent settlement at a site known as Mormon Station, later Genoa, on the Carson River emigrant route. Appropriately enough, Nevada's first printing press was also established there, but not until more than eight years after the first residents had come. Two earlier newspapers had been published in what was then still a part of western Utah Territory, the *Gold Cañon Switch* at Johntown and the *Scorpion* at Mormon Station; but both were handwritten and of interest here only because they indicate the absence of printing equipment in the mid-fifties. In the late summer or early fall of 1858—there is some disagreement over the exact time—the citizens of Carson Valley learned through publication of a prospectus that they were soon to have a newspaper and would no longer have to depend on Salt Lake City and California papers for news of their area. In November of that year W. L. Jernegan and Alfred James had a secondhand press hauled over the Sierra Nevada from Placerville to Genoa and on December 18 issued the first number of the *Territorial Enterprise* from their print shop in the Nevada Hotel on Main Street. According to the late Lucius Beebe, in *Comstock Commotion* (p. 6), the equipment used in Nevada's first printing venture was the "acorn" model of Hoe's Washington press.

TERRITORIAL ENTERPRISE. *Genoa, Utah Territory*. Prospectus. [Placerville, California: Mountain Democrat?] 1858.   [L1]
Beebe (p.3) quoted a prospectus for the *Enterprise* with the title "A Journal for the

Eastern Slope,'' but did not document his source. In response to an inquiry from the author, Beebe's long-time associate, Charles Clegg, wrote on July 23, 1975, that he could not recall Beebe's ever mentioning his discovery of the prospectus, although it was his wont to speak of such things delightedly when he found them. And it would have been unusual for him to say nothing, since he and Clegg were, respectively, publisher and editor of a resurrected version of the paper in the 1950s. Effie Mona Mack, in ''Nevada's First Newspapers,'' *Nevada Magazine,* I (1945), p.7, noted that a prospectus was issued in August of 1858, but her source was not documented, either; a search of her papers at NvHi revealed no clues. Beebe's quotation indicated that the newspaper would commence ''on the first week of November next, 1858, at Carson City, Eagle Valley,'' but that calls into question Mack's statement that it was issued in August, since Carson City's site was not laid out until September. Dan De Quille, the *Enterprise*'s editor and local for many years, writing in the San Francisco *Examiner* of January 22, 1893, on the passing of the *Enterprise,* noted that there had indeed been a prospectus that announced the first issue ''for a much earlier date than that on which it appeared,'' but that it had not mentioned Carson City as the town in which the newspaper was to be published. The *Enterprise* finally appeared on December 18 in Genoa. The prospectus would have had to be printed outside of western Utah Territory, since the press and material did not arrive there until November. It is as good a guess as any that it was printed at the Placerville *Mountain Democrat,* the paper from which the material and press were purchased; that paper's first mention of the *Enterprise* was on November 13, but it said nothing of a prospectus.

❧1859❧

Almost from the time of its earliest settlement the western portion of Utah had been trying to break away politically from the territorial government in Salt Lake City. In 1851 a squatter government had been set up; in 1853 and again in 1856 the Legislature of California had been urged to accept attachment of the area for judicial purposes; a provisional territorial constitution had been drawn up in 1854; and a petition had been sent to Washington, D.C., asking for a separate territory in 1857. The reason for all of this activity was as much religious as it was political: the government in Salt Lake City was dominated by Mormons, and the largely Gentile population of western Utah's Carson County resented what they considered to be sectarian rule. So again in 1859 an unauthorized constitution was written, a delegate was sent to Washington to lobby for separation from Utah, and a provisional governor was elected. The constitution was duly published in the July 30 issue of the *Territorial Enterprise,* but it is not known whether it was issued separately as a pamphlet. The shortage of paper that caused the *Enterprise* to miss several issues during its first year may well have militated against separate publication.

The *Enterprise* continued to be the only press in the area in 1859, but it underwent a change of location as well as a change in ownership. The paper moved from Genoa to Carson City between its issues of November 5 and November 12. One of its cofounders, Alfred James, had before that time sold his interest to Jonathan Williams. The other original proprietor, W. L. Jernegan, soon proved to have less business acumen than was required, his creditors seized his interest, and Williams became sole owner.

TERRITORIAL ENTERPRISE. *Carson City, Utah Territory.* Extra. December 27, 1859.   [L2]

Enterprise, December 31, 1859: "From our Extra of Tuesday. Arrival of the J. L. Stephens. San Francisco, Dec. 27th—8 P.M." The steamer *Stephens* had arrived in San Francisco on the previous day, carrying news from New York to the 5th of the month. The most important news reported was of the hanging of John Brown on December 2.

UTAH TERRITORY. *District Court. Second Judicial District (Carson County).*

Report | of the | Grand Jury | of the | Second District of Utah Territory, | September Term, 1859. | [*filet*] | Carson Valley: | Printed at the Office of the Territorial Enterprise. | [*short dotted rule*] | 1859.   [3]

4 p. 23 x 15 cm.

Genoa was situated in Carson Valley, but the owners apparently used the latter name here and in the newspaper's masthead to indicate that they intended to reach a wider audience.

W. L. Jernegan had been active in the movement to gain separate territorial status for his part of Utah, and in July of 1859 had been a delegate to the unofficial constitutional convention that drew up a document to submit to officials in Washington, D.C. His former partner on the *Enterprise,* Alfred James, was Clerk of the Court. As a result of these circumstances the publication of this piece could almost be expected. The report, addressed to the Hon. John Cradlebaugh, the District Judge assigned to Carson County, was issued on October 25. In it the Grand Jury complained bitterly of what it called the "Theocratic Tyrany [*sic*]" of the Salt Lake City government, the lack of regular terms of the court, inadequate defense against the Indians, and problems with the boundary between California and Utah Territory. The creation

31

of a Territory of Nevada to redress the grievances was suggested in the strongest terms: "In view . . . of the dissimilar tastes and interests, and of the discordant sentiments, religious and political, of the people, and of the outrages above enumerated, we submit that the best interests of the Government in this Territory imperatively require some remedial legislation on the part of Congress."

Check List: 1 located a copy at NvHi and another in the private collection of William Robertson Coe. The latter copy is now at CtY; the copy at NvHi is a positive photostat.

CtY. DNA. NvHi (photostat). NvU (microfilm).

WOODFORDS, CALIFORNIA. *Christmas Ball.*

Christmas Ball. | [*filet*] | The pleasure of your company | is respectfully solicited to attend a | Ball at Woodford's Hotel, at | the Mouth of Carson Can-|yon, | Monday, December 26, 1859. | [*filet*] | . . . | [*rule*] | Territorial Enterprise Print, Carson City. [4]

[4] p., printed on p. [1] only. 17 x 11 cm. Printed in blue, partly in script type. Embossed border. Facsimile following p. 314.

This earliest known piece of Carson City printing was probably issued within a month of the *Enterprise*'s move from Genoa. It may not have been the only invitation printed during that season, however, since the December 17 issue of the paper included notices in its advertising columns for two other Christmas parties. One of them was scheduled for December 23 in Susanville, California, which was rather a long distance for Carsonites to travel; the other was to be held in Carson City itself on Christmas night. Both founders of the newspaper are listed as managers of the ball on the present invitation, W. L. Jernegan in Carson City, and Alfred James in Genoa.

A peculiar bit of irony attaches to this Nevada printing of an invitation to a party in California—even if just barely so—considering the later practice of sending printing orders of Nevada origin to California to be executed.

The provenance of the recorded copy of the invitation is remarkably complete for so ephemeral a piece. A young Genoa schoolteacher, who had been there since 1858, left for Salt Lake City with her family in early 1860, shortly after the ball, taking the invitation with her. Her father was not a devotee of the Mormon Church and, refusing to become a member, soon left with his family for their original home in Iowa. The invitation, which had been kept in the family Bible, remained there until given by a relative to a niece in Independence, Missouri. On a 1971 trip to Nevada the niece presented it to the institution that now owns it, in the city of its origin. NvMus.

❧1860❧

Prospecting for ores of various kinds had for some years brought men, some of them disillusioned by the worked-out placers in California, to western Utah in the hope of one day finding the mine that would allow them to retire in luxury. The discovery in 1859 of the enormously rich vein of silver and gold that became known as the Comstock Lode quickly changed the area's economic base from one founded primarily on agriculture to one that was almost exclusively dependent on hardrock mining and its attendant industries. Printing needs changed, too, as forms for deeds and other legal instruments to record claims and the often-changing ownership of mining property came into demand. The *Territorial Enterprise* moved again in its peripatetic search for an ever larger circulation by going at the end of October to Virginia City, the center of all the mining activity. The departure of the *Enterprise* from Carson City did not, however, leave a journalistic void there, since it was replaced almost immediately by the *Silver Age,* a newspaper founded by John C. Lewis. But the long struggle to break away from the Salt Lake City government was not lessened by the obsessive search for silver. It was in fact strengthened by the rapidly growing dependence on California financing for the mines and the need of an exploding population for more local control over its own affairs.

CARSON COUNTY, UTAH TERRITORY. *Citizens.*

Petition. | [*short wavy rule*] | To the | Hon. the Senators and Representatives of the U.S., | in Congress Assembled: | . . . | [Carson City? 1860?]   [5]

Broadside. 122 x 20 cm. Two columns for signatures, separated by a vertical double rule.

If the petition was printed in western Utah Territory it would have to have been executed by the *Territorial Enterprise* or the *Silver Age,* the only two presses in the area at the time. Handwritten on the verso of the located copy: "1861 Jany. 29, Referred to the Com. on Post Offices and Post Roads." The petition was likely printed in late 1860 because of the large number of signatures, which would have taken time to gather, and the time it would have taken to transmit it to Washington. The petition requests daily mail service between Placerville in California, and

Genoa, Carson City, Silver City, and Virginia City in Utah Territory; it also asks for semi–weekly service between these western Utah towns, the Esmeralda district (then thought to be in California), and Monoville in the Walker River Mines. DNA. NvU (microfilm).

CARSON COUNTY, UTAH TERRITORY. *Citizens.*

To the Senate, | And House of Representatives of the United States. | [*thick-thin rule*] | Your petitioners, residents of Western Utah, in the proposed new Territory of Nevada, would respectfully represent:— | . . . | [*thick-thin rule*] | Names. Names. | [*double rule*] | [Carson City: 1860?]   [6]

Broadside. 26 x 21 cm. Two columns for signatures. Two of the three located copies, all at DNA, have sheets attached for signatures. Handwritten on the verso of one of these copies: "1861 Feby 11, Referred to the Com. on Territories."

The petition asks for passage of bills pending before Congress that would create a Territory of Nevada, citing the distance from Salt Lake City (over 600 miles) and the consequent difficulty in enforcing the laws, Indian troubles, the large amount of capital in the area because of the Comstock mines, and the growing population ("Union loving people") as reasons. DNA. NvU (microfilm).

CARSON COUNTY, UTAH TERRITORY. *Forms, blanks, etc.*

Bill of Sale. | [*thick-thin rule*] | For and in Consideration of the Sum of [*dotted rule*] | [*dotted rule*] Dollars, to me in hand paid by [*dotted rule*], the receipt whereof is hereby | acknowledged, [*blank*] have this day Bargained Sold and Conveyed, And By These Presents | do Bargain, Sell and Convey unto [*dotted rule*] all of my right, title and interest in and to a certain | piece or parcel of Mining Ground or Quartz Lode, and described as follows, to–wit: | . . . | [*rule*] | Printed at the "Territorial Enterprise" Office, Carson City, N.T. | [1860?]   [7]

Broadside. 31 x 20 cm. Printed on blue paper.

"Carson County, Utah Territory" is mentioned in the printed text. The "N.T." in the imprint, rather than the expected and more correct "U.T.," is perhaps explained by the fierceness of the desire of local residents to have their own government separate from that in Salt Lake City.

The earliest of the recorded copies, at CtY, is hand–dated March 2, 1860. CtY. NvHi. NvU.

CARSON COUNTY, UTAH TERRITORY. *Forms, blanks, etc.*

This Indenture, Made the [*blank*] day of [*blank*] in | the year of our Lord one thousand, eight hundred and sixty [*blank*] | Between [*rule*] | . . . | Printed and Sold by Wm. B. Cooke, Importing and

Jobbing Stationers, 158 Montgomery Block, San Francisco. |
[1860?]   [8]

[4] p., printed on p. [1-2, 4] only. 35? x 22 cm. The bottom of the recorded copy is
cropped at an angle, leaving only small portions of the imprint intact. Triple rule
border, with imprint below the border. Printed on blue paper.

"Carson County, Utah Territory" is mentioned in the printed text. The recorded
copy is dated by hand: June 19, 1860.

NvHi.

CARSON COUNTY, UTAH TERRITORY. *Forms, blanks, etc.*

This Indenture, Made the [*blank*] day of [*blank*] | in the year of our
Lord one thousand, eight hundred and sixty [*blank*] | Between
[*rule*] | . . . | Mining Deed—No. 3. Printed and sold by Wm. B.
Cooke and Co., Importing and Jobbing Stationers, 158 Montgom-
ery Street, Montgomery Block, San Francisco. | [1860?]   [9]

[4] p., printed on p. [1, 4] only. 35 x 22 cm. Triple rule border, with imprint below the
border. Printed on blue paper.

"County of Carson, Territory of Utah" is mentioned in the printed text. The
recorded copy is dated by hand: February 25, 1860.

NvU.

CARSON COUNTY, UTAH TERRITORY. *Forms, blanks, etc.*

This Indenture, Made this [*blank*] day of [*blank*] | in the year of our
Lord one thousand, eight hundred and sixty [*blank*] | Between [*bro-
ken rule*] | . . . | Sold by Wilson & Keyes, Virginia City, U.T.
| [1860?]   [10]

[4] p., printed on p. [1, 4] only. 36 x 22 cm. Triple rule border, with "imprint"
below the border. Printed on blue paper.

"Carson County" is mentioned in the printed text. Dated by hand on the recorded
copy: December 14, 1860.

NvHi.

CARSON COUNTY, UTAH TERRITORY. *Forms, blanks, etc.*

This Indenture, Made this [*blank*] day of [*blank*] in | the year of our
Lord one thousand, eight hundred and sixty [*blank*] | Between
[*rule*] | . . . | Mining Deed—No. 2. Printed and Sold by Wm. B.
Cooke, Importing and Jobbing Stationers, 158 Montgomery Block,
San Francisco. | [1860?]   [11]

[4] p., printed on p. [1, 4] only. Triple rule border, with imprint below the border.
Printed on blue paper.

The printed text mentions the "County of Carson, Territory of Utah." The recorded
copy is dated by hand: April 20, 1860.

NvHi.

CARSON COUNTY, UTAH TERRITORY. *Probate Court.*

Election Notice. | [*thick-thin rule*] | To the People of Carson County, Utah Territory: | Greeting:--- | . . . | John S. Child, | Probate Judge of Carson County, Utah Territory. | Attest, George McNeir, Clerk. | [*thick-thin rule*] | [Carson City:] Territorial Enterprise Job Print. | [1860.]   [12]

Broadside. 40 x 20 cm.

The notice sets the first Monday in August of 1860 as the date for the election, names the offices to be filled, defines precinct boundaries, and lists a number of the laws that are applicable to the election.

NvHi.

TERRITORIAL ENTERPRISE. *Carson City, Utah Territory.* Extra. April 12, 1860.   [L13]

Enterprise, April 14, 1860: "From our Extra of Thursday. Arrival of the Pony Express!! 8 days and 20 Hours from St. Joseph, Missouri. Dates from St. Joseph, Mo., to April 3d, 6 P.M. The Rubicon is Passed! The Pony Express is a Success!! No Fears for the Future!" A synopsis of the Senate bill for formation of a Nevada Territory was included.

TERRITORIAL ENTERPRISE. *Carson City, Utah Territory.* Extra. May 15, 1860.   [L14]

Enterprise, May 19, 1860: "From our Extra of Tuesday." The regular issue of the 19th noted that the extra had contained ten columns; since the paper usually had five columns per page, the extra was probably issued as a half sheet. The most significant local news involved the "Indian Fight at Pyramid Lake," a celebrated battle that marked the beginning of the end of Indian hostilities in the Territory. The death of Major William M. Ormsby, after whom the county in which Carson City was situated was later named, was mentioned. There was also the "Latest from the Prize Fight," a forty-two-round draw between John C. Heenan and Tom Sayers in London on April 17, and news of the adjournment of the Democratic convention at Charleston, South Carolina, to Baltimore.

TERRITORIAL ENTERPRISE. *Virginia City, Utah Territory.*

Territorial Enterprise. | Arrival of the Pony! Extra. | Virginia City, N.T., Nov. 7, 1860.   [L15]

Broadside. Description from *Check List:* 2, which included the item on the basis of a description in a catalog of the American Art Association, January 31, 1921.

UTAH TERRITORY. *Forms, blanks, etc.*

Quit-Claim Deed. | [*double rule*] | Know All Men By These Presents, That [*broken rule*] | [*broken rule*] | [*broken rule*], of the First Part, for and in consideration of the sum of | [*broken rule*] | to [*blank*] in hand paid by [*broken rule*] | [*broken rule*] of [*broken rule*] | [*broken rule*]

Territory aforesaid, of the Sedond [*sic*] Part, the receipt whereof is hereby | acknowledged, ha[*blank*] Bargained, Sold and Quit-Claimed, And By These Presents | do[*blank*] Bargain, Sell and Quit-Claim unto the said [*broken rule*] | [*broken rule*] and to [*blank*] heirs and assigns, forever, all [*blank*] right, title, interest, estate, claim and | demand, both in law and equity, as well in possession as in expectancy, of, in and to all that certain piece or | parcel of land lying, bounded and described as follows, to-wit: [*dotted rule*] | . . . | [*rule*] | Printed at the "Territorial Enterprise" office, Carson City, N.T. | [1860?]   [16]

[4] p., printed on p. [1] only. 31 x 20 cm. Printed on blue paper. Note "N.T." in the imprint; see also Nos. 7 and 17.

Of the four copies recorded (two at CSmH, two at CSt), only one at CSt, hand-dated January 16, 1860, has the error in line 6. Three of the copies are hand-dated between the 16th and the 20th of January; these early dates suggest the possibility of a late 1859 printing.

CSmH. CSt.

Utah Territory. *Forms, blanks, etc.*

Quit-Claim Deed. | [*thick-thin rule*] | Know All Men By These Presents, That [*dotted rule*] | [*dotted rule*] | [*dotted rule*], of the First Part, for and in consideration of the sum of | [*dotted rule*] | to [*blank*] in hand paid by [*dotted rule*] | [*dotted rule*] of [*dotted rule*] | [*dotted rule*] Territory aforesaid, of the Second Part, the receipt whereof is hereby | acknowledged, ha[*blank*] Bargained, Sold and Quit-Claimed, And By These Presents | do[*blank*] Bargain, Sell and Quit-Claim unto the said [*dotted rule*] | [*dotted rule*] and to [*blank*] heirs and assigns, forever, all [*blank*] right, title, interest, estate, claim and | demand, both in law and equity, as well in possession as in expectancy, of, in and to all that certain piece or | parcel of land lying, bounded and described as follows, to-wit: [*dotted rule*] | . . . | [*rule*] | Printed at the "Territorial Enterprise" Office, Carson City, N.T. | [1860?]   [17]

Broadside. 30 x 19 cm. Note "N.T." in the imprint, as in Nos. 7 and 16.

The recorded copy with the earliest handwritten date, at NjP, is dated March 3, 1860.

CSt. CU-B. CtY. NjP. NvU (microfilm).

Utah Territory. *Forms, blanks, etc.*

This Indenture, Made this [*blank*] day of [*blank*] | in the year of our Lord one thousand eight hundred and sixty [*blank*] | Between [*rule*] | . . . | [*double rule*] | Printed for and sold by Harned & Wilcox, Main street, Silver City. | [1860?]   [18]

[4] p., printed on p. [1, 4] only. 31 x 20 cm.
The transaction on the recorded copy is dated, by hand, March 9, 1860.
CtY. NvU (microfilm).

UTAH TERRITORY. *Forms, blanks, etc.*

This Indenture, Made this [*blank*] day of [*blank*] | in the year of our
Lord one thousand eight hundred and sixty [*blank*] | Between
[*rule*] | . . . | Mining Deed—No. 1. Printed and Sold by Batters &
Waters, Virginia City. | [1860?]   [19]

[4] p., printed on p. [1, 4] only. 35 x 22 cm. Last line below a thick-thin rule border.
Printed on blue paper. No other evidence has been found to link the firm of Batters
& Waters with the printing trade.
The recorded copy is dated by hand: November 26, 1860.
NvU(NvMus).

❧1861❧

Western Utah Territory finally achieved its long-sought freedom
from Salt Lake City's domination on March 2, 1861, when President
James Buchanan signed the act creating the Territory of Nevada. The
boundaries included the former Carson and Humboldt counties of
Utah Territory, an area that was enlarged to the east in 1862 and 1866
and to the south in 1867. Buchanan left office two days later, leaving
to his successor, Abraham Lincoln, the task of appointing officials
for the new territory. James W. Nye of New York was selected to be
Governor, while the post of Secretary went to Orion Clemens, a
printer and lawyer from Keokuk, Iowa, who had earlier read law in
the St. Louis office of Lincoln's Attorney General, Edward Bates.
Clemens was joined on the overland journey to Carson City, the
territorial capital, by his younger brother Samuel, who hoped to
become a secretary to the Secretary. The junior Clemens did actually
receive a salary from the federal government for a short time until it
was discovered that no such position had been authorized. He then
engaged in several unsuccessful mining ventures, during one of
which he contributed short, humorous pieces, signed Josh, to the
Territorial Enterprise. He later became a regular reporter for the paper
and adopted there his more familiar pseudonym of Mark Twain.
Many of his older brother's tribulations with federal and other ter-

ritorial officials, including some involving the public printing, were amusingly recounted in his *Roughing It*.

John C. Lewis took on a partner, E. F. McElwain, at his *Silver Age,* but before the end of the year McElwain was replaced by G. T. Sewall. The Territory's third newspaper was established in March, when the *Washoe Times* began publication in Silver City; it lasted only until September. Shortly before the demise of the *Times* the owners of the Territory's three newspapers were asked by Secretary Clemens to respond to a series of "Inquiries Relative to Printing in the Territory of Nevada" so that it could be determined which of them was best qualified to take on the public printing that would be required when the Legislative Assembly began its first session in October. The *Times* disqualified itself because of inadequate equipment, but Clemens obtained replies from the *Enterprise* and the *Silver Age* and forwarded them to Elisha Whittlesey, whose duty it was as First Comptroller of the U.S. Treasury Department to oversee official printing in the territories. The responses indicated that the *Enterprise* owned a Ruggles job press large enough for foolscap and a Washington hand press that Clemens supposed must be a double medium because of the size of the newspaper. The *Silver Age* had a No. 4 Washington hand press; in addition, Sewall had gone to San Francisco at the time of the Secretary's letter to Whittlesey to obtain a power press for book and job work (RG217: Clemens to Whittlesey, August 21, 1861). Sewall purchased "certain printing materials" there from the firm of Faulkner & Son for $526.34, paying $14.25 cash with the remainder to be remitted on payment from the Territory (Jean Webster McKinney Papers at NPV: Lorenzo Sawyer to Clemens, March 1, 1862). When the federal government's rates were made known the *Enterprise* dropped out of consideration and the firm of Lewis & Sewall was chosen to act as public printer. But a squabble between the partners in the middle of the session resulted in the sale of the newspaper to an organization of workers in the shop, the Age Association, which apparently continued to print minor pieces for the Territory, but ceased work on the journals of the two legislative houses. See the 1863 Summary for a discussion of the resolution of the difficulty.

CARSON COUNTY, UTAH TERRITORY. *Forms, blanks, etc.*

Printed at the Office of the "Territorial Enterprise." | [*thick-thin rule*] | This Indenture, Made this [*blank*] day of | [*blank*] one thousand eight hundred and sixty [*blank*] | Between [*blank*] | . . . | [Virginia City? 1861?]   [20]

[4] p., printed on p. [1-2] only. 32 x 20 cm. Mostly script type. Printed on blue lined paper.

The recorded copy is dated by hand February 8, 1861. The *Enterprise* began publishing in Virginia City on November 3, 1860.

CSmH.

CARSON COUNTY, UTAH TERRITORY. *Forms, blanks, etc.*

Territory of Utah, County of Carson---ss. | On this [*blank*] day of [*blank*] A.D. 186[*blank*], before me, E.C. Dixson, a Justice of the Peace in and | for Carson County, 4th Precinct, U.T., duly commissioned and sworn, personally appeared the within named | . . . | [1861?]   [21]

Broadside. 11 x 21 cm.

The recorded copy is hand-dated March 15, 1861.

CSt.

CARSON COUNTY, UTAH TERRITORY. *Forms, blanks, etc.*

This Indenture, Made the [*wavy rule*] day of [*wavy rule*] | In the year of our Lord, one thousand eight hundred and sixty [*blank*] | Between [*rule*] | . . . | "Territorial Enterprise" Print, A St., Virginia City, U.T. | [1861?]   [22]

[4] p., printed on p. [1, 4] only. 35 x 22 cm. Last line below a border of rules. Printed on blue paper.

The printed text refers to the "County of Carson, Territory of Utah." The recorded copy is dated by hand: March 17, 1861.

NvU.

CARSON COUNTY, UTAH TERRITORY. *Forms, blanks, etc.*

This Indenture, Made the [*rule*] day of [*rule*] | in the year of our Lord one thousand, eight hundred and sixty [*blank*] | Between [*rule*] | . . . | Mining Deed—No. 1. Printed and sold by Wm [*sic*] B. Cooke & Co., Importing and Jobbing Stationers, 158 Montgomery St., San Francisco. | [1861?]   [23]

[4] p., printed on p. [1, 4] only. 35 x 21 cm. Last line below a border of rules. Printed on blue paper.

The printed text refers to the "County of Carson, Territory of Utah." CSt has two copies, the earlier one dated by hand January 1, 1862, the later one February 18, 1862; in both copies there are handwritten changes to make the text read "Storey County" and "Nevada Territory," since Nevada became a territory on March 2, 1861.

CSt.

CARSON COUNTY, UTAH TERRITORY. *Forms, blanks, etc.*

This Indenture, Made the [*rule*] day of [*rule*] | in the year of our Lord, one thousand, eight hundred and sixty [*blank*] | Between [*rule*] | . . . | Quit-Claim Deed for Mining—No. 2. Printed and sold by Wm. B. Cooke & Co., Importing and Jobbing Stationers, 158 Montgomery Street, San Francisco. | [1861?]   [24]

[4] p., printed on p. [1-2, 4] only. 35 x 22 cm. Last line below a border of rules. Printed on blue paper.

Both "Carson County, Utah Territory" and "Territory of Utah, County of Carson" are mentioned in the printed text.

CSt has two copies, with one hand-dated May 23, 1861, the other September 30, 1861; both have appropriate handwritten alterations to reflect the change from Utah to Nevada Territory, but the name of the county has not been changed.

CSt.

CARSON COUNTY, UTAH TERRITORY. *Forms, blanks, etc.*

This Indenture, Made this [*blank*] day of [*blank*] | in the year of our Lord, One Thousand Eight Hundred and Sixty-[*blank*] | Between [*rule*] | . . . | [1861?]   [25]

[4] p., printed on p. [1, 4] only. 29? x 22 cm. The recorded copy has been cropped at the foot.

The recorded film copy is dated by hand: May 25, 1861. "County of Carson, Territory of Utah," which appears in the printed text, is crossed out and made to read "Mono County, California."

CU-B (microfilm).

CARSON COUNTY, UTAH TERRITORY. *Forms, blanks, etc.*

This Indenture, Made this [*blank*] day of [*blank*] | in the year of our Lord one thousand, eight hundred and sixty [*blank*] | Between [*rule*] | . . . | Mining Deed—No. 1. Printed and sold by A. Fleishhacker & Co., Carson City and Virginia City | [1861?]   [26]

[4] p., printed on p. [1-2, 4] only. 35 x 22 cm. Last line below a border of rules. Printed on blue paper. On p. [2], a recorder's form, the following appears in type: "Territory of Utah, County of Carson." There is no other evidence that Fleishhacker was involved in the printing trade.

Both copies at NvU are dated by hand: March 25, 1861. The CSt copy is hand-dated April 23, 1861.

CSt. NvU.

CARSON COUNTY, UTAH TERRITORY. *Forms, blanks, etc.*

This Indenture, Made this [*blank*] day of [*blank*] | in the year of our Lord one thousand, eight hundred and sixty [*blank*] | Between [*rule*] | . . . | Mining Deed—No. 1. Printed and sold by Lewis & McElwain, "Silver Age" Office, Carson City, Utah Territory. | [1861.]   [27]

[4] p., printed on p. [1-2, 4] only. 31 x 20 cm. Thick-thin rule border.

The recorded film copy mentions "Esmeralda Mining District," then thought to be in California, in the printed text; "Mono County, California" is filled in by hand. The date, September 30, 1861, is also filled in by hand. E. F. McElwain was a partner on the *Silver Age* in 1861 only.

CU-B (microfilm).

CARSON COUNTY, UTAH TERRITORY. *Forms, blanks, etc.*

This Indenture, Made this [*blank*] day of [*blank*] in | the year of our Lord one thousand, eight hundred and sixty [*blank*] | Between [*rule*] | . . . | Mining Deed—No. 1. Printed and sold by Wm. B. Cooke, Importing and Jobbing Stationers, 158 Montgomery Block, San Francisco. | [1861?]   [28]

[4] p., printed on p. [1, 4] only. 35 x 22 cm. Last line below a border of rules.

"County of Carson, Territory of Utah" is mentioned in the printed text. The recorded copy is dated January 28, 1862, by hand, but would have been printed earlier because of Nevada's admission as a territory on March 2, 1861. Samuel L. Clemens was one of the parties to the transaction recorded on the located copy.

CU-B(MT).

CARSON COUNTY, UTAH TERRITORY. *Forms, blanks, etc.*

This Indenture, Made this [*blank*] day of [*blank*] | in the year of our Lord one thousand, eight hundred and sixty [*blank*] | Between [*rule*] | . . . | Mining Deed—No. 1. Printed and sold by Wm. B. Cooke & Co., Importing and Jobbing Stationers, 158 Montgomery Street, Montgomery Block, San Francisco. | [1861?]   [29]

[4] p., printed on p. [1, 4] only. 34 x 22 cm. Last line below a border of rules.

The printed text mentions the "County of Carson, in the Territory of Utah." The recorded film copy is hand-dated February 11, 1861.

CU-B (microfilm).

CARSON COUNTY, UTAH TERRITORY. *Forms, blanks, etc.*

This Indenture, Made this [*blank*] day of [*blank*] | in the year of our Lord one thousand eight hundred and sixty [*blank*] | Between [*blank*] | . . . | Mining Deed—No. 3. Printed and Sold by Carl & Flint, Montgomery Street, San Francisco. | [1861?]   [30]

[4] p., printed on p. [1, 4] only. 35 x 22 cm. Border of rules. Printed on blue paper.

The printed text mentions the "County of Carson, Territory of Utah." The recorded copy is dated by hand November 13, 1861, after Nevada became a territory;

"Utah" is crossed out and changed to "Nevada," but "County of Carson" is allowed to remain.

CU-B(MT).

EAGLE AND WASHOE VALLEY MINING DISTRICT. *Ordinances, local laws, etc.*

Laws of Eagle & Washoe Valley Mining District. | . . . | Parker H. Pierce, Recorder. | [Carson City: Silver Age? 1861.]   [31]

Broadside. 19 x 14 cm. Printed in two columns; probably reprinted from the same type as in the *Silver Age,* the only press in Eagle Valley in 1861, but appropriate issues have not been located.

The district was organized in 1859; these laws reflect changes in the original laws, made at a meeting in Carson City on November 9, 1861. The 1859 laws have not been found.

NvCR.

ESMERALDA COUNTY, NEVADA TERRITORY. *Forms, blanks, etc.*

This Indenture, Made the [*dotted rule*] day of [*dotted rule*] | in the year of our Lord one thousand eight hundred and sixty [*blank*] | Between [*dotted rule*] | . . . | [1861?]   [32]

[4] p., printed on p. [1, 4] only. 35 x 22 cm. Decorative thick-thin-thin rule border. Printed on blue paper.

"Esmerelda [*sic*] Mining District, in the County of Mono, State of California" is mentioned in the printed text; until an 1863 survey the district and part of Esmeralda County were thought to be in California.

The recorded copy is hand-dated September 30, 1861.

CBriM.

NEVADA TERRITORY. *Governor, 1861-1864 (James Warren Nye).*

First | Message | of | Gov. James W. Nye, | Submitted to the | Council and House of Representatives | of | Nevada Territory, | October 2, 1861. | [*filet*] | Lewis & Sewall, Legislative Printers, | "Silver Age" Office, Carson City, N.T. | [*short dotted rule*] | 1861.   [33]

12 p. 22 x 14 cm. Wrapper title, in double rule border. The message also appears in JC, 1861, p. 14-25, and in JHR, 1861, p. 14-24; both are from different type settings than the issue described here. Facsimile of wrapper in Wegelin (see below).

Voucher 29, Session of 1861, in RG217 notes for October 8 the printing of 2,000 copies, for which $165.12 was charged; when the bill was audited in 1864 the printers were allowed $128.

The year following the publication of *Check List* a brief article by Oscar Wegelin on this *First Message* appeared in the *Quarterly Bulletin of the New York Historical Society* ("An Early Nevada Imprint," QBNYHS, XXIV, 1940, p. 124-125). He noted its absence in *Check List* and speculated that it "may be the earliest specimen of typog-

raphy, excepting the newspaper, that came from a press in Carson City'' (but see Nos. 4, 7, 12, 16, 17, etc.). One of the two NHi copies mentioned by Wegelin is uncut and unopened and measures 25.7 x 16.1 cm., while the untrimmed page size is 23.2 cm. high and ranges from 14.3 to 15.7 cm. wide; in the middle the width is 15.2 cm. See Armstrong, ''Early Printing in Carson City, Nevada: The Record Corrected,'' *Nevada Historical Society Quarterly*, XXI (1978), p. 152-156.
CU-B. CtY. DLC. DNA. NHi. NjP. NvU (microfilm).

NEVADA TERRITORY. *Governor, 1861-1864 (James Warren Nye).*

United States of America. | [*short thick-thin rule*] | Territory [*cut of eagle*] of Nevada. | [*short thick-thin rule*] | To All To Whom These Presents Shall Come Greeting: | Know Ye, That, reposing special confidence in the capacity, integrity, fidelity and patriotism | of [*broken rule*] a Citizen of [*rule*] | I, James W. Nye, Governor, and Ex-Officio Commander=in=Chief of the Territory of Nevada, by the authority in | me vested, do, by these presents Appoint and Commission him, the said [*rule*] | . . . | [Lewis & Sewall, Legislative Printers, ''Silver Age'' Office, Carson City, N.T. 1861.] [34]

Broadside. 35 x 43 cm. Partly script type. Handwritten on the verso of the recorded copy: ''No. 1. Military Commissions.''

The recorded copy, which has not been filled in, is in a packet at DNA with other documents from 1861. Voucher 28, Session of 1861, in RG217 notes that 50 copies were billed by Lewis & Sewall on September 4, for which a charge of $10 was made. When audited in 1864 the charge was allowed to stand.
DNA. NvU (microfilm).

NEVADA TERRITORY. *Governor, 1861-1864 (James Warren Nye).*

United States of America. | [*short thick-thin rule*] | Territory [*cut of eagle*] of Nevada. | [*short thick-thin rule*] | To All To Whom These Presents Shall Come, Greeting: | Know Ye, That, reposing special trust and confidence in the integrity and ability | of [*broken rule*] a Citizen of [*broken rule*] | I, James W. Nye, Governor of the Territory of Nevada have nominated, and in behalf of the People of said | Territory do Commission him [*rule*] | . . . | [Lewis & Sewall, Legislative Printers, ''Silver Age'' Office, Carson City, N.T.? 1861?] [35]

Broadside. 35 x 43 cm. Partly script type.

Although this form does not appear on an 1861 voucher in RG217, it may probably be assumed that it was printed at about the same time as No. 34, and by the same printer, because of the typefaces used and because it is in the same packet at DNA with other dated 1861 documents.
DNA. NvU (microfilm).

NEVADA TERRITORY. *Legislative Assembly. House of Representatives.*

[Legislative bills. First session, 1861. Lewis & Sewall, Legislative

Printers, "Silver Age" Office, Carson City, N.T. 1861.] The bills recorded here were among the documents sent to the First Comptroller of the U.S. Treasury, Elisha Whittlesey, by Territorial Secretary Orion Clemens so that the federal government could be assured that it was not being done in by the locals. The government's auditor, when he got to them in 1864, apparently saw a good deal of creative bookkeeping on the part of Lewis & Sewall, because in every instance he reduced the amount the printers were to be allowed, usually by a sizable figure. His computations appear on many of the recorded copies, all at DNA, but they do not always agree with the amounts allowed on Vouchers 29 and 30, Session of 1861, in RG217 (see, for instance, No. 39). Nor are the allowable charges always consistent with the strictures in Whittlesey's 1855 circular (see Appendix A), which inveighed against the practice of charging for more pages than were printed. Other numbers that I originally thought referred to entry numbers on the vouchers also appear on most of the bills, but they are apparently a kind of arcane shorthand of the auditor's. I shall leave it to a student of the federal bureaucracy to sort out these apparent inconsistencies.

During the early part of the session, when the first bills were introduced, the House had not yet decided how many of each were to be printed. Beginning with bill No. 4, fifty copies was the "usual number." Charges for bills 1-5 are on Voucher 29; the remainder are on Voucher 30. The government allowed $1.50 per thousand ems and $1.50 per token, but allowed paper charges to vary because of local conditions.

In a letter dated December 24, 1861, now in RG217, Clemens indicated to Whittlesey that, in an effort to save the inadequate printing fund, only one Council bill had been printed; apparently no copy of it has survived.

No. 1. To provide for the formation of corporations for certain purposes. October 10, 1861. 11 p. 29 x 23 cm. One of two copies at DNA has penciled corrections throughout; there are also two small sheets pasted at separate spots, with handwritten changes on them. A note in pen appears on the verso of p. 11: "House of Rep. Oct. 15th 1861. Considered on Com Whole & amended as within." The other copy incorporates some, but not all, of these changes. The "P" in "Provide" is upper case in this variant; line endings are slightly different. There are penned notes throughout: "Altered in 'House Bill A.'" House bill B is also derived from this bill. See Nos. 37, 38. The printers billed the government for $86.23 on October 11. House bills A and B and corrections on this bill are not listed separately on the voucher, so it seems at least possible that Lewis & Sewall consolidated all of their changes under one heading. Nonetheless, the government auditor reduced the charges to $39.58. DNA. NvU (microfilm).   [36]

No. A. To provide for the formation of corporations for certain purposes. 12 p. 29 x

23 cm. Although this bill and No. B are chronologically later than No. 1, No. A seems to have been used to make the initial computations regarding the number of ems per page. There were 65 lines of 36 ems apiece, or 2,340 ems per page; at 12 pages, the total was 28,080 ems. On the recorded copy there are handwritten notes on p. [1] and p. 10-12: "Altered from 'No.1.' " See Nos. 36 and 38. DNA. NvU (microfilm). [37]

No. B. To provide for the formation of corporations for certain purposes. 11 p. 29 x 23 cm. A handwritten note appears on p. [1] and on p. 10-11 of the recorded copy: "Altered from 'No. 1' & 'House Bill A.' " When the Council considered the version of the bill passed by the House on October 31, it ordered 200 copies, with amendments, for its own use (JC, 1861, p. 107); because the Council, like the House, seldom referred to bills by number, however, it is impossible to determine whether that order was carried out and, if it was, whether this was the result. See Nos. 36, 37. DNA. NvU (microfilm). [38]

No. 3 [sic]. For securing liens to mechanics and others. October 11, 1861. 7 p. 29 x 23 cm. This bill was probably intended to be No. 2, as it is dated earlier than the other bill with the same number (see No. 40). It is not referred to by number in the printed journal, possibly because of the confusion in numbering that may have come about because of the several printings of Nos. 1, A, and B. On p. [1] of the recorded copy, by hand: "Abstract C, Voucher No. 30." Charges for the bill, dated October 13, actually appear on Voucher 29. The confusion continues. The printers asked $58.10, which on the audited voucher was reduced to $30.31. But the auditor's figures on the recorded copy show 8 pages of 2,340 ems, or 18,720 ems; at $1.50 per thousand the charge was $28.08. For 4 tokens of press work the charge was $6; for 4 quires of paper, $3; and for folding, $2.50; for a total of $39.58. It should also be noted that while only 7 pages were printed, 8 pages were allowed, a seeming violation of the government's own strictures. DNA. NvU (microfilm). [39]

No. 3. For the better observance of the Lord's day. October 14, 1861. [2] p. 29 x 23 cm. As computed by the government auditor, the charge for composing 2 pages of 2,340 ems apiece, at $1.50 per thousand, was $7.02; 1 token of press work was $1.50; and 2 quires of paper were $1.50; for a total of $10.02. The voucher, however, shows that the printers on October 15 charged $18.78 and that only $5.76 was allowed. DNA. NvU (microfilm). [40]

No. 4. Relating to elections, and the mode of supplying vacancies. October 15, 1861. 17 p. 29 x 23 cm. 18 pages of 2,340 ems each, at $1.50 per thousand, were $63.18; 9 tokens of press work were $13.50; 10 quires of paper were $7.50; and folding was $5; for a total of $89.18, the figure that appears on the voucher. On October 16, however, Lewis & Sewall had charged $136.25. DNA. NvU (microfilm). [41]

No. 5. For the government and protection of Indians. October 17, 1861. [2] p. 29 x 23 cm. Handwritten on p. [1] of the recorded copy: "Specimens of Printing, Nevada Territory." The printers on October 16 charged $18.77 for printing the bill; the government allowed them $5.76. DNA. NvU (microfilm). [42]

No. 6. Creating the Board of County Commissioners, and defining their duties. October 16, 1861. 7 p. 29 x 23 cm. Lewis & Sewall asked on October 17 for $58.10, but the government allowed only $39.58: 8 pages of composition,

$28.08; 4 tokens of press work, $6; 4 quires of paper, $3; and folding, $2.50. DNA. NvU (microfilm). [43]

No. 7. To exempt the Homestead and other property from forced sale in certain cases. October 17, 1861. 4 p. 29 x 23 cm. Penciled corrections throughout on the recorded copy. The government allowed $19.04: 4 pages of composition, $14.05; 2 tokens of press work, $3; 2 quires of paper, $1.50; and folding, 50¢. On October 17 the printers had asked $28.05. DNA. NvU (microfilm). [44]

No. 8. Relating to the support of the poor. October 19, 1861. 5 p. 29 x 23 cm. Handwritten on p. [1] of the recorded copy: "Abstract C, Voucher 29." Charges and audited corrections actually appear on Voucher 30. Lewis & Sewall charged $50.60 on October 19, but this amount was reduced by the government auditor to $30.31: 6 pages of composition, $21; 3 tokens of press work, $4.50; 3 quires of paper, $2.25; and folding, $2.50. DNA. NvU (microfilm). [45]

No. 9. To provide for the establishment of a hospital for the indigent sick and insane in the Territory of Nevada. October 19, 1861. 6 p. 29 x 23 cm. As with No. 45, the printers' charges of $50.60 were reduced to $30.31. DNA. NvU (microfilm). [46]

No. 10. In relation to the books of the Recorder of Carson County, Utah Territory. October 19, 1861. Broadside. 30 x 23 cm. On October 19 the printers asked for $18.78 for printing the bill. The audited voucher shows that $10.02 was allowed, but the computations on the recorded copy of the bill are $3.51 for composition, $1.50 for press work, and 75¢ for paper, for a total of $5.76. DNA. NvU (microfilm). [47]

No. 11. To create a Board of Examiners, and to define their powers and duties. October 24, 1861. 5 p. 29 x 23 cm. Lewis & Sewall asked for $46.80 on November 8, but the government allowed only $21.06 for 6 pages of composition, $4.50 for 3 tokens of press work, $2.25 for 3 quires of paper, and $2.50 for folding, for a total of $30.31. DNA. NvU (microfilm). [48]

No. 12. To create counties, and establishing the boundaries thereof. October 30, 1861. 4 p. 29 x 23 cm. The printers asked on November 8 for $25.90, but the government auditor allowed only $19.04. DNA. NvU (microfilm). [49]

No. 13. In relation to common jails, and the prisoners thereof. November 2, 1861. 4 p. 30 x 23 cm. Lewis & Sewall charged the same amount, and received the same reduction, as for No. 49. DNA. NvU (microfilm). [50]

NEVADA TERRITORY. *Legislative Assembly. House of Representatives.*

Rules | and | Orders | of the | House of Representatives | of | Nevada Territory, | Adopted October 3, 1861. | [*filet*] | Lewis & Sewall, Legislative Printers, | "Silver Age" Office, Carson City, N.T. | [*short dotted rule*] | 1861. [51]

11 p. 22 x 15 cm. Wrapper title, in double rule border.

Lewis & Sewall's bill, dated October 9, was for $48.62 for printing 250 copies, but the auditor's notes on the rear wrapper of the recorded copy and the voucher that was audited in 1864 show that only $44.50 was allowed: $30 for composition, $4.50 for press work, $7.50 for paper, and $2.50 for folding (Voucher 29, Session of 1861,

in RG217).
DNA. NvU (microfilm).

NEVADA TERRITORY. *Legislative Assembly. House of Representatives. Committee on Incorporations.* Report on corporation bill. Lewis & Sewall, Legislative Printers, "Silver Age" Office, Carson City, N.T. 1861. [L52]

The Committee reported to the House on October 10 its recommendation that the bill, as amended by the Committee, should be passed (JHR, 1861, p. 51), but there is no order to print the report. Perhaps because of legislative inexperience with printing, however, it may have been assumed that it should be printed. Lewis & Sewall billed the government $23 for 200 copies on the same date (Voucher 29, Session of 1861, in RG217), but when the voucher was audited in 1864 only $20 was allowed—even though Secretary Clemens had "not sent" a copy to be examined by the Treasury Department.

NEVADA TERRITORY. *Secretary.*

General Instructions. | [*short rule*] | Secretary's Office, | Carson City, Nevada Territory, | October 10th, 1861. | To the Hon. House of Representatives: | . . . | [Lewis & Sewall, Legislative Printers, "Silver Age" Office, Carson City, N.T. 1861.] [53]

3 p. 22 x 15 cm. Caption title. Lines 3-4 connected by brace.

Lewis & Sewall printed 250 copies on October 12, for which a charge of $17 was made; when audited in 1864, however, the bill was reduced to $12.50 (Voucher 29, Session of 1861, in RG217). The latter figure is handwritten on p. [1] of the recorded copy.

Page [1]: "In response to your resolution, I proceed to give a brief summary of my instructions from the Treasury Department." The instructions largely concern such matters as per diem, travel, and the like, but the following appears on p. 2. "*Public Printing.*—The Treasury Department claims and exercises the right to regulate the price and quantity of the Territorial Printing. The Comptroller says: 'the limits of the annual appropriation, aside from any other consideration, would not admit of indefinite action in this respect, by the Assembly. You will therefore suggest to the presiding officer of each House, that memorials, petitions, and documents having no necessary connection with the duties of legislation, or the dissemination of useful information among the people, will be excluded, and not printed at the expense of the United States." And on p. 3: " 'The number of copies of the Journal of either House should not exceed, at any session, more than two hundred and fifty, as this number will be amply sufficient for all purposes. The laws should be limited to fifteen hundred copies for the first session, and one thousand after that.' It will be the personal duty of the Secretary of the Territory, if the labor of his office will possibly permit of it, to make the necessary indices to these documents, and to superintend their printing."
DNA. NvU (microfilm).

PALMER & DAY, *Assayers. Gold Hill, Nevada Territory.*

Chas. T. H. Palmer. Roger Sherman Day. | Palmer & Day, | [*or-*

nament] | Assayers | of | Gold, Silver | and | Ores, | Gold Hill, N.T. | [*filet*] | . . . | Gold Hill, N.T., Sept. 1st, 1861. | Towne & Bacon, Printers, San Francisco.   [54]

Broadside. 33? x 26? cm. The recorded copy is framed. Line 2 in an arch over the ornament and line 3. The imprint is below a decorative rule border. Printed in gold ink.
CSfWF-H.

STEAMBOAT SPRINGS, NEVADA TERRITORY. *Grand Opening Ball.*

A Grand | Opening Ball | Will be Given at | Cameron's Steamboat Springs Hotel, | On Thursday Evening, July 18th, 1861. | [*filet*] | M[*broken rule*] | The pleasure of your com=|pany is respectful-ly solicited. | [*filet*] | . . .   [55]

[4] p., printed on p. [1] only. 16 x 10 cm. Partly script type. Embossed edges.

The list of managers includes men from Virginia City, Silver City, Washoe Valley, Pleasant Valley, Gold Hill, Carson City, Galena Hill, and Truckee Meadows. The invitation was probably printed by the *Territorial Enterprise* in Virginia City or by the *Silver Age* in Carson City. The Silver City *Washoe Times,* the only other press in the Territory at the time, is also a possibility, but seems unlikely because of geographical factors.
Pvt.

UNITED STATES. *36th Congress, 1st Session.* An act to organize the Territory of Nevada. [Lewis & Sewall, Legislative Printers, "Silver Age" Office, Carson City, N.T. 1861.]   [L56]

Bills for the formation of a Territory of Nevada were introduced by California's two Senators shortly after the Confederate States of America was organized in early February of 1861. Two and a half weeks later the Senate passed a bill that had been written by Missouri's Senator James S. Green. On the day that a companion bill passed the House of Representatives, March 2, President James Buchanan signed it, thus bringing into the Union fold another anti-slavery territory. Perhaps because of the speed with which the Organic Act was written and considered it is less than clear concerning boundaries, a confusion that resulted in disputes with California throughout Nevada's territorial period. Lewis & Sewall's bill for 250 "Organick Acts," dated October 8, was $28; when the voucher was audited in 1864, the amount was reduced to $25 (Voucher 29, Session of 1861, in RG217).

UTAH TERRITORY. *District Court. Second Judicial District (Carson County).*

Territory of Utah, | County of Carson. | I, Alfred James, Clerk of the Distirct [*sic*] Court | of the United States, in and for the 2nd Judicial District, in said Territory . . . | . . . | Witness my hand and seal of said Court, this [*dotted rule*] | day of [*dotted rule*] A.D. 186[*blank*]. | . . . | [1861?]   [57]

Broadside. 10 x 20 cm. Lines 1-2 connected by brace. Mostly italic type.

The court was organized in September 1859 and continued until February 1861. The recorded copy, dated by hand September 7, 1861, has been altered to read Nevada Territory.

Nv-Ar.

UTAH TERRITORY. *Forms, blanks, etc.*

This Indenture, Made the [*blank*] day of [*blank*] | In the year of our Lord, one thousand eight hundred and sixty [*blank*] | Between [*rule*] | . . . | "Territorial Enterprise" Print, A St., Virginia City, U.T. | [1861?]   [58]

[4] p., printed on p. [1, 4] only. 35 x 22 cm. Imprint below a border of rules. Printed on blue paper.

The recorded copy is dated, by hand, February 16, 1861.

NvU.

UTAH TERRITORY. *Forms, blanks, etc.*

This Indenture, Made this [*blank*] day of [*blank*] | in the year of our Lord, one thousand, eight hundred and sixty [*blank*] | Between [*rule*] | . . . | S. Wasserman & Co. | Depot for | Cigars, Tobacco and Stationery, | B Street, Virginia, U.T. | [1861?]   [59]

[4] p., printed on p. [1-2, 4] only. Last 4 lines from p. [4]. Printed on blue paper.

"Territory of Utah" is mentioned in the printed text of the recorded copy, which is hand-dated September 27, 1862, more than a year and a half after Nevada became a territory.

NvU.

❧1862❧

Although the federal government exercised strict control of public printing in the territories, the new legislature of Nevada Territory apparently neither understood nor fully respected that power. The Council, or upper house, decided during the first week of its first session to make its own printing arrangements, and later on even adopted a resolution requiring that its proceedings "be printed as ordered by the Secretary of the Council, regardless of any dictation whatever from any other party or parties" (JC, 1861, p. 115). The House of Representatives, too, objected to control from the Treasury Department, but the joint committee of the two houses that was appointed to settle the matter could not agree on the proper action and finally proposed that the matter be turned over to Secretary Orion Clemens—a mandate that had been his, as Washington's local factor, from the beginning. Late in the session, however, the Legislative Assembly was able to agree that the Secretary should be "authorized and required" to contract with one or more California printers for the printing of the laws and journals (LTN, 1861, p. 294). Clemens could not, in fact, be "required" to follow legislative orders in this regard, but the lack of local printers who were either willing or able to take on the job forced him to do so anyway (but see No. 67). It should be noted, though, that in sending the Territory's printing out of Nevada the Secretary was violating the federal requirement that "Public Printing must be executed in the Territory" (RG217: First Comptroller to Clemens, November 25, 1862). The dilemma thus forced upon the harried Secretary by Washington may have resulted in the ruse adopted by later territorial and state printers, that of having their own names printed on title pages or wrappers while actually sending the printing to be done in California.

The situation was obviously less than amusing for Clemens, but his younger brother was able to see it from a different perspective in 1872.

> The matter of printing was from the beginning an interesting feature of the new government's difficulties. The Secretary was sworn to obey his volume of written "instructions," and these commanded him to do two certain things without fail, viz.:
>
> 1. Get the House and Senate journals printed; and,
> 2. For this work, pay one dollar and fifty cents per "thousand" for composition, and one dollar and fifty cents per "token" for presswork, in greenbacks.
>
> It was easy to swear to do these two things, but it was entirely impossible to do more than one of them. When greenbacks had gone down to forty cents on the dollar, the prices regularly charged everybody by printing establishments were one dollar and fifty cents per "thousand" and one dollar and fifty cents per "token," in *gold*. The "instructions" commanded that the Secretary regard a paper dollar issued by the government as equal to any other dollar issued by the government. Hence the printing of the journals was discontinued. Then the United States sternly rebuked the Secretary for disregarding the "instructions," and warned him to correct his ways. Wherefore he got some printing done, forwarded the bill to Washington with full exhibits of the high prices of things in the Territory, and called attention to a printed market report wherein it would be observed that even hay was two hundred and fifty dollars a ton. The United States responded by subtracting the printing-bill from the Secretary's suffering

salary—and moreover remarked with dense gravity that he would find nothing in his "instructions" requiring him to purchase hay!

This simplified narrative from Mark Twain's *Roughing It* (p. 188-189) generally agrees with the Secretary's accounts and correspondence at DNA and Nv-Ar. For a fuller discussion of the printing in 1862 of the laws and journals of the first session, see Armstrong, "The Only Alternative Course: An Incident in Nevada Printing History," *Nevada Historical Society Quarterly*, XV (1972), p. 31-39.

Secretary Clemens was not allowed to rest for long between his problems with the first session and preparations for the Legislative Assembly's second meeting in November, for which a new Territorial Printer had to be found. This time he was able to convince the proprietors of the *Territorial Enterprise,* Joseph T. Goodman and Denis E. McCarthy, to take on the public printing, an arrangement that lasted only through the second session. But it could be equally as true that it was Clemens who was persuaded by filial considerations, for earlier in the year his brother Samuel had begun his journalistic career as a reporter for the *Enterprise;* he was, in fact, that paper's legislative correspondent during the session. In a letter that appears in the manuscript journals of the Council (p. 67), the *Enterprise* proprietors offered to execute legislative printing at $1.50 per thousand ems, $2 per token, and $20 per ream of paper; these figures may have been fairly typical for the area, but no evidence has survived to show that the Secretary queried other local printers to discover what they might charge. Nor is there evidence to show that the incidental printing for the second session was executed in Carson City, where imprints on the larger pieces indicate they were done. Because there was no press in Carson City during the session, the *Silver Age* having sold its plant to the Virginia City *Union,* the chances are good that the printing was done at the *Enterprise* job office in Virginia City. Other presses in the Territory during the year were at Aurora and Washoe City.

CAPTAIN JIM, *Chief of the Washoes.*

Annual Message of Captain Jim, | Chief of the Washoes, and Governor (de facto) of Nevada, | Delivered Before the Third House of the Territorial Legislature, Friday, November | Fourteenth, One Thousand Eight Hundred and Sixty-Two. | [*double rule*] | On motion of Mr. S. Myth, of King's Canon, Five Hundred Thousand Million Copies of the Message were ordered to be | printed and circulated throughout the fertile Realm of Sage Brush and Sand, for the

better Enlightenment of the Benighted, Deluded | and Hetero-
geneous Inhabitants thereof. | To the Officers and Members of the
Third House of the Terri- | torial Legislature of Nevada: | . . .
| [*rule*] | Barney Woolf, Printer to the Third House, Carson
City.   [60]

Broadside. 61 x 23 cm. Lines 1-7 extend across the sheet; lines 8-9 are in the first of two
columns; the imprint is at the foot of column 2. The text is reprinted in Angel, p.
82-84, and in Claude M. Simpson, Jr., ''Captain Jim and the Third House,'' *Western
Folklore,* IX (1950), p. 101-110. In a report on the legislative session written on
November 15, Andrew J. Marsh wrote that he had ''been favored with a copy,'' and
quoted briefly from it (Sacramento *Union,* November 18, 1862). Facsimile following
p. 314.

The Third House, in early California and later in Nevada and other Western territories, was a good-natured gathering of newspapermen, legislative attachés, and
occasionally some of the legislators themselves, that was designed to poke fun at the
seriousness of the session and generally to lighten the atmosphere at the capitol. In a
somewhat altered form the tradition continues in Nevada today. The first known
Nevada example of the genre occurred during the second session of the territorial
Legislative Assembly, when the address described here was delivered. Its humor is
heavy-handed and at times rather dense, but it shows nonetheless the practiced
journalistic hand of one—or perhaps more—of the newspapermen covering the
session.

Simpson dismissed Captain Jim, who was in fact a Washo chief, as the author. He
speculated that it may have been written by J. Ross Browne (but Browne was just
then preparing to return to the United States after two years in Europe); by Dan De
Quille, the doyen of the *Territorial Enterprise* staff; or most likely by Clement T.
Rice, whom Mark Twain had dubbed ''The Unreliable.'' Twain himself was not
considered by Simpson to be a serious possibility as the author because ''the familiar
Mark Twain touch is missing here, and in its place is a more labored, less spontane-
ous play of grotesquerie, hyperbole, and local allusion.'' The argument is not convincing on that basis alone since Twain had only a short time before begun his
newspaper career and had not yet developed the sureness that characterized his later
writing. What seems more likely, however, is that the message was a pastiche,
perhaps drafted by a single writer but brought to its final state by a number of
people, probably including Twain and his ''Unreliable'' colleague.

The joke appears to have extended even into the imprint. Although Collins's 1864-
1865 directory (No. 182) lists a D. B. Woolf as ''prop'r 'Old Piute' Office'' (p. 215)
in Virginia City, thereby giving him at least a loose connection with the trade,
Kelly's 1862 and 1863 directories (Nos. 62 and 156) list him as, respectively, a clerk
with G. T. Davis, who sold groceries and dry goods (p. 91), and as owner of a cigar
and tobacco shop (p. 117). Both earlier occupations were in Carson City and the first
places him there—if, in fact, D. B. and Barney Woolf were the same person—at the
time of the second legislative session. But there is no evidence to show that he had at
the time any experience with the press. Since the *Silver Age* had ceased operations in
Carson City earlier in the month and the material went immediately to the Virginia
City *Union,* it is likely that the broadside was not even printed in Carson City, much
less by Barney Woolf. Yet there is a tantalizing entry in Orion Clemens's accounts at
DNA, showing that a draft for $231 was drawn on December 27, 1862, in favor of

D. B. Woolf (RG217: Clemens to Assistant Treasurer, San Francisco)—and one doubts the legislators' ability, in a forty-day session, to smoke that many cigars. MH. NvHi. (negative photostat).

GENOA, NEVADA TERRITORY. *Grand Anniversary Ball.*

Grand Anniversary Ball. | [*cut of Revolutionary soldier with flag and upraised sword*] | M[*blank*] and Lady: | The pleasure of your Company is respectfully solicited at a | Ball to be given at the Union Hall, Genoa, N.T., on the Fourth | day of July, 1862. | [*filet*] | . . . | Music by a Full Quadrille Band. | Dancing to commence at eight o'clock, precisely.   [61]

[4] p., printed on p. [1] only. 21 x 13 cm. Line 1 in an arch over cut. Printed in red and blue inks. Decorative rule border.

There was no press in Genoa in 1862. The closest press, in Carson City, was the *Silver Age* job office. Eberstadt 121:244 gives San Francisco as the printing site; Greenwood:1650 cites Eberstadt.

CtY. NvU (microfilm).

KELLY, JAMES WELLS.

First Directory | of | Nevada Territory, | Containing: | The Names of Residents | in the Principal Towns; | A Historical Sketch, the Organic Act, | and Other Political Matters of Interest; | Together with a | Description of All the Quartz Mills; | Reduction Works, and All Other Industrial Estab-|lishments in the Territory; | as Also of | the Leading Mining Claims; | and Various | Mineral Discoveries, Works of Internal Improvement, etc. | With a | Table of Distances, List of Public Officers, | and Other Useful Information. | [*short rule*] | Compiled from the Most Recent and Authentic Sources, | By J. Wells Kelly. | [*short rule*] | San Francisco: | Commerical Steam Presses: Valentine & Co., | 517 Clay and 514 Commercial Streets. | [*short dotted rule*] | 1862.   [62]

xvi, [2], 266 p. 24 x 15 cm. Quarter-leather binding; printed boards. Verso of title page: "Entered according to act of Congress, in the Year of our Lord 1862, By J. Wells Kelly, In the Clerk's Office of the District Court of the First District of the Territory of Nevada." Facsimile reprint, with an introduction by Richard Lingenfelter, Los Gatos, Calif.: Talisman Press, 1962. Facsimile of title page in Greenwood, p. 457.

C. CHi. CSmH. CU-B. CtY. DLC. MB. MH. MWA. Nv. NvHi. NvU.

NEVADA TERRITORY. *Governor, 1861-1864 (James Warren Nye).*

Second | Annual Message | of | Governor James W. Nye, | to the | Legislature of Nevada Territory, | November 13, 1862. | [*short rule*] | Together with | Reports of Territorial Auditor, Treasurer, and Superintendent | of Public Instruction. | [*filet*] | Carson City: | J. T [*sic*] Goodman & Co., Territorial Printers. | 1862.

[63]

48 p. 25 x 15 cm. Wrapper title, in thick-thin rule border. Pages [1]-30: Governor's Message; p. [31]-36: Report of the Superintendent of Public Instruction; p. 36-43: Auditor's Report; p. [44]-48: Treasurer's Report. Some copies have a period after the "T" in the imprint and presumably represent a later state.

1,000 copies of the message and accompanying documents were ordered printed for the use of the Council (JC, 1862, p. 61-62); 1,000 copies ordered printed for the use of members of the House and an additional 500 for the use of the Governor (JHR, 1862, p. 33). 2,500 copies were printed and on December 19 Goodman submitted a bill for 58,800 ems of small pica, 23,310 ems of breviere, and 11,985 ems of nonpareil, for a total of 94,095 ems and $188.19; 72 tokens of press work, $144; 7 reams and 16 quires of paper, $156; $50 for covers; and $150 for folding, stitching, covering, etc.; the total bill of $688.19 was figured at the rate of $2 per thousand ems and $2 per token. The First Comptroller's office, however, allowed only 72,088 ems and 60 tokens and used the correct figure of $1.50 for both computations, thus reducing the bill by $134.07. Secretary Clemens paid $500 to Goodman for this and other work on May 21, 1863 (RG217: Abstract C, Voucher 14, Session of 1862).

C. CU. DLC (incomplete). ICN (lacks wrapper). NN. NvU (microfilm).

NEVADA TERRITORY. *Governor, 1861-1864 (James Warren Nye).*

United States of America. | [*thick-thin rule*] | Territory of Nevada. | [*thick-thin rule*] | To All To Whom These Presents Shall Come Greeting: | Know Ye, That reposing special trust and confidence in the integrity and | ability of [*broken rule*] I, James W. Nye, Governor | of the Territory of Nevada, in the name and by the authority of the people thereof, do hereby | appoint him, the said [*broken rule*] | [*broken rule*] | under the laws of this Territory, . . . | . . . | . . . Done at Carson City | this [*broken rule*] day of [*broken rule*] in the year of our | Lord, one thousand eight hundred and sixty [*blank*] | [Carson City? 1862?]

[64]

Broadside. 36 x 29 cm. Printed on grey paper.

A catch-all form for appointments. The appointment in this case was made on December 22, 1862, and was signed by Governor Nye and Orion Clemens, Territorial Secretary.

NvU(NvMus).

NEVADA TERRITORY. *Governor, 1861-1864 (James Warren Nye).*

United States of America. | [*short thick-thin rule*] | Territory [*cut of eagle*] of Nevada. | [*short thick-thin rule*] | To All To Whom These Presents Shall Come Greeting: | Know Ye, That reposing special trust and confidence in the capacity, integrity, | fidelity and patriotism of [*rule*]a citizen of | [*rule*] I, James W. Nye, Governor and | Commander in Chief of the Military of the Territory of Nevada, by the authority in me | vested, do, by these presents, Appoint and Commission him, the said [*rule*] | . . . | [Carson City? 1862?]   [65]

Broadside. 37 x 29 cm.

The recorded copy, the appointment of H[enry] P[ierrepont] Russell as Adjutant General, is hand-dated January 7, 1862; the early date in the year suggests the possibility that the form was printed in 1861.

CSmH.

NEVADA TERRITORY. *Laws, statutes, etc.*

Laws | of the | Territory of Nevada, | Passed at the | First Regular Session | of the | Legislative Assembly, | Begun | the First Day of October and Ended on the Twenty-ninth Day | of November, 1861, at Carson City. | [*short rule*] | Printed under the Supervision of | Wm. Martin Gillespie. | [*short rule*] | San Francisco: | Valentine & Co.: Commercial Steam Printing Establishment, | Nos. 517 Clay and 514 Commercial Streets. | 1862.   [66]

xviii, [2], 608 p. 24 x 16 cm. 100 copies in half-leather; 200 in full leather (RG217: Valentine's bill, March 1, 1862). The make-ready was inadequate in setting up the title page, causing the "W" in line 11 to disappear in some copies.

Although he was not authorized to send any of the public printing out of Nevada Territory, Secretary Clemens found it necessary to do so because of circumstances he could not control. The *Washoe Times* could not print the laws because of inadequate equipment, the *Territorial Enterprise* would not print them because of inadequate compensation, and the *Silver Age* refused to give the bond of $20,000 required by the Legislative Assembly. Since there were no other presses in the Territory the Secretary wrote on November 19, 1861, to three San Francisco printing houses to determine their ability and willingness to do the job under territorial and federal conditions (Nv-Ar: Letterbook). Clemens's incoming correspondence has not survived, nor have the records of two of the firms to which he wrote, but on December 16, James Towne of Towne & Bacon wrote to the Secretary expressing an interest and implying strongly that there had been other communications between the two (CSt: Towne & Bacon Letterbook, I, p.140). By then, however, Clemens had already concluded an agreement with William Martin Gillespie, who had been Clerk of the House of Representatives during the first session, that authorized Gillespie to go to California and, on the basis of responses to the "Inquiries Relative to Printing in the Territory of Nevada," select the printer that could provide the most for the least. For whatever reasons, Valentine got the job.

Valentine presented a bill for $2,557.55, which included $1,374.35 for 531 2/3 pages of small pica and nonpareil, 2,068 ems per page, 1,099,486 ems at $1.25 per thousand; $20.70 for 6 pages of brevier plain, 2,760 ems per page, 16,560 ems at $1.25 per thousand; $2.30 for 1/3 page of brevier, 921 ems at $2.50 per thousand; $386.10 for 88 pages of minion plain, 3,510 ems per page, 308,880 ems at $1.25 per thousand; $17.55 for 2 pages of minion, 3,510 ems per page, 7,020 ems at $2.50 per thousand; $17.55 for 4 pages of minion reset because of an error, 3,510 ems per page,

14,040 ems at $1.25 per thousand; $158 for 158 tokens of press work, 86 forms, at $1 per token; $156 for 13 reams of paper at $12; $125 for 100 copies half-bound at $1.25; and $300 for 200 copies full-bound at $1.50 (RG217: Valentine's bill, March 1, 1862). The Secretary paid two-thirds of the bill from federal funds available to him on May 5 and June 2, 1862; after auditing in Washington the remainder was allowed and was paid on May 20, 1863. There were other expenses as well: $1.50 to Gillespie for a "leather carpet bag" in which to carry the manuscript laws to San Francisco on December 11; $9.75 to Wells, Fargo on January 2, for expressage; $100 to Gillespie for his services on March 5 (later withdrawn); and $104.67 to S. T. Gage on March 7 for freight on the finished laws (RG217: Clemens's accounts).

The United States did not get its money's worth. There is a letter tipped into one of NvU's copies in which the University Librarian, J. D. Layman, noted on June 5, 1912, that both copies in the library were lacking eight gatherings and asked the Secretary of State whether he could replace them. The Secretary, George Brodigan, replied two days later that "the copies of the Laws of the Territory of Nevada all seem to have been printed with several forms left out. The ones you have are just as good as any that we have. Have looked over several and have found the same mistakes so think you had better keep the ones you now have." The problem was caused by the binder, who made the cases too small. When the volumes were put together a sufficient number of gatherings was put into each case, seemingly at random, to make a comfortable fit. NvU has attempted to gather together as many copies as possible for purposes of comparison; of those now there, no two appear to have been bound with the same sections missing. On those few copies that are complete, including one at NvU, the hinges are invariably split because of the extra pressure of the sheets. No copy with the half-leather binding has been located.

For further discussion of the printing of the laws, see Armstrong, "The Only Alternative Course," *Nevada Historical Society Quarterly*, XV, (1972), p. 31-39.

Az. C. CHi. CLU. CSfCP. CSmH. CU. CU-B. CtY. CtY-L. DLC. ICU. IU. M. MBS. MH-L. MWA. NN. Nv. NvC. NvEHi. NvGM. NvHi. NvLC. NvLN. NvRW. NvRWL. NvSC. NvU. NvVSR. NvYLR. OrU-L. ViU. WHi.

NEVADA TERRITORY. *Legislative Assembly.*

Journal | of the | House of Representatives | of the | First Legislative Assembly | of the | Territory of Nevada, | Begun on the | First Day of October and Ended on the Twenty-Ninth Day of November, | 1861, at Carson City. | [*short rule*] | Printed by Authority, | Under the Supervision of | Wm. Martin Gillespie. | [*short rule*] | San Francisco: | Valentine & Co.: Commercial Steam Printing Establishment, | Nos. 517 Clay and 514 Commercial Streets. | 1862.

[67]

295 p. 22 x 15 cm. Half-leather binding. The Council journal is followed in the same volume, as issued, by:

Journal | of the | House of Representatives | of the | First Legislative Assembly | of the | Territory of Nevada, | Begun on the | First Day of October and Ended on the Twenty-Ninth Day of November | 1861, at Carson City. | [*short rule*] | Printed by Authority, | Under the Supervision of | Wm. Martin Gillespie. | [*short rule*] | San Francisco: | Valentine & Co.: Commercial Steam Printing Establishment, | Nos. 517 Clay and 514 Commercial Streets. | 1862.

422 p. Page 413 is misnumbered 414; p. 414 is misnumbered 314. Page [393], Appendix; p. [395]-396, Order to Take the Census; p. [397]-403, Census Report; p. [405]-422, Proclamations of the Governor (No. 1, Organizing Territorial Government; No. 2, Defining Judicial Districts and Assigning Judges; No. 3, Ordering an Election; No. 4, Ordering Term of Court in First Judicial District; No. 5, Creating Election Precinct No. 3, District No. 3; No. 6, Changing Election Poll in Precinct No. 1, District No. 2; No. 7, Anouncing [*sic*] Election of Delegate to Congress; No. 8, Announcing Result of Election). 240 copies printed (RG217: Valentine's bill, March 1, 1862).

The Journals for the second and third sessions were not published.

As with so much of Nevada's public printing, the imprints on these journals are not altogether honest; parts of both were actually printed in Carson City in 1861. Secretary Clemens apparently took seriously the admonition in Elisha Whittlesey's 1855 circular regarding printing in the territories (see Appendix A, §5th) that printing of legislative journals be undertaken on a daily basis, for he authorized Lewis & Sewall of the *Silver Age* to print sheets for the journals whenever enough copy was available. Dissolution of the partnership in mid-session, however, and the refusal of the successors to continue the job without payment each week of two-thirds of the money owing them—a demand that was impossible to meet because of the Treasury Department's governmentally slow methods of payment—made it necessary to wait until the Legislative Assembly had adjourned and to send the remaining copy to San Francisco to be printed. The freight bill for the manuscript journals was $8 for 16 pounds. Clemens had intended to retain the sheets that had already been printed and have them bound with those done by Valentine when they were sent to Carson City. On February 15, 1862, however, he wrote to William Martin Gillespie, who had been retained to superintend the printing in California, that the Carson City binder whom he had planned to employ to bind the journals in wrappers was leaving town and that it would be necessary to send the Lewis & Sewall sheets to be bound with Valentine's in San Francisco (Nv-Ar: Letterbook, p. 68). Shipping, at 50¢ per pound, was $52.50 (ibid., p. 128). When the sheets were received by Valentine it was discovered that a printer in the *Silver Age* office had set "October 8th" instead of "October 25th" on the last section printed there of the House journal. Since the last date on the Carson City sheets of the Council journal is October 8th, it may be surmised that the same compositor set them both, setting first the Council proceedings and then unthinkingly setting the same date on the outside form of those for the House. Valentine reset the entire 8-page section (ibid., p. 128, 130). Valentine matched the type well with that used by Lewis & Sewall, but minor differences in format and a larger one in choice of paper make it possible to identify p. [5]-44 of the Council journal and p. [5]-100 of the House journal as those printed in Carson City. The remainder of the volumes, including the 4-page title sections in each, was printed by Valentine.

Lewis & Sewall submitted a bill for $403 for printing 152 pages (those noted above, the section that was later reset, and probably two 4-page title sections) (RG217: First Comptroller to Clemens, August 19, 1862). This total was reduced by $21.21 for the section that required resetting and was paid to the printers in two installments (ibid., Clemens to First Auditor, April 4, 1863). Valentine's claim included $805.14 for 497 pages of small pica, 1,296 ems per page, 644,112 ems at $1.25 per thousand; $308.85 for 87 pages of minion, 2,840 ems per page, 247,080 ems at $1.25 per thousand; $112.50 for 75 tokens of press work at $1.50 per token; $100 for 10 reams of paper at $10; and $250 for half-binding 200 of the 240 copies; for a total of $1,576.49. Clemens deducted $26.51 for a 10-page overcharge and paid two-thirds of the bill on May 5 and June 2, 1862 (ibid., Valentine's bill). The bills of both printers later underwent severe bureaucratic niggling in Washington and approval of payment was temporarily suspended, but eventually the First Auditor and First Comptroller agreed that they were legitimate and should be paid in full; Valentine received the final payment on May 20, 1863 (ibid., Abstract C, Voucher 12, Session of 1862).

For further discussion of the printing of the journals, see Armstrong, "The Only Alternative Course," *Nevada Historical Society Quarterly,* XV (1972), p. 31-39.

C. CSfCP. CSmH. CU. CtY-L. DLC. ICU. M. NN. Nv. NvHi. NvU. WHi.

Nevada Territory. *Legislative Assembly. Council.* Committees and order of business. [Carson City: J. T. Goodman & Co., Territorial Printers. 1862.]   [L68]

Fifty cards were invoiced on November 29, 1862, at $12; reduced to $8 by the Treasury Department (RG217: Abstract C, Voucher 62, Session of 1862).

Nevada Territory. *Legislative Assembly. Council.*

[Concurrent resolutions. Second session, 1862. Carson City: J. T. Goodman & Co., Territorial Printers. 1862.]

No. 1. That a committee of the two houses be appointed to inform his Excellency, James W. Nye, that they have completed their organization and are now ready to receive any communication which he may be pleased to make. November 12, 1862. Goodman submitted a bill, dated November 27, for 15,990 ems, $31.98, which was disallowed in its entirety by the Treasury Department; 2 tokens of press work, $4, which was raised to $4.50; and $11 for paper, folding, and stitching, of which only $3.75 was allowed; his bill of $46.98 was thus reduced to a mere $8.25 (RG217: Abstract C, Voucher 61, Session of 1862).   [L69]

Nevada Territory. *Legislative Assembly. Council.*

[Legislative bills. Second session, 1862. Carson City: J. T. Goodman & Co., Territorial Printers. 1862.] On November 26 Secretary Clemens sent a letter to Goodman (Nv-Ar: Letterbook) in which he included an extract from his instructions from the Treasury Department: "The bills should not be printed in type of less than small pica, with a blank space of the same width between the lines. In their printing you will discourage any attempts, should they be made, at constructive composition, by means of a large open heading, and wide blanks between the lines—so that two pages are made of what should constitute but one." Information regarding printing costs is from RG217: Abstract C, Vouchers 13, 61, and 62, Session of 1862. On some of the vouchers the results of the federal audits are entered alongside the figures claimed by the printer; the First Comptroller's office usually reduced these claims, sometimes drastically (probably because of the "constructive composition" that is evident on the bills that have been examined), but on occasion would actually raise the amount. But the audits apparently did not take place until 1869, nearly five years after the Territory had ceased to exist. Clemens had already paid the bills, so the First Comptroller, R. W. Taylor, wrote to Clemens, by then living in St. Louis, dunning him for the overpayments (RG217: Taylor to Clemens, June 9, 1869). The ex-Secretary replied on October 4 (CU-B: Mark Twain Papers) that "it is rather severe to require me to refund all the profits those printers ever got." On the same date he drafted letters to the printers asking them to remit the amount of overpayment "unless you wish, through the influence of your Senators and Representatives, to attempt to get that amount or your whole bill allowed by the Comptroller, in which case I would like you to notify me as well as the Comptroller immediately." No records have been found that would suggest a resolution to the problem.

Bills numbered 2-6 have been examined at DNA. No reliable evidence has been found that would provide titles for the others. Bill registers at Nv-Ar assign numbers only by order of introduction; since not all bills were printed these numbers cannot be used. Neither is there an adequate record in the General Orders file at Nv-Ar, as there is for the House of Representatives.

No. 1. [Title unknown.] The printer submitted a claim, dated November 24, for 10,660 ems, $21.32, which was raised to $23.62; 1 token of press work, $2, raised to $4.50; and $4 for paper and folding, reduced to $3.75: Goodman's claim of $27.32 was thus actually raised to $31.87.   [L70]

No. 2. Providing for the erection of county buildings in Storey County. November 29, 1862. 4 p. 30 x 24 cm. In his claim of December 1, Goodman asked for $21.32 for 10,660 ems, reduced to $15.74; $2 for 1 token press work, raised to $3; and $4 for paper and folding, reduced to $2: $20.74 was allowed of the $27.32 claim. DNA.   [71]

No. 3. To amend an act entitled "An act to regulate proceedings in civil cases in courts of justice of the Territory of Nevada," approved Nov. 29th, 1861. November—, 1862. 4 p. 30 x 24 cm. The claim, dated December 2, was the same as for No. 71 and suffered the same reductions. DNA.   [72]

No. 4. Amendatory of an act entitled "An act defining the judicial districts, fixing the terms of the supreme and district courts of the Territory, locating the county seats of the several counties of this Territory, and providing for the transfer and trial of actions," approved November 29th, 1861. December 4, 1862. 3 p. 31 x 24 cm. The December 6 claim was for 7,995 ems, $15.99, reduced to $11.81; 1 token press work, $2, raised to $3; and $4 for paper and folding, reduced to $2: Goodman's claim was thus reduced to $16.81 from $21.99. DNA.   [73]

No. 5. To provide for the confirmation and transfer of judgments, and in relation to actions at law, now pending in the courts of California, affecting persons and property within the counties of Esmeralda, Lake, and Mono, and any other territory that may hereafter become a part of the Territory of Nevada. December 5, 1862. 3 p. 31 x 24 cm. The printer's claim, dated December 7, was exactly the same as for No. 73 and was altered in exactly the same ways. DNA.   [74]

No. 6. To frame a constitution and state government for the state of Washoe. December 8, 1862. 4 p. 31 x 24 cm. The claim, submitted on December 9, was the same as for No. 71, with the same alterations by the Treasury Department. This is the act under whose authority a constitutional convention met in Carson City in late 1863. See no. 166. DNA.   [75]

No. 7. [Title unknown.] No individual auditing is shown for this bill, although the entire voucher was reduced considerably; the claim, dated December 11, is for 10,660 ems, $21.32; 1 token press work, $2; and paper and folding, $5.44: the total claimed was $28.76. 175 copies were printed.   [L76]

No. 8. [Title unknown.] As with No. L76, no individual auditing is shown on the voucher. Goodman claimed 15,990 ems, $31.98; 2 tokens press work, $4; and $9.88 for paper and folding: the total was $45.86. 175 copies were printed. [L77]

NEVADA TERRITORY. *Legislative Assembly. Council.* Roll calls. Carson City: J. T. Goodman & Co., Territorial Printers. 1862.   [L78]
300 copies were invoiced on December 19 at a charge of $7 (RG217: Abstract C, Voucher 13, Session of 1862).

NEVADA TERRITORY. *Legislative Assembly. Council. Committee on Corporations.* Report. Carson City: J.T. Goodman & Co., Territorial Printers. 1862.   [L79]
250 copies were printed, for which Goodman submitted an invoice on December 11 in the amount of $8.40 for 4,200 ems; $4 for 2 tokens press work; and $14.33 for paper, folding, and stitching: the total was $26.73

NEVADA TERRITORY. *Legislative Assembly. House of Representatives.*

[Legislative bills. Second session, 1862. Carson City: J. T. Goodman & Co., Territorial Printers. 1862.] Printing costs provided below are from RG217: Abstract C, Vouchers 13, 60-62, Session of 1862. Titles for "lost" bills are from the General Orders file at Nv-Ar; late in the session, however, the clerk who kept the file apparently ran out of time to keep it up to date, because no printed bill numbers appear with the titles after bill No. 50. See the note regarding Council bills for the 1862 session.

No. 1. Memorial to Congress relating to expenses of the Indian War and depredations committed by Indians. Goodman submitted a claim on November 20 for 5,330 ems, $10.66, reduced to $8; 1 token press work, $2, reduced to $1.50; and $4 for folding and paper, reduced to $2: the $16.66 bill was thus reduced to $11.50.
      [L80]

No. 2. For the relief of insolvent debtors and the protection of creditors. The claim, dated November 20, was for 23,985 ems, $47.97, reduced to 13,220 ems and $14.83; 3 tokens press work, $6, reduced to $4.50; and $14 for paper, folding, and stitching, reduced to $3.75: the bill for $67.97 was thus reduced to $23.08. [L81]

No. 3. Providing for submitting the question of the removal of the county seat of Humboldt County to a vote of the qualified electors thereof. Goodman's claim of November 20 was the same as for No. L80 and suffered the same reductions.
[L82]

No. 4. To repeal "An act to provide compensation for the Supreme Judges of the Territory for the transaction of territorial business," approved Nov. 29th, 1861. The claim of November 20 shows that Goodman asked $5.33 for 2,665 ems, reduced to $4; $2 for 1 token press work, reduced to $1.50; and $4 for paper and folding, reduced to $2: the reduction was from $11.33 to $7.50. [L83]

No. 5. Joint memorial to Congress concerning the office of Surveyor General of the Territory of Nevada. The printer's November 20 claim was for the same amount and underwent the same reductions as for No. L80. [L84]

No. 6. Defining the rights of husband and wife. Goodman's claim of November 20 was for 10,660 ems, $21.32, reduced to 10,496 ems and $15.74; 1 token press work, $2, raised to $3; and $4 for paper and folding, reduced to $2: his bill for $27.32 was thus lowered to $20.74. [L85]

No. 7. Providing for marks instead of signatures. The claim is for the same amounts as for No. L83, as are the reductions. [L86]

No. 8. To provide increased compensation to the Governor, Justices of the Supreme Court, and other officers in the Territory of Nevada. The claim, dated November 22, is the same as for No. L80; the reductions are also the same. [L87]

No. 9. Concerning judgments of the probate court of Storey County. The claim and reductions are the same as for No. L83; it is dated November 22. [L88]

No. 10. Extending the jurisdiction of the probate courts of Storey County. Goodman presented a claim on November 22 for 7,995 ems, $15.99, which was reduced to 7,872 ems and $11.81; 1 token press work, $2, raised to $3; and $4 for paper and folding, reduced to $2: the total of $21.99 was lowered by the First Comptroller to $16.81. [L89]

No. 11. Providing for the appointment of elisors. The November 22 claim was for the same amounts, with the same reductions, as for No. L80. [L90]

No. 12. Amendatory of "An act creating boards of county comissioners and defining their duties," passed at the first session of the Legislative Assembly of the Territory of Nevada. The claim, dated November 22, was the same as for No. L80, and was reduced by the same amounts. [L91]

No. 13. To provide for the selection of probate judges and prosecuting attorneys and defining their duties. The November 22 claim involved the same amounts as for No. L89; the same reductions and raise were made by the Treasury Department.
[L92]

No. 14. Fixing the time for electing a Delegate to the House of Representatives of the United States. Goodman's claim of November 23 was the same as for No. L83, as were the reductions. [L93]

No. 15. In relation to fences. The November 23 printer's claim was the same as for

No. L85, with the same raise and reductions. [L94]

No. 16. Concerning wills. Goodman's November 23 claim was for 13,325 ems, $26.65, reduced to 13,220 ems and $19.83; 2 tokens press work, $4, reduced to $3; and $11 for paper, folding, and stitching, reduced to $3.75: the $41.65 total thus became $26.58. [L95]

No. 17. To provide for the formation of corporations for certain purposes. The claim, dated November 23, was for 31,980 ems, $63.96, reduced to 31,488 ems and $47.23; 3 tokens press work, $6, raised to $9; and $14 for paper, folding, and stitching, reduced to $8.50: the amount allowed was $64.73 instead of the $83.96 claimed. [L96]

No. 18. [Title unknown.] The charges were the same, as were the reductions, as for No. L83 on Goodman's claim of November 23. [L97]

No. 19. To prevent the trespassing of animals upon private property. Goodman's claims and the Treasury Department's reductions were the same as for No. L80; the claim was dated November 23. [L98]

No. 20. Changing the name of Lake County to that of Roop County. The November 24 printer's claim was the same as for No. L83, with the same reductions. [L99]

No. 21. To amend an act entitled "An act to exempt the Homestead and other property from forced sale in certain cases." The printer's claim, dated November 27, was the same as for No. L85, with the same reductions and raise. [L100]

No. 22. For the relief of persons imprisoned on civil process. Goodman's claim, dated November 27, was the same as for No. L89, with the same raise and reductions. [L101]

No. 23. Supplementary to an act concerning conveyances. The claim, dated November 27, was the same as for No. L80; the reductions were also the same, except that the charge for paper and folding was lowered from $4 to $1.50. [L102]

No. 24. Prescribing the manner of applying for pardons. Goodman's claim of November 27 was the same as for No. L89, with the same raise and reductions. [L103]

No. 25. To authorize the formation of limited partnerships. The claim, dated November 27, was the same as for No. L95, except that the price for 2 tokens of press work was raised to $4.50 by the First Comptroller. [L104]

No. 26. Providing for the appointment of a district attorney for Humboldt County. The November 27 claim was the same as for No. L102, with the same reductions by the Treasury Department. [L105]

No. 27. To prohibit the collection of accounts for liquors sold at retail. The printer's claim, dated November 27, was the same as for No. L83, except that the charge for paper and folding was reduced from $4 to $1.50. [L106]

No. 28. To provide for the obtainment and preservation and distribution of vaccine matter. The claim, dated November 26, was the same as for No. L102, with the same reductions. [L107]

No. 29. Supplementary to and amendatory of an act authorizing D. D. Kingsbury and James M. McDonald to establish and maintain a toll road. Goodman's claim, dated November 27, was the same as for No. L85, with the same raise and reductions.   [L108]

No. 30. Explanatory of section 1 of an act entitled an act relative to bills of exchange and promissory notes. The claim, dated November 27, was the same as for No. L106, with the same reductions.   [L109]

No. 31. To amend chap. 64 of the Laws entitled "An act to regulate surveyors and surveying." The November 27 claim was the same as for No. L106, with the same reductions by the First Comptroller.   [L110]

No. 32. To audit the claim of Edwin A. Sherman and to provide for the payment of the same. Goodman's claim was the same as for No. L106, with the same reductions.   [L111]

No. 33. Prohibiting justices of the peace from acting as notaries. The claim, dated November 27, was the same, as were the reductions, as for No. L106. [L112]

No. 34. For the relief of purchasers at sales of real estate by public officers. The charges and reductions on the November 27 bill were the same as for No. L106. [L113]

No. 35. To repeal an act entitled an act for the better observance of the Lord's day. The printer's claim, dated November 27, was the same as for No. L106, with the same reductions by the Treasury Department.   [L114]

No. 36. To change the time of meeting of the Legislative Assembly. The claim submitted by the printer on November 28 was the same as for No. L106, with the same disallowances by the First Comptroller.   [L115]

No. 37. Concerning unlawful stock. The claim, dated November 28, was the same as for No. L85, with the same raise and reductions.   [L116]

No. 38. For the better protection of the mines, and mining claims, in the Territory of Nevada. November —, 1862. 2 p. 30 x 24 cm. Goodman's claim, dated November 29, was the same as for No. L102, with the same reductions. DNA.
                                                                                    [117]

No. 39. To provide for the conveyance of mining claims. November 28, 1862. 2 p. 31 x 24 cm. The December 1 claim was the same as for No. L102, with the same reductions by the Treasury Department. DNA.   [118]

No. 40. To amend an act entitled "An act concerning roads and highways." November 28, 1862. 2 p. 31 x 24 cm. The printer's claim, dated December 1, was the same as for No. L102, with the same reductions. DNA.   [119]

No. 41. Memorial to Congress praying for amendment to Organic Act, so that the annual session of the Legislative Assembly may have authority to sit ninety instead of forty days. The claim, dated December 1, was the same as for No. L102, with the same reductions.   [L120]

No. 42. Concerning roads and highways. December 1, 1862. 12 p. 31 x 24 cm. The December 1 claim was the same as for No. L96, with the same raise and reductions. DNA.   [121]

No. 43. To prohibit the sale of ardent spirits, firearms, or ammunition to the Indians. Goodman's December 1 claim was the same as for No. L102, with the same reductions.   [L122]

No. 44. To authorize certain parties to supply the town of Carson City with water.

December 1, 1862. 3 p. 30 x 24 cm. The claim submitted by the printer on December 1 was the same as for No. L89, with the same raise and reductions. DNA. [123]

No. 45. For the protection of agricultural lands. December 2, 1862. 2 p. 30 x 24 cm. The December 3 claim was the same as for No. L102, with the same reductions by the First Comptroller. DNA. [124]

No. 46. To provide for the establishment of a hospital for the indigent sick and insane in the Territory of Nevada. December 3, 1862. 6 p. 30 x 24 cm. Goodman's claim, dated December 3, was the same as for No. L69; the alterations by the Treasury Department were also the same, except that $23.62 was allowed for composition, thus reducing the bill from $46.98 to $31.87. DNA. [125]

No. 47. To amend an act entitled "An act to grant the right to construct a toll road from Virginia City to Truckee Meadows and Steamboat Valley, in Storey and Washoe counties," approved November 29th, 1861. December 3, 1862. 2 p. 32 x 24 cm. The printer's claim of December 5 was the same as for No. L102, with the same reductions. DNA. [126]

No. 48. To amend, and supplemental to, an act to provide for the assessing and allocating county and territorial revenue. December 4, 1862. 58 p. 30 x 24 cm. The claim, dated December 5, was for 154,570 ems, $309.14, reduced to 152,192 ems and $228.29; 15 tokens press work, $30, raised to $43.50; and $65 for paper, folding, and stitching, reduced to $45: the printer's total of $404.14 was thus reduced to $316.79. DNA. [127]

No. 49. To provide for the improvement of navigation on the Carson and Humboldt rivers. December 4, 1862. 3 p. 31 x 24 cm. The December 8 claim was the same as for No. L89, with the same raise and reductions. DNA. [128]

No. 50. To amend an act entitled "An act to regulate the settlement of the estates of deceased persons," approved November 29, 1861. December 4, 1862. 2 p. 30 x 24 cm. Goodman's claim, dated December 8, was the same as for No. L102, with the same reductions. DNA. [129]

No. 51. [Title unknown.] The December 10 claim was the same as for No. L69, but specific reductions by the Treasury Department do not appear on the invoice for this bill or for any of the remaining 1862 House bills. [L130]

No. 52. [Title unknown.] The claim, dated December 10, was the same as for No. L89; see No. L130. [L131]

No. 53. [Title unknown.] The printer's claim of December 10 was the same as for No. L95; see No. L130. [L132]

No. 54. [Title unknown.] Goodman's claim, dated December 10, was for 23,985 ems, $47.97; 3 tokens press work, $6; $13.33 for paper; and $10 for folding and stitching: the total, for 175 copies, was $77.30. See No. L130. [L133]

No. 55. [Title unknown.] The December 11 claim was the same as for No. L80; see No. L130. [L134]

No. 56. [Title unknown.] The claim submitted on December 13 was for 29,315 ems, $58.63; 3 tokens press work, $6; and $14 for paper, folding, and stitching: the total was $78.63. See No. L130. [L135]

No. 57. [Title unknown.] The claim, dated December 13, was the same as for No.

L85; see No. L130. [L136]

No. 58. [Title unknown.] Goodman's claim, dated December 14, was the same as for No. L85; see No. L130. [L137]

No. 59. [Title unknown.] The printer's claim of December 15 was the same as for No. L85; see No. L130. [L138]

No. 60. [Title unknown.] Goodman's December 15 claim was the same as for No. L80; see No. L130. [L139]

No. 61. [Title unknown.] The claim, dated December 15, was for 45,305 ems, $90.61; 5 tokens press work, $10; and $20 for paper, folding, and stitching: the total was $120.61. See No. L130. [L140]

No. 62. [Title unknown.] The December 16 claim was the same as for No. L85; see No. L130. [L141]

No. 63. [Title unknown.] Goodman's claim of December 16 was the same as for No. L80; see No. L130. [L142]

No. 64. [Title unknown.] The claim, dated December 17, was the same as for No. L80; see No. L130. [L143]

No. 65. [Title unknown.] The claim of December 18 was the same as for No. L89; see No. L130. [L144]

No. 66. [Title unknown.] The December 18 claim was the same as for No. L89; see No. L130. [L145]

NEVADA TERRITORY. *Legislative Assembly. House of Representatives.* Roll calls. Carson City: J. T. Goodman & Co., Territorial Printers. 1862. [L146]

1,000 copies were invoiced on November 11 at a charge of $14, of which $13 was allowed by the Treasury Department (RG217: Abstract C, Voucher 40, Session of 1862).

NEVADA TERRITORY. *Legislative Assembly. House of Representatives. Committee on Incorporations.* Corporation act and report. Carson City: J. T. Goodman & Co., Territorial Printers. 1862. [L147]

250 copies in pamphlet form, in addition to those provided for in No. L96, were ordered on November 22 (JHR, 1862, p. 100). They were invoiced on November 24, with charges for 19,600 ems, $39.20, but composition was raised to 21,500 ems and the price lowered to $32.25 by the Treasury Department; 4 tokens press work, $8, reduced to $3; paper, $5.25, allowed; and $15 for folding and stitching, reduced to $5: Goodman's total of $67.45 was therefore lowered to $45.50 (RG217:Abstract C, Voucher 61, Session of 1862).

REESE RIVER MINING DISTRICT. *Ordinances, local laws, etc.*

Mining Laws | —of the— | Reese River Mining District, | Reese River, Nevada Territory. | [*filet*] | . . . | [1862.] [148]
Broadside. 30 x 19 cm. Printed in three columns.

The laws are those adopted at a meeting on July 17, 1862, replacing "a few rules" passed on the previous May 10.
NvALR.

TOPLIFFE'S THEATRE. *Virginia City, Nevada.*

Topliffe's Theatre! | [*thin-thick-thin rule*] | . . . | [*thick-thin rule*] | Grand Complimentary Benefit | Tendered by the Citizens of Virginia City to | Mrs. W.H. | Leighton. | [*thick-thin rule*] | Monday Evening, - - - - - Sept. 22, 1862, | . . . | [*thick-thin rule*] | To-Morrow, Benefit of "Virginia City Guards!" | . . . | Territorial Enterprise Job Print, C Street, Virginia City. [149]

Broadside. 40? x 21? cm. Description from a facsimile, printed on rose-colored paper and probably reduced, in "Pioneer Western Playbills," Keepsake Series of the Book Club of California (San Francisco: 1951); also reproduced in Margaret G. Watson, *Silver Theatre* (Glendale, California: Arthur H. Clark, 1964), p. 212, and in William C. Miller, "Drama for the Comstockers," *Nevada Highways and Parks*, XVIII (1958), p. 29. Imprint below a thick-thin rule border. Printed on silk.
Pvt.

UNITED STATES. *Army. Second California Cavalry.*

Ho, for the Second Cavalry | [*thick-thin rule*] | [*cut of eagle holding banner, with:*] E Pluribus Unum. | [*thick-thin rule*] | Wanted | A Few More | Good Men | for the | Second Cavalry | California Vol., now on the way to Salt Lake. | None But Good Men Need Apply! | [*filet*] | Office: | B Street, Virginia City, N.T. | [*filet*] | Capt. D. McLean, | Recruiting Officer. | Virginia City, N.T., August 16th, 1862. [150]

Broadside. 39? x 39? cm. The recorded copy has been trimmed on all sides.

Ten days before this recruiting poster was issued Colonel P. Edward Connor of the California Volunteers assumed command of the District of Utah, headquartered at Fort Churchill, N.T., and comprising the territories of Nevada and Utah. No one in Nevada was authorized to raise military companies until the following year.
Pvt.

❧1863❧

S ince there was no meeting of the Legislative Assembly in 1863, the public printing was limited to publication of the laws enacted by the session of 1862 (the legislative journals were not printed) and the proposed state Constitution that was later to be defeated. The Nevada press was nevertheless busy, and in fact a number of newspapers were founded during the year. Aurora acquired another paper in April and Carson City, which had been without a press for nearly nine months, acquired one in late July. Austin, Gold Hill, and Unionville each had a newspaper by year's end. Virginia City's two papers were joined by two more, one of which had only a brief existence; the *Enterprise* and the *Union* both acquired new steam presses for newspaper and job work. The Comstock Lode's metropolis also got its first pure job press, the Commercial Printing Office, which was owned by Frank Hastings. Washoe City's only newspaper ceased to publish in early December, with its material passing to a successor there. But the most significant development was the founding in June of one of the area's first labor organizations, the Washoe Typographical Union, made up of sixty-two journeyman printers from Storey County. The union was a strong and active advocate throughout the period for fair wages and working conditions for local printers.

AMERICAN BASIN COMPANY.

Office American Basin Company. | [*filet*] | Virginia, September 26th, 1863. | . . .   [151]

Broadside. 23? x 18? cm. The recorded copy is cropped all around.

Announcement to stockholders of an assessment for completion of a tunnel to facilitate work on the company's mine. Only the offices were in Virginia City; the mine was located in Humboldt County.

NvHi.

DAILY TERRITORIAL ENTERPRISE. *Virginia City, Nevada Territory.* Extra. July 1863.   [L152]

The *Reese River Reveille* of July 8, 1863, noted receipt "yesterday" of the *Enterprise* extra, which included news of the Battle of Gettysburg through July 3 at 3:30 P.M.

DAILY TERRITORIAL ENTERPRISE. *Virginia City, Nevada Territory.* Extra. December 2, 1863.   [L153]

The Gold Hill *News,* an afternoon paper, reported in its issue of December 2 that the news it had received the night before regarding the retreat of Confederate General Braxton Bragg toward Atlanta had been published as an extra by the morning *Enterprise.*

ESMERALDA MINING DISTRICT. *Ordinances, local laws, etc.*

Mining Laws | of | Esmeralda District, | Mono County, California. | From August 30th, 1860, to July 1st, 1864. | [*short rule*] | San

Francisco: | Printed by Towne & Bacon, Book and Job Printers. | No. 536 Clay Street, opposite Leidesdorff. | 1863. [154]

8 p. 21 x 14 cm.

The laws were amended on July 8, 1861, June 1, 1862, and June 15, 1863. Until an official boundary survey later in 1863 the Esmeralda District was thought to be in California.

CU-B. NvHi.

HUMBOLDT REGISTER. *Unionville, Nevada Territory*. Carrier's address. New Year's Day, 1864. 1863. [L155]

The *Register*'s issue of January 2, 1864, reprinted the address that had been "distributed yesterday," and presumably printed in the last days of 1863. The carrier's address was a time-honored journalistic custom, but it apparently did not catch on in Nevada until shortly before it began to die out elsewhere. It was usually distributed at New Year's with the day's newspaper. Characteristically, the address was a description in clumsy verse of the wonders of the area or an expression of hope for what the coming year would bring. Always, though, there was a pitch, overt or muted, for a gratuity for past services. Although the address form no longer exists as such, the custom lingers on with the delivery to homes at Christmastime of commercial greeting cards by garbage collectors, elevator operators, milkmen, and anyone else who thinks an end-of-the-year bonus is due him.

KELLY, JAMES WELLS.

Second Directory | of | Nevada Territory; | Embracing a | General Directory of Residents | of all the principal Towns; | Business Directory of Advertisers; | Quartz Mills, Reduction Works, Toll Roads, Etc.; | Officers of the Masonic, Odd Fellows and Sons of Tem-|perance Associations; Members Washoe Stock Board | of Exchange; Fire Department; | Incorporation Acts of Virginia and Gold Hill; | and All Other Information Connected with the Progress and Present | Condition of the Territory; | also, | An Accurate Table of Distances; List of Public Officers; and | Principal Mining Laws of Different Districts; With | the Residents and Principal Mines, Mills, | Etc. of the | Reese River Region. | [*short rule*] | Compiled from the Most Recent and Authentic Sources, | By J. Wells Kelly. | [*short rule*] | Virginia: | [*short dotted rule*] | 1863. | [*short rule*] | Printed by Valentine & Co., 517 Clay and 514 Commercial Streets, San Francisco. [156]

xliv, [4], viii, 486 p. 23 x 15 cm. Quarter-leather binding; printed boards. The first series of roman numerals precedes the title page; advertisements on colored paper. Facsimile of front cover in Hershel V. Jones, *Adventures in Americana* (New York: William Edwin Rudge, 1928), II, p. 289.

The Virginia City *Bulletin* of August 7, 1863, acknowledged receipt of a copy of the directory from Kelly and noted that it was for sale at Bernhard Franz's music store in

Virginia City. The militantly chauvinistic *Reese River Reveille* complained vigorously in its issue of August 8 that Austin and environs had at least tripled in size since Kelly's census-taking in May.

CHi. CSmH. CU-B. CtY. ICN. MWA. NvHi. NvU. WHi.

MARYSVILLE MINING DISTRICT. *Ordinances, local laws, etc.*

Reese River Reveille. | [*double rule*] | Austin, Lander County, N.T., October 28, 1863. | [*double rule*] | Supplement | [*double rule*] | . . . [157]

[2] p. 30 x 22 cm. Lines 1-2 printed across the sheet; line 3 in the first of three columns.

The first page contains general news; on the verso, covering approximately one and three-quarters columns, are the by-laws of the mining district: [*thick-thin rule*] | By-Laws of Marysville Mining | District. | [*short rule*] | Adopted October 13, 1863. | [*short rule*].

CtY. NvU.

MERCHANTS' EXCHANGE. *Virginia City, Nevada Territory.* Circular. August 18, 1863.   [L158]

The Virginia City *Bulletin* reprinted the circular in its issue of August 19; it called for a meeting to form a Merchants' Exchange at eight o'clock on the evening of the 19th at the Probate Court room in Virginia City.

NEVADA TERRITORY. *Governor, 1861-1864 (James Warren Nye).* Proclamation for a national day of thanksgiving, August 6, 1863. [L159]

Reese River Reveille, August 5, 1863: "Gov. Nye has issued a proclamation requesting the people of this Territory to observe the national day of Thanksgiving, to-morrow, the 6th inst. We can only do so in our grateful hearts and the sagebrush—having no churches as yet." Nye's proclamation, which may not have been issued separately from its almost certain newspaper publication, probably echoed the one issued on July 15 by Abraham Lincoln, in which the President set aside August 6 as a day to thank God for bringing "to the army and navy of the United States victories on land and on the sea," and asked the people "to assemble on that occasion in their customary places of worship." The battles of Gettysburg and Vicksburg had been completed earlier in July.

NEVADA TERRITORY. *Governor, 1861-1864 (James Warren Nye).*

Thanksgiving Proclamation. | [*filet*] | Executive Department, [*brace*] | Carson City, Nevada Terrritory [*sic*], [*brace*] | November 17th, 1863. [*brace*] | . . . | . . . I, James W. Nye, Governor of the Territory of Nevada, do hereby appoint | Thursday, The 26th Day of November Instant, | As a day of Public Thanksgiving to Almighty God . . . | . . . | [Carson City? 1863.]   [160]

Broadside. 36 x 43 cm. Facsimile following p. 314.

CtY. DLC. ICN. M. NvHi (photostat). NvU (microfilm).

NEVADA TERRITORY. *Governor, 1861-1864 (James Warren Nye).*

United States of America. | [*filet*] | Territory of Nevada. | [*short thin-scalloped rule*] | To All to Whon [*sic*] these Presents Shall Come, Greeting: | Know Ye, That reposing special trust and confidence in the integrity and ability of [*broken rule*] | I, James W. Nye, Governor of the Territory of Nevada . . . do hereby ap-||point him the said [*rule*] . . . and I do authorize him to | discharge, according to law, the duties of said office . . . | . . . | [Carson City? 1863?] [161]

Broadside. 31 x 39 cm. Partly script type.

The recorded copy is hand-dated December 17, 1863. It appoints Artemus Ward as "Speaker of Pieces" to the People of Nevada Territory, "for the term of his natural life." The popular humorist had arrived in the Territory for his first visit a few days before.

IU.

NEVADA TERRITORY. *Governor (Acting), 1863 (Orion Clemens).*

One Thousand Dollars | Reward!! | [*thin-thick-thin rule*] | Territory of Nevada, Executive Department, | Carson City, February 19, 1863. | . . . | $1,000 Reward | for the apprehension of | Edw'd W. Richardson, | charged with Murder and Robbery, and | Horace F. Swazey | charged with Murder; both of whom escaped last night from the Ormsby County jail. | [*thick-thin rule*] | . . . | Orion Clemens, | Acting Governor. | [*thick-thin rule*] | "Washoe Times" Print, Washoe City. [162]

Broadside. 53 x 35 cm. Facsimile following p. 314.

Carson City had no press between early November of 1862 and late July of 1863, and it was necessary to send official printing elsewhere. The *Washoe Times* had the closest press, but there was perhaps an even more compelling reason for sending the printing of this piece there: barely three weeks earlier Swazey (also spelled Swayze) had shot and killed the paper's proprietor, G. W. Derickson. Governor Nye was frequently out of the Territory attending to a long catalog of illnesses, politics, and business interests; in his absence Secretary Clemens was authorized to act in his stead.

NvHi.

NEVADA TERRITORY. *Laws, statutes, etc.*

Laws | of the | Territory of Nevada, | Passed at the | Second Regular Session of the Legislative Assembly, | Begun | the Eleventh Day of November, and Ended on the Twentieth Day of | December, Eighteen Hundred and Sixty-two, at Carson City. | [*short *double rule*] | Virginia: | J.T. Goodman & Co., Territorial Printers. | [*short rule*] | 1863. [163]

xiv, [2], 215 p. 23 x 15 cm. Leather binding.

About three weeks after adjournment of the second session, Secretary Clemens inquired of Goodman when he intended to print the laws (Nv-Ar: Letterbook, January 9, 1863). But the old bugaboo of uncertainty about payment from the federal government led Goodman to question Clemens regarding "probable compensation for doing the work" (RG217: Goodman to Clemens, January 28, 1863). The Secretary replied eight days later, advising Goodman to begin printing as soon as practicable; he wrote to the Treasury Department the same day, enclosing a copy of his letter to Goodman and asking what the government's terms would be (ibid., Clemens to Goodman and Elisha Whittlesey, February 5, 1863). The response from Washington was unequivocal: "that the prices to be allowed by you for the Territorial printing, as fixed by the Department, are $1.50 per thousand ems and $1.50 per token; and these rates will not be departed from." Some latitude was to be allowed for paper prices; government notes were to be the only bases for payment (ibid., Wm. Hemphill Jones to Clemens, March 5, 1863). In the meantime Clemens had sent the usual interrogatories to owners of presses in the Territory regarding their pricing policies and, on their return, forwarded them to Washington. Goodman's response showed that the prices he paid his employees for composition and press work were half those allowed by the government (ibid., Goodman to Clemens, February 16, 1863); the difference was apparently considered sufficient to provide a fair profit, even after discounting of greenbacks, because Goodman did undertake the printing in June. But in order to get his agreement to do it Clemens had to promise to pay on delivery the whole amount of the bill instead of the half to two-thirds authorized by the government prior to auditing. Goodman charged $900.16 for 193 1/2 p. long primer with nonpareil marginal notes (2,326 ems per page), 450,081 ems at $2; $30.61 for 8 p. long primer plain (1,914 ems per page), 15,312 ems at $2; $407.96 for 30 1/2 p. minion rule and figure work (3,344 ems per page), 101,992 ems at $4; $174 for 87 tokens press work at $2; $264 for 11 reams fine book paper at $24; $600 for binding 300 copies in full law style at $2; $450 for binding 300 copies in half law style at $1.50; and $300 for preparing the index and marginal notes. His total bill was $3,126.73 (ibid., Voucher 7, Session of 1864). There is no record of Goodman's receipt of more than the $2,457.06 for which he signed on October 26, 1863, but the difference between that amount and his total charge, $669.67, was the exact amount demanded of Clemens as overpayment in 1869 (ibid., R. W. Taylor to Clemens, June 9, 1869). See note preceding No. L70.

The Virginia City *Bulletin* of September 10, 1863, had the following: "In reply to the inquiry published in yesterday's *Bulletin,* relative to the Territorial Statutes, the Enterprise informs us that the laws of the Territory are all printed, and as soon as bound will be ready for distribution. The delay in their publication was owing to the depreciation of 'greenbacks.' " Clemens, too, was concerned. On September 21 he wrote to Goodman asking "what in the world is the matter that the laws don't come? I have heard for several days of our Territorial laws of 1862 being advertised for sale in San Francisco. Do you suppose [the binder] is keeping back the Government copies till he sells his own?" Finally, in its issue of October 17, the *Humboldt Register* of Unionville acknowledged receipt of a copy, "Printing and binding done in good shape. J. T. Goodman & Co., of the Territorial Enterprise, printers."

No copy bound in half-leather has been located.

Az. CSmH. CU-B. CtY. CtY-L. DLC. IU. MBS. MH-L. NIC. NN. Nv. Nv-Ar.
NvEuC. NvGoEC. NvHi. NvRNC. NvRWL. NvSC (rebound). NvU.'OrU-L.
ViU-L.

NEVADA TERRITORY. *Supreme Court.*

[Briefs. 1863.]

Sparrow & Trench vs. Clark et al. Brief of appellants, Sparrow & Trench. 37 p. 23 x
15 cm. Imprint on wrapper: San Francisco: Printed by Towne & Bacon, Book
and Job Printers. No. 536 Clay Street, opposite Leidesdorff. 1863. Nv-Ar. [164]

Van Valkenburg et al vs. Hoff. Brief of appellants, Henry Van Valkenburg et al. 11
p. 22 x 14 cm. Imprint on wrapper: Virginia City, N.T., Democratic Standard
Book and Job Printing Office. 1863. Nv-Ar.   [165]

NEVADA. *Constitution.*

The | Constitution | of the | State of Nevada | to be | Submitted
to the People for Ratification | Tuesday, January 19th, 1864. | [*fi-
let*] | Official Copy. | [*filet*] | Virginia, N.T. | Printed by John
Church & Co., Daily Union Office. | [*short dotted rule*] | 1863. [166]

14 p. 24 x 16 cm. Printed in two columns; possibly printed from the same type as in
the newspaper, but appropriate issues of the *Union* have not been located. The
recorded copy is sewn and unopened.

No Congressional authorization had been given for the convention that drew up the
constitution; it was held only under authority of a legislative act "to frame a Constitution and State Government for the State of Washoe" (LTN, 1862, p. 128-130).
See No. 75. During the meeting, which lasted from November 4 to December 11, it
was decided not to use Washoe as the name of the prospective state. The convention,
which met in Carson City, spent a great deal of time debating the advantages and
disadvantages of various methods of getting the public printing done. The debates,
as reported by Andrew J. Marsh, were occasionally humorous, but were generally
repetitive and marked by little understanding of the subject at hand. But Mark
Twain wrote a letter on December 12, 1863, which was published three days later in
the *Enterprise;* it sums up the matter rather better than Marsh was able to do. "This
subject worried the Convention some. In the first place, the Standing Committee
reported an article providing for the election of a State Printer, whose compensation
was to be fixed by law, etc. The members, without even showing the Committee
the courtesy of discussing the matter, snubbing them very pointedly, by pitching the
bill overboard without offering the semblance of an apology for their conduct. They
substituted an article providing for printing State work by contract. That was debated to death, and duly buried with its stillborn predecessor. Then they tried a
Superintendent of Public Printing. That plan appeared to suit them. They adopted
it, and looked upon the work of their hands and pronounced it good. There the
matter rested until last night, when [former California] Governor [J. Neely] Johnson
got up and asked unanimous consent to substitute the original State Printer article
for the Superintendent. He pointed out to the Convention that the office of Superintendent would be turned into a mere sinecure, and its incumbent would accomplish
no good to the State—and behold, without a word of objection, the change was

made! Verily, it is vastly better to yield to wisdom at last, than not at all'' *(Reports of the 1863 Constitutional Convention of the Territory of Nevada.* Carson City: Legislative Counsel Bureau, 1972, p. 488-489).

This first attempt at a constitution was overwhelmingly defeated because of a provision taxing the mines, the Territory's principal industry.

CSmH.

NEVADA. *Constitution.*

[*Thick-thin rule*] | Humboldt Register--Supplement. | [*double rule*] | Unionville: Saturday, December 26, 1863. | [*thick-thin rule*] | [Official.] | The Constitution of the State | of Nevada. | [*short rule*] | . . .   [167]

Broadside. 70 x 51 cm. Lines 1-2 in columns 2-8 of 9 columns; columns 1 and 9 begin immediately below the first thick-thin rule. Line 3 printed in brackets. The Constitution covers 7 full columns and 33 lines of the 8th; the remainder is unrelated news.

The copy at CU-B is torn, affecting the text.

Register, December 26, 1863: "THE CONSTITUTION prepared by the Carson Convention we issue in supplement to day. Read it, and study it. It is exactly correct as we issue it—certified by the officers of the convention." *Register,* April 9, 1864: THE UNION ON THE CONSTITUTION &C.—The Virginia Union of the 31st ult. had something to say as to why the late legislature did not make appropriations to pay newspapers for publishing the constitution proposed last Winter for the State of Nevada. It said: Now, we have been informed that one issue of the Territorial Enterprise contained the State Constitution by the authority of the Convention, and that it presented a bill of *nine* hundred dollars; that the Enterprise printed the Constitution in supplement form for several other papers, and stipulated with them for one-half of what each should receive from the Legislature for thus promulgating the Constitution; that each of those papers presented a bill of *nine* hundred dollars; and that, seeing these outrageous bills, the Committee of the Legislature naturally 'suspected something,' and bundled them all out as a vile pack of claims which ought not to be paid. As the Union does not specify the papers which entered into the arrangement of which it had been 'informed,' and as we published the document in question, we choose to reply in part to the fling the weathercock makes at the press of the Territory. The publishers of the Union offered to print the constitution in supplement form for us, for a consideration. The Enterprise people never made any proposition to us concerning it. We published the constitution as ordered by the convention, and charged for it as we charge for other advertising. Sent in the bill. It was considerably less than $900. Nobody in with us. The bill was not paid. The Enterprise of the 1st April denounces the whole statement of the oscillator as untrue; and concludes: It may be very well for the Union to denounce the legitimate accounts of its cotemporaries 'as a vile pack of claims which ought not to be paid,' but the account charged by this paper was only what would have been demanded of a private individual, and we presume the same was the case with the other newspaper publishers. But the Union is rather complimentary to its cotemporaries than otherwise. To receive its denunciation is a greater honor than to be the recipients of its praises.''

See Nos. 166 and 168.

CU-B. DLC. NvU (microfilm).

NEVADA. *Constitution*.

[*Thick-thin rule*] | Reese River Reveille--Supplement. | [*double rule*] | Austin, N.T., Saturday, December 26, 1863. | [*thick-thin rule*] | [Official.] | The Constitution of the State | of Nevada. | [*short rule*] | . . .   [168]

Broadside. 69 x 51 cm. Lines 1-2 in columns 2-7, below the top of columns 1 and 9. Line 3 printed in brackets. The Constitution covers 7 full columns and 35 lines of the eighth, the remainder of that column and all of column 9 being dispatches from other papers.

The film copy at Nv and one of two film copies at NvU are deficient, with approximately one-third of the first column unreadable; the bottom has been cropped, affecting the text.

See Nos. 166 and 167.

CtY. Nv (microfilm). NvU (microfilm).

NICKERSON, BENJAMIN ROLLIN.

A Statement | of the | Grounds of the Claim | of the | Grosch Consolidated | Gold and Silver Mining Company, | to the | Comstock Mine in Nevada Territory: | Together with Their Reply to the | Attacks of the Press. | By Benj. R. Nickerson. | San Francisco: | Printed by Towne & Bacon, Book and Job Printers, | No. 536 Clay Street, opposite Leidesdorff. | 1863.   [169]

22 p. 22 x 15 cm. Printed wrapper.

A defense of the company's claims to three-fourths of the 3,750 feet of the Comstock Lead.

C. CSmH. CU-B. CtY. NvRW.

REESE RIVER MINING DISTRICT. *Ordinances, local laws, etc.*

Mining Laws | of Reese River Mining District. | [*rule*] | . . . | [Austin: Reese River Reveille. 1863.]   [170]

Broadside. 45 x 20 cm. Printed in three columns, from the same type as in several issues of the *Reveille*.

Contains the "Mining Laws of Reese River District," formulated July 17, 1862, and the "Revised Mining Laws of Reese River," dated at Clifton, April 20, 1863. The *Reveille* noted in its issue of October 14, 1863, that it had "on hand and for sale, at this office, a few copies of the Mining Laws of Reese River District—old and new—which are going off like hot cakes. If you are in want of the article, come along immediately."

CtY. NvU (microfilm).

REESE RIVER REVEILLE. *Austin, Nevada Territory*. Extra. July 19, 1863.
                                    [L171]

The *Reveille*'s issue of July 22 reprinted approximately one and one-half columns "From our Extra of Sunday" about a mining accident and the mayhem committed by a drunken, berserk miner.

REESE RIVER REVEILLE. *Austin, Nevada Territory*. Prospectus. Virginia City: Daily Union. 1863. [L172]

In its first issue, on May 16, 1863, the *Reveille* noted that "In a prospectus issued by us from the Virginia Union office, we used the name of 'Reese River Miner' for this paper; afterward, when that name was 'set up' it did not seem to 'look well' (mechanically speaking) and was not altogether satisfactory to our friends."

UNION LEAGUE OF AMERICA. *Nevada Territory. Grand Council.*

Proceedings | of the | Grand Council | of the | Union League of America | for the | Territory of Nevada | at its | Sessions | Held in | Virginia, October 5th, November 5th, 1863. | [*short wavy rule*] | Virginia: | Published by Order of the Grand Council. | 1863. [173]

10 p. 21 x 13 cm. The recorded copy has been disbound; there is no trace of a wrapper. The constitution is on p. 3-4.

The Union League was a national organization formed to encourage loyalty to the United States during the Civil War. One of the "Grand Vice Presidents" of the Council in Nevada Territory was Orion Clemens, territorial Secretary.
NvU.

VIRGINIA CITY, NEVADA TERRITORY. *Ordinances, local laws, etc.* Ordinances, charter, rules of the Board of Aldermen. 1863. [L174]

In its issue of August 19, 1863, the Virginia City *Bulletin* noted that the Board of Aldermen had "ordered the printing, in pamphlet form, of five hundred copies" on the previous evening. The issue of September 29 reported that the "Aldermen have had the city ordinances published in pamphlet form."

WASHOE AGRICULTURAL, MINING AND MECHANICAL SOCIETY. *Carson City, Nevada Territory*. Poster. San Francisco: Valentine & Co. 1863. [L175]

Issues of September 19, 1863, and continuing, of the Unionville *Humboldt Register* contain an advertisement for the "First Annual Fair" of the organization, to be held in Carson City on the 12th through the 16th of October. "For premiums, see posters." An advertisement by Valentine & Co., San Francisco, appeared in the issue of November 6, and following, of the Virginia City *Bulletin,* which said: "Printing in Colored Inks. See the late Posters of the Washoe Agricultural, Mining and Mechanical Society, for Specimens of our Work in that Department."

WASHOE TYPOGRAPHICAL UNION.

Constitution | and | By-Laws | of the | Washoe Typographical

Union, | No. —, | Including | The Scale of Prices | and | List of Members. | [*short rule*] | Organized June 28th, 1863. | [*short rule*] | Virginia, N.T.: | Standard Book and Job Printing Office. | [*short dotted rule*] | 1863. [176]

31, [1] p. 14 x 9 cm. Printed wrapper. Title and text pages in single rule borders.

Page [3]: "For the better protection of the interests of the trade in Storey County, Nevada Territory, the Printers of Virginia, in convention assembled, have resolved to establish a Union of all the journeymen printers who are now or may hereafter be employed at the printing business in this county." The scale of prices to be charged covers p. [24]-31; see Appendix B.

CtY. NvU (microfilm).

WHITE, ALBERT F.

A | Discourse | Delivered on | Thanksgiving Day, | By | Rev. A. F. White, A.M. | Pastor of the First Presbyterian Church, | Carson City, Nevada Territory. | November 27th, 1862. | [*short rule*] | Published by Request. | [*short rule*] | San Francisco: | Printed by Towne & Bacon, Book and Job Printers. | No. 536 Clay Street, opposite Leidesdorff. | 1863. [177]

19 p. 22 x 14 cm. Printed? wrapper.

CU-B (bound without a wrapper). NvHi (has traces of a wrapper).

❧1864❧

The lack of a legislative session in 1863 was more than compensated for in 1864, when the territorial Legislative Assembly sat for its third and final time early in the year and the state Legislature met for its first session in mid-December. In between, in July, the second Constitutional Convention met and produced, finally, a document that was acceptable to the electorate. President Lincoln was anxious to have Nevada's electoral votes as well as its congressional votes on the antislavery amendment, so he approved the Constitution immediately on receiving it, and Nevada, after only three and a half years as a territory, became the thirty-sixth state on October 31.

Israel Crawford of the Carson City *Independent* was named Territorial Printer for the third session and was no luckier than his predecessors in dealing with the federal government's leisurely methods of auditing and payment. He did, though, devise a canny means to beat the discounting of greenbacks on the West Coast. On January 30 he wrote to the chairmen of the two printing committees in the Legislative Assembly with the following suggestion (JC, p. 115-116): "The Federal Government allows for Printing $1 50/100 Dollars per thousand Ems, and $1 50/100 Dollars per token for press work. This price was established by the Government at a time when currency was at little or no discount on this Coast. The general rates for composition in this Territory is [sic] $1.— per thousand in Coin—United States Currency is at a discount of some 35 cents on the dollar, which would amount to only 97 1/2 cents per thousand, an amount less than is paid to compositors, and making a difference of 52 1/2 cents per thousand less than Government price in Coin. You will readily perceive that the undersigned cannot do the work for the price paid by the Government if forced to take U.S. Currency at a discount of from 35 to 40 cents on the Dollar without submitting to heavy loss. I would therefore ask that the difference be made up (by appropriation) by your Honorable Bodies equivalent to $1 50/100 per thousand ems additional per thousand to the price paid by the government in currency. Respectfully Israel Crawford." A week later the Council's Committee on Claims reported out "An Act for the Relief of Israel Crawford" (ibid., p. 163); after passage by both houses it was returned with the Governor's approval on February 20 (ibid., p. 309). But when it came time to print the laws enacted at the session, Secretary Clemens chose the firm of John Church & Co., proprietors of the Virginia City *Union,* to do the job. He objected to the "miserable style of printing" done by Crawford (RG217: Clemens to R. W. Taylor, March 16, 1864), but may also have been influenced by Church's intention "to print [the laws] in the Territory" (see No. 208). As after the 1862 session, the legislative journals were not printed.

The first state Legislature did not get around to passing a bill relating to the state's official printing until early in 1865 and could not until then select a State Printer; nevertheless, there was printing to be done and, according to the Virginia City *Constitution* of December 23, "The [Carson City] Post has succeeded in getting at least a tea-cup of the public pap; both Houses having concluded to give them what little printing is imperatively necessary to be done, anterior to the selection of a State Printer."

In March one of the two newspapers in Aurora suspended, but another replaced it immediately. There was only a single press in Carson City at both the beginning and the end of the year, although three different papers published there in 1864. Amid much fanfare— brass band, anvil chorus, and a great deal of bibulousness—a press arrived in Como in March; by early July it had been sent, much more quietly, to Dayton. The Gold Hill *News* had a rival, briefly, in late spring. The new county of Nye had two newspapers, both at Ione; one died after a few issues and the other suspended shortly after its establishment, reappearing in 1865. The press in Virginia City was particularly active, with seven new papers—two of them printed in German—but only two of the newcomers survived to the end of the year; another paper that had begun the year there suspended operations in May. The Commercial Printing Office in Virginia City was in operation at least until late January, when Clemens inquired of its owner, Frank Hastings, whether he might execute the Legislative Assembly's incidental printing (Nv-Ar: Letterbook, Clemens to Hastings, January 26, 1864); neither the firm's name nor that of its owner appears in Collins's directory (No. 182) that was published later in the year. Washoe City had one paper in the beginning of January and one at the end of December, but they were not the same ones, although they used the same material.

AMADOR MINING DISTRICT. *Ordinances, local laws, etc.* Mining laws. 1864?   [L178]

Reese River Reveille, January 23, 1864: "Mining Laws of Reese River and Amador Districts, for sale at this office." The Amador district, which was situated immediately to the north of the Reese River district, was later incorporated into the latter district. The Reese River laws mentioned here are probably the 1863 revision; see No. 170.

AURORA, NEVADA TERRITORY. *Citizens.*

[*Thick-thin rule*] | To His Excellency, James W. Nye, Governor of the Territory of Nevada, Carson City. | Your petitioners, residents and citizens of Aurora, Esmeralda County, Territory of Nevada, would most respectfully represent: | . . . | Aurora, March 3d, 1864. | [*thin-thick rule*].   [179]

Broadside. The recorded film copy does not locate the original. Two columns for signatures, each headed: Names.

The petitioners complain that a vigilante group, "The People's Safety Committee," had arrested an Aurora police officer, John M. Prendergrast, and ordered him to leave town. "We therefore, your petitioners, earnestly urge upon your Excellency, to adopt some measures by which our society may be held and protected within the law; the imminent danger of a disastrous outbreak and bloodshed be avoided, and the rights of all be protected and secured." The vigilante action was undoubtedly a continuation of that described in the note to No. L180, but the account in Angel (p. 422-425) does not mention this incident and contemporary Aurora newspapers are not available. A second microfilm copy has handwritten notations changing the place to Carson City and the date to March 7; it contains signatures of Carson City citizens.

NvU (microfilm).

AURORA, NEVADA TERRITORY. *Citizens' Safety Committee.* Handbill. February 3, 1864. [L180]

The Gold Hill *News* of February 8, 1864, quoting the February 3 issue of the Aurora *Times,* said: "Handbills were stuck around town this morning calling a meeting of the 'Citizens Safety Committee,' at Armory Hall, 7 o'clock, to-night. It is signed 'No. 7, Secretary.' Rumor has it that a Vigilance Committee is in full blast in our midst." The report of the Esmeralda County Grand Jury for the March Term, 1864—released on March 31, 1864, and published in the *Esmeralda Daily Union* of that date—said, as quoted in Angel (p. 423-425), that the Committee was found to be "composed of over six hundred of our best, most substantial and law-abiding citizens." Nevertheless, it also found that the Committee was responsible for the public hanging of four men, an action it could not bring itself to condemn because of the salutary effect it had on the community. For several months Aurora's citizens had been living in terror of a gang of thugs and rowdies whose chief pleasure seemed to be getting drunk and shooting people. Witnesses who reported these crimes became themselves the gang's victims, and juries could not be found that would convict the criminals for fear of retribution. On the first of February the affair came to a head with the murder and immolation of W. R. Johnson by John Dailey (spelled Daly in the *Union*'s report of the Grand Jury proceedings), James Masterson, John McDowell ("Three-Fingered Jack"), and William Buckley. The Citizens' Safety Committee was then formed to combat the lawlessness. Besides capturing the miscreants, it took into custody a number of law officers whose inability to maintain order had infuriated them. The four murderers were tried and convicted, and when Governor Nye inquired on the ninth of February as to the state of affairs in Aurora, a county commissioner telegraphed in reply: "All quiet and orderly. Four men will be hung in half an hour." They were. The account in Angel concludes (p. 423): "The effect of this wholesome exhibition of justice and the absence of the bad characters warned out of town, was a quiet and orderly community for some time, and a considerable modification of lawlessness ever after." The same affair is described very briefly in Joseph Wasson's *Bodie and Esmeralda* (San Francisco: Spaulding, Barto & Co., 1878, p. 49-51).

BIG CREEK MINING DISTRICT. *Ordinances, local laws, etc.*

Laws of Big Creek | Mining District, | Adopted Feb. 13th, 1864. | [*thick-thin rule*] | . . . | [Austin: Reese River Reveille?]

[181]

Broadside. 30 x 14 cm. Caption title. Printed in two columns; at the bottom of column 2: C. F. Newcomb, Ch'n.

Two-column printing often suggests an earlier newspaper appearance, but in this case the laws did not appear in the county's only paper, the *Reveille.* Rather, the laws appear to have been printed for use at the district's February 13 meeting, with the type held for later newspaper publication. The *Reveille*'s issue of February 18, however, contained a notice that the laws had been voted down.

ICN. NvU (microfilm).

COLLINS, CHARLES.

Mercantile Guide | and | Directory | for | Virginia City, Gold Hill, Silver City | and | American City, | Comprising | A General Business and Resident Directory | for those Cities, with Sketches of | their growth, development | and resources. | Also Containing | Valuable Historical and Statistical Matter | of Unusual Interest, | Together with the Only | Accurate Mining Directory | Yet Published, | Giving the name of the mine, number of feet in each | claim, the District in which the same is located, | and the names of Secretaries, with their | respective places of business. | [*filet*] | Compiled by | Charles Collins. | [*filet*] | Virginia: | 1864-5. | [*short rule*] | Printed by Agnew & Deffebach, Book and Job Printers, 511 Sansome Street, S.F. | [1864.]   [182]

viii, 386 p. 24 x 15 cm. Quarter-leather binding; printed boards. Colored paper used for advertisements on p. 1-7 only.

The Gold Hill *News* reported on the 26th of April, 1864, that canvassing for the directory would begin the next day in Gold Hill and that two canvassers were already at work in Virginia City. On the 10th of May the *News* called upon those who had not been contacted by the canvassers to leave their names and addresses at the newspaper office if inclusion in the directory was desired. The *News* reported the directory "now ready for delivery" on the 7th of July, and acknowledged receipt of a copy on the ninth. An advertisement in the July 16 issue of the *News,* and continuing, stated that the work "will be delivered by the canvassers to-day."

C. CHi. CSmH. CU-B. DLC. NvHi. NvU.

COMO, NEVADA TERRITORY. *Independence Day Celebration.* Poster. Como: Sentinel. June 20, 1864.   [L183]

The June 19 entry in Alf Doten's *Journals* noted that "Evening J B Witherell & I & Hunt got up draft for posters for the 4th of July"; his entry for the following day is: "evening I got the 4 of July posters from the printing office, and stuck some of them up round town — left the rest with Witherell to distribute."

COMO TRI-WEEKLY DELTA. *Como, Nevada Territory.* Prospectus. 1864
                                                                       [L184]

Gold Hill *News,* January 6, 1864: "Edward & Rosenbergh have issued the prospectus of a paper to be published at Como, called the 'Como Tri-Weekly Delta.' " No newspaper was issued from Como until the following April when the Como *Sentinel* began publication.

CROSS'S HALL. *Como, Nevada Territory.* Playbill. July 11, 1864.[L185]

Doten Diaries, July 11, 1864: "PM busy at Cross's hall fixing & fitting up for a grand fun performance tonight & ball by Como Amateurs . . . also sent bills down to Palmyra & other places — doors open at 7 1/2 — performance commenced at 8 o'clock — All about same bill as our last in Dayton — some variations in the doings of the first part — We had about two hundred of an audience — all were very well pleased indeed, especially with our burlesque circus . . . they passed round the hat and only collected $1.25 for each of us — rather poor pay." The *Sentinel* moved from Como to Dayton between the 9th and 16th of July, 1864.

DOYLE'S THEATRE. *Dayton, Nevada Territory.*

Grand | Concert | to be given at | Doyle's Theatre! | Dayton, | on Friday Even'g! | June 10th, 1864, for the | Benefit of the M.E. Church. | . . . | Dayton, June 9th, 1864. ('Como Sentinel' Print.)
[186]

Broadside. 36 x 15 cm. Decorative border.
NvU.

DOYLE'S THEATRE. *Dayton, Nevada Territory.*

I'm Here! | at the | Dayton | Theatre! | [*thick-thin rule*] | The | Como Amateurs | will give a Performance | at Doyle's Theatre! | Dayton, on | Thursday Evening | June 30th, 1864, | . . . | . . . ('Como Sentinel' Print.)
[187]

Broadside. 36 x 15 cm. Line 1 appears in a banner held at one end by an elephant's trunk and at the other end by a ring around the elephant's tail; lines 2-4 on a blanket on the elephant's back. Decorative border.
NvU.

DOYLE'S THEATRE. *Dayton, Nevada Territory.*

I'm Here! | at the | Dayton | Theatre! | [*thick-thin rule*] | "Again with Songs We Greet You." | [*rule*] | The | Como Amateurs | will give their Second Performance | at Doyle's Theatre! | Dayton, on | Tuesday, Even'g! | July 5th, 1864, | . . . | . . . ('Como Sentinel' Print.)
[188]

Broadside. 36 x 15 cm. Line 1 appears in a banner held at one end by an elephant's trunk and at the other end by a ring around the elephant's tail; lines 2-4 on a blanket on the elephant's back. Decorative border. Facsimile following p. 314.

Another copy at NvU has the following penciled changes by Alf Doten. "Dayton" on the elephant's blanket is crossed out and replaced with "Como"; "their Second" is replaced with "*free*"; "Doyle's Theatre" becomes "Como"; "Tuesday" is replaced with both "Monday" and "This evening."; "5th" is crossed out and not replaced. At the bottom, before the imprint, the price schedule is crossed out, and below the border is written "*Admittance free.*" No copy of a printed version with these changes has been located.
NvU.

GOLD HILL, NEVADA. *Ladies' Festival.*

Ladies' | Festival | at the | Theatre Hall, Gold Hill, | on the |

Evenings of November 15, 16, 17, & 18. | [*filet*] | Order of Exercises | For this Tuesday Evening, November 15th, 1864. | [*filet*] | Music, by the [*dotted rule*] Virginia Glee Club | [*filet*] | . . . | [*rule*] | Printed at the Office of the Gold Hill News.   [189]

Broadside. 15 x 10 cm.

NvHi.

GOLD HILL DAILY NEWS. *Gold Hill, Nevada Territory.* Extra. May 16, 1864.   [L190]

The *News* of May 17, 1864, reported that the extra had announced ''the important and cheering news of the victorious onward march of our armies under [Generals Ulysses S.] Grant and [George H.] Thomas and [John M.] Schofield.

HUMBOLDT REGISTER. *Unionville, Nevada.* Extra. November 10, 1864.   [L191]

Register, November 12, 1864: ''Thursday [i.e., November 10] we received by telegraph the gratifying news of the general bent of the election in California and the East, also the cheering accounts from [General William Tecumseh] Sherman, and of the capture of the pirate Florida. This was got into shape as soon as the second dispatch arrived, and an extra printed for the Humboldt Express Co. . . . Westerfield told us his thousand copies of the Extra were to be in Idaho City at 8 o'clock Sunday morning, or the route marked out with dead horses.'' Part of the news from the extra was reprinted in the issue of the 12th; the intention to issue a second extra the following Monday was announced, if ''any news can be got to justify.''

MCCUMBER'S HALL. *Como, Nevada Territory.*

The Como | Amateurs | will give a | Concert! | At [*rule*] | —on— | Saturday Even'g, | June 4th, 1864, for the | Benefit | —of the— | Como School Fund! | [*thick-thin rule*] | . . . | Como, May 28th, 1864. Sentinal Job Press.   [192]

Broadside. 27 x 15 cm. Decorative border.

The blank in the recorded copy is filled in with ''Como N T'' in brown pencil. Alf Doten's Diaries for June 5 noted that the printer's bill was donated.

NvU.

MCCUMBER'S HALL. *Como, Nevada Territory.*

Ho! for the War! | [*double rule*] | Again With Song We Greet You! | [*thick-thin rule*] | The | Como Amateurs | will give their Second Performance | at McCumber's Hall! | —on— | Saturday Evn'g | June 18th, 1864, in aid of | The Sanitary Fund! | . . . | Como, June 13th, 1864. ('Sentinel' Job Press.)   [193]

Broadside. 33 x 15 cm. Decorative border. Facsimile in Doten *Journals*, following p. 394.

Penciled along the right side of the recorded copy, in Alf Doten's hand, is: Martin

the Wizard will also appear.
NvU.

MAGUIRE'S OPERA HOUSE. *Virginia City, Nevada Territory.*

Maquire's Opera House | [*thick-thin rule*] | . . . | [*thick-thin rule*] | The Greatest Success! | —:Ever Achieved in This City, is the Engagement of:— | Miss Adah Isaacs | Menken | . . . | [1864.]

[194]

Broadside. Description from a probably reduced facsimile in *Nevada Highways and Parks,* XVIII (1958), p. 29.
The *Territorial Enterprise* of September 13, 1863, published a letter from Mark Twain, who was staying in San Francisco, saying that he had seen Menken in *Mazeppa* there and that she would be leaving directly for Virginia City. She did not arrive, however, until the following March and could not perform *Mazeppa* until the seventh of the month because her horse and scenery had not arrived. Until then she entertained Virginia City audiences with *The French Spy.*
Pvt.

MOUNT AIRY MINING DISTRICT. *Ordinances, local laws, etc.*

Reveille--- Supplement. | [*thick-thin rule*] | Vol. I. Austin, Thursday, April 21, 1864. Number 118. | [*double rule*] | . . .   [195]

[2] p. 30 x 20 cm. Text printed in three columns, with the banner across all three. The by-laws of the district, which was in Lander County, are in the first column of the verso; they were adopted at Mount Airy House on March 25, 1864.
CtY. NvU (microfilm).

MUSIC HALL. *Virginia City, Nevada Territory.*

Music Hall! | [*thick-thin rule*] | . . . | [*thick-thin rule*] | [*cut of minstrel group, signed:*] Loomis | [*thick-thin rule*] | [*fist*] First Appearance of— | Miss Florence | The Sweet Balladist. | [*thick-thin rule*] | [*fist*] Re-Appearance of— | Harry Taylor, | In connection With All the— | Old Favorites | Now Performing at this Popular Place of Public Resort. | [*thick-thin rule*] | Monday Evening, Sept. 26th. | . . . | [*thick-thin rule*] | Enterprise Job Print. | [1864.]   [196]

Broadside. 52 x 18 cm.
Date established from Doten *Journals,* p. 805-806, in which Doten refers to "Sutliffes music hall."
NvU.

NEVADA TERRITORY.

Annual Reports | of the | Secretary of the Territory, | Territorial Auditor, | Treasurer, | Superintendent of Public Instruction, | and | Adjutant-General. | January 13, 1864. | [*filet*] | Carson City:

| Israel Crawford, Territorial Printer. | 1864.   [197]

6, 11, 12, 9, 6 p. 23 x 15 cm. Wrapper title, in thick-thin rule border.

The copy at CtY has a variant wrapper: Annual Reports | of the | Territorial Auditor, | Treasurer, | Superintendent of Public Instruction, | and | Adjutant-General. | January 13, 1864. | [*filet*] | Carson City: | Israel Crawford, Territorial Printer. | 1864. The copy includes all of the reports; the wrapper is probably an earlier one that was rejected because it failed to mention the report of the Secretary.

Note on wrapper at NvHi: ". . . to accompany Voucher No. 42, from item 'judicial report' to item 'Annual Reports Territorial Officers,' inclusive. March 8/64." On that voucher, in RG217, Crawford's charges are listed as follows: $282.85 for composition, $82.50 for press work, $25 for folding, $25 for stitching, and $147 for paper; the total was $568.35 (error in printer's addition; should have been $562.35). 600 copies were printed.

CSmH (traces of a wrapper). CU-B(MT). CtY. DHEW. M. NN. NvHi. NvU (microfilm of variant). WHi.

NEVADA TERRITORY. *Adjutant General.*

Report | of the | Territorial Adjutant-General, | For the Year 1863. | [Carson City: Israel Crawford, Territorial Printer. 1864.]
[L198]

6 p. Description from caption title in No. 197.

The *Reese River Reveille* of February 6, 1864, noted receipt of a copy.

NEVADA TERRITORY. *Auditor.*

Report | of the | Territorial Auditor, | For the Year 1863. | [Carson City: Israel Crawford, Territorial Printer. 1864.]   [L199]

11 p. Description from caption title in No. 197.

The Unionville *Humboldt Register,* in noting receipt of this report and those of the Treasurer and Superintendent of Public Instruction in its issue of February 13, 1864, said that they were "three as efficient samples of abominably bad printing as need be."

NEVADA TERRITORY. *Commissioner of the Boundary Survey.*

Report | of | Butler Ives, | Commissioner of the | Boundary Survey, | Between | Nevada Territory | and | California. | 1863. | [*filet*] | Carson City: | Israel Crawford, Territorial Printer. | 1864.
[200]

8 p. 23 x 14 cm. Wrapper title, in decorative rule border. Printed from the same type as the 23 p. issue, No. 201, but here line numbering has been eliminated, lines have been lengthened, leads have been removed, and typographical errors have been corrected. These changes do not go very far toward explaining the $20.38 Crawford charged for composition, when he had already charged a sizable amount for that task on the issue that was printed for use during the legislative session; he also asked $9 for press work, $5 for folding, $10 for sewing and pasting, and $3.50 for paper. His

total bill was for $47.88. 500 copies were printed (RG217, Voucher 42, Session of 1864).

The survey, conducted jointly by California and Nevada Territory, settled the dispute over which entity had jurisdiction in Aurora, placing it a few miles inside Nevada. The new boundary had the effect of halting the bothersome practice of electing two sets of officials there, one for Mono County, California, and the other for Esmeralda County, Nevada Territory. It did not, however, stop interstate squabbling over the boundary north of Lake Tahoe; in mid-1980 the U.S. Supreme Court finally decided an occasionally rancorous dispute between the states by upholding the results of an 1872 survey.

CSmH. CU-B(MT). CtY (rebound, without wrapper). DNA. M. MH-L. NHi. NvHi. NvU (microfilm). WHi.

NEVADA TERRITORY. *Commissioner of the Boundary Survey.*

Territory of Nevada. | [*broken wavy rule*] | February 12, 1864. | [*short rule*] | Report of the Boundary Survey between | California and Nevada Territory, 1863: | To the Honorable the Legislative Assembly of the Territory of Nevada: | . . . | [Carson City: Israel Crawford, Territorial Printer. 1864.]   [201]

23 p. 30 x 21 cm. Caption title. Page 23: "Butler Ives, Commissioner."

This issue was the predecessor of No. 200, and was designed to acquaint members of the Legislative Assembly with the findings as soon as possible so that they could be taken into account during the session. Lines are numbered and there is heavy leading between lines, as with legislative bills. Crawford charged $44.85 for composition, $18 for press work, $3 for folding, $3 for stitching, and $5.25 for paper, for a total of $74.10; 100 copies were printed (RG217: Voucher 42, Session of 1864). Receipt of a copy was acknowledged in the *Reese River Reveille* of February 23, but it is not clear whether it was this issue or the 8 p. issue, No. 200.

NvHi.

NEVADA TERRITORY. *District Court. First Judicial District (Storey County).*

Argument | of | Judge James H. Hardy, | in the Case of | The Potosi G. & S.M. Co. | versus | The Bajazet & Golden Era | Gold and Silver Mining Co. | [*filet*] | Before R. S. Mesick, Esq., Referee. | [*filet*] | Virginia, Nevada: | Goodman & M'Carthy, Enterprise Job Printing Office. | [*short rule*] | 1864.   [202]

40 p. 22 x 14 cm. Printed wrapper. Text printed in two columns.

CSmH.

NEVADA TERRITORY. *District Court. First Judicial District (Storey County).*

. . . | Gould & Curry Silver Mining Co., | Plaintiff, | vs. | North Potosi Gold and Silver Mining Co. | Defendant. | [*filet*] | Opinion of Referee, | August 22, 1864. | [*filet*] | Virginia, N.T.: | Goodman & M'Carthy, Printers, Enterprise Office. | [*short rule*] | 1864.

[203]

12 p. 22 x 14 cm. Printed wrapper. Text printed in two columns.

CU-B. CtY. DLC. ICN. MH-L. NvU (NvMus).

NEVADA TERRITORY. *District Court. First Judicial District (Storey County).*

. . . | Overman Consolidated Gold | and Silver Mining Co. | vs. | Robert Apple et als. | [*short rule*] | Opinion of J. B. Harmon, Referee. | [*short rule*] | San Francisco: | Towne & Bacon, Book and Job Printers, 536 Clay Street, opposite Leidesdorff Street. | 1864.

[204]

95 p. 24 x 16 cm. Wrapper title, in decorative rule border.

CU-B.

NEVADA TERRITORY. *Governor, 1861-1864 (James Warren Nye).* Proclamation ordering an election. May 2, 1864.

[L205]

Gold Hill *News,* May 5, 1864: "Elsewhere in our columns will be found the Proclamation of Governor Nye, ordering an election on the State Government Question. It was not sent to us as an advertisement, owing probably to our expressed disinclination to being henceforth honey-fuggled by the Circumlocution Office. It being a matter of public information, we publish it gratis. The Territory of Nevada, owes this establishment all that it ever will, if we can keep it." The proclamation, which may not have been issued separately, ordered an election for delegates to a constitutional convention.

NEVADA TERRITORY. *Governor, 1861-1864 (James Warren Nye).*

Third | Annual Message | of | Governor James W. Nye, | to the | Legislature of Nevada Territory, | January 13, 1864. | [*filet*] | Carson City: | Israel Crawford, Territorial Printer. | 1864.

[206]

11 p. 25 x 16 cm. Wrapper title, in thick-thin rule border.

1,000 copies ordered printed, with 200 for use of the Governor, 200 for the Council, and 600 for the House (Virginia City *Bulletin,* January 22, 1864). For printing those 1,000 copies, Crawford charged $41.89 for composition, $44.50 for press work, $10 for folding, $25 for sewing and pasting, and $43.75 for paper, for a total of $165.14 (RG217: Voucher 42, Session of 1864).

CoD. CtY. DLC (rebound, without wrapper). DNA. NvU (microfilm). WHi.

NEVADA TERRITORY. *Laws, statutes, etc.*

The | Common School Laws | of | Nevada Territory. | Compiled by the Superintendent of Public Instruction. | With Forms and Di-

rections fqr [*sic*] the Different School Officers and | Teachers of the
Public Schools. | [*filet*] | Virginia, N.T. | [*short rule*] | Daily Union
Print. | [*short rule*] | 1864.   [L207]

17 p. 20 cm. Wrapper title. *Check List:* 17 described this title in full, but did not locate
a copy. NUC 412 describes it briefly (including the error in line 6) and locates three
copies; inquiries at those three institutions indicate that they do not now own copies.

NEVADA TERRITORY. *Laws, statutes, etc.*

Laws | of the | Territory of Nevada, | Passed at the | Third Regu-
lar Session of the Legislative Assembly, | Begun | the Twelfth Day
of January, and Ended on the Twentieth Day of | February, Eigh-
teen Hundred and Sixty-four, at Carson City. | [*short double
rule*] | Virginia: | John Church & Co., Territorial Printers. | [*short
rule*] | 1864.   [208]

xiv, [2], 180 p. 24 x 15 cm. Leather and half-leather bindings.

By the third session of the Legislative Assembly, Secretary Clemens was familiar
enough with the insistence of local printers that they be paid local going rates that he
no longer bothered to consult with the holders of the purse strings in Washington,
D.C. He sent out his usual "Interrogatories," made a decision immediately on their
return, and concluded a contract with John Church of the Virginia City *Union.*
Perhaps his dilemma was eased by Church's promise to do the printing in the
Territory, as required by Clemens's instructions (Nv-Ar: Letterbook, Clemens to
Church, February 24, 1864); there is, however, no evidence to show whether it was
actually done there. On March 29 Clemens signed a contract with Church (ibid.)
providing for the printing of 600 copies, half to be bound in full leather and the
others to be half-bound; Church was to be paid $1.50 per thousand ems, $1.50 per
token, $250 for indexing, a table of contents, and supervising the printing (perhaps a
clue that the printing was done elsewhere), and "a fair profit" on paper and binding.
Church agreed to accept payment in greenbacks. Church billed the Secretary $900
for composition, side notes and index included; $250 for indexing and supervising;
$123 for 82 tokens of press work; $600 for 300 full-bound volumes and another $450
for the 300 volumes that were half-bound; and $200 for 11 reams of paper. The total
was $2,523, of which the Secretary paid $2,300 on June 2 (ibid.). As was its wont,
the Treasury Department dawdled until 1869 before auditing the account, then
reduced the amount by $625 to $1,898, thus leaving Clemens owing the government
$402. See the note preceding legislative bills of the Council for 1862.

The Gold Hill *News* acknowledged receipt of a copy on June 15, 1864. The Unionville *Humboldt Register* of June 25 thanked Secretary Clemens "for a copy of this
creditably done and very useful catalogue of toll-road franchises." Throughout its
brief history the Legislative Assembly had frequently been chastised in the press for
paying more attention to private bills, including particularly toll road franchises,
than to public business.

Az. CSmH. CU-B. CtY. CtY-L. DLC. MBS. MH-L. NIC. NN. Nv. NvC.
NvEC. NvHi. NvLN. NvSC. NvU. NvVSR. NvYLR. OrU-L. ViU-L.

NEVADA TERRITORY. *Legislative Assembly.* Joint rules. Carson City:

Israel Crawford. 1864. [L209]

For printing 100 copies, Crawford charged $3.93 for composition, $1.50 for press work, and $4 for paper, for a total of $9.43 (RG217: Voucher 42, Session of 1864).

NEVADA TERRITORY. *Legislative Assembly. Council.*

[Legislative bills. Third session, 1864. Carson City: Israel Crawford, Territorial Printer. 1864.] The correct session for bills without dates in their titles was verified in the manuscript journals at Nv-Ar. Data regarding charges are from RG217, Voucher 42, Session of 1864. 100 copies of each bill were printed. Totals for some bills may appear to be incorrect because Crawford used a rounding-off method when the total included a half cent, going up to the next full cent for some bills and dropping the half cent for others. The total for Voucher 42—for Council and House bills, reports, messages, and some other pieces—was $3,331.86. Crawford signed for $2,000 in part payment on February 17, 1864. When the voucher was finally audited on June 7, 1869, $1,000 of the total was disallowed, leaving $331.86 owing to Crawford, but there is no indication on the voucher which pieces were discounted or why. There are no vouchers at DNA for any other 1864 Council bills than the ones recorded here; since no bills not on the voucher have been located, it may seriously be questioned whether any others were printed. *Check List* described No. 210 as an 1863 imprint, and Nos. 212 and 217 as 1861 imprints.

No. 5 To encourage the discovery and manufacture of minerals. 3 p. 29 x 21 cm. The printer charged $5.85 for composition, $3 for press work, 50¢ for folding, and 87 1/2¢ for paper, for a total of $10.23. NvHi. [210]

No. 18. To amend an act, entitled "An act to regulate proceedings in the courts of justice in this Territory." 12 p. 22 x 16 cm. The charges were $23.40 for composition, $9 for press work, $2 for folding, $2 for stitching, and $2.62 1/2 for paper, for a total of $39.02. NvHi. [211]

No. 24. Amendatory of an act entitled an act to exempt the Homestead and other property from forced sale in certain cases, approved November 1861. 7 p. 29 x 21 cm. Charges were $13.65 for composition, $6 for press work, $1 for folding, $2 for stitching, and $1.75 for paper; the total was $24.40. NvHi. [212]

No. 25 [House of Representatives Bill No. 86]. To incorporate the Bullion Insurance Company. January 30, 1864. 11 p. 30 x 22 cm. Crawford entered this bill under one heading on Voucher 42, indicating that the usual 100 copies were printed; he probably printed only half as many for the Senate, the smaller body by half, varying the headings for each house. See No. 265. Charges for composition were $17.05, for press work $7.50, for folding $1, for stitching $1, and for paper $1.75; the total was $28.30. DNA. NvHi. [213]

No. 28. For the relief of insolvent debtors and protection of creditors. January 25, 1864. 18 p. 30 x 21 cm. Crawford charged $35.10 for composition, $15 for press work, $3 for folding, $3 for stitching, and $4.38 for paper, for a total of $60.48.

NvHi. [214]

No. 32. To amend an act entitled an act to regulate proceedings in civil cases in the courts of justice of the Territory of Nevada. January 26, 1864. 15 p. 29 x 21 cm. The printer's charges were $29.25 for composition, $12 for press work, $2 for folding, $2 for stitching, and $3.50 for paper; the total was $48.75. NvHi. [215]

No. 35. To amend an act entitled "An act to regulate proceedings in civil cases in the courts of justice of this territory," approved November 21st, 1861. January 23, 1864. 3 p. 31 x 22 cm. Charges were $5.85 for composition, $3 for press work, 50¢ for folding, and 87 1/2¢ for paper, for a total of $10.22. NvHi. [216]

No. 36. To amend an act, entitled "An act to regulate proceedings in civil cases in the courts of justice of this territory," approved Nov. 29, 1861. 3 p. 30 x 21 cm. The printer charged the same as for No. 210. NvHi. [217]

No. 49. To amend an act entitled "An act to provide for the formation of corporations for certain purposes" approved December 20th, 1862. January 28, 1864. 7 p. 30 x 21 cm. Crawford asked the same amounts as for No. 212. NvHi. [218]

No. 52. Authorizing and empowering county commissioners to grant franchises. 8 p. 31 x 21 cm. Charges were $15.60 for composition, $6 for press work, $1 for folding, $1 for stitching, and $1.75 for paper, for a total of $25.35. DNA. NvHi. [219]

No. 58. To exempt firemen from militia service and jury duty. January 29, 1864. 3 p. 29 x 21 cm. Crawford's charges were the same as for No. 210. NvHi. [220]

No. 59. To provide for incorporating the Fireman's Charitable Fund Association of the City of Virginia. January 29, 1864. 3 p. 29 x 21 cm. The printer charged the same as for No. 216. NvHi. [221]

No. 60. To regulate the fire department of the City of Virginia. January 29, 1864. 17 p. 31 x 22 cm. Charges were $33.10 for composition, $13.50 for press work, $2 for folding, $2 for stitching, and $3.50 for paper, for a total of $54.10. NvHi. [222]

No. 64. To amend an act entitled "An act establishing a common school system for the Territory of Nevada," approved November 29th, 1861. February 2, 1864. 6 p. 31 x 22 cm. Crawford charged $11.70 for composition, $6 for press work, $1 for folding, $2 for stitching, and $1.75 for paper; the total asked was $23.45 (error in printer's addition; should have been $22.45). NvHi. [223]

No. 71. For the appointment of a Master in Chancery for the First Judicial District. February 2, 1864. 15 p. 31 x 22 cm. Charges were $29.25 for composition, $12 for press work, $3 for folding, $3 for stitching, and $3.50 for paper; the total was $50.75. NvHi. [224]

No. 73. To provide for the maintenance of a Territorial Prison. February 2, 1864. 4 p. 30 x 22 cm. The printer charged the same as for No. 210. NvHi. [225]

No. 84 [sic]. To supply the Town of Austin with water. 2 p. 30 x 21 cm. Crawford asked $3.90 for composition, $1.50 for press work, 50¢ for folding, and 87¢ for paper; his total was $6.77. Check List: 28 describes in some detail a 2-p. bill with the same number, title, and size, and locates a copy at NvHi; that item has not been found. The copy recorded here differs from Check List:28 in omitting details regarding introduction and committee assignment in the title. See No. 227.

DNA. NvHi. [226]

No. 84 [*sic*]. To supply the towns of Austin and Clifton with' water. February 6, 1864. 5 p. 30 x 21 cm. Charges were $9.75 for composition, $4.50 for press work, $1 for folding, $2 for stitching, and $1.75 for paper; the total was $19. There is no indication in the Council journal as to why the same number was used twice; see No. 226. NvHi. [227]

No. 86. To regulate fees and costs. February 4, 1864. 29 p. 31 x 22 cm. Crawford charged $56.55 for composition, $24 for press work, $4 for folding, $4 for stitching, and $7 for paper; his total was $95.55. NvHi. [228]

No. 113. Prescribing the rules and regulations for the execution of the trust arising under the act of Congress, entitled an act for relief of citizens upon lands of the United States under certain circumstances. February—, 1864. 19 p. 31 x 22 cm. The Council journal shows February 9 to be the date of introduction. The printer charged $37.55 for composition, $15 for press work, $3 for folding, $3 for stitching, and $4.37 1/2 for paper, for a total of $62.92. NvHi. [229]

No. 116. To grant the right to construct a toll road from Gold Hill to the City of Virginia, and to lay down railroad tracks in said cities. February 10, 1864. 15 p. 31 x 22 cm. The printer asked the same as for No. 224. NvHi. [230]

No. [122]. To prevent disloyal persons from holding franchises. February 10, 1864. 3 p. 31 x 22 cm. The bill number is from the Council journal. Crawford charged the same as for No. 216. NvHi. [231]

No. —. To incorporate the Aurora and Walker River Railroad Company. February 15, 1864. 14 p. 30 x 22 cm. Crawford's bill refers to the bill by title; the Council journal does not list a number. Charges were $27.30 for composition, $10.50 for press work, $2 for folding, $2 for stitching, and $3.50 for paper; the total was $44.80 (error in printer's addition; should have been $45.30). DNA. NvHi. [232]

NEVADA TERRITORY. *Legislative Assembly. Council.*

Standing Committees of Council. | [*ornament*] | . . . | [Carson City: Israel Crawford, Territorial Printer. 1864.] [233]

Broadside. 34 x 28 cm. Card stock. The copy at DNA has a penciled note: "no charge."
The membership of committees is made up entirely of 1864 Council members.
DNA. NvHi.

NEVADA TERRITORY. *Legislative Assembly. Council.* Union joint resolutions. Carson City: Israel Crawford, Territorial Printer. 1864. [L234]

When the Council's concurrent resolution expressing devotion to the Union cause reached the House of Representatives it was assigned for study to the Committee on Federal Relations, which was chaired by William M. Gillespie. On January 16 he recommended that the House pass the resolution as amended by his committee; his further recommendation that his committee's report be printed was passed. The resolution was debated at some length on January 20, with the members showing considerable familiarity with the resolution, so it may be supposed that they had each had access to the text, probably a printed one (Ms. House journal, at Nv-Ar). RG217, Voucher 42, Session of 1864, shows that the printer charged $5.85 for composition, $3 for press work, and 87 1/2¢ for paper, for a total of $9.72; 100 copies were printed.

NEVADA TERRITORY. *Legislative Assembly. House of Representatives.*

Concurrent Resolutions. | [*short rule*] | Resolved, By the House, the Council concurring: . . . | . . . | Memorial Relative to the Judicial System of Nevada Terri-|tory. | . . . | [Carson City: Israel Craw-ford, Territorial Printer. 1864.]   [235]

3 p. 30 x 21 cm.

An earlier version of No. 296. On p. [1] of the NvHi copy, in pen: "Samples of Printing to accompany voucher No. 42, from item 'House Bill 27 substitute' to item 'concurrent Resolution'—inclusive. March 5/64." Crawford's charge for printing the item, recorded in RG217, Voucher 42, Session of 1864, was $4.65 for composition, $3 for press work, 50¢ for folding, and 87¢ for paper; the total was $9.02. DNA. NvHi.

NEVADA TERRITORY. *Legislative Assembly. House of Representatives.*

[Legislative bills. Third session, 1864. Carson City: Israel Crawford, Territorial Printer. 1864.] See note preceding 1864 Council bills.

No. 2. For the relief of Mason and Huff. January 26, 1864. 2 p. 31 x 22 cm. Crawford's charges were $3.90 for composition, $1.50 for press work, 50¢ for folding, and 87 1/2¢ for paper, for a total of $6.77. NvHi.   [236]

No. 3. Concerning official bonds. January 16, 1864. 16 p. 31 x 22 cm. The printer charged $31.20 for composition, $12 for press work, $2 for folding, $3 for stitching, and $3.50 for paper; his total bill was $51.70. NvHi.   [237]

No. 4. Providing for the order in which territorial and county warrants shall be paid, and the rate of interest they shall bear. January 21, 1864. Broadside. 31 x 22 cm. Charges were $1.95 for composition, $1.50 for press work, 50¢ for folding, and 87 1/2¢ for paper; the total was $4.82. NvHi.   [238]

No. 6. To provide for the appointment of notaries public and defining their duties. January 23, 1864. 9 p. 31 x 22 cm. The printer's charges were $16.55 for composi-tion, $7.50 for press work, $1 for folding, $2 for stitching, and $2 for paper, for a total of $29.05. NvHi.   [239]

No. 7. Repealing an act, amendatory of section thirty-four of an act entitled an act defining the time of commencing civil actions, approved Nov. 21st, 1861. January 16, 1864. Broadside. 31 x 22 cm. Composition was $2.56, press work $1.50, folding 50¢, and paper 87 1/2¢, for a total of $5.44. NvHi.   [240]

No. 8. [To create the County of Nye.] Title from Ms. House journal, p. 160, at Nv-Ar. Crawford charged $9.21 for composition, $3 for press work, 50¢ for folding, and $1.75 for paper; the total was $14.46.   [L241]

No. 11. To amend an act, entitled an act to regulate proceedings in criminal cases in courts of justice, approved November 26th, 1861. January 23, 1864. 3 p. 31 x 22 cm. Charges were $5.85 for composition, $3 for press work, 50¢ for folding, and 87 1/2¢ for paper; the total was $10.22. NvHi. [242]

No. 13. Relating to the sale of real estate, and mining claims belonging to the estate of deceased persons. January 16, 1864. 3 p. 31 x 22 cm. The printer asked the same amounts as for No. 242. NvHi. [243]

No. 14. To provide for the location of coal lands. January 26, 1864. 2 p. 31 x 22 cm. Charges were the same as for No. 236. NvHi. [244]

No. 15. Prescribing the manner of commencing and maintaining actions by or against counties. January 23, 1864. 2 p. 31 x 22 cm. Crawford's charges were the same as for No. 236. NvHi. [245]

No. 18. To amend an act, entitled an act to regulate proceedings in civil cases in the courts of justice of the Territory of Nevada. January 23, 1864. 3 p. 31 x 22 cm. The charges were $5.85 for composition, $3 for press work, 50¢ for folding, and 87 1/2¢ for paper, for a total of $10.23. NvHi. [246]

No. 23. To encourage enlistments and give bounties and extra pay to our volunteer soldiers. January 21, 1864. 15 p. 31 x 22 cm. The printer's charges were $29.25 for composition, $10.50 for press work, $2 for folding, $2 for stitching, and $3.50 for paper; the total was $47.25. NvHi. [247]

No. 27. Supplementary to, and amendatory of an act entitled "An act to establish a seminary of learning in Carson City," approved November 21st, 1861. January 22, 1864. 5 p. 31 x 22 cm. House bill 27 appears twice on Voucher 42; it is not known whether this is an error in entry or if the bill underwent enough amendments to justify reprinting it. This latter possibility is perhaps the stronger one in view of the existence of a substitute for the bill, No. 249. In one set of charges the printer asked $11.70 for composition, $4.50 for press work, $1 for folding, $2 for stitching, and $1.75 for paper, for a total of $20.75 (error in printer's addition; should have been 20.95); in the other he asked $9.75 for composition, $3 for press work, $1 for folding, $2 for stitching, and $1.75 for paper, with a total of $17.50. NvHi. [248]

No. 27, Substitute. To provide for the establishment and support of the Sierra Seminary and Polytechnic College in the Territory of Nevada. 11 p. 30 x 22 cm. The bill itself is not identified as a substitute, but it is referred to as such on p. 427 of the Ms. House journal at Nv-Ar. Crawford charged $21.45 for composition, $9 for press work, $2 for folding, $2 for stitching, and $2.62 for paper; the total was $37.07. DNA. [249]

No. 28. Amendatory of "An act defining the judicial district, fixing the terms of the supreme and district courts of the Territory, locating the county seats of the several counties of the Territory and providing for the transfer and trial of actions, approved Nov. 29th, 1863." January 23, 1864. 4 p. 31 x 22 cm. Charges were the same as for No. 242. NvHi. [250]

No. 33. Relating to county prosecuting attorneys. January 25, 1864. 3 p. 31 x 22 cm. The printer charged the same amounts as for No. 242. NvHi. [251]

No. 33, Substitute. Relating to county prosecuting attorneys. February —, 1864. 6 p. 31 x 21 cm. Crawford asked $11.70 for composition, $6 for press work, $1 for folding, $2 for stitching, and $1.75 for paper, for a total of $22.45. NvHi. [252]

No. 41. To authorize the County Commissioners of Lander County to provide means to build a court house and jail. January 25, 1864. 13 p. 31 x 22 cm. Charges were $27.30 for composition, $10.50 for press work, $2 for folding, $2 for stitching, and $3.50 for paper, for a total of $45.30. NvHi.   [253]

No. 46. Amendatory of an act to amend an act entitled an act, establishing a common school system, for the Territory of Nevada. Approved November 29th, 1861; approved December 20th, 1862. January 29, 1864. 4 p. 31 x 22 cm. The charges were $7.80 for composition, $3 for press work, 50¢ for folding, and 87 1/2¢ for paper; the total was $12.17. NvHi.   [254]

No. 56. Providing for the building of a court house and jail for the County of Lyon, in the Territory of Nevada. January 29, 1864. 6 p. 31 x 22 cm. Crawford charged the same amounts as for No. 252. NvHi.   [255]

No. 57. [Authorizing county recorders to appoint deputies.] Title from Ms. House journal, p. 238, at Nv-Ar. The printer charged the same as for No. 242. See No. 257.   [L256]

No. 57, Substitute. Authorizing ministerial officers to appoint deputies. January 29, 1864. 3 p. 31 x 22 cm. There is no record of a printer's charge on Voucher 42; it is possible that the charges designated for No. L256 are actually for this bill. NvHi.   [257]

No. 58. Supplementary to, and amendatory of an act relating to elections, and the mode of supplying vacancies, approved November 1st, A.D. 1861. January 27, 1864. 4 p., with p. 1 and 4 reversed. 31 x 22 cm. As with House bill 27, this bill appears twice on Voucher 42; it is not known whether the double entry is the result of an accounting error. The charges in both entries are the same, and are identical to those for No. 254. NvHi.   [258]

No. 60. To authorize certain parties to construct a railroad in the County of Storey. January 27, 1864. 12 p. 31 x 22 cm. Charges were $23.40 for composition, $9 for press work, $1.50 for folding, $2 for stitching, and $2.62 1/2 for paper; the total was $38.50 (error in printer's addition; should have been $38.52). NvHi. [259]

No. 61. To organize the County of Churchill, and other purposes. January 29, 1864. 5 p. 31 x 22 cm. Crawford asked the same amounts as in the second set of charges for No. 248. NvHi.   [260]

No. 64. Amendatory of and supplementary to an act entitled "An act to authorize the incorporation of the City of Virginia," approved December 19th, 1862. January 27, 1864. 22 p. 31 x 22 cm. Charges for composition were $42.90, for press work $18, for folding $2, for stitching $3, and for paper $5.25; the total was $71.15. NvHi.   [261]

No. 78. Describing the duties and powers of the Police Magistrate in and for the City of Virginia, County of Storey. January 30, 1864. 4 p. 31 x 22 cm. The charges were the same as for No. 246. NvHi.   [262]

No. 83. In relation to probate judges and prosecuting attorneys of Lyon and Churchill, Lander and Ormsby counties. January 30, 1864. 3 p. 31 x 22 cm. Crawford charged the same amounts as for No. 246. NvHi.   [263]

No. 84. To provide for the assessing and collecting county and territorial revenue. January 30, 1864. 121 p. 31 x 21 cm. Charges were $235.95 for composition, $91.50 for press work, $5 for folding, $5 for stitching, and $26.25 for paper, for a total of $363.70. NvHi. [264]

No. 86 [Council bill No. 25]. To incorporate the Bullion Insurance Company. January 30, 1864. 11 p. 31 x 21 cm. See No. 213. NvHi. [265]

No. 91. Concerning franchises. February 1, 1864. 2 p. 31 x 22 cm. Charges were the same as for No. 236. NvHi. [266]

No. 93. [In relation to contracts payable in coin.] Title from Ms. House journal, p. 303, at Nv-Ar. The printer asked the same amounts as for No. 242. [L267]

No. 95. To amend an act entitled "An act to authorize the county commissioners of the several counties to cause the county lines to be established," approved December 19th, 1862. February 15, 1864. 4 p. 30 x 21 cm. Crawford asked the same amounts as for No. 254. DNA. NvHi. [268]

No. 96. To legalize the assessment of real and personal property, as made by the Board of Commissioners of Lyon and Churchill counties, for the year eighteen hundred and sixty-three. February 2, 1864. 3 p. 31 x 22 cm. The printer charged the same amounts as for No. 242. NvHi. [269]

No. 98. For the encouragement of mining. February 2, 1864. 5 p. 31 x 22 cm. Charges were the same as the second set of charges for No. 248. NvHi. [270]

No. 99. To amend an act entitled "An act creating board of county commissioners, and defining their duties." February 2, 1864. 5 p. 31 x 22 cm. Crawford asked the same amounts as in the second set of charges for No. 248. NvHi. [271]

No. 100. To amend an act, to provide increased compensation to justices of the Supreme Court and other officers in the Territory of Nevada. Approved December 19th, 1862. February 2, 1864. 2 p. 31 x 22 cm. The printer charged the same amounts as for No. 236. NvHi. [272]

No. 101. To amend an act entitled an act relating to wild game, and fish approved November 21st, 1861. February 2, 1864. [2] p. 31 x 22 cm. Crawford asked the same amounts as for No. 236. NvHi. [273]

No. 102. To provide for the registration of qualified electors, and to secure the purity of elections. February [3], 1864. 17 p. 31 x 22 cm. Date from Ms. House journal at Nv-Ar. Charges were $33.15 for composition, $15 for press work, $3 for folding, $3 for stitching, and $4.38 for paper, for a total of $58.53. NvHi. [274]

No. 106. To grant to Wm. V. Kingsbury and others, the right to construct and maintain a toll road in Roop County. February 4, 1864. 3 p. 31 x 22 cm. The charges were the same as for No. 246. NvHi. [275]

No. 122. To provide for funding the outstanding indebtedness of Lander County. February 5, 1864. 8 p. 30 x 21 cm. The printer charged $14.05 for composition, $6 for press work, $1.50 for folding, $2 for stitching, and $1.75 for paper, for a total of $25.30. NvHi. [276]

No. 123. To supply the Town of Dayton in Lyon County with water, and to protect the town against fire. February 12, 1864. 4 p. 31 x 22 cm. Crawford's charges were the same as for No. 254. NvHi. [277]

No. 124. To incorporate the City of Austin. February 5, 1864. 21 p. 30 x 21 cm. The printer asked $40.95 for composition, $18 for press work, $3 for folding, $3 for stitching, and $5.25 for paper, for a total of $70.20. NvHi.   [278]

No. 128. Amendatory of and supplementary to an act entitled "An act to provide for the formation of corporations for certain purposes, approved December 20th, 1862." February 5, 1864. 11 p. 31 x 22 cm. The printer's charges were $21.45 for composition, $9 for press work, $1.50 for folding, $2 for stitching, and $2.62 for paper, for a total of $37.57 (error in printer's addition; should have been $36.57). NvHi.   [279]

No. 129. Requiring county recorders to give bonds. February 6, 1864. 2 p. 31 x 21 cm. Crawford charged the same as for No. 236. NvHi.   [280]

No. 130. To establish and support a polytechnic college in the Territory of Nevada. February 6, 1864. 7 p. 31 x 22 cm. Charges were $15.60 for composition, $6 for press work, $1 for folding, $2 for stitching, and $1.75 for paper, for a total of $26.35. NvHi.   [281]

No. 131. To amend an act entitled "An act to provide for the election of probate judges and prosecuting attorneys, and defining their duties," approved December 19th, 1862. February 8, 1864. 3 p. 31 x 22 cm. The printer requested the same amounts as for No. 246. NvHi.   [282]

No. 132. For the relief of H. L. Joachimsen. February 8, 1864. 2 p. 31 x 22 cm. Printer's charges were the same as for No. 236. NvHi.   [283]

No. 133. To provide for taking the census and statistics of the Territory, and for the apportionment of representation in the Legislative Assembly. February 8, 1864. 9 p. 31 x 21 cm. Charges were $17.75 for composition, $9 for press work, $1.50 for folding, $2 for stitching, and $2.62 1/2 for paper, for a total of $32.87. NvHi.
[284]

No. 135. To audit the claim of Wellington Stewart, and to provide for the payment of the same. February 8, 1864. 2 p. 30 x 21 cm. Charges were the same as for No. 236. NvHi.   [285]

No. 136. To provide for the publication of the decisions of the Supreme Court, and the appointment of a reporter. February 8, 1864. 4 p. 30 x 21 cm. Crawford asked for the same amounts as in the second set of charges for No. 248. The decisions of the Supreme Court of Nevada Territory were never published. NvHi.   [286]

No. 156. To increase the salary of the probate judges of Esmeralda County. February 10, 1864. 2 p. 31 x 22 cm. Charges were for the same amounts as for No. 236. NvHi.   [287]

No. 160. To audit the claim of L. E. Crane, and to provide for the payment of the same. February 12, 1864. 2 p. 31 x 22 cm. Printer's charges were the same as for No. 254. See No. L290. NvHi.   [288]

No. 160. Substitute for Council bill No. 126, for the relief of certain persons. To provide for certain expenses incurred by the Constitutional Convention. February 16, 1864. 4 p. 30 x 22 cm. Neither Council bill 126 nor House bill 160, Substitute, appear on Voucher 42. DNA. NvHi.   [289]

No. 169. [To audit the claim of L. E. Crane and to provide for the payment of the same.] Title from Ms. House journal, p. 521, at Nv-Ar; see No. 288. The printer asked the same amounts as for No. 236.   [L290]

No. 172. To provide for a Territorial Prison. February 12, 1864. 5 p. 31 x 21 cm.

Crawford asked for the same amounts as in the second set of charges for No. 248.
NvHi. [291]

No. —. Mr. Clagett's amendments to the revenue bill. February 15, 1864. 13 p.
30 x 22 cm. Charges were $23.35 for composition, $10.50 for press work, $2 for
folding, $2 for stitching, and $3.50 for paper; the total was $43.55 (error in
printer's addition; should have been $41.35). DNA. NvHi. [292]

No. —. To repeal an act entitled an act to authorize and require the County
Commissioners of Esmeralda County, to procure the necessary books and station-
ary [sic]—authorize the County Recorder of Mono County, California, to transfer certain records and indexes of records of said County of Mono. February 15,
1864. 2 p. 31 x 22 cm. Charges were the same as for No. 236. The bill was needed
because of the findings of an 1863 survey; see Nos. 200, 201. DNA. NvHi.
[293]

No. 212. To provide compensation to the attaches of the Legislative Assembly.
February 17, 1864. 2 p. 31 x 22 cm. The printer asked $4.25 for composition, $1.50
for press work, 50¢ for folding, and 87¢ for stitching; the total was $7.12. DNA.
NvHi. [294]

NEVADA TERRITORY. *Legislative Assembly. House of Representatives.*

Rules and Orders | of the | House of Representatives | of the |
Territory of Nevada. | [short rule] | . . . | [Carson City: Israel
Crawford, Territorial Printer. 1864.] [295]

10 p. 22 x 15 cm. Caption title. The names of Wm. M. Gillespie and Wm. H.
Brumfield, as the committee to draw up the rules, appear on p. 10; both men were in
the House only during the third session.
100 copies ordered printed in pamphlet form (JHR, 1864, p. 66). Crawford's charges
were $29.50 for composition, $9 for press work, $2 for folding, $2 for stitching, and
$2.62 1/2 for paper; the total was $45.12 (RG217: Voucher 42, Session of 1864).
NvHi.

NEVADA TERRITORY. *Legislative Assembly. House of Representatives.*

Territory of Nevada. | [short rule] | House of Representatives,
| February 9, 1864. | [short rule] | Hon. Mr. Clagett offered the
following which was ordered | printed: | To the Honorable the
Senate and House of Representatives in | Congress Assembled:—
| . . . | [Carson City: Israel Crawford, Territorial Printer. 1864.]
[296]

5 p. 31 x 21 cm. Page 5: "Dated at Carson City, N.T., February 3d, 1864."
A concurrent resolution requesting authorization for two more judges because of the
rapid growth of the Territory, and requesting gubernatorial authority to call special
sessions for this and other purposes. See No. 235. The printer asked $9.75 for
composition, $4.50 for press work, $1 for folding, $2 for stitching, and $1.75 for
paper, for a total of $19; 100 copies were printed (RG217: Voucher 42, Session of
1864).
NvHi.

NEVADA TERRITORY. *Legislative Assembly. Joint Committee on Territorial Prison.*

Territory of Nevada. | [*broken wavy rule*] | Report of Joint Committee on Territorial | Prison. | . . . | [Carson City: Israel Crawford, Territorial Printer. 1864.]   [297]

7 p. 30 x 21 cm. Caption title. Signed by members of the 1864 Legislative Assembly; *Check List:* 7 described this title as an 1862 imprint.

For printing 100 copies the printer charged $13.65 for composition, $6 for press work, $1.50 for folding, $2 for stitching, and $1.75 for paper, for a total of $24.90 (RG217: Voucher 42, Session of 1864).

NvHi.

NEVADA TERRITORY. *Politics.* Poster. Dayton: Sentinel. August 1864.
                              [L298]

The entry in Alf Doten's *Journals* for August 17, 1864, has the following: ". . . Evening I received a bundle of posters from Dayton announcing to the gaping public that C A Witherell is up for Councilman & Alfred Doten for the Assembly." He added that "All the different independent candidates are putting out their posters. . . ." The *Sentinel* was the only press in Dayton in 1864.

NEVADA TERRITORY. *Prison.*

$500 | Reward! | For the arrest of | Thomas Boulton. | Who escaped from the Territorial Prison on the even-|ing of August the 15th, 1864. . . . | . . . | R. M. Howland, | Warden Territorial Prison. | Carson City, Nevada Territory, August 15, 1864. | [Carson City: Israel Crawford, Territorial Printer?]   [299]

Broadside. 39? x 29? cm. The recorded copy has been framed, obscuring the outside dimensions.

At the bottom of the recorded copy, in Howland's hand: "The only Escape while I was Warden, 1864 & Part of 1865." He also wrote: "Prisoner Returned Nov 12th 64 by Sheriffs of Siskiyou Co. Cal." If he noticed the irony in the escapee's surname he did not record it.

NvMus.

NEVADA TERRITORY. *Secretary.*

Report | of the | Territorial Secretary, | For the Year 1863. | [Carson City: Israel Crawford, Territorial Printer. 1864.]   [L300]

6 p. Description from caption title in No. 197.

It is questionable whether this report was ever issued separately, apart from No. 197, although other reports included in that document appear to have been sent out as separates. The Secretary's own copy, at CU-B(MT), is an extract from the collected issue.

NEVADA TERRITORY. *Superintendent of Public Instruction.*

Report | of the Superintendent of Public Instruction. | [Carson City:
Israel Crawford, Territorial Printer. 1864.]   [L301]

9 p. Description from caption title in No. 197.

Receipt of a copy was acknowledged in the February 13, 1864, issue of the Unionville
Humboldt Register.

NEVADA TERRITORY. *Supreme Court.*

[Briefs. 1864.]

Hamilton et al. vs. Kneeland & Requa et al. Brief of respondents, A. C. Hamilton et
al. 39 p. 20 x 14 cm. Imprint on wrapper: Virginia, N.T. John Church & Co.,
Printers. Pages 33-36 have been taken out of the recorded copy. Nv-Ar. [302]

NEVADA TERRITORY. *Treasurer.*

Report | of the | Territorial Treasurer, | For the Year 1863.
| [Carson City: Israel Crawford, Territorial Printer. 1864.] [L303]

12 p. Description from caption title in No. 197.

The Unionville *Humboldt Register* acknowledged receipt of a copy on February 13,
1864.

NEVADA. *Constitution.*

Constitution of State of Nevada, | To be submitted to the people on
Wednesday, September 7th, 1864. | [*double rule*] | Official. | [*short
rule*] | The | Constitution | of the | State of Nevada, | Together
with the | Resolutions and Ordinances, | as Passed by the | State
Constitutional Convention | Thursday, July 28th, 1864. | . . . |
[Virginia City: 1864.]   [304]

[2] p. 46 x 30 cm. Printed in five columns. Lines 1-2 extend across the sheet; the
remainder is in column 1. On the verso, in column 5: J. Neely Johnson, | President
of the Convention, and Delegate from | Ormsby County. | Wm. M. Gillespie,
Secretary. The signatures are followed by: [*rule*] | Hair, Plaster and Cement!!! |
[*short rule*] | Hair, Plaster and Cement. | For sale by | Gartrell & Murray, |
jy123od. 74 South C st., Virginia.

During the Constitutional Convention (*Official Report of the Debates and Proceedings*
. . . San Francisco: Frank Eastman, 1866, p. 775-777) a Storey County delegate,
Samuel A. Chapin, introduced a resolution that provided for the majority of the
printed copies of the proposed Constitution to be sent to newspapers for distribution.
In the ensuing discussion he said, "My intention [is] to procure the printing of all the
copies at one office, and then distribute them to the various newspapers, to the *Washoe
Star,* the *Carson Independent,* the *Esmeralda Daily Union,* and so on, requesting the
editors of those newspapers to distribute them to their subscribers, which I presume
they would cheerfully do." No action on the resolution is recorded, but it is likely that
it was at least informally adopted, for on August 17 the *Union* noted that "To-day we
send to each of our subscribers, enclosed in our paper, a copy of the Constitution lately
framed for the State of Nevada." The printing of 10,000 copies was authorized by

another resolution, with the expense of printing and distribution to "be certified . . . to the next session of the State or Territorial Legislature, as may be, for payment." A committee authorized by the latter resolution was made up entirely of Storey County delegates to the convention, since it was the feeling of most members that the printing could be done cheaper there than elsewhere in the Territory. It is unknown whether copies distributed outside of Storey County contained Gartrell & Murray's advertisement, but the copy at DNA shows signs of an attempt at erasure.
CU-B(MT). DNA.

NEVADA. *Governor (Acting), 1864 (James Warren Nye).*

Thankgiving Proclamation. | [*short thick-thin rule*] | Executive Department, | Carson City, Nevada, November 14, 1864. | . . . | . . . I, James W. Nye, Governor of the State of Nevada, do | hereby apppoint [*sic*] and fix | Thursday, The 24th Day of November Inst., | as a day of Public Thanksgiving and Prayer, . . . | . . . | [Carson City: 1864.] [305]

Broadside. 29 x 40 cm. Lines 2-3 connected by a brace. The state seal, which had not yet been adopted, is represented by a circle with the word "Seal" printed in the center.

The officers of the new state had not yet been sworn in, so the leftover officers from the territory, James W. Nye and Orion Clemens, had the task of conducting state business; the names of both men appear on the proclamation.
NvHi. NvMus.

NEVADA. *Governor, 1864-1871 (Henry Goode Blasdel).*

Inaugural Address | —of— | H. G. Blasdel, | Governor of the State of Nevada, | Delivered at Carson City, Dec. 5, 1864. | Also, | First Annual Message, | Delivered to the Legislature, in Carson City, | December 14, 1864. | [*filet*] | Carson City: | Printed at the Office of the Daily Morning Post. [306]

12 p. 20 x 15 cm. Printed wrapper. The inaugural address in on p. [3]-5; the annual message covers p. [6]-12. The message is also in JA, 1864-5, p. 21-28, and appears in a separate 1865 issue along with the inaugural address; each of the three is from different type. See Nos. 339 and 345.
DLC.

NEVADA. *Homographic Charts.*

First Organization. | Homographic Chart | of the | State Officers and Legislature | of the State of Nevada. | . . . | December 12, A.D. 1864. | Gold Hill News Print. [L307]

Broadside. Description from a photograph at NvHi; the location of the original, formerly in a private collection, is unknown. Line 2 in a reverse arch under line 1. Decorative border. Line 1 in a compartment imbedded in the border; the imprint is in a compartment imbedded in the border.

ODD FELLOWS, INDEPENDENT ORDER OF. *Virginia City, Nevada Territory. Nevada Lodge No. 7.*

Constitution, | By-Laws and Rules of Order | of | Nevada Lodge, No. 7, | I.O. of O.F., | of the | Territory of Nevada. | [*filet*] | Instituted at Virginia, N.T., Jan. 15, 1864. | [*filet*] | [*lodge emblem*] | Sacramento: | H. S. Crocker & Co., Printers, 107 J Street. | 1864. [308]

65 p. 13? x 9? cm. The recorded copy has been rebound and trimmed. Title and text pages in double rule borders.
C.

REESE RIVER REVEILLE. *Austin, Nevada Territory.* Extra. May 15, 1864.
[L309]

The *Reveille*'s issue of May 17, 1864, reprinted war news from various places, dated May 13 and 14, "From our Extra of Sunday, May 15th."

REESE RIVER REVEILLE. *Austin, Nevada Territory.* Extra. May 17, 1864.
[L310]

The *Reveille* of May 19, 1864, reprinted war news of the 12th and 15th of May, "From our Extra of Tuesday, May 17th."

REPUBLICAN PARTY. *Douglas County, Nevada Territory.*

Douglas County | Regular | Union Nominations. | [*short rule*] | For Delegates to Congress, | . . . | Constitution, yes. | [1864.]
[311]

Broadside. 20 x 8 cm. Slip pasted in after line 4 of the recorded copy: "Judge Cradlebaugh."

Nominees are those who ran in the election of September 7, 1864, at which time the second Constitution was also before the electorate. John Cradlebaugh won narrowly as an Independent Republican over the Democrat, A. C. Bradford, and by a larger margin over the regular Republican, Thomas Fitch. Because of the overwhelming acceptance of the Constitution, however, Cradlebaugh's election as the Territorial Delegate was negated; after formal admission to the Union the following month, Nevada elected a voting member to the U.S. House of Representatives in the November election.
NvU.

REPUBLICAN PARTY. *Douglas County, Nevada Territory.*

For Delegates | —To The— | Constitutional Convention. | [*filet*] | Regular Union Nominees | For Douglas County, | A. T. Hawley, | J. W. Haines. | [1864.] [312]
Broadside. 10 x 8 cm.

Hawley and Haines were both elected to the second Constitutional Convention in 1864.
NvU.

REPUBLICAN PARTY. *Douglas County, Nevada.*

Nevada Union State Ticket. | [*short rule*] | . . . | Abraham Lincoln, | . . . | Andrew Johnson. | . . . | [*short rule*] | For Governor, | H. G. Blasdel, of Storey county. | For Lieutenant-Governor, | J. S. Crosman, of Lyon county. | . . . | [*filet*] | Douglas County Ticket. | [*short rule*] | . . . | [1864.]   [313]

Broadside. 12? x 6? cm. The recorded copy is cropped all around.

The national election in 1864 was on November 8; Nevada's admission to the Union only slightly more than a week earlier made necessary the rapid assembling of a slate of nominees for state offices.
NvU.

REPUBLICAN PARTY. *Esmeralda County, Nevada.*

Regular Union Ticket. | [*short rule*] | . . . | County Ticket. | [*filet*] | . . . | [1864.]   [314]

Broadside. 19 x 7 cm. On the recorded copy the name of the county has been filled in by hand, but the names of nominees who ran in Esmeralda County in the election of November 1864 are printed.
NvHi.

REPUBLICAN PARTY. *Roop and Washoe Counties, Nevada.*

Regular | Union Ticket. | [*filet*] | . . . | [1864.]   [315]

[2] p. 18 x 9 cm. On verso, printed in blue: "Lincoln and Johnson."

The heading before names of county nominees is simply "County Ticket," but the printed names correspond to those of men elected from Roop and Washoe counties in November 1864. The two counties voted as a single district until 1883, when Roop became a part of Washoe County.
NvU.

REPUBLICAN PARTY. *Storey County, Nevada.*

Regular Union Nominees. | [*short rule*] | . . . | [*double rule*] | Storey County Ticket. | . . . | [1864.]   [316]

Broadside. 23 x 6 cm.

Names of county nominees who ran in the election of November 1864 are printed.
NvHi.

REPUBLICAN PARTY. *Storey County, Nevada.*

Regular Union Ticket. | [*short rule*] | Lincoln and Johnson. | [*short rule*] | . . . | [*filet*] | Nevada Union State Ticket | [*short rule*] | . . . | [*filet*] | Storey County Union Ticket. | . . . | [1864.]

[317]

Broadside. 11? x 8 cm. The recorded copy is cropped at the bottom. Printed in blue ink.

NvU.

REPUBLICAN PARTY. *Storey County, Nevada.*

Regular Union Ticket. | [*short rule*] | Lincoln and Johnson. | [*short rule*] | . . . | [*filet*] | Nevada Union State Ticket | [*short rule*] | . . . | [*filet*] | Storey County Union Ticket. | . . . | [1864.]   [317a]

[2] p. 11 x 8 cm. Recto printed in blue ink; verso, with cut of U.S. flag, Constitution, clasped hands, etc., printed in red ink.

CU-B.

SUMNER, CHARLES ALLEN.

Odd-Fellowship. | [*filet*] | Oration | by | Charles A. Sumner. | [*filet*] | Delivered at Dayton, N.T., | on the Occasion of I.O.O.F. | Anniversary and Dedicatory Ceremonies, | April 26th, 1864. | [*filet*] | Published by request of Dayton Lodge, No. 5. [*filet*] | Virginia: | J. T. Goodman & Co., Printers, Enterprise Office. | 1864.   [318]

24 p. 23 x 15 cm. Printed wrapper.

C. CSmH. CtY. MH. NjP. Nv. NvU.

WASHOE AGRICULTURAL, MINING AND MECHANICAL SOCIETY. *Carson City, Nevada Territory.* Poster. October 1864.   [L319]

An item in the Gold Hill *News* of October 28, 1864, said that "We notice that posters are out for the State Fair, which commences carnival at Carson October 31st., and will continue until November 5th." Either the local of the *News* or the Society, which sponsored the event, must have been supremely confident that there could be a "State" fair; Nevada was admitted to the Union on the fair's opening day.

≈1865≈

Early in the year the Legislature agreed on a means to get the state's printing done by enacting a law providing for election of a State Printer by a joint convention of the Senate and Assembly; at the 1866 general election and every two years thereafter a State Printer was to be chosen by the state's qualified electors. His bond was to be $10,000. The law went on to say that "whenever any message, report or other document in book form is ordered printed by either house, two hundred copies in addition to the number ordered shall be struck off and be retained in sheets by the printer, to be bound with the journals of the house ordering, as an appendix. Whenever any bill is ordered printed, one hundred copies shall be deemed the number ordered, unless the house ordering the same specially order a different number" (SSN, 1864-65, p. 90-94). Six hundred copies of the laws and 200 of the legislative journals were to be printed. The law was very specific regarding style and payment:

> The laws, journals, messages and other documents in book form, shall be printed "solid," in long primer type, on good white paper, each page, except the laws, shall be thirty-three "ems" wide and fifty-eight "ems" long, including title, blank line under it and foot line; the laws to be of the same length as the journals, and twenty-nine "ems" wide, exclusive of marginal notes, which notes shall be printed in nonpareil type, and be seven "ems" wide; figure work, and rule and figure work, in messages, reports and other documents, in book form, shall be on pages corresponding in size with the journals, providing it can be brought in by using type not smaller than minion, and whenever such work cannot be brought into pages of the proper size by using type not smaller than minion, it shall be executed in a form to fold and bind with the volume it is intended to accompany; bills, and other work of a similar character, shall be printed with long primer type, on white, plain cap paper, commencing the heading one fourth of the length of the sheet from its top, and when said printing does not occupy more than two pages of such sheet, or less, the same shall be printed upon half sheets, and the State Printer shall only charge for the same, and in like ratio for a greater amount, and be forty-six "ems" wide and seventy-three "ems" long, including running head, blank line under it and foot line, and between each printed line there shall be a white line corresponding with four lines of the body of the type, and each printed line shall be numbered; blanks shall be printed in such form, and on such paper, and with such sized type as the officers ordering them may direct. The laws shall be printed without chapter headings, and with no blank lines, with the exception of one head line, one foot line, two lines between the last section of an Act and the title of the next Act; *provided,* that when there shall not be space enough between the last section of an Act to print the title and enacting clause and one line of the following Act upon the same page, such title may be printed on the following page. The journals shall be printed with no blank lines, with the exception of one head line, one foot line, and ten lines between the journal of one day and that of the following day. In printing the "yeas" and "nays," the word "yeas" shall be run in with the names, and the

word "nays" shall be run in with the names. Folding shall also be allowed and charged on any bill or document, and no bill or document not exceeding four pages shall be stitched. When stitching and folding is required on bills oa [*sic*] documents ordered by either House, one sixteenth of one per cent. per page shall be allowed for such folding and stitching; *provided,* that no folding or stitching shall be allowed on the laws or journals. For all work executed and material furnished under this Act by the State Printer he shall be allowed as follows, which allowance shall include all the charges he shall make for the work, well executed, and delivered in good order at the seat of Government, excepting only the cost of paper, as herein provided, which shall be furnished to him by the Secretary of State, and an appropriation made by the Legislature therefor; For composition, per one thousand "ems," one dollar and sixty cents; figure work, per one thousand "ems," two dollars; rule work, per one thousand "ems," two dollars and fifteen cents; rule and figure work, per one thousand "ems," two dollars and twenty-five cents. Press work, per token of two hundred and forty impressions, one dollar and fifty cents. For all proclamations, orders, notices, and advertisements, authorized by section five of this Act to be published in the State papers, he shall be allowed one dollar per square of three hundred "ems" for composition and the first insertion, and fifty cents for each subsequent insertion; but no charge shall be made for a greater number of such subsequent insertions than may be ordered or directed by law, or by the Governor of the State. For binding the laws of each session, in full binding and lettering the same, two dollars per volume; for binding the journals of the Senate and Assembly in half binding, leather backs, and corners in junk board marbled, and lettering the same, one dollar and seventy-five cents per volume. *Provided,* no charge shall be made or allowed for composition for blank pages under the provisions of this Act.

A Board of Commissioners was created, made up of the Governor, the Secretary of State, and a Printing Expert, to measure the State Printer's work prior to auditing. But Section 16 of the law, one of the shortest, is as significant as any of the others, for it provides that "the Printing for the Legislature *during its session* shall be done at the capital" [emphasis added]. It thus seems probable that the area's printers had made it clear to the lawmakers that the larger pieces of the public printing could not profitably be executed in Nevada.

Five men, all local newspapermen, presented themselves as candidates for the job as State Printer: T.W. Abraham, John Church, Joseph T. Goodman, John C. Lewis, and Philip Lynch. With so many men vying for the position the election was both difficult and protracted, but on the second day of the joint convention, January 11, Church was finally chosen, despite unspecified objections that he might be constitutionally ineligible.

The 1878 report of the State Controller (p. 30) shows warrants drawn on the State Printing Fund in the amount of $25,042.20 during the fiscal year 1865, which ran from November 1, 1864, to December 31, 1865.

Aurora lost one of its newspapers in April and Carson City's single paper lasted only into May, but it was replaced immediately by another. Genoa, which had been without a press since 1859, saw two papers established in late 1865; neither of them still existed at the end of the year. Ione's paper, which had suspended in 1864, began publishing again at mid-year. Two of Virginia City's newspapers suspended early in January; two others started—and stopped—in April. Washoe City began and ended 1865 with one newspaper in town, but the year saw three papers printed there.

AUSTIN, NEVADA. *Citizens.*

The Funeral | Ceremonies | in Honor of | Abraham Lincoln, | President of the United States of America, | Held at | Austin, Lander Co., Nevada, | On Wednesday, April 19, A.D. 1865. | [*fi-let*] | J.D. Fairchild & Co., Printers: | [*filet*] | Austin.   [320]

22 p. 30? x 13? cm. The recorded copy has been rebound and trimmed. Printed wrapper. Cut of a Lincoln bust on verso of title page. Text pages in decorative rule borders. Includes: "Preamble and Resolutions," adopted by a committee of city aldermen; "Funeral Oration," by D. R. Ashley, Nevada's U.S. Representative; "An Elegy," by Myron Angel; and "Sermon," by the Reverend A. N. Fisher. J. D. and O. L. C. Fairchild were lessees of the *Reese River Reveille.*

The ceremonies took place on the same day as Lincoln's funeral in Washington, D.C.

CSmH.

CENTRAL PACIFIC RAILROAD COMPANY.

Central Pacific Railroad. | [*filet*] | Reply | to the | Letter of L. L. Robinson. | [*filet*] | February 14, 1865.   [321]

10 p. 23 x 14 cm. Wrapper title, in double rule border. Also appears, set in different type, on p. [129]-139 of *Evidence Concerning Projected Railways . . . 1865;* see No. 349. Sacconaghi:48 identifies the present issue as a Sacramento imprint.

CSmH. CSt. CU-B.

CENTRAL PACIFIC RAILROAD COMPANY.

Central Pacific Railroad Company. | [*filet*] | Statement | Made to | Senate Committee | of the | Nevada Legislature. | [*filet*] | January 14, 1865.   [322]

15 p. 22 x 14 cm. Wrapper title, in a thin-thick-thin rule border. Caption title: Railroad Resolutions | of the | State of Nevada. Also appears, set in different type, on p. [7]-22 of *Evidence Concerning Projected Railways . . . 1865;* see No. 349. Sacconaghi:52 identifies the present issue as a Sacramento imprint.

C. CLU. CSmH. CSt. CU-B. CtY. MH. NvU (rear wrapper missing). UU. WyU.

DAILY EVENING POST. *Carson City, Nevada.*

Post-Extra | [*funerary rule*] | Carson City, Satuuday [*sic*] April 15, 3 P.M. | [*funerary rule*] | Assassination of | President Lincoln | and | William H. Seward. | [*filet*] | . . . | [1865.]   [323]

Broadside. 41 x 16 cm. Lines 1-2 extend across the sheet; the remainder is in the first of two columns.

The extra tells the story of Lincoln's visit to "Forbes' Theatre," the shooting, and his subsequent death. Perhaps the *Post* received a garbled version, confusing the name of the President's footman, Charles Forbes, with the name of the theater in which the shooting occurred. It also describes the separate attempt on the life of Secretary Seward, but incorrectly states that he, too, had died, even giving the exact time of day, of three stab wounds in the neck. A call is given for a meeting of the citizens of Carson City to prepare for a public expression of sorrow.

NvHi. NvU(NvMus).

DAILY TERRITORIAL ENTERPRISE. *Virginia City, Nevada.* Extra. April 10, 1865.   [L324]

The April 10 entry in Alf Doten's *Journals* describes the surrender of Robert E. Lee and says that the "papers all got out an extra," mentioning specifically the *Enterprise* and the Virginia City *Union.*

DAILY TERRITORIAL ENTERPRISE. *Virginia City, Nevada.* Extra. April 15, 1865.   [L325]

The entry in Alf Doten's *Journals* for this date says "about 10 AM the news of the assassination of Lincoln was received . . . At 2 PM the Enterprise and Union each issued extras, containing particulars of the assassination . . . never saw such a stir in the 'extra' line."

FREEMASONS. *Dayton, Nevada. Valley Lodge No. 9.*

Constitution | of the | M.˙. W.˙. Grand Lodge | of | Free and Accepted Masons | of the | State of Nevada, | and | Lodge By-Laws; | Together with | The Ancient Charges, | The Twenty-Five Landmarks of Freemasonry, | and | A Funeral Service. | [*filet*] | San Francisco: | Frank Eastman, Printer, 415 Washington Street. | 1865.   [326]

61, [2] p. 17 x 11 cm. Leather binding; in gold stamping on the front cover: Valley Lodge, No. 9, F. & A.M. A list of members of Valley Lodge is on p. [63].

NvLN.

FREEMASONS. *Nevada. Grand Lodge.*

Constitution | of the | M.˙.W.˙.Grand Lodge | of | Free and Ac-
cepted Masons | of the | State of Nevada, | and | Uniform Code of
By-Laws; | Together with | The Ancient Charges, | The Twenty-
Five Landmarks of Freemasonry, | and | A Funeral Service. | [*fi-
let*] | San Francisco: | Frank Eastman, Printer, 415 Washington
Street. | 1865.   [327]

61 p. 17 x 11 cm. Printed wrapper.

Proceedings, October 1865, p. 63: "Constitutions, on account, (balance due, $82.89)
. . . 91.40."

CHi. DSC. ICSR. MBFM. NvHi.

FREEMASONS. *Nevada. Grand Lodge.*

Proceedings | of the | Convention to Organize | the | M.˙. W.˙.
Grand Lodge | of | Free and Accepted Masons | of the | State of
Nevada, | and of the | First Grand Communication | of the
| Grand Lodge; | Held at Masonic Hall, in the City of Virginia,
| January 16, 17, and 18, A.L. 5865. | [*filet*] | San Francisco: |
Frank Eastman, Printer, 415 Washington Street. | 1865.   [328]

[3], 4-51, [1] p. 23 x 14 cm. Printed wrapper. An index is on p. [52]; this page is blank
in copies bound later, and is a cancel. See No. 685.

600 copies ordered, with an additional 300 to be left with the printer for future
binding (Proceedings, October 1865, p. 16); reported printed (p. 60), at a cost of $216
(p. 63).

DSC. IaCrM. NvHi (microfilm). NvMus (microfilm). NvRFM. NvU (microfilm).

FREEMASONS. *Nevada. Grand Lodge.*

Proceedings | of the | M.˙.W.˙.Grand Lodge | of | Free and Ac-
cepted Masons | of the | State of Nevada, | at its | First Annual
Grand Communication, | Held at Masonic Hall, in the City of Vir-
ginia, | October 10, 11, 12, and 13, A.L. 5865. | [*filet*] | San Fran-
cisco: | Frank Eastman, Printer, 415 Washington Street. | 1865.

                                                                   [329]

[3], 56-113, iii p. 23 x 14 cm. Printed wrapper. An index is on the pages set in roman
numerals. Page [i] is on the verso of p. 113: it is not present in the bound volume, and
is a cancel.

A total of $850 was designated for "printing proceedings and expenses of Grand
Secretary's Office" (p. 900). 800 copies were printed, of which 300 were retained in
sheets by the printer for future binding (Proceedings, 1866, p. 123), at a cost of
$329.40 (ibid., p. 126). But see No. 685.

DSC. IaCrM. NvHi (lacks front wrapper). NvMus (microfilm). NvRFM. NvU
(microfilm).

FREEMASONS. *Virginia City, Nevada. Virginia Lodge No. 3.*

Constitution | of the | M.˙.W.˙. Grand Lodge | of | Free and Accepted Masons | of the | State of Nevada, | and | By-Laws | of | Virginia Lodge, No. 3, | Together with | The Ancient Charges, | The Twenty-Five Landmarks of Freemasonry, | and | A Funeral Service. | [*filet*] | San Francisco: | Frank Eastman, Printer, 415 Washington Street. | 1865.   [330]

61 p. 18 x 11 cm. Cloth binding. Basically the same type as in No. 326.
CHi.

GOLD HILL, NEVADA. *Citizens.*

Remonstrance. | [*filet*] | The Undersigned, Taxpayers and Citizens of Gold Hill, respectfully remonstrate against any Consolidation of Storey | county—Virginia City and Gold Hill, or any Consolidation of the last mentioned places—desiring to remain as now, a Corporation | known as Gold Hill: | [*double rule*] | . . . | [Gold Hill? 1865.]   [331]

Broadside. 32 x 20 cm. Printed on blue-lined paper.
The attempt at consolidation was defeated in the 1865 Legislature.
NvHi.

HARRINGTON, WILLIAM P. Directory of the City of Austin. Prospectus. June 1865.   [L332]

Reese River Reveille, June 22, 1865: "It is the intention oi [*sic*] Mr. W. P. Harrington to compile and publish a directory of this city. From the prospectus of the work we learn . . ." The directory was not published until 1866; see No. 374.

HASKELL, DUDLEY HAINES.

Pacific Railroad. | [*filet*] | Second Speech of the | Hon. D. H. Haskell, | Before the Nevada Legislature, | February 21st, 1865. | [*filet*] | . . .   [333]

16 p. 23 x 14 cm. Caption title. Page [12]-16: "Extracts from the Speech of the Hon. H. [*sic*]. A. Young, Before the Nevada Legislature, February 21, 1865." Young's first initial was "R."
C. CLU. CSmH. CSt. CU-B. CtY. NvU (microfilm).

HASKELL, DUDLEY HAINES.

Speech | of | Hon. D. H. Haskell, | on the | Pacific Railroad Resolutions | Before the | Nevada Legislature. | [*filet*] | . . . | [1865].   [334]

16 p. 22 x 14 cm. Caption title. Pages 15-16, "Remarks of Hon. D. H. Brown, of Humboldt."

CSmH. CSt. CU-B. CtY. NvU (microfilm).

NEVADA TERRITORY.

Reports | of the | Territorial | Treasurer, Auditor, | and Board of | Prison Commissioners, | to the | Legislature of the State of Nevada. | [*filet*] | Carson City: | John Church, State Printer. | [*short dotted rule*] | 1865.   [335]

22 p. 23 x 15 cm. Wrapper title, in thick-thin rule border. The report of the Treasurer covers p. [3]-10, the Auditor's report is on p. [11]-17, and the report of the Prison Commissioners is on p. [19]-22.

Check List: 67, 50, and 51 describe the three parts of this piece as separate documents of the state government; the only separate parts located are extracts from AJS, 1865, Nos. [3], [4], and [5].

CSmH. CU-B. CtY. NvU (lacks rear wrapper).

NEVADA TERRITORY. *Adjutant General.*

[*Thick-thin rule*] | Report | of the | Adjutant General | of Nevada. | [*thin-thick rule*] | [Carson City:] John Church, State Printer. | [1865.]   [336]

13 p. 23 x 15 cm. Wrapper title. Issued also as [No. 6] in AJS, 1865.

The report is that of H[enry] P[ierrepont] Russell, Adjutant General of Nevada Territory, for 1864. *Check List:* 49 describes the piece as a state document, apparently because it was issued by the State Printer. See No. 353.

CSmH. ICN. ICU. MH. Nv. NvHi. NvU(microfilm). WHi.

NEVADA TERRITORY. *Superintendent of Public Instruction.*

Report | of the | Superintendent | of | Public Instruction, | of the | Territory of Nevada, | for | the School Year Ending October 31st, 1864. | [*short double rule*] | Carson City, | John Church, State Printer, | 1865.   [337]

19 p., and a folding table. 23 x 15 cm. Printed wrapper. "Errata and Emendata" slip precedes p. [3]. Issued also, printed from a different type setting on 20 p., as [No. 7] in AJS, 1865.

The school year did not end on October 31, but the Superintendent's responsibilities did because of the admission of Nevada to the Union on that date. *Check List:* 65 describes the piece as a document of the state government because it was issued by the State Printer.

DHEW. ICU. M. MH. Nv. NvHi. NvU (microfilm).

NEVADA. *Constitution.*

Constitution | of the | State of Nevada, | Together with the | Resolutions and Ordinances | as Passed by the | State Constitutional Convention, | Thursday, July 28th, 1864. | [*filet*] | Carson City: | John Church, State Printer. | [*short dotted rule*] | 1865.   [338]

42 p. 23 x 14 cm. Printed wrapper. Folding homographic chart of the Convention precedes the text.

LTN, 1864 (p. 155) authorized $450 to John Church & Co. for printing the Constitution "in pamphlet form." Both houses of the first state Legislature passed resolutions to have 240 copies printed in pamphlet form; the Assembly's copies were to be for the use of the Legislature and state officers (JA, 1865, p. 81), while the Senate wanted 240 copies for its own use (JS, 1865, p. 257). The Unionville *Humboldt Register* acknowledged receipt of "pamphlet copies" of the Constitution in its issue of February 20, 1865.

CSmH. CU. CU-B. CtY. MH-L. NHi. NvU.

NEVADA. *Governor, 1864-1871 (Henry Goode Blasdel).*

Inaugural Address | of | H. G. Blasdel, | Governor of the State of Nevada, | Delivered at Carson City, Dec. 5, 1864. | Also | First Annual Message | Delivered to | The Legislature, in Carson City, | December 14, 1864. | [*filet*] | Carson City: | John Church, State Printer. | [*short dotted rule*] | 1865.   [339]

26 p. 22 x 15 cm. Printed wrapper. The message is also printed in JA, 1865, p. 21-28; both the address and the message appear in an 1864 issue. The three issues are from different type. See Nos. 306 and 345.

There were separate resolutions to print 500 copies of the address and message in the Assembly (JA, 1865, p. 28, 96); the Senate's resolution (JS, 1865, p. 237) was to print 500 copies of both, and the same number of copies of the reports of territorial officers to accompany them.

MWA. NvU (microfilm). WHi (has traces of a wrapper).

NEVADA. *Governor, 1864-1871 (Henry Goode Blasdel).*

State of Nevada. | [*short thick-thin rule*] | Proclamation | by | Henry G. Blasdel, Governor | [*short thick-thin rule*] | . . . | Done at Carson City, this sixteenth day of May, A.D., one thousand eight hundred and sixty-five.   [340]

Broadside. 43 x 36 cm. Facsimile in *Quarterly Journal of the Library of Congress*, July 1968, p. 239.

"Whereas, great grief has been suddenly brought upon our land and nation by the untimely death of our Chief Ruler, Abraham Lincoln; and whereas, in this time of national sorrow, we should look up to a higher source than man for relief and consolation; and whereas, it is right and proper at all times to acknowledge God as our Supreme Ruler, and the giver of all good gifts; therefore, let us humble ourselves before our Heavenly Father, with fasting; and sincerely pray for His protection and guidance in this time of great affliction. And to this end, and in accordance with the Proclamation of the President of the United States, and the wishes of a heart stricken

people, I do appoint Thursday, the First Day of June, A.D. 1865, As a Day of Fasting, Humiliation and Prayer, to Almighty God, throughout the State of Nevada.''
CSmH. DLC.

NEVADA. *Governor, 1864-1871 (Henry Goode Blasdel).*

Thanksgiving Proclamation | [*state seal*] | By His Excellency, H. G. Blasdel, Governor of Nevada. | [*thick-thin rule*] | . . . | . . . Done at Carson City, this 17th day of November, A.D. 1865.   [341]

Broadside. 35 x 28 cm. Line 1 in an arch over state seal and line 2. December 7, 1865, was set aside for Thanksgiving.
NHi. NvU.

NEVADA. *Laws, statutes, etc.*

State of Nevada. | [*filet*] | School Law. | [*filet*] | Published by the Department of Public Instruction, | for the use of | School Officers. | [*cut of eagle, banner, stars, etc.*] | John Church & Co., Printers, | Office of the ''Virginia Daily Union,'' Virginia, Nevada. | [*short dotted rule*] | 1865.   [342]

20 p. 22 x 14 cm. Printed wrapper. The recorded copy is imperfect: p. 9-10, 13-14, and 15-16 have been clipped.

The Virginia City imprint may indicate that Church actually did the printing there instead of farming it out to a California printer.
DLC.

NEVADA. *Laws, statutes, etc.*

Statutes | of the | State of Nevada | Passed at the | First Session of the Legislature, | 1864-5, | Begun December 12th, 1864, and ended March 11th, 1865. | [*state seal*] | Carson City, Nevada: | John Church, State Printer.   [343]

xii, 528 p. 23 x 15 cm. Leather binding. 600 copies authorized.

The Unionville *Humboldt Register,* a Democratic paper, complained throughout July of the slowness of the Republican State Printer in delivering the statutes, while the Virginia City *Union,* Church's own paper, was understandably apologetic and reluctant to criticize. By mid-August, according to the Carson City *Appeal,* the volumes had begun to arrive at the office of the Secretary of State. The *Register*'s editor had still not seen a copy by the time of his issue of August 19, but he quoted the *Territorial Enterprise* as follows: ''The Statutes of Nevada, embracing the laws of the last Legislature, have at length been published. We have seen a copy of them, and unhesitatingly assert, that for bungling composition—for grammatical, orthographical, and typographical errors—they stand without a parallel. They are a disgrace to the State. They are partially corrected in four pages of 'errata' at the conclusion of the volume, but had every error been referred to, including inaccuracies in punctuation, the pages of 'errata' would have outnumbered those of the laws. We shall devote our first leisure hours to a careful examination of the volume, and ascertain whether or not if can be used in our courts. Many lawyers inform us that its errors render it almost worthless. . . . We trust the State Printer will be able to offer a reasonable excuse for the bungling work under notice. It is due, at least, to every printing office in Nevada, that Mr. Church should publicly acknowledge that the Statutes were not printed in this State.'' The *Register* got off its final shot on September 9. "Chauncey N. Noteware, Secretary of State, but a gentleman, favors us with a copy of the Statutes enacted at the first session of the Legislature of the State of Nevada. Section 7th, of the law defining duties of the Secretary of State, to which attention is called, directs him to send statutes, journals, and things, to such associations and publishers as will be likely to respond with works suitable to be placed in the State Library. It is a good idea. To get off these miserably done statutes for something fit to be placed in the State Library is a big thing for the Library. We commend Uncle Chauncey's strategy." The volume is indeed not a very lovely example of printing, but the journalistic sniping would seem to reflect political differences as much as professional criticism. The last sentence of the *Enterprise*'s comment, however, is notable as the earliest published indication that the state's printing was being done in another state.

Az. CSmH. CU-B. CtY. CtY-L. DLC. IU. MBS. MH-L. NN. NNLI. NjP. Nv. NvEHi. NvEuC. NvHi. NvLN. NvPLC. NvRWL. NvSC. NvU. OrU-L. PU. RPL. WHi.

NEVADA. *Legislature*.

Transmountain Railways. | [*short rule*] | Discussion | on the | Railroad Resolutions | in the | Legislature of the State of Nevada. | [*short rule*] | First Session, 1865. | [*short rule*] | San Francisco: | Alta California Book and Job Printing Oefice [*sic*], | 1865.

[344]

31 p. 23 x 15 cm. Printed wrapper. The error in the imprint also appears on the wrapper.

Page [3], "The Railroad Resolutions Asking for $10,000,000 bonus by Congress to the first Company building a Railroad from Navigable tide waters in California to the base of the Eastern slope of the Sierra Nevadas"; p. [4]-10, "Speech of the Hon. J. A. Rigby, of Storey County"; p. [11]-15, "Speech of Hon. D. H. Brown, of Humboldt"; p. [16]-19, "Speech of Hon. E. P. Sine, of Lander"; p. [20]-25, "Speech of Hon. Cyril Hawkins, of Esmeralda"; p. [26]-31, "Letter of L. L. Robinson, Civil Engineer."

A resolution to have the "usual number" (i.e., 240) of the railroad resolutions printed is in JS, 1865, p. 54.

CSmH. M. NvU (microfilm).

NEVADA. *Legislature. Assembly*.

The | Journal of the Assembly | During | the First Session | of the | Legislature of the State of Nevada | 1864-5. | Begun on Monday, the Twelfth Day of December, and Ended | on Saturday the Eleventh Day of March. | [*state seal*] | Carson City: | John Church, State Printer. | [*short rule*] | 1865. [345]

524 p. 23 x 15 cm. Half-leather binding.

Printing of 200 copies was authorized (SSN, 1865, p. 92). On the 21st of November, 1865, the editor of the Gold Hill *News* wrote: "We have seen a copy of the last Assembly journals. The book, we know, is actually printed. It has no table of errata, and in this respect differs, by several pages, from its predecessors—the Senate Journal and Appendix. It is well printed, and makes an end of the Public State Documents of the year—unless there is an Appendix to come, which we suppose there is not, as the Governor's full Message is here."

CtY. CtY-L. DLC. M. MH. NN. Nv-Ar. NvHi. NvLC. NvLN. NvRWL. NvSC. NvU. UPB. WHi.

NEVADA. *Legislature. Assembly. Committee on Federal Relations.*

House | Concurrent Resolutions No. 5, | Majority and Minority | Reports | of the | Committee on Federal Relations, | on Resolutions Concerning The | Latrobe Railroad. | [*filet*] | Carson City: | Printed at the Independent Office, | 1865.   [346]

8 p. 21? x 13? cm. The recorded copy has been bound and trimmed. Wrapper title, in thick-thin rule border.

Pages [1]-2, "House Concurrent Resolutions No. 5, on The Latrobe Railroad; Introduced by Hon. W. M. Cutter, of Storey, December 21st, 1865"; p. [3]-7, "Majority Report of Committee on Federal Relations, on Resolutions Respecting the Latrobe Railroad. Hon. Mr. Haskell, Chairman"; p. 8, "Minority Report of Committee on Federal Relations on Resolutions Respecting the Latrobe Railroad."

Three of the five committee members recommended that the railroad receive federal aid because of existing track from Freeport to Latrobe in California, only a short distance from Carson City, and because the Central Pacific's total track length at the time was only thirty miles. The minority did not disagree, but recommended a delay so that representatives of the Latrobe Railroad could demonstrate how they would do a better job than the Central Pacific.

The Carson City *Independent* ceased publication with its issue of October 11, 1864, its material going to the *Carson Valley Farmer* in Genoa. The *Farmer* did not begin publishing until nearly a year later, however, so the *Independent* office may have been kept in Carson City during the legislative session in order to pick up some printing jobs. It may also have subcontracted the work to a California printer, as so many Nevada offices did both then and later.

CSmH.

NEVADA. *Legislature. Senate.*

Appendix | to | Journals of Senate | of the | First Session of the Legislature | of the | State of Nevada. | [*filet*] | Carson City: | John Church, State Printer. | [1865.]   [347]

10, [15]-18, 10, [11]-17, [19]-22, 13, 20, 5, 5, 5, 7, 16, 256 p. 23 x 15 cm. Half-leather binding.

The table of contents lists the Joint Rules of Assembly and Senate, which are not present in any of the examined copies; the order of binding differs in minor respects from the order called for in the table of contents. The volume contains the following, listed in the order in which they are bound, each with its own half title or title page and each paged separately, except as indicated. [No. 1], First Annual Message of H. G. Blasdel, Governor of the State of Nevada, 10 p.; [No.2], Address of Hon. J. S. Crosman, President of the Senate, p. [15]-18, continuing the pagination of the Governor's message; [No. 3], Report of the State [i.e., Territorial] Treasurer, 10 p.; [No. 4], Report of [Territorial] Auditor, p. [11]-17, continuing the pagination of the Treasurer's report; [No. 5], Report of the [Territorial] Board of Prison Commissioners, p. [19]-22, continuing the pagination of the Treasurer's and Auditor's reports; [No. 6], Report of the [Territorial] Adjutant General, 13 p.; [No. 7], Report of the [Territorial] Superintendent of Public Instruction. For the School Year Ending October 31, 1864, 20 p. and a folding table; [No. 8], Report of the Warden of the State Prison, 5 p.; [No. 9], Minority Report on Memorial to Congress, 5 p.; [No. 10], Proceedings of Senate Special Committee [to Inquire into the Existence and Authenticity of the Decisions of the Supreme Court of the Territory of Nevada], 5 p.; [No. 11], Report of Committee on Ways and Means, 7 p.; [No. 12], Standing Rules of the Senate, 16 p.; [No. 13], Evidence Concerning Projected Railways Across the Sierra Nevada Mountains, From Pacific Tide Waters in California, and the Resources, Promises and Action of Companies Organized to Construct the Same; Together with Statements Concerning Present and Prospective Railroad Enterprises in the State of Nevada, Procured by the Committee on Rail Roads of the First Nevada Legislature, 256 p.

200 copies of all messages, reports, etc., ordered by either house were authorized to be printed for use in the appendix (SSN, 1865, p. 91).

DLC. ICU. M. MH. NN. Nv. NvHi. NvU. WHi.

NEVADA. *Legislature. Senate.*

The | Journal of the Senate | During | the First Session | of the | Legislature of the State of Nevada, | 1864-5. | Begun on Monday, the Twelfth Day of December, and Ended | on Saturday the Eleventh Day of March. | [*state seal*] | Carson City: | John Church, State Printer. | [*short rule*] | 1865.   [348]

470 p. 23 x 15 cm. Half-leather binding.

The printing of 200 copies was authorized in SSN, 1865, p. [92].

Az. CtY. CtY-L. DLC. ICN. M. MH. NN. Nv. Nv-Ar. NvHi. NvLN. NvRWL. NvSC. NvU. WHi.

NEVADA. *Legislature. Senate. Committee on Railroads.*

Evidence | Concerning | Projected Railways | Across the | Sierra Nevada Mountains, | from | Pacific Tide Waters in California, | and the | Resources, Promises and Action of Companies | Organized to Construct the Same; | Together with | Statements Concerning Present and Prospective | Railroad Enterprises in the | State of Nevada, | Procured by the | Committee on Rail Roads | of the First Nevada Legislature. | [*short rule*] | Printed by

Order of Senate. | [*short rule*] | Carson City: | John Church, State
Printer. | [*short rule*] | 1865. [349]

256 p. 23 x 15 cm. Printed wrapper. Issued also as [No. 13] in AJS, 1865.

Each section has a separate half title. Pages [3]-5, Railroad Resolutions Appointing a
Committee of the Senate; p. [7]-22, Statement of the Central Pacific Railroad Com-
pany of California; p. [23]-45, Recent Report of the Acting Chief Engineer of the
Central Pacific Railroad Company; p. [47]-51, Report of the Secretary of the
C.P.R.R. Co.; p. [53]-71, Speech of Leland Stanford, President of the Central Pacific
R.R. Co., in the Nevada Constitutional Convention; p. [73]-102, Report of the Chief
Engineer of the Placerville and Sacramento Valley R.R. Company; p. [103]-120,
Report of the Chief Engineer of the San Francisco and Washoe Railroad Company; p.
[121]-127, Letter of L. L. Robinson; p. [129]-139, Reply of Leland Stanford, Pres't
C.P.R.R. Co. to Letter of L. L. Robinson; p. [141]-151, Answer of L. L. Robinson, C.
E. to the Letter of Leland Stanford; p. [153]-167, Testimony of F. A. Bee; p.
[169]-179, Testimony of A. J. Lockwood and C. E. DeLong; p. [181]-195, Testimony
of Joseph Kloppenstein; p. [197]-214, Evidence of L. L. Robinson, C.E., and F. A.
Bishop, C.E., and William J. Lewis, C.E.; p. [215]-219, Questions Addressed to
Leland Stanford, Pres't C.P.R.R. Co.; p. [221]-228, Statement of the Action of the
First Nevada Legislature on Joint Resolutions Concerning Trans-Sierra Railways; p.
[229]-232, Statement of I. E. James, Chief Engineer of the Virginia and Truckee R.R.
Co.; p. [233]-256, Pacific Railroad Bills Passed by the Congress of the United States.

The reports were ordered printed in the Senate (JS, 1865, p. 405-406) and by a joint
committee in the Assembly (JA, 1865, p. 484-485), but in neither case was the
number to be printed specified.

C. CSmH. CU-B. CtY. DBRE. DLC. ICU. MH. NN. Nv. NvHi. WHi.

NEVADA. *Legislature. Senate. Committee on Ways and Means.*

State of Nevada. | [*rule*] | Report | of | Committee on Ways and
Means, | Hon. W. W. Hobart, Chairman. | [*short rule*] | Report Re-
ceived, Jan. 20, 1865. | [*short rule*] | [*short dotted rule*] | Carson,
Nevada: | John Church, State Printer, | 1865. [350]

7 p. 23 x 16 cm. Printed wrapper. Issued also as [No. 11] in AJA, 1865.

A report by A. W. Nightingill, State Controller, regarding taxable property, estimated expenses, etc., appears on p. 6-7.

CU-B.

NEVADA. *Office of Superintendent of Public Instruction.*

State of Nevada. | [*filet*] | Public School Register | of | [*dotted rule*]
District No. [*dotted rule*], County of [*dotted rule*] | [*short dotted
rule*] | Instructions to teachers: | . . . | [1865.] [351]

[98] p. 32 x 21 cm. Caption title. Page 2, "Department of Public Instruction, July,
1865."

NvHi.

NEVADA. *State Library*.

·Catalogue | of the | Nevada State Library, | for the Year 1865. | [*filet*] | C. N. Noteware, Secretary of State, | and | Ex Officio State Librarian. | [*state seal*] | Carson City: | John Church, State Printer. | [*short rule*] | 1865.   [352]

32 p. 23 x 14 cm. Printed wrapper. Title and text pages in double rule borders.

Includes: p. [3]-6, Rules of the Library; p. [7]-12, An Act in Relation to the State Library. A copy of the Senate journal for the first session is catalogued but the Assembly journal is not, indicating that copy for the pamphlet was sent to the printer between receipt of the two volumes in the Library. The Carson City *Appeal,* in its issue of July 28, 1865, acknowledged receipt of a copy: "It is just from the hands of the State printer, is in pamphlet form, is printed in large plain type on inferior paper."

"Paid for Printing Catalogue, $113.34" (Reports of Directors of State Library and Librarian of the State of Nevada, For the Year 1865, p. 6).

In. M. NvU (microfilm).

NEVADA. *State Prison*.

State of Nevada. | [*double rule*] | Report | of | Robert M. Howland, | Warden | of | Nevada State Prison | [*short double rule*] | Carson City, | John Church, State Printer. | 1865.   [353]

6 p. 21 x 14 cm. Printed wrapper. Issued also, in a different type setting, as [No. 8] in AJS, 1865.

It is tempting to call this a territorial document, since it is dated December 9, 1864—only four days after state officials were sworn in—and because it is a description of an addition to the prison, a task that would have had to be done before statehood. Unlike the report of the Adjutant General (No. 336), however, it was issued over the name of a state officer, and to ignore the prominent use of "Nevada State Prison" on the wrapper would unquestionably infuriate a good many library catalogers.

CSmH.

ODD FELLOWS, INDEPENDENT ORDER OF. *Virginia City, Nevada. Mount Davidson Lodge No. 3.*

Constitution, | Laws and Regulations | of | Mount Davidson Lodge | No. 3, | I.O.O.F. | [*filet*] | Instituted at Virginia City, Nevada Territory, April 23, 1862. | [*filet*] | San Francisco, Cal. | Wm. P. Harrison's Print, No. 417 Clay Street, | 1865.   [354]

65, [1] p. 15 x 10 cm. Title and text pages in single rule borders. Cloth binding, with blind-stamped border and gold-stamped title: Constitution & By-Laws of Mount Davidson Lodge No. 3. I.O.O.F. There is a short leaf (13cm.) tipped in between p. 28-29 of the recorded copy: Article 5 1/2 [of the by-laws]; tipped in on p. 30: Amendment adopted at a regular meeting: Article VI.

CSmH.

ODD FELLOWS, INDEPENDENT ORDER OF. *Virginia City, Nevada. Pioneer Encampment No. 1.*

Constitution, | By-Laws and Rules of Order | of | Pioneer Encampment | No. 1, I.O.O.F., | Nevada. | [*filet*] | Instituted at the City of Virginia, Nevada, July 17, A.D. 1864. | [*filet*] | San Francisco: | W. P. Harrison's Print, No. 417 Clay Street. | 1865. [355]

28, [4] p. 14 x 9 cm. Printed wrapper. Title and text pages in single rule borders. Page [3]: "Organized under Right Worthy Grand Encampment of California." NvRW.

ORMSBY COUNTY, NEVADA. *Board of Registration.*

Voters of Ormsby County. | [*double rule*] | Following are the Names of Persons Registered by the Board | of Registration of Ormsby County, Nevada, for the Year A.D. 1865, as qualified electors of | said County: | . . . | Dated at my office in Carson City, Nevada, this 13th October, 1865. | By Order of the Board of Registration of Ormsby County, | H. B. Pomroy, Clerk of said Board. | By M. J. Ashmore, Deputy. [356]

Broadside. 36 x 21 cm. Printed in six columns.

"In pursuance of law, and as required by the Board of Registration, I hereby give notice, That an adjourned Meeting of the Board of Registration of Ormsby County, Nevada, will be held at the office of the Clerk of said Board, in the Court House, in Carson City, on Friday, the 20th of October. [*sic*] 1865, for the purpose of receiving objections to the right to vote, of any person or persons, registered as aforesaid." The list includes voters of Carson City, Empire City, and Clear Creek precincts. CU-B (MT). NvCR.

ROBINSON, LESTER LUDYAH.

Transmountain Railways. | [*double rule*] | Letter | --of-- | L. L. Robinson, Civil Engineer, | --to the-- | Joint Committee on Railroads | of the | Nevada Legislature. | [*short double rule*] | Dated Feb. 3d. 1865. | [*short double rule*] | Carson City, Nevada: | John Church, State Printer. | 1865. [357]

7 p. 21 x 15 cm. Issued also, in a different type setting, in *Evidence Concerning Projected Railways . . . 1865* (No. 349), p. [121]-127. CSmH. CtY. NvU (microfilm).

ROBINSON, LESTER LUDYAH.

Washoe | and | San Francisco Railroad. | [*filet*] | Answer | to the | Statements of Leland Stanford, | President of Central Pacific R.R, [*sic*] | by | L. L. Robinson, | Civil Engineer, | [*filet*] | To the | Joint Committee Legislature of Nevada, | on | Railroads. | [*fi-

let] | February 23, 1865. [358]

10 p. 23 x 16 cm. Printed in two columns. Streeter IV:2338 mentions "facsimile printed wrappers," but neither of the recorded copies shows evidence of ever having had a wrapper; both are unsewn and unopened. Dated, p. 10: "Sacramento February 23rd, 1865." Issued also, in a different type setting, in *Evidence Concerning Projected Railways . . . 1865* (No. 349), p. [141]-151.
CLU. CSmH.

STANFORD, LELAND.

Pacific Railroad. | [*filet*] | Speech | of | Hon. Leland Stanford, | in the | Constitutional Convention | of the State of Nevada, | On Wednesday, July 13th, 1864. | [*filet*] | Andrew J. Marsh, Official Reporter. | [*filet*] | San Francisco, Cal. | Printed by Francis, Valentine & Co., 517 Clay Street. | [*short dotted rule*] | 1865. [359]

12 p. 22? x 14? cm. The recorded copy has been bound and trimmed. Printed in two columns. The text appears also on p. 290-300 of the *Official Report of the Debates and Proceedings in the Constitutional Convention* (No. 381), and in *Evidence Concerning Projected Railways . . . 1865* (No. 349), p. [53]-71; each is from a different type setting.
CSmH.

SUMNER, CHARLES ALLEN.

The | Celebration | of the | Eighty-Eighth Anniversary | of the | Declaration of Independence | July 4th, 1865. | At | Virginia and Gold Hill, Nevada. | [*short rule*] | Poem by J. T. Goodman: | Oration by Charles A. Sumner. | [*short rule*] | San Francisco: | Commercial Steam Presses: Francis, Valentine & Co. | 517 Clay Street, 510, 512 and 514 Commercial Street. | [*short rule*] | 1865. [360]

35 p. 23 x 15 cm. Printed wrapper.
Footnote, p. [3]: "The description of the Procession, and the remarks upon the Exercises, are taken from the 'Virginia Daily Union.'"
CSmH (bound without wrapper). CtY. MH. NvU (microfilm).

SUTRO TUNNEL COMPANY.

Virginia, Nevada, October 1st, 1865. | To the Presidents, Trustees and Stockholders of the | Mining Companies on the Comstock Ledge. | [*filet*] | Gentlemen: | . . . | [Virginia City? 1865.] [361]

[4] p. 28 x 22 cm. Partly script type. Signed as trustees by Wm. M. Stewart, D. E. Avery, Louis Janin, Jr., H. K. Mitchell, and A. Sutro.
A letter to accompany the contract between the company and Comstock mining firms (see No. 418); the contract is reproduced on p. [3-4]. The advantages of the tunnel and of signing the contract are given in some detail.
CU-B.

TOZER, CHARLES W.

Pacific Railroad. | [*filet*] | Speech of the | Hon. C. W. Tozer, | Speaker of the Nevada Assembly, | February 6, 1865. | [*filet*].
[362]

14 p. 22 x 14 cm. Caption title.
C. CSmH. CSt. CU-B. CtY (rebound). NvU.

VIRGINIA CITY, NEVADA. *Eagle Engine Company No. 3.*

Constitution | and | By-Laws | of | Eagle Engine Company | No. 3, | Virginia, Nevada. | [*filet*] | San Francisco: | Printed by Francis, Valentine & Co. | [*short dotted rule*] | [1865.]   [362a]

22 p. 15 x 10 cm. Printed wrapper. Title and text pages in double rule borders. Cut of fire wagon on verso of title page.

The examined copy is in the cornerstone of the capitol building in Carson City. The recorded microfilm copies were made during renovation of the building in 1978-1979.
NvHi (microfilm). NvMus (microfilm). NvU (microfilm).

VIRGINIA DAILY UNION. *Virginia City, Nevada*. Extra. April 10, 1865.
[L363]

See No. L324.

VIRGINIA DAILY UNION. *Virginia City, Nevada.*

[*Thick-thin rule*] | The Virginia Daily Union. | [*double rule*] | Vol. 5. Virginia, Nevada, Saturday Morning, April 15, 1865. No. 137. | [*thick-thin rule*] | The Daily Union. | [*thick-thin rule*] | Extra! | [*funerary rule*] | Saturday, April 15---2 P.M. | [*funerary rule*] | Assassination of | President Lincoln! | and | Secretary Seward!!! | [*short thick-thin rule*] | Full Particulars! | [*short thick-thin rule*] | Proclamation of the Mayor! | [*short thick-thin rule*] | . . .   [364]

[2] p. 60 x 45 cm. The first thick-thin rule and line 1 extend across the sheet; the double rule and line 2 extend across columns 2-7; the following thick-thin rule covers all eight columns; lines 3-11 are in column 6. Advertising columns of the regular April 15 issue, with column 7 and part of column 8, are replaced by the extra; the verso is p. [4] of the regular issue. The columns are separated by vertical funerary rules on p. [1] only.

This is one of the extras referred to by Alf Doten in his *Journals*; see No. L325. Doten was a local for the *Union* at the time. The news of the death of Seward is incorrect, as in No. 323.
NvU.

VIRGINIA DAILY UNION. *Virginia City, Nevada*. Extra. April 15, 1865.
Second edition.   [L365]

Cited and quoted in the *Union* extra of April 17, 1865; see No. 368.

VIRGINIA DAILY UNION. *Virginia City, Nevada.* Extra. April 16, 1865.
[L366]

Cited and quoted in the *Union*'s extra of April 17, 1865; see No. 368.

VIRGINIA DAILY UNION. *Virginia City, Nevada.* Extra. April 16, 1865.
Second edition. [L367]

Cited and quoted in the *Union*'s extra of April 17, 1865; see No. 368.

VIRGINIA DAILY UNION. *Virginia City, Nevada.*

The Virginia Daily Union. | [*rule*] | Vol. X. Virginia, Nevada, Monday Morning, April 17, 1865. No. 63. | [*rule*] | . . . [368]

[2] p. 53 x 35 cm. Printed in six columns, with vertical funerary rules separating them. The six columns on the recto contain news of the assassination of President Lincoln; part of the first column on the verso quotes comment in other newspapers, also on the assassination, with the remainder made up of advertisements.

The size and misnumbering of the volume (see Nos. 364 and 369) suggest that the extra may have been printed in another newspaper office. The volume numbering is closer to that of the *Territorial Enterprise*.

The extra quotes from the *Union*'s extra of Saturday, the second edition of the Saturday extra, and the first and second edition extras of Sunday (Nos. 364 and L365-L367). It includes a request from Virginia City Mayor Pembroke Murray not to publish newspapers on Sunday in order that the people may mourn.
NvU.

VIRGINIA DAILY UNION. *Virginia City, Nevada.*

[*Thick-thin rule*] | The Virginia Daily Union. | [*double rule*] | Vol. 5. Virginia, Nevada, Wednesday Morning, April 19, 1865. No. 135. | [*thick-thin rule*] | Extra! | [*thick-thin rule*] | Tuesday, April 18---5 P.M. | [*double rule*] | . . . | Further Particulars of the | Assassination! | . . . [369]

[2] p. 60 x 45 cm. The first thick-thin rule and line 1 extend across the sheet; the double rule and line 2 extend across columns 2-7; the following thick-thin rule covers all eight columns; lines 3-5 are in column 6. News of the assassination is in columns 6-7 of the recto; the other columns contain advertisements from the regular issue of the paper; on the verso are advertisements and legal notices from p. [4] of the regular edition of the day.
NvU.

WINTON, NELSON W.

Pacific Railroad. | [*filet*] | Speech of the | Hon. N. W. Winton, | in the | Nevada Senate, | February 27th, 1865. | [*filet*] | . . . | [Sacramento? 1865.]   [370]

16 p. 22 x 15 cm. Caption title.

Gold Hill *News,* March 11, 1865: "WINTON'S SPEECH!!! In the [San Francisco] *American Flag* of last Wednesday [i.e., March 8], appears three columns of solid matter, entitled 'The Speech of Senator Winton, delivered in the Nevada Senate, February 27th.' The speech is a good one; but the idea of it being *Winton's* speech, is a joke so broad, so rich, so rare, so side-splitting, as to be only appreciated by those who know the 'man.' Winton has neither the brains to conceive a speech, nor sense enough to commit one to memory. The speech was written and printed in Sacramento, and 'attributed' to Winton on account of his 'piety and respectability,' and if Jake Smith had been as much of a psalm-singer, and less of a 'hully-kryster,' he might have been wearing the laurels now worn by his invertebrated colleague."

Jacob Smith was a member of the Assembly from Storey County during the first session; Winton was also from Storey County, where the *News* was located.

CSmH. CSt. CU. CU–B. CtY (rebound and trimmed). NvU.

~1866~

The 1864 Constitution provided for biennial sessions of the Legislature, but it also stipulated that for the first three years they should be annual so that the new state could get off to a good start. One of the first bills introduced in the second session amended the 1865 law regarding the office of State Printer. Among the amendments were provisions for changing the number of extra copies of messages and reports for the appendix from 200 to 300, and for a like change in the number of legislative journals; no changes were made in the number of bills or laws to be printed (SSN, 1866, p. 49-51). Another law affecting the State Printer required that he file with the Secretary of State an itemized duplicate of his accounts (ibid., p. 139); these accounts appear not to have survived.

The State Controller's report for 1878 (p. 30) indicates that between January 1 and December 31, 1866, a total of $18,683.66 was charged to the State Printing Fund.

In November, Joseph E. Eckley, proprietor of the *Nye County News* in Ione, a Republican, defeated the Democrat Orlando E. Jones of the Virginia City *Union* for the two year term as State Printer.

Carson City's single press was joined briefly by another paper in May and there was another unsuccessful attempt to establish a

German-language newspaper in Virginia City toward the end of the year. Dayton lost its only press in July. All other papers that were active at the end of 1865 published throughout the year.

DEMOCRATIC PARTY. *Storey County, Nevada.*

[*Cut of flag, Constitution, clasped hands, stars, etc.*] | National Union Democratic | State Ticket. | [*filet*] | . . . | [*thick-thin rule*] | Storey County Ticket. | . . . | [1866.]   [371]

[2] p. 19 x 7 cm. The recorded copy is pasted in a scrapbook; the verso cannot be read, but there is printing on it.

There was some Copperhead sentiment in Nevada during and after the Civil War, but the majority of Democrats favored the Union cause and identified themselves with the Union Democratic faction.

NvI Ii.

FENIAN BROTHERHOOD. *Gold Hill, Nevada.* Poster. June 1866. [L372]

Gold Hill *News*, June 9, 1866: "FENIAN CALL.—Posters are out calling upon the friends of Ireland—as in fact upon all who sympathize with the Fenian movement—to meet at the Gold Hill Theater Sunday evening; eloquent speeches, spirited resolutions and all the attendant circumstances of a first-rate meeting will take place."

FREEMASONS. *Carson City, Nevada. Carson Lodge No. 1.*

By-Laws | of | Carson Lodge, No. 1, | of | Free and Accepted Masons, | Held at | Carson City, Ormsby County, | State of Nevada; | Being the Uniform Code | Recommended by the Grand Lodge: | With | The Funeral Service, | as Arranged by | The V.˙. W.˙. Bro. Alex. G. Abell, | Grand Secretary of the Grand Lodge of California; | and | A Funeral Dirge and Other Odes. | [*short rule*] | San Francisco: | Frank Eastman, Printer, Franklin Office, 509 Clay Street. | 1866.   [372a]

23 p. 14 x 9 cm. Printed wrapper.

The examined copy is in the cornerstone of the capitol building in Carson City. The recorded microfilm copies were made during renovation of the building in 1978-1979.

NvHi (microfilm). NvMus (microfilm). NvU (microfilm).

FREEMASONS. *Nevada. Grand Lodge.*

Proceedings | of the | M.˙. W.˙. Grand Lodge | of | Free and Accepted Masons | of the | State of Nevada, | at its | Second Annual Grand Communication, | Held at Masonic Hall, in the City of Virginia, | September 18, 19, 20, and 21, A.L. 5866; | and | Special Grand Communication to Lay Corner-Stone of U.S. | Branch Mint, Held at Carson City, Sept. 24, A.L. 5866. | [*short rule*] | San

Francisco: | Frank Eastman, Printer, 509 Clay Street. | 1866. ⌊373⌋

[3], 118-205, [1], iii p. 22 x 14 cm. Wrapper title, in decorative rule border. Title page printed from the same type as the wrapper, with the semicolon at the end of line 11 replaced by a period and lines 12-14 omitted. Caption title of the special proceedings, p. [193], is: Proceedings of the M∴ W∴ Grand Lodge of F. & A.M. of the State of Nevada, at a Special Grand Communication, September 24, A.L. 5866.

The amount of $1,010 was recommended "For printing proceedings, and expenses of Grand Secretary's office" (p. 173). 800 copies, including the September 24 special communication, were printed; 300 of them were left "uncut" with the printer for future binding (1867 Proceedings, p. 214-215) at a cost of $464 (ibid., p. 218), but on p. 126 of the 1867 Proceedings is the following curious note: $329.40 "For printing proceedings of last communication."

CSmH (lacks wrapper). CU-B. NvHi (microfilm). NvMus (microfilm). NvRFM. NvRW (lacks wrapper). NvU (microfilm).

HARRINGTON, WILLIAM P.

Harrington's | Directory | of the | City of Austin, | for the Year | 1866. | With a Historical and Statistical Review | of | Austin, | and the | Reese River Mining Region, | By Myron Angel. | [*filet*] | Austin: | Printed by J. D. Fairchild & Co., Daily Reese River Reveille, | Book and Job Printing Office. | 1866.[374]

119 p. 22 x 14 cm. Quarter-leather binding; printed boards. A prospectus was issued in 1865; see No. L332. *Check List*: 70 described the DLC copy, which has the first gathering bound at the end.

Territorial Enterprise, August 19, 1866: "The book is credited to the *Reveille* office, and is neatly printed and substantially bound. Price, $3."

C. CU-B. CtY. DLC. NN. NvU.

MAGUIRE'S OPERA HOUSE. *Virginia City, Nevada.*

Maguire's Opera House | [*double rule*] | . . . | [*thick-thin rule*] | Benefit | —of the— | Odd Fellows' Library! | [*thick-thin rule*] | First Array of Amaetures [*sic*] in This State! | [*thick-thin rule*] | . . . | [*thick-thin rule*] | Monday Evening, March 12th. | [*double rule*] | The performance will commenee [*sic*] with an original poem, written by | Alf. Doten! | [*thick-thin rule*] | To be followed by Benjamin Webster's thrilling Drama, in two acts, of the | Golden Farmer! | . . . | [Virginia City? 1866.]   [375]

Broadside. 45 x 19 cm.

The Gold Hill *News* of March 24, 1866, noted that "a clear profit of $850" was made at the library benefit.

NvHi. NvU.

MUSIC HALL. *Virginia City, Nevada.*

Music Hall. | [*double rule*] | . . . | [*thick-thin rule*] | Look at This!

| Sunday Night's Bill! | [*thick-thin rule*] | Don't Fail to See It! | [*thick-thin rule*] | Great Success | Of the Beautiful Sensation Play of the | Corrigan Brothers! | A Parody, Not a Burlesque, in | Two Acts and Five Tableaux! | [*short double rule*] | . . . | [*thick-thin rule*] | Sunday Evening, Sept. 23. | [*double rule*] | . . . | [Virginia City:] From the "Enterprise" Book and Job Printing Establishment. | [1866.]   [376]

Broadside. 47 x 16 cm.

On the located copy, in the hand of Alf Doten, the words "The Last Of " are printed in pencil above the first line; below the last line he has written, also in pencil, the words "Music Hall 'join in.' " The Gold Hill *News* for September 24, 1866, explained the notations as follows: "MUSIC HALL BURNT.—Last Night, a few minutes past ten o'clock, one of the camphene lamps, or foot-lights, on the stage of Musice [*sic*] Hall, in Virginia City, burst, scattering a large quantity of ignited burning fluid over the stage and underneath. Alarm and consternation seized the audience, which was very large, and it rushed pell-mell out of the theater. The actors, however, seized upon all the water which was available, and extinguished the fire upon the stage; but the camphene penetrated underneath, and in a short time the place below was all in a blaze, and before assistance from the fire department arrived, the interior of the theater was all in a blaze, when it was found impossible to extinguish it—the premises being entirely constructed of wood, many thousands of feet of lumber being contained therein. The firemen, we are informed, worked gallantly to subdue the devouring element, but the whole place being very dry, it was impossible to save it." An account in the Virginia City *Union* for the same date added that the fire on the stage was spread when members of the audience, in an attempt to help the actors extinguish the flames, broke several other footlights.

NvU.

MUSIC HALL. *Virginia City, Nevada.* Playbill. February 9, 1866.

[L377]

Gold Hill *News*, February 9, 1866: "We notice huge bills out for Amanda Lee's benefit, and we also notice that all the talent in Virginia has been secured. . . . Remember, it is to-night." An advertisement in the same issue states that Amanda Lee was appearing at the "Virginia Music Hall"; there is a notice in the next day's issue concerning the benefit of the previous evening.

NEVADA. *Adjutant General.*

[*Thick-thin rule*] | Annual Report | of the | Adjutant-General | of the | State of Nevada, | For 1865. | [*thin-thick rule*] | [Carson City:] John Church, State Printer. | [1866.]   [378]

46 p. 23 x 15 cm. Wrapper title. Issued also as [No. 6] in AJS, 1866.
A Senate concurrent resolution authorized the printing of 640 copies (JS, 1866, p. 36; concurred in, JA, 1866, p. 39). Unionville *Humboldt Register,* February 10, 1866: "ADJUTANT GENERAL'S REPORT.—Col. [William] Cradlebaugh has indulged himself, without restraint, and publishes a good-sized pamphlet."

CSmH. DLC. MH. NvU (microfilm). PHi. PP.

NEVADA. *Adjutant General.*

[*Rule-wavy rule-rule*] | Roster | of | First Battalion Nevada Volunteer Cavalry | and | First Battalion Nevada Volunteer Infantry | For the Years 1863-1866. | [*rule-wavy rule-rule*] | [1866?]   [379]

[27]-55 p. 23 x 15 cm. Wrapper title. Reprinted from different type and with some emendations, including dates of and reasons for discharge, from p. [21]-46 of the Adjutant General's report for 1865 (No. 378). It is not clear whether the pages preceding p. [27] in the document described here were issued separately, or indeed what they might have been. The last mustering-out dates are in mid-1866.
NvMus.

NEVADA. *Citizens.*

[*Thick-thin rule*] | Petitions | from | Citizens of Esmeralda and Lander Counties, | in Favor of an Appropriation for the Relief of the | Orphan Asylum at Virginia City. | [*thick-thin rule*] | . . . | [1866.]   [380]

[4] p., printed on p. [1, 3-4] only. 32 x 21 cm. The names of the petitioners, thirteen from Esmeralda and twenty-five from Lander, are printed. See Nos. L391 and 416-L417.

The petition relates to Senate Bill 41 of the 1866 session, "An Act Appropriating Moneys for the Benefit of the Orphan Asylum Conducted by the Sisters of Charity at Virginia City," and was but one of several expressions of support for the bill. A flurry of petitions praying for passage was presented to the Senate on February 13, 1866, this one among them (JS, 1866, p. 146). When the bill reached the Assembly its Committee on Ways and Means submitted a blistering report (JA, 1866, p. 246-249) on a rival Assembly bill that would appropriate funds to support the St. Paul's Episcopal Parish School in Virginia City, and came out strongly in favor of state support for the Sisters' asylum. The orphans' support bill eventually passed both houses but was vetoed as unconstitutional by Governor Blasdel; the attempt to override was unsuccessful (JS, 1866, p. 252-253).
NvHi.

NEVADA. *Constitutional Convention, 1864.*

Official Report | of the | Debates and Proceedings | in the | Constitutional Convention | of the | State of Nevada, | Assembled at Carson City, July 4th, 1864, | to | Form a Constitution and State Government. | [*short rule*] | Andrew J. Marsh, Official Reporter. | [*short rule*] | [*state seal*] | San Francisco: | Frank Eastman, Printer. | 1866.   [381]

xvi, 943, [1] p. 23 x 16 cm. Leather binding. Printed in two columns. Page [944]: Errata.
Page 852: "At the first regular session of the Legislature, to convene under the

requirements of this Constitution, provision shall be made by law for paying for the publication of six hundred copies of the debates and proceedings of this Convention, in book form." Authorization was duly provided in SSN, 1865, p. 168. J. Neely Johnson, who had been President of the convention, advertised for bids, specifying that 600 copies of 1,000 pages "more or less" would be wanted; that they should be printed on "40 lb. book paper, Clear and White, 24 x 38 inches," in 16-page sections; press work to be paid per token of 240 impressions; "Type to be used, Brevier and Nonpareil solid, Resolutions, Extracts, &c being in Nonpareil, set in double columns, the page to be 48 brevier ems wide (including the central column rule) and 72 brevier ems long, type to be new or as good as new." The work was to be done under the supervision of the convention's official reporter, Andrew J. Marsh, who was to be allowed ten days after receiving revised proofs to submit speeches of members to them for their revisions (Nv-Ar: Nevada Contracts, p. 1-3; also published in Report of the Special [Assembly] Committee Concerning the Publication of Debates of the Constitutional Convention, JA, 1866, p. [21]-32 following p. 375). Eastman submitted the lowest bid, and he and Johnson agreed to the following terms: composition at 95¢ per thousand ems; alterations at 60¢ per hour; paper at $10.50 per ream; press work at 85¢ per token; binding at 95¢ per copy; with transportation from San Francisco to Carson City "by one of the Fast Freight Lines," at 10¢ per pound. The contract was amended at the end to alter the quality of paper; it was "to be of the same weight specified to wit 40 lb. paper but more highly finished and sized and cullendered than as herein specified and to be at the additional cost to the State of $1 00 per ream, to wit at Eleven 50/100 Dollars per ream." Payment was to be "in Gold Coin of the United States of the Standard of A.D. 1861 or its equivalent." The contract was signed on February 28, 1865, and filed in the office of the Secretary of State on March 24, 1865.

Work apparently began immediately, since the Controller issued a warrant for $483.33 for composition of the first 150 pages on April 25, and another for $460.99 on June 27 for the second 150 pages (Report of the Special Committee, p. [23]). Soon after this time Eastman was informed that the treasury would have no money to pay him until December; because he could get no more than sixty cents on the dollar for his warrants in San Francisco, he stopped the printing. In a letter to the Assembly committee on January 23, 1866, Eastman stated that he considered the contract to have been broken by the state, and that he could not complete the work even if money were available to pay him, citing the increased costs of printing and paper in the year since the contract was signed (ibid., p. 30). On February 1, Eastman continued his plaint and repeated his inability to complete the contract, citing this time the rise in rates for composition to $1.25 per 1,000 ems, press work to $1.20 per token, and time work to $1 per hour. Because these rates had not yet been ratified by the printers, however, he stated his willingness to finish the work at $1.10 per 1,000 ems, $1 per token, 85¢ per hour, $16 per ream for paper, and 5¢ more per copy for binding. He suggested that an additional $475 would be needed for the balance of the work (ibid., p. 31). The committee responded (p. [22]) by recommending that an extra $500 be granted to Eastman; the Legislature agreed, formalizing the recommendation by enacting a law authorizing an additional payment "in gold coin" on completion of the work (SSN, 1866, p. 183). Payments to Eastman then resumed, with warrants issued for $457.54, $473.54, $479.60, and $481.65 during 1866 (Comptroller's Report, 1866, p. 27). The additional $500 recommended by the committee was paid in 1867 (ibid., 1867, p. 93) on completion of the work. Eastman's total was $3,336.51. However, the Controller's Report for 1867 also reported payment of

$2,035.55 for "Debates of Constitutional Convention," some of which may have been paid to Eastman, although a large part of the original $10,000 appropriation was paid to Marsh for reporting the convention, transcribing his shorthand notes for the printer, and superintending the printing.

C. CU-B. CtY. CtY-L. DLC. ICN. ICU. In. In-SC (rebound). M. MB. MH. MH-L. NN. NjP. Nv. NvC. NvHi. NvLN. NvMiD. NvRNC. NvRW. NvRWL. NvSC. NvU. PU-L. UU.

NEVADA. *Governor, 1864-1871 (Henry Goode Blasdel).*

Second | Annual Message | of | H. G. Blasdel, | Governor of the State of Nevada, | Delivered to the Legislature, | in Carson City, January, A.D., 1866. | [*short double rule*] | Carson City: | John Church, State Printer. | 1866.   [382]

20 p. 23 x 15 cm. Printed wrapper. Printed from the same type in the appendix to JA, 1866, p. [3]-20.

Most of the printing of this issue must have been done in late 1865, since the Gold Hill *News* of January 2, 1866, reported receiving "an advance copy . . . just at noon to-day," the day the message was delivered. The next day's issue of the Carson City *Appeal* said that "we are enabled to put each one of our readers in possession of his Annual Message to the Legislature, in the pamphlet form in which it comes from the hands of the State Printer." If Church was following by this time the later practice of farming out his printing to a California firm, the entire message would have had to be printed in 1865, despite the date on the title page—which, after all, would have been in those circumstances less than truthful about the printer's identity as well. But if this is one of the few state pamphlets actually printed in Nevada, at least the finishing touches may have been performed in the year claimed on the title page.

Early in the legislative session the Senate passed a concurrent resolution authorizing the printing of 1,500 copies (JS, 1866, p. 36), which was concurred in by the lower house (JA, 1866, p. 39). The authority to print may have been merely an ex post facto recognition of the existence of that many copies.

CSmH. CoD. CtY (has remnants of a wrapper). DLC. NvU (microfilm). WHi.

NEVADA. *Governor, 1864-1871 (Henry Goode Blasdel).*

Thanksgiving Proclamation | [*state seal*] | By H. G. Blasdel, Governor of the State of Nevada. | [*filet*] | I do Hereby Appoint | Thursday, November 29th, A.D. 1866, | As a day of Public Thanksgiving . . . | . . . | . . . Done at Carson City, this the 10th day of November, A.D. 1866. | . . . | [Carson City: John Church, State Printer. 1866.]   [383]

Broadside. 36 x 29 cm. Line 1 in an arch over state seal and line 2.
CSmH. CtY. NvU.

NEVADA. *Homographic Charts.*

Homographic Chart, | —of the— | State Officers and Members of the Second Nevada Legislature, | Convened at Carson City, January,

1866. | [*thick-thin rule*] | . . .   [384]

Broadside. 43 x 36 cm. Decorative rule border.
CSmH. NvHi.

NEVADA. *Laws, statutes, etc.*

Nevada State Mining Law. | [*rule*] | An Act | Concerning the Loca-
tion and Possession | of | Mining Claims. | [*filet*] | . . . | [1866.]
                                                                        [385]

7 p. 22 x 14 cm. Imprint on p. 7: Printed by J. D. Fairchild & Co., Daily Reese River
Reveille Office. Austin, Nevada. The located copy has been disbound.
Reese River Reveille, March 19, 1866: "To MINERS.—The State Mining Law is for sale
at Frank Drake's and at this office." The price was fifty cents.
ICN. NvU (microfilm).

NEVADA. *Laws, statutes, etc.*

Statutes | of the | State of Nevada | Passed at the | Second Session
of the Legislature, | 1866, | Begun on Monday, the First Day of
January, and | Ended on Thursday, the First Day of March. | [*state
seal*] | Carson City: | John Church, State Printer. | [*short rule*]
| 1866.   [386]

ix, [3], 315 p. 23 x 15 cm. Leather binding. Page [301]-315: Annual Report of the State
Treasurer of the State of Nevada, For the Year 1865.

The Legislature authorized the printing of 600 copies (p. 50) and appropriated $1,000
to cover costs, but warrants for only $314.08 were issued (Controller's report, 1866,
p. 26). That much is clear; it is equally clear that many more than 600 copies were
printed. The Secretary of State received batches of 197 and 407 copies on the 11th and
20th of June, respectively (Carson City *Appeal,* June 12 and 21, 1866). But a Virginia
City bookseller, H. Levison, had copies on hand and for sale by May 17; he also
distributed copies to at least two newspapers (*Territorial Enterprise,* May 18; Gold Hill
News, May 19), and the *Appeal* acknowledged a copy from the State Printer in its issue
of May 23. The affair is confused even more by the report in Carson City's *Nevada
State Journal* of May 22 that indicated receipt of copies by the Secretary of State, and
continued: "We understand the State Printer now has on hand, and for sale, at
Virginia, a few of the advance copies."
Az. CSmH. CU-B. CtY. CtY-L. DLC. IU. MBS. MH-L. NN. NNLI. NjP. Nv.
NvEC. NvEHi. NvEuC. NvHi. NvLN. NvPLC. NvPLR. NvRNC. NvRWL.
NvSC (rebound). NvU. NvVSR. OrU-L. WHi.

NEVADA. *Legislature. Assembly.*

The | Journal of the Assembly | During | the Second Session | of
the | Legislature of the State of Nevada, | 1866. | Begun on Mon-
day, the First Day of January, and | Ended on Thursday, the First
Day of March. | [*state seal*] | Carson City: | John Church, State
Printer. | [*short rule*] | 1866.   [387]

375, 32 p. 23 x 15 cm. Leather binding. Appendix, made up of three reports, following p. 375, each with a separate half title: Annual Message from Governor H. G. Blasdel, p. [3]-16; Statement of State Indebtedness, p. [17]-20; Report of the Special Committee Concerning the Publication of Debates of the Constitutional Convention, p. [21]-32. The first 20 pages are printed from the same type as the separate issue of the Governor's message; see No. 382.

300 copies were authorized (SSN, 1866, p. 50). The Gold Hill *News* reported receipt of a copy from the Secretary of State in its issue of June 29, 1866.

CtY. CtY-L. DLC. M. MH. NN. Nv. Nv-Ar. NvHi. NvLC. NvLN. NvRWL. NvSC (rebound). NvU. UU-L. WHi.

NEVADA. *Legislature. Senate.*

The | Journal of the Senate | During | the Second Session | of the | Legislature of the State of Nevada, | 1866. | Begun on Monday, the First Day of January, and | Ended on Thursday, the First Day of March. | [*state seal*] | Carson City: | John Church, State Printer. | [*short rule*] | 1866.   [388]

291, 22, 15, 5, 23, 12, 46, 83, 31, 5, 8, 6 p. 23 x 15 cm. Half-leather binding.

Reports of state officers and legislative committees follow p. 291. Each has a separate half title, and each is paged separately. Numbers have been assigned according to the position of the reports in the volume, as there is no table of contents. The general half title is: Appendix to Senate Proceedings. [No. 1], First Annual Report of the Controller of the State of Nevada, For 1865, 22 p.; [No. 2], Annual Report of the State Treasurer, of the State of Nevada, For the Year 1865, 15 p.; [No. 3], Annual Report of the Secretary of State, For the Year 1865, 5 p.; [No. 4], First Annual Report of the Sup't of Public Instruction, of the State of Nevada, For the School Year Ending August 31, 1865, 23 p. and two folding tables; [No. 5], Report of J. S. Crosman, Warden of the Nevada State Prison, For the Fiscal Year Ending December 31, 1865, 12 p. and a folding table; [No. 6], Report of the Adjutant-General of the State of Nevada, for 1865, 46 p.; [No. 7], Annual Report of the Surveyor-General of the State of Nevada, For the Year 1865, 83 p. (includes: Appendix to Report of Surveyor-General, p. [29]-34; Reports of County Surveyors and County Assessors, p. [35]-78; Communications. Forest and Timber Trees, p. [79]-83. Lacks errata leaf present in separate issue); [No. 8], Reports of Directors of State Library and Librarian of the State of Nevada, For the Year 1865, 31 p.; [No. 9], Report of the Special Committee Appointed to Examine the Books of the State Board of Examiners, 5 p.; [No. 10], Report of the Special Committee Appointed to Examine the Books of the State Board of Examiners, and into the Matters Set Forth in the Report of the Special Committee Previously Appointed for the Same Purposes, 8 p.; [No. 11], Report of the Joint Committee Appointed to Examine into Matters Relating to the State Prison, 6 p.

Printing of 300 copies was authorized (SSN, 1866, p. 50). The Carson City *Appeal* of June 27, 1866, reported that the Secretary of State had received his copies "yesterday."

CtY. CtY-L. DLC. ICU. M. MH. NN. Nv. Nv-Ar. NvHi. NvLC. NvLN. NvRW (rebound). NvRWL. NvSC. NvU. UU-L. WHi.

NEVADA. *Legislature. Senate.*

Roll Call—Senate. | [*double rule*] | . . . | [Carson City: John Church State Printer. 1866.]   [389]

Broadside. 21 x 10 cm. Eighteen names of members of the 1866 state Senate in one column, with two additional columns for recording votes.
NvMus.

NEVADA. *Legislature. Senate. Committee on Mines and Mining Interests.*

[*Thick-thin rule*] | Report | of the | Senate Committee | on | Mines and Mining Interests, | on | Assembly Bill No. 22: | "An Act Concerning the Location and Pos-|session of Mining Claims." | [*thin-thick rule*] | [Carson City:] John Church, State Printer. | [1866.]   [390]

10 p. 21 x 13 cm. Wrapper title and title page are identical. Dated, p. [3]: Feb. 23, 1866.
The report strongly recommends adoption of the bill.
MH-BA. NvU (microfilm).

NEVADA. *Legislature. Senate. Committee on State Affairs.* Report. Carson City: John Church, State Printer. 1866.   [L391]

JA, 1866, p. 247: "Senate Bill No. 41 is recommended by the Senate Committee on State Affairs, in an elaborate and convincing report, to which, inasmuch as it is printed for general circulation, we presume we violate no parliamentary propriety in refer-ring." SB41 was the bill appropriating money for the orphan asylum in Virginia City that received so much attention from petitioners during the session. See Nos. 380 and 416-L417. The Gold Hill *News* referred to the report on February 3, 1866, but did not specifically mention having seen a pamphlet issue.

NEVADA. *Legislature. Senate. Special Committee on State Board of Examiners.*

[*Thick-thin rule*] | Report | of the | Special Committee | Appoint-ed | to Examine the Books | of the | State Board of Examiners. | [*thin-thick rule*] | [Carson City: John Church, State Printer. 1866.]   [L392]

5 p. Description from half title in AJS, 1866, where it is [No. 9].

Carson City *Appeal,* February 17, 1866: "We have a copy of the report in pamphlet form of the Special Committee appointed to examine the books of the State Board of Examiners." Two days later the Gold Hill *News* had the following: "We have before us a 'Report of the Special Committee appointed to examine the Books of the State Board of Examiners.' We have read the document, in the light of a certified transcript from the office of the Board, and we are compelled, in honor and duty to declare that this so-called report is untrue and libellous in many statements and calculated—all its remarks and estimates—to do injustice. We presume that the 'Report' is the hand-iwork of F. M. Proctor, Copperhead, (the only Cop. in the Legislature,) and C.

Lambert, of Washoe." The *News* went on to call for the appointment of another committee, which was, in fact, appointed. The report of the second committee was issued as [No. 10] in AJS, 1866, but no separate issue of the latter report has been located, nor has a mention of one been found in contemporary newspapers.

NEVADA. *Office of Superintendent of Public Instruction.*

[*Thick-thin rule*] | First Annual Report | of the | Sup't of Public Instruction, | of the | State of Nevada, | for the School Year Ending August 31, 1865. | [*thin-thick rule*] | [Carson City:] John Church, State Printer. | [1866.]   [393]

23 p. and two folding tables. 23 x 15 cm. Wrapper title. Issued also as [No. 4] in AJS, 1866.

The letter of transmittal, p. [3], is dated November 25, 1865. The Gold Hill *News* of January 23, 1866, acknowledged receipt of "Legislative documents" from Senator Winton, Chairman of the Senate Committee on Education; the following day's issue specifically acknowledged receipt, from Winton, of this document.

CSmH. CtY. DHEW. DLC. Nv. NvHi. NvU (microfilm). PU. WHi.

NEVADA. *Secretary of State.*

[*Thick-thin rule*] | Annual Report | of the | Secretary of State, | for | the Year 1865. | [*thin-thick rule*] | [Carson City: John Church. State Printer. 1866.]   [L394]

5 p. Description from half title in AJS, 1866, [No. 3].

JS, 1866, p. 39, contains a concurrent resolution to print 480 copies; concurrence is noted on p. 46. Carson City *Appeal,* January 30, 1866: "We yesterday received a copy of the Report of the Secretary of State of the year 1865. The Report shows for itself that it was made in due season; but it seems to have been delayed in the hands of somebody who ought to have had it printed three or four weeks ago."

NEVADA. *State Controller's Office.*

[*Thick-thin rule*] | First Annual Report | of the | Controller | of the | State of Nevada, | For 1865. | [*thin-thick rule*] | [Carson City:] John Church, State Printer. | [1866.]   [395]

22 p. 23 x 14 cm. Wrapper title. Issued also as [No. 1] in AJS, 1866.
Senate concurrent resolution to print 1,000 copies (JS, 1866, p. 61); concurred in by the Assembly (JA, 1866, p. 88). The Carson City *Appeal* of February 18, 1866, acknowledged receipt of a copy "in pamphlet form." An Assembly concurrent resolution to print extra copies (JA, 1866, p. 108) was defeated after amendment in the Senate (JS, 1866, p. 87).
DLC. MH.

Nevada. *State Library.*

[*Thick-thin rule*] | Reports of | Directors of State Library | and | Librarian | of the State of Nevada, | For the Year 1865. | [*thin-*

thick rule] | [Carson City:] John Church, State Printer. | [1866.]
[396]

31 p. 23 x 15 cm. Wrapper title. The Librarian's report consists of a catalog of the Library. Issued also as [No. 8] in AJS, 1866.

Senate concurrent resolution to print 500 copies (JS, 1866, p. 81); amended to 720 copies (ibid., p. 85) and concurred in by the Assembly (JA, 1866, p. 128). The Carson City *Appeal* reported receipt of a copy in its issue of February 18, 1866.

M. NvU (microfilm).

NEVADA. *State Prison*.

[*Thick-thin rule*] | Report | of | J. S. Crosman, | Warden of the Nevada State Prison, | for the Fiscal Year Ending December 31, 1865. | [*thin-thick rule*] | [Carson City: John Church, State Printer. 1866.]
[L397]

12 p. and a folding table. Description from half title in AJS, 1866, [No. 5].

Senate concurrent resolution to print 500 copies (JS, 1866, p. 36); concurred in by the Assembly (JA, 1866, p. 39). The Carson City *Appeal* acknowledged receipt of a copy in its issue of January 19, 1866; the Gold Hill *News* referred to the report in its issue of the previous day, but did not say whether its copy was separately issued.

NEVADA. *Supreme Court*.

[Briefs. 1866.]

Carson River Lumbering Co. vs. Bassett et al. Addendum to argument of respondent, Carson River Lumbering Co. 4 p. 20 x 15 cm. Handwritten on one of two copies at Nv-Ar: "Filed May 28th 1866 Alfred Helm Clerk." Same typefaces as in No. 399. Nv-Ar.
[398]

Carson River Lumbering Co. vs. Bassett et al. Brief and argument of respondent, Carson River Lumbering Co. 36 p. 21 x 14 cm. Imprint on wrapper: Virginia, Nev.: Territorial Enterprise Book and Job Printing Office, 24 South C St. 1866. Nv-Ar.
[399]

Chase vs. Savage Mining Co. Brief of appellant in reply on rehearing, Charles C. Chase. 30 p. 25 x 18 cm. Imprint on wrapper: San Francisco: Printed at the Alta Book and Job Office, No. 538 Sacramento Street, 1866. Nv-Ar.
[400]

Chase vs. Savage Mining Co. Brief of respondent on rehearing, Savage Mining Co. 32 p. 20 x 14 cm. Imprint on wrapper: Virginia, Nev.: Printed at the "Territorial Enterprise" Book and Job Office. 1866. CSmH. Nv-Ar.
[401]

McCurdy vs. Alpha Gold Hill Mining Co. et al. Brief and points of respondent, John A. McCurdy. 34 p. 26 x 18 cm. Imprint on wrapper: Sacramento: Russell and Winterburn, Printers—Union Book and Job Office. 1866. Nv-Ar.
[402]

NEVADA. *Supreme Court*.

Reports of Cases | Determined in the | Supreme Court | of the | State of Nevada, | Reported by the Judges of the Court | During the Year 1865. | [*short rule*] | Volume 1. | [*short rule*]

| Edward I. Robinson, | Publisher. | [*short rule*] | Sacramento: |
James Anthony & Co., Printers. | 1866.   [403]

667 p. 23 x 15 cm. Leather binding.

The first session of the Legislature authorized the publication of 300 copies, plus
enough additional copies to supply the bar of Nevada (SSN, 1864-5, p. 404). In an
agreement dated August 21, 1865, the state of Nevada contracted with James Anthony
& Co., Robert Robinson, and Edward I. Robinson for the preparation and printing of
the volumes (Nv-Ar: Nevada Contracts, p. 4-5). The contract specified that the
Reports were to be printed "on the same kind and quality of paper as is the twenty
fifth volume of the California Reports," and that it was to be printed "in the same
style with the same quality of type and bound in a manner not inferior" to the
California volume. Delivery was to be made "either at Sacramento or San Francisco
as may be most convenient to the parties of the second part," i.e., Anthony and the
Robinsons. For this work the state agreed to pay to Anthony the sum of $1,400 "in
United States gold coin," and further agreed to pay interest at the rate of 1 1/4% per
month if the state was not ready to pay the full amount on delivery. If the volume
exceeded the estimated 700 pages, the state would pay Anthony $2 for each additional
page, but if it were more than twenty pages short of 700 pages, a reduction would be
made "equal to the cost of composition and paper which is saved . . .
by such diminution of the volume." For their part in the publication, consisting
of preparing a title page, a table of cases, and an index, correcting proof, and
superintending the printing, the Robinsons were authorized "to contract with James
Anthony & Co. for whatever number of copies of said edition . . . they may think
best. That they shall be entitled to the control of the entire edition of said work over
and beyond the three hundred volumes furnished to the State of Nevada and may in
their discretion take any necessary steps to secure the copyright of said volume." The
Robinsons agreed to "furnish in the Towns of Virginia City, Carson City and Austin
a sufficient number, not exceeding one hundred & fifty (150) of volumes of said work
to supply the demand therefor at a retail price not exceeding ten ($10) Dollars in
United States gold coin per volume at those places." They agreed further that they
would "never attempt by reason of any copyright they may obtain in this book to
prohibit or interfere with the publication of any one or more of the decisions contained
in said volume but may assert any legal right they have to prevent the republication
copying or printing the syllabi, table of cases or index of said volume."

The number of pages in the volume was less than the estimated 700 and it would seem
that the provision mandating a reduction in cost would have come into effect. But the
1866 Treasurer's report (p. 6) indicates a total disbursement from January 1 to
December 31, 1866, of $1,977.80 for "Publishing Decisions of Supreme Court."
Perhaps a supplementary agreement was executed between the state and Anthony to
cover rising costs of printing and paper, as was the case with the Debates and
Proceedings of the 1864 Constitutional Convention (see No. 381). A further anom-
aly arises with the notice in the March 6, 1866, issue of the Carson City *Appeal* that
Supreme Court Justice H. O. Beatty had left Carson City for Sacramento the day
before "to supervise the printing of the first volume of Reports for this State." Beatty
was gone for nearly two months (*Appeal,* May 1, 1866) and it may be conjectured that
the Robinsons had reneged on their part of the contract; yet the name of Edward I.
Robinson appears on the title page of the volume, and the *Appeal* acknowledged
receipt of a copy from him on May 22.

The *Territorial Enterprise* of May 5, 1866, had the following: "Dale & Co., No. 76

South C street, have received a few copies of the first volume of the Supreme Court Reports of Nevada—the first, we believe, in the market. The volume embraces all the decisions of 1865, and is gotten up in a very handsome style."

If the Robinsons obtained the copyright they were authorized to get (there is no notice in the book), they apparently did not exercise their consequent right to prevent republication of certain parts of it, since this first volume was reissued with volume 2 by A. L. Bancroft & Co. of San Francisco in 1877 (see No. 915) in a stereotyped edition, again by Bancroft-Whitney in 1887, and has been reissued as well in the twentieth century. See also No. 404.

Az (lacks title page). CU-B (rebound). DHEW. DLC. In-SC (rebound). M. Nv-Ar. NvHi. NvRWL. NvU (rebound).

NEVADA. *Supreme Court.*

Reports of Cases | Determined in | The Supreme Court | of the | State of Nevada, | Reported by the | Judges of the Court, | During the Year 1865. | Volume 1. | San Francisco: | Sumner [*sic*] Whitney, | Law Bookseller, Publisher and Importer, | Nos. 19 and 20 Montgomery Block. | 1866.   [404]

667 p. 23 x 14 cm. Leather binding; the recorded copy has been rebound since the first examination. The printer's name is usually seen as Sumner, Whitney & Company.

Robert and Edward I. Robinson, by virtue of a contract with the state of Nevada (see No. 403), were granted the privilege to "control . . . the entire edition of said work over and beyond the three hundred volumes furnished to the State of Nevada and . . . to secure the copyright of said volume." Although no copyright notice appears in the present volume, it appears that the Robinsons may have exercised the privilege to have more than 300 copies produced. The title page of this issue is a cancel, with the remainder printed from the same type as the Sacramento issue of James Anthony & Co.; there is also some rearrangement of the preliminary pages, with an errata leaf that appears on p. [2] in the present volume appearing on p. [16] in the Anthony issue.

Nv (rebound).

NEVADA. *Surveyor General.*

[*Thick-thin rule*] | Annual Report | of the | Surveyor-General | of the | State of Nevada, | For the Year 1865. | [*thin-thick rule*] | [Carson City:] John Church, State Printer. | [1866.]   [405]

83 p. 23 x 15 cm. Wrapper title. Half title printed from different type. An errata leaf follows the front wrapper in the copy at CSmH; it is after the contents page at NvRW. Page [29]-34: Appendix to Report of Surveyor-General; p. [35]-83: Reports of County Surveyors and County Assessors. Issued also as [No. 7] in AJS, 1866.

The Senate Committee on Printing reported a probable cost of approximately $450 and not more than $500 (JS, 1866, p. 143), whereupon a Senate concurrent resolution to print 2,500 copies in pamphlet form, with 1,000 to the Legislature and the remainder to the Secretary of State for distribution, was passed (SSN, 1866, p. 271). The Carson City *Appeal* acknowledged receipt of a copy "in pamphlet form," on March 11, 1866.

The Gold Hill *News* had the following comment on March 31, 1866: "The pamphlet consists of eighty-three pages, and is neatly covered and printed—but there is an 'errata' appendage, in manuscript, which the General has sent, indicating that either the original manuscript or the proof-reader had a plentiful lack of correctness. The 'errata,' which the General has sent us, occupies four full sheets of legal-cap paper—which, in that sense, may be set down 'errata' enough for a volume of statutes consisting of six hundred pages. The Report itself is the finest State paper, from that office, that has yet appeared, and merits general perusal. Let the public read the Report, General—the 'errata' will not be noticed." It was noticed, though. Unionville's *Humboldt Register* commented on April 7 that it had received "a corrected copy." It stated further that the report, "as originally printed, is full of glaring errors, showing extreme negligence either in its preparation or printing. We can not see how it was possible for such errors to escape the watchfulness of the most ordinary proof reader." S. H. Marlette, the Surveyor General, noticed them, too. In his report for the following year (p. 49) he carried on at great length about the errors: "Last year's report was so full of errors, by fault of copying clerk of the compositor, as to be comparatively worthless. I paid $10 coin to the 'Enterprise' for printing 2,500 copies of 'errata,' nearly 2,000 of which I sent to the Secretary of State. Some of these were used, but none were inserted in the appendix to the Journals. But the Board [of Examiners] deemed the 'charge' an 'improper one.' The Board allowed three dollars freight on reports from Carson, and three dollars for distributing the same in this city [i.e., Virginia City], but would not allow $10 for correcting an otherwise almost worthless document. Was the Board guided by law or by whim?" The *News* of May 8, 1867, noted that the Legislature of that year had finally allowed Marlette's claims.

CSmH (has errata). MH. MH-Z. MWA (lacks rear wrapper). NHi. NjP. NvHi. NvRW. NvU (has errata; lacks rear wrapper). WHi.

NEVADA. *Treasury Department.*

[*Thick-thin rule*] | Annual Report | of the | State Treasurer, | of the | State of Nevada, | For the Year 1865. | [*thin-thick rule*] | [Carson City: John Church, State Printer. 1866.]   [406]

15 p. 23 x 15 cm. The recorded copy is sewn and shows no sign of extraction from AJS, [No. 2]; issued without wrapper? Issued also, from the same type, in SSN, 1866, p. [301]-315.

Senate concurrent resolution to print 250 copies (JS, 1866, p. 36); returned from the Assembly, with concurrence (JA, 1866, p. 41). Attempts to authorize the printing of extra copies were lost (JA, 1866, p. 108; JS, 1866, p. 74 and 87).

NvU.

ORMSBY COUNTY, NEVADA. *Board of Registration.*

Registered Voters of Ormsby County. | [*filet*] | . . . | [Carson City? 1866.]   [407]

Broadside. 38? x 26? cm. The recorded copy is trimmed on all sides. Printed in four columns. Handwritten note at the top of the recorded copy: "October 1866." Includes Carson, Empire, and Brunswick Mill precincts.

Nv-Ar.

ORMSBY COUNTY, NEVADA. *Board of Registration.*

Registered Voters of Ormsby County. | [*filet*] | . . . | [Carson City? 1866.] [408]

Broadside. 33 x 25 cm. Printed in eight columns, with each of the columns separated by three vertical rules. Handwritten note at the top of the recorded copy: "1866." Includes Carson, Empire, and Brunswick Mill precincts.
NvCR.

REPUBLICAN PARTY. *Lyon County, Nevada.*

Union | State Ticket. | [*filet*] | . . . | [*filet*] | Lyon Co. Legislative Union Ticket. | [*short rule*] | . . . | [*rule*] | Lyon County People's Ticket. | [*short rule*] | . . . | [1866.] [409]

Broadside. 17 x 6 cm.
NvHi.

REPUBLICAN PARTY. *Nevada. State Central Committee.* Poster. Gold Hill: Gold Hill News. 1866. [L410]

Gold Hill *News,* October 27, 1866: "We have just printed for the Union State Central Committee, a six-foot poster, containing the State Ticket—intended for distribution in the different counties of the State. It is the neatest and cleanest poster ever turned out of any printing office on this side of the mountains—so pronounced by those who have seen it." The *News,* a Republican paper, used "the Democracy" or "Copperheads" when writing of the Democratic Party; "Union" used alone referred invariably to the Republican Party.

REPUBLICAN PARTY. *Ormsby County, Nevada.*

Regular | Union Tickets. | [*filet*] | Nevada Union State Ticket. | [*filet*] | . . . | [*filet*] | Ormsby County Union Ticket | [*filet*] | . . . | [Carson City? 1866.] [411]

Broadside. 20 x 7 cm. Geometrical design on verso.
The ticket contains names of candidates who ran in 1866.
NvMus.

REPUBLICAN PARTY. *Storey County, Nevada.* Regular Union Assembly ticket. Gold Hill: Gold Hill News. 1866. [L412]

Gold Hill *News,* November 6, 1866 (election day): "To UNION VOTERS.—A sad error occurred in printing the Regular Union Assembly ticket for Storey county. Hugh Twining was the nominee of the County Convention, but he subsequently withdrew, and the County Central Committee placed in his stead the name of J. L. Swaney. In the printing of the tickets, (there being four full tickets on one sheet) the name of Mr. Twining was accidentally printed upon one instead of that of Mr. Swaney. As soon as the error was discovered this morning, we sent messengers to all the different wards to withdraw that portion of the tickets containing Mr. Twining's name, as there were plenty of the others in the field, which was accordingly done; and we presume the error, although very provoking to Mr. Swaney as well as ourself, will not materially affect the result of the election. Of all the candidates on the ticket, Mr. Swaney has been our particular choice—and it was through our instrumentality more than any other man [i.e., Philip Lynch, proprietor of the *News*], in our capacity as a County Central Committee member, that he was placed there. Therefore, such a mishap, happening as it did in our own printing office, and knowing how prone men are with their tongues of slander and insinuation to attribute wrong motives for accidents, we have felt sorely grieved and vexed." Swaney won.

REPUBLICAN PARTY. *Storey County, Nevada.* Regular Union ticket. 1866.   [L413]

Gold Hill *News*, November 6, 1866 (election day): "FRAUDS.—The Copperheads have attempted various tricks to counterfeit our Regular Union Tickets, by printing poor imitations. Let every Union man beware when he takes a Ticket, and be sure to examine all the names. DON'T VOTE A SCRATCHED TICKET!" On the previous day the *News* had issued a warning to avoid tickets with opposition names pasted over those of Union nominees; it was a general statement, however, and no mention was made of specific instances.

RICKARD, WILLIAM THOMPSON.

Silver Ores, | —and— | Their Modes of Reduction, | [*filet*] | A Lecture, | Delivered at the Gold Hill, Nevada, U.S., Literary and Scientific Society, | November 30th, 1865, | —by— | W. T. Rickard, | Fellow of the Chemical Society, and Member of the Microscopical Society and | Geologist Association, London. | [*double rule*] | Price [*dotted rule*] Fifty Cents. | [*double rule*] | Virginia, Nev.: | Printed at the "Territorial Enterprise" Book and Job Office. | [*short rule*] | 1866.   [414]

9 p. 22 x 15 cm. Printed wrapper, from same type as the title page. Text printed in two columns, possibly from same type as in the *Enterprise*, but the appropriate issues have not been located.
CU-B.

STOREY COUNTY, NEVADA. *Board of Education.* Address. February 14, 1866. 12 p.   [L415]

Gold Hill *News*, February 15, 1866: "A very neat pamphlet, of twelve pages, was issued yesterday, containing an address to the parents and guardians of pupils in our Public Schools, by the Storey county Board of Education, with other important documents relating to the subject matter of the address, and the excellent annual report of Colonel [John A.] Collins, County Superintendent of Public Schools. This address was called forth in answer to a series of disgraceful attacks made upon the Board of Education and upon the character of the Public Schools, school houses, school furniture and school yards, by that mendacious sheet known as the Virginia Daily *Union*."

STOREY COUNTY, NEVADA. *Citizens.*

To His Excellency, Henry G. Blasdel. | [*filet*] | We, the under-signed citizens of Storey County, most respectfully petition your Excellency not to | withhold your sanction from the bill now before you in aid of the Orphan Asylum of the Sisters of Charity | in Virginia. We pray your Excellency to concur in the noble action of the Legislature in aid of so humane | a purpose: | [*double rule*] | . . . | [1866.] [416]

[4] p., printed on blue-lined paper on p. [1] only. 31 x 20 cm.

The bill, SB41 of the 1866 session, was enrolled on February 27 and returned with the Governor's veto message on March 1. See also Nos. 380, L391, and L417.

NvHi.

SUMNER, CHARLES ALLEN. Bill, petition, report and veto in Senate and Assembly concerning the Orphan Asylum conducted by the Sisters of Charity, at Virginia City, Storey County, Nevada. 1866. [L417]

Washoe City *Eastern Slope,* quoted in the Unionville *Humboldt Register,* March 17, 1866: "We are indebted to Mr. Sweeny, of Carson City, for a copy of a pamphlet, edited by Senator Sumner . . . with the request that we would carefully read and prayerfully consider. It lacks but one thing to make it perfect. The work should have contained the veto, which in our estimation is worth all the balance; were that added, the book would be invaluable as an electioneering document—as it is, it is well calculated to purify the Union party, by driving from its ranks such aspirants for office as are unwilling to trust entirely to that party for political success." See Nos. 380, L391, and 416 for other items dealing with Senate Bill 41 of the 1866 session. There is no mention of this publication in JS, 1866, so it probably was not printed and paid for by the state. The comment regarding omission of the veto message is a curious one, since it is mentioned in the title cited by the *Register.* The Unionville paper may not, however, have quoted correctly from the *Eastern Slope.*

SUTRO TUNNEL COMPANY.

Agreement. | The Sutro Tunnel Company with the [*blank*] | Articles of Agreement, Made and entered into this [*blank*] A.D. one thousand eight hundred and sixty-six, by and between William M. Stewart, D. E. Avery, Louis Janin, Jr., H. K. Mitchell, and A. Sutro. | Trustees for the Sutro Tunnel Company, parties of the first part, and the [*blank*] Mining Company, a corporation doing business in the County of Storey, State of Nevada, party of the second part. | . . . | [San Francisco: Towne & Bacon, Book and Job Printers. 1866.] [418]

Broadside. 71 x 52 cm.

200 copies on "news paper," 50 on "fine paper," and 60 on "Parchment" were printed by Towne & Bacon; the bill for $187.75, including an unspecified amount for "alterations," was entered on March 31, 1866, in the company's daybook, volume 15 at CSt. The parchment issue is 65 x 55 cm. and has minor variations in

text and forms for signatures at the bottom: Agreement. | The Sutro Tunnel Company with [*blank*] | Articles of Agreement, Made and entered into this [*blank*] A.D. one thousand eight hundred and sixty-six, by and between William M. Stewart, D. E. Avery, Louis Janin, Jr., H. K. Mitchell, and A. Sutro | Trustees for the Sutro Tunnel Company, parties of the first part, and [*blank*] doing business in the County of Storey, State of Nevada, parties of the second part.

See also No. 361.

COMus. CtY. NvRH (parchment). NvU (paper and parchment).

UNITED STATES. *Army. District of Nevada.*

General Orders | Headquarters District of Nevada, | No. 8. | Camp McGarry, Nevada, Dec. 31, 1866. | . . .   [419]

[2] p. 18 x 12 cm. Caption title. Lines 1 and 3 connected by a brace.

The document reports on the success of operations against hostile Indians during 1866: "one hundred and seventy-two killed and one hundred and fifty-five taken prisoners; a total loss of three hundred and twenty-seven." Only one Army death is reported.

Camp McGarry was established in late 1865 in order to protect emigrants and other travelers in northwestern Nevada; it was closed about three years later. No evidence has been found to indicate the presence of a press at any military post in Nevada.

ICN. NvU (microfilm).

VIRGINIA CITY, NEVADA. *Politics.* Poster. April 20, 1866.   [L420]

Alf Doten's *Journal* entry of April 21, 1866, contains the following: "posters stuck up round City as sort of electioneering documents against John Piper, who is Candidate for Mayor — created considerable discussion & stir, as they were clandestinely posted, no one knowing by whom, the night before." Piper was elected.

YELLOW JACKET SILVER MINING COMPANY. Annual report. 1866.

[L421]

Gold Hill *News,* July 24, 1866: "The Yellow Jacket Silver Mining Company's Board of Trustees have just published their Annual Report, in a neat pamphlet form. It was issued to stockholders and others this morning." A July 12 entry in Towne & Bacon's records shows a billing to Philip Lynch of Gold Hill, proprietor of the *News,* of $35 for 250 copies of the pamphlet; it is likely, then, as with later Yellow Jacket reports (see Nos. 458 and 496-497), that this one bore the imprint of the *News* job office. A marginal note at the entry indicates that the reports were sent by Wells, Fargo & Company, with the "bill inclosed [*sic*]."

YELLOW JACKET SILVER MINING COMPANY.

Semi-Annual Report | —of the— | Operations | —of the— | Yellow Jacket | Silver Mining Company, | —for the— | Six Months Ending December 31st, 1865; | —and the— | Financial Condition, | January 1st, 1866. | [*filet*] | [Virginia City:] Territorial Enterprise Book and Job Printing House, No. 24 South C Street.

[422]

[4] p. 20 x 12 cm. Line 1 in an arch over line 2. Title page in decorative rule border; text pages in double rule borders. Page [4]: "Gold Hill, Nevada, January 1st, 1866." CtY. NvU (microfilm).

❧1867❧

Nevada had not just one legislative session in 1867; it had two. During the regular session the legislators neglected to enact provisions in the revenue law that would assure payment of interest on the state debt, so the Governor called them back for a twenty-day special session to repair the omission. The regular session produced the first of several controversies connected with the office of State Printer and the first portents of later suggestions that the position be abolished. The journals are silent on the matter, referring in only the tersest way to Senate Bill 194, "An Act to Provide for Certain Public Printing for the State of Nevada," but Henry R. Mighels had some revealing things to say in his paper, the Carson City *Appeal,* on March 6. Ostensibly, the bill provided that the State Printer be paid in gold coin, a view that Mighels supported as "a piece of justice that ought to prevail." But there were apparently also attempts "by certain owl headed legislators" to abolish the office outright because they believed it to be "an unnecessary encumbrance and expense to the State." Mighels, who ten years later successfully pushed an abolition bill through the Legislature, had not yet come to that view, stating that "it is something of a bull to abolish that office at the tail end of the session, after all the 'fat takes' have been set up." He did, however, support the idea of "putting the business of contracting for the printing of the Statutes and Journals into the hands of the Secretary of State," calling it "a promising plan which may prove beneficial to the tax payers" and an action that would "take [State Printer Joseph E.] Eckley's elephant off his hands." The bill passed the Senate but was indefinitely tabled and allowed to die in the Assembly.

The State Controller's 1878 report (p. 30) shows that during fiscal year 1867, $22,253.40 was expended from the State Printing Fund. Records at Stanford University's Jackson Library of Business indicate that the de facto State Printer for Nevada in 1867 and 1868 was the San Francisco firm of Towne & Bacon.

Belmont got its first press at the end of March and a single issue of a newspaper may have been published in Empire City in January, although the likelihood of a hoax is high. Ione lost its paper in May, with its press going to Belmont, and one of Virginia City's newspapers died in early February, to be replaced the next day by another, using the same press. All other papers that were active at the end of 1866 published throughout the year.

ESMERALDA COUNTY, NEVADA. *Citizens.*

Petition for Land Office. | To His Excellency the President, and to the Hon. Commissioner of | the General Land Office of the United States: | Your Petitioners of | [*blank*] county, State of [*blank*], pray that a new | Land District be organized, comprising the county of Esmeralda, State | of Nevada, and also the counties of Mono and Inyo, State of California, | . . . | [Aurora? 1867.]   [423]

Broadside. 40 x 21 cm. Dated at bottom: "December, 1867." The printer apparently ran short of upper case S's; those in the last third of the petition are set in bold face and in a larger size than the bulk of the printing. Facsimile following p. 314.

The petitioners asked that a new land district be established at Aurora for the convenience of the citizens, all three counties being east of the Sierra Nevada range. The land office for Esmeralda County was in Carson City. The county is here described as "embracing the prosperous mining districts of Aurora, Esmeralda, Pine Grove, Washington, Silver Peak, Columbus, Palmetto, and other mining districts, and the Walker River and other valleys."

Gold Hill *News,* February 1, 1868, copied from the Aurora *Esmeralda Union:* "Most of the petitions for the establishment of a Land Office at Aurora, that have been circulated through the counties of Mono and Inyo, of California, and Esmeralda, Nevada, have been returned, and forwarded to Washington." A U.S. Land Office was established in Aurora on August 24, 1868. It continued there until February 27, 1873, when its Nevada functions were returned to the office in Carson City; on the same date the California portion of the land office's duties was consolidated into the land office at Independence, California.

CtY. DNA.

FERGUSON, ROBERT D.

Introductory Address | of the | Hon. R. D. Ferguson, | Speaker Elect of the | House of Representatives | of the State of Nevada. | [*short rule*] | Delivered January 7, 1867. | [*filet*] | Carson City: | J.E. Eckley, State Printer. | [*short rule*] | 1867.   [424]

7 p. 22 x 14 cm. Printed wrapper.

The Carson City *Appeal* of January 20, 1867, noted receipt of a copy "in pamphlet form."

The speech occasioned great hilarity in the local newspapers. On the 26th of January the *Territorial Enterprise* devoted a long article to it, declaring in part: "Speaker Ferguson's introductory address to the Assembly has been published—very extensively published. It first appeared in the Legislative reports of the *Enterprise,* and occupied about a half column of space, in a type known to printers as nonpareil. It was a laborious production. It was brought forth after days of travail; but Mr. Ferguson loved it, and the Assembly ordered a thousand copies printed in pamphlet form at the expense of the State for the use of the author! It makes a pamphlet—that half column of twaddle—of twelve pages, including the cover. We are thankful that it was not issued in three volumes, with the title-page repeated through two-thirds of each. But the thousand copies provided by the Assembly for the use of Mr. Ferguson, constitute but a small part of the number actually printed. We are informed that not less than forty thousand copies have been furnished by the State Printer—thirty-nine thousand of them on the private order of Mr. Ferguson—and that the printer has been instructed to keep the forms standing, as several thousand more may possibly be required. Complaints reach us from both Houses of the tardiness of the State Printer in furnishing printed copies of the Governor's message and department reports, and a committee was appointed last Wednesday to inquire into the cause of the delay. The committee discovered—although it was not so reported—that since the meeting of the Legislature the presses of the printer had been almost constantly employed in working off Ferguson's pamphlets. . . . We need scarcely explain what Mr. Ferguson has done and is still doing with his pamphlets. Upon them are based his hopes of political advancement, and they are being distributed, of course. The boxes of the Post-office in this city are overflowing with them, and the same may be said of every other Post-office in the State. A copy has been directed to the name of every person on the face of the earth known to the author, and the publication of a fresh letter list brings to the office from which it emanates another supply of Ferguson's pamphlets. They are beginning to make their appearance as wrappers to pill boxes, but druggists should use them exclusively for emetics." The Gold Hill *News* had its fun, too, reporting on the 24th of January: "We have not, as yet, received any printed bills, resolutions or reports; so we cannot say much in detail of Legislation inaugurated up to or within date. We *have,* however, a copy of the Inaugural Address of our esteemed Representative, Mr. Speaker Ferguson. Of this production, it would be a sufficient compliment to herald the fact that 1,000 copies were ordered printed by the Assembly, on motion of Mr. [Thomas J.] Tennant, of Lander—Mr. F.'s competitor for the Speaker's chair;—and so earnest was the desire of the members to secure copies of this neat speech that the whole edition was exhausted before Mr. Ferguson had an opportunity to supply himself with due proportion of the issue. The House even ignored the rule of printing limitation in its eagerness to secure a handsome edition of the Address. . . . This Inaugural is contained in an eight-page pamphlet—two pages and a half being occupied with the speech, the balance being devoted to title page, Mr. Tennant's resolution, and the profit-margin of the printer. It has a cover; the covers are sometimes of one color, and sometimes of another. We should be pleased to dwell longer on this first formal, printed production from the Legislature of 1867, but we must sail away from it, for a space." The *News* returned to the subject two days later, noting that a "new edition of 1,500 copies . . . has been ordered," and on the 5th of February got in its final dig: "Last night was a gala-time for the Good Templars [in Carson City]. . . . While the Lodge was being opened, before the ceremonies . . . commenced, many visitors stood at the foot of the stairs waiting the opening of the doors. Mr. Mason enlivened the outsiders with extempore lectures, in one of which he remarked that his professional conclusion was that there were at present four great, crying evils in society—Tobacco, Ardent Spirits, Syphilis, and Ferg's Inaugural."

The speech was, in fact, a trite and turgid potboiler. Its opening lines are: "Man is frail; and I do not claim to be free from his errors and his weaknesses. But let me assure you, gentlemen, that if sincerity of purpose, coupled with honest intent, can guide and direct me in this responsible position, clear from the shoals and quicksands of personal prejudice, which have unfortunately stranded so many upon the barren reefs of discourtesy, and rendered the position of members intolerable by giving vent to personal spleen, then will I assuredly pass safely over the angry waves of strife and dissension, which may possibly arise during the course of our deliberations." The "Man is frail" portion was picked up and bandied about by many newspapers during and after the session.

CSmH. CtY. ICN. NvU.

FREEMASONS. *Nevada. Grand Lodge.*

Proceedings | of the | M.˙. W.˙. Grand Lodge | of | Free and Accepted Masons | of the | State of Nevada, | at its | Third Annual Grand Communication, | Held at Masonic Hall, in the City of Virginia, | September 17, 18, and 19, A.L. 5867. | [*short rule*] | San Francisco: | Frank Eastman, Printer, 509 Clay Street. | 1867. [425]

[3], 210-309, [1], iii p. 23 x 14 cm. Printed wrapper.

The Grand Lodge provided $800 "For printing proceedings, postage, expressage, and expenses of Grand Secretary's office" (p. 285). 800 copies were printed, with the "usual number," i.e., 300, left "uncut" with the printer for future binding (1868 Proceedings, p. 318), at a cost of $523.36 (ibid., p. 320).

NvHi (microfilm). NvMus (microfilm). NvRFM. NvU (microfilm).

GOLD HILL, NEVADA. *School for Girls.* Circular. 1867.   [L426]

Gold Hill *News,* September 10, 1867: "A School for Girls has recently been opened by Mrs. Conrad Wiegand, on the Tunnel Road near Fort Homestead. . . . A circular can be obtained by calling at the Gold Hill Assay office." The assay office was owned by Conrad Wiegand.

HAYNIE, JOHN W.

Report | Relating to | Finances | —of— | Douglas County, Nevada, | —from— | Its Organization | —to— | January 7th, 1867. | [*filet*] | "Alpine Miner" Book and Job Printing Office, Monitor. | [1867?]   [426a]

8 p. 16 x 12 cm. Wrapper title, in wavy-thin rule border.

It is not clear why the report was printed in the small mountain town of Monitor, particularly because in order to get there one had first to pass through another California town with an active press. In the other direction, Carson City was much closer over much less uncertain winter terrain.

Douglas County's Board of County Commissioners had hired Haynie, whose name appears only at the end of the report, to sort through the jumble that county records had become in the five years since establishment. There were apparently suspicions on the part of the Commissioners that all was not well, but it is difficult to trace the origins of those suspicions because there had not been a newspaper in Douglas County for over a year and Carson City's paper was preoccupied with legislative happenings.

Haynie's findings could not have been heartening to the Commissioners. He noted, for instance, that the county had an *apparent* outstanding indebtedness in excess of $22,650—apparent, but not certain, since the County Auditor had not troubled himself to keep a record of warrants issued. In addition, former officials were said to owe the county, for unexplained reasons, anywhere from roughly $7,625 to nearly $8,200, in amounts ranging from $1.33 to over $3,250. Haynie drew no direct conclusions of his own, but it is clear from the manner of his presentation what kind of decisions he expected the Commissioners to reach.

NvHi.

HILLER, FREDERICK.

Medical | Truth and Light | for the Million, | —or— | Homoeopathy | vs. | Allopathy. | By F. Hiller, M.D. | [*filet*] | Dr. F. Hiller's Homoeopathic Pharmacy, No. 68 South C Street, | Virginia, Nevada. | [*filet*] | Virginia, Nev.: | Territorial Enterprise Book and Job Printing Office, 24 South C St. | [*short rule*] | 1867.   [427]

16 p. 22 x 14 cm. Printed wrapper. Described in *Check List:* 112 as an 1869 imprint. The Diaries of Alf Doten show him to be the ghost-writer of this first medical treatise printed in Nevada. The appropriate entries are as follows. May 25, 1867: "PM called on Dr Hiller awhile & got items & material for the compilation of a pamphlet for him; being a treatise on Homeopathy as compared with allopathy"; May 28: "At home all day busy on Dr Hiller's pamphlet"; May 29: "Worked hard all day on Dr Hiller's pamphlet"; May 30: "Completed Dr. Hiller's pamphlet at one o'clock today, and took it to him — He was much pleased with the job — 18 pages legal cap"; June 6: "at Hiller's office I stopped & corrected proof of his pamphlet — took it to the Enterprise job office — Sam Leonard . . . set it up, & I read it over by copy"; June 11: "Hiller's pamphlets were finished & published in due form today"; June 13: "Dr Hiller has 2,000 pamphlets now printed, & is distributing them freely all about town, & everywhere else — 16 pages, & got up tolerable neatly."

CSmH. CU-B. NvU.

HUMBOLDT COUNTY, NEVADA. *Surveyor and Assessor.*

Report | of the | County Surveyor | and | County Assessor | of | Humboldt County. | [*filet*] | 1867. | [*short rule*] | Virginia, Nev.: | Enterprise Steam Printing Office.   [428]

16 p. 21 x 14 cm. Printed wrapper. *Check List:* 108 identifies this as an 1868 imprint, apparently confusing the imprint date with the period covered in the report.

The report contains a general description of the county and specific descriptions of mining districts.

CSmH. MBC.

NEVADA. *Governor, 1864-1871 (Henry Goode Blasdel).*

[*Thick-thin rule*] | Message | —of— | H. G. Blasdel, | Governor of the State of Nevada. | To the Legislature, convened in Special Session, by Proclamation, | issued March 12th, 1867. Delivered March 15th, 1867. | [*thin-thick rule*] | [Carson City:] J. E. Eckley, State Printer.   [429]

4 p. 22 x 13 cm. Printed wrapper.

The message deals with the failure of the Legislature in its regular session to enact a revenue law to provide for payment of a $500,000 debt, which it had authorized the state to borrow.

NN. NvU (microfilm). WHi.

NEVADA. *Governor, 1864-1871 (Henry Goode Blasdel).*

Proclamation by the Governor, | [*state seal*] | For a day of Public Thanksgiving. | [*short wavy rule-short rule*] | . . . | . . . I | recommend that | Thursday, the 28th instant, | be set apart and appropriately observed as a day of Special Thanksgiving . . . | . . . | . . . Done at Carson City, this the 14th day of | November, A.D. 1867. | . . .   [430]

[4] p., printed on p. [1] only. 25 x 20 cm. Line 1 in an arch over state seal and line 2.
CSmH. CtY. M. NvMus. NvU (microfilm). ViU.

NEVADA. *Governor, 1864-1871 (Henry Goode Blasdel).*

Second | Inaugural Address | —of— | H. G. Blasdel, | Governor of the State of Nevada. | Delivered January 8th, 1867, | Before the Senate and Assembly, in Joint Convention. | [*short rule*] | —Also— | First Biennial Message. | Delivered to the Legislature, January 10th, 1867. | [*filet*] | Carson City: | J. E. Eckley, State Printer. | [*short rule*] | 1867.   [431]

22 p. 23 x 15 cm. Printed wrapper. Page [3]-7: Second Inaugural Address; p. [9]-22: Biennial Message. Issued also, from a different type setting, as [Nos. 1-2] in AJS, 1867.

Senate concurrent resolution to print 1,000 copies (JS, 1867, p. 18); concurred in (JA, 1867, p. 32). Report of the Senate Printing Committee (JS, 1867, p. 54): "The Message of the Governor has been printed, and will be ready for distribution this day [i.e., January 24]." The Gold Hill *News* reported on January 11, in an article containing an abstract of the message, that "a thousand extra copies of the Message have been ordered printed for general distribution." Presumably these "extra" copies were the ones referred to in JS and JA and not those printed for AJS.

CSmH. CoD. CtY. DLC. ICN. NN. NvU. PP. WHi (remnants of wrapper remain).

NEVADA. *Laws, statutes, etc.*

Laws | Relating to Revenue | of the | State of Nevada, | Passed at | The Third And Special Sessions | of the Legislature, 1867. | [*filet*] | Carson, Nevada: | Printed at the office of the "Daily

Appeal," Second Street. | [*short rule*] | 1867.   [432]

26, [1] p. 22 x 15 cm. Printed wrapper.

Senate concurrent resolution of the special session to print 500 copies in pamphlet form (SSN, 1867, p. 184). Gold Hill *News*, April 27, 1867: "Hon. C. N. Noteware, Secretary of State, will please accept our acknowledgment of a copy of the new 'Laws Relating to Revenue.' It is a neatly printed and covered pamphlet of thirty pages, issued from the *Appeal* office."

CSmH.

NEVADA. *Laws, statutes, etc.*

School Law | of the | State of Nevada, | As Amended at the | Third Session of the Legislature. | [*short rule*] | Published by the | Department of Public Instruction, | For the Use of School Offi-cers. | [*short rule*] | Carson City: | Joseph E. Eckley, State Printer. | 1867.   [433]

23, [1] p. 22 x 14 cm. The recorded copy lacks a wrapper. *Check List:* 95 located a copy at the U.S. Office of Education Library, now part of DHEW, and indicated that it had a wrapper. That copy was transferred in early 1969 to DLC, which discarded it. See Introduction, p. 10-11.

Towne & Bacon's records for May 3, 1867, indicate that 600 copies were printed at a cost of $45.65. An acknowledgment for receipt of a copy is in the Gold Hill *News* of May 27, 1867.

WHi.

NEVADA. *Laws, statutes, etc.*

Statutes | of the | State of Nevada, | Passed at the | Third Session of the Legislature, | 1867, | Begun on Monday, the Seventh Day of January, and Ended on | Thursday, the Seventh Day of March. | [*short rule*] | Special Session, | Begun on Friday, the Fifteenth Day of March, and Ended on | Wednesday, the Third Day of April, 1867. | [*state seal*] | Carson City: | Joseph E. Eckley, State Printer. | 1867.   [434]

xiii, [3], 216 p. 23 x 15 cm. Leather binding. Pages [199]-216, Annual Report of the State Treasurer of the State of Nevada for the Year 1866; printed from the same type as in No. 452, and [No. 4] in No. 438.

Towne & Bacon's records for June 24, 1867, show that 675 copies were printed at a cost of $819.46. Carson City *Appeal*, June 28, 1867: "State Printer Eckley, who arrived here from California yesterday, reports copies of the Laws and House Journal of the last session of the Legislature on the way to the office of the Secretary of State. They were forwarded on the 20th. As they are coming by fast freight they are now due at this place." An advertisement for H. C. Lillie & Co. of Virginia City, dated June 24 but appearing for the first time in the Gold Hill *News* of June 25, announced the "Laws of Nevada of 1867" as "Just Received."

Az. CSmH. CU-B. CtY-L. DLC. MBS. MH-L. NN. NNLI. NjP. Nv. NvEuC.

NvGoEC. NvHi. NvLC. NvLN. NvRNC. NvRWL (rebacked). NvSC. NvU. NvYLR. OrU-L. WHi.

Nevada. *Legislature.*

United States of America. | [*short rule*] | Joint | Memorial and Resolutions | of the | Nevada Legislature, | Asking Government Aid in the Construction | of the | Sutro Tunnel. | Together with the Report of the "Senate Committee on Fed-|eral Relations," Showing the Importance of the Proposed | Work; the Benefits Which Result to the People of | the United States by the Increased Production | of the Precious Metals; the Consequent | Increase of Taxable Property, and | its Bearing on the | Payment of the National Debt. | San Francisco: | Towne & Bacon, Book and Job Printers. | 1867.
[435]

32 p. 28 x 22 cm. Printed wrapper. A facsimile of No. 439, which folds out to 43 x 36 cm., is tipped in on the inside rear wrapper.

This pamphlet, unlike other documents issued by the state, bears openly the imprint of Towne & Bacon. It was not, in fact, issued by the state, but ordered and paid for by Adolph Sutro himself, no doubt as a part of his campaign to impress potential backers of his tunnel project. An entry in Towne & Bacon's Journal E for January 29, 1867, shows that there was to be an extra charge "for difference bet. usual style of printing such reports, and style adopted for Mr. S." This entry was voided, however, and the entry for January 31 shows only that the piece was printed on 56-lb. paper rather than the usual 40-lb. stock and cost Sutro $352.60 for 200 copies.

CHi. CLU. CSmH. CU. CU-B. CtY. DLC. ICN. MH. MWA. NN. Nv (lacks facsimile; cropped to 22 x 22 cm.). NvHi (lacks facsimile). NvU. WHi.

Nevada. *Legislature. Assembly.*

Journal of the Assembly | During | the Third Session | of the | Legislature of the State of Nevada, | 1867, | Begun on Monday, the Seventh Day of January, and Ended | on Thursday, the Seventh Day of March; | and | Special Session, | Begun on Friday, the Fifteenth Day of March, and Ended | on Wednesday, the Third Day of April. | [*state seal*] | Carson City: | Joseph E. Eckley, State Printer. | 1867.
[436]

398 p. 23 x 15 cm. Half-leather binding.

The printing of 300 copies at a cost of $870.44 is noted in the Towne & Bacon records for June 24, 1867. The Carson City *Appeal* of June 28, 1867, noted a report from the State Printer that the Journal had been forwarded by fast freight from San Francisco on June 20; receipt of a copy was acknowledged in the July 6 issue of the *Appeal*.

CSmH. CtY. CtY-L. DLC. M. MH. NN. Nv-Ar. NvHi. NvLC. NvLN. NvRWL. NvSC. NvU. UU-L. WHi.

Nevada. *Legislature. Assembly. Select Committee on Toll Roads and Bridges.*

[*Thick-thin rule*] | Report | of the | Special Committee | on | Toll Roads and Bridges | Within this State. | [*thin-thick rule*] | [Carson City:] J. E. Eckley, State Printer. | [1867.]   [437]

9 p. 23 x 15 cm. Printer wrapper. Motion to print 500 copies (JS, 1867, p. 202).

"We most respectfully recommend, to the favorable consideration of this House, Assembly Bill No. 107, entitled 'An Act to enforce the payment of two per cent. of the gross proceeds of all Toll Roads and Bridges, as provided by law, to the General School Fund of this State,' introduced February 18th, 1867, by Mr. [Thomas] Parker." The committee is referred to as "Select," both at the end of the report itself and in JA, 1867.

CSmH.

NEVADA. *Legislature. Senate.*

Journal of the Senate | During | the Third Session | of the | Legislature of the State of Nevada, | 1867, | Begun on Monday, the Seventh Day of January, and | Ended on Thursday, the Seventh Day of March; | and | Special Session, | Begun on Friday, the Fifteenth Day of March, and Ended | on Wednesday, the Third Day of April. | [*state seal*] | Carson City: | Joseph E. Eckley, State Printer. | 1867.   [438]

365, 5, [7]-16, 36, 16, 45, 15, 12, 12, 95, 151 p. 23 x 15 cm. Half-leather binding. Two legislative committee reports follow the Journals of the regular and special sessions: Report of Committee on Ways and Means, of the Receipts and Expenditures for the Third, Fourth and Fifth Fiscal Years, p. [321]-325; and Report of Joint Committee of the Senate and Assembly, on State Prison, p. [327]-336. An index to the Journals is on p. [337]-365. Following p. 365 is a general half title: Appendix to Senate Proceedings. Each of the ten reports in the Appendix has a separate half title and/or title page and each is paged separately unless otherwise indicated. Numbers have been assigned according to position of the reports in the volume, since there is no table of contents. [No. 1], Second Inaugural Address of Hon. H. G. Blasdel, Governor of the State of Nevada, Delivered January 8th, 1867, Before the Senate and Assembly, in Joint Convention, 5 p.; [No. 2], First Biennial Message of Governor H. G. Blasdel, Delivered to the Legislature of Nevada, January 10, 1867, p. [7]-16, continuing pagination of the Inaugural Address; [No. 3], Annual Report of Controller of the State of Nevada, for 1866, 36 p.; [No. 4], Annual Report of the State Treasurer of the State of Nevada, for the Year 1866. Carson City: Joseph E. Eckley, State Printer. 1867, 16 p.; [No. 5], First Biennial Report of the Superintendent of Public Instruction of the State of Nevada, for the School Year Ending August 31, 1866. Carson City: Joseph E. Eckley, State Printer. 1867, 45 p. and two folding tables; [No. 6], Annual Report of the Warden of the Nevada State Prison, for the Fiscal Year Ending Dec. 31, 1866. J. S. Crosman, Warden. Carson City: Joseph E. Eckley, State Printer. 1867, 15 p. and folding table; [No. 7], Third Annual Report of the State Library, 12 p.; [No 8], Report of Committee on Federal Relations in Relation to Joint Memorial and Resolutions Asking Government Aid in the Construction of the Sutro Tunnel. Carson City: Joseph E. Eckley, State Printer. 1867, 12 p.; [No. 9], Report of the Surveyor General of Nevada for 1866, 95 p., including two folding tables; [No. 10], Nevada State Mineralogist's Report for 1866, 151 p., including a folding table.

Towne & Bacon's records for June 24, 1867, show the printing of 300 copies at a cost of $836.60; the printer's overrun of 300 copies for many of the reports contained in this volume was presumably not included in this cost but was added to the cost of printing each report. The Carson City *Appeal* and the Gold Hill *News* both said in their issues of June 27, 1867, that the Secretary of State had received 100 copies of the Senate journal; the *News* acknowledged receipt of a copy on July 8.

CtY. CtY-L. DLC. M. MH. NN. Nv. Nv-Ar. NvHi. NvLC. NvLN. NvRWL. NvSC. NvU. WHi.

NEVADA. *Legislature. Senate.*

United States of America. | State of Nevada. | Senate Concurrent Resolutions. | No. 70. | In Relation to | Adolph Sutro. | [*filet*] | Resolved, by the Senate the Assembly concurring, | . . . | [1867.] [439]

Broadside. 58 x 43 cm. Lines 1-2 in banner compartment; line 3 in an arch over line 4. Ornaments around lines 3-7. In decorative thin-thick-thin rule border. Text in script type. Also issued on vellum, 48 x 37 cm.

Considering Sutro's penchant for self-puffery, his willingness to spend money to boost his enterprises (see No. 435), and a previous history of printing on vellum (see No. 418), it may be reasonable to conjecture that he ordered and paid for at least a part of the edition of this resolution, if not all of it.

The resolution, dated January 25, 1867, thanks Sutro for originating the plan of the Sutro Tunnel and expresses confidence that he will find financing to undertake its construction. Confidence in Sutro did not last for long, however; see No. 547.

CHi (paper). CU-B (paper). NvU (vellum).

NEVADA. *Legislature. Senate. Committee on Federal Relations.*

Report | of | Committee on Federal Relations | in Relation to | Joint Memorial and Resolutions Asking | Government Aid in the Construction | of the Sutro Tunnel. | [*short rule*] | Carson City: | Joseph E. Eckley, State Printer. | 1867. [440]

vi, [3]-12 p. 23 x 15 cm. Printed wrapper. Only p. vi of the preliminaries, which include an index and the text of the Joint Memorial and Resolutions, is numbered. A variant issue lacks the pages with roman numerals; it was issued also as [No. 8] in AJS, 1867. In the variant the title page is p. [1]; in the issue described here it is p. [i] and there is consequently no p. [1-2]. Neither issue contains the "Legislative proceedings" that are indicated in the index to begin on p. 13.

2,000 copies were ordered printed (JS, 1867, p. 49-50); Towne & Bacon's Journal E for January 28, 1867, shows that 2,000 copies were printed on 40-lb. book paper at a cost of $137.27. There is no clue in the record as to the reason for the different issues, although the variant may have been brought about by a press overrun of the issue intended for AJS.

C (variant). CHi (prelims). CU-B (prelims). CtY (both issues). DLC. M. MWA (prelims). NvHi (variant). NvU (prelims; microfilm of both issues). WHi (variant).

NEVADA. *Legislature. Senate. Committee on Ways and Means.*

[*Thick-thin rule*] | Report | of the | Senate Committee | on | Ways and Means, | In Connection With The Loan Bill, | —of the— | Receipts and Expenditures | for the | Third, Fourth and Fifth Fiscal Years. | [*thin-thick rule*] | [Carson City:] J. E. Eckley, State Printer. | [1867.]   [441]

6 p. 22 x 14 cm. Printed wrapper. Issued also, printed from the same type, in JS, 1867, p. [321]-325.

400 copies ordered printed (JS, 1867, p. 58).

CSmH.

NEVADA. *Office of Superintendent of Public Instruction.*

First Biennial Report | of the | Superintendent of Public Instruction | of the | State of Nevada, | for the | School Year Ending August 31, 1866. | [*short rule*] | Carson City: | Joseph E. Eckley, State Printer. | 1867.   [442]

45 p. and two folding tables. 23 x 14 cm. Printed wrapper. Issued also as [No. 5] in AJS, 1867.

500 copies ordered printed (SSN, 1867, p. 143). The record in Towne & Bacon's Journal E for January 22, 1867, indicates that 800 copies were printed; the extra 300 were for the AJS issue. Towne & Bacon charged $116.89 for 133,588 ems, $15 for 24 tokens of press work, $46.67 for 1,600 sheets of 40-lb. book paper, $4.40 for 250 sheets of cover paper, $6.87 for binding, $1 for boxing, and 75¢ for cartage, for a total of $191.58.

The Carson City *Appeal* of February 12, 1867, acknowledged receipt of a copy.

CtY. DHEW. DLC. M. NvU (microfilm).

NEVADA. *State Controller's Office.*

Annual Report | of | The Controller | of the | State of Nevada, | for the | Second Fiscal Year, Ending December 31, 1866. | A. W. Nightingill, | State Controller. | [*short rule*] | Carson City: | Joseph E. Eckley, State Printer. | 1867.   [443]

36 p. 23 x 14 cm. Printed wrapper. Issued also as [No. 3] in AJS, 1867.

Towne & Bacon's Journal E for February 1, 1867, indicates that 540 copies were printed; the entry for March 29 shows a cost of $144.07.

DLC.

NEVADA. *State Library.*

Catalogue | of the | Nevada State Library, | for the Year 1867. | [*short rule*] | C. N. Noteware, Secretary of State, | and | Ex Officio State Librarian. | [*state seal*] | Carson City: | Joseph E. Eckley, State Printer. | 1867.   [444]

37 p. 23 x 15 cm. Printed wrapper. Title and text pages in single rule borders.

Towne & Bacon's Journal E for January 11, 1867, indicates that 500 copies were printed: 84,448 ems at 87½¢ per thousand ems, $73.90; 4 tokens press work, $5; 638 sheets of 40-lb. book paper, $18.60; 130 sheets cover paper, $2.30; binding, $5; and boxing and cartage, $1; for a total of $105.80. The small cartage fee probably means that the pamphlets were sent to a local shipping firm for transshipment and that the State Printer was charged an additional amount for sending them from San Francisco to Carson City.

The Carson City *Appeal* of February 6, 1867, acknowledged receipt of a copy from "the gentlemen of the Secretary of State's office."

CSmH. Nv-Ar.

NEVADA. *State Library.*

Third Annual Report | of the | Board of Directors | of the | State Library, | for the | State of Nevada. | [*short rule*] | Carson City: | Joseph E. Eckley, State Printer. | 1867.   [L445]

12 p. Description from title page in AJS, 1867, [No. 7].

Senate concurrent resolution to print 240 copies (SSN, 1867, p. 150). Journal E for February 4, 1867, in the Towne & Bacon records indicates that 400 copies were printed at a cost of $35.75.

NEVADA. *State Mineralogist.*

Annual Report | of the | State Mineralogist | of the | State of Nevada | For 1866. | Carson City: | Joseph E. Eckley, State Printer. | 1867.   [446]

151 p., including a folding table. 23 x 14 cm. Printed wrapper. Pages [105]-112, Appendix "A." On the Causes of the Decay of Mining Enterprises in Many Portions of the State; p. [113]-119, Appendix "B." Hints for the Use of Prospectors and Persons Engaged in the Early Development of Mining Property; p. [121]-132, Appendix "C." Catalogue of the Principal Minerals Found in Nevada; p. [133]-138, Appendix "D." Analyses of Nevada Minerals; p. [139]-147, Appendix "E." Journal of Explorations in Southern Nevada in the Spring of 1866, by His Excellency Governor Blasdel, of Nevada. R. H. Stretch; p. 148-151, List of Mills in Nevada. Issued also as [No. 10] in AJS, 1867.

2,000 copies ordered printed (SSN, 1867, p. 144). Towne & Bacon's Journal E entry for March 8, 1867, indicates that 2,300 copies were printed at a cost of $826.67; the 300 extra copies were for AJS.

Gold Hill *News,* March 22, 1867: "We are indebted to Assemblyman [A. K.] Potter for a copy of the Annual Report of the State Geologist. It is a handsomely printed pamphlet of one hundred and fifty-five pages, and is filled with highly useful and interesting reading and statistical matter; one of latter productions being a tabular statement of the amount of bullion products of this State for the year 1866, first compiled for and published in the Gold Hill NEws in January, and stolen bodily by the State Geologist without a word of credit. For Shame! Stretch." R. H. Stretch was the State Mineralogist in 1866.

C. MH-Z. MWA. NvHi. NvU.

Nevada. *State Prison.*

Annual Report | of | The Warden | of the | Nevada State Prison, | for the Fiscal Year Ending Dec. 31, 1866. | J. S. Crosman, | Warden. | [*short rule*] | Carson City: | Joseph E. Eckley, State Printer. | 1867.   [447]

15 p. and a folding table. 23 x 14 cm. Printed wrapper. Issued also as [No. 6] in AJS, 1867.

750 copies ordered printed (SSN, 1867, p. 144). Towne & Bacon's Journal E entry for January 22, 1867, shows a charge for 1,050 copies; the 300 extra copies were for the AJS issue. The firm charged $39.45 for 45,086 ems, $8.75 for 15 tokens of press work; $24.29 for 1,196 sheets of 40-lb. book paper; $14.65 for 265 sheets of cover paper; $5 for binding; and $1 for boxing and cartage; for a total of $93.14.

The Carson City *Appeal* of February 9, 1867, reported receipt of a copy.

CSmH. CtY. NvU (microfilm).

Nevada. *Supreme Court.*

[Briefs. 1867.]

Lucich et al. vs. Medin. Brief of appellants, Andreanna Lucich et al. 33 p. 25 x 17 cm. Imprint on wrapper: [San Francisco:] Mullin, Mahon & Co., Printers, 505 Clay street, cor. Sansome. Handwritten on wrapper of the recorded copy: Filed January 22d A D 1867 Alfred Helm Clerk. Nv-Ar.   [448]

Stonecifer vs. Yellow Jacket Silver Mining Co. Petition for rehearing. 10 p. 19 x 13 cm. Imprint on wrapper: Virginia, Nevada: Territorial Enterprise Book and Job Printing Office, 24 South C Street. 1867. Nv-Ar.   [449]

Nevada. *Supreme Court.*

Reports of Cases | Determined in the | Supreme Court | of the | State of Nevada, | During the Year 1866. | Reported by | Alfred Helm, Clerk of the Court. | [*short rule*] | Volume 2. | [*short rule*] | San Francisco: | Towne & Bacon, Book and Job Printers, Excelsior Office, | No. 536 Clay Street, just below Montgomery. | 1867.   [450]

416 p. 23 x 14 cm. Leather binding.

The printing of 500 copies was authorized (SSN, 1867, p. 114). Helm's contract with Towne & Bacon on April 20, 1867 (Nv-Ar: Nevada Contracts, p. 12-13), stipulated that the work was to contain approximately 496 p. of printed matter "to be printed on what is known as 56 lb. paper of the best quality." The amount of printed matter on each page and the type "shall, as far as practicable, be the same as that of the 1st volume of Nevada Reports, and the binding shall in no respect be inferior to said 1st Nevada Reports." On delivery to Helm in Carson City of the first 100 copies, he agreed to pay to the printers $500 "in gold coin of the United States"; on receipt of the remaining copies he agreed to pay the remainder of the contract price, $990. In case of a delay in payment, Towne & Bacon would receive interest at a rate of 1.5 percent per month; the firm did, in fact, add an interest charge of $68.50 on June 28, 1867 (CSt:

Towne & Bacon, vol. 12, p. 72). If the work turned out to be over the estimated 496 pages, the state would pay $2.50 for each excess page; if it was short of the estimate, $1.50 per page would be deducted. On May 31 the printer deducted $120 because the volume was 80 pages smaller than estimated (ibid., p. 38). Helm retained the copyright, as the state had failed to do in the case of the first Reports (see Nos. 403-404), "and no copies . . . shall be published except by order of "Helm. Towne & Bacon's total charge for printing was $1,438.50, including interest (ibid., p. 72). Helm paid $63.08 in freight charges for 300 copies, as noted in the printers' records of July 2, 1867 (ibid., p. 80).

On June 1, 1867, the Carson City *Appeal* reported receipt of the first 100 copies by the Secretary of State's office "yesterday"; receipt of another 375 copies "yesterday" was noted in the *Appeal* of June 13. The Gold Hill *News* of June 3 rhapsodized over the "elegantly gotten up" volume, "the type and the paper being of a most excellent character." The *News* speculated that "if anything in the way of printing could induce a disinterested person to read the decisions in this book, Towne & Bacon have afforded the seductive publication."

Reissued with volume 1 in a stereotype edition by A. L. Bancroft & Co. of San Francisco in 1877 (see No. 914), and again by Bancroft-Whitney in 1887; it has also been reissued in the twentieth century.

Az. CU-B. DHEW. DLC. In-SC (rebound). M. Nv. Nv-Ar. NvHi. NvRWL. NvU.

NEVADA. *Surveyor General.*

Annual Report | of the | Surveyor General | of the | State of Nevada | for the Year A.D. 1866. | Carson City: | Joseph E. Eckley, State Printer. | 1867.   [451]

viii, [9]-95, including two folding tables. 23 x 14 cm. Printed wrapper. Issued also as [No. 9] in AJS, 1867.

Printing of 2,000 copies was authorized (SSN, 1867, p. 151). The entry for March 9, 1867, in Towne & Bacon's Journal E shows that 2,300 copies were printed at a cost of $658.44; the overage was for the AJS issue.

The Carson City *Appeal* acknowledged receipt of a copy in its issue of April 23, 1867. Four days later the Gold Hill *News* editorialized that "if the State expended more money in the printing and circulation of such a State paper, and less in the printing of nonsensical productions of some other State officers and reports of committees during the session of the Legislature, the people would derive more solid benefit from the taxes which they pay into the State treasury."

CU-B. MH-Z. Nv-Ar. PP.

NEVADA. *Treasury Department.*

Annual Report | of the | State Treasurer | of the | State of Nevada, | for the Year 1866. | [*short rule*] | Carson City: | Joseph E. Eckley, State Printer. | 1867.   [452]

16 p. 23 x 15 cm. Printed wrapper. Issued also as [No. 4] in AJS, 1867, and from the same type in SSN, 1867, p. [199]-216.

240 copies ordered printed (SSN, 1867, p. 147). Journal E for January 24, 1867, in the Towne & Bacon records shows that 540 copies were printed; the extra 300 copies were

for the AJS issue. The journal indicates only that 40-lb. book paper was used and that the total charge for the work was $71.58.

CSmH

ODD FELLOWS, INDEPENDENT ORDER OF. *Carson City, Nevada. Carson Lodge No. 4.*

Constitution | and | By-Laws | of | Carson Lodge, No. 4, | I.O. of O.F. | of the | State of Nevada. | [*filet*] | [*lodge emblem*] | [*filet*] | Sacramento: | H. S. Crocker & Co., Printers and Stationers. | 1867.

[452a]

72 p. 14 x 9 cm. Printed wrapper. Title and text pages in thick-thin rule borders.

The examined copy is in the cornerstone of the capitol building in Carson City. The recorded microfilm copies were made during the renovation of the building in 1978-1979.

NvHi (microfilm). NvMus (microfilm). NvU (microfilm).

ODD FELLOWS, INDEPENDENT ORDER OF. *Nevada. Grand Lodge.*

Proceedings | of the | Convention to Organize | the | R.W. Grand Lodge, I.O.O.F. | of the | State of Nevada, | and of the | First Communication | of the | Grand Lodge, | Held at | Odd Fellows' Hall, Virginia, | January 21st, 22d and 23d, 1867. | [*short rule*] | Sacramento: | H.S. Crocker & Co. Steam Printers and Stationers. | 1867.

[453]

107, v p. 23 x 14 cm. Printed wrapper. The title page for the first annual communication, June 4-6, 1867, is on p. [31].

The Grand Secretary was instructed during the first communication to determine the cost of printing 480 copies of the proceedings (p. 19); he apparently inquired also about the cost of having the organization's constitution printed. During the June communication he reported (p. 41-42) that Frank Eastman of San Francisco had bid at $3.60 per page for proceedings of 32 p., or $115.20, and constitutions of 22 p. at the same price, or $79.20; H. S. Crocker of Sacramento had bid at $2.90 per page for proceedings of 24 p., or $69.60, and at $3.375 per page for constitutions of 22 p., or $74.25; and W. J. Forbes of Virginia City had bid at $4 per page for proceedings of 32 p., or $128, and $5 per page for constitutions of 22 p., or $110. Eastman, a large part of whose business was the printing of fraternal proceedings and constitutions, was the only bidder to specify the quality of paper to be used. The Committee on Finance recommended that the contract be given to Crocker as the low bidder (p. 59), and $225 was allocated for printing the constitutions and journals (p. 60). A later decision, not recorded here, seems to have been to substitute printing of the June proceedings for the constitution, since 480 copies of 107 pages, "exclusive of the index and cover" were received; 200 were "covered," with the remainder retained by the Grand Lodge for future binding (1868 Proceedings, p. 121). The printing bill was $364.67 (ibid., p. 142), which was paid on June 9, 1868 (1869 Proceedings, p. 206). The examined copy is in the cornerstone of the capitol building in Carson City. The recorded microfilm copies were made during renovation of the building in 1978-1979.

NvHi (microfilm). NvMus (microfilm). NvU (microfilm).

WASHOE TYPOGRAPHICAL UNION.

Constitution | and | By-Laws | of the | Washoe Typographical Union | No. 65; | Including | The Scale of Prices | and | List of Officers and Members. | [*short rule*] | Organized June 28th, 1863. | [*short rule*] | Virginia, Nev.: | Enterprise Book and Job Printing Office, | 24 South C Street. | 1867.   [454]

30, [2] p. 14 x 9 cm. Printed wrapper. Title and text pages in single rule borders. Scale of prices on p. [23]-30, [31]; see Appendix B.

CtY. NvU (microfilm).

WIEGAND, CONRAD AARON?

Radical Reconstruction | on the Basis of | One Sovereign Repub-lic, | With | Dependent States and Territories, | Uniformly Consti-tuted Throughout the Public Domain, | and with the | Corruptions of Party Politics Abolished, | Being | An Address | Delivered at an Interior Town in Nevada, | and Printed by Request as | An Appeal to All Americans | for | New Nationality with | The South and Russian America, | Looking Also to Union with | Mexico and Canada. | [*short rule*] | Sacramento: | Russell & Winterburn, Printers—Union Book and Job Office. | [*short rule*] | 1867.   [455]

17 p. 21 x 14 cm. Printed in two columns.

The Gold Hill *News* of May 9, 1867, noted that the *Reese River Reveille* had received a copy of the pamphlet and had ridiculed it; the issue of the *Reveille* containing the notice was unavailable for inspection. There is no certain proof that the author was Wiegand, but a handwritten note on the recorded copy suggests that it might have been, and the subject and style of the address are not unlike Wiegand's; see, for example, No. 633.

NvHi.

YELLOW JACKET SILVER MINING COMPANY. Annual Report. 1867.
[L456]

Gold Hill *News,* July 31, 1867: "The annual report of the Trustees and Secretary of the Yellow Jacket Mining Company has just made its appearance, in elegantly printed form. It shows the receipts and expenditures for the fiscal year ending June 30, 1867, and the financial condition of the company. . . . We wish this report, as published in beautiful pamphlet form, could have a general circulation." The ecstat-ic description may indicate that the report bore the imprint of the *News* job office, as the earlier semi-annual report did (see No. 458). There is further support for this theory, but it also indicates that the *News* did not actually do the printing. On July 17 Towne & Bacon entered in their records a charge of $30 for printing 200 copies of the report. The entry was under "P. Lynch. 'Gold Hill.' "; Philip Lynch was the proprietor of the *News*. The entry also shows that half of the copies were to be sent to

Gold Hill and the other half to the Bank of California, which controlled the mining company.

YELLOW JACKET SILVER MINING COMPANY. By-Laws. 1867.   [L457]

Towne & Bacon's records for July 18, 1867, show a charge to "P. Lynch. 'Gold Hill.'" of $20 for 100 copies of the Yellow Jacket's by-laws. The involvement of Lynch, the proprietor of the Gold Hill *News*, suggests that the by-laws had the imprint of the *News*.

YELLOW JACKET SILVER MINING COMPANY.

Semi-Annual | Report | of the Operations of the | Yellow Jacket S.M. Co. | —for the— | Six Months Ending Dec. 31, 1866; | —and the— | Financial Condition | of the Company | January 1st, 1867. | Printed at the Office of the Gold Hill Daily News. | [1867.]
                                                                      [458]

[4] p. 20 x 13 cm. Title in decorative single rule border. See No. L456. NvHi.

❧1868❧

The constitutional section providing for biennial sessions of the Legislature came into play in 1868 for the first time since statehood and there was no meeting in Carson City. Even conventional political activity, the choosing of men for office, was limited—the state's principal officers had been elected to four-year terms in 1866 and there were few statewide races of consequence. Henry R. Mighels of the Carson City *Appeal,* running as a Republican, defeated the Democratic candidate for State Printer, Charles L. Perkins.

The San Francisco firm of Towne & Bacon, which had acted as Nevada's de facto State Printer in 1867, had little to do for the state in 1868 because of the lack of legislative printing; its only job was printing the Supreme Court Reports under a direct contract with the Court. The 1878 report of the State Controller (p. 30) indicates no expenditures at all from the State Printing Fund during fiscal 1868.

The transcontinental railroad reached Nevada from the west in 1868 and its effect was immediately felt. For example, Washoe City, which was to remain the seat of government in Washoe County for another three years, lost its last remaining newspaper in mid-year to

Reno, a town that did not exist until the railroad reached its site in late spring. Winnemucca, also on the Central Pacific route, had a paper as well, albeit briefly. Aurora's press lasted only until October; Austin had a competitor, briefly, for its newspaper; one paper went out of business and another began in Belmont; Pine Grove had a short-lived fling at journalism; and the new eastern town of Treasure City saw the beginnings of two newspapers in December, only one of which lasted to year's end. Virginia City had a net gain of one press, with a paper dying and two starting up, although one of the latter may have been printed at the office of the venerable *Territorial Enterprise.* All other papers that were active at the end of 1867 continued to publish throughout the year.

BACHELORS' CLUB OF VIRGINIA. *Virginia City, Nevada.*

[*Ornament*] | [*ornament*] The Bachelors of Virginia [*ornament*] | Present Compliments to | M[*broken rule*] | And will be glad to be honored with | [*broken rule*] company on the Evening | of Friday, the 31st inst., at Athletic | Hall, at 8 1/2 o'clock. [*ornament*] | [*ornament*] Dancing. [*ornament*] | [*ornament*] | [1868.]   [459]

[4] p., printed on p. [1] only. 16 x 10 cm. Mostly script type; embossed edges. The recorded copy is in an envelope with a ticket giving the date as "Friday Evening,— January 31, '68."
CSmH.

CARSON THEATER. *Carson City, Nevada.*

Theater | [*thick-thin rule*] | . . . | [*thick-thin rule*] | The Manager respectfully informs the public that the Theater will | Open on Saturday Evening, Dec. 19, 1868, | For the Winter Season with a | Brilliant Array of Talent. | A new Stage has been laid, two commodious Stage or Proscenium pri-|vate Boxes, and new Scenery will be painted to suit each piece as it may be | required. No expense will be spared to produce the plays in a manner ac-|ceptable to the patrons. | [*thin-thick-thin rule*] | Saturday Evening, December 19th, | Will be produced Victor Hugo's Romantic, Thrilling and Musical Tragic | Drama, in 3 Acts, entitled: | Lucretia | Borgia | Or, The Doom of the Poisoner. | . . . | [*thick-thin rule*] | Daily Appeal Print, Carson City, Nevada.   [460]

Broadside. 37 x 15 cm.
CtY. NvU (microfilm).

DAILY TERRITORIAL ENTERPRISE. *Virginia City, Nevada.* Extra. October 21, 1868.   [L461]

Enterprise, October 22, 1868, concerning an earthquake in San Francisco: "At last our office was able to communicate with San Francisco, and soon the cry of *'Enterprise Extra!'* was heard from the throats of a squad of nimble-footed youngsters on every street." Alf Doten's *Journal* entry of October 21 puts the time of issuance of the extra in the afternoon.

DeLong, Charles Egbert.

Life | and | Confession | of | John Millian, | (Properly, Jean Marie A. Villain,) | Convicted as the | Murderer of Julia Bulette, | as Given By Him to His Attorney. | [*filet*] | Virginia: | Lammon, Gregory & Palmer. | 1868.   [462]

6, [5], 14-16 p. 21 x 14 cm. Printed wrapper. The typesetter apparently became confused in numbering pages; if the wrapper title had been counted as p. [1], rather than the title page, the pagination would have come out correctly. Reproduced in facsimile from the copy at NvU and sent out as the Winter 1960, issue of the *Nevada Historical Society Quarterly*. In preparing the original for the camera it was marked up heavily with a dark pencil to indicate the order in which the pages were to appear. Another facsimile reprint was issued in·1973 by Dave's Printing & Publishing of Sparks, Nevada.

Julia Bulette, a resident of Virginia City's D Street, the local prostitutes' row, was discovered dead in her bed on January 20, 1867. Her throat had been cut. The death of a prostitute might ordinarily have attracted little attention, but Jule, as she was known, was no ordinary prostitute. She was well known on the Comstock for her benevolence and kindness of heart, and enjoyed the genuine esteem of many of the area's leading citizens. She was buried by Virginia Engine Company No. 1, of which she had been an honorary member, with a funeral oration delivered by a clergyman. No evidence concerning her assailant's identity was found, but four months later John Millian was arrested on a charge of the attempted murder of another woman. While he was in jail a number of clues were found to link him to Jule's death, among them the discovery of a trunk that had belonged to her in a bakery where Millian was said to have left it. Much of the evidence presented at his trial seems to have been circumstantial, but he was convicted of first degree murder and sentenced to die. It is reported that during the period between sentencing and execution some of the ladies of Virginia City made regular trips to the jail with home-cooked victuals for the condemned man, in thanks for his service in ridding the community of its best-known prostitute.

Charles E. DeLong, a respected Virginia City attorney and later U.S. Minister to Japan, represented Millian at his trial. After his conviction Millian prepared, with DeLong, a confession and brief autobiographical statement, but later asked to have it back and subsequently refused to release it. DeLong then wrote down what he could remember of the "confession," and it is this version that appears here. In it Millian implicated two other men and admitted to an involvement in the case, but adamantly denied that he had done the killing. The document was released on April 23, 1868; Millian was hanged the next day. His speech on the scaffold, translated from the French, is in the *Territorial Enterprise* of April 26.
NvU.

Democratic Party. *Ormsby County, Nevada.*

The Const ution [*sic*] and the Union | [*cut of national Democratic nominees, with flags, eagle, etc.*] | . . . | [*filet*] | Democratic | State Ticket; | [*short rule*] | . . . | [*short rule*] | Ormsby County | Democratic Ticket. | [*short rule*] | . . . | [*short rule*] | Carson Precinct. | . . . | [1868.]   [463]

Broadside. 19? x 6? cm. The recorded copy is cropped all around. Line 1 in a streamer. Printed on lavender paper.
NvHi.

DEMOCRATIC PARTY. *Storey County, Nevada.*

[*Cut of national Democratic nominees, with flags, eagle, etc.*] | [*filet*] | Democratic State Ticket | . . . | [*short rule*] | Storey County Democratic Ticket | . . . | Township Officers. | . . . | [1868.]
                                                                            [464]

[2] p. 30 x 9 cm. Printed in red ink. The national ticket on the verso is printed in green in a decorative rule border.
NvU.

FREEMASONS. *Nevada. Grand Lodge.*

Proceedings | of the | M.˙. W.˙. Grand Lodge | of | Free and Accepted Masons | of the | State of Nevada, | at its | Fourth Annual Grand Communication, | Held at Masonic Hall, in the City of Virginia, | September 15, 16, and 17, A.L. 5868. | [*filet*] | San Francisco: | Frank Eastman, Printer, 509 Clay St., & 508 Commercial St. | 1868.   [465]

[3], 314-429, ii p. 22 x 14 cm. Printed wrapper.
The Grand Lodge allocated $600 "For printing proceedings of this session" (p. 409). The "usual number," i.e., 800, were printed, with 300 of them left "uncut" with the printer for future binding (1869 Proceedings, p. 439), at a cost of $577.31 (ibid., p. 441).
NvHi. NvMus (microfilm). NvRFM. NvU (microfilm).

FREEMASONS. *Virginia City, Nevada. Escurial Lodge No. 7.*

Roll | of the | Members | of | Escurial Lodge, | No. 7, F. & A. M., | Virginia, Storey County, Nevada. | Also, | A Short History of the Lodge, | To December 1st, 1867. | [*filet*] | San Francisco: | Frank Eastman, Printer, | 1868.   [466]

23, [1] p. 16 x 10 cm. Printed wrapper. Title and text pages in red decorative rule border. Initials in line 6 printed in red; remainder of the title and text pages printed in blue.
CU-B.

GEE, G. J.

Canticles | for | Morning and Evening Prayer, | Arranged for | Saint Paul's Church, | Virginia, Nevada, | by | G. J. Gee, Organist. | [*filet*] | San Francisco: | Frank Eastman, Printer, 509 Clay Street. | 1868. [467]

10 p. 17? x 11? cm. The recorded copy has been trimmed and bound. Printed wrapper. CU-B.

GELATT'S STAGE LINE.

R. Gelatt's | Lake Tahoe | [*cut of stage*] | Stage Line | [*thick-thin rule*] | On and after July 1, 1868, Stages will leave the Ormsby House, Carson | City at 5 o'clock p.m., on the arrival of Billy Wilson's Stages from Virginia | and H. D. Gelatt's Stages from Silver Mountain. | . . . | [Carson City? 1868.] [L468]

Broadside. Description from a reduced facsimile in Edward B. Scott, *Saga of Lake Tahoe* (Crystal Bay, Nevada: Sierra-Tahoe Publishing Company, 1957), p. 248. Scott cites NvHi as the source for his illustration, but the copy cannot be located there.

GILLIS, WILLIAM ROBERT.

The | Nevada Directory, | For 1868-9: | Containing a Full List of the | Residents, Mining and Business Men | of | Virginia, Gold Hill, Silver City, Carson, Washoe, | Dayton, Empire City, Reno and Genoa; | With a | Historical Sketch of the Principal Places; | Also, | Carefully Prepared Statistical Tables | of the Mining Interests of the State: | To Which is Appended, | Masonic and Odd-Fellows' Intelligence, List of State Officers, | The Judiciary, State Representatives, Members of | the Legislature, Notaries Public, Terms | of the Several Courts, Etc., Etc. | Together with a Correct List of | Virginia Officials, Rules of the Board of Aldermen, | and City Ordinances Thereof. | [*short rule*] | Compiled and Published by | William R. Gillis, | Virginia. | [*filet*] | San Francisco: | M. D. Carr & Co., Book and Job Printers, | No. 411 Clay Street. | 1868. [469]

xxviii, 309 p. 23 x 15 cm. Title page, p. [xvii], in a single rule border. The last numbered page is the rear paste-down. Quarter-leather binding; printed boards.

On April 26, 1868, the *Territorial Enterprise* announced that Gillis would begin canvassing for the directory on the following day; the issue of June 20 contains the statement that he had completed his work and would soon leave for San Francisco to have it printed. His actual date of departure was the 29th (*Enterprise,* June 30). A long delay in publication was explained in the *Enterprise* of September 16: "We received a letter last evening from William Gillis, the gentleman who is engaged in getting up the Virginia and Gold Hill Directory, informing us that we were wrong in stating that the delay in the publication of said work was on account of delay in the printing. He says he has been sick nearly all the time he has been in San Francisco, and besides had the misfortune to lose a number of names of residents of Gold Hill, which being furnished were carried and deposited in a letter box of a vacant house, where they remained (with other letters) until discovered by a new tenant, who, in prospecting about the premises, found them. This was the latter part of last week; being all right at last, the book will be out and Mr. Gillis will be here with it in two weeks—unless San Francisco is swallowed up by an earthquake.'' It nearly was. The Gold Hill *News* of October 30 had the following: "Subscribers to the new directory . . . are informed that Mr. Gillis will be up from San Francisco with the books the 1st of next week, ready for distribution. The recent earthquake down there delayed it some'' (see Nos. L461 and L472). Publication was announced in a notice in the San Francisco *Times* and reprinted in the Carson City *Appeal* of November 14. Finally, on the 18th of November, the *News* was able to announce that "Wm. R. Gillis . . . arrived from San Francisco last evening, with some of the books. More will arrive to-night ready for public distribution and purchase to-morrow.'' Alf Doten, the editor of the *News,* noted also that he had seen a copy that morning. The sketch of Gold Hill that appears on p. [82]-85 of the directory was written by Doten (Diaries, June 24-27, 1868). C. CSmH. CU-B. MWA. NHi. Nv. NvHi. NvMus. NvRW (rebound). NvU.

Gold Hill, Nevada. *Fire Department.*

Constitution | and | By-Laws | of the | Fire Department | of | Gold Hill, Nevada. | [*filet*] | Organized May 22d, 1867. | [*cut of fire wagon*] | Sacramento: | H. S. Crocker & Co., Printers and Stationers. | 1868.   [470]

30 p. 14 x 9 cm. Printed wrapper. Title and text pages in thick-thin rule borders. C. NvHi.

Gold Hill, Nevada. *Social Party.*

Social Party. | [*cut of couple dancing*] | [*filet*] | The pleasure of | M[*broken rule*] | Company is respectfully solicited | —at a— | Social Party, | —to be Given at— | Homestead Hall, | On Friday Evening, June 19, 1868, | [*broken rule*] Secretary.   [471]

[4] p., printed on p. [1] only. 17 x 11 cm. Line 1 in an arch over the cut. Printed in gold ink, partly in script type, on lavender paper.

Tentatively identified as a Nevada item because of the presence of the recorded copy with similar materials from Nevada at CSmH. There was a Homestead Hall in Gold Hill in 1868; the Gold Hill *News,* which often mentioned such affairs in its local columns, did not mention the party. CSmH.

Gold Hill Daily News. *Gold Hill, Nevada.* Extra. October 21, 1868. [L472]

Alf Doten's *Journals,* October 21, 1868: "Morning, news of great earthquake at San Francisco & other contiguous places — After noon both the *Enterprise* & *News* issued extras.'' The *Territorial Enterprise,* in reporting its own extra of October 21 on October 22 (see No. L461), said that ''Afterward the Gold Hill *News* extra came up with additional particulars. . . .''

GOLD HILL DAILY NEWS. *Gold Hill, Nevada.* Extra. November 4, 1868.   [L473]

An announcement of the intention to issue an extra the next day was made in the *News* of November 3, election day. The issue of November 4 had the following: ''EXTRTRAS [*sic*].—An Extra Gold Hill NEWS, with all the latest election returns from the Eastern States, was issued at 11 o'clock this forenoon. . . .''

GOLD HILL DAILY NEWS. *Gold Hill, Nevada.* Extra. November 4, 1868. Second edition.   [L474]

News, November 4, 1868: ''An Extra Gold Hill NEWS . . . a second edition, with additional returns from the East, California, and some from several counties in this State, was again issued at 1 o'clock. . . . Hundreds of copies were sold by the newsboys.'' Alf Doten's *Journal* entry for the date corroborates the issuance of two extras (see also No. L473) at the times stated.

GOLD HILL DAILY NEWS. *Gold Hill, Nevada.* Extra. November 5, 1868.   [L475]

News, November 5, 1868: ''We issued an EXTRA NEWS at 1 o'clock to-day, containing all the latest election returns received in Gold Hill up to that hour.''

GOLD HILL DEMOCRATIC CLUB. *Gold Hill, Nevada.*

Constitution | of the | Gold Hill Democratic Club, | Gold Hill, Storey County, Nevada. | [*filet*] | . . . | [San Francisco Daily Examiner print.] | [1868?]   [476]

[4] p., printed on p. [1-2] only. 28 x 21 cm. Imprint, from p. [2], printed in brackets. A handwritten letter on p. [3-4] of the recorded copy, from G. W. Cassidy to C. C. Cassidy, dated February 28, 1868, suggests that the constitution was a recent one. CU-B.

HILLER, FREDERICK.

Common Sense | versus | Allopathic Humbuggery; | or, | Chloroform and Apoplexy | Duly Considered | in Connection with Certain Allopathic Luminaries. | [*filet*] | By F. Hiller, M.D. | [*filet*] | Virginia, Nevada, July 25, 1868. | [*filet*] | 1868. | Virginia, Nevada: | Enterprise Book and Job Printing Office.
                                                                                     [477]

15 p. 20 x 14 cm. Printed wrapper. Text printed in two columns, from the same type as the original publication in the *Territorial Enterprise* of July 26, 1868.

A man named John Gray had died on the first of July while Hiller was administering

chloroform in preparation for an operation on a broken shoulder. At the inquest the testimony of a number of Virginia City doctors was heard; all of them questioned Hiller's methods, and the finding was that Gray had died "by the administration of chloroform" (p. 11). Hiller, whose several years of practicing homeopathic medicine in Virginia City were marked by frequent controversy with his allopathic colleagues, engaged Colonel John A. Collins to draft a reply to their finding. Collins's effort was too wordy for Hiller, however, so he turned again to Alf Doten, who had written a pamphlet for him the previous year (see No. 427). Doten spent parts of three days revising the Collins draft; it was delivered to the *Enterprise* office on July 23, proof was corrected on the 25th, and it appeared in three columns in the issue of the 26th, titled "Hiller vs. Humbug," but with the ignominious heading of "Advertisement," indicating that Hiller probably had to pay to have it published. On the 11th of August Doten said in his Diary: "I got $25 from Albert Hiller," the doctor's brother, presumably in payment for his labors with the article. Doten did not mention the pamphlet publication, but it was probably issued within a few days of the newspaper appearance (Doten Diaries, July 1-August 11, 1858). The proceedings of the inquest cover p. [3]-11; the Hiller-Collins-Doten response is on p. 11-15.
DNLM.

HILLER, FREDERICK.

Small-Pox and Vaccination. | [*short rule*] | Reprinted from the "Daily Territorial Enterprise," Dec. 27, 1868. | [*short rule*] | By F. Hiller, M.D. | [*short rule*] | [1868?]   [478]

4 p. 23 x 15 cm. Caption title. Printed in two columns, from the same type as the newspaper appearance. Identified as an 1869 imprint in *Check List:* 113, but it was more probably issued as a separate immediately after the newspaper article was printed.

"Vaccination as the antagonist of small-pox, is a Don Quixote war against an unconquerable windmill, and has nothing in common with science or material wisdom. It is a visionary, fallacious practice which cannot be too soon abandoned for the benefit of the human race, as totally unworthy the enlightened age in which we live" (p. 4).

The article was brought about by Hiller's objections to the widespread use of vaccination during a local smallpox epidemic. For this last, quixotic tilt at his colleagues before leaving Virginia City for San Francisco, he again engaged Alf Doten, as with Nos. 427 and 477, to do the ghost-writing chores (Doten Diaries, December 6-26, 1868). "The Hiller-Doten article on 'Small pox and Vaccination' appeared in the Enterprise this morning — made nearly two columns very fine print" (ibid., December 27, 1868).

NNNAM. NvHi (microfilm). NvMus (microfilm). NvU (microfilm).

INDEPENDENT ORDER OF GOOD TEMPLARS. *Virginia City, Nevada. Crystal Lodge No. 12.*

Virginia, April [*broken rule*] 1868. | M[*broken rule*] | The pleasure of your company | is solicited at a | Masquerade Fancy Dress Sociable, | To be held at Good Templars' | Hall, on Friday Evening,

17th | inst. | . . . | [*broken rule*] | On behalf of Invitation Commit-
tee of Members of | Crystal Lodge. No. 12. I.O.G.T. | [*fi-
let*] | N.B.—All are expected to attend Masked. [479]

[4] p., printed on p. [1] only. 16 x 10 cm. Partly script type; edges embossed. The
recorded copy is in an envelope.
CSmH.

NEVADA. *Governor (Acting), 1868 (James S. Slingerland).*

Thanksgiving Proclamation. | [*state seal*] | . . . | . . . I, the Acting
Governor of the State of Nevada, do hereby appoint and set | apart, as
a Day of Public Thanksgiving and Prayer, | Thursday, the 26th Day
of November, A.D. 1868. | . . . | . . . Done at Carson City, this
the 23d day of October, A.D. 1868. | . . . | [Carson City: Joseph
E. Eckley, State Printer. 1868.] [480]

Broadside. 43 x 32 cm. Line 1 in an arch over state seal.
M. NvU (positive photostat).

NEVADA. *Supreme Court.*

[Briefs. 1868.]

Nevada vs. Anderson. Brief for the state. 33 p. 25 x 19 cm. Imprint on wrapper:
Austin, Nevada: O. L. C. Fairchild, Printer. (Reese River Reveille.) 1868. Nv-Ar.
[481]

NEVADA. *Supreme Court.*

Reports of Cases | Determined in | The Supreme Court | of the
| State of Nevada, | During the Year 1867. | Reported by Alfred
Helm, | Clerk of the Court. | [*short rule*] | Volume III. |
[*short rule*] | San Francisco: | Towne & Bacon, Book and Job Print-
ers, Excelsior Office, | 536 Clay Street, just below Montgom-
ery. | 1868. [482]

616 p. 23 x 15 cm. Leather binding.
Helm's contract with Towne & Bacon (Nv-Ar: Nevada Contracts, p. 15), dated
November 22, 1867, called for the printers "to print, bind, furnish general index, or
pay for said index the sum of one hundred and fifty dollars if furnished by [the state],
(to remain at the option of [the state])" a total of 500 copies, to be delivered to the
Secretary of State in Carson City; the printers were to pay the freight. For their labors
Towne & Bacon were to receive on delivery $1,460 "in Gold Coin of the United
States" for a volume of 496 pages; fifty cents was to be deducted for each page under
496, and two dollars added for each page over that amount. Interest at the rate of 1.5
percent per month was to be paid for a delay in payment. The state retained the
copyright, and "no additional copies over and above the five hundred volumes above
mentioned shall be published." The contract was recorded on February 22, 1868.
Because the volume was vastly larger than the estimate, and perhaps also because of a

delay in payment, the amount expended was $3,276.75 (Controller's Report, 1867-1868, p. 36). The only reference to the work in the extant records of Towne & Bacon was recorded on April 16, 1868: "To Balance for Third Vol. Sup. Ct. Reports . . . 616 pp., $1,152.10."

The Carson City *Appeal* of April 28 called the book "the handsomest volume of reports yet issued, being very beautifully printed, on heavy, white paper and very nicely bound." The ever-enthusiastic Gold Hill *News* called attention the next day to its typographical execution, designating it "very superior, and decidedly creditable to Towne & Bacon."

The volume was reissued in a stereotype edition in 1877 by A. L. Bancroft & Co. in combination with volume 4, and again in 1887 by Bancroft-Whitney; it has also been reissued in the twentieth century.

CU-B. DHEW. In-SC (rebound). Nv. NvHi. NvRWL (rebound). NvU.

ODD FELLOWS, INDEPENDENT ORDER OF. *Dayton, Nevada. Dayton Lodge No. 5.*

Constitution | and | By-Laws | of | Dayton Lodge, No. 5, | I.O. O.F. | [*short rule*] | Adopted December 10th, 1867. | [*short rule*] | Sacramento: | H.S. Crocker & Co., Printers and Stationers. | 1868. [483]

65, [3] p. 14 x 9 cm. Printed wrapper. Title and text pages in thick-thin rule borders. NvU.

ODD FELLOWS, INDEPENDENT ORDER OF. *Nevada. Grand Lodge.*

Proceedings | of the | Second Annual Communication | of the | R. W. Grand Lodge | of the | Independent Order of Odd Fellows, | of the | State of Nevada, | Held at | Odd Fellows' Hall, Carson City, | June 2d, 3d, and 4th, 1868. | [*short wavy rule*] | Sacramento: | H. S. Crocker & Co., Steam Printers and Stationers. | 1868. [L484]

[3], 112-180, v p. Description from title page in bound volume for 1867-1873; see No. 723. Printed? wrapper.

The estimated cost for 480 copies was $280 (p. 142). Crocker again got the contract because he offered to remit the interest on the unpaid bill for the previous year's printing. His bill was $218.75, or $2.45 per page—45¢ per page lower than the year before; it was paid on August 18 (1869 Proceedings, p. 207). 200 copies were "covered and trimmed for distribution," with the remainder retained by the Grand Lodge for future binding (ibid., p. 204).

ODD FELLOWS, INDEPENDENT ORDER OF. *Virginia City, Nevada. Odd Fellows' Library Association.*

By-Laws, | Rules and Regulations | of the | Virginia Odd Fellows' | Library Association. | [*filet*] | Virginia City, Nevada. | Instituted November 17, A.D. 1865. | [*filet*] | Adopted November 26,

1867. | [*short rule*] | Sacramento: | H. S. Crocker & Co., Printers and Stationers. | 1868. [485]

15 p. 14 x 9 cm. Printed wrapper. Title and text pages in thick-thin rule borders.

"The objects of this Association are the establishment of a Library, Reading Room and Museum, to consist of specimens and curiosities from the animal, vegetable and mineral kingdoms, and works of art, particularly from the State of Nevada; to stimulate, encourage and cultivate among the membership of the Order a taste for reading and a spirit of inquiry in the departments of literature, art and science, with a view to their moral and intellectual elevation" (p. 5).

CSmH.

ODD FELLOWS, INDEPENDENT ORDER OF. *Virginia City, Nevada. Olive Branch Lodge No. 12.*

Constitution, | By-Laws and Rules of Order | of | Olive Branch Lodge, No. 12, | of the | Independent Order of Odd Fellows, | of Nevada. | [*filet*] | Instituted at Virginia City, April 4th, 1867. | [*filet*] | Sacramento: | H.S. Crocker & Co., Steam Printers and Stationers. | 1868. [486]

71, [2] p. 14 x 9 cm. Printed wrapper. Title and text pages in thick-thin rule borders.

NvRW.

ORMSBY COUNTY, NEVADA. *Board of Registration.*

Registered Voters of Carson Precinct. | [*broken wavy rule*] | Official List For 1868. | [*wavy rule*] | . . . | L. C. McKeeby. | Registry Agent for Carson Precinct, Ormsby County. . [487]

Broadside. 34 x 19 cm. Printed in five columns, each separated by three vertical dotted rules.

NvCR.

PAGE, J. D.

Dialect | of [*cut*] the | Sho [*cut*] shone | Indi [*cut*] ans. | Edited & [*cut*] Published | —by— | Page & Butterfield. | [*filet*] | Belmont: | O. L. C. Fairchild & Co., Printers, Reporter Office. | 1868. [488]

30, [2] p. 11 x 7 cm. A single cut of an Indian separates the letterpress in lines 2-5. Running head: The Shoshone Dialect Arranged | by J. D. Page & H. Butterfield. Printed wrapper. Facsimile following p. 314.

The March 28, 1868, *Silver Bend Reporter,* in whose office the dictionary was printed, commented: "SHOSHONE TALK'EM.—Page and Butterfield have recently published a neat little pamphlet of the 'Shoshone Dialect.' It is a useful affair for any one traveling or living in this section of the country. It is for sale at the Post. Office."

CtY. NvU (microfilm).

PIPER'S OPERA HOUSE. *Virginia City, Nevada.* Poster. October 19, 1868.   [L489]

Gold Hill *News,* October 19, 1868: "Posters about town say that Colonel [Charles Allen] Sumner will address a meeting at Piper's Opera House this evening, on politics."

REPUBLICAN PARTY. *Lyon County, Nevada.*

National Union Republican | Ticket. | [*cut of eagle with banner in beak*] | . . . | [*thick-thin rule*] | Lyon County Union Ticket. | [*rule*] | . . . | [*thick-thin rule*] | Silver City Precinct. | . . . | [1868.]
[490]

[2] p. 20 x 9 cm. NvHi has two copies; both are pasted in a scrapbook, but one is loose enough to identify a red thick-thin rule border enclosing letterpress on the verso. National candidates are those who ran in 1868.
NvHi.

REPUBLICAN PARTY. *Storey County, Nevada.*

Regular | Union Republican Ticket! | [*cut of U.S. flag*] | . . . | [*short rule*] | Storey County Nominations. | [*short rule*] | . . . | [*short rule*] | Township Nominations. | [*short rule*] | [1868.] [491]

[2] p. 25 x 5 cm. On the verso, printed in blue and red, is a cut, signed W. C. Butler, of cannon firing to defend a monument symbolizing the Constitution. National candidates are those who ran in 1868.
NvU.

VIRGINIA CITY, NEVADA. *Fancy Dress and Masquerade Party.*

Mr. [*broken rule*] | You are respectfully invited to become a Sub-|scriber to a | Fancy Dress and Masquerade Party, | To be given at Athletic Hall, Friday Evening, | May 1st, 1868. [*ornament*] | Subscription, $10—to be paid to Mr. Jas. | Webster, at the Bank of California, on or before | April 28th. [*ornament*] | . . .   [492]

[4] p., printed on p. [1] only. 18 x 12 cm. Partly script type. Embossed edges; corners rounded. The recorded copy is in an envelope.
Athletic Hall was in Virginia City.
CSmH.

VIRGINIA CITY, NEVADA. *Masquerade and Fancy Dress Party.*

M[*broken rule*] | You are respectfully invited to attend a Mas-|querade and Fancy Dress Party, at Athletic | Hall, on Tuesday Evening, December 22d, 1868. | . . . | [*ornament*] | Ladies will please

come Masked. Each person will be required | to unmask to a member
of the Committee at the door. | . . .   [493]

[4] p., printed on p. [1] only? 16? x 10? cm. Description from a facsimile in the Book
Club of California Keepsake Series, 1968; probably reduced. Mostly script type.
Embossed and scalloped edges.

This invitation is the version intended for women; the men's version is described in
No. 494. Following line 4 is a list of committee members; the list is printed from the
same type on No. 494.

Pvt.

VIRGINIA CITY, NEVADA. *Masquerade and Fancy Dress Party.*

Mr [*broken rule*] | You are respectfully invited to participate in | a
Masquerade and Fancy Dress Party, to be | given on Tuesday Eve-
ning, December 22nd, | 1868. . . . | . . . | Tickets, $10.00. |
[*ornament*] | [*fist*] No person admitted without a Mask.   [494]

[4] p., printed on p. [1] only. Mostly in two faces of script type.
The recorded copy is in an envelope.

This is the men's version of an invitation to the party; the women's version, lacking
the price of tickets and notification of where to buy them, is described in No. 493.

CSmH.

VIRGINIA CITY, NEVADA. *Ordinances, local laws, etc.*

Ordinances | of the | City of Virginia, | Storey County, State of
Nevada, | Compiled by | Wm. T. Barbour and David E. Baily,
| and Approved by the | Mayor | and | Board of Aldermen.
| July, 1868. | [*short wavy rule*] | [Virginia City:] Printed at the
Office of the Daily Trespass.   [495]

50, iv p. 22 x 13 cm. Printed wrapper.

The *Trespass* ceased publication on October 3, 1868.

NN. NvU (microfilm).

YELLOW JACKET SILVER MINING COMPANY.

Annual Report | of the | Trustees and Secretary | of the | Yellow
Jacket Silver Mining Co. | Showing the | Receipts and Expenditures
for the Fiscal | Year Ending June 30th, 1868, | and the | Financial
Condition of the Company | July 1st, 1868. | [*filet*] | Gold Hill,
Nevada: | Printed at the Office of the Gold Hill Daily News. | 1868.
                                                              [496]

10 p. 22 x 15 cm. Printed wrapper. Title and text pages in single rule borders.

The October 2, 1868, issue of the *News* noted publication of the report.

NvHi.

Yellow Jacket Silver Mining Company.

Semi-Annual | Report | of the Operations of the | Yellow Jacket S.M. Co. | —for the— | Six Months Ending Dec. 31, 1867; | —and the— | Financial Condition | of the Company, | January 1, 1868. | [*filet*] | Printed at the Office of the Gold Hill Daily News.

[497]

[4] p. 20 x 13 cm. Title page in decorative single rule border; text pages in double rule borders.
NvHi.

❧1869❧

Shortly after his election as State Printer, Henry R. Mighels went to San Francisco to purchase a new press and material so he could carry out his duties when the Legislature met in January. In the December 22, 1868, issue of his newspaper, the Carson City *Appeal,* the following statement appeared: "A press and furniture and printing material in ample quantities to enable the State Printer elect to perform all the work that may devolve upon him have been received at this office. The laws, journals, etc., will be printed here." The "laws, journals, etc." were not, of course, printed in Carson City, as Mighels later admitted (see Introduction, p. 1).

At about the same time, agitation began among the state's newspaper editors to amend the law relating to the State Printer. An editorial by E. F. McElwain of the Belmont *Mountain Champion,* published on December 12, 1868, and quoted in the *Appeal* six days later, suggested that the two-year term of office, in view of the brief legislative sessions, was far too short to allow the State Printer a fair profit. It continued:

> To perform the work in accordance with the law necessitates the expenditure of a considerable amount of money for material which is of but little value in a newspaper office in this State. At the adjournment of the Legislature the State Printer must sell his type, "slugs," etc., for babbit-metal at a loss of from twenty to forty cents per pound, or store it with the view of selling it to the next incumbent of the office, who, of course, will take advantage of the knowledge that it is not saleable material for any other purpose than that of State work. The above,

however, it not the most objectionable feature of the law; its scale of prices are [*sic*] entirely too low. At the figures allowed by law there is but one character of the State's printing which will pay a decent profit upon the work. The printing of "bills" for the Legislature is profitable at the figures allowed, but, usually, there is not enough of this kind of work to balance the losses sustained in printing the reports and messages of the State officers, large blanks, journals of the two Houses and the statutes of the State.

The theme was picked up by the *Territorial Enterprise* on the following February 20, after introduction of a bill in the Senate that was designed to amend the State Printer act of 1865. Its view of proper compensation, however, was rather different from that of the *Champion*.

It provides for the election of a State Printer in 1870, and every four years thereafter. This officer is now elected for the term of two years. Printing materials to the value of some thousands of dollars are required at the Capital to properly do the State work, and as our Legislative sessions are biennial and of but sixty days' duration, the present extravagant prices for State printing scarcely warrant the necessary outlay for materials for the profits of a single term of two years. The longer the term of office, the cheaper the work may be done. We should not object to see the State Printer elected for a term of eight years, and to have his prices regulated from year to year by the scale of rates of the Typographical Unions of the State. These rates are higher here than in any other State in the Union—possibly higher than in any other part of the world—and as they must eventually suffer something of a decline, it would be proper to regulate the prices of State work by them. The State Printer should of course be allowed a profit on these Typographical Union rates—the profit of a fixed per centage—and then his compensation would be uniform, and the State would reap some of the advantages of the coming decline in printing tariffs.

The bill increases the bond of the State Printer from ten to twenty thousand dollars, to correspond with the increased term of office, compels State officers to designate the length of time for which their notices are to be published in the official journal, and restricts the number of copies of messages, reports and bills to be ordered by the Legislature. It also regulates and somewhat shortens the time for the publication of the laws and journals after the adjournment of the Legislature, and allows the Secretary of State the sum of five hundred and forty dollars for copying and indexing the journals of each regular session, and one-third of that sum for performing a similar service after any special session. It further provides that "the laws shall be bound in one volume, or in two volumes, as the Secretary of State may determine, having in view the proper number of pages for convenience and durability. Whenever a special session of the Legislature shall be convened within forty days after the adjournment of any regular session, all laws, joint and concurrent resolutions and memorials passed at such special session shall be printed and included in the same volume or volumes with the laws of the previous regular session; but in case a special session shall be convened at a later period, or too late to include the laws, resolutions and memorials passed at such special session in the volume with the laws of the preceding regular session, then they shall be printed and bound in a separate volume; and the journals of the two Houses of such special session shall be printed and bound with the journals of the succeeding regular session; *Provided,* That whenever the laws of any special session shall be printed and bound with those of the preceding regular session, the State Printer shall be allowed thirty days additional time in which to deliver the bound volumes of said laws to the Secretary of State.

The manner of performing the various styles of printing, and the prices to be paid therefor, are the next features of the bill, and here a very considerable saving to the state is provided for. Owing to the wide "spacing" between the lines, the bills as now authorized and printed contain but fourteen lines to the page, and the pages are paid for as "solid" matter. There should be some space between the lines, of course, for the accommodation of interlineations during the consideration of bills in the Legislature, but the space of four blank lines between the printed lines for this purpose is entirely too great. The bill proposes to reduce this blank space to the value of two lines, which would almost double the capacity of each page. In this connection, we would suggest to the author of the bill a still further improvement, by providing for just such bills, typographically, as are in use in Congress. These bills are exceedingly neat, and offer a desirable model.

All the prices are very materially lessened. Plain composition is to be paid for at the rates of $1.20 per thousand "ems"—it is now $1.60. Figure work, $1.75—now $2. Rule work, $1.90—now $2.15. Rule and figure work, $2—now $2.25. Binding and lettering the journals (half binding, leather backs and covers, junk board, marbled) $1—now $1.75. Prices for blanks not now mentioned are also provided for, and the Attorney General is substituted for the "Expert" now belonging to the Board of Printing Commissioners.

In conclusion, the State Printer is allowed to sell copies of the laws, by furnishing his own paper, at a price not to exceed one-third more than the actual cost. The Act is to go into effect from and after the first Monday in January, 1871. Hence, the present incumbent is not to be affected thereby. The bill, or something similar to it, should become a law.

It did not. A very much diluted bill was approved a week later; it altered only slightly the provisions in the section relating to the Board of Printing Commissioners (SSN, 1869, p. 90-91).

The 1878 report of the State Controller (p. 30) indicated that $20,069.31 was expended from the State Printing Fund in 1869.

Presses that had been active at the end of the previous year in Austin, Carson City, Gold Hill, Reno, and Treasure City continued to publish newspapers in 1869. Belmont lost its paper in April, as did Unionville in the following month. But the railroad town of Elko saw the first issue of a newspaper in June, a paper was begun at Hamilton, and two started at Shermantown—although only one of them lasted to the end of the year. Unionville lost its paper; Winnemucca had two entries, one of which was still publishing at year's end. The press in Virginia City was reduced to a single entry by the disappearance of two of its papers early in the year.

CARSON DAILY APPEAL. *Carson City, Nevada.* Extra. April 7, 1869.

[L498]

Gold Hill *News,* April 8, 1869: "About noon, yesterday, a telegram was sent to Brother [Henry R.] Mighels of the Carson *Appeal,* containing brief details of our local calamity in the mines, and he immediatly issued an *Extra Appeal.* The excitement at Carson was intense, and several gentlemen came up in buggies and on horseback to ascertain further particulars." The "local calamity" was a disastrous fire in the Yellow Jacket, Kentuck, and Crown Point mines. See Nos. L511 and 514.

CARSON THEATER. *Carson City, Nevada.*

Carson Theater! | [*thick-thin rule*] | . . . | [*thick-thin rule*] | Engagement of the Eminent Artistes: | Miss Lucille Western! | —and— | Mr. J. A. Herne | Supported by a brilliant | Combination Star Company! | [*thick-thin rule*] | Thursday Evening, February 11th, 1869, | In consequence of the unanimous request of all who witnessed the first | Representation, and a large number of patrons who were unable | to attend the Theater on that occasion, the Management | have concluded to repeat Boucicault's Sensa-|tional Drama, entitled: | Rip Van Winkle! | [*rule*] | . . . | [*thin-thick-thin rule*] | Daily Appeal Print, Carson City, Nevada.   [499]

Broadside. 38 x 15 cm.

CtY. NvU (microfilm).

CARSON THEATER. *Carson City, Nevada.*

Carson Theater! | [*thick-thin rule*] | . . . | [*thick-thin rule*] | Friday Evening, February 12th, 1869, | Will be presented Augustin Daly's Great Sensational Play in 5 Acts, | entitled: | Leah! | The Forsaken! | . . . | [*thin-thick-thin rule*] | Daily Appeal Print, Carson City, Nevada.   [500]

Broadside. 39 x 15 cm.
CtY. NvU (microfilm).

CARSON THEATER. *Carson City, Nevada.*

Carson Theater! | [*thick-thin rule*] | . . . | [*thick-thin rule*] | In con-
sequence of the great demand for an early repetition of | East Lynne,
| Miss Lucille Western | Has selected it for the occasion of her
| Benefit! | [*thick-dotted rule*] | Monday Evening, February 15th,
1869, | Will be presented Miss Braddon's Great Dramatization
of | East Lynne | Or, The Elopement; | in which | Miss Lucille
Western | Will sustain her unequalled Representation in the Duel [*sic*]
Role of | Lady Isabel and Madame Vine! | . . . | [*thin-thick-thin
rule*] | Daily Appeal Print, Carson City, Nevada.   [501]

Broadside. 38 x 15 cm.
CtY. NvU (microfilm).

CARSON THEATER. *Carson City, Nevada.*

Carson Theater! | [*thick-thin rule*] | . . . | [*thick-thin rule*] | Last
Week | of the Engagement of the | Eminent and Popular Trage-
dian, | James Stark! | Supported by the | Combination Star Com-
pany! | [*thick-thin rule*] | Monday Evening, March 8th, 1869,
| Will be presented Dion Boucicault's great Sensation in 5 Acts,
entitled: | The Octoroon! | Or, Life in Louisiana. | . . . | [Daily
Appeal Print, Carson City, Nevada?]   [502]

Broadside. 28? x 15 cm. The recorded copy has been cropped at the bottom, destroying a possible imprint. The format, the printing by the Daily Appeal Print of other
Carson Theater playbills in 1869, and the fact that it was the only job press in town at
the time strongly suggest the *Appeal* as the printer.
NvMus.

CARSON THEATER. *Carson City, Nevada.*

Carson Theater! | [*thick-thin rule*] | . . . | [*thick-thin rule*] | Monday
Evening, January 18th, 1869, | Will be presented the great sensational
Play, in Five Acts, entitled: | Under the Gaslight! | . . . |
[*rule*] | Daily Appeal Print, Carson City, Nevada.   [503]

Broadside. 40 x 15 cm.
CtY. NvU (microfilm).

CARSON THEATER. *Carson City, Nevada.*

Carson Theater! | [*thick-thin rule*] | . . . | [*thick-thin rule*] | Satur-
day Evening, February 13th, 1869, | Will be presented Buckstone's

Sensational Drama in three Acts, entitled | Victorine! | Or, A Life's Dream! | [rule] | . . . | [thin-thick-thin rule] | Daily Appeal Print, Carson City, Nevada. [504]

Broadside. 38 x 15 cm.

CtY. NvU (microfilm).

CARSON THEATER. *Carson City, Nevada.*

Carson Theater! | [thick-thin rule] | . . . | [thick-dotted rule] | Thursday Evening, February 18th, 1869, | Will be presented the Serio Comic Drama, entitled: The | Rag Picker | —of— | Paris! | . . . | [thin-thick-thin rule] | Daily Appeal Print, Carson City, Nevada. [505]

Broadside. 39 x 15 cm.

CtY. NvU (microfilm).

CARSON THEATER. *Carson City, Nevada.*

Theater | [thick-thin rule] | . . . | [thick-thin rule] | First Night of the Great Sensation | After Dark | [thick-thin rule] | Notice to the Public.—The manuscript of this truly great Play | was obtained direct from the Author, Dion Bourcicault [sic], by Mr. D. C. Ander-|son while in London; also, the models of the scenery. | Miss Sallie | Hinckley! | Has purchased the copy-right from Mr. Anderson and is the only person | authorized to produce it on this Coast outside of San Francisco . . . | . . . | [thick-thin rule] | Friday Evening, January 8th, 1869, | Will be presented the Great Sensation of | After Dark! | . . . | [thick-thin rule] | Daily Appeal Print, Carson City, Nevada. [506]

Broadside. 38 x 15 cm. Facsimile following p. 314.

CtY. NvU (microfilm).

FREEMASONS. *Genoa, Nevada. Douglas Lodge No. 12.*

By-Laws | of | Douglas Lodge, No. 12, | of | Free and Accepted Masons, | Held at | Genoa, Douglas County, | State of Nevada; | Being the Uniform Code | Recommended by the Grand Lodge; | With | The Funeral Service, | as Arranged by | the V.∴ W.∴ Bro. Alex G. Abell, | Grand Secretary of the Grand Lodge of California; | and | A Funeral Dirge and Other Odes. | [short rule] | San Francisco: | Frank Eastman, Pr., Franklin Office, 509 Clay Street. | 1869. [506a]

23 p. 14 x 10 cm. Printed wrapper.

The examined copy is in the cornerstone of the capitol building in Carson City. The recorded microfilm copies were made during renovation of the building in 1978-1979. NvHi (microfilm). NvMus (microfilm). NvU (microfilm).

FREEMASONS. *Gold Hill, Nevada. Silver Star Lodge No. 5.*

By-Laws | of | Silver Star Lodge, No. 5, | of | Free and Accepted Masons, | Held at | Gold Hill, Nevada, | with | The Funeral Service, | as Arranged by | The M. ˙. W. ˙. Grand Lodge of Nevada, | and | A Funeral Dirge and Other Odes, | Approved July 23, A.L. 5869. | [*short rule*] | San Francisco: | H. H. Bancroft and Company. | 1869   [507]

15, [1] p. 18 x 11 cm. Title and text pages in single rule borders. Cloth binding, with gold-stamped title: By-Laws of Silver Star Lodge, No. 5 of Free and Accepted Masons, Gold Hill, Nev. The examined copy is in a private collection.

500 copies ordered printed (NvRFM: Silver Star Lodge Minute Book, April 11, 1863-December 17, 1870, p. 391 and 394); the cost was $114 (ibid., p. 417).

Even here, as with so many Nevada publications, the facts give the lie to the imprint, since Bancroft had no book manufacturing capability until the following year (John Walton Caughey, *Hubert Howe Bancroft: Historian of the West.* Berkeley and Los Angeles: University of California Press, 1946, p. 53); see also No. 550.

NvU (microfilm).

FREEMASONS. *Nevada. Grand Lodge.*

Proceedings | of the | M. ˙. W. ˙. Grand Lodge | of | Free and Accepted Masons | of the | State of Nevada, | at its | Fifth Annual Grand Communication, | Held at Masonic Hall, in the City of Virginia, | Sept. 21, 22, and 23, A.L. 5869. | [*filet*] | San Francisco: | Frank Eastman, Printer, 509 Clay Street. | 1869.   [508]

[3], 434-531, [1], ii p. 23 x 14 cm. Printed wrapper.

$600 was allocated for printing, less $227 already paid on account (p. 508, but $227.50 on p. 441). The "usual number," i.e. 800, were printed, with 300 kept by the printer for future binding (1870 Proceedings, p. 11), at a cost of $516, i.e. $288.50 plus the $227.50 already paid (ibid., p. 13).

CSmH. NvHi (microfilm). NvMus (microfilm). NvRFM. NvU (microfilm).

FREEMASONS. *Reno, Nevada. Reno Lodge No. 13.*

By-Laws | of | Reno Lodge, No. 13, | of | Free and Accepted Masons, | Held at | Reno, Washoe County, | State of Nevada; | Being the Uniform Code | Recommended by the Grand Lodge. | [*short rule*] | San Francisco: | Frank Eastman, Pr., Franklin Office, 509 Clay Street. | 1869.   [509]

8 p. 14 x 9 cm. Wrapper title.

CU-B.

GOLD HILL, Nevada. *Liberty Engine Company No. 1.*

Constitution | and | By-Laws | of | Liberty Engine Company, No. 1, | Gold Hill, Nevada. | [*cut of fire-fighting equipment*] | Sacramento: | H. S. Crocker & Co., Printers and Stationers. | 1869.

[510]

17, [1] p. 14 x 10 cm. Title and text pages in thick-thin rule borders.
C. NvHi (microfilm). NvMus (microfilm). NvU (microfilm).

GOLD HILL DAILY NEWS. *Gold Hill, Nevada.* Extra. April 10, 1869.

[L511]

News, April 10, 1869: "About noon to-day, we issued an EXTRA, containing full and correct particulars of the late calamity, as published in Wednesday, Thursday and Friday's regular editions of our paper [i.e. April 7-9], with such additional matters of interest as have transpired since last evening. Hundreds of copies have been sold, to be sent to California, to the Eastern States, and to Europe. We have still on hand several hundred copies which can be obtained from our agents and carriers." Doten Diaries, April 10, 1869: "We issued about 1,000 *extras* at noon today giving full account of disaster from 1st to last — delayed last issue of paper till after 5 o'clock PM." The *News* had indicated in its issue of the previous day that it would issue an extra, whose price would be twenty-five cents. The "late calamity" was a fire in the Yellow Jacket, Kentuck, and Crown Point mines, which had begun on April 7 and ultimately resulted in thirty-nine deaths. See Nos. L498 and 514.

GOLD HILL DAILY NEWS. *Gold Hill, Nevada.* Extra. November 14, 1869.

[L512]

News, November 15, 1869: "Our faithful special reporter at Sacramento City, John F. Allen, Esq., yesterday afternoon telegraphed us a portion of the particulars of the sad calamity which happened on the Western Pacific Railroad. Of course it was a private telegram to the GOLD HILL NEWS, and on our announcing that Judge [Alexander W.] Baldwin, of our U.S. District Court, was killed, and that Will Campbell, our U.S. District Attorney, had a leg broken, the public became greatly excited for further particulars, which we accordingly obtained at Sacramento, and issued an EXTRA NEWS at six o'clock last evening, which were [*sic*] extensively circulated around Gold Hill, Virginia and Silver City." Doten Diaries, November 14, 1869: "News arrived of great railroad collision near San Antonio, Cal., whereby 13 persons were killed, among them Judge AW Baldwin, U S Dist Judge, of Virginia." See No. L513.

GOLD HILL DAILY NEWS. *Gold Hill, Nevada.* Extra. November 14, 1869. Second edition.

[L513]

News, November 15, 1869: "At nine o'clock we issued another Extra, containing more and fuller particulars [of the train wreck in California that killed Judge Alexander W. Baldwin; see No. L512]—the contents of both Extras being embodied in our issue of to-day, with such further information as we have been able to obtain up to three o'clock this afternoon."

GOLD HILL DAILY NEWS. *Gold Hill, Nevada.*

[Thick-thin rule] | Gold Hill News Extra. | *[double rule]* | Gold Hill, Nevada: Thursday Morning, April 15, 1869. | *[thick-thin rule]* | The Gold Hill Disaster | *[short rule]* | Full Particulars of | the Calamity. | *[short rule]* | . . .   [514]

[2] p. 59? x 43? cm. Both recorded copies have been trimmed and bound. The first rule extends across the sheet; lines 1-2 extend across columns 2-6 of 7 columns; lines 3-4 are in column 1. All of p. [1] and more than two columns of p. [2] are devoted to a recapitulation of the fires in the Yellow Jacket, Kentuck, and Crown Point Mines of the preceding week. Mostly quotes from the *News,* but comments from other papers are also included. The remainder is advertisements.

News, April 14, 1869: "Owing to the great demand for the full particulars of the great mining calamity in Gold Hill, another EXTRA, with everything which has transpired concerning the disaster up to Wednesday evening, April 14th, will be published on Thursday morning, April 15th. Price, 25 cents." *News,* June 29, 1869, and continuing sporadically through July 15: "A few copies of the EXTRA NEWS of April 15, containing a full account of the Mining Calamity in Gold Hill on the 7th of April—suitable for future reference—can be obtained by applying at this office." Doten Diaries, April 14, 1869: "Evening wrote short letter . . . enclosed the Gold Hill News Extra for tomorrow morning." See Nos. L498 and L511.

CU-B. NvU.

HILLYER, CURTIS JUSTIN.

Woman Suffrage. | *[filet]* | Speech | of | Hon. C. J. Hillyer, | Delivered in the Assembly of the State of Nevada | Tuesday, February 16, 1869. | *[filet]* | Carson City: | Henry R. Mighels, State Printer. | *[short rule]* | 1869.   [515]

19 p. 21 x 13 cm. Printed wrapper. Facsimile of wrapper following p. 314.

Resolution to distribute ten copies to each member of the Senate and Assembly and five copies to each attaché; the remainder of the edition was to go to Hillyer for his own use (JA,1869, p. 238), but the number of copies to be printed is not given. Issued also, on 15 p. from different type, in AJA, 1869.

Though strewn with the popular prejudices of the day, the speech is a remarkable one for its early statement of the desirability of truly universal suffrage. Hillyer was at times witty, occasionally eloquent, but at all times a strong proponent of the right of half the population to vote. On the conclusion of his arguments he was greeted with a long and loud ovation—and immediate rejection of the constitutional amendment he supported. It was not until the Legislatures of 1911 and 1913 struck the word "male" from the Constitution's voting qualifications, an action ratified in 1914 by the state's male voters, that Nevada women finally achieved the suffrage right.

CSmH. CU-B.

MINERS' UNION OF VIRGINIA CITY.

Special Notice. | *[thick-thin rule]* | The Members of the Virginia | and Gold Hill Miners' Union, | are requested to attend a Special | Meeting, to be held at the District | Court Room on | Wednesday Evening, August 25, | at 7.30 [*sic*] o'clock. | [*short thick-thin rule*] | All Members of the Union who | can possibly attend will please do | so, as there is Business of Great Im-|portance to be considered. | J. D. Bethel, | Sec'y, G.H.M.U. | Alex. Miot, | Sec'y, V.M.U. | Virginia, August 23, 1869. [516]

Broadside. 42 x 29 cm.
CSmH.

NEVADA. *District Court. Sixth Judicial District (Lander County).*

[Briefs. 1869.]

Nevada, ex rel. Dawley vs. Irwin. Brief for plaintiff. Austin: 1869. 23 p. Wrapper.
Norris:2805. The only press in Austin in 1869 was at the *Reese River Reveille.*
[L517]

NEVADA. *Governor, 1864-1871 (Henry Goode Blasdel).*

Second | Biennial Message | of | H. G. Blasdel, | Governor of Nevada.| [*filet*] | Delivered to the Legislature, January, 1869. | [*filet*] | Carson City: | Henry R. Mighels, State Printer. | [*short rule*] | 1869. [518]

23 p. 23 x 14 cm. Printed wrapper. AJS, 1869, contains as [No. 1] a 14 p. issue of the message, printed from a different type setting.
The *Reese River Reveille* of February 17, 1869, expressed thanks for a copy of the message.
DLC. NN. NvU (microfilm). WHi.

NEVADA. *Governor (Acting), 1869 (James S. Slingerland).*

Thanksgiving Proclamation. | [*state seal*] | . . . | I, the Acting Governor of the State of Nevada, do hereby appoint | Thursday, the 18th Day of November, A.D. 1869, | As a day of Public Thanksgiving and Praise. | . . . | [Carson City: Henry R. Mighels, State Printer. 1869.] [519]

Broadside. 43 x 32 cm. Line 1 in an arch over state seal. Issued on the "20th day of October, A.D. 1869."
NvHi.

NEVADA. *Laws, statutes, etc.*

School Law | of the | State of Nevada, | As Amended at the | Fourth Session of the Legislature. | [*short rule*] | Published by the | Department of Public Instruction, | For the Use of School Officers. | [*short rule*] | Carson City: | Henry R. Mighels, State Printer. | 1869. [520]

21, [2] p. 22 x 14 cm. Printed wrapper.

Gold Hill *News,* March 29, 1869: "The last Legislature amended the School Law in several particulars, which is important to be generally known. We are informed that State Superintendent [S. N.] Fisher is now preparing a pamphlet edition of said law as amended, for general circulation; but one or two items of amendatory legislation need to be made public before this pamphlet can be printed and distributed."

The DHEW copy noted in *Check List:* 117 was transferred in 1969 to DLC, where it was discarded. See Introduction, p. 10-11.

Nv.

NEVADA. *Laws, statutes, etc.*

Statutes | of the | State of Nevada | Passed at the | Fourth Session of the Legislature, | 1869, | Begun on Monday, the Fourth Day of January, and Ended on | Thursday, the Fourth Day of March. | [*state seal*] | Carson City: | Henry R. Mighels, State Printer. | 1869.

[521]

xiii, [3], 376 p. 23 x 15 cm. Leather binding. Page [343]-376, printed from the same type as in Nos. 524 and 535: Reports of the State Treasurer of Nevada for the Fiscal Years 1867 and 1868.

Carson City *Appeal,* June 24, 1869: "The Laws passed at the last session of the Legislature of this State—that of 1869—have been printed in book form and received in Carson City. Copies can now be obtained on application to the State Printer at the office of the Carson Daily Appeal. The volume contains 376 pages. Price $5." The *Appeal* of the following day, however, stated that only 200 of the authorized 400 copies had been received, and it was not until July 8 that Mighels could announce in the paper he owned that all copies had been received.

Az. CU-B. CoD. CtY-L. DLC. IU. MBS. MH-L. NN. NNLI. Nv. NvEuC. NvGoEC. NvHi. NvPLC. NvRNC. NvRWL. NvU. NvVSR. OrU-L. WHi.

NEVADA. *Legislature.*

Standing Rules, | Joint Rules, | and | Standing Committees | of the | Senate and Assembly | of the | State of Nevada. | [*short rule*] | Fourth Session—1869. | [*short rule*] | Carson City: | Henry R. Mighels, State Printer. | [*short rule*] | 1869.   [522]

32 p. 18 x 11 cm. Printed wrapper.

500 copies ordered printed by Senate concurrent resolution (SSN, 1869, p. 297).

NvU.

NEVADA. *Legislature. Assembly.*

Journal of the Assembly | During | the Fourth Session | of the | Legislature of the State of Nevada, | 1869, | Begun on Monday, the Fourth Day of January, and Ended on | Thursday, the Fourth Day of March. | [*state seal*] | Carson City: | Henry R. Mighels, State Printer. | 1869.   [523]

330, [2], 15 p. 23 x 15 cm. Half-leather binding. In an appendix following p. 330 is the speech of C. J. Hillyer called "Woman Suffrage" that is described in No. 515; the two are from different settings of type.

Az. CtY. CtY-L. DLC. ICU. M. MB. MH. NN. Nv-Ar. NvHi. NvLC. NvLN. NvRWL. NvSC. NvU. WHi.

NEVADA. *Legislature. Senate.*

The | Journal of the Senate | During | the Fourth Session | of the | Legislature of the State of Nevada, | 1869, | Begun on Monday, the Fourth Day of January, and | Ended on Thursday, the Fourth Day of March. | [*state seal*] | Carson City: | Henry R. Mighels, State Printer. | 1869.   [524]

331, [3], 14, 124, 33, 43, 96, 37, 161, 7, [1] p. 23 x 15 cm. Half-leather binding.

Half title following p. 331: General Appendix. Each of the reports has a separate title page and each is paged separately. Numbers have been assigned according to the position of the reports in the volume, since there is no table of contents. [No. 1], Second Biennial Message of H. G. Blasdel, Governor of Nevada. Delivered to the Legislature, January, 1869, 14 p.; [No. 2], Biennial Report of the Controller of the State of Nevada, for the Third and Fourth Fiscal Years 1867 and 1868. W. K. Parkinson, State Controller, 124 p.; [No. 3], Report of the State Treasurer of Nevada for the Fiscal Years 1867 and 1868, 33 p.; [No. 4], Biennial Report of the Warden of the Nevada State Prison for the Years 1867 and 1868, 43 p. and three folding tables; [No. 5], Nevada State Mineralogist's Report for the Years 1867 and 1868, 96 p.; [No. 6], Fourth Annual Report of the Superintendent of Public Instruction of the State of Nevada for the School Year Ending August 31, 1868, 37 p.; [No. 7], Biennial Report of the Surveyor General and State Register of the State of Nevada, For 1867 and 1868, 161 p. and three folding tables (see No. 534); [No. 8], First Biennial Report of the Secretary of State in Relation to the Indigent Insane, 7, [1] p.

Az. CtY. CtY-L. DLC. ICU. M. MB. MH. NN. Nv. Nv-Ar. NvHi. NvLN. NvRWL. NvSC. NvU. WHi.

NEVADA. *Office of Superintendent of Public Instruction.*

Fourth Annual Report | of the | Superintendent of Public Instruc- tion | of the | State of Nevada | for the | School Year Ending Au- gust 31, 1868. | [*filet*] | Carson City: | Henry R. Mighels, State Printer. | 1869.   [525]

37 p. 23 x 15 cm. Printed wrapper. Issued also as [No. 6] in AJS, 1869.

Superintendent S. N. Fisher was confused about the numbering of his report, and remained confused throughout his tenure as the state's head educator. It is in fact the second biennial report, covering the school years 1866 to 1868; there was no third annual report in printed form, although Fisher apparently wrote one that he later incorporated into this one. See Nos. 442 and 615.

1,000 copies of the report "and accompanying documents, excluding nos. 6, 7, and 8," ordered printed by Senate concurrent resolution; 700 were for the use of the Legislature, 25 were to go to the Secretary of State, and the remaining copies were for the Superintendent (SSN, 1869, p. 298). Receipt of a copy was acknowledged in the

February 17, 1869, issue of the *Reese River Reveille*.
DHEW. M. NvU (microfilm).

NEVADA. *Secretary of State.*

First | Biennial Report | of the | Secretary of State | in Relation to the Indigent Insane. | [*state seal*] | Carson City: | Henry R. Mighels, State Printer. | [*short rule*] | 1869.   [526]

8 p. 23 x 15 cm. Printed wrapper. Issued also as [No. 8] in AJS, 1869.

The *Territorial Enterprise* acknowledged receipt of a copy in its issue of February 13, 1869.

CSmH.

NEVADA. *State Controller's Office.*

Biennial Report | of the | Controller of the State of Nevada, | for the | Third and Fourth Fiscal Years 1867 and 1868. | W. K. Parkinson, | State Controller. | [*short rule*] | Carson City, Nevada: | Henry R. Mighels, State Printer. | 1869.   [527]

124 p. 23 x 14 cm. Printed wrapper. Issued also as [No. 2] in AJS, 1869.

1,500 copies ordered printed by Senate concurrent resolution (SSN, 1869, p. 298); another Senate concurrent resolution authorized 200 copies for the Controller's use (ibid., p. 300), but it is not clear whether they were part of the original order or extra copies.

DLC. MH. NN. Nv-Ar.

NEVADA. *State Mineralogist.*

Report | of the | State Mineralogist | of Nevada | for the Years 1867 and 1868. | [*short rule*] | Carson City, Nevada: | Henry R. Mighels, State Printer. | 1869.   [528]

96 p. 23 x 14 cm. Printed wrapper. Issued also as [No. 5] in AJS, 1869.

1,500 copies ordered printed by Senate concurrent resolution (SSN, 1869, p. 299). The State Mineralogist was empowered to take his report to San Francisco to superintend its printing (JS, 1869, p. 40). The *Territorial Enterprise* acknowledged receipt of a copy on February 21, 1869.

C. CU-B. CtY.

NEVADA. *State Prison.*

Biennial Report | of | the Warden | of the | Nevada State Prison | for the | Years 1867 and 1868. | [*short rule*] | Carson City, Nevada: | Henry R. Mighels, State Printer. | 1869.   [529]

43 p. and three folding tables. 23 x 15 cm. Printed wrapper. Issued also as [No. 4] in AJS, 1869.

Senate concurrent resolution to print 1,000 copies in pamphlet form for the Warden's use (SSN, 1869, p. 299). Receipt of a copy was acknowledged in the *Reese River*

Reveille of March 2, 1869.

NvHi. NvMiD (has remnants of a wrapper).

NEVADA. *Supreme Court.*

[Briefs. 1869.]

Nevada vs. McCluer. Brief of appellant, State of Nevada. 21 p. 25 x 18 cm. Imprint on wrapper: San Francisco: Printed by Turnbull & Smith, Law Printers, No. 516 Sacramento street, below Leidesdorff. 1869. Nv-Ar. [530]

Robinson et al. vs. Imperial Silver Mining Co. Brief of appellant, Imperial Silver Mining Co. 38 p. 22 x 14 cm. Imprint on wrapper: Daily Safeguard Print: Virginia, Nev., 1869. Nv-Ar. [531]

Sime et al. vs. Armstrong. Brief of appellants, John Sime et al. 14 p. 21 x 14 cm. Imprint on wrapper: Daily Safeguard Print: Virginia, Nev., 1869. Nv-Ar. [532]

NEVADA. *Supreme Court.*

Reports of Cases | Determined in | The Supreme Court | of the | State of Nevada, | During the Year 1868. | Reported by Alfred Helm, | Clerk of the Court. | [*short rule*] | Volume IV. | [*short rule*] | San Francisco: | Bacon & Company, Book and Job Printers, Excelsior Office, | 536 Clay Street, just below Montgomery. | 1869. [533]

615 p. 23 x 16 cm. Leather binding.

600 copies authorized (SSN, 1869, p. 48); no more than 600 were to be printed so that the state could have the entire edition. The estimate for printing Reports during 1869 and 1870 was $7,500 (Controller's Report, 1867-1868, p. 56); $3,700 was appropriated and spent during 1869 (ibid., 1869-1870, p. 99). The estimate and appropriation probably included all costs, not only that of printing. Both the Carson City *Appeal* and the Gold Hill *News* acknowledged receipt of copies on July 20, 1869.

Reissued in a stereotype edition in 1877, with volume 3, by A. L. Bancroft & Co., and again in 1887 by Bancroft-Whitney; it has also been reissued in the twentieth century.

CU-B. DHEW. DLC. In-SC (rebound). M. Nv-Ar. NvRWL (rebound). NvU.

NEVADA. *Surveyor General.*

Biennial Report | of the | Surveyor General and State Register | of the | State of Nevada, | For 1867 and 1868. | [*state seal*] | Carson City: | Henry R. Mighels, State Printer. | [*short rule*] | 1869. [534]

6, [5], 4-158 p. and three folding tables. 26 x 16 cm. Printed wrapper. Issued also as [No. 7] in AJS, 1869, with 161 p.

This separate, which was printed from the same type as the AJS issue, corrects for the most part the peculiar imposition of the latter. In all examined copies of the AJS document the first folding table is counted in the pagination as *one* page, bringing about a following even-numbered recto page. Folding charts thereafter are not counted and the confusion continues to p. 161, a verso. In the separate, none of the folding tables is counted and pagination is corrected, except for p. 41 which follows an unnumbered page and precedes two folding tables and two unnumbered pages, and is a recto. There is also a rearrangement of preliminaries in the separate issue that makes necessary the counting of the wrapper as p. [1]. The three "extra" pages in the AJS issue are therefore the result of typographical tomfoolery and not additional printed matter. The oddity in that issue suggests that untrained or perhaps bibulous printers had a hand in it, and that the press of business and the necessity for speed during the legislative session militated against normal checking for errors until a number of copies had been printed. These copies may have been reserved for AJS in the hope that the errors would be less noticeable there.

1,000 copies ordered printed by Senate concurrent resolution (SSN, 1869, p. 299). MWA. NN (rebound). Nv-Ar. WHi.

NEVADA. *Treasury Department.*

Report | of the | State Treasurer of Nevada | for the | Fiscal Years 1867 and 1868. | [*short rule*] | Carson City, Nevada: | Henry R. Mighels, State Printer. | 1869. [535]

33 p. 23 x 15 cm. Printed wrapper. Issued also as [No. 3] in AJS, 1869, and from the same type in SSN, 1869, p. [343]-376.

1,500 copies ordered printed by Senate concurrent resolution, for the use of the Legislature (SSN, 1869, p. 298).
DLC. Nv-Ar.

ODD FELLOWS, INDEPENDENT ORDER OF. *Genoa, Nevada. Genoa Lodge No. 15.*

Semi-Centennial Anniversary, | I.O.O.F. | Ball. | At Genoa, April 26, 1869. | [*filet*] | The pleasure of your company, with Ladies, is respectfully so-|licited to a Ball, to be given by the Genoa Lodge U.D., | I.O.O.F., on Monday, April 26th, 1869. | [*filet*] | . . . [536]

[4] p., printed on p. [1] only. 18 x 12 cm. Line 1 in an arch over line 2. Edges embossed and scalloped.
There was no press in Genoa in 1869.
NvHi. NvU.

ODD FELLOWS, INDEPENDENT ORDER OF. *Gold Hill, Nevada. Parker Lodge No. 13.*

Constitution, | By-laws and Rules of Order | —of— | Parker Lodge, No. 13, | of the | Independent Order of Odd Fellows, | of Nevada. | [*short rule*] | Instituted at Gold Hill, Oct. 8th, 1868. | [*lodge emblem*] | Sacramento: | H. S. Crocker & Co., Printers and Stationers. | 1869. [537]

71, [1] p. 13? x 9? cm. The recorded copy has been trimmed and bound without a

wrapper. Title and text pages in thick-thin rule borders.
C.

ODD FELLOWS, INDEPENDENT ORDER OF. *Nevada. Grand Lodge.*

Proceedings | of the | Third Annual Communication | of the | R. W. Grand Lodge | of the | Independent Order of Odd Fellows, | of the | State of Nevada, | Held at Odd Fellows' Hall, Virginia City, | June 8th, 9th and 10th, 1869. | [*filet*] | Sacramento: | H.S. Crocker & Co., Steam Printers and Stationers. | 1869.
[538]

[3], 184-288, iii p. 21 x 14 cm. Printed wrapper.

The estimate for printing proceedings was $300 (p. 257); the number of copies was not specified, but it was probably 480 as in previous years. On January 20, 1870, $346.15 was paid "for printing"; an additional $20 was paid out for the same purpose on the following April 24, but this smaller amount may have been for incidental printing (1870 Proceedings, p. 312).

The examined copy is in the cornerstone of the capitol building in Carson City. The recorded microfilm copies were made during renovation of the building in 1978-1979.

NvHi (microfilm). NvMus (microfilm). NvU (microfilm).

ODD FELLOWS, INDEPENDENT ORDER OF. *Reno, Nevada. Truckee Lodge No. 14.*

Constitution | By-Laws and Rules of Order | —of— | Truckee Lodge, No. 14, | of the | Independent Order of Odd Fellows, | at Reno, State of Nevada. | [*short rule*] | Adopted January 19th, 1869. | [*short rule*] | Sacramento: | H.S. Crocker & Co., Printers and Stationers. | 1869.
[539]

70, [1] p. 13? x 9? cm. The recorded copy has been trimmed and bound without a wrapper. Title and text pages in thick-thin rule borders.
C.

ODD FELLOWS, INDEPENDENT ORDER OF. *Shermantown, Nevada. White Pine Association.*

Celebration | of the | Fiftieth Anniversary | of | Odd Fellowship in the United States, | under the Auspices of the | White Pine Association, I.O.O.F. | at Shermantown, | White Pine County, Nev., April 26, 1869. | [*short rule*] | Published by Order of the White Pine I.O.O.F. Association. C. G. Hubbard, | Chairman Committee of Arrangements. | [*short rule*] | Sacramento: | Russell & Winterburn, Steam Printers, Corner of J and Third Sts. | [*short rule*] | 1869.
[540]

26 p. 22 x 14 cm. Printed wrapper.
CSmH. CU-B.

PEOPLE'S TRIBUNE. *Gold Hill, Nevada*. Address to the people. November 1869.   [L541]

Gold Hill *News*, November 3, 1869: "THE PEOPLE'S TRIBUNE.—Our versatile neighbor, Conrad Wiegand, issued this morning the prospectus or first number of his proposed newspaporial effort, which will bear the above title, although the present issue—served up on the half shell, or rather half sheet—is entitled 'Address to the People.' This number is well filled with assorted moralizing, outcroppings, indications, etc., is well printed on good paper, and will be read with interest by all who are addicted to this style of reading. . . . The prospectus says that the 'second number will shortly be published, supported by a private, non-sectarian and non-partizan association of men and women, having for its purpose the emancipation of our community as a part of mankind from ignorance, prejudice, injustice and error, for the reclamation of the fallen, and for the People's defense.' " The "Address" was apparently a true prospectus, since the *People's Tribune* began its six-month run in January 1870 with volume 1, number 1.

PEOPLE'S TRIBUNE ASSOCIATION.

The People's Tribune Sunday Meeting, | —at— | Piper's Opera House | Sunday Afternoon, at 2 o'clock. | [*filet*] | Tickets of Admission, Free--At Morrill's Drug Store. | Reserved Seats, 50 Cents Each, at the Opera House. | [*filet*] | Benefit of Orphan Asylum. See Advertisement in Enterprise | [*filet*] | . . . | Conrad Wiegand, | Publisher of People's Tribune. | [1869.]   [542]

Broadside. 17 x 11 cm.

Doten Diaries, November 14, 1869: "PM, at 3 I went to Wiegand's second entertainment at Opera House — good house." Issues of the *Enterprise* for the period are unavailable.
NvU.

PEOPLE'S TRIBUNE ASSOCIATION.

Programme | —of the— | People's Tribune Meeting, | —at— | Piper's Opera House, | —on— | Sunday Afternoon, November 7, | At 2 1-2 o'clock. | [*filet*] | Tickets of Admission, Free—at Morrill's Drug Store | Where also Copies of Wiegand's Address to | the People, explaining the nature | of these Meetings, may be | obtained. | [*filet*] | . . . | [*wavy rule*] | See Advertisements in Enterprise and News. | [Virginia City: Territorial Enterprise? 1869.]   [543]

Broadside. 22 x 13 cm.

The Gold Hill *News* of November 5, 1869, reported that the program had been published. The "Address to the People" was Conrad Wiegand's prospectus for his proposed *People's Tribune;* see No. L541. The tentative identification of the *Territorial Enterprise* as the printer is based on information provided by that paper's business manager when the *Enterprise* refused to do any more work for Wiegand early in 1870; see No. 573.

The *News* for November 4 contained an advertisement for the meeting, headed "Fiat Justitia Ruat Coelum [*sic*]!" It announced that at the first meeting of the association, held on November 3, it had been decided to hold a public meeting on the following Sunday, in keeping with the by-laws of the organization. It was also announced that Wiegand would address the meeting on "The Morals of Nevada, and the Future of the Comstock Mines."

NvU.

PIPER'S OPERA HOUSE. *Virginia City, Nevada.*

Piper's Opera House. | [*double rule*] | . . . | [*thick-thin rule*] | Saturday Evening, August 7. | [*thick-thin rule*] | First Night of the Great Sensational Artiste, Miss | Emma Forrestell! | The Wonderful Female Contortionist, | Who will appear in some of her remarkable Performances and the same | Startling Acts of Contortion and Gymnastic Feats that | have astonished the Public of all the Principal | Cities of Great Britain and America, | and been pronounced by | the Public as the | Wonder of Wonders! | . . . | [Virginia City: Territorial Enterprise? 1869.]   [544]

Broadside. 28? x 10? cm. Description from *Nevada Highways and Parks*, No. 3 (1958), p. 29; probably reduced. The *Enterprise*, the only newspaper in town at the time, reviewed the performance in its issue of August 8, 1869.

Pvt.

REESE RIVER MINING DISTRICT. *Ordinances, local laws, etc.*

Mining Laws | of | Reese River District, | with | Revisions and Amendments. | [*filet*] | Austin: | Reveille Printing Office. | 1869.   [545]

4 p. 24 x 15 cm. Wrapper title, in decorative rule border. Text printed in two columns, from the same type as in the *Reveille*'s issue of March 23, 1869.

Reveille, March 25, 1869: "The REVEILLE has just printed a pamphlet of the 'Mining Laws of the Reese River District, with all the Revisions and Amendments.' . . . They comprise the Mining Laws passed July 17, 1862; Revised Laws passed April 20, 1863; and June 4, 1864; and Amendments passed June 27, 1864." Two days earlier the *Reveille* had published the laws in the paper, with the comment that "we have had frequent applications for copies of these laws, which we can now supply in quantity." The demand may not have been as heavy as anticipated; there were still copies available, "Price 50 cents per copy," on February 12, 1872.

CU-B. NvALR.

SUTRO, ADOLPH HEINRICH JOSEPH. Awake! Arm! Arm! Virginia City: Territorial Enterprise. October 1869.   [L546]

Territorial Enterprise, October 17, 1869: "A BLUNDER.—In the poster issued by Mr.

Sutro, the printer headed it 'Awake! Arm! Arm!' instead of 'Awake! Arise!' as it should have been.'' The error may not have been a printer's blunder, considering the antipathy of the *Enterprise,* then controlled by the Bank of California, toward Sutro. See No. 547.

SUTRO, ADOLPH HEINRICH JOSEPH.

Miners! Laboring Men! | Mechanics! Rally! | [*thin-thick-thin rule*] | Great Mass Meeting | at | [*blank*] | [*thick-thin rule*] | Adolph Sutro | Will address the Citizens of | [*blank*] | Subject: "The Sutro Tunnel and the Bank of California." Admission | Free. Seats reserved for Ladies. Come one! Come all! | [1869.]

[547]

Broadside. 46 x 61 cm. Facsimile in Robert E. Stewart, Jr., and Mary Francis Stewart, *Adolph Sutro: A Biography* (Berkeley, California: Howell-North, 1962), following p. 46.

The Stewarts focus on Sutro's presentation at Piper's Opera House in Virginia City on September 20, 1869, and most of the copies that have been examined show, in black crayon, that they were used on that occasion. The blanks clearly indicate, however, that the broadside was intended for use elsewhere as well. No copy has been found with another time and place filled in and it is not known whether he gave the speech elsewhere. The copy at NvU has not been filled in. Sutro had much of his Sutro Tunnel printing done outside of Nevada and it cannot be said where this piece was printed; Streeter IV:2351 suggests Carson City as a printing site.

Sutro had tried for years to raise enough money to dig a tunnel to be used for draining water and removing ore from the Comstock mines—and, in emergencies, to remove men—and had at first achieved considerable success. As time passed, however, the Bank of California, to which many of the mine owners were indebted, saw that it could increase its political and economic control of the area by withdrawing its initial support of the tunnel idea. One of its methods was to build a railroad from Carson City to Virginia City, thereby denying Sutro the franchise to move ore for processing at the Carson River mills. Because of the bank's sway over many of the mine owners, money that had been pledged to the tunnel project went instead to the Virginia and Truckee Railroad, which by late 1869 had reached the southern end of the Comstock in Gold Hill. The local factor of the bank, William Sharon, saw that Sutro's position had been mightily weakened and determined to drive him out of the country. Sutro had retained his abundant influence with the miners, though, and a disastrous mine fire early in April, in which forty-five men died because they could not get above ground, gave him and his project even more credibility. After brooding through the summer about his shrinking resources and opportunities, he decided to take his case directly to the miners. The address at Piper's caused a sensation. He told of his many efforts to locate backing and funds; he spoke at length of the bank's mismanagement of the mines it controlled and its attempts to humiliate and degrade him; he requested his listeners to give him not only moral support but monetary support, through their subscriptions to stock in the tunnel. The miners received his two-hour speech with enthusiasm, but the bank's opposition continued and it was to be another ten years before the tunnel finally reached the mines—long after they had been largely worked out and the primary reason for digging the tunnel had ceased to exist. See No. 548. C. COMus. CSmH. CtY. NvU.

Sutro, Adolph Heinrich Joseph.

The Sutro Tunnel and the Bank of California. | [*double rule*] | Virginia City, Nev. | [*double rule*] | Tuesday [*dotted rule*] Sept. 20, 1869. | [*double rule*] | Speech of Adolph Sutro, | On the Sutro Tunnel and the Bank of | California. | [*short rule*] | Delivered at Piper's Opera House, Vir-|ginia City, September 20, 1869. | [*short rule*] | [Virginia City: Daily Territorial Enterprise. 1869.] [548]

[2] p. 49? x 35? cm. The recorded copy has been cropped on all sides. Line 1 extends across the sheet on both sides. Text printed in six columns, from the same type used for the *Enterprise* of September 22, 1869.

This is the speech announced in the poster recorded in No. 547.

CSmH.

Sutro Tunnel Company.

Virginia City, Nev. | [*double rule*] | Monday [*dotted rule*] Octob r [*sic*] 4, 1869. | [*thick-thin rule*] | Sutro Tunnel Company. | [*short rule*] | . . . [549]

Broadside. 40 x 18 cm. In column 1 of three columns. Signed, at the foot of column 3: Adolph Sutro, For the Sutro Tunnel Company. Virginia, Nevada, October 1, 1869. The error in line 2 of the NvU copy is corrected in other recorded copies.

Reprints two powers of attorney and a trust deed.

CSmH. CtY. NvU.

Taylor, Robert H.

Masonic Addresses | and | Poems. | By Robert H. Taylor. | [*filet*] | "Urbem fecisti quod primus orbis erat." | [*short rule*] | "—the faith we follow teaches us to live in bonds of charity with | all mankind, and die with hope of bliss beyond the grave."—Sheridan. | [*filet*] | Virginia, Nevada: | 1869. [550]

50 p. 23 x 14 cm. Wrapper title, in decorative rule border: Masonic Addresses | and | Poems. | By Robert H. Taylor. | [*filet*] | San Francisco: | H. H. Bancroft and Company. | 1869. See No. 507.

C. CU-B. IaCrM. MBFM. NNFM (lacks wrapper).

White Pine Mining District. *Ordinances, local laws, etc.*

Mining Laws | of | White Pine District. | [*short rule*] | Published and for Sale by | McCann & Company, | Stationers and Newsmen, | Main Street, Treasure City, Nev. | [*short rule*] | Sacramento: | H. S. Crocker & Co., Steam Printers and Stationers. | 1869. [551]

10, [1] p. 14 x 9 cm. Printed wrapper. Wrapper, title page, and text pages in thick-thin rule borders. Cut of a mill on verso of title page.

The laws are those that took effect October 10, 1865, as amended July 20, 1867. CtY. NvU (microfilm).

WIEGAND, CONRAD AARON? Awake to danger. San Francisco? August 2, 1869. [L552]

Territorial Enterprise, August 3, 1869: "Something of a sensation was created in the city last evening by the distribution of a large quantity of handbills, embodying a lengthy address 'to the people of Storey County,' under the rather startling heading of 'Awake to Danger.' The bills were distributed by a long-haired, cadaverous-looking individual who moved nervously about his work, and might have been mistaken for one of Brigham Young's Destroying Angels. The bills were printed in San Francisco, we think, and fifteen hundred, we are informed, were received for circulation. The address is a tirade against the Virginia and Truckee Railroad Company—a corporation referred to as a 'foul body of conspirators,' 'headed by the chief agent of the Bank of California in Virginia.' The burden of the complaint is, that these 'foul conspirators have received the promise of assistance to the extent of $575,000 from Storey, Ormsby and Lyon counties; that they employ more Chinese than white men as laborers; that they have bribed the press . . . ; that when the road is completed, it will ruin the teaming business, blacksmithing, saloons, boarding-houses, merchants, mechanics, and almost everybody else.' The address concludes by appealing to the people to assemble in mass meeting 'and demand that not a dollar shall be paid nor a bond issued by the Commissioners of the county until this railroad shall be completed to the Truckee [River], as the directors originally agreed.' The inference is, that the 'completion of the road to the Truckee' will in a great measure relieve blacksmiths, teamsters and saloon-keepers from the danger menacing them with Carson as the terminus! But we did not start out with the view of giving anything like a synopsis of the address. Having designated its character, we take pleasure in being able to announce, by authority, that it was not issued by the authority or the consent or knowledge of the Miners' Unions of this county. The author or authors are unknown to the officers of the Unions, by whom we are requested to state that, in behalf of these associations and for themselves, they repudiate the address in toto. As the Workingmen's Convention was in session at the time of the circulation of the address, it was supposed by many to be an official proclamation of that body." The Gold Hill *News* of the same date had the following: "The American Flat Toll Road sticks out so prominently in the contents of this anonymous handbill, that it is needless to make any further comment. The poster, which has been thrown around loosely in Gold Hill, has not attracted one-tenth the interest that Tom Thumb's handbills have." The rhetoric and subject are so similar to other Wiegand pronouncements that it is not unlikely he was the author. See No. 553.

WIEGAND, CONRAD AARON.

Freemen of Storey | Awake! | [*thick-thin rule*] | Worse than Highway Rob-|bery is abroad! | [*thick-thin rule*] | The Officers of the Law have become the Agents | of Plunder! Not alone the cheap thing by dream-|ers called Liberty is in danger, but your | very precious Coin And Pockets | are now in immediate Peril! | [*thick-thin rule*] | Friendly Warning To Tax-Payers. | [*filet*] | . . . | [1869.] [553]

Broadside. 31 x 19 cm. Signed at the bottom: Conrad Wiegand. Facsimile following p. 314.

Gold Hill *News*, October 30, 1869: " 'Awake!'—Neighbor Conrad Wiegand, assayer, etc., etc., had circulated in Gold Hill and Virginia City, this morning, a handbill with the above eye-opener as a heading. The contents of the handbill are a protest against the payment of the small amount of special tax to defray the interest on the Railroad Bonds which Storey County is to issue in aid of the Virginia and Truckee Railroad. We are inclined to believe that Mr. Wiegand is not actuated so much by a desire to see people save the small amount of railroad tax which each one of us are called upon to pay, as it is to give vent to a private revenge he has against the Bank of California, to Mr. [William] Sharon, the business manager, and to the Union Mill Company; and he therefore makes this railroad tax business simply a pretense of excuse for stepping forth as the would-be champion against an imaginary wrong." The *News* of November 1 reprinted most of the circular, with additional comment. See No. L552.
CSmH.

~1870~

Printers' rates in Nevada had always been related to those in California, at least since creation of the Washoe Typographical Union in 1863, so when in early March of 1870 the Eureka Typographical Union of San Francisco acceded to the demands of two of that city's newspapers to lower the rates for composition there was an immediate request for reduced rates from Nevada newspapers (Gold Hill *News*, March 5). A lowered pay scale was in fact agreed to by the Nevada union in mid-month (ibid., March 14) and, although newspaper rates were given the publicity, it may be supposed that job rates were affected as well. Then on August 1, printers in California and Nevada struck for a return to the old scale (*Territorial Enterprise*, August 5). Some California papers agreed, others did not. In Nevada the demand was for a rather modest increase, which was granted. But the California papers that refused to raise the scale eventually won the battle and it was again lowered; in a show of solidarity, the Washoe Typographical Union also agreed to a reduced scale (ibid., August 16).

A radical reduction in state printing costs was brought about by the lack of a legislative session in 1870; the 1878 report of the State Controller (p. 30) indicates that only $2,695.47 was spent from the State Printing Fund during the 1870 fiscal year.

Henry R. Mighels's bid for a second term as State Printer was denied by Charles L. Perkins, the Democrat whom Mighels had defeated two years earlier. Perkins then bought the Carson City *Appeal* from Mighels, changed its name to the *Daily State Register,* and used its facilities to execute the public printing for the next two years.

Elko's newspaper had competition for about six months beginning in June, and early in the year two papers unsuccessfully challenged the supremacy of the *News* in Gold Hill. Hamilton had a new paper, but also saw an old one suspend, then die. Shermantown lost its only press in June, and Treasure City in January. But Eureka and Pioche welcomed their first newspapers, Unionville acquired one after a hiatus of nearly a year, and Reno's single press was joined by another in late November. Presses that were active in Austin, Virginia City, and Winnemucca at the end of 1869 continued to publish throughout the year.

BACHELORS' CLUB OF VIRGINIA. *Virginia City Nevada.*

Bachelors' Club | ....of.... | Virginia. | Mr [*dotted rule*] | The pleasure of your company is respectfully requested | . ..at a.... | Soiree Dansante! | to be Given on | Friday Evening [*dotted rule*] 187 [*dotted rule*] | at Athletic Hall, Virginia. | J. P. Smith, President. | L. S. Graves, Secretary. | [*filet*] | Tickets, $5 to be Obtained from | . . . | Dancing will commence at 9 o'clock. | [1870.] [554]

[4] p., printed on p. [1] only. 16 x 10 cm. Line 1 in an arch over line 2. Dots in lines 2 and 6 are textual, including the missing dot in line 6. Edge-embossed.

One of two copies at CSmH is hand-dated December 16, 1870; the other, identical except for variant embossing, is hand-dated January 20, 1871.
CSmH.

BACHELORS' CLUB OF VIRGINIA. *Virginia City, Nevada.*

Mr [*broken rule*] | The "Bachelors' Club of Virginia," | will be happy to be favored with your company and Ladies | to a Social at Athletic Hall, on Friday Evening, Janu-|ary 28, 1870. | A. L. Edwards, President. | J. H. T. Martin, Secretary. | [*fist*] Tickets $5, to be obtained from the Secretary, on or | before the 26th instant. | Dancing will commence promptly at half=past | 8 o'clock.
[555]

[4] p., printed on p. [1] only. 16 x 10 cm. Printed in blue ink, partly in script type. Edge-embossed; corners rounded. The recorded copy is in an envelope.
CSmH.

CARSON THEATER. *Carson City, Nevada.*

Entertainment | —by the— | Carson Dramatic Association, |

—at the— | Carson Theater, | On Tuesday Evening, Dec. 6th, 1870, | On which occasion will be presented the beautiful melo-drama, entitled: | Michael Erle | Or, The Maniac Lover. | . . . | [Daily Appeal Print, Carson City?]   [556]

Broadside. 31? x 15? cm. The recorded copy has been cropped at head and foot, destroying a possible imprint. The *Appeal* and its immediate successor, the *Daily State Register,* had the only press in Carson City in 1870; both printed playbills for the Carson Theater.

NvMus.

CARSON THEATER. *Carson City, Nevada.*

Entertainment | in Aid of the | Public School, | at the Carson Theater, on | Saturday Evening, Oct. 22, 1870 | [*thick-thin rule*] | . . . | [*rule*] | Daily Appeal Print, Carson City.   [557]

Broadside. 36 x 12 cm.

NvMus.

DAILY TERRITORIAL ENTERPRISE. *Virginia City, Nevada.* Extra. August 8, 1870.   [L558]

The entry in Alf Doten's *Journals* for this date mentions the issuance of an extra by the *Enterprise* ''a little later'' than the extra put out by the Gold Hill *News.* It contains news of the fighting in the Franco-Prussian War. See No. L564.

DAILY TERRITORIAL ENTERPRISE. *Virginia City, Nevada.* Extra. September 3, 1870.   [L559]

News of the surrender of Napoleon III and Marshal McMahon: Doten *Journals,* September 3, 1870.

DEMOCRATIC PARTY. *Storey County, Nevada.*

For Governor, | L. R. Bradley. | . . . | State Printer [*broken rule*] Chas. L. Perkins | . . . | [*short rule*] | Storey County | Democratic Ticket | [*short rule*] | . . . | [1870.]   [559a]

[2] p. 14 x 8 cm. Verso, with eagle, clasped hands, and word ''Union'' in decorative compartment, printed in red ink.

CU-B.

ELY MINING DISTRICT. *Ordinances, local laws, etc.*

Laws | of | Ely Mining District, | Lincoln County, Nev., | Adopted March 11, 1867. | [*filet*] | Hamilton, Nev.: | White Pine Daily News Print—Corner Hamilton and Pine Streets. | 1870.
                                                                              [560]

10 p. 24 x 15 cm. Printed wrapper.

CU-B.

FREEMASONS. *Nevada. Grand Lodge.*

Ceremonies | at the | Laying of Foundation-Stones; | Adopted by | Grand Lodge of Nevada. | [*filet*] | . . . | [1870?]   [560a]

7 p. 18 x 11 cm. Caption title.

The pamphlet could have been printed anytime between the formation of the Grand Lodge of Nevada in 1865 and the laying of the cornerstone of the State Capitol in 1870.

The examined copy is in the cornerstone of the capitol building in Carson City. The recorded microfilm copies were made during renovation of the building in 1978-1979.

NvHi (microfilm). NvMus (microfilm). NvU (microfilm).

FREEMASONS. *Nevada. Grand Lodge.*

Proceedings | of the | M.˙.W.˙. Grand Lodge | of | Free and Accepted Masons | of the | State of Nevada, | at its | Sixth Annual Grand Communication, | Held at Masonic Hall, in the City of Virginia, | Sept. 20, 21, and 22, A. L. 5870; | Also at its | Special Grand Communication, Held at Carson City, | June 9th, 5870, to Lay the Foundation-|Stone of the State Capitol. | [*filet*] | San Francisco: | Frank Eastman, Printer, 509 Clay Street. | 1870.   [561]

192, ii p.; erratum slip between p. 166 and 167. 22 x 14 cm. Printed wrapper. Pages [179]-192: Returns of the Subordinate Lodges Under the Jurisdiction of the Grand Lodge of Nevada, On July 15th, A.L. 5870, and Sept. 1st, A.L. 5870.

NvHi and NvU have issues that end on p. 177. On a slip preceding the title page at NvU, not present at NvHi: "Notice. The Report of Committee on Correspondence not having been printed in time for the Annual Communication, these copies are issued in advance for general distribution and circulation among the Lodges. The regular number of copies of the proceedings will be furnished all entitled to them as soon as the same are completed." This issue lacks a wrapper and the erratum slip. The "Notice" suggests that the latter portion of the pamphlet was printed in 1871; the possibility is just as strong, however, that the printer used the 1870 date on the wrapper of the complete issue so the volume would not be confused with the one issued after the 1871 communication.

$700 was set aside for printing the proceedings (p. 165); the amount paid was $897.31 (1871 Proceedings, p. 205). The number of copies printed is not specified, but in the following year and in all preceding years 800 were printed, with 300 of that amount saved for future binding. There were probably more in 1870 because of the advance issue described above.

NvHi (177 p.). NvRFM (192 p.). NvU (both issues).

FREEMASONS. *Silver City, Nevada. Amity Lodge No. 4.*

Constitution | of the | M.˙.W.˙. Grand Lodge | of | Free and Accepted Masons | of the | State of Nevada, | and | By-Laws | of | Amity Lodge No. 4, | Together with | The Ancient Charges, | The Twenty-Five Landmarks of Freemasonry, | and a | Funeral Service. | [*short rule*] | Springfield: | H. G. Reynolds, Jr., Printer,

Masonic Trowel Office. | 1870.   [562]

67, [1] p. 19 x 12 cm. Line 1 in an arch over line 2; line 3 in a reverse arch under line 2. Cloth binding, with gold-stamped title: Amity Lodge No. 4, F. & A. Masons. The by-laws begin on p. [64]; a list of officers and members of Amity Lodge is on p. [68]. H. G. Reynolds, Jr., was the publisher of the monthly *Masonic Trowel* in Springfield, Illinois.

NvU (microfilm).

FREEMASONS. *Virginia City, Nevada. Royal Arch Masons. Virginia Chapter No. 2.*

By-Laws | of | Virginia Chapter, | No. 2, | Royal Arch Masons, | Virginia, Nevada; | with | Extracts from the Constitution of the General Grand | Chapter of Royal Arch Masons for the | United States of America. | [*filet*] | San Francisco: | Frank Eastman, Printer, 509 Clay Street. | 1870.   [563]

25 p. 15 x 10 cm. Printed wrapper. Title and text pages in single rule borders.
CU-B.

GOLD HILL DAILY NEWS. *Gold Hill, Nevada.* Extra. August 8, 1870.
[L564]

News, August 8, 1870: "At eleven o'clock this morning we published an extra, containing a very lively account of the late battle between the Prussians and the French, a large number of copies being sold by the newsboys in Gold Hill, Virginia City and Silver City." Alf Doten's *Journals* for the date noted that this was the "first *extra* of the war."

GOLD HILL DAILY NEWS. *Gold Hill, Nevada.* Extra. September 3, 1870.   [L565]

News, September 3, 1870: "The Gold Hill NEWS issued an EXTRA at precisely half-past ten o'clock this morning, containing the intelligence from France that the French armies, (including the Emperor himself,) had surrendered yesterday afternoon, at Sedan. The news created the greatest excitement in Gold Hill, Virginia City and Silver city [*sic*]. The intelligence being generally acceptable to those communities, and especially the German population, our newsboys sold a great many copies of the EXTRA."

GOSLING, JOSEPH.

Specifications | of the | Labor and Materials | Requisite for the Erection and Completion of the | Nevada State Capitol | at Carson City. | By | Joseph Gosling, | . . . | San Francisco: Excelsior Press, Bacon and Company, Printers, | No. 536 Clay Street, just below Montgomery. | 1870.   [565a]

12 p. 25 x 18 cm. Wrapper title, in thick-thin-thin rule border.

Gosling, a San Francisco architect, received a fee of only $250 for designing the building that, with some additions and renovations, is still used as Nevada's Capitol. The Board of Capitol Commissioners chose the Carson City firm of Peter Cavanaugh & Son to construct the building; costs were kept relatively low by furnishing the building stone to the contractor, free of charge, from the State Prison quarry. The cornerstone was laid on June 9, 1870, and the building was ready, except for a few minor details, for the January 1871 meeting of the Legislature (Frederick C. Gale, *The History of the Capitol Building and Governor's Mansion, State of Nevada*. Carson City: State Printing Office, 1968, p. 6, 11).

The examined copy is in the cornerstone of the capitol building in Carson City. The recorded microfilm copies were made during renovation of the building in 1978-1979.

NvHi (microfilm). NvMus (microfilm). NvU (microfilm).

Lyon County, Nevada. *Board of Registration.*

List of Voters | Registered for the General Election, | Tuesday, November 8, 1870, | Dayton Precinct, Lyon County, Nevada. | [*thick-thin rule*] | . . .   [566]

Broadside, 28 x 19 cm. Text printed in six columns. The recorded copy has been damaged, with parts of columns 1 and 6 torn out, affecting the text.

There was no press in Lyon County in 1870.

NvMus.

Lyon County, Nevada. *Board of Registration.*

Lyon County | [*short thick-thin rule*] | Registered Voters. | [*short rule*] | Official list of Regis-|tered Voters for Silver City Precinct, | entitled to vote at the general election to be | held November 8th, A.D. 1870. | . . .   [567]

Broadside. 17? x 13? cm. The recorded copy has been cropped on all sides. Line 1 extends across the sheet; lines 2-6 extend across columns 1-2 of four columns. See No. 566.

NvMus.

NEVADA. *Governor, 1864-1871 (Henry Goode Blasdel).*

Thanksgiving Proclamation. | [*cut: in a banner held in an eagle's beak:*] Nevada. | [*ornament*] State of Nevada, Executive Department. [*ornament*] | [*filet*] | . . . | . . . I, H. G. Blasdel, Governor of Nevada, do hereby recommend that the National Thanksgiving pro=| claimed by U.S. Grant, President of the United States of America, namely: | Thursday, November 24th, 1870, | Be observed by the People of this Commonwealth, as a day of heartfelt praise to Almighty God, for His | manifold and great mercies toward the children of men. | . . . | . . . Done at Carson City, this the 31st day of October, A.D. 1870. | [Carson City: Henry R. Mighels, State Printer.]   [568]

Broadside. 43 x 36 cm. Line 1 in an arch over the cut and line 2. Partly script type. Printed state seal at bottom left.

CSmH.

NEVADA. *Laws, statutes, etc.*

An Act | To Provide for the Erection of a State Capitol at Carson City. | [*filet*] | . . . | Approved February 23d, 1869. | . . . | [Carson City: Henry R. Mighels, State Printer? 1870.]   [568a]

Broadside. 50 x 40 cm. Printed on vellum. Gold state seal at bottom left. Contains the printed date June 9, 1870, when Secretary of State C. N. Noteware certified the piece as "a correct copy" of the 1869 act.

The examined copy is in the cornerstone of the capitol building in Carson City. The recorded microfilm copies were made during renovation of the building in 1978-1979.

NvHi (microfilm). NvMus (microfilm). NvU (microfilm).

NEVADA. *Supreme Court.*

[Briefs. 1870.]

Nevada vs. Central Pacific Railroad Co. Opening brief of appellant, Central Pacific Railroad Co. 86 p. 25 x 17 cm. Imprint on wrapper. [Sacramento:] H. S. Crocker & Co., Printers, 42 and 44 J Street. 1870. CHi. Nv-Ar.   [569]

NEVADA. *Supreme Court.*

Reports of Cases | Determined in | the Supreme Court | of the | State of Nevada, | During the Year 1869. | Reported by | Alfred Helm, Clerk of Supreme Court, | and | Theodore H. Hittell, Esq. | [*short rule*] | Volume V. | [*short rule*] | San Francisco: | Bacon & Company, Book and Job Printers, Excelsior Office, | 536 Clay Street, just below Montgomery. | 1870.   [570]

504 p. 23 x 15 cm. Leather binding. See No. 533.

The *Reese River Reveille* acknowledged receipt of a copy in its issue of May 17, 1870.

Reissued in a stereotype edition in 1879, with volumes 6 and 7, by A. L. Bancroft & Co., and in 1887 by Bancroft-Whitney; issued several times in the twentieth century.

Az. CU-B. DHEW. DLC. In-SC (rebound). M. Nv. Nv-Ar. NvEuC. NvRWL (rebound). NvU. U-L.

ODD FELLOWS, INDEPENDENT ORDER OF. *Nevada. Grand Lodge.*

I.O.O.F. | Office of the Grand Secretary | of the | R.W. Grand Lodge of Nevada, | Carson City, Nev., July 1st, 1870. | To all Lodges Subordinate to the R.W. Grand Lodge, State of Nevada: | . . .   [571]

Broadside. 26 x 21 cm. Line 1 in a compartment. Grand Lodge seal to the left of lines 1-4.

Lists reinstatements, expulsions, rejections, and suspensions from the order.
NvHi.

ODD FELLOWS, INDEPENDENT ORDER OF. *Nevada. Grand Lodge.*

Proceedings | of the | Fourth Annual Communication | of
the | R.W. Grand Lodge | of the | Independent Order of Odd Fel-
lows, | of the | State of Nevada, | Held at Odd Fellows' Hall, Vir-
ginia City, | June 7th, 8th, 9th and 10th, 1870. | [*filet*] | Sac-
ramento: | H. S. Crocker & Co., Steam Printers and Station-
ers. | 1870.   [L572]

[3], 292-387, [1], iv p. Description from title page in bound volume for 1867-1873; see
No. 723. Printed? wrapper.

The Grand Secretary was instructed to get proposals for printing, stitching, and
covering 400 copies, and authorized to contract with the lowest bidder (p. 348).
Payments of $20, $135, and $135 were made to Crocker between September 11, 1870,
and February 3, 1871 (1871 Proceedings, p. 388), but it is not indicated whether the
entire bill was for printing the proceedings.

PEOPLE'S TRIBUNE. *Gold Hill, Nevada.*

The People's Tribune---Extra! | [*double rule*] | Freemen to the
Rescue! | [*thick-thin rule*] | The Voice of the People Stifled | [*fi-
let*] | Is the Press Free? | [*filet*] | Do the People Rule in Storey?
| [*filet*] | When Ridicule and Violence fail to Intimidate a | Puny
Man, should "Legal Advice" | Terrify the Press? | [*filet*] | Will not
Every True Man in Storey Insist upon | His Right to Read the True
Voice of the | People in their own Papers? | [*filet*] | . . . | [1870.]
                                                                [573]

Broadside. 34 x 18 cm. Lines 1-2 extend across the sheet; the remaining lines are in the
first of two columns.

Conrad Wiegand published the *People's Tribune* from his assay office in Gold Hill
from January to June 1870, as an organ for his seemingly unquenchable capacity for
indignation at one thing or another. *Territorial Enterprise,* February 1, 1870: "Mr.
Wiegand is acting foolishly. . . . The management of the job office of the ENTER-
PRISE does not seem to suit him, and he devoted the most of his hours of yesterday to
the distribution of printed circulars, under the heading of 'The People's Tribune—
Extra'—the greater part of the matter referring to the refusal of the bookkeeper and
business manager of the ENTERPRISE to do his (Mr. Wiegand's) press-work for any
further issues of *The People's Tribune,* and with an unusual flourish of display type
insinuating that the ENTERPRISE is disposed to crush him! . . . The business manager
of the ENTERPRISE furnishes us with the following facts: A considerable amount of
work has been done for Mr. Wiegand and 'The People's Tribune Association' during
the past two or three months, consisting of cards, circulars, programmes, posters and
advertisements—for all of which the regular rates have been paid. The first number of
The People's Tribune was 'worked off' in the ENTERPRISE press room, Mr. Wiegand
furnishing the 'forms' and paper for the edition." The editorial continues on to say

that the *Enterprise* had refused to print further issues of the *Tribune* because of the contents of the first number, which the *Enterprise* said it considered to be libelous, thus opening it to law suits. Others agreed. Shortly after distribution of the first issue Wiegand was summoned to an audience with John B. Winters, a Gold Hill mining superintendent whose integrity had been called into question in the paper. After failing to get a satisfactory retraction, Winters administered a severe flogging to the intransigent publisher. The whipping incident was described in a long letter from Wiegand to the *Enterprise* on January 20. The letter, with a few changes, was reprinted in the February issue of the *Tribune* and was used later by Mark Twain in *Roughing It*.
NvU.

PIPER'S OPERA HOUSE. *Virginia City, Nevada.*

. . . | First Grand Concert | Given by | Miss Adelaide Phillipps, | With the Assistance of | Mr. J. Levy, | Acknowledged by the Press to be the greatest Cornet Player in the World, | Mr. C. W. Rayner and Mr. E. J. Pasmore | [*filet*] | . . . | [1870.]   [574]

Broadside. 17? x 12 cm. The recorded copy has been cropped at head and foot. Alf Doten, whose copy this was, noted in his *Journals* for Friday, June 17, 1870, that the performance was at Piper's that evening.
NvU.

PIPER'S OPERA HOUSE. *Virginia City, Nevada.*

Piper's Opera House! | [*thick-thin rule*] | Programme. | . . . | [*thick-thin rule*] | Novel Act----Revolving Orbs. | By the Gregory Brothers. | [*thick-thin rule*] | M'lle Gertrude | and Her Troupe of | Wonderful Trained Dogs. | [*thick-thin rule*] | The Flying Men of the Air. | With the Perilous Aerial Somersaults by the Inventors, | Jean, Albert and Arthur. | [*thick-thin rule*] | . . . | [1870.] [575]

Broadside. 20? x 10? cm. The recorded copy has been cropped on all sides.
The Gregorys were in Virginia City from January 17 to 22, 1870, according to entries in Alf Doten's *Journals.*
NvU.

PIPER'S OPERA HOUSE. *Virginia City, Nevada.*

. . . | [*thick-thin rule*] | Thursday Evening, June 16 | Programme. | . . . | [*thick-thin rule*] | [1870.]   [576]

Broadside. 20? x 15 cm. The recorded copy has been cropped at head and foot.
Doten Diaries, June 16, 1870: "Even'g took Mrs. M[orton] to Professor [G. J.] Gee's Complimentary benefit at [Piper's] Opera House."
NvU.

REESE RIVER REVEILLE. *Austin, Nevada.* Extra. August 8, 1870.
          [L577]

Reveille, August 8, 1870: "Our extra of to-day was set up in a hurry and was full of typographical errors, some of which altered the sense. Thus in one case the word 'Prussians' should have read 'prisoners,' and in another, speaking of French losses, the figures were 40,000 whilst they should have read 4,000. These are all corrected in to-day's issue, but we will not vouch for the correctness of names of places and commanders." In the same issue, "From our Extra of this morning" covers approximately four columns.

REESE RIVER REVEILLE. *Austin, Nevada.* Extra. August 15, 1870.
[L578]

Reveille, August 16, 1870: "In order to gratify the feverish interest excited by the short dispatch which appeared in yesterday's REVEILLE we issued an extra containing all the dispatches received up to 8 o'clock last evening. To those of our readers who expected to hear of the complete annihilation of the French army it proved rather unsatisfactory. This is not our fault, and had not public expectation been on such a *qui vive* we would not have issued an extra at all." In the same issue are approximately two columns "From our Extra of last night." The *Reveille* had announced its intention in the previous day's issue to put out an extra about the battle of Metz if the particulars "arrive at any reasonable hour."

REESE RIVER REVEILLE. *Austin, Nevada.* Extra. August 21, 1870.
[L579]

The *Reveille* of August 22 contains more than five columns "From our Extra of yesterday afternoon" on the Franco-Prussian War.

REESE RIVER REVEILLE. *Austin, Nevada.* Extra. August 22, 1870.
[L580]

Reveille, August 23, 1870: "Since the beginning of the European war we have issued four extras. . . . An idea seems to prevail in the minds of certain people that we are responsible for the character of the news received. . . . The extra we issued last night called forth an unusual amount of abuse from both sides. Some of the German sympathizers declared that it was a trick of ours to make a few dollars whilst the friends of the other side appeared to come to the same conclusion, adding that we gave the French the advantage on this occasion, so as to flatter the interests of all parties. Others again pronounced it a trick of Mr. Clark, the [telegraph] operator." The same issue contains nearly two columns "From our Extra of last night."

REESE RIVER REVEILLE. *Austin, Nevada.* Extra. September 3, 1870.
[L581]

Reveille, September 3, 1870: "The extraordinary news of to-day, which we published in an extra at noon, almost passes belief. . . . The whole French army at Sedan surrendering; the imperious Cesar of the French voluntarily walking into the arms of his lately condemned enemy!" The same issue contains brief paragraphs "From our Extra of to-day."

REPUBLICAN PARTY. *Douglas County, Nevada.*

Republicans of Douglas County! | Read! [*cut of eagle*] Read! | Do not be Misled by Misrepresentations of Bolters from the Party! | [*fi-let*] | Resolutions, Adopted by the Union Republican Convention of | Douglas County, September 17th, 1870, and the Candidates whose | names are attached hereto are pledged to oppose all Legislation in | conflict herewith. | . . . | [*short rule*] | Daily Appeal Print, Carson City. [582]

Broadside. 30 x 24 cm. Line 1 in an arch over line 2.

Endorses candidates and expresses opposition to a proposed consolidation of Douglas and Ormsby counties, taxation for railroad purposes, and any diversion of Carson River water that would injure Douglas County agricultural interests.

NvGM. NvU (microfilm).

REPUBLICAN PARTY. *Nevada.*

Roll Call | of the | Republican State Convention, | Assembled in Elko, | Wednesday, September 21, 1870. | [*double rule*] | . . . [583]

Broadside. 47? x 6? cm. Both recorded copies are cropped on all sides and torn in two pieces.

NvHi. NvMus.

SUTRO, ADOLPH HEINRICH JOSEPH.

The Sutro Tunnel | And the Bank of California. | [*double rule*] | [*double rule*] | Speech of Adolph Sutro | to the | Miners of Nevada | on | The Sutro Tunnel and the Bank of | California. | [*short rule*] | [1870?] [584]

[2] p. 75 x 52 cm. Lines 1-2 extend across columns 2-7 of eight columns; the remaining lines are in column 1.

The speech covers all eight columns on the recto and four and one-half columns on the verso; the remainder is general news reprinted from newspapers. The last date mentioned in the speech is 1870.

CU-B.

UNITED STATES. *Laws, statutes, etc.*

Carson | Daily Appeal. | [*filet*] | Vol. XII. [*brace*] Carson City, Nevada, Nov. 25, 1870. [*brace*] No. 9. | [*filet*] | Acts and Resolutions | of the | United States of America, | Passed at the Second Session | of the | Forty-First Congress. | [*filet*] | Carson City: | Henry Mighels, Publisher. | 1870. | [Washington, D.C.: Government Printing Office.] [585]

480 p. 22 x 14 cm. Printed wrapper; cloth spine.

On front wrapper: "In order to partially compensate our subscribers for a non issue of our paper in its regular form to-day, we have, at much expense, arranged for the publication and circulation in the form of a compact pamphlet, of the Acts and Resolutions passed at the Second Session of the Forty-First Congress, the Appeal having been selected by authority in Washington to perform such publication. . . . These pages will be found printed in our best type; and the entire contents of the work have been indexed with much care and at no little trouble and expense. As a specimen of book work, hastily executed, we flatter ourselves that this will compare with anything ever done in this state." But it was not "done in this State." On one of two copies at Nv-Ar, Mighels's wrapper imprint has been torn off, revealing below it the imprint of the Government Printing Office in Washington, D.C. Thus, the only work "done in this State" on the 480 page "pamphlet" was the bogus wrapper that was pasted over the original one and the cancel title page described above. Mighels had had a government contract, as one of two publishers in each state, to publish the laws of the second session in the *Appeal,* a job he began on April 27, 1870. But unlike his fellow Nevada contractor, Philip Lynch of the Gold Hill *News,* Mighels published only a few of the laws, choosing instead to print the same material over and over through the spring and summer, possibly to avoid the expense of composition as new laws arrived. Federal inquiries, or perhaps even reprimands, may have caused him to seek another means to satisfy his contractual obligation. And he may have hit upon the device of issuing the pamphlet laws as an issue of the *Appeal* when the State Department sent single copies to all of its contractors on October 3. As a loyal supporter of the Republican Party he may have been able to acquire enough extra copies to send to *Appeal* subscribers through one or more of Nevada's three Republican members of Congress. His ruse seems to have worked, because on December 10 the State Department issued a check to Mighels for $764, the same amount sent to Lynch two weeks later (RG59: Publishers of the Laws, 1861-1870).
Nv-Ar.

VIRGINIA CITY, NEVADA. *Concert.*

Camilla Urso's | Last | Concert | at the | Methodist Church, | Thursday Evening, April 28, 1870. | [*filet*] | . . . | [*wavy rule*] | Doors open at 7. Concert commences at 8 o'clock. | [*short wavy rule*] | Tickets—$1 50 [*dotted rule*] Children Full Price | [*filet*] | Tickets for Sale at Dale & Co.'s, Lillie & Co.'s and Burrall's.

[586]

Broadside. 20 x 13 cm. Decorative rule border. All of the ticket outlets named on the broadside were in Virginia City.
NvU.

VIRGINIA CITY, NEVADA. *Fat Men's Ball.*

Fat Men's Ball. | [*ornament*] | Virginia, April 28th, 1870. | Mr. [*broken rule*] and Ladies. | You are respectfully invited to attend a | Fat Men's Ball, | (Burlesque on New York,) | To be given on Thursday Evening, May Fifth, | [*dotted rule*] at [*dotted rule*] | Athletic

Hall, | Virginia. | [*filet*] | . . . | This invitation is issued by a Committee appointed | by the Fat Men of this city. | Fatty, | Chairman of said Committee. [587]

Broadside. 20 x 13 cm. Line 1 in an arch over line 2; line 6 in a pointed arch. Printed in light brown ink. Decorative rule border. The recorded copy is in an envelope, as issued. Facsimile following p. 314.

"You will be required to dress in such a manner as to personate a fat man, and give your weight at any figure from two hundred and fifty pounds to four hundred and eighty pounds—to be recorded at the door as you enter the Hall; the record of which will be sent to the New York papers, unless you wish your name withheld."
CSmH.

VIRGINIA CITY, NEVADA. *Fifteenth Amendment Celebration.* Programme. April 7, 1870. [L588]

Territorial Enterprise, April 6, 1870: "The colored citizens of Virginia will meet at the Union Club on the 7th instant, where they will have a grand jubilee over the ratification of the Fifteenth Amendment. . . . A full programme of the exercises for that day is published in another column, as well as printed and distributed in various parts of the city."

VIRGINIA CITY, NEVADA. *Masquerade Ball.*

Virginia, Nev. Nov. 23, '70. | M [*rule*] | Sir: There will be a grand | Masquerade Ball | given on the evening of the 28th | Dec. at Athletic Hall, Vir=| ginia, under the immediate super=| vision of Prof. A. Farini. | . . . [589]

[4] p., printed on p. [1, 3] only. 20 x 13 cm. Line 4 in a horizontal S-curve. Mostly script type. First page printed in red ink, the third in lavender. Printed pages in thick rule border.
CSmH.

WHITAKER, OZI WILLIAM. Report of the Missionary Bishop of Nevada and Arizona. San Francisco: Cubery, [1870]. 8 p. [L590]

Eberstadt 127:338. Whitaker visited the four Nevada parishes of the Protestant Episcopal Church in Virginia City, Carson City, Gold Hill, and Hamilton, but did not go to Arizona because of Indian unrest there.

❧1871❧

The 1871 Legislature made an attempt to repeal part of the act creating the office of State Printer, but the bill was defeated (JS, 1871, p.

134). One change was made in his duties, however, when the requirement that he submit duplicate copies of claims against the state to the Secretary of State was altered to make it necessary henceforth that he file duplicate accounts with the State Board of Examiners (SSN, 1871, p. 70); the accounts have apparently not survived.

Expenditures from the State Printing Fund totalled $20,988.36 in 1871, according to the 1878 report of the State Controller (p. 30).

An advertisement on p. cii of *The Pacific Coast Business Directory for 1871-1873* (San Francisco: Henry G. Langley, 1871) indicates that the California Type Foundry Company of San Francisco had furnished type to the J. T. Goodman Job Printing House of Virginia City. Goodman ran his job printing operation in connection with the *Territorial Enterprise,* of which he was proprietor.

All of the newspapers that were active at the end of 1870 continued to publish throughout the year.

BACHELORS' CLUB OF VIRGINIA. *Virginia City, Nevada.*

Mr [*dotted rule*] | The pleasure of your company is respectfully requested at a | Calico Party! | To be given by the | B.C.V. | At National Guard Hall, | Friday Evening, [*dotted rule*] 1871. | J. P. Smith, President. | L. S. Graves, Secretary. | Dancing will commence at 9 o'clock. [591]

[4] p., printed on p. [1] only. Printed in lavender ink, on lavender paper. The recorded copies are in envelopes, as issued.

Two copies at CSmH; one is hand-dated February 17, the other April 14, both in 1871. CSmH.

CARSON CITY JOCKEY CLUB. *Carson City, Nevada.* Poster. October 1871. [L592]

Carson City *State Register,* October 17, 1871: "In printing the posters for the races at the Fall meeting of the Carson City Jockey Club (commencing to-day), the usual announcement that, to constitute a race, 'three or more must enter and two or more start,' was inadvertently omitted."

CARSON THEATER. *Carson City, Nevada.*

Carson Theater! | [*thick-thin rule*] | . . . | [*thin-thick-thin rule*] | Engagement, for Most Positively Six Nights Only, of the | Brilliant Young Tragedienne, | Miss Fanny B. Price! | She will make her First Appearance this evening in Carson, in her great and | everywhere successful impersonation of | Fanchon, | Assisted by Mr. J. Proctor's Talented Company. | [*thick-thin rule*] | This Evening, Monday, Jan. 23, | Will be presented, the beautiful drama, in five acts, entitled | Fanchon! | The Cricket. | . . . [*rule*] | [Carson City:] Daily State Register Print. | [1871.]   [593]

Broadside. 40 x 15 cm.

Reviewed in the Carson City *State Register* on January 24, 1871.

CtY. NvU (microfilm).

CARSON THEATER. *Carson City, Nevada.*

Carson Theater! | in Aid of the | School Building Fund! | On Saturday Evening, July 8th, 1871. | [*thick-thin rule*] | Programme: | To commence with the Extravaganza of | Cinderella! | Or, The Glass Slipper! | . . . | [*rule*] | Daily State Register Print, Carson City.

[594]

Broadside. 39? x 15 cm. The recorded copy is torn in two near the bottom; some of the text is lost.

NvMus.

CARSON THEATER. *Carson City, Nevada.*

Carson Theatre. | [*double rule*] | . . . | [*thick-thin rule*] | The Citizens of Carson are respectfully informed that the manager has, at considerable expense, ef-|fected an engagement with the celebrated | Musical Wonders! | [*dotted rule*] the [*dotted rule*] | Hyers Sisters! | (Colored,) | Who Will Appear in | Two Grand Concerts Only, | In English and Italian. | [*thick-thin rule*] | . . . | On Thusrday [*sic*] & Friday, July 27th and 28th | . . . | [1871.]   [595]

Broadside. 50 x 17 cm.

Issues of the Carson City *State Register,* which had previously printed playbills for the theater, are no longer extant, but Virginia City's *Territorial Enterprise,* in reviewing the performance there in its issue of July 27, 1871, noted that "To-night they appear in Carson City." The variant spelling of "Theater" in line 1 may indicate that the bill was printed by someone who was not familiar with it, perhaps elsewhere than in Carson City.

NvRH.

COUNTY DIRECTORY PUBLISHING COMPANY.

Storey, Ormsby, Washoe | and Lyon Counties | Directory, | Including the Cities and Towns of | Virginia City, Gold Hill, Carson City, Dayton, | Silver City, Empire City, Washoe City, Reno, | Wadsworth, Crystal Peak, Ophir, etc., | For 1871—72, | Containing | the Names, Business and Location | of | Merchants, Miners, Farmers, Manufacturers, Professional Men, | Book-keepers, Salesmen, Clerks, and all Adult Male | Citizens of the County. | Also, | Railroads, Stage Lines, Corporations, | Companies, Mills, Schools, Churches, etc. | Together with a | Sketch of the Cities and Towns Mentioned Above. | [fi-let] | Complete General and Business Directory | of the Residents of Storey, Ormsby, Washoe and Lyon Counties. | [filet] | Published by | County Directory Publishing Company. | [filet] | Sacramento: | H. S. Crocker & Co., Stationers and Printers. | 1871.   [596]

16, [3], 26-471, [1] p. 23 x 15 cm. Title and text pages in single rule borders. Quarter-leather binding; printed boards. Page [1] is on the front board; p. 2 is the front paste-down; p. 471 is the rear paste-down; p. [472] is on the rear board. Advertisements throughout, with a few on colored paper.

The odd use of the singular in line 14 probably is a reflection of the company's usual practice of dealing with one county at a time. The publisher was L. M. McKenney, who published West Coast directories for many years.

Canvassing began sometime before the 13th of July 1871, as stated in the Gold Hill News of that date; Reno's Nevada State Journal acknowledged receipt of a copy in its issue of September 23, 1871.

CSmH. CU-B. CtY. NvHi.

DAGGETT, ROLLIN MALLORY.

The | Psychoscope. | A Sensational Drama in Five Acts. | [fi-let] | By R. M. Daggett and J. T. Goodman. | [filet] | Virginia, Nev.: | Printed by the Authors for Private Circulation. | 1871.

[597]

60 p. 21 x 14 cm. Printed wrapper. On verso of title page: Territorial Enterprise. [sic] Print. Virginia, Nevada. The copies at CSmH and NvHi are interleaved, with the former copy containing many handwritten alterations throughout; it was probably used as a rehearsal copy.

Rollin M. Daggett fancied himself something of a literary light, and indeed he was not without credentials. In 1852 he helped to found San Francisco's Golden Era, one of the most influential literary journals in California history, and was not only a partner but a contributor until 1860. When he moved to Virginia City in 1862 he formed a brokerage firm and the next year was elected to the territorial Council, but his journalistic experience soon brought him to the Enterprise, first as a part-time reporter, later as editor. There were few celebrations or holidays that did not merit a long poem from Daggett; he later wrote a novel and, with King Kalakaua, a book on Hawaiian legends learned during his service as U.S. Minister to Hawaii. From 1879 to 1881 he was Nevada's lone Congressman. Joseph T. Goodman had worked as a printer for Daggett on the Golden Era and knew him well. It was through Goodman, by then part owner of the Enterprise, that Daggett became associated with Comstock journalism. Goodman was a versifier too, and he and his former employer had for many years a more or less cordial rivalry in that line. Goodman finally won a timed poetry-writing contest and became known thereafter as "Boss Poet of the Comstock."

The play on which the two men collaborated was a sensational drama that was fairly typical of the times, distinguished neither by fine writing nor fine dramaturgy. One scene, in a brothel, caused considerable comment, but the play's notoriety was brought about principally because its authors were so well known locally. It was revived in the 1950s at Piper's Opera House in Virginia City by a University of Nevada troupe.

CSmH (lacks p. 3-4). CtY. NvHi (lacks wrapper). NvRW.

DAILY STATE REGISTER. *Carson City, Nevada.* Extra. September 18, 1871. [L598]

Register, September 19, 1871: "Our readers were yesterday informed by our extra of the prominent facts respecting the break at the State Prison on Sunday Evening."

DETTER, THOMAS.

Nellie Brown | —or— | The Jealous Wife, | —with— | Other Sketches, | Written and Published by | Thomas Detter, (Colored,) | of Elko, Nevada. | [*filet*] | This work is perfectly chaste and moral in every particular. | [*filet*] | San Francisco: | Cuddy & Hughes, Printers, 511 Sansome Street. | [*short rule*] | 1871. [599]

160 p. 20 x 12 cm. Wrapper title printed from same type as title page, but with line 7 reset to eliminate mention of Detter's race. Copyright on verso of title page. Facsimile of wrapper in Stanley W. Paher, ed., *Nevada: Official Bicentennial Book* (Las Vegas: Nevada Publications, 1976), p. 210.

James de T. Abajian, in *Blacks and Their Contributions to the American West: A Bibliography and Union List of Library Holdings Through 1970* (Boston: G. K. Hall, 1974), p. 247, called this pamphlet the "first known book of fiction authored by a black person in the West." Its distinction ends there. *Nellie Brown* is set in antebellum Virginia, an area that Detter knew because of his Washington, D.C., origin. The story is a weak one built around a divorce trial, and is not helped by the turgid, unnatural speech of the white characters or the fawning, obsequious dialogue of the blacks, which can perhaps be best described as akin to that favored by contemporary white writers who had not visited the South. The final third of the book is given over to short stories and brief essays on blacks, towns in Idaho, and the Central Pacific Railroad. In the railroad sketch, a paean to the transportation moguls, Detter devotes a single paragraph to Elko, damning it with ironic praise; a tribute to barbers—his own calling—appears in a piece on Idaho City. Detter later became a thoughtful and effective voice for black equality in public addresses and black newspapers in San Francisco.

C. CHi. CLU. CU-B.

EUREKA, NEVADA. *St. Patrick's Ball.*

St. Patrick's Ball! | [*3 ornaments*] | M [*rule*] | The pleasure of your company is solicited | to attend St. Patrick's Ball, to be given | at Mint Hall, on the 17th of March, | 1871. | . . . | Eureka, March 4, 1871. [600]

Broadside. 21 x 13 cm.
NvU.

EUREKA DAILY SENTINEL. *Eureka, Nevada.* Carrier's address. New Year's Day, 1872. 1871. [L601]

Reese River Reveille, January 3, 1872: "We have received a copy of the Sentinel

Carrier's New Year's Address. It is a splendid 'poem' and bears the ear marks of the Sentinel's blond Senior [i.e., George W. Cassidy]."

FREEMASONS. *Nevada. Grand Lodge.*

Proceedings | of the | M.˙.W.˙. Grand Lodge | of | Free and Accepted Masons | of the | State of Nevada, | at its | Seventh Annual Grand Communication, | Held at | Masonic Hall, in the City of Virginia, | September 19, 20, 21, and 22, A.L. 5871. | [*filet*] | San Francisco: | Frank Eastman, Printer, 509 Clay Street. | 1871. [602]

[3], 196-353, iii p. 22 x 14 cm. Printed wrapper. Page [i] is on the verso of p. 353; p. [ii] is a recto page and p. [iii] a verso. Chart between p. 292 and 293 folds out to 59 x 22 cm.

$700 was budgeted for printing the proceedings (p. 329). 800 copies were printed, with 300 left with the printer for future binding (1872 Proceedings, p. 365), at a cost of $785.90 (ibid., p. 370). But, on p. 210 of the 1873 proceedings the cost of printing of the 1871 volume "and other printing" is given as $773.28; this is probably a misprint for the 1872 proceedings.

NvRFM.

GOLD HILL DAILY NEWS. *Gold Hill, Nevada.* Extra. March 25, 1871. [L603]

Doten *Journals*, March 25, 1871: "Arthur Perkins was hung about 1 or 2 oclock this morning by the Vigilance Committee . . . 'Extra' *News* this morning issued."

GOLD HILL DAILY NEWS. *Gold Hill, Nevada.* Extra. September 18, 1871. [L604]

News, September 18, 1871: "Terrible News from the State Prison! The Prisoners in Possession of the Armory—The Prison Guard Shot Down! One Man Killed and the Warden Seriously Wounded! Twenty-Nine Prisoners Escape with Henry Rifles and Ammunition! The National Guards of Virginia Gone to the Prison! Pursuit of the Escaped Prisoners! (From our Extra of this morning.) Gold Hill, Monday, Sept. 18—9 o'clock A.M.''

MINERS' UNION OF GOLD HILL.

Constitution, | By-Laws, Order of Business, | and | Rules of Order, | of | The Miner's [*sic*] Union, | of Gold Hill, Nev. | [*filet*] | Organized December 8th, 1866. | [*filet*] | 1871. | [Virginia City:] Printed at the Enterprise Office. [605]

10 p. 17 x 9 cm. Wrapper title, in decorative rule border.

CU-B. CtY. NvHi. NvRW. NvU (microfilm).

NEVADA. *Governor, 1864-1871 (Henry Goode Blasdel).*

Third | Biennial Message | of | Henry G. Blasdel, | Governor of Nevada. | [*filet*] | Delivered to the Legislature, January, 1871.

| [*filet*] | Carson City: | Charles L. Perkins, State Printer. | 1871. [606]

39 p. 23 x 15 cm. Cloth binding, with gold-stamped title: Third Biennial Message of H. G. Blasdel Governor of Nevada Delivered Jany. 3d 1871. Copies at C and WHi are unbound. Issued as [No. 1] in AJS, 1871, from different type, on 19 p.

Senate concurrent resolution to print 1,000 copies, with 250 for the Governor, 250 for the Senate, and 500 for the Assembly (SSN, 1871, p. 174). The *Reese River Reveille* acknowledged receipt of a copy on January 19, 1871; the Reno *Nevada State Journal* reported receipt of "a bound copy" on January 28.

C. CU-B. DLC. NN. NvU (microfilm). WHi.

NEVADA. *Homographic Charts.* Homographic chart. Fifth legislative session, 1871. [L607]

On January 7 the Carson City *State Register* outlined the general plan of the chart, which was then in preparation by William M. Gillespie, and announced in its issue of January 31 that the chart "will be ready for distribution to-day." An Assembly concurrent resolution passed on January 14 ordered printed "ten copies for each member and attaché of the Legislature, and two hundred and fifty copies to the Secretary of State for distribution among the State officers aud [*sic*] public libraries" (SSN, 1871, p. 169). The *Territorial Enterprise,* in quoting from the *Register* of February 3, noted that "in the homographic chart of the Nevada State government, just issued, the various State officers and members of the Legislature are classified as single, married or widower, except Senator W. N. Hall of Gold Hill, whose state in life is put down as 'comfortable.' "

NEVADA. *Laws, statutes, etc.*

Instructions and Laws | for the | Purchase of Land | from the | State of Nevada. | [*filet*] | Dated March 5, 1871. | [*filet*] | [*state seal*] | Carson City: | Charles L. Perkins, State Printer. | 1871. [608]

22, [1] p. 21 x 14 cm. Printed wrapper.

One of the very few items mentioned by title in PSPC for 1871 is this pamphlet, possibly indicating that the State Printer actually printed it; type faces differ from most of the other work executed during the session of the Legislature. The 2,000 copies printed on April 26 cost $63.36 for composition, $54 for 36 tokens of press work, and $30 for folding and stitching 48,000 pages; no charge for paper is given.

CSmH. DLC. NvHi. NvU.

NEVADA. *Laws, statutes, etc.*

School Laws | of the | State of Nevada, | Compiled and Published by the Superintendent of Public Instruction, | For the | Use of School Officers. | [*state seal*] | Carson City: | Charles L. Perkins, State Printer. | 1871. [L609]

24, [1] p. 21 x 15 cm. Wrapper title. Description adapted from *Check List:* 133, which located a copy at the U.S. Office of Education Library, now a part of DHEW. That copy was transferred in early 1969 to DLC, which destroyed it. See Introduction, p. 10-11.

The State Printer put in his claim for payment to the Board of State Printing Commissioners on July 3, 1871, as follows: 500 copies [composition], $68.84; 8 tokens press work, $12; and folding and stitching, $22.50; for a total of $103.34; no charge for paper is given (PSPC, 1871). It was part of a larger claim totaling over $1,300, which the Board reduced by $189.17; it is not indicated which part(s) of the claim brought about the reduction. The Carson City *State Register* reported on May 18, 1871, that the laws "have been issued."

NEVADA. *Laws, statutes, etc.*

Statutes | of the | State of Nevada | Passed at the | Fifth Session of the Legislature, | 1871, | Begun on Monday, the Second Day of January, and Ended | on Thursday, the Second Day of March. | [*state seal*] | Carson City: | Charles L. Perkins, State Printer. | 1871. [610]

xii, [3], 6-231 p. 23 x 15 cm. Leather binding. On pages [189]-207: Reports of the State Treasurer of Nevada. For the Fiscal Years 1869 and 1870.

PSPC, 1871, records a claim on July 10, 1871, for the printing of 600 copies at $2,706.61: 857,262 ems at $1.60, or $1,371.61; 90 tokens of press work at $1.50, or $135; and binding, $1,200.

The State Printer, who also published the Carson City *State Register,* had the following long comment in the issue of February 19: "It has been charged on the outside that the present legislative body had 'economy on the brain' to such an extent that it was liable to fall into parsimonious measures and defeat the passage of just claims against the State. The action of the Legislature, however, a few days ago in appropriating one thousand dollars for the purchase of one hundred copies of the statutes of this State of 1861, does not sustain this assumption. A bill passed the Senate appropriating one thousand dollars for the statutes named, and was sent to the House, where it was referred to the Committee on Judiciary. While in the hand [*sic*] of that committee, a proposition was received from the State Printer to publish 600 copies of all the general laws unrepealed, in the volume of 1861, and bind the same with the statutes of 1871, for the same sum of money—the Supreme Judges to designate the laws which were still in force. The Judiciary Committee reported the facts as above stated to the House, and recommended that the proposition of the State Printer be accepted, instead of the one providing for the purchase of 100 copies which had passed the Senate. The House, however, refused to accept the proposition made by the State Printer, and voted to pay ten dollars per copy for one hundred copies, instead of one dollar and sixty-six and two-thirds cents for six hundred volumes. After this exhibition of princely liberality on the part of the Assembly, no further fears need be entertained that they will run economy into the ground. So far as the State Printer is concerned, he is not, of course, disposed to complain, as the price was put so low that there was but little if any margin for profit in the work. His principal object was to have the volume of the statutes for 1871 swelled to an average size, which, from present appearances, it will not be, as but ten or a dozen laws have been enacted so far. As there was no money in the offer, he can well afford to have the proposition rejected by the Legislature, if it thinks it is representing the true interests of the State in so doing." Three days later the *Register* reported that Governor Bradley had vetoed the bill, stating that the State Printer's proposition "will be of more practical benefit to the State, and better meet its requirements" because many of the 1861 laws had expired or been repealed, and one hundred copies was insufficient anyway. However, the 1871 Statutes do not include the 1861 laws.

On June 17th the *Register* reported that the Secretary of State had been busy "for a day or two" sending the Statutes to county officials. It said also, understandably but indiscreetly, that the "statutes of 1871 make but little showing in book form, but are well printed and neatly bound."

Az. CU-B. CoD. CtY. CtY-L. DLC. MBS. MH-L. NN. NNLI. Nv. NvEC. NvEuC. NvGoEC. NvHi. NvLN. NvPLC. NvRNC. NvRWL (rebound). NvSC. NvU. NvYLR. OrU-L. WHi.

NEVADA. *Legislature.*

Standing Rules, | Joint Rules, | and | Standing Committees | of the | Senate and Assembly | of the | State of Nevada. | [*filet*] | Fifth Session—1871. | [*filet*] | Carson City: | Charles L. Perkins, State Printer. | 1871.   [611]

35 p. 22 x 14 cm. The recorded copy is sewn but has no wrapper. The copy located at Ia-HA by *Check List:* 135 is no longer in its catalog (letter to the author, August 3, 1971).

C.

NEVADA. *Legislature. Assembly.*

The | Journal of the Assembly | During | the Fifth Session | of the | Legislature of the State of Nevada, | 1871, | Begun on Monday, the Second Day of January, and Ended | on Thursday, the Second Day of March. | [*state seal*] | Carson City: | Charles L. Perkins, State Printer. | 1871.   [612]

257, [1], xxii p. 23 x 15 cm. Half-leather binding.

Perkins's own paper, the Carson City *State Register,* reported on November 16, 1871, that the Assembly Journal "has been printed in a neat volume, which is now ready for distribution."

CtY. CtY-L. DLC. M. MH. NN. Nv-Ar. NvHi. NvLC. NvLN. NvRWL. NvSC. NvU. UU-L. WHi.

NEVADA. *Legislature. Senate.*

The | Journal of the Senate, | During | the Fifth Session | of the | Legislature of the State of Nevada, | 1871, | Begun on Monday, the Second Day of January, and Ended | on Thursday, the Second Day of March. | [*state seal*] | Carson City: | Charles L. Perkins, State Printer. | 1871.   [613]

333, [3], 19, 144, 15, 24, 45, 128, 26, 19, 4, xxiv p. 23 x 15 cm. Half-leather binding.

Half title following p. 333: Appendix to Proceedings of Senate. Each of the messages and reports has a separate half title and each is paged separately. Numbers have been assigned according to the position of the reports in the volume, since there is no table of contents. [No. 1], Third Biennial Message of Gov. Henry G. Blasdel, Delivered to the Legislature, January, 1871, 19 p.; [No. 2], Biennial Report of the State Controller, for the Fifth and Sixth Fiscal Years, 1869 and 1870, 144 p.; [No. 3], Reports of the State Treasurer of Nevada, for the Fiscal Years 1869 and 1870, 15 p.; [No. 4], Report of the Surveyor-General and State Land Register, 24 p. and two folding tables; [No. 5], First Biennial Report of the Superintendent of Public Instruction, for the School Years 1869 and 1870, 45 p.; [No. 6], Third Biennial Report of the State Mineralogist, 128 p. and folding table; [No. 7], Second Biennial Report of the Warden of Nevada State Prison. 1869 and 1870, 26 p. and folding table; [No. 8], Report of Committee on the Defalcation in the State Treasury, 19 p.; [No. 9], Report of Committee on Asylum for the Insane, 4 p.

The Carson City *State Register,* Perkins's paper, reported on October 19, 1871, that the Senate Journal had been published and was "ready for distribution." The Gold Hill *News* commented on October 26 that the volume "is neatly and substantially bound, excellently printed, arranged and indexed, and is a creditable piece of work from the hands of State Printer Perkins."

CtY. CtY-L. DLC. M. MH. NN. Nv. Nv-Ar. NvHi. NvLC. NvLN. NvRWL. NvSC (rebound). NvU. UU-L. WHi.

NEVADA. *Legislature. Senate. Select Committee on Annexation of Utah Territory.* Report. 1871. [L614]

Territorial Enterprise, February 10, 1871: "We have before us the report of the Select Committee of the Senate to whom was referred the subject of the annexation of Utah Territory to Nevada." Noting that the report recommended against annexation, the *Enterprise* stated that it "is little else than a special plea for polygamy," and that "it would take some proof to convince us that it was not prepared under the eye and dictation of Brigham Young."

NEVADA. *Office of Superintendent of Public Instruction.*

First Biennial Report | of the | Superintendent of Public Instruction | of the | State of Nevada | for the | School Years 1869 and 1870. | [*filet*] | Carson City: | Charles L. Perkins, State Printer. | 1871. [615]

45 p. 22 x 14 cm. Wrapper title, in thick-thin rule border. Issued also as [No. 5] in AJS, 1871.

S. N. Fisher, the Superintendent, compounded the confusion begun two years earlier by calling this the "First Biennial Report." In his own mystifying terms it is indeed *his* first, since he had erroneously called the earlier one the "Fourth Annual Report." Actually, the report described here is the third issued by the office, and Fisher's second. See Nos. 442 and 525.

Senate concurrent resolution to print 720 copies (SSN, 1871, p. 176).

CtY. DHEW. M. NvU (microfilm).

NEVADA. *Office of Superintendent of Public Instruction.* Public school register. 1871. [L616]

At its meeting of May 3, 1871, the Board of State Printing Commissioners received the following bill from the State Printer (PSPC, 1871): "No. 34, dated March 24, 1871. 300 School Registers. 1 Blk 42 pgs each 12600 Blks @ $7, $91; 1 Blk 41 pgs each 12300 Blks @ $7, $91; 1 Blk 5 pgs each 1500 Blks @ $7, 14; 5 Blks 4 pgs each @ $7, $70; Title page & Instrns 15180 Ems @ $1.60, $24.29; Binding 300 Books @ 50¢, $150; 135 Tokens Press Work Double @ $3.20, $432; 100 Printed Slips for Supt. Pubn, $7; total, $879.29."

NEVADA. *State Controller's Office.*

Biennial Report | of the | Controller of the State of Nevada, | for the | Fifth and Sixth Fiscal Years 1869 and 1870. | Lewis Doron, | State Controller. | [*filet*] | Carson City: | Charles L. Perkins, State Printer. | 1871. [617]

144 p. 23 x 14 cm. Wrapper title, in thick-thin rule border. Issued also as [No. 2] in AJS, 1871.

Senate concurrent resolution to print 1,500 copies (SSN, 1871, p. 178).

C. DLC. M. NvU (microfilm).

NEVADA. *State Mineralogist.*

Report | of the | Mineralogist of the State of Nevada | for the | Years 1869 and 1870. | [*filet*] | Carson City: | Charles L. Perkins, State Printer. | 1871. [618]

128 p. and folding table. 23 x 14 cm. Wrapper title, in thick-thin rule border. Includes, p. [116]-128: A Catalogue of Nevada Flora, by C. L. Anderson, M.D. Issued also as [No. 6] in AJS, 1871.

Senate concurrent resolution to print 1,500 copies, with 900 for the Assembly, 500 for the Senate, and 100 for the State Mineralogist (SSN, 1871, p. 174).

C. MH-Z. NjP. NvLC. NvU.

NEVADA. *State Prison.*

Second | Biennial Report | of the | Warden | of the Nevada State Prison, | for the | Years 1869 and 1870. | [*filet*] | Carson City: | Charles L. Perkins, State Printer. | 1871. [619]

26 p. and folding table. 23 x 15 cm. Wrapper title, in thick-thin rule border. Issued also as [No. 7] in AJS, 1871.

Receipt of a copy was acknowledged in the *Territorial Enterprise* of April 11, 1871. CU-B.

NEVADA. *Supreme Court.*

[Briefs. 1871.]

Caples vs. Central Pacific Railroad Co. Points and authorities of appellant, Central Pacific Railroad Co. 15 p. 25 x 18 cm. Imprint on wrapper: Sacramento: H. S. Crocker & Co., Printers, 42 and 44 J Street. 1871. Nv-Ar. [620]

Clute vs. Steel et al. Brief of respondents, James Steel et al. 8 p. 25 x 14 cm. Printed on title page: January Term, 1871. Imprint on title page: White Pine Daily News Print—Hamilton, Nevada. Nv-Ar. [621]

Nevada vs. Ah Tong. Brief of appellant, Ah Tong. 17 p. 25 x 18 cm. Imprint on wrapper: Sacramento: H. S. Crocker & Co., Printers and Stationers. 1871. Nv-Ar. [622]

Nevada vs. Central Pacific Railroad Co. Opening brief of appellant, Central Pacific Railroad Co. 86 p. 25 x 17 cm. This is Supreme Court case No. 487, with the preceding and following cases dated in 1871. Nv-Ar. [623]

Ophir Silver Mining Co. vs. Carpenter et als. Brief of appellants, C. Carpenter et als. 26 p. 25 x 18 cm. Imprint on wrapper: E. G. Jefferis' Law Printing Office, Second Story, "Union" Building, Third Street, Sacramento. Handwritten on the pamphlet: Filed February 28th A D 1871 Alfred Helm Clerk. Nv-Ar. [624]

NEVADA. *Supreme Court.*

Reports of Cases | Determined in | The Supreme Court | of the | State of Nevada, | During the Year 1870. | Reported by | Alfred Helm, Clerk of Supreme Court, | and | Theodore H. Hittell, Esq. | [*short rule*] | Volume VI. | [*short rule*] | San Francisco: | Bacon & Company, Book and Job Printers, Excelsior Office, | 536 Clay Street, just below Montgomery. | 1871. [625]

459 p. 23 x 15 cm. Leather binding.

$3,700 was appropriated for the sixth and seventh Nevada Reports (SSN, 1871, p. 109); $3,700 was paid out during the seventh fiscal year (Controller's report, 1871, p. 159). A copy was reported received in the Reno *Nevada State Journal* of August 19, 1871.

Reissued with volumes 5 and 7 in 1879 by A. L. Bancroft & Company in a stereotype edition, and in 1887 by Bancroft-Whitney.

Az. CU-B. DHEW. DLC. In-SC (rebound). M. Nv. Nv-Ar. NvEuC. NvRWL. NvU. U-L.

NEVADA. *Surveyor General.*

Report | of the | Surveyor General | and State Land Register, | of the State of Nevada, | for the | Years 1869 and 1870. | [*filet*] | Carson City: | Charles L. Perkins, State Printer. | 1871. [626]

24 p. and two folding tables. 23 x 15 cm. Wrapper title, in thick-thin rule border. Issued also as [No. 4] in AJS, 1871.

Senate concurrent resolution to print 1,500 copies (SSN, 1871, p. 178). MH. WHi.

NEVADA. *Treasury Department.*

Annual Report | of | C. C. Batterman, | State Treasurer of Nevada, | for the | Years 1869 and 1870. | [*filet*] | Carson City: | Charles L. Perkins, State, Printer. | 1871. [627]

15 p. 23 x 15 cm. Wrapper title, in thick-thin rule border. Issued also as [No. 3] in AJS, 1871, and in SSN, 1871, p. [189]-207 from the same type.

The *Territorial Enterprise* acknowledged receipt of a copy on February 24, 1871.

C.

ODD FELLOWS. INDEPENDENT ORDER OF. *Nevada. Grand Lodge.* Annual report of the Most Worthy Grand Master, to the Right Worthy Grand Lodge of Nevada. 1871.   [L628]

Carson City *State Register,* June 9, 1871: "We are under obligations to Grand Secretary F. G. Ludlow, for copies of the 'Annual Report . . . I.O.O.F.' "

ODD FELLOWS, INDEPENDENT ORDER OF. *Nevada. Grand Lodge.*

Proceedings | of the | Fifth Annual Communication | of the | R. W. Grand Lodge | of the | Independent Order of Odd Fellows, | of the | State of Nevada, | Held at Odd Fellows' Hall, Virginia City, | June 6th, 7th, 8th and 9th, 1871. | [*filet*] | Sacramento: | H. S. Crocker & Co., Stationers and Printers. | 1871. [L629]

3], 368-485, [1], v p. Description from title page in bound volume for 1867-1873; see No. 723. Printed? wrapper. The 1870 Proceedings were paged through p. [388].

The estimated cost for printing was $400 (p. 424). On September 29, $389.55 was paid out, with another $18.50 paid on November 15 (1872 Proceedings, p. 511); the latter figure may have been for incidental printing. The Reno *Nevada State Journal* reported that the proceedings "will be out in a few days, as the MS. is all in the hands of the printer and no doubt, ere this in type," on August 19, 1871;' a week later the *Journal* reported receipt of a copy.

ODD FELLOWS, INDEPENDENT ORDER OF. *Virginia City, Nevada. Colfax Degree of Rebekah Lodge No. 1.*

Constitution | and | By-Laws | of | Colfax Degree of Rebekah Lodge | No. 1, | of the | Independent Order of Odd Fellows, | of the State of Nevada. | [*filet*] | Instituted at Virginia, March 4, 1869. | [*filet*] | Sacramento: | H, [*sic*] S. Crocker & Co., Steam Printers. | 1871.   [630]

28, [2] p. 14 x 10 cm. Printed wrapper, with the error in the imprint corrected. Title and text pages in thick-thin rule borders.

CSmH. NvHi.

SPRUCE MOUNTAIN MINING DISTRICT. *Ordinances, local laws, etc.*

Miners Meeting, | and the | By Laws | Adopted for the Government of Spruce Mountain Mining District. | [1871?]   [631]

Broadside. 39 x 18 cm. Text printed in two columns.

"These laws shall take effect on and after September 26th, A.D. 1871." The district was in Elko County.
NvMus.

UNITED STATES. *Circuit Court. District of Nevada (Ninth Circuit).*
[Briefs. 1871.]

Cole Silver Mining Company vs. Virginia and Gold Hill Water Company et als. In equity. Points and authorities for complainant, Cole Silver Mining Company, on motion to dissolve injunction. Sacramento: Crocker & Co., printers, 1871. 24 p. Talisman 3:373. [L632]

WIEGAND, CONRAD AARON.

The | Reorganized Republic. | By a Citizen. | [*short rule*] | Reprinted from the Radical. | [*short rule*] | Virginia City, Nevada. | 1871. | [Boston: The Radical.] [633]

14, [2] p. 23 x 15 cm. Printed wrapper; p. [1] is the wrapper title. Printed from the same type as p. 417-427 of the July 1871 issue of *The Radical,* published in Boston, with several changes. In the reprint the type column is shorter, and the order of two sections—"The Abolition of the State" and "Preservation of Land for Settlers"—is reversed. One line has been reset: line 14 on p. 424 of the serial publication, "selves to a sensible point to be determined by law; to a third, repre-" becomes "selves to a point to be sensibly determined by law; to a third, repre-" on line 25 of p. 10 of the reprint. Also, the *Radical* article is signed, "CONRAD WIEGAND. *Virginia City, Nevada, April 17, 1871*"; the only indication of authorship in the reprint is in a listing, on the inside of the rear wrapper, of recent articles appearing in the magazine.

The piece is a typically Wiegandish screed calling for the abolition of all governments subordinate to the federal government.
DLC. MBC. NvHi. PPL (lacks wrapper).

ᴂ1872ᴂ

According to the report of the State Controller for 1878 (p. 30), costs for state printing during 1872 were $4,372.67.

The Republicans regained the office of State Printer for 1873 and 1874 when Charles A. V. Putnam defeated Democrat John C. Lewis in the November election. With his public printing responsibilities finished, Charles L. Perkins sold the *Daily State Register* back to its original owner, Henry R. Mighels, who returned its politics to Republican and its name to the *Appeal.* In anticipation of increased job orders, Mighels bought half-medium and eighth-medium Globe presses and a two-horsepower Baxter steam engine to run them (*Appeal,* September 17, October 28, December 21). When the half-medium press arrived Mighels was ecstatic, describing it in his newspaper of September 17 as "one of the most perfect pieces of printing machinery ever invented," and speculating that it might be "one of the best if not actually the most superior job press in the State of Nevada." The Gold Hill *News,* too, ran a puff for its job printing capabilities in the issue of October 30: "Having received an extensive assortment of the latest styles of type from Painter & Co.'s type foundry, San Francisco, we are prepared to do better job work than ever. Poster work, hand-bills, dodgers, tickets, etc., printed for political parties in the most approved style. Also bill-heads, circulars, all kinds of cards and similar printing done to order with neatness and dispatch, and on the most reasonable terms."

In addition to the *Register-Appeal* change, Carson City gained yet another paper in July. Pioche had a competing paper that suspended immediately after the November election. A newspaper was begun in Schellbourne in July, and the *Territorial Enterprise* picked up two competitors in Virginia City. All other presses that had been active at the end of 1871 continued to publish throughout the year.

DELAVAN, JAMES.

To the Voters of Storey County! | [*filet*] | What I Know About J. P. Jones. | [*filet*] | . . . | [Virginia City? 1872.]   [634]

Broadside. 27? x 12? cm. The recorded copy has been cropped on all sides. Proof, with proofreader's notations in margins. Facsimile following p. 314.

The text makes it clear that Jones was not yet a United States Senator from Nevada; his first attempt at the office was during the legislative election campaign of 1872. Delavan carries on at some length about Jones's alleged dishonesty, calling him the "prince of Oily Gammons" and suggesting that if he were elected "it will be regretted and repented of in sackcloth and ashes, except [by] those perhaps who may be bought to vote for him." Delavan's peroration is: "Voters of Nevada, will you place yourselves in a situation to be ashamed of what you have done? Will you be the dupes of a faithless politician, and be held up to ridicule by our sister States? God forbid! If you would not be thus ashamed and ridiculed, do not cast your votes where they will conduce to the elevation of JOHN P. JONES to the United States Senate." Despite Delavan's admonition, the 1873 Legislature elected Jones to the Senate, where he remained for thirty years. See No. 703.
NvU.

DEMOCRATIC PARTY. *Lyon County, Nevada.*

Democratic | —and— | Liberal Republican Ticket | [*short rule*] |

. . . | [*filet*] | Lyon County Ticket. | [*short rule*] | . . . | Justice
of the Peace, Dayton Precinct, W. W. Harris | [1872.]   [635]

Broadside. 17 x 7 cm. Partial use of the same type as in No. 636; same type as in Nos.
637-639. There was no press in Lyon County in 1872.

Dissatisfaction with President Grant during his first term brought about the formation in 1872 of the Liberal Republican party, whose support for resumption of specie
payments prompted great interest in a state whose economy was based largely on
silver mining. When the Democrats selected the same national ticket of Horace
Greeley and B. Gratz Brown there was some expectation in Nevada that the coalition
would be successful. There were few statewide contests in 1872, however, and local
races engendered the most excitement. The Legislature was to elect a U.S. Senator the
following year, and voters found themselves tempted less by ideological considerations than by the large amounts of money made available by senatorial candidate
John P. Jones. The Democratic-Liberal Republican partnership thus had a lesser
impact on Nevada than might have been expected; political tickets are among the few
remaining proofs that it ever existed. But see No. 735.
NvMus.

DEMOCRATIC PARTY. *Lyon County, Nevada.*

Democratic and | Liberal Republican | Ticket. | [*short rule*] | . . .
| [*filet*] | Lyon County Ticket. | [*short rule*] | . . . | [*short rule*]
| Dayton Precinct. | [*short rule*] | . . . | [1872.]   [636]

Broadside. 20 x 7 cm. See No. 635.
NvMus.

DEMOCRATIC PARTY. *Lyon County, Nevada.*

Democratic and | Liberal Republican | Ticket. | [*short rule*] | . . .
| [*filet*] | Lyon County Ticket. | [*short rule*] | . . . | [*short rule*]
| Sutro Precinct. | [*short rule*] | . . . | [1872.]   [637]

Broadside. 20 x 7 cm. See No. 635.
NvMus.

DEMOCRATIC PARTY. *Storey County, Nevada.*

Democratic and Liberal | Republican Ticket. | [*filet*] | . . . |
Justices of the Peace—Virginia: | . . . | Constables—Virginia:
| . . . | [1872.]   [638]

Broadside. 25 x 9 cm. See No. 635.
NvMus.

DEMOCRATIC PARTY. *Storey County, Nevada.*

Democratic | —and— | Liberal Republican Ticket | [*short rule*] |

. . . | [*filet*] | Storey County Ticket | [*short rule*] | . . . | [1872.]

[639]

Broadside. 20 x 7 cm. See No. 635.

NvMus.

DEMOCRATIC PARTY. *Washoe County, Nevada.*

Democratic and Liberal Republican | National Ticket. | . . . | For state Printer, C. A. V. Putnam. | [*double rule*] | County Ticket. | For state senator, William Thompson. | . . . | [1872.]   [640]

Broadside. 10 x 6 cm. Thick-thin rule border. Printed on gray paper.

Thompson was from Washoe County; a variant at NvHi lists the name of Theodore Winters for the office. The Democratic-Liberal Republican coalition was eroded somewhat in Washoe County by the selection of Putnam, who was a regular Republican. See No. 635.

NvHi.

EUREKA, NEVADA. *Rescue Hose Company No. 1.*

Constitution | and | By-Laws | of | Rescue Hose Company, No. 1, | Eureka, Nevada. | [*filet*] | Organized May 30th, 1872. | [*filet*] | Eureka, Nev.: | Eureka Sentinel Print. | 1872.   [641]

16, [1] p. 15 x 10 cm. Printed wrapper. Title and text pages in single rule borders.

CU-B.

FREEMASONS. *Elko, Nevada. Elko Lodge No. 15.*

Constitution | of the | M.˙. W.˙. Grand Lodge | of | Free and Accepted Masons of the | State of Nevada, | and | By-Laws of | Elko Lodge, No. 15, | Together with | The Ancient Charges, | The Twenty-Five Landmarks of Freemasonry, | and a | Funeral Service. | [*short rule*] | Chicago: | J. W. Middleton, Stationer and Steam Printer, | 6 & 7 East Randolph Street. | [*short rule*] | 1872.   [642]

62, [1] p. 17 x 12 cm. Cloth binding, with gold-stamped cover: Elko Lodge, No. 15. F. & A.M.

CU-B.

FREEMASONS. *Nevada. Grand Lodge.*

Constitution | of the | M.˙. W.˙. Grand Lodge | of | Free and Accepted Masons | of the | State of Nevada: | Together with | The General Regulations, | The Ancient Landmarks, | and | A Digest of the Decisions | Rendered at the Several Annual Grand Communications | of the M.˙. W.˙. Grand Lodge of Nevada, from its | Organization in 1865, to and including | The Annual Communication of 1872: | With | A Complete General Index. | [*filet*] | Virginia, Nevada: | Compiled by Robert H. Taylor, Grand Secretary. | 1872. [643]

[v], vi-xxii, 68 p. 19 x 12 cm. Cloth binding, with gold-stamped title: Constitution Grand Lodge, Nevada. The examined copy is in a private collection.

1,500 copies were authorized, at an estimated cost of $400 (1872 Proceedings, p. 499); the actual cost was $371, with an additional charge of $50 for "Preparing index revised Constitution" (ibid., 1873, p. 210).

The authorized number of copies probably included enough to satisfy the needs of subordinate lodges. For instance, the minutes of Washoe Lodge No. 2 of Washoe City (at NvRFM) for December 2, 1872, acknowledge a notice from the Grand Secretary to the effect that local lodges could have their by-laws printed with the Constitution of the Grand Lodge. NvU has a microfilm copy of the Constitution, also from a private collection, with Washoe Lodge's by-laws substituted for the Uniform Code of By-Laws on p. [65]-68; it is in every other respect identical to the Grand Lodge Constitution, except for a binder's title that reads: Constitution Grand Lodge Nevada, and By Laws Washoe Lodge, No. 2. The minutes of Washoe Lodge's meeting of March 8, 1873, record the presentation of a bill for $26.75 "for furnishing 50 Copies of the Constitution and By Laws of this Lodge, and the Express charges on the same," indicating that local lodges were charged only for resetting the final few pages. Constitutions containing by-laws for other subordinate lodges have not been located.

IaCrM. NvU (microfilm).

FREEMASONS. *Nevada. Grand Lodge.*

Proceedings | of the | M.˙. W.˙. Grand Lodge | of | Free and Accepted Masons | of the | State of Nevada, | at its | Eighth Annual Grand Communication, | Held at | Masonic Hall, in the City of Virginia, | September 17, 18, and 19, A.L. 5872. | [*filet*] | San Francisco: | Frank Eastman, Printer, 509 Clay Street. | 1872. [644]

[3], 358-526 p. 23 x 15 cm. Printed wrapper. Erratum slip between p. 166 and 167.

The 1872 communication allocated $800 for printing the proceedings (p. 367). The cost for this job "and other printing" was $773.28 (1873 Proceedings, p. 210), although there is another entry on the same page for $23.50 for "Printing miscellaneous proceedings." 800 copies were printed and "disposed of in accordance with previous custom and the requirements of this Grand Lodge" (ibid., p. 221), i.e. 500 were issued in wrappers and the remaining 300 were retained by the printer for future binding.

NvHi. NvRFM. NvU.

KNIGHTS OF THE ANCIENT UNIVERSAL BROTHERHOOD. *Belmont, Nevada. Retreat No. 5.* Constitution and by-laws of Retreat No. 5, K.A.U.B. Belmont, Nye Co., Nev., 1872. 16 p. Printed wrapper. [L645]

Dawson 208:838. The *Reese River Reveille* of April 13, 1872, recorded receipt of a copy.

LIBERAL REPUBLICAN PARTY. *Storey County, Nevada.*

Liberal Republican and Demo-|cratic Ticket. | In Union is Strength | . . . | School Trustees, Gold Hill—J. W. L. Hunt, | S. W. Chubbuck, O. T. Barber. | [1872.]   [646]

Broadside. 22 x 7 cm. Line 3 in banner held by eagle poised above clasped hands. Essentially the same candidates as the Storey County regular Republican ticket described in No. 673, but printed from different type.
NvMus.

LIBERAL REPUBLICAN PARTY. *Washoe County, Nevada.*

Liberal Republican & Dem-|ocratic Ticket. | [*short rule*] | . . . | [*filet*] | County Ticket. | [*short rule*] | For State Senator, | Theo-dore Winters. | . . . | [1872.]   [647]

Broadside. 17 x 6 cm. Printed on yellow paper.
Winters was from Washoe County.
NvHi.

LYON COUNTY, NEVADA. *Board of Registration.*

List of Voters | Registered for the | General Election, | —on— | Tuesday, Nov. 5th, 1872. | [*filet*] | Spring Valley Precinct, Lyon Co., Nev. | . . .   [648]

Broadside. 10? x 8 cm. The recorded copy has been cropped at head and foot. List printed in two columns. There was no press in Lyon County in 1872.
NvMus.

LYON COUNTY, NEVADA. *Board of Registration.*

List of Voters | Registered for the | General Election, Tuesday, Nov. 5, 1872 | [*filet*] | Dayton Precinct, Lyon County, Nev. | . . .   [649]

Broadside. 19 x 11 cm. List printed in four columns. See No. 648.
NvMus.

METHODIST EPISCOPAL CHURCH. *Conferences. Nevada.*

Minutes | of the | Nevada Annual Conference | of the | Methodist Episcopal Church, | Eighth Session, | Held in | Sierraville, Cal., Aug. 15-18, A.D. 1872. | [*short rule*] | San Francisco: | Cubery & Company, Book, Job and Ornamental Printers, | 536 Market Street, Just Below Montgomery. | 1872.   [650]

11, [2] p. 21? x 13? cm. Both recorded copies are in bound volumes with other minutes.

The minutes of the first session in 1865 may not have been printed; minutes of the second through fifth sessions, 1866-1869, were issued with the minutes of the California Conference. Minutes for the sixth and seventh sessions in 1870 and 1871 have not been located, while those for the ninth session, held in 1873 at Truckee, California, exist only in typed form at CBPac. The Nevada Conference included several California counties that lay to the east of the Sierra Nevada mountains.

CBPac. NcLjUM.

NEVADA. *State Library*.

Catalogue | of the | Nevada State Library, | 1872. | [*filet*] | J. D. Minor, Secretary of State, | and | Ex-Officio State Librarian. | [*state seal*] | Carson City: | Charles L. Perkins, State Printer. | 1872.

[651]

116 p. 23 x 14 cm. Issued with printed wrapper and in blind-stamped cloth binding. Title, half titles, and text pages in single rule borders.

DLC. In (wrapper). M. Nv (cloth). WHi.

NEVADA. *Supreme Court*.

[Briefs. 1872.]

Leahigh vs. White. Brief of respondent, E. A. White. 21 p. 25 x 18 cm. Imprint on wrapper: San Francisco: Carr, Dunn & Newhoff, Printers, N.E. Corner Sacramento and Leidesdorff Streets. 1872. Nv-Ar.   [652]

Mosier & Guptil vs. Caldwell & Wilson. Respondents' brief on rehearing, Caldwell & Wilson. 10 p. 25 x 18 cm. Imprint on wrapper: C. A. Murdock & Co., Printers, 532 Clay Street, San Francisco. Handwritten on the pamphlet: Filed March 18th 1872 Alfred Helm Clerk. Nv-Ar.   [653]

Welland et al. vs. Huber. Brief of appellants, Henry Welland et al. 13 p. 26 x 19 cm. Imprint on wrapper: San Jose Mercury Steam Job Printing Office: 1872. Nv-Ar.

[654]

NEVADA. *Supreme Court*.

Reports of Cases | Determined in | The Supreme Court | of the | State of Nevada, | During the Year 1871. | Reported by | Alfred Helm, Clerk of Supreme Court, | and | Theodore H. Hittell, Esq. | [*short rule*] | Volume VII. | [*short rule*] | San Francisco: | Bacon & Company, Book and Job Printers, Excelsior Office, | 536 Clay Street, just below Montgomery. | 1872.   [655]

518 p. 23 x 15 cm. Leather binding. See No. 625.

The *Reese River Reveille* acknowledged receipt of a copy on July 2, 1872. Reissued with volumes 5-6 in 1879 by A.L. Bancroft & Company in a stereotype edition, and in 1887 by Bancroft-Whitney.

Az. CU-B. DHEW. DLC. In-SC (rebound). M. Nv. Nv-Ar. NvEuC. NvRWL. NvU. U-L. UU-L.

ODD FELLOWS, INDEPENDENT ORDER OF. *Eureka, Nevada. Eureka Lodge No. 22.*

Constitution, | By-Laws and Rules of Order | of | Eureka Lodge, No. 22, | of the | Independent Order of Odd Fellows | of the | State of Nevada. | [*filet*] | Instituted at Eureka, March 14, 1872. | [*filet*] | Eureka: | Eureka Sentinel Print. | 1872.　　　[656]

72 p. 14? x 10? cm. The recorded copy has been trimmed and bound. Printed wrapper. Membership certificate, not counted in pagination, precedes title page; title and text pages in single rule borders.

CU-B.

ODD FELLOWS, INDEPENDENT ORDER OF. *Nevada. Grand Lodge.*

Fifty-Third Anniversary | I.O.O.F. | The pleasure of your Company with Ladies is respectfully solicited | at an Anniversary Ball of the Independent Order of | Odd Fellows, to be given at | Dyer's Hall, Reno, on Friday Evening, April 26, 1872. | [*filet*] | . . .
　　　[657]

[4] p., printed on p. [1] only. 19 x 12 cm. Line 1 in an arch over line 2; line 2 in an ornamental compartment. Printed in red ink; edge-embossed.

NvHi.

ODD FELLOWS, INDEPENDENT ORDER OF. *Nevada. Grand Lodge.*

Proceedings | of the | Sixth Annual Communication | of the | R.W. Grand Lodge | of the | Independent Order of Odd Fellows, | of the | State of Nevada, | Held at Odd Fellows' Hall, Reno, | June 4th, 5th, 6th and 7th, 1872. | [*filet*] | Sacramento: | H. S. Crocker & Co., Printers and Stationers. | 1872.　　　[658]

[3], 490-630, vi p. 22 x 14 cm. Printed wrapper.

The estimated cost of printing was $400 (p. 585). On October 5, 1872, $502 was paid to Crocker; on January 27, 1873, another $29; and on May 30, 1873, $10 (1873 Proceedings, p. 666). The latter two amounts may have been for incidental printing. A copy was included in the cornerstone of the Virginia City Odd Fellows' Hall (Gold Hill *News*, October 16, 1872).

CU-B.

PIPER'S OPERA HOUSE. *Virginia City, Nevada.*

Piper's Opera House! | [*thick-thin rule*] | . . . | [*thick-thin rule*] | First Appearance of Mr. Lawrence | Barrett! | Supported by | Henry Edwards, | Mr. John Wilson | Eben Plympton, | of the California Theatre, and | Mr. and Mrs. Bates | Miss Mandeville, | Mrs. E. F. Stewart, | Mrs. C. Edmonds, | And Miss Nelly Cummings. | [*thick-thin rule*] | Monday Evening, July 1st, 1872, | Shakspeare's immortal tragedy of | Hamlet! | . . . | [*thick-thin rule*] | [*fist*] To-Morrow Evening— | Romeo and Juliet. | [Virginia City: Territorial Enterprise? 1872.] [659]

Broadside. 51 x 17 cm. See No. 661.
NjP.

PIPER'S OPERA HOUSE. *Virginia City, Nevada.*

Piper's | Opera HousE [*sic*] | [*thick-thin rule*] | . . . | [*thick-thin rule*] | Last Night but Three of the | Dramatic Season | [*thick-thin rule*] | Engagement of Mr. Lawrence | Barrett | Supported by | Mr. Henry Edwards, | And Mr. John Wilson, | of the California Theatre, and | Mrs. F. M. Bates! | [*thick-thin rule*] | Thursday Evening, July 4 | The Beautiful Drama, Entitled | Rosedale! | Or, The Rifle Ball! | . . . | [*double rule*] | To-morrow Evening, | Divorce! | [*thick-thin rule*] | On Saturday Afternoon, at 2 o'clock, | Grand Barrett Matinee | [*rule*] | [Virginia City:] "Evening Chronicle" Print. | [1872.] [660]

Broadside. 54 x 20 cm. Facsimile following p. 314.

Advertisement in the Gold Hill *News,* July 3, 1872.
NjP.

PIPER'S OPERA HOUSE. *Virginia City, Nevada.*

Piper's Opera House! | [*thick-thin rule*] | . . . | [*thick-thin rule*] | Immense Success | —of the— | Psychoscope! | [*thick-thin rule*] | Last Night But One | of Mr. John | M'Cullough | Supported by the | California Theatre Company | —and— | Mrs. F. M. Bates! | [*thick-thin rule*] | Sunday Evening, August 18th, 1872, | For the Last Time, R. M. Daggett and J. T. Goodman's Great Sensational Play, | The Psychoscope | . . . | [*thick-thin rule*] | [*fist*] Monday Evening, August 19,— | Farewell Benefit | and Last Appearance of | Mr. John M'Cullough | When a Monster Bill of Attraction will be given | [Virginia City: Territorial Enterprise? 1872.] [661]

Broadside. 51 x 17 cm.

The play, written by the proprietors of the *Territorial Enterprise* (see No. 597), had its first performance four days earlier. Not unsurprisingly, it was reviewed favorably in the *Enterprise,* but the Gold Hill *News* found it to be flawed. Since most performances on the Comstock received uniformly good notices in local newspapers, the *News* review may have been more a reflection of the rivalry between the two papers than anything else. It seems probable, considering the play's authorship, that the playbill was printed by the job press of the *Enterprise;* format similarities between this and the one described in No. 659 suggest that the latter bill was printed there as well.
CSmH.

REESE RIVER REVEILLE. *Austin, Nevada.* Extra. November 30, 1872.
[L662]

Reveille, November 30, 1872: "Death of Horace Greeley.—Our dispatches to-day contain the mournful intelligence of the death of the above named eminent journalist, philosopher and philanthropist, whose spirit forsook its mortal tenement at half-past 6 o'clock last evening. Immediately upon the receipt of the news we issued an extra, containing the dispatch, which we circulated gratuitously throughout the city."

REPUBLICAN PARTY. *Esmeralda County, Nevada.*

Republican | National Ticket. | [*filet*] | . . . | [*filet*] | Esmeralda County Ticket. | [*short rule*] | . . . | [1872.]   [663]

Broadside. 22 x 10 cm. There was no press in Esmeralda County in 1872.
The ticket contains the names of 1872 Republican national candidates.
NvMus.

REPUBLICAN PARTY. *Lyon County, Nevada.*

Delegates to | Republican County Convention | [*filet*] | Dayton Precinct. | . . . | [1872?]   [664]

Broadside. 13 x 7 cm. There was no press in Lyon County in 1872.
Tentatively dated as 1872 because surrounding items in the scrapbook in which the recorded copy is mounted are from 1872.
NvMus.

REPUBLICAN PARTY. *Lyon County, Nevada.*

For Pr[esident] | Ulysses S. [Grant] | . . . | [*short rule*] | Lyon County | Union Republican Ticket. | . . . | [1872.]   [665]

Broadside. 21 x 8 cm. The top right corner of the recorded copy has been torn off, affecting the text. See No. 664.
NvU.

REPUBLICAN PARTY. *Lyon County, Nevada.*

For State Senator, | Theodore S. Davenport. | [*filet*] | Delegates to | Union Republican County Convention | [*short rule*] | . . . | [1872.]   [666]

Broadside. 8? x 8? cm. The recorded copy has been cropped all around. See No. 664.
Davenport was the winning candidate for the state Senate from Lyon County in 1872.
NvMus.

REPUBLICAN PARTY. *Lyon County, Nevada.*

Union Republican Primary Ticket. | [*filet*] | Dayton Precinct. | [*short rule*] | Delegates. | . . . | [1872?]   [667]

Broadside. 8? x 7? cm. The recorded copy has been cropped all around. Printed on purple paper. See No. 664.

On the recorded copy the name of C. F. Chatterton has been crossed off and R. Midgley penciled in. Tentatively dated as 1872 because surrounding items in the scrapbook in which the recorded copy is mounted are from 1872.
NvMus.

REPUBLICAN PARTY. *Lyon County, Nevada.*

Union Republican Ticket | [*short rule*] | . . . | For State Senator, | T. S. Davenport. | For Assemblymen, | James Crawford, B. F. Carrick, | James W. Dillon. | . . . | [1872.]   [668]

Broadside. 21 x 8 cm. Same type as on tickets described in Nos. 671-673. See Nos. 664 and 666.

There are at least three variants, all mounted in the same scrapbook in which the present ticket is pasted. A presumably earlier version (16 x 8 cm.) omits the names of some of the candidates listed above; another lists different names for some offices than either the present ticket or the earlier version. Neither of these variants has a name after the office of Justice of the Peace; yet another does not list the office at all. This last variant has a period after line 1.
NvMus.

REPUBLICAN PARTY. *Lyon County, Nevada.*

Union Republican Ticket | [*cut of U.S. flag*] | Hurrah for Grant and Wilson! | [*filet*] | For Delegates to the County Con-|vention in Dayton Precinct, Lyon | County: | . . . | [1872.]   [669]

Broadside. 12 x 7 cm. See No. 664.
NvMus.

REPUBLICAN PARTY. *Lyon County, Nevada.*

Union Republican | Ticket. | [*filet*] | . . . | Lyon County | Un-ion Republican Ticket. | . . . | [1872.]   [670]

Broadside. 20 x 7 cm. See No. 664.
NvMus.

REPUBLICAN PARTY. *Storey County, Nevada.*

Union Republican Ticket. | [*short rule*] | . . . | For State Sena-tors, | C. C. Stevenson, W. S. Hobart. | . . . | [1872.]   [671]

Broadside. 20 x 8 cm. See Nos. 668 and 672.
Stevenson and Hobart, who won their races, were from Storey County.
NvMus.

REPUBLICAN PARTY. *Storey County, Nevada.*

Union Republican Ticket. | [*short rule*] | . . . | For State Senators, | Jewett W. Adams, W. E. F. Deal | . . . | [1872.]   [672]

Broadside. 21 x 8 cm. See Nos. 668 and 671.

The spirit of ecumenism brought about by the Democratic-Liberal Republican coalition in 1872 was manifested also in this regular Republican ticket: Adams and Deal, both from Storey County, were Democrats; both men lost.
NvMus.

REPUBLICAN PARTY. *Storey County, Nevada.*

Union Republican Ticket. | [*short rule*] | . . . | For State Senators, | Jewett W. Adams, W. E. F. Deal. | . . . | School Trustees, Gold Hill—J. W. L. Hunt, | S. W. Chubbuck, O. T. Barber. | [1872.]
[673]

Broadside. 21 x 7 cm. See Nos. 646 and 671-672.
NvMus.

REPUBLICAN PARTY. *Washoe County, Nevada.*

For Delegates | —to the— | Washoe County Republican | Convention | to be Holden in | Reno, September 18, 1872: | . . .
[674]

Broadside. 10 x 6 cm. Printed on purple paper.
NvHi.

REPUBLICAN PARTY. *Washoe County, Nevada.*

National | Union Republican Ticket. | [*short rule*] | . . . | [*short rule*] | Washoe County | Union Republican Ticket. | [*short rule*] | . . . | [1872.]   [675]

Broadside. 18 x 7 cm.

National Republican candidates for 1872 are listed on the ticket. The candidate for State Printer was C. A. V. Putnam; one of two copies at NvHi has the printed name of J. C. Lewis pasted over Putnam's name and other printed and manuscript changes.
NvHi.

SPRUCE MOUNTAIN MINING DISTRICT. *Ordinances, local laws, etc.*

Mining Laws | of | Spruce Mountain Mining District. | Elko County, Nevada. | [*filet*] | Also: | Mining Laws of the United States, | Embraced in | An Act of Congress | for the Development of Mining Resources of the | United States. | [*filet*] | San Francisco: | Printed by B. F. Sterett, No. 532 Clay Street, Opposite Leidesdorff. | [*short rule*] | 1872.   [676]

8 p. 23 x 14 cm. Wrapper title, in thick-thin rule border.
CtY. NvU (microfilm).

UNITED STATES. *Laws, statutes, etc.* Laws of the 42nd Congress, 2nd Session: supplements to the Gold Hill *News*. Salem, Oregon: Oregon Statesman, 1872. [L677]

Doten Diaries, May 1, 1872: "I published supplement of the United States Laws passed at 42nd Congress — First I have published — Got them from Oregon from S A Clarke — of the Oregon *Statesman* — 250 of them — Sent them out folded in each copy of the *News*." Clarke began issuing laws supplements with the weekly editions of the *Statesman* on March 20 and sent out twelve more supplements through November 12. At least as early as 1870, Clarke had furnished the laws as supplements for other papers as well as issuing them with the *Statesman*. On September 27, 1870, he wrote to Oregon Senator Henry Winslow Corbett, commenting that he wanted "all papers made out so that you can collect the amounts due for the several papers I am publishing supplements for" (OrHi: Corbett Papers). There is no evidence that Clarke printed the laws for Nevada papers in 1870, since records at DNA indicate direct payments from the U.S. State Department to the proprietors of the two newspapers in Nevada that were authorized to print the laws and not, as in 1872, to Corbett *for* the papers (RG59: Publishers of the Laws, 1861-1870); the same is true for 1871 and for the brief period after 1872 when local papers printed federal laws (ibid., 1871-1874). On November 14 Doten sent his affidavit and bill to the State Department, which issued a check for $776 payable to Corbett on December 6 (ibid.), and on December 17 Doten received a personal check from Corbett "for $388 in currency, being my pay for printing the U S Laws of the last session of Congress, or my half, dividing with S A Clarke of Salem, Oregon, who did the printing for me." Doten was able to cash the check at the Bank of California in Gold Hill for only 88½¢ on the dollar, or $343.38.

It is almost certain that supplements issued with the *News* bore no identification of the *Statesman* office as printer, since in 1870 the *Statesman* had supplied supplements to the Albany (Oregon) *Register* bearing the *Register*'s name. It is also likely that Clarke attempted, through stop-press alterations, to duplicate the typography of the identifying lines for each of the papers, since each of them was almost certainly an exchange of the *Statesman* and he would know the type faces used by each. But there are perhaps more questions to be asked than are answered here. Very little that Alf Doten did escaped mention in his Diaries, so it is both unusual and perplexing that he did not say how he learned of Clarke's stable of newspapers for which supplements were furnished. It is also puzzling that he received half of the $776 paid for issuing the supplements when Clarke did all of the work unless, as seems probable, part of the arrangement was that Doten kick back a portion of his pay to Corbett and Clarke. See No. L678.

UNITED STATES. *Laws, statutes, etc.* Laws of the 42nd Congress, 2nd Session: supplements to the Reno *Nevada State Journal*. Salem, Oregon: Oregon Statesman, 1872. [L678]

Records at DNA (RG59: Publishers of the Laws, 1871-1874) indicate that the U.S. State Department on December 6, 1872, issued a check to Oregon Senator Henry

Winslow Corbett for "[W. H. H.] Fellows & [C. C.] Powning" of the *Nevada State Journal* for issuing the laws of the second session of the 42nd Congress; see No. L677.

UNITED STATES. *Marshal. Nevada.*

Notice | [*thick-thin rule*] to [*thick-thin rule*] | Illegal Voters! | [*filet*] | Owing to reliable information I have received, and which I have in my | possession, that many men have been illegally registered, I hereby give | notice that in pursuance of an Act of Congress, approved May 31, 1870, | entitled "An Act to enforce the rights of Citizens of the United States to | vote in the several States of this Union, and for other purposes," I shall | cause the arrest of any person illegally registered who votes or attempts | to vote, or any person voting or attempting to vote in the name of any other | person, whether living, dead, or fictitious; or who shall vote or attempt | to vote more than once in this County, on the 5th day of November, 1872. | . . . | Geo. I. Lammon, | U.S. Marshall [*sic*] for District Nevada.   [679]

Broadside. 13? x 20? cm. The recorded copy has been cropped on all sides. NvMus.

VIRGINIA CITY, NEVADA. *Fire Department.*

Laws | of the | Virginia Fire Department, | Comprising | The Acts of the Legislature of the State of Nevada | In Relation to the Fire Department. | Also, | The Laws Passed by the Board of Delegates for | the Government of the Department, | Together with the | Act of Incorporation of the Virginia City Fire | Department Charitable Fund. | [*filet*] | Sacramento: | H. S. Crocker & Co., Steam Printers, J Street, Near Second. | 1872.   [680]

26 p. 18 x 11 cm. Printed wrapper. NvHi.

YELLOW JACKET SILVER MINING COMPANY.

Annual Report | of the | Yellow Jacket Silver Mining Co. | July 1st, A.D. 1872. | [*filet*] | Gold Hill, Nevada: | Printed at the Office of the Daily News. | 1872.   [681]

12 p. 22 x 14 cm. Printed wrapper, printed in blue ink. Title and text pages in a red decorative single rule border.

The *News* reported on August 3, 1872, that it had been "furnished with a copy," which may have been the manuscript; two days later the *News* reported that the "Yellow Jacket report is issued in pamphlet form, as usual."
CSmH. NvHi.

～1873～

In mid-1872, before the political parties had named their choices for statewide offices, the *Reese River Reveille* in Austin called upon them to nominate men who were practical printers for State Printer, noting on June 18 that "the emoluments of the office properly belong to the members of the craft and we trust that they will see in the future that the office supports no outside paupers." It is not altogether clear what the reasons were for these comments by the Democratic *Reveille,* since the incumbent, Charles L. Perkins, was both a Democrat and a practical printer. But after Republican Charles A. V. Putnam won the job over Democrat John C. Lewis in the November election—and even though he, too, was a practical printer—the *Reveille* recommended that the office be abolished and that state work be given by contract to the lowest bidder. In an editorial on February 1 the *Reveille* claimed that

> that office is simply a reward for partizan services given to parties who never expect to do the work themselves, but screw down the printer who really does it to the lowest possible notch, the State official pocketing all the profits without any further trouble. Whatever money he makes out of it is just so much squandered by the State without any benefit to the craft. The talk about the outlay for material which the State Printer elect is compelled to make in order to execute the work is the veriest bosh; the Carson Appeal, Virginia Enterprise, and probably other establishments in the western part of the State are in possession of ample material to do it without the purchase of an additional dollar's worth, and as a simple act of justice to them as well as to the State they ought to have the chance of competing for it without the intervention of a third party who does not own as much as a composing stick.

The legislative correspondent of the Gold Hill *News,* Toby Green [pseudonym of Fred H. Hart], noted on February 15 the "wide-spread complaint throughout the session of the dilatoriness of the State Printer in completing and returning the State Work," and wrote that Senator J. B. Moore had given notice of a bill to abolish the office. Ten days later Green wrote to the *News* that Moore had introduced his bill and added that "there are, undoubtedly, abuses in the office of the State Printer, but I think they will be remedied by legislation, without the abolition of the office." Indeed the office was not abolished and the Legislature instead passed an Assembly bill increasing the term of office of the State Printer from two years to four (SSN, 1873, p. 52). In commenting on the latter bill before its passage, the legislative reporter of the Reno *Nevada State Journal* declared on January 18 that "if the term were four years the State Printer would be enabled to have all the material necessary to perform the work here in Carson, whereas now a great portion is sent to San Francisco, thus causing the delay complained of." But by the following August 22 the *Journal* had apparently become disillusioned and suggested that the office either be abolished and the work let out to the lowest bidder, or that the Legislature should "reduce the fees of the office at least one-half," claiming that by following the latter course "the State of Nevada can be saved thousands of dollars annually—at least $5,000." The editorialist added that "the last Legislature should have attended to the matter." It was to be four more years, however, before the office was abolished by legislative action.

The 1878 State Controller's report (p. 30) noted the expenditure during 1873 of $29,792.48 from the State Printing Fund.

On September 2 the Gold Hill *News* published the following: "NEW JOB PRINTING OFFICE.—J. D. Bethel & Co. [of Virginia City] have just received from San Francisco four new presses, several fonts of type and other appliances necessary to a first-class job printing establishment. Mr. Bethel was formerly Superintendent of the Sutro Tunnel Company and late business manager of the Virginia *Chronicle*. The printing of the *Footlight* will be done hereafter in this establishment. We wish the new firm success." And on December 2 the *Reese River Reveille* noted that "we have just received a full assortment of job stock, placing us in a condition to print billheads, letter heads, circulars, cards, etc., in the best style, which will be done at living rates."

But there was also turmoil on the job printing scene. In June the *Territorial Enterprise* job office purchased a complete new plant and engaged a San Francisco printer, George Daly, to set it up. These facts are not in dispute, but nearly everything else surrounding the situation is. On November 4 the *Enterprise* published a long editorial in which it was asserted that members of the Washoe Typographical Union had refused to work with Daly because he did not belong to a printers' union, that his application for membership in the local union had been denied, that the union printers on the *Enterprise* were given some time to resolve the difficulty, and that on failure to do so were fired and replaced with a non-union crew from San Francisco. The next day an even longer article appeared in the Gold Hill *News* over the signatures of J. C. Harlow, President, and three other members of the Washoe Typographical Union's Board of Directors, which refuted many of the claims made in the *Enterprise*. It declared also that international union rules prevented Daly's acceptance because he had been expelled from a San Francisco printers' union as a "rat." Daly himself then joined the fracas, publishing "A Card to the Directors of the Printers' Union" in the *News* of November 6, in which he made uncomplimentary statements about Harlow, whom he had replaced as foreman of the *Enterprise* job office, and another member of the union's Board of Directors, J. E. Eckley; the next day he retracted part of his comments concerning Eckley in an item in the *News*. Also on November 7, the *Enterprise* published a follow-up editorial, the tone of which can perhaps be best ascertained from the following: "The misrepresentations we foresaw are already being busily scattered abroad. We do not refer particularly to the card of the printers; for, though that was a mass of perverted facts and gratuitous assumptions, altogether false in so far as they differed materially from our statement of the case; yet its general tone was more moderate than might have been expected of a set of men who had stupidly opposed their own interests and that of an employer who had labored with them for four months to effect some arrangement by which they might retain the situations they finally lost through sheer obstinacy." Resolution of the problem is not mentioned in available files of Comstock newspapers, although Daly still ran the *Enterprise* job office as late as 1879.

Presses that were active at the end of 1872 in Austin, Carson City, Elko, Eureka, Gold Hill, Hamilton, Pioche, Reno, Unionville, Virginia City, and Winnemucca continued to publish throughout the year, although the plant of the Eureka *Sentinel* was nearly totally lost in a fire that destroyed much of the town in November (see No. L682). Battle Mountain got its first paper late in December, and a paper was started in Columbus in August. Elko's single paper was joined briefly in January by another one, and two new papers in Virginia City published for short periods during the year. Schellbourne's newspaper lasted only into January.

EUREKA DAILY SENTINEL. *Eureka, Nevada.* Eureka Daily Sentinel. Friday, Nov. 21, 1873. We Still Live! Slightly Disfigured, But Still in the Ring!   [L682]

A note in the Carson City *Appeal* of November 25, 1873, said: "We reproduce, as follows, a copy of the entire issue of the Eureka *Sentinel* of Friday Last." The article, which takes up less than one column of the *Appeal*, reported a fire in Eureka on November 20 that destroyed most of the *Sentinel* office. Probably an extra.

FREEMASONS. *Nevada. Grand Lodge.*

Proceedings | of the | M.˙.W.˙. Grand Lodge | of | Free and Ac-
cepted Masons | of the | State of Nevada, | at its | Special Grand
Communication, | Held at Reno, October 15, A.L. 5872; | Also at
its | Special Grand Communication, | Held at Genoa, November
13, A.L. 5873; | Also at its | Ninth Annual Grand Communica-
tion, | Held at | Masonic Hall, in the City of Virginia, | November
18, 19, 20, and 21, A.L. 5873; | Also at its | Special Grand Com-
munication, held at Reno, | December 25th, A.L. 5873. | [fi-
let] | San Francisco: | Frank Eastman, Printer, 509 Clay Street.
| 1873.   [683]

[3], 4-247 p. 23 x 15 cm. Wrapper title, in decorative rule border. The complex
contents are arranged under two title pages.
On p. [1]: Proceedings | of the | M.˙. W.˙. Grand Lodge | of | Free and Accepted
Masons | of the | State of Nevada, | at its | Special Grand Communication,
| Held at | Reno, October 15th, A.L. 5872; | Also at its | Special Grand Com-
munication, | Held at | Genoa, November 13th, A.L. 5873. | [filet] | San Fran-
cisco: | Frank Eastman, Printer, 509 Clay Street. | 1873.
On p. [9]: Proceedings | of the | M.˙.W.˙. Grand Lodge | of | Free and Accepted
Masons | of the | State of Nevada, | at its | Ninth Annual Grand Communica-
tion, | Held at | Masonic Hall, in the City of Virginia, | November 18, 19, 20, and
21, A.L. 5873; | Also at its | Special Grand Communication, held at Reno, | De-
cember 25th, A.L. 5873. | [filet] | San Francisco: | Frank Eastman, Printer, 509
Clay Street. | 1873.
800 copies were printed, with 300 retained by the printer for future binding (1874
Proceedings, p. 258), at a cost of $1,059.95 (ibid., p. 264).
NvHi. NvRFM. NvU.

FREEMASONS. *Nevada. Grand Lodge.*

[*Thick-thin rule*] | Proceedings | of the | M.˙. W.˙. Grand Lodge
| of | Free and Accepted Masons | of the | State of Nevada, |
For the Years 1870, 1871 and 1872. | [*short rule*] | Vol. II. |
[*short rule*] | [*thin-thick rule*] | [San Francisco: Frank Eastman, Print-
er, 509 Clay Street, 1873.]   [684]

[3], 4-192, [i]-ii, [3], 196-353, [4], 358-523, [2], ii-iv p. 22 x 15 cm. Erratum slip
between p. 166 and 167; folding table, not counted in the pagination, folds out to 22 x
60 cm. The binder has inserted leaves between the parts of the volume. Leather
binding. On a red leather patch at the top of the spine: Proceedings of the Grand Lodge
of Nevada; black leather patch at the bottom: Vol. II. 1870-1872. Between the patches:
F. & A.M. Of the 300 copies that were authorized for binding, only 271 were bound
because of damage sustained to the remaining 29, apparently at Eastman's office (1874
Proceedings, p. 258-259). See Nos. 561, 602, and 644 for separate parts of the volume.
See No. 685 for cost of binding.
DSC. ICSR. MBFM (rebound). NNFM. NvRFM. NvU.

FREEMASONS. *Nevada. Grand Lodge.*

Proceedings | of the | M.˙. W.˙. Grand Lodge | of | Free and Ac-
cepted Masons | of the | State of Nevada, | from its Organization,
in 1865, | up to and including the | Fifth Annual Communication, in
1869. | [*filet*] | San Francisco: | Frank Eastman, Printer, 509 Clay
Street, | 1873.   [685]

[3], 4-51, [5], 56-113, [4], 118-205, [4], 210-309, [4], 314-429, [4], 434-531, [2], ii-iv p.
22 x 16 cm. The binder has inserted a leaf between proceedings of the first and second
annual communications. Leather binding. On a red leather patch at the top of the
spine: Proceedings of the Grand Lodge of Nevada; black leather patch at the bottom:
Vol. I. 1865-1869. Between the patches: F. & A.M.

The Grand Lodge had regularly authorized Eastman to print and retain in sheets an
extra 300 copies of each year's proceedings for later binding. The 1872 communication allocated $125 to bind the 1865-1869 volume (1872 Proceedings, p. 367), but it
was reported the next year (ibid., 1873, p. 19) that Eastman was unable to locate the
sheets for the October 1865 session and therefore could not complete the binding
order. Nevada's Masons were anxious to have their bound volume and ordered that
the missing proceedings be reprinted (ibid., p. 207) but, incredibly, agreed to pay
Eastman—again—rather than to insist that he replace them at his own expense. The
title page of the reprinted proceedings, complete with the printer's 1865 street address
in the imprint but with slightly different lineation from the first printing (see No.
329), is: Proceedings | of the | M.˙. W.˙. Grand Lodge | of | Free and Accepted
Masons | of the | State of Nevada, | at its | First Annual Grand Communica-
tion, | Held at | Masonic Hall, in the City of Virginia, | October 10, 11, 12, and 13,
A.L. 5865. | [*filet*] | San Francisco: | Frank Eastman, Printer, 415 Washington
Street. | 1865. The three pages of index at the end of the wrappered issue are not
included here. Based on the initial 1865 cost for printing 800 copies of the proceedings,
the 300 missing copies had cost Nevada's Masons approximately $125; Eastman billed
the Grand Lodge an additional $174 for the second printing (ibid., 1874, p. 264),
bringing the total bill for printing the proceedings twice to just under $300. It cannot
be certainly determined whether the reprinting was done in late 1873 or in early 1874,
since existing Grand Lodge records note only the day of payment of Eastman's bill.
For further discussion of this bizarre episode, see Armstrong, "Frank Eastman and the
Nevada Masons: A Note for Printing Historians," *Nevada Historical Society Quarterly,*
XIV (1971), p. 39-41.

In addition to losing the proceedings of one year, Eastman apparently allowed sheets
from other years to become damaged, because only 281 copies of the first volume
were bound (1874 Proceedings, p. 258-259). The total cost of binding the first two
volumes was $282.50; freight was an additional $24 (ibid., p. 264). Most of the bound
copies of the first two volumes that were still held by the Grand Lodge in 1875 were
destroyed in the Virginia City fire in October of that year (ibid., 1879, p. 350).

See Nos. 328-329, 373, 425, and 508 for separate parts of the volume.

DSC. ICSR. MBFM (rebound). NNFM. NvU.

GOLD HILL, NEVADA. *Public Schools.*

[*Thick-thin rule*] | Rules | and | Regulations | for the | Govern-
ment | of the | Gold Hill Public Schools. | [*thin-thick rule*] | [1873?]
                                                                   [686]

[4] p., printed on p. [1-3] only. 20 x 13 cm. Page [3]: Extracts from Compulsory School Law, Approved February 25, 1873.
NvHi.

GOLD HILL DAILY NEWS. *Gold Hill, Nevada.* Extra. September 20, 1873. [L687]

News, September 22, 1873: "We notice that all of our San Francisco cotemporaries published, telegraphically, in full our account of the recent fatal disaster in the Yellow Jacket mine, as published in our extra of Saturday, and we also notice that all except the *Call* gave us the proper credit: 'From the Gold Hill NEWS EXTRA.'" Alf Doten's *Journal* entry for September 20 has the following: "Rose at alarm of fire at 3 AM — fire in Yellow Jacket — 6 killed & lots asphyxiated — I was on hand & saw all the items — Wrote up account of it — got out 'extra' at PM — Sold about 300 extras."

GOLD HILL MINING DISTRICT. *Ordinances, local laws, etc.*

Laws | —of— | Gold Hill Mining District. | [*thick-thin rule*] | [1873?] [688]

[2] p. 36 x 21 cm. Text printed in two columns, but only about a third of the verso is printed. The meeting at which the laws were adopted was held on October 8, 1873.
CSmH.

HUMBOLDT AGRICULTURAL, MINING AND MECHANICAL SOCIETY. *Winnemucca, Nevada.*

F A [*cut of trotting horse and sulky*] I R ! | [*thick-thin rule*] | The First Annual Fair | of the | Humboldt | Agricultural, Mining & Mechanical Society | Will be Held at Winnemucca, Humboldt County, Nevada, Thursday, Friday and Saturday; | Oct. 23-4-5, 1873. | [*thick-thin rule*] | . . . | [*short rule*] | [Winnemucca:] Humboldt Register Print. [689]

Broadside. 92 x 61 cm. The recorded copy is badly damaged.
NvHi.

HUMBOLDT AGRICULTURAL, MINING AND MECHANICAL SOCIETY. *Winnemucca, Nevada.*

First Annual Ball | of the | Humboldt Agricultural, Mining | —and— | Mechanical Society, | to be held in | El Dorado Hall, | Winnemucca, Nevada, | Friday Evening, October 24, 1873. [690]

[2] p. 10 x 7 cm. Line 1 in an arch over line 2. Embossed border; scalloped edges.
NvHi.

KNIGHTS OF PYTHIAS. *Carson City, Nevada. Damon Lodge No. 2.*

Constitution | [*dotted rule*] and [*dotted rule*] | By-Laws | [*dotted rule*] of [*dotted rule*] | Damon Lodge, | [*lodge emblem*] | No. 2, | Knights of Pythias, | Carson City, Nevada. | [*filet*] | . . . | [*filet*] | Carson Appeal Steam Print, Carson City, Nevada, [*sic*] | [1873?]

[691]

29 p. 15 x 10 cm. Printed wrapper. Page [4]: Charter Members of Damon Lodge No. 2, K. of P. Instituted July 18th, 1873. The list contains nineteen names, two of which were misspelled; on the recorded copy the errors are corrected on paste-over slips. CtY. NvU (microfilm).

MAMMOTH SWINDLING CORPORATION. Big bonanza! Invest while you can at current prices! Unionville, July 15, 1873. Broadside.   [L692]

Check List: 146 called the poster a narrow folio and said that the copy described had had the top portion torn off, but that "Mammoth Swindling Corporation" had been supplied in handwriting. It said further that the broadside had been exhibited at Long Beach, California, before the earthquake of 1933, but that its present location was unknown. It also said: "Before July 15, 1873, all printers of Unionville had removed to Winnemucca. After the county seat of Humboldt County was removed, it would appear that rumors of a big bonanza were circulated in order to arrest the declining prices of Unionville real estate."

MEASURE FOR MEASURE. *Battle Mountain, Nevada.* Prospectus. October 1873.   [L693]

Reese River Reveille, October 20, 1873: "MEASURE FOR MEASURE—A WEEKLY JOURNAL.—Citizens of Battle Mountain, desiring to better make known to the world the facilities and resources of this part of Lander county for trade, agriculture and mining, have engaged the undersigned [*sic*] to conduct the publication of a newspaper, the first number of which will be issued early next month—as soon as the material can be put into operation. . . . W. J. Forbes, Editor. Battle Mountain, Nev., Oct. 17, 1871 [*sic*]. The above is the prospectus and name of the new paper to be established at Battle Mountain." The paper began publication on December 26, 1873.

NEVADA. *Board of Commissioners for the Care of the Indigent Insane.*

[*Thick-thin rule*] | Report of the Commissioners | for | The Care of the Indigent Insane | of the | State of Nevada, | to the | Legislature, at its Sixth Session. | [*thin-thick rule*] | [Carson City: Charles A. V. Putnam, State Printer. 1873.]   [L694]

12 p. Description from half title in AJS, 1873, No. 13.

PSPC, 1873, indicates that 240 copies were printed on February 12, 1873, at the following cost: "Comp. 8 pages L.P. plain 15,212 Ems, $24.33; Comp. 2 pages L.P. R.&F. 3,838 Ems, $8.61; Comp. 2 pages Nonp'l R.&F. 10,450 Ems, $23.51; Press Work 3 Tokens, $4.50; Folding and Stitching 3,840 pages, $2.40"; for a total of $63.35.

NEVADA. *Constitution.*

Constitution. | [*short rule*] | [1873?]   [695]

171 p. 21 x 12 cm. Caption title.

Both recorded copies lack wrapper, title page, and possibly preliminary pages. The last date mentioned in the text cites an act of the 1873 Legislature.

DLC. NvHi.

NEVADA. *District Court. Sixth Judicial District (Eureka County).*

Testimony | of | Clarence King, | in the Case of | Eureka Consolidated Mining Company | vs. | Richmond Mining Company, | of Eureka, Nevada, | at the March Term of the Sixth Judicial District Court, | 1873. | [*filet*] | Eureka Sentinel Print.   [696]

16 p. 23? x 13? cm. The recorded copy has been trimmed and bound. Printed wrapper. Wrapper title and title page in double rule borders. Text printed in two columns.

CSmH.

NEVADA. *District Court. Seventh Judicial District (Lincoln County).*

[*Thick-thin rule*] | The Raymond & Ely | —vs.— | The Kentucky Mining Co. | [*short rule*] | Judge Beatty's Decision. | [*thin-thick rule*] | [1873?]   [697]

7 p. 22 x 15 cm. Wrapper title. Text printed in two columns. In caption title on p. [1]: "State of Nevada, County of Lincoln—In the District Court of the Seventh District."

The decision is signed by W. H. Beatty, District Judge, and dated at Hamilton, December 1, 1873. Judge Beatty found for the plaintiff, The Raymond & Ely Mining Company, after determining that the Kentucky company had located claims in a Raymond & Ely vein.

NvHi.

NEVADA. *Governor, 1871-1879 (Lewis Rice Bradley).*

First Biennial Message | of | L. R. Bradley, Governor of Nevada, | Delivered to the | Legislature, January 8, 1873. | [*state seal*] | Carson City: | Charles A. V. Putnam, State Printer. | 1873.

[698]

21 p. 23 x 15 cm. Wrapper title, in decorative rule border. Issued also as No. 1 in AJS, 1873.

Senate concurrent resolution to print 1,000 copies (SSN, 1873, p. 228). PSPC, 1873, shows that 1,000 copies were printed on July [i.e., January] 17: "Comp. 18 1/2 pages L.P. 1,914 Ems to page, 25,409 Ems @ 1.60, $56.65; Comp. 1 1/2 pages L.P. R.&F. 2,871 Ems @ 2.25, $6.46; Comp. 2 pages Min. R.&F. 6,776 Ems @ 2.25, $15.24; Press Work 25 tokens @ 1.50, $37.50; Folding and Stitching 28,000 pages @ 1/16%, $17.50." The Gold Hill *News* acknowledged receipt of copies "neatly bound in pamphlet form, convenient for reference," on January 18, 1873.

CSmH. CtY. NN. NvU (microfilm). PHi.

NEVADA. *Homographic Charts.*

Homographic Chart | of the | Nevada State Government | [ornament] A.D. 1873. [ornament] | . . .   [699]

Broadside. 57 x 26 cm. Decorative rule border.

Gold Hill *News,* February 27, 1873: "With the compliments of Ed. Kiesele, the compiler thereof, we have received a homographic chart of the Nevada State Government, including the executive, judicial, and legislative departments, and giving the names, age, nativity, profession, matrimonial condition, etc., of each officer and member. It is neatly arranged and printed, and both valuable and convenient for reference. Thanks, Ed."

CSt. NvU(NvMus).

NEVADA. *Laws, statutes, etc.*

The | Compiled Laws | of the | State of Nevada. | Embracing | Statutes of 1861 to 1873, Inclusive. | [*short rule*] | Published Under Authority of Law, by | M. S. Bonnifield and T. W. Healy, | Compilers. | [*short rule*] | In Two Volumes. | Vol. I. [II.] | [*state seal*] | Carson City: | Charles A. V. Putnam, State Printer. | 1873.   [700]

cxli, [3], 591; lxi, [3], 683 p. Leather binding. An errata slip follows p. 591 of Volume I.

Two proposals were made to the Legislature for a compilation of the laws, one by Bonnifield and Healy, and a competing one by a California man named Robert Desty. The Joint Committee on Compilation of Laws recommended Desty (JS, 1873, p. 230-231) for, among other reasons: (1) Desty would furnish 600 bound volumes for $7,200 or 1,000 for $10,000; (2) Bonnifield and Healy wanted $8,000 for their manuscript or $10,000 for 1,000 volumes (500 copies), bound; (3) Bonnifield and Healy's compilation would make 1,800 pages, with typesetting at $3.34 per page, $6,012; press work, 282 tokens, $423; binding, 1,200 volumes (600 copies, 2 volumes each), $2,400; paper, 70 reams, $350; total, $9,185; (4) this cost, added to the cost of the manuscript, would come to $17,185, or $28.64 per copy, and would be $9,985 more than the same number of copies from Desty; (5) Bonnifield and Healy's alternate proposal would work out to $20 per copy, while Desty's would be $10 per copy. But a minority of the committee found Bonnifield and Healy's manuscript to be more desirable because it contained fewer errors and was arranged better. Moreover, it held that the price estimates of the majority were incorrect, citing $3,750 to $4,000 as the estimate of San Francisco's Bacon & Co. (ibid., p. 236-237). In response, the majority issued a bitterly worded reply, which appeared as No. 16 in AJS, 1873. It did no good; the minority opinion prevailed, and the Secretary of State, Attorney General, and Clerk of the Court were authorized and directed to contract with Bonnifield and Healy to purchase their manuscript of the compiled laws, the price not to exceed $6,000 (SSN, 1873, p. 222). The number of copies to be printed was not specified.

On June 20 the Carson City *Appeal* noted that the "Compiled Laws are now being printed by Crocker & Co., with whom State Printer Putnam has made arrangements for the execution of the work." By September 4 the *Appeal* was able to report that the "first volume of the Compiled Laws of the State of Nevada, is printed, and we have seen an advance copy of the same. It is a book of 591 pages, beautifully printed. Volume 2 is now passing through the press. When completed, these volumes will embrace all the Statutes of this State, 1861 to 1873, inclusive, except Special Franchise

Acts, and a few Local Acts, not of general interest. Reference will be found to the latter. They will contain a full alphabetical index, head notes, and analysis of contents of chapters; also numerous references and notes of decisions. All amendments are incorporated in the Acts amended." The *Reese River Reveille* noted on October 7 that the Lander County Recorder had received "to-day" a number of copies "for distribution to the various county officers."

CU-B. CoD. CtY-L. DLC. ICU. IU. M. MBS. MH-L. NNLI. NjP. Nv-Ar. NvHi. NvLC. NvRNC. NvRWL. NvSC. NvU. PU. RPL. UPB. ViU-L.

NEVADA. *Laws, statutes, etc.*

Instructions and Laws | for the | Purchase of Land | from the | State of Nevada. | [*short rule*] | Dated March 5th, 1873. | [*short rule*] | Carson City: | Charles A. V. Putnam, State Printer. | [*short rule*] | 1873. [701]

20, [2] p. 24 x 15 cm. Printed wrapper. Addenda slips tipped in before and after title page.

CU-B. Nv. Nv-Ar. NvU.

NEVADA. *Laws, statutes, etc.*

Statutes | of the | State of Nevada, | Passed at the | Sixth Session of the Legislature, | 1873. | Begun on Monday, the Sixth Day of January, and Ended | on Thursday, the Sixth Day of March. | [*state seal*] | Carson City: | Charles A. V. Putnam, State Printer. | 1873. [702]

xiii, [1], 424 p. 23 x 15 cm. Leather binding. On p. [241]-378, from the same type as in AJS, 1873, and the separate issue: Report of the State Treasurer of the State of Nevada, for the Seventh and Eighth Fiscal Years, 1871 and 1872.

Carson City *Appeal*, June 6, 1873: "State Printer Putnam showed us yesterday a copy of the Statutes for 1873. . . . Put is doing his work splendidly and with great promptness."

Az. CU-B. CoD. CtY. CtY-L. DLC. IU. MBS. MH-L. NN. NNLI. NjP. Nv. Nv-Ar. NvEC. NvGoEC. NvHi. NvLN. NvRNC. NvRWL. NvSC. NvU. NvYLR. OrU-L.

NEVADA. *Legislature.*

Proceedings of the Joint Convention | of the | Nevada Legislature, | Held on | January 22d, 1873. | Also, The | Address of Senator John P. Jones, | Then Delivered. | [*state seal*] | Carson City: | Charles A. V. Putnam, State Printer. | 1873. [703]

14 p. 22 x 15 cm. Wrapper title, in decorative rule border. Issued also as No. 12 in AJS, 1873.

The proceedings deal with the election of a U.S. Senator. Jones's speech accepts the Senatorship and defends his campaign against those who had attacked him for buying his seat.

Senate concurrent resolution to print 2,500 copies in pamphlet form (SSN, 1873, p. 230). 2,500 copies were printed on February 12, according to PSPC, 1873: "Comp. 15 pages L.P. = 28,710 Ems @ 1.60, $45.93; Press Work = 33 Tokens @ 1.50, $49.50; Folding and Stitching 3,840 pages 50,000 pages 1/16, $31.25"; for a total of $126.68.

Gold Hill *News,* February 17, 1873: "Thanks to Assemblymen Stern, Gray and several others for numerous copies of Senator J. P. Jones' noted speech before the Legislature. What have we done?"

NjP. NvHi (lacks rear wrapper).

NEVADA. *Legislature. Assembly.*

[*Thick-thin rule*] | Assembly. | [*short rule*] | Standing Rules | of the | Assembly of Nevada, | and | Joint Rules of the Senate and Assembly. | [*short rule*] | Sixth Session—1873. | [*thin-thick rule*] | [Carson City: Charles A. V. Putnam, State Printer. 1873.]

[L704]

23 p. Description from half title, p. [353], in JA, 1873.

PSPC, 1873, indicates that 400 copies of the Assembly rules were printed on February 1: "Comp. 20 pages L.P. = 38,280 Ems @ 1.60, $61.24; Comp. 2 pages Minion R.&F. @ 2.25, $15.24; Press Work — 8 Tokens @ 1.50, $12.00; Folding and Stitching 11,200 pages, $7.00"; for a total of $95.48.

NEVADA. *Legislature. Assembly.*

The | Journal of the Assembly | of the | Sixth Session | of the | Legislature of the State of Nevada, | 1873. | Begun on Monday, the Sixth Day of January, and Ended | Thursday, the Sixth Day of March. | [*state seal*] | Carson City: | Charles A. V. Putnam, State Printer. | 1873. [705]

352, 23, 34 p. 23 x 15 cm. Half-leather binding. Following p. 352, on 23 p.: Assembly. Standing Rules of the Assembly of Nevada, and Joint Rules of the Senate and Assembly. Sixth Session—1873. Following the Assembly rules, on 34 p.: List of General Deficiency Claims Reported to the Sixth Nevada Legislature, by the Controller of State.

The Carson City *Appeal* of July 23, 1873, reported that the volume had been delivered to the Secretary of State by the State Printer.

CtY. CtY-L. DLC. M. MH. NN. Nv. Nv-Ar. NvHi. NvLC. NvLN. NvRWL. NvSC. NvU. UU-L. WHi.

NEVADA. *Legislature. Assembly.*

Roll Call. Assembly. | [*double rule*] | . . . | [Carson City: Charles A. V. Putnam, State Printer. 1873.] [706]

Broadside. 40 x 8 cm. Double rule border. Names of members of the 1873 Assembly are printed in column 1, followed by two unheaded columns for recording votes. NvMus.

NEVADA. *Legislature. Joint Committee on Compilation of Laws.* Majority and minority reports. Carson City: Charles A. V. Putnam, State Printer. 1873. 8 p.   [L707]

PSPC, 1873, has the following entry for February 24: "composition, 8 pages L.P., 15,312 ems @ $1.60 = $24.49; press work, 6 tokens @ $1.50 = $9.00; folding and stitching, 5,760 pages @ 1/16 = $3.60"; the total was $37.09 for 400 copies. It would seem that a great amount of "fat" would have had to be built into the publication to make eight pages of it, since the majority report covers only slightly more than a page in JS, 1873, p. 230-231, while the minority report covers about a page and a half in the same volume, p. 236-237. It may have been padded with half titles for each report, a not uncommon practice. The majority issued a supplementary report in AJS, 1873, that, with inclusion of a half title, made four pages of somewhat less than two pages of printed matter.

The *Territorial Enterprise* reported receipt of a copy on February 25.

NEVADA. *Legislature. Joint Committee on Insane Asylum.* Report. Carson City: Charles A. V. Putnam, State Printer. 1873.   [L708]

PSPC, 1873, has the following: " Feby 17, 480 Copies Report on Insane Asylum. Comp. 5 pages L.P. = 9,570 Ems. @ 1.60, $15.31; Press Work, 6 Tokens @ 1.50, $9.00; Folding and Stitching 3,840 pages, $2.40"; the total was $26.71.

Gold Hill *News,* February 18, 1873: "We are indebted . . . for . . . a copy of the report of the special committee sent to visit the Insane Asylum at Woodbridge, Cal."

NEVADA. *Legislature. Senate.*

Appendix | to the | Journal of the Senate | of the | Sixth Session | of the | Legislature of the State of Nevada. | [*state seal*] | Carson City: | Charles A. V. Putnam, State Printer. | 1873.
[709]

21, 23, 227, 138, 42, 43, xii, [4], 191, 34, 26, 4, 31, 14, 11, 9, 9, 4 p. 23 x 15 cm. Half-leather binding.

Each report has a separate half title or title page and each is paged separately. Numbering follows the table of contents. No. 1, First Biennial Message of L. R. Bradley, Governor of Nevada, Delivered to the Legislature, January 8, 1873, 21 p.; No. 2, Senate. Standing Rules of the Senate of Nevada, and Joint Rules of the Senate and Assembly. Sixth Session—1873, 23 p.; No. 3, Report of the Controller of State of the State of Nevada, for the Years 1872 and 1871, 227 p.; No. 4, Report of the State Treasurer of the State of Nevada, for the Seventh and Eighth Fiscal Years, 1871 and 1872. Jerry Schooling, Treasurer, 138 p.; No. 5, Second Biennial Report of the Superintendent of Public Instruction of the State of Nevada, for the School Years 1871 and 1872, 42 p.; No. 6, Report of the Surveyor General and State Land Register of the State of Nevada for the Years 1871 and 1872, 43 p.; No. 7, Biennial Report of the State Mineralogist of the State of Nevada, for the Years 1871 and 1872, xii, [4], 191 p.; No. 8, Report of the Warden of the Nevada State Prison, for the Years 1871--1872, 34 p.; No. 9, Report of the Board of Directors of the State Orphans' Home, for the Seventh and Eighth Fiscal Years. Transmitted to the Honorable the Assembly of the State of Nevada, January 30th, 1873, 26 p.; No. 10, Report of Special Committee Appointed to Visit The Nevada Orphan Asylum at Virginia City, February 1st, 1873, 4 p.; No. 11, Report of the Board of Directors of the Nevada State Library, for the Years 1871 and 1872, 31 p.; No. 12, Proceedings of the Joint Convention of the Nevada Legislature, Held on January 22d, 1873. Also, the Address of Senator John P. Jones, Then Delivered, 14 p.; No. 13, Report of the Commissioners for The Care of the Indigent Insane of the State of Nevada, to the Legislature, at its Sixth Session, 11 p.; No. 14, Report of Select Committee on Centennial Exhibition of 1876. Nevada Legislature, Sixth Session, 1873, 9 p.; No. 15, Extract from Report of Committee on Ways and Means on Senate Bill No. 87, "An Act to Create a Board of Tax Commissioners and Define the Duties Thereof," 9 p.; No. 16, Supplementary Report of Majority of Joint Committee on Examination of Compilation of Laws, at the Sixth Session of the Nevada Legislature, 4 p.

Receipt of a copy was acknowledged in the Reno *Nevada State Journal* on July 26, 1873.

Az. DLC. M. MH. Nv-Ar. NvHi. NvLN. NvU. WHi.

NEVADA. *Legislature. Senate.*

The | Journal of the Senate | of the | Sixth Session | of the | Legislature of the State of Nevada, | 1873. | Begun on Monday, the Sixth Day of January, and Ended | Thursday, the Sixth Day of March. | [*state seal*] | Carson City: | Charles A. V. Putnam, State Printer. | 1873.   [710]

375 p. 23 x 15 cm. Half-leather binding.

The Carson City *Appeal* reported on July 23, 1873, that the State Printer had delivered the Journal to the Secretary of State; the Reno *Nevada State Journal* acknowledged receipt of a copy three days later.

CtY. CtY-L. DLC. M. MH. NN. Nv. Nv-Ar. NvHi. NvLC. NvLN. NvRWL. NvSC. NvU. UU-L. WHi.

NEVADA. *Legislature. Senate. Select Committee on Centennial Exhibition of 1876.*

[*Thick-thin rule*] | Report of Select Committee | on | Centennial Exhibition of 1876. | [*short rule*] | Nevada Legislature, Sixth Session, | 1873. | [*thin-thick rule*] | [Carson City: Charles A. V. Putnam, State Printer. 1873.]   [L711]

9 p. Description from half title in AJS, 1873, No. 14.

PSPC, 1873, records on February 14 the printing of 960 copies, as ordered by a Senate concurrent resolution (SSN, 1873, p. 231): "Composition 10 pages L.P. plain 19,140 Ems, $30.62; Press Work 10 Tokens, $18.00; Folding and Stitching 13,440 pages, $8.40"; for a total of $57.02.

The Gold Hill *News* of February 21 reported receipt of a copy.

NEVADA. *Office of Superintendent of Public Instruction.*

Second Biennial Report | of the | Superintendent of Public Instruction | of the | State of Nevada, | for the | School Years 1871 and 1872. | [*state seal*] | Carson City: | Charles A. V. Putnam, State Printer. | 1873. [712]

42 p. 23 x 15 cm. Wrapper title, in decorative rule border. Issued also as No. 5 in AJS, 1873.

Superintendent S. N. Fisher achieved some measure of consistency, if not accuracy, in his numbering of this report, since he had called the one of two years earlier the first. It is not the first, but the third; the one recorded here was the fourth report issued by the office, and Fisher's third. See Nos. 525 and 615.

PSPC, 1873, records on February 8 the printing of 1,000 copies, as ordered by Senate concurrent resolution (SSN, 1873, p. 228): "composition 22 pages L.P. plain 42,108 Ems, $67.37; composition 9 pages L.P. R.&F. = 17,126 Ems, $38.53; composition 10 pages Min. R.&F. 33,880 Ems, $76.23; press work 35 tokens, $52.50; folding and stitching 46,000 pages @ 1/16 %, $28.75"; for a total of $263.38.

Receipt of a copy was acknowledged in the Gold Hill *News* of February 14, 1873. DHEW. M. NvU (microfilm).

NEVADA. *State Controller's Office.*

Biennial Report | of the | Controller of State | of the | State of Nevada, | Transmitted | Monday, January 13th, 1873. | [*state seal*] | Carson City: | Charles A. V. Putnam, State Printer. | 1873. [713]

227 p. 23 x 15 cm. Wrapper title, in decorative rule border. Issued also in a cloth binding, with blind-stamped border front and rear and gold-stamped title. The 1872 report precedes that for 1871. Issued also as No. 3 in AJS, 1873.

1,200 copies were ordered printed by Senate concurrent resolution (SSN, 1873, p. 229). PSPC, 1873, records for February 1 the printing of 1,200 copies: "Comp 29 pages L.P. plain 55,506 Ems, $88.80; Comp. 189 pages L.P. R.&F. 361,646 Ems, $813.70; Comp. 1 page Min. R.&F. 3,388 Ems, $7.62; Press Work 150 Tokens, $225.00; Folding and Stitching 278,400 pages, $174"; for a total of $1,309.12.

The Gold Hill *News* acknowledged receipt of a copy on February 6, 1873.

DLC (wrapper). NN (wrapper). NvHi (cloth). NvU (cloth, and microfilm of wrappered issue).

NEVADA. *State Controller's Office.*

[*Thick-thin rule*] | List | of | General Deficiency Claims | Reported to the | Sixth Nevada Legislature, | by the | Controller of State. | [*thin-thick rule*] | [Carson City: Charles A. V. Putnam, State Printer. 1873.] [L714]

34 p. Description from half title at end of JA, 1873.

PSPC, 1873, records for February 24 the printing of 240 copies: "Comp. 8 pages L.P. = 13,398 Ems plain, $21.43; Comp. 27 pages L.P. R. and F. = 51,678 Ems, $129.19; Press Work 6 Tokens, $9.00; Folding and Stitching 9,120 pages, $5.70"; for a total of $165.32.

The date in PSPC was apparently that of entry rather than of printing, because the *Reese River Reveille* acknowledged receipt of the "pamphlet" on January 30, 1873.

NEVADA. *State Mineralogist.*

Biennial Report | of the | State Mineralogist | of the | State of Nevada, | for | The Years 1871 and 1872. | [*state seal*] | Carson City: | Charles A. V. Putnam, State Printer. | 1873.   [715]

xii, [4], 191 p. 23 x 15 cm. Wrapper title, in decorative rule border. Issued also in a cloth binding, with blind-stamped border and gold-stamped title. Issued also as No. 7 in AJS, 1873.

Senate concurrent resolution to print 2,000 copies, of which 500 were to be bound in cloth at a cost not to exceed 25¢ extra per copy (SSN, 1873, p. 232). PSPC, 1873, for February 21, records the printing of 2,000 copies: "Comp. 142 pages L.P. plain 271,788 Ems, $434.86; Comp. 15 pages L.P. R.&F. 28,710 Ems, $64.59; Comp. 47 pages Min. R.&F. 159,236 Ems, $358.28; Press Work 225 Tokens, $337.50; Folding and Stitching 294,000 pg. @ 1/16 %, $183.00 [error in printer's addition; should be $183.75]; Binding 500 copies in Cloth, $125.00"; for a total of $1,503.23.

The Gold Hill *News* acknowledged receipt of a copy on February 25, 1873.

C (cloth). CSfCP (cloth). CU-B (wrapper). MH-Z (wrapper). NvHi (both). NvRW (cloth). NvU (cloth). PPL (wrapper). UU (cloth).

NEVADA. *State Orphans' Home.*

Report of the Board of Directors | of the | State Orphans' Home, | for the | Seventh and Eighth Fiscal Years. | [*short rule*] | Transmitted to the Honorable the Assembly of the State | of Nevada, January 30th, 1873. | [*state seal*] | Carson City: | Charles A. V. Putnam, State Printer. | 1873.   [716]

26 p. 23 x 14 cm. Wrapper title, in decorative rule border. Issued also as No. 9 in AJS, 1873.

PSPC, 1873, records for February 14 the printing of 480 copies, as ordered by Assembly concurrent resolution (JA, 1873, p. 74; concurred in, JS, 1873, p. 109): "Comp. 11 pages L.P. plain 21,054 Ems, $33.68; Comp. 10 pages R.&F. = 19,140 Ems, $43.06; Comp. 4 pages Minion R.&F. 14,552 Ems, $32.74; Folding and Stitching 14,400 pages @ 1/16, $9.00; Press Work 10 Tokens, $15.00" for a total of $133.48.

The Gold Hill *News* acknowledged receipt of a copy on February 25, 1873.

Nv-Ar.

NEVADA. *Supreme Court.*

[Briefs. 1873.]

Boylan vs. Huguet et al. Brief of appellants, H. Huguet et al. 28 p. 23 x 14 cm. Imprint on wrapper: Virginia City, Nevada: Virginia Evening Chronicle Print. 1873. Nv-Ar.   [717]

NEVADA. *Supreme Court.*

Reports of Cases | Determined in | The Supreme Court | of the | State of Nevada, | During the Year 1872. | Reported by | Alfred Helm, Clerk of Supreme Court, | and | Theodore H. Hittell, Esq. | [*short rule*] | Volume VIII. | [*short rule*] | San Francisco: | Frank Eastman, Printer, No. 509 Clay Street. | 1873. [718]

424 p. 23 x 15 cm. Leather binding. Reissued, with volume 9, in a stereotype edition in 1887 by Bancroft-Whitney.

$4,500 was authorized for printing 1,000 copies (SSN, 1873, p. 192); $4,500 paid out (Controller's report, 1873, p. 18). The Carson City *Appeal* of September 3, 1873, reported receipt of a copy.

Az. CU-B. DHEW. DLC. In-SC (rebound). M. Nv. NvEuC. NvHi. NvRNC. NvRWL. NvU. OrU-L. U-L.

NEVADA. *Surveyor General.*

Report of the Surveyor General | and | State Land Register | of the | State of Nevada, | for | The Years 1871 and 1872. | [*state seal*] | Carson City: | Charles A. V. Putnam, State Printer. | 1873.

[719]

43 p. 23 x 15 cm. Wrapper title, in decorative rule border. Issued also as No. 6 in AJS, 1873.

Senate concurrent resolution to print 1,200 copies (SSN, 1873, p. 234); PSPC, 1873, records on February 14 the printing of 1,200 copies: "Comp 22 pages L.P. plain, 32,538 Ems, $52.06; Comp. 9 pages L.P. R.&F. 45,936 Ems, $103.35; Comp 1 page Min. R.&F. 3,388 Ems, $7.62; Press Work 35 Tokens, $52.50; Folding & Stitching, 57,600 pages, $36.00" for a total of $251.53. Note the discrepancy between the number of pages charged for and the number in the report.

The Gold Hill *News* acknowledged receipt of a copy of February 21, 1873.

CU-B. NvHi. NvU.

NEVADA. *Treasury Department.*

Report | of the | State Treasurer | of the | State of Nevada, | for the | Seventh and Eighth Fiscal Years, 1871 and 1872. | [*short rule*] | Jerry Schooling, Treasurer. | [*state seal*] | Carson City: | Charles A. V. Putnam, State Printer. | 1873. [720]

138 p. 23 x 15 cm. Wrapper title, in decorative rule border. Issued also as No. 4 in AJS, 1873, and in SSN, 1873, p. [241]-378, from the same type as here.

Senate concurrent resolution to print 1,200 copies (SSN, 1873, p. 229); PSPC, 1873, records on February 8 the printing of 1,200 copies: "Comp. 12 pages L.P. plain 22,968 Ems, $36.74; Comp. 171 pages L.P. R.&F. 231,594 Ems, $521.08; Comp. 1 page Min. R.&F. 3,388 Ems, $7.62; Press Work 95 Tokens, $142.50; Folding and Stitching 170,400 p. @ 1/16 %, $106.50"; for a total of $814.44.

The Gold Hill *News* acknowledged receipt of a copy "in pamphlet form" on February 12, 1873.

C. DLC.

Odd Fellows, Independent Order of. *Dayton, Nevada. Dayton Lodge No. 5.*

Constitution | and | By-Laws | of | Dayton Lodge, No. 5, | I.O.O.F. | [*short rule*] | Adopted October 9th, 1873. | [*short rule*] | Virginia, Nevada: | J. D. Bethel & Co., Printers, Cor. C and Taylor Streets. | 1873. [721]

73, [2] p. 14 x 10 cm. Printed wrapper. Title and text pages in double rule borders. NvU.

Odd Fellows, Independent Order of. *Dayton, Nevada. Garden Valley Encampment No. 6.*

Constitution, | By-Laws and Rules of Order | of | Garden Valley Encampment, No. 6, | Independent Order of Odd Fellows | of Nevada. | [*filet*] | Instituted at Dayton, Nevada, Dec. 13th, 1872. | [*filet*] | San Francisco: | Winterburn & Co., Book and Job Printers, | 417 Clay Street, near Sansome. | 1873. [722]

33, [3] p. 15 x 10 cm. Printed wrapper. Title page in a single rule border. NvU.

Odd Fellows, Independent Order of. *Nevada. Grand Lodge.*

[*Thick-thin rule*] | Journal of | Proceedings | [*thin-thick rule*] | I | [*thick-thin rule*] | R. W. Grand Lodge | of Nevada. | 1867-1873. | [*thin-thick rule*] | [1873?] [723]

30, [3], 34-107, [1], ii-v, [3], 112-180, [1], ii-v, [4], 184-288, [1], ii-iii, [4], 292-387, [2], ii-iv, [3], 368-485, [2], ii-v, [4], 490-630, [1], ii-vi, [3], 634-764, [1], ii-vi p. 22 x 15 cm. Leather binding. Binder's title: lines 1-2 in gold on red leather patch; lines 4-6 in gold on black leather patch; line 3 in gold between patches. The copy at Nv lacks line 3 and the periods after lines 5 and 6, suggesting that two dies were used in stamping the title. There are title pages and indexes for each of the separate proceedings, but no volume title page or volume index. For separate parts of the volume, see Nos. 453, L484, 538, L572, L629, 658, and 724.

During the 1874 communication the Grand Secretary reported (1874 Proceedings, p. 786) that "One hundred and twenty copies of the extra Journals, reserved for the purpose, have been elegantly and substantially bound in law style. One hundred copies (of Session, 1870), of these reserved Journals have been lost or destroyed, rendering the remaining hundred of each other Session valueless. I have searched diligently for these lost Journals, but can discover no trace of them, nor have I been able to ascertain to a certainty when nor [*sic*] how they were lost. They were stored in the ante-room of Odd Fellow's [*sic*] Hall, at Gold Hill, for some years, and are reported burned, by mistake, in kindling fires—the Janitor presuming them to be waste and valueless." In the same issue of the Proceedings (p. 792), the Grand Treasurer noted that a warrant for $60 had been drawn in favor of Bartling & Kimball, a San Francisco binder, on January 8, 1874. Because the warrant was dated so early in the year it seems reasonable to assume that binding had been completed and the volumes delivered before the end of 1873.

The organization's second bound volume collects the proceedings from 1874 through 1879, but no evidence has been found to suggest its issuance before the end of 1880.

Nv. NvLN (microfilm). NvU (microfilm).

ODD FELLOWS, INDEPENDENT ORDER OF. *Nevada. Grand Lodge.*

Proceedings | of the | Seventh Annual Communication | of the | R.W. Grand Lodge | of the | Independent Order of Odd Fellows, | of the | State of Nevada, | Held at Odd Fellows' Hall, Carson City, | June 3d, 4th, 5th and 6th, 1873. | [*filet*] | San Francisco, Cal. | Joseph Winterburn & Co., Printers and Electrotypers, | No. 417 Clay Street, between Battery and Sansome. | 1873. [724]

[3], 634-764, vi p. 23 x 15 cm. Printed wrapper.

The Gold Hill *News* of August 16, 1873, reported receipt of a copy; Reno's *Nevada State Journal* specifically acknowledged receipt of a copy "in pamphlet form" four days later. A warrant was drawn to Winterburn on September 11, 1873, for $376.50 (1874 Proceedings, p. 792), $355 of which was for printing these Proceedings (ibid., p. 830).

On p. 829-830 of the 1874 Proceedings is the following rather plaintive report of the Committee on Printing: "Your 'Committee on Printing' respectfully report: that immediately after the adjournment of your last annual session, we entered upon what we conceived to be the proper discharge of our duties, by inviting proposals for printing 720 copies of the Proceedings of said session, 500 of which were to be folded, stitched, covered and trimmed, for distribution; and 220 copies to be folded and stitched only, being the usual number kept in reserve for binding. In the absence of any definite instructions as to the number of copies required, we concluded that the number obtained for the year next preceding, would be sufficient. Messrs. H. S. Crocker & Co. asked the same price as we paid them for the work the year preceding, viz: $2.65 per page, with a variety of additional charges for 'rule and figure work,' 'marginal notes,' 'covers,' etc., which made the preceding Journal cost $2.85 per page. Messrs. Joseph Winterburn & Co., of San Francisco, offered to do the work at $2.50 per page, without any extras or et ceteras, and to them we awarded the contract, saving thereby some $50, while the general appearance of the work is better than heretofore. Conceiving it to be within the scope of the power intended to be delegated to us, we in due time invited proposals for binding 150 copies of the entire Proceedings of the Grand Lodge, from its organization up to and including its last annual session, the highest bid being sixty cents, and the lowest fifty cents, per volume. We awarded the work to Bros. Bartling & Kimball at the latter price. We have, from time to time, audited all bills for printing that have been presented to us, viz: H. S. Crocker & Co., for one ream of official letter-heads for the M.W. Grand Master, $6.50. Joseph Winterburn & Co., printing Proceedings, $355; Circular of Delinquents, etc., $5; three reams official letter-heads, $16.50; 1,250 copies of Amendments of Constitution of Subordinate Lodges, per Order of the Grand Master, $6; having razed [*sic*] their bills $8 in all for erroneous charges. What other printing has been obtained, or by whom done, or at what price, during the past year, we are unable to report, not having been consulted in the matter, or had any bills submitted for our approval. As before

stated, we let the contract for binding the Proceedings at fifty cents per copy or volume, but how many volumes were bound, or what sum was paid for the work, we are unable to report, not having seen any bill. We suggest that it will be much pleasanter for the members of this new standing committee who may be selected to succeed us, if the powers and duties both of the committee and of the General Secretary, in the premises, can be plainly defined, by resolution or otherwise.''
CU-B.

ODD FELLOWS, INDEPENDENT ORDER OF. *Reno, Nevada. Truckee Lodge No. 14.*

I.O.O.F. | [*arched rule*] | Anniversary Ball | [*two arched rules*] | [*cut of dancers*] | Under the Auspices of | Truckee Lodge | No. 14, I.O.O.F. | Will be Given at | Reno, Nevada, | —:(on):— | Tuesday Evening, October 28, 1873, | —:(at):— | Dyer's Hall. | [*filet*] | Yourself and Ladies are respectfully invited to attend. | [*filet*] | . . . [725]

[4] p., printed on p. [1] only. 18 x 12 cm. Line 2 in an arch over the cut. Embossed border. On the recorded copy the right-hand portion of both filets is missing because of poor inking or make-ready.
NvHi.

UHLHORN, JOHN F.

The | Virginia and Truckee | Railroad Directory, | 1873-74, | Embracing a | General Directory of Residents | of | Virginia City, Gold Hill, Silver City, Dayton, Carson, | Franktown, Washoe City and Reno, | Together With a | Business Directory, | Also | an Appendix, | Giving | Statistics of State, and Storey, Lyon, Ormsby and Washoe | Counties. | [*short rule*] | Compiled by John F. Uhlhorn. | [*short rule*] | H. S. Crocker & Co., | Printers, Publishers, Wholesale and Retail Stationers, Sacramento and San Francisco. | 1873. [726]

lii, 416 p. 23 x 15 cm. Quarter-leather binding; printed boards. Title page in a single rule border. Pages in roman numerals precede title page. Advertisements throughout, some on colored paper.

Uhlhorn canvassed from at least February 20 to April 9 (*Territorial Enterprise* and Reno *Nevada State Journal* of the respective dates); the Gold Hill *News* reported receipt of a copy on June 4, 1873.
C. CHi. CSmH. CU-B. DLC. ICN (mutilated). NjP (rebound). Nv. NvHi. NvU.

UNIONVILLE, NEVADA. *Horse Races.* Poster. June 1873. [L727]

The Unionville *Silver State* of June 28, 1873, contains an advertisement for the races to be held July 4 and 5 "Over Unionville Course! See Posters!"

WIEGAND, CONRAD AARON.

"Show me the tribute money. And they brought to him a pen- | ny." | [*short rule*] | A Protest and Petition | Addressed to the | Congress of the United States | by the Present and Former | Assayers' of Nevada, | Against | Unlawful Practices | at the | Carson City Branch Mint, | and Praying for | Remedial Legisla- | tion. | [*short rule*] | January 1, 1873. | [*short rule*] | Appendix Part | I.—To Hon. Secretary of Treasury. | Appendix Part II.—To H. R. | Linderman, Esq. | [*short rule*] | "Whose image and superscription is | this?" "In God we trust." | [San Francisco: Women's Union Print, | 424 Montgomery Street. 1873.]   [728]

60 p. 23 x 15 cm. Printed wrapper. The second and third words in line 4 are printed in a vertical S-curve, as are single rules above and below them. Wrapper title lacks the quotations at top and bottom; imprint from wrapper. Each of the appendixes has a title page. On p. [19]: Part I. of Appendix. | [*short rule*] | An Appeal | to the | Hon. Secretary of the Treasury. | Soliciting the | Suspension of Unlawful Practices | at the | Carson City Branch Mint, | Pending Congressional Action in relation there- to. | [*filet*] | . . . | By Conrad Wiegand, | Formerly Melter and Refiner, but later Assayer | of the | U.S. Branch Mint at San Francisco, California. | [*filet*] | San Francisco. | Women's Co-Operative Print, 424 Montgomery Street. | [*short rule*] | 1873. On p. [39]: Part II. of Appendix. | [*short rule*] | An Epistolary Re- view | of the | Carson Mint Errors, | Addressed to | Hon. H. R. Linder- man | Formerly Director of the U.S. Mint, | and Later, | Special Agent of the Treasury. | [*filet*] | By Conrad Wiegand, | Formerly Melter and Refiner, but later Assayer | of the | U.S. Branch Mint at San Francisco, California. | [*filet*] | San Francisco: | Women's Co-Operative Print, 424 Montgomery Street. | [*short rule*] | 1873. *Check List:* 468, in describing the copy at MB, noted the variant imprint on the first appendix, but said the imprint on the second appendix was the same as on the wrapper; both located copies are as described here. An errata slip is pasted on p. 29; another with an additional paragraph to be inserted is pasted on p. 37.

The protest stated that the Carson City Mint assayed for the public and made silver bars at low, non-competitive rates, for which there was no basis in law. It asked for relief and suggested the form of an act to correct the situation. Wiegand's assaying business in Gold Hill no doubt had suffered because of these alleged practices, and his more or less constant outrage brought forth this pamphlet.

C. MB.

❧1874❧

Expenditures from the State Printing Fund during 1874 totaled only $207.52, according to the Report of the State Controller for 1878 (p. 30).

After a brief two-year period in the hands of the Republicans, the office of State Printer was returned to the Democrats when John J. Hill defeated C. C. Powning in November. Hill was the only State Printer to be elected to a four-year term under the 1873 law; the office was abolished by the 1877 Legislature.

An entry in Alf Doten's *Journal* for May 22 indicated that his paper, the Gold Hill *News*, was to have the local job printing for the Society of Pacific Coast Pioneers. The June 12 issue of the Winnemucca *Humboldt Register* had the following: "We have just added to the HUMBOLDT REGISTER Office nearly $2,000 worth of new job material, in addition to that we already had. We now have a new Gordon Job Press, and an abundant supply of type and other material to do any kind of job printing required; and are now fully 'armed and equipped as the law directs,' to turn out, at the shortest notice, all kinds of job work, from the finest visiting or wedding cards, to threble [*sic*] sheet posters, at San Francisco prices. Come on with your job work!"

After a hiatus of several years, Belmont and Silver City acquired presses in February and July, respectively. The Eureka *Sentinel* lost part of its material in a flood in July; the plant of a rival paper that had begun in March was totally destroyed and it did not start over again. Gold Hill had two papers for a brief time in October, and the papers in Pioche and Winnemucca were joined by competitors late in the year. Unionville lost its last press and Virginia City acquired its fourth and fifth newspapers, one of which died quickly. All other papers that were active at the end of 1873 published throughout the year.

ANCIENT ORDER OF DRUIDS. *Virginia City, Nevada*. Constitution and by-laws. Gold Hill "Daily News" Print? 1874.　　　　　　[L729]

Doten *Journals,* November 7, 1874: "Evening read proof on a Constitution & By Laws for Ancient Order of Druids, at Virginia City — Took about 3 hours." Doten had become proprietor of the *News* in 1872 after the death of the former owner, Philip Lynch.

AUSTIN, NEVADA. *Masquerade Ball*. Invitation. January 1874. [L730]

Reese River Reveille, January 16, 1874: "Tickets and invitations for the masquerade ball, which takes place on the 29th instant, are now ready." The ball was to take place at International Hall in Austin.

CARSON CITY, NEVADA. *Independence Day Ball*.

[*Cut of eagle and flag*] | M [*broken rule*] | The pleasure of your company and | [l]adies is respectfully solicited at a | Fourth of July Ball | [t]o be given at Carson City, on the even[ing] | of July 4th, 1874, at Moore [& | Par]ker's Hall.　　　　　　[731]

Broadside? 10? x 6? cm. The recorded copy is cropped on all sides, obliterating parts of the reconstructed words in the transcription; pasted on the back of a photograph. Partly script type. Cut printed in gold and blue inks.
NvMus.

DAILY CUPEL. *Eureka, Nevada.* Extra. July 13, 1874. [L732]

Reese River Reveille, July 15, 1874: "An extra issued from the *Cupel* office, Eureka, July 13, states that that paper has suspended as a daily issue, but will appear semi-weekly from and after Wednesday of next week."

DEMOCRATIC PARTY. *Lyon County, Nevada.*

Democratic | State Ticket. | [*filet*] | . . . | [*filet*] | Lyon County Independent Ticket! | [*filet*] | . . . | [1874.] [733]

Broadside. 22 x 10 cm.

Adolph Sutro's attempts to locate backing for his Sutro Tunnel project (see No. 547) had been consistently frustrated by a cabal made up of William Sharon, local agent of the Bank of California, and Comstock mine owners who were beholden to the bank. He was likewise disappointed in his try for national support for the idea by his defeat in the U.S. Senate election in 1872. In 1874 he tried again for the senatorship, but this time his chief rival was Sharon himself. Sharon had the support of the Republican party and was reasonably certain that he could count on Democratic legislators as well. So Sutro formed his own Independent or Dolly Varden party in several counties, with strong backing in Lyon County, the site of the proposed tunnel. His Virginia City *Independent* was his campaign's organ. The Independents nominated some of the candidates from the two regular parties, but also named a few of their own. In Lyon County local Independents were listed on the Democratic ticket. None of the party's statewide candidates won election and Sutro's bid for the Senate was again defeated.
NvHi.

DEMOCRATIC PARTY. *Storey County, Nevada.* Combination ticket. 1874. [L734]

Gold Hill *News*, November 2, 1874: "Bogus tickets appeared yesterday. Tom Williams had them distributed. He proposes to trade off the whole Democratic State and county ticket to elect his legislative nominees. Friends of the Democratic party, now owned by Tom Williams & Co., will look out for this *combination ticket*." The same issue of the *News* had the following: "Republicans, look to your tickets. See that the names are the same as those published in this paper under the head of 'Republican State and County Ticket.' Tom Williams and Sutro have gotten up a compromise ticket, with the Republican State nominees at its head. Look out for it. It is anti-Republican. It is a fraud." Thomas H. Williams, a prominent Storey County politician and mining man, was a Democratic candidate for the U.S. Senate in 1867, 1872, and 1874. See No. 733.

DEMOCRATIC PARTY. *Storey County, Nevada.*

For Governor, | L. R. Bradley. | [*thick-thin rule*] | Democratic Liberal Primary | Virginia City. | [*double rule*] | . . . | [1874.]   [735]

Broadside. 18 x 8 cm. Cut of a miner printed in green ink as a background on the top third of the ticket.

The Democratic platform and slate of nominees that were published in Nevada newspapers immediately after the party's convention appeared under the banner of the Democratic and Liberal Party. Contemporary editorial comment preferred the shorter Democratic Party. Standard histories of Nevada refer to intraparty factionalism between Copperheads and Union Democrats but, like the newspapers, use Democratic Party when speaking of the whole. It is probable that the addition of "Liberal" to the 1874 title was an attempt to hold together the Democratic-Liberal Republican coalition of 1872. See No. 635.

NvU.

DYER'S THEATER. *Reno, Nevada.*

Dyer's Theater. | [*thick-thin rule*] ¦ . . . | [*thin-thick-thin rule*] | Engagement of | Mr. Barton Hill | and the | California Theater | Company. | [*thin-thick-thin rule*] | . . . | [*thick-thin rule*] | Wednesday Evening, June 10, 1874, | Byron's Drama, in 5 acts, entitled The | Lancashire Lass! | . . .   [736]

Broadside. 25? x 13? cm. The recorded copy has been cropped on all sides.
NvHi.

FOOTLIGHT. *Virginia City, Nevada.*

"Foot-Light"   Extra. | [*thick-thin   rule*] | The   Scrap! | [*filet*] | Rodda   Winner! | [*filet*] | Time,   Two   Hours   and | Twenty Minutes. | [*filet*] | Full   Account | of   the   Difficulty. | [*filet*] | . . . | [1874.]   [737]

Broadside. 30 x 18 cm. Line 1 extends across the sheet; the remaining lines are in the first of three columns.

An account of a prize fight between two Cornishmen, James Rodda and James Tickell, said to be a grudge match between former friends. The fight was held on the morning of September 10, 1874, at Five-Mile House north of Virginia City. The Gold Hill *News,* an evening paper, carried a brief account on the day of the fight, and the *Territorial Enterprise* had a longer story on the following morning.

NvU.

FREEMASONS. *Nevada. Grand Lodge.*

Proceedings | of the | M.'. W.'. Grand Lodge | of | Free and Accepted Masons | of the | State of Nevada, | at its | Special Grand Communication, | Held at | Belmont, August 28, A.L. 5874; | Also at its | Special Grand Communication, | Held at | the City of Virginia, September 27, A.L. 5874; | Also at its | Tenth Annual Grand Communication, | Held at | Masonic Hall, in the City of Virginia, | November 17, 18, 19, and 20, A.L. 5874. | [*filet*] | San

Francisco: | Frank Eastman, Printer, 509 Clay Street. | 1874. [738]

[3], 248-405, [1], iii p. 23 x 15 cm. Printed wrapper.

$1,000 was set aside for printing (p. 261). The "usual number," i.e. 800, were printed, with the proceedings of the special communications; 250 were set aside for future binding (1876 Proceedings, p. 431). The cost of printing was $808.27 (ibid., p. 434). NNFM (lacks wrapper). NvHi. NvRFM. NvU.

FREEMASONS. *Nevada. Royal Arch Masons. Grand Chapter.*

Proceedings | of the Convention to Organize the | M.E. Grand Royal Arch Chapter | of the | State of Nevada, | and of the | First Grand Convocation | of the | Grand Chapter, | Held at Masonic Hall, in the City of Virginia, | November 18th, 20th, 21st, 22d, A.D. 1873, A.I. 2403; | Also at its | Second Grand Convocation, | Held at Masonic Hall, in the City of Virginia, | November 16th, 17th, and 18th, A.D. 1874, A.I. 2404. | [*filet*] | San Francisco: | Frank Eastman, Printer, No. 509 Clay Street. | 1874. [739]

[3], 4-48 p. 22 x 15 cm. Printed wrapper.

IaCrM.

FREEMASONS. *Virginia City, Nevada. Scottish Rite. Silver Lodge of Perfection No. 1.*

By-Laws | —of— | Silver Lodge | —of— | Perfection, No. 1. | [*short double rule*] | Adopted June, 1874. | [*short double rule*] | Virginia City, Nevada: | Brown & Mahanny, Book and Job Printers. | 1874. [740]

14, [1] p. 15 x 10 cm. Printed wrapper. Title page in a double rule border.

NvU.

HUMBOLDT AGRICULTURAL, MINING AND MECHANICAL SOCIETY. *Winnemucca, Nevada.*

Annual Fair | of the | Humboldt Agricultural, Mining and | Mechanical Society. | [*filet*] | The Board of Directors of the Humboldt | Agricultural, Mining and Mechanical Soci-|ety, respectfully announce to the Public that | The Annual Fair, | of this society will be held in Winnemucca | on the 12th, 13th & 14th days of October, | 1874. . . . [741]

Broadside. 23 x 15 cm. Printed on yellow paper.

CU-B.

INDEPENDENT PARTY. *Storey County, Nevada.*

Rooms of Committee on Organization, under Miners' Union Hall, Virginia, Nev. | Citizens of Nevada! | . . . | By order of the

Committee on Organization. | M. J. McCutchan, Chairman. | W. G. Orrick, Secretary. | Virginia, Nev., August 31, 1874.   [742]

Broadside. 26 x 20 cm. Printed in two columns.

Possibly printed at the office of the *Daily Independent,* a newspaper financed by Adolph Sutro to promote his interests. The handbill is an attempt to discredit William Sharon as a senatorial candidate, and asks citizens to elect an independent Legislature that will shun him and therefore be free of the influence of the railroads, the California Bank, and the purchased press. See No. 733.

NvMus.

METHODIST EPISCOPAL CHURCH. *Conferences. Nevada.*

Minutes | of the | Nevada Annual Conference | of the | Methodist Episcopal Church, | Tenth Session, | Held in | Carson City, Neva-da, | September 3-5, A.D. 1874. | [*short rule*] | San Francisco: | Cubery & Co., General Book, Job and Ornamental Printers, | 414 Market Street, below Sansome, | 1874.   [743]

17, [3] p. 21? x 13? cm. The recorded copies are trimmed and bound without wrappers.

CBPac. NcLjUM.

NASH, ORISON E.

Orison E. Nash | Independent Candidate | [*thick-thin rule*] for [*thick-thin rule*] | County Assessor. | Subject to the Votes of the | People. | [1874.]   [744]

Broadside. 9? x 17? cm. The recorded copy has been cropped all around.

Nash ran and was elected in Lyon County as an Independent in 1874; in 1876 he was involved with the "Nash Democratic" and "Nash Republican" tickets. See Nos. 829 and 855.

NvMus.

NEVADA. *Elections.* Circular. October 15, 1874.   [L745]

Gold Hill *News,* October 15, 1874: "A HUMBUG TICKET.—A printed circular, posted in various conspicuous places in Virginia City this morning, cautions candidates and voters against paying any attention to a ticket called the 'Citizens,' gotten up by one Geo. C. Eldridge, a political adventurer, for the purpose of obtaining money from candidates. There is no such organization as the 'Citizens' party' in existence." Eldridge apparently held no grudge against Alf Doten, proprietor of the *News,* for less than a month later he "came and waterproofed the roof of the *News* office with a sort of asphaltum tar preparation for $50" (Doten *Journals,* November 13, 1874).

NEVADA. *Governor, 1871-1879 (Lewis Rice Bradley).*

State of Nevada. | [*filet*] | By the Governor: | A Proclama-tion. | [*filet*] | . . . | I do, therefore, in pursuance of an established custom appoint | Thursday, the 26th day of November, instant, | to be observed as a day for the annual offerings of Thanksgiving and Praise. | . . . | Given under my hand and the Great Seal of the State | at Carson City, this ninth day of November, | A.D. 1874. | . . . | [Carson City: Charles A. V. Putnam, State Printer. 1874.]   [746]

Broadside. 25 x 20 cm.

M. NvU (microfilm).

NEVADA. *State Controller's Office.*

Annual Report | of the | Controller | of the | State of Nevada. | [*filet*] | W. W. Hobart, State Controller. | [*filet*] | Transmitted January 25, 1874, [*sic*] | [*state seal*] | Carson City: | Charles A. V. Putnam, State Printer. | 1874.   [747]

88 p., including a folding table, which folds out to 61 x 56 cm. 23 x 15 cm. Wrapper title, in decorative border. Issued also as No. 2 in AJSA, 1875.

1,200 copies in pamphlet form were ordered by the Legislature (SSN, 1873, p. 175). Acknowledgment for a copy is in the Gold Hill *News,* November 12, 1874.

C. Nv-Ar.

NEVADA. *State Library.*

Catalogue | of the | Nevada State Library, | 1874. | [*filet*] | J. D. Minor, Secretary of State, | and | Ex-Officio State Librarian. | [*state seal*] | Carson City: | C. A. V. Putnam, State Printer. | 1874.
[748]

132 p. 23 x 15 cm. Printed wrapper. Title and text pages in single rule borders.

Copies at Nv and NvU in half-leather bindings and interleaved with blue-ruled leaves; they were probably for use at Nv in recording additions to the collection.

DLC. In. M. NjP. Nv. NvU.

NEVADA. *Supreme Court.*

[Briefs. 1874.]

420 Mining Co. vs. Bullion Mining Co. Brief of respondent, Bullion Mining Co. 42 p. 25 x 18 cm. Imprint on wrapper: San Francisco: Francis & Valentine, Book and Job Printers, Engravers, etc. No. 517 Clay Street and 514 Commercial Street. Handwritten on the recorded copy: Filed April 3d A D 1874, Alfred Helm, Clerk. Nv-Ar.   [749]

Nevada vs. Central Pacific Railroad Co. et al. Points and authorities of appellants, Central Pacific Railroad Co. et al. 19 p. 25 x 18 cm. Imprint on wrapper: Sacramento: Gardiner & Henry, Printers, Corner Third and J Streets. 1874. Nv-Ar.
[750]

Schafer vs. Bidwell. Points and authorities of appellant, Julius A. Bidwell. 7 p. 26 x 18 cm. Imprint on wrapper: Owen & Cottle, Printers, San Jose, Cal. The case, No. 652, is preceded and followed by 1874 cases. Nv-Ar. [751]

NEVADA. *Supreme Court.*

Reports of Cases | Determined in | The Supreme Court | of the | State of Nevada, | During the Year 1873-4. | Reported by | Alfred Helm, Clerk of Supreme Court, | and | Theodore H. Hittell, Esq. | [*short rule*] | Volume IX. | [*short rule*] | San Francisco: | Frank Eastman, Printer, No. 509 Clay Street. | 1874.

[752]

456 p. 23 x 15 cm. Leather binding. Reissued with volume 8 in a stereotype edition by Bancroft-Whitney of San Francisco in 1887.

The 1873 Legislature appropriated $4,500 for printing 1,000 copies (SSN, 1873, p. 192); $4,500 was paid out (Controller's report, 1874, p. 31). 1,000 copies were received by the Secretary of State during January and February 1875 (Secretary's report, 1875-1876, p. 7-8). The Carson City *Appeal* acknowledged receipt of a copy on January 16, 1875.

Az. CU-B. DHEW. DLC. In-SC (rebound). M. Nv. NvEuC. NvHi. NvLN. NvRNC. NvRWL. NvU. OrU-L. U-L.

NEVADA. *Treasury Department.*

[*Thick-thin rule*] | Report | of the | State Treasurer | of the | State of Nevada, | for the | Ninth Fiscal Year, 1873. | [*short rule*] | Jerry Schooling, Treasurer. | [*thin-thick rule*] | [Carson City: Charles A. V. Putnam, State Printer. 1874.] [L753]

56 p. Description from half title in AJSA, 1875, No. 4; it also appeared, from the same type, in SSN, 1875, p. [185]-234.

The 1873 Legislature authorized 1,200 copies in pamphlet form (SSN, 1873, p. 174). Both the Carson City *Appeal* and the Gold Hill *News* acknowledged receipt of the "pamphlet" on April 22, 1874.

NEVADA. *University.* Circular. October 1874. [L754]

Gold Hill *News,* October 9, 1874: "We are this morning in receipt of a circular, issued by Prof. D. R. Sessions, Principal of the Nevada State University at Elko, which we print below. It will be noticed that the standard of qualifications is not placed so high as to exclude any who will be likely to avail themselves of the advantages contemplated by the establishment of this institution, and yet a candidate for admission must be a pretty fair scholar to pass muster. The University will be opened next Monday." The University was authorized by the Constitution of 1864, but was not established until 1874—and then only as a preparatory school. In 1886 it moved to Reno and began offering college level courses. The circular lists requirements for admission.

NEVADA. *University.*

University Ball! | [*filet*] | —To be given in the— | State University

Hall, | Elko, Nevada, | On Monday Evening, February 23d, 1874. | [*filet*] | Tickets, Including Supper, $6 oo. [755]

Ticket. 6 x 9 cm. Line 1 in an arch over line 2. Embossed, scalloped border. Facsimiles in Samuel Bradford Doten, *An Illustrated History of the University of Nevada* (Reno: University of Nevada, 1924), p. 22, and in James G. Scrugham, ed., *Nevada* (Chicago: American Historical Society, 1935), I, p. 306.

A letter in the University Archives at NvU from W. T. Adams to geology professor J. Claude Jones, dated January 25, 1922, at Alberton, Montana, gives a brief history of the ball. "You will please find enclosed a souvenir of the first days of the State University of Nevada in the shape of a Ball ticket which was purchased by my Father in Jan 1874, and no doubt but a little old time history would be interesting to you. Nevada's first University was built in 1873 on a little hill just outside of Elko, and was built of brick and was the most handsome Structure in all the State. Money to carry on the school was not very plentiful at the time, as the Building cost much more than they thought it would, so this Grand Ball was given in order to raise funds to purchase the needs of the School, such as furniture and ect [*sic*]. So the tickets were offered for sale in every town in the State, and those who could afford to buy one, did. The Music consisted of a Violin and Guitar, and the dances were most all Quadrilles. The music was donated and so was the supper. The night was bitter cold, better than 40 below, but there was a large crowd there. It was some big doings. There was no door keeper and the tickets were never taken up—it was free for all, and those who did not buy tickets were just as welcome as those who did. I was there myself and what took my eye the most was the large quantities of Cakes and pies and Candy."
NvU.

NEVADA STATE AGRICULTURAL, MINING AND MECHANICAL SOCIETY. *Reno, Nevada.*

Inauguration and First Fair | of the | Nevada | State Agricultural, Mining | and | Mechanical Society, | to be held on | Tuesday, Wednesday, and Thursday, | October 20, 21, and 22, 1874. | At Reno. | [*filet*] | Please Circulate, and bring a copy with you to the Fair. | [San Francisco:] Eastman, Printer. [756]

31 p. 23 x 14 cm. Wrapper title, in decorative rule border, with imprint below the border. One of two copies at NvHi lacks the imprint on the wrapper. Includes the certificate of incorporation, by-laws, and rules and arrangements for the fair.
NvHi.

NEVADA STATE AGRICULTURAL, MINING AND MECHANICAL SOCIETY. *Reno, Nevada.*

The Nevada State | Agricultural, Mining, and Mechanical | Society. | [*thick-thin rule*] | Speed Contest! | [*cut of race track, with horses prepared to start, grandstands, etc.*] | [*thick-thin rule*] | Programme for the Season 1874. | [*filet*] | Inauguration: Reno, Nevada. | [*filet*] | . . . | Reno, Sept. 22, 1874. | [*thick-thin rule*] | Frank Eastman, Printer, 509 Clay Street, S.F. [757]

Broadside. 48 x 20 cm. The same cut is used in the 1875 poster; see No. 817.
NvHi.

ODD FELLOWS, INDEPENDENT ORDER OF. *Nevada. Grand Lodge.*

Proceedings | of the | Eighth Annual Communication | of the | R.W. Grand Lodge | of the | Independent Order of Odd Fellows, | of the | State of Nevada, | Held at Odd Fellows' Hall, Virginia City, | June 2nd, 3d, 4th, and 5th, 1874. | [*filet*] | San Francisco, Cal.: | Jos. Winterburn & Co., Printers and Electrotypers, | No. 417 Clay Street, between Sansome and Battery. | 1874.

[L758]

[3], 768-907, [2], ii-viii p. Description from title page in bound volume for 1874-1879. Printed wrapper?

The Committee on Printing recommended setting aside $425 for printing, probably to include incidental printing (p. 866); Winterburn printed 720 copies of the Proceedings at $2.50 per page, for a total of $385 (1875 Proceedings, p. 976). The Gold Hill *News* acknowledged receipt of a copy on September 24, 1874.

PIPER'S OPERA HOUSE. *Virginia City, Nevada.*

Piper's Opera House! | [*wavy rule*] | . . . | [*thick-thin rule*] | Last Night | of Mr. | Charles Pope | M'lle Bonfanti! | Marie Gaugain, | and Corps de Ballet. | [*decorative rule*] | Sunday Evening, May 31st, 1874, | Will be Aresented [*sic*] Schiller's Great Play of | The Robbers! | . . .

[759]

Broadside. 22? x 10? cm. The recorded copy has been cropped on all sides.
NvHi.

REPUBLICAN PARTY. *Churchill County, Nevada.*

Republican | State   Ticket | [*filet*] | . . . | [*filet*] | Churchill County Republican Ticket. | [*short rule*] | . . . | [1874.]   [760]

Broadside. 25 x 11 cm. There was no press in Churchill County in 1874.

Dated by list of candidates; the name of gubernatorial candidate J. C. Hazlett is misspelled Haskell.
NvHi.

REPUBLICAN PARTY. *Storey County, Nevada.* Delegates to county and state conventions. Gold Hill first ward. Gold Hill: News. 1874.

[L761]

Doten *Journals,* September 15, 1874: "Evening a caucus of Republican Citizens at Yellow Jacket Engine House — I attended — Selected list of delegates to County & State Conventions, to be voted for at the Primary election tomorrow in Gold Hill — A similar meeting in the lower ward — After meeting was over we got ticket ready for the press — Took till 1 oclock before got fully to press — 6,000 wanted — 4,000 for 1st

Ward & 2,000 for 2nd Ward — Bed at 2." See No. L729.

REPUBLICAN PARTY. *Storey County, Nevada.* Delegates to county and state conventions. Gold Hill second ward. Gold Hill: News. 1874.

[L762]

See No. L761.

REPUBLICAN PARTY. *Storey County, Nevada.*

Union Republican | City Primary Ticket. | [*filet*] | April 18, 1874. | [*filet*] | . . . | [Virginia City? 1874.]   [763]

Broadside. 16 x 8 cm.

The election was for Virginia City offices.

NvU.

SOCIETY OF PACIFIC COAST PIONEERS. *Nevada.*

Constitution and By-Laws | of | The Society | of | Pacific Coast Pioneers | State of Nevada | [*short rule*] | Organized at Virginia City, June 22d, 1872. | [*short rule*] | Gold Hill "Daily News" Print. | 1874.   [764]

19 p. 20 x 13 cm. Printed wrapper.

In the Society's minute book, 1872-1877, at NvU, is a July 23, 1874, notation that a committee had been appointed to have 800 copies of the revised constitution, by-laws, and rules of order printed. The Doten *Journals* have the following entries: "Sent copy to A L Bancroft & Co of new Constitution and By Laws for the Pacific Coast Pioneers — 1,000 of them — Wish them to print the lot for me." (July 28, 1874); the copies were received between the 18th and 24th of August: "Presented my bill to the Pioneers this evening for printing 1,000 copies of Constitution and By-Laws $95" (August 27, 1874).

CU-B. NvHi.

SOCIETY OF PACIFIC COAST PIONEERS. *Nevada.* Poster. Gold Hill "Daily News" Print. October 1874.   [L765]

Doten *Journals,* October 18, 1874: "Worked in office all day with Andy [Andrew J. Graham] and Morris [Davis] on job work — Did 100 full sheet posters for the Pioneers — Ball and annual celebration Oct 30 & 31."

STOREY COUNTY, NEVADA. *Board of Registration.*

List of Registered Voters, of Virginia, Storey County, Nevada. | Election, Tuesday, November 3d, 1874. | [*short thick-thin rule*] | . . .   [766]

Broadside. 50 x 30 cm. Lines 1-2 extend across the sheet, with the list printed below in ten columns. At the head of the first two columns: List of Registered Voters in the

First and Second Districts of the County of Storey, Comprising the First and Second Wards of the City of Virginia and Township No. 2 of Storey County.
NvMus.

SUTRO, ADOLPH HEINRICH JOSEPH.
[*Thick-thin rule*] | The Daily Independent --- Supplement. | [*double rule*] | Virginia City, Nevada, Saturday, October 31, 1874. | [*thick-thin rule*] | Lecture | —on— | Mines and Mining, | —delivered by— | Adolph Sutro, | at Piper's Opera House, Virginia | City, and in all the Princi-|pal towns and Mining | Camps in the State of Nevada. | [*short rule*]. [767]

[4] p. 61 x 47 cm. Lines 1-2 extend across the first recto; the remainder is in column 1 of eight columns. Thirty-seven cuts, including a facsimile of the 1867 Senate Concurrent Resolution No. 70; see No. 439.
CSmH. CSt. CU-B. CtY. NvHi. NvRH. NvRW. NvU.

VIRGINIA AND TRUCKEE RAILROAD COMPANY.
Virginia and Truckee Railroad | [*short thick-thin rule*] | Shop Rules. | [*short thin-thick rule*] | . . . | [*at left:*] Carson, Nev., February 1st., 1874. | Approved: H. M. Yerington, Gen'l Sup't. | [*at right:*] J. W. Bowker, M. M. [768]

Broadside. 46 x 31 cm. Line 1 in an arch over line 2. Thick-thick-thin rule border. Printed in brown ink.
NvHi.

VIRGINIA CITY, NEVADA. *Funerals, etc.* Funeral notice: Ellen, wife of Thomas Diamond, aged 21 years. 1874. [L769]

Alta California 18:47.

~1875~

The session of the Legislature that convened in January 1875 devoted itself to several matters relating to the state printing, including passage of a law changing the usual number of legislative bills to be printed from 100 to 240 (SSN, 1875, p. 46). It also passed "An Act for the Relief of C. A. V. Putnam," which allowed the former State Printer the sum of $91.50, apparently for an unpaid claim during his term in 1873 and 1874 (ibid., p. 133). But the most far-reaching enactment involved repeal of the state's law regarding publication of the Supreme

Court Reports and its replacement by an act providing that a contract be awarded "to the lowest competent and responsible bidder, for a term of not less than five nor more than eight years." The law further required the contracting printer "to sell six hundred copies of each of said volumes of Reports to the State at the price stipulated in the contract, said price not to exceed three dollars per volume, and to keep on hand and for sale, at the price fixed in the contract, a sufficient number of copies of each volume to supply all demands for eight years from the publication thereof; and said publisher shall give bond for the fulfillment of the terms of the contract, in the sum of ten thousand dollars, which bond shall be filed with [the] Clerk of the Supreme Court, and approved by the Justices of the Supreme Court, or by a majority thereof " (ibid., p. 72-74). An article in the Carson City *Appeal* of May 7 noted that "it may be an item of interest to the legal fraternity of this State to know that they can obtain the future Reports of Decisions of the Supreme Court at the low rate of two dollars per volume. Proposals were opened Monday last, there was considerable competition and bids varied from two dollars to two dollars and eighty cents. The houses of Sumner, Whitney & Co. and A. L. Bancroft & Co., of San Francisco, proposed to print them for the same price—two dollars. The contract was awarded to the latter house for eight years." The Reno *Nevada State Journal* added, on May 13, that "the State, by the public printing process, has not heretofore been able to produce these reports for less than $8 to $10 a volume." The *Journal* did not mention, however, that the reports had never been published "by the public printing process," but had always been contracted for directly by the Supreme Court.

The new State Printer, John J. Hill, began a practice of placing his imprint on the verso of half titles, thus creating what *Check List* (p. x) called "a title page in embryo." The practice continued throughout his four-year term. It should be remembered, however, that Hill did not actually print these pieces and that his innovation was merely carried out by the California printer with whom he contracted.

Charges to the State Printing Fund during 1875, according to the report of the State Controller in 1878 (p. 30), were $25,226.70.

The Winnemucca *Humboldt Register* of September 10 took a mild slap, probably related to the printing of No. 781, at the practice of sending job work out of state in the following item: "The only place you can get Job Printing done in Humboldt County is at the REGISTER Office, which has the only Job Office in Winnemucca. We do as fine work, and as cheap, as it can be done in San Francisco. We do the work ourselves, and do not send it abroad to be done, then charge our patrons two or three prices for it, besides the expressage."

Presses that were active at the end of 1874 in Austin, Belmont, Carson City, Columbus, Elko, Eureka, Gold Hill, Hamilton, Pioche, Silver City, and Winnemucca continued to publish throughout the year. Battle Mountain's newspaper ceased publication in October. Carson City had a third paper for a brief period in late summer; Genoa, after ten years without one, got a press in February. One of Reno's two newspapers died in June, passing its press along to another paper there; the new entry did not last the year. Another attempt at a German-language paper in Virginia City was made in March; it lasted until December. The Virginia City *Independent* suspended operations in January but was reincarnated in July, using the same plant as the Sutro *Independent*.

AUSTIN, NEVADA. *Funerals, etc.* Obituary notice. Austin: Reese River Reveille. December 1875. [L770]

Reveille, December 10, 1875: "At the request of many friends of the late Mr. Andrew Casamayou, a few extra copies of the obituary notice published in Wednesday's REVEILLE have been printed, which may be obtained, free of cost, by those desiring them, on application at this office." Casamayou was the owner of the *Reveille* at the time of his death; the original notice was published in the December 8 issue.

AUSTIN HARMONIE. *Austin, Nevada.* Concert program. Austin: Reese River Reveille? November 4, 1875. [L771]

Reveille, November 3, 1875: "The committee having the matter in charge have concluded to have printed programmes of the concert, to-morrow night, which will be distributed to the audience present thereat." An advertisement in the same issue stated that the concert was to be held at International Hall for the "Relief of the Sufferers by the Recent Fire in Virginia City." The *Reveille* made no further mention of the programs, but it is likely that, as the only press in Austin, it had already printed them. The issue of November 5 noted that $182 was taken in.

BETHEL, JOHN D., & COMPANY.

A General Business | —and— | Mining Directory | —of— | Storey, Lyon, Ormsby, | —and— | Washoe Counties, Nevada, | Embracing | Virginia City, Gold Hill, Silver City, Dayton, Sutro, | Empire, Carson City, Reno, Franktown, Washoe | City, and Steamboat Springs. | —Compiled by— | John D. Bethel & Co. | [*short rule*] | Price, Five Dollars. | [*short rule*] | Virginia City: | John D. Bethel & Co., Publishers. | 1875. | Francis & Valentine, Printers, 517 Clay St., S.F. [772]

[4], lxv, [1], 355 p. 23 x 15 cm. Quarter-leather binding; printed boards. Title page in a single rule border. Two unnumbered pages precede title page.

Canvassing for the directory took place at least from March 11 to May 4, 1875 (Gold Hill *News* and Carson City *Appeal* for the respective dates); the *Territorial Enterprise* reported receipt of a copy on August 10. Gold Hill *News,* August 11, 1875: "The public may consider that the new directory appears only by a scratch, for an accident occurred to the copy after everything was in a state of forwardness that came within one of destroying it. The publishing houses in San Francisco are infested by rats, and in order to protect manuscript, etc., from their depredations, it is necessary to have everything of the kind put away in boxes. Bethel had, just after a vast deal of labor, succeeded in getting the greater portion of the names arranged, and pasted in their proper order on large sheets of brown paper. These he packed away in boxes, unlil [*sic*] he could get another list of names, for which he was waiting, from his assistant, who had not finished canvassing Gold Hill. On looking at his copy in a couple of weeks after packing it away, he found that instead of being all right, as he expected, it was mildewed and great portions of the paper consumed. Strange to relate, the pencil marks where the names were written seemed to preserve the paper immediately around them, and with great difficulty the names were all restored. Two or three days longer waiting would very likely have sealed the fate of the new directory. The book is now being worked off as fast as possible by the publisher, and two hundred copies are expected in Virginia to-morrow."

CHi. CSfCP. CtY (rebound). ICN. NvHi. NvU.

CARSON DAILY APPEAL. *Carson City, Nevada.*

. . . | Carrier of the Carson Daily "Appeal" | To His Patrons. | . . . | [1875.]   [772a]

Broadside. 23? x 18? cm. The recorded copy has been cropped all around, probably destroying at least one line before the first line recorded here. Printed in three columns, separated by vertical double rules. The text makes it clear that the address was to be distributed on New Years Day, 1876; it was probably printed in the last days of 1875.

NvU.

DAILY EVENING HERALD. *Carson City, Nevada.* Prospectus. August 1875.   [L773]

Carson City *Appeal,* August 4, 1875: "By a hand-bill of modest dimensions issued a day or two since we are informed that the new Carson paper, about which there have been some whisperings of late, 'will make its appearance in a few days' and will be named the 'Daily Evening Herald.' We are further informed that it will be a live newspaper and the largest paper in Carson City. We are also made acquainted with the fact that Wells Drury & Co. are the publishers. The office of this new paper is in the second story of the APPEAL building." C. A. V. Putnam, former State Printer, was editor in chief.

DENNIS, JOHN HANCOCK. Oration. July 4, 1874. San Francisco: 1875. [L774]

Eureka *Sentinel*, April 15, 1875: "VIOLATION OF A COPYRIGHT.—Somebody in San Francisco has had printed in pamphlet form the oration delivered by our junior last Fourth of July, before the Hoodlum Association of Austin. The literary pilferer had not even the grace to credit the author with the production, but had the assurance to send him a copy by mail, thus adding insult to injury. The author assures us that the right to print the speech was long since secured at an enormous expense by the Sazerac Lying Club of Austin, which powerful association will prosecute to the bitter end all violators of the copyright." Dennis, who had left the *Reese River Reveille* in Austin late in 1874 to become the junior partner at the *Sentinel*, had given the Fourth of July address before the Ancient and Honorable Order of Hoodlums in that year; his oration, covering nearly two columns of tomfoolery, appeared in the *Reveille* of July 7. The notice in the *Sentinel* may very well have been an attempt to match the successful formula used by the editor of the *Reveille,* Fred H. Hart, who had recently begun a series of stories built around well-known citizens of the Austin area. The tales were of the tallest kind and many of them featured the misspellings and outrageous dialect that were so popular at the time. Hart called his series "The Sazerac Lying Club," honoring a local watering spot, the Sazerac Saloon. The *Sentinel* story (or hoax) may have given Hart the idea of publication in a more substantial form; in 1878 he collected the series and some of his more ephemeral pieces in a 240-page book published in San Francisco by Henry Keller & Co., called *The Sazerac Lying Club: A Nevada Book*. It is altogether possible that Dennis was himself responsible for the San Francisco printing of his oration.

EAGLE AND WASHOE VALLEY MINING DISTRICT. *Ordinances, local laws, etc.*

Revised Laws of Eagle and | Washoe Valley Mining | District. | [*short rule*] | Carson City, Nov. 1, 1875. | . . . | [Carson City: Carson Daily Appeal.]   [775]

Broadside. 29 x 19 cm. Printed in three columns from the same type as in the *Appeal* of November 4, 1875, but with three articles added to the laws.
NvCR.

EUREKA, NEVADA. *Horse Races*. Posters. April 1875.   [L776]

Eureka *Sentinel,* April 23, 1875: "THE RACES.—Posters distributed about town announce that the meeting over the Willows Course will commence on June 17th and continue four days."

FREEMASONS. *Virginia City, Nevada. Virginia Lodge No. 3.*

The Masons on the Mountains. | [*cut of Masonic parapher-nalia*] | From the Virginia (Nevada) Territorial Enterprise, Sept. 9th, 1875. | [*thick-thin rule*] | The Meeting of Virginia Lodge, No. | 3, Upon the Top of Mount David-|son—The Highest Lodge Ever | Opened in the United States, if | Not in the World—The Cause of | this Unusual Proceeding—The | Improvised Altar, Chairs, Etc.— | The Doings, Speeches, Attend-|ance—Etc. | [*short rule*] | . . . | [Virginia City: Daily Territorial Enterprise. 1875.]   [777]

Broadside. Printed in blue on silk, 62 x 62 cm., and in black on paper, 47 x 35 cm. Both printings from the same type, but different from that in the newspaper; type column is 42 x 29 cm. Reprinted in 1892 and later. Line 1 in an arch over line 2; following lines in the first of five columns. Some copies have ornamentation preceding line 1 and on either side of the cut. Decorative rule border.

The Masonic Hall in Virginia City had burned on May 19, 1875, and between that time and the following September 3 the Virginia Lodge held its meetings in the hall owned by the local Odd Fellows. On the latter date, though, the Odd Fellows' Hall also burned. The Masons then decided to hold their next meeting atop Mt. Davidson, on the lower reaches of which Virginia City was built. The resultant publicity in the *Enterprise* gave them the opportunity to have the account reprinted as a means of raising funds to rebuild the meeting hall. But the big Virginia City fire of the next month that destroyed much of the town caused considerable postponement of these plans.

The *Enterprise* of September 11 had the following account of the separate printing: "Yesterday the experiment of printing on handkerchiefs, etc., the account of the meeting of Virginia Lodge, No. 3, F. and A.M., upon Mount Davidson was tried and resulted most successfully. The form is about seventeen by twelve inches, and will be kept standing to-day, and any one wishing the impression put upon handkerchiefs, aprons or the like, can be accommodated, and thus a keepsake and a memento of the occasion be had for preservation. The time will come when these mementos will be prized very highly, and they can be secured now at very little cost and inconvenience." A letter with a copy at MBFM, dated January 11, 1879, suggests that copies on silk may have been sent to Grand Lodges in other states. The silk copies that have been examined vary slightly in size, but most have the characteristic handkerchief stripes around the edges. No copy has been found on an apron.

DSC (silk). MBFM (silk). NvHi (paper). NvMus (silk and paper). NvRFM (silk).

GOLD HILL, NEVADA. *Independence Day Celebration.* Fantastic programs. Gold Hill: News. July 4, 1875.   [L778]

Doten *Journals*, July 4, 1875: "Had Andy [Andrew J. Graham], Morris [Davis], and Tom Watts at work in office part of the day — Sent out about 1,000 of the Fantastic programmes to Va & Gold Hill." The Fantastics were a fun-loving group that seemed to exist only to march in parades.

GOLD HILL, NEVADA. *Independence Day Celebration.* Proclamation by Grand Marshal. Gold Hill: News. July 4, 1875.   [L779]

Doten *Journals*, July 4, 1875: "PM sent out about 1000 Chief Marshals 'Proclamations' to Va & Gold Hill." The same printers as in No. L778 were involved.

GOLD HILL DAILY NEWS. *Gold Hill, Nevada.* Extra. August 31, 1875.
[L780]

News, August 31, 1875: "Shortly after 9 o'clock this morning special dispatches to the Gold Hill NEWS from our reporters in San Francisco conveyed the welcome news that the Bank of California would resume business at an early day. . . . Our reporters in San Francisco were at once instructed by telegraph to procure and transmit all reliable intelligence concerning a matter of such vital interest to the citizens of this section. The result was that about 11 o'clock an extra Gold Hill NEWS was issued, containing dispatches confirming the statements first received. In addition to this, and desiring to be absolutely certain, we telegraphed to Senator [William] Sharon as to the correctness of the reports we had received. His answer was published in our extra, and will be found in the telegraphic columns of to-day's issue." Doten *Jour-*

nals for the same date: "I got out an 'extra' at noon, 2000 of them, & distributed them free throughout Va & Gold Hill." The bank, which had financial dealings with most of the mines on the Comstock, had failed and been closed for several months. It did not open until October 2.

HUMBOLDT DISTRICT AGRICULTURAL, MINING AND MECHANICAL SOCI-ETY. *Winnemucca, Nevada.*

Inauguration and First Fair | of the | Humboldt District Agricultur-al, | Mining and Mechanical | Society, | to be Held on | Wednesday, Thursday, Friday and Saturday, | Oct. 13th, 14th, 15th and 16th, | at | Winnemucca, Nevada. | Competition Open to All the State. | For Rules governing the Fair, Exhibitions and | Track, and also the Premiums, Speed | Programme, etc., see Posters. | [*short rule*] | San Francisco: | A. L. Bancroft & Co., Printers, 721 Market St. | 1875. [781]

18 p. 14 x 9 cm. Printed wrapper. Contains only the certificate of incorporation and by-laws of the Society.

Winnemucca *Humboldt Register,* July 9, 1875: "The first meeting of the Directors of the Humboldt Agricultural Mining and Mechanical Society, under the new corpora-tion was held at the office of the Secretary last Saturday [i.e., July 3], at which time a permanent organization was effected." The group was in fact the same one that had presented previous fairs (see, for example, No. 740), but was newly incorporated. *Register,* August 6, 1875: "The Trustees of the Humboldt Agricultural Mining and Mechanical society held a meeting last Saturday [i.e., July 31]. . . . Bancroft & Co. were awarded the contract for printing the By-Laws, and annual announcements for the Society, their bid being the lowest presented."

CU-B.

HUMBOLDT DISTRICT AGRICULTURAL, MINING AND MECHANICAL SOCI-ETY. *Winnemucca, Nevada.* Poster. Winnemucca: Humboldt Register, 1875. [L782]

Register, August 27, 1875: "The large treble sheet posters of the Humboldt Agricul-tural Mining and Mechanical Society, have just been completed at the REGISTER Office, and will be distributed without delay." *Register,* October 8, 1875: "In the Annual Circular of the Humboldt Agricultural, Mining and Mechanical Society, containing their Programme and List of Premiums, an error occurs in Group IX, Class 45. It should read 'Best Group of *Five,* fat cattle,' instead of 'Fine, fat cattle.' " See No. 781.

KNIGHTS OF PYTHIAS. *Eureka, Nevada. Beatific Lodge No. 7.* Constitu-tion and by-laws of Beatific Lodge No. 7, Knights of Pythias, Eureka, Nevada. Organized September 21, 1874. Virginia, Nev.: Brown & Mahanny, Printers. 1875. 34, [1] p. Wrapper. [L783]

Dawson 208:874; and Eberstadt 134:472.

LAVENDER, B. ALSTON.

The | Millenium: | A | Masonic Lecture | by | B. Alston Laven-
der. | Respectfully Inscribed to | Hon. J. C. Currie, | of Virginia
City. | [*short rule*] | Price, Twenty-Five Cents. | [*short rule*] | Vir-
ginia, Nev.: | Brown & Mahanny, Book and Job Printers. | 1875.
[784]

16 p. 21 x 13 cm. Printed wrapper. On p. [10]-13: An Ancient and Very Interesting
Judean Document; p. [14]-16: Divine Hymn of the Christian's Battle. Questions for
Atheists.

Douglas C. McMurtrie identified this pamphlet as a Virginia City, Montana, imprint on the basis of information from a bookseller's catalog (*Montana Imprints,
1864-1880*. Chicago: Black Cat Press, 1937. No. 88a, p. 52).

CtY. NvU (microfilm).

METHODIST EPISCOPAL CHURCH. *Conferences. Nevada.*

Minutes | of the | Nevada Annual Conference | of the | Methodist
Episcopal Church, | Eleventh Session, | Held in | Reno, Neva-
da, | September 2, A.D. 1875. | [*short rule*] | San Francisco: | Cub-
ery & Company, | General Book and Job Printer, | 414 Market
street, below Sansome. | 1875.   [785]

16, [4] p. 21? x 13? cm. Both recorded copies have been trimmed and bound without
wrappers.

The conference continued through September 6.

CBPac. NcLjUM.

NEVADA. *Board of Commissioners for the Care of the Indigent Insane.*

[*Thick-thin rule*] | Report of the Commissioners | for the | Care of
the Indigent Insane | of the | State of Nevada, | for | the Years
1873 and 1874. | [*thin-thick rule*] | [Carson City: John J. Hill, State
Printer. 1875.]   [L786]

10 p. Description from half title in AJSA, 1875, No. 16.

Senate concurrent resolution to print 500 copies (SSN, 1875, p. 176); 250 copies
printed February 10 (Report of Assembly Printing Committee, JA, 1875, p. 310).
The *Reese River Reveille* of February 15, 1875, reported receipt of a copy.

NEVADA. *Bond Commissioners.*

Report | of the | Bond Commissioners | of the | State of Neva-
da. | [*short rule*] | Seventh Session of the Legislature of Nevada,
1875. | [*state seal*] | Carson City: | John J. Hill, State Printer.
| 1875.   [787]

9 p. 23 x 15 cm. Wrapper title, in decorative rule border.

Senate concurrent resolution to print 500 copies (SSN, 1875, p. 176); 250 copies printed February 10 (Report of the Assembly Printing Committee, JA, 1875, p. 310). Issued also as No. 21 in AJSA, 1875.

Nv-Ar.

NEVADA. *Governor, 1871-1879 (Lewis Rice Bradley).*

Second Biennial Message | of | L. R. Bradley, Governor of Neva-da, | Delivered to the | Legislature, January 6, 1875. | [*state seal*] | Carson City: | John J. Hill, State Printer. | 1875.   [788]

26 p. 22 x 15 cm. Wrapper title, in decorative rule border.

Senate concurrent resolution to print 1,500 copies (SSN, 1875, p. 174). Issued also as No. 1 in AJSA, 1875. The Gold Hill *News* acknowledged "advanced sheets of the Message" on January 6, and the pamphlet issue on January 25, 1875.

CtY. MWA. NN. NvU (microfilm). WHi.

NEVADA. *Governor (Acting), 1875 (Jewett W. Adams).* Veto message. Seventh session, 1875. Carson City: John J. Hill, State Printer. 1875.

[L789]

Reese River Reveille, February 6, 1875: "Plague on the printer who first invented 'fat.' We would like to shampoo him with a shooting stick. We yesterday got one of those January fat head lines at the head of the Governor's message, and that accounts for our present wrath." Acting Governor Adams had vetoed a bill that would have authorized a railroad between Austin and Battle Mountain. The bill was a highly popular one in Austin, and it is as likely that the *Reveille*'s "wrath" was brought about as much by the action as the format of the veto message.

NEVADA. *Homographic Charts.* Homographic chart. Seventh session, 1875.   [L790]

Reno *Nevada State Journal,* February 26, 1875: "We have received a homographic chart of the Nevada State Government, with the compliments of the publisher, Ed. Kiesele, for which we return our thanks." Kiesele was a Committee Clerk in the Assembly during the 1875 session.

NEVADA. *Laws, statutes, etc.*

Statutes | of the | State of Nevada, | Passed at the | Seventh Session of the Legislature, | 1875. | Begun on Monday, the Fourth Day of January, and Ended | on Thursday, the Fourth Day of March. | [*state seal*] | Carson City: | John J. Hill, State Printer. | 1875.   [791]

xiv, 323 p. 23 x 15 cm. Leather binding. On p. [185]-284: Reports of the State Treasurer of the State of Nevada, for the Ninth and Tenth Fiscal Years, 1873 and 1874. Jerry Schooling, Treasurer.

The 1875-1876 report of the Secretary of State notes on p. 6 the receipt of 600 copies. The *Nevada State Journal* of Reno acknowledged receipt of a copy on May 20, 1875.

Az. CU-B. CoD. CtY. CtY-L. DLC. MBS. MH-L. NN. Nv-Ar. NvEC. NvEuC.

NvHi. NvLN. NvPLC. NvRNC. NvRWL (rebound). NvSC. NvU. NvVSR. OrU-L. WHi.

NEVADA. *Legislature.*

Appendix | to | Journals of Senate and Assembly, | of the | Seventh Session | of the | Legislature of the State of Nevada. | [*state seal*] | Carson City: | John J. Hill, State Printer. | 1875.

[792]

26, 88, 128, 56, 50, 7, 33, 16, 4, 50, 5, [3], 78, 19, 5, viii, 191, 10, 9, 8, 5, 15, 9, 14 p. 22 x 15 cm. Half-leather binding. Numbering follows the table of contents. No. 1, Second Biennial Message of L. R. Bradley, Governor of Nevada, Delivered to the Legislature, January 6, 1875, 26 p.; No. 2, Annual Report of the Controller of the State of Nevada. W. W. Hobart, State Controller. Transmitted January 25, 1874, 88 p. and folding table; No. 3, Annual Report of the Controller of the State of Nevada. W. W. Hobart, Controller. Transmitted January 11th, 1875, 128 p.; No. 4, Report of the State Treasurer of the State of Nevada, for the Ninth Fiscal Year, 1873. Jerry Schooling, Treasurer, 56 p.; No. 5, Report of the State Treasurer of the State of Nevada, for the Tenth Fiscal Year, Ending December 31, 1874. Jerry Schooling, Treasurer, 50 p.; No. 6, Exhibit Showing Manner in Which Appropriations have been Expended by the Secretary of State, Appertaining to His Office, During the Ninth and Tenth Fiscal Years, 7 p.; No. 7, Report of the Superintendent of Public Instruction of the State of Nevada, for the Years 1873 and 1874, 33 p.; No. 8, Majority and Minority Reports of the Board of Regents of the State University, 16 p.; No. 9, Report of Joint Special Committee Appointed to Visit the State University at Elko, 4 p.; No. 10, Report of the Surveyor General and State Land Register of the State of Nevada, for the Years 1873 and 1874, 50 p.; No. 11, Majority and Minority Reports of Committee on Counties and County Boundaries on Assembly Bill No. 68, 5, [3] p.; No. 12, Biennial Report of the Warden of the Nevada State Prison, for the Years 1873 and 1874, 78 p.; No. 13, Majority and Minority Report of Joint Special Committee Appointed to Visit the New State Prison Grounds at Reno, 19 p.; No. 14, Report of Committee on Assembly Bill No. 86, An Act to Perfect the Title to the State Prison, 5 p.; No. 15, Biennial Report of the State Mineralogist of the State of Nevada, for the Years 1873 and 1874, viii, 191 p.; No. 16, Report of the Commissioners for the Care of the Indigent Insane of the State of Nevada, for the Years 1873 and 1874, 10 p.; No. 17, Report of Special Committee to Investigate the Condition of Our Insane at the Asylum at Woodbridge, California, and Our Deaf and Dumb at the Deaf, Dumb, and Blind Institute of California, 9 p.; No. 18, Majority and Minority Reports of Special Committee on Assembly Bill No. 73, 8 p.; No. 19, Report of Standing Committee on Corporations and Railroads on Assembly Bill No. 49, 5 p.; No. 20, Communication of the Superintendent of the U.S. Mint, at Carson, Nevada, 15 p.; No. 21, Report of the Bond Commissioners of the State of Nevada, 9 p.; No. 22, Report of the Directors of the State Orphans' Home, for the Ninth and Tenth Fiscal Years, 14 p.

300 copies were authorized (SSN, 1875, p. 46). The Carson City *Appeal* acknowledged receipt of a copy on May 15, 1875, but other newspapers did not report receiving copies until late August or early September. When its copy did arrive, however, the *Territorial Enterprise* had some tart words to say (September 2, 1875): "We have been furnished by the Secretary of State . . . with a stupendous volume

called an 'Appendix to the Journals of the Senate and Assembly.' [It] strikes us as little less than a robbery of the State Treasury for the benefit of the State Printer. It embraces matter never before included either in the Journals or Appendix of a State Legislature. It not only reproduces in expensive form all the biennial reports of the State Officers—reports of which from twenty-five hundred to three thousand copies each were printed and circulated when presented—but gives in full a large number of reports of Legislative Committees on bills disposed of by the Legislature. This is monstrous. The volume is neither paged nor indexed, and is a bald fraud and imposition, costing the State several thousands of dollars. We are content that the State Printer should do well, but protest against his becoming a millionaire in a single year from the profits of unnecessary work. From the fact that several reports and messages are separately paged, while the volume itself is not, we infer that extra copies of the documents were struck off and laid aside when first printed, and then put together and bound as an 'Appendix' of seven or eight hundred pages—the State paying for it, to some extent, as new work. The Journals are indexed, but as the Appendix could not be paged as it was printed, it was necessary to omit the index, and pitch it before the public in the manner in which it reaches us. We should be pleased to know who authorized the publication of all of this trash.''

DLC. M. MBS. MH. NN. Nv-Ar. NvHi. NvLN. NvRW. NvU. WHi.

NEVADA. *Legislature. Assembly.*

The | Journal of the Assembly | of the | Seventh Session | of the | Legislature of the State of Nevada, | 1875. | Begun on Monday, the Fourth Day of January, and Ended | on Thursday, the Fourth Day of March. | [*state seal*] | Carson City: | John J. Hill, State Printer. | 1875.   [793]

364 p. 23 x 15 cm. Half-leather binding.

The Gold Hill *News* reported receipt of a copy on July 30, 1875.

CtY. CtY-L. DLC. M. MH. NN. Nv-Ar. NvHi. NvLC. NvLN. NvRWL. NvSC. NvU. UPB. UU-L. WHi.

NEVADA. *Legislature. Assembly. Committee on Corporations and Rail-roads.*

[*Thick-thin rule*] | Report | of | Standing Committee on Corporations and Railroads | on | Assembly Bill No. 49. | [*thin-thick rule*] | [Carson City: John J. Hill, State Printer. 1875.]   [L794]

5 p. Description from half title in AJSA, 1875, No. 19.

The printing of 240 copies on February 16, 1875, is noted in the report of the Assembly Committee on Printing (JA, 1875, p. 310). AB49 was entitled "An Act to Regulate Fares and Freights on Railroads in the State of Nevada."

NEVADA. *Legislature. Assembly. Committee on Counties and County Boundaries.*

[*Thick-thin rule*] | Majority and Minority Reports | of | Committee on Counties and County Boundaries | on | Assembly Bill No.

68. | [*thin-thick rule*] | [Carson City: John J. Hill, State Printer. 1875.]   [L795]

5, [3] p. Description from half title in AJSA, 1875, No. 11.

The printing of 240 copies on February 20, 1875, is noted in the report of the Assembly Committee on Printing (JA, 1875, p. 310); the Winnemucca *Humboldt Register* reported receipt of a copy on February 26, 1875. AB68 was entitled "An Act to Create the County of Buena Vista, and Provide for the Organization Thereof."

NEVADA. *Legislature. Assembly. Committee on State Prison.*

[*Thick-thin rule*] | Report of Committee | on | Assembly Bill No. 86, | An Act | To Perfect the Title to the State Prison. | [*thin-thick rule*] | [Carson City: John J. Hill, State Printer. 1875.]   [L796]

5 p. Description from half title in AJSA, 1875, No. 14.

The printing of 240 copies on February 26 was noted in the report of the Assembly Committee on Printing (JA, 1875, p. 310).

NEVADA. *Legislature. Assembly. Special Committee on Assembly Bill No. 73.*

[*Thick-thin rule*] | Majority and Minority Reports | of | Special Committee | on | Assembly Bill No. 73. | [*thin-thick rule*] | [Carson City: John J. Hill, State Printer. 1875.]   [L797]

8 p. Description from half title in AJSA, 1875, No. 18.

The printing of 240 copies on February 16 was noted in the report of the Assembly Committee on Printing (JA, 1875, p. 310). AB73 was entitled "An Act to Divide Churchill County, and Annex the Portions Thereof to Adjacent Counties, and Provide for the Government of the Same."

NEVADA. *Legislature. Joint Committee on Insane Asylum.*

[*Thick-thin rule*] | Report of Special Committee | to Investigate the | Condition of Our Insane | at the Asylum at Woodbridge, California, | and | Our Deaf and Dumb | at the | Deaf, Dumb, and Blind Institute of California. | [*thin-thick rule*] | [Carson City: John J. Hill, State Printer. 1875.]   [L798]

91 p. Description from half title in AJSA, 1875. No. 17.

The printing of 240 copies on February 22 was noted in the report of the Assembly Committee on Printing (JA, 1875, p. 310).

NEVADA. *Legislature. Joint Committee on State Prison.*

[*Thick-thin rule*] | Majority and Minority Report | of | Joint Special Committee | Appointed to Visit the | New State Prison Grounds | at Reno. | [*thin-thick rule*] | [Carson City: John J. Hill, State Printer. 1875.]   [L799]

19 p. Description from half title in AJSA, 1875, No. 13.

Senate concurrent resolution to print 240 copies (SSN, 1875, p. 183); the Reno *Nevada State Journal* of February 18, 1875, reported that it "has been printed."

NEVADA. *Legislature. Joint Committee on University.*

[*Thick-thin rule*] | Report | of | Joint Special Committee | Appointed to Visit the | State University at Elko. | [*thin-thick rule*] | [Carson City: John J. Hill, State Printer. 1875.]   [L800]

4 p. Description from half title in AJSA, 1875, No. 9.

The printing of 240 copies on February 19 was noted in the report of the Assembly Committee on Printing (JA, 1875, p. 310).

NEVADA. *Legislature. Senate.*

The | Journal of the Senate | of the | Seventh Session | of the | Legislature of the State of Nevada, | 1875. | Begun on Monday, the Fourth Day of January, and Ended | on Thursday, the Fourth Day of March. | [*state seal*] | Carson City: | John J. Hill, State Printer. | 1875.   [801]

329 p. 23 x 15 cm. Half-leather binding.

The Gold Hill *News* reported receipt of a copy on August 30, 1875.

CtY. CtY-L. DLC. M. MH. NN. Nv. Nv-Ar. NvHi. NvLC. NvLN. NvRWL. NvSC. NvU. UU-L. WHi.

NEVADA. *Legislature. Senate.*

[Legislative bills. Seventh session, 1875. Carson City: John J. Hill, State Printer. 1875.]

No. 46. To grant to certain persons the right of way to construct a railroad track from the north end of Carson Street [in Carson City] to the south end or terminus of Carson Street, and to intersect at Carson Street and Fifth Street, and thence to the Warm Springs within the County of Ormsby and State of Nevada, and to run horse-cars thereon. February 3, 1875. 6 p. 30 x 23 cm. Receipt of a copy is noted in the Gold Hill *News* of February 6, 1875. CU-B.   [802]

No. 80. To grant the Nevada and Oregon Railroad Company the right of way for a railroad and telegraph line from Virginia City, Nevada, to the northern boundary of this state, and to encourage the construction of said railroad and telegraph line to Umatilla, Oregon. February 16, 1875. 19 p. 30 x 23 cm. CSt.   [803]

NEVADA. *Office of Superintendent of Public Instruction.*

Report | of the | Superintendent of Public Instruction | of the | State of Nevada, | for | the Years 1873 and 1874. | [*state seal*] | Carson City: | John J. Hill, State Printer. | 1875.   [804]

33 p. 23 x 15 cm. Wrapper title, in decorative rule border.

Senate concurrent resolution to print 1,000 copies (SSN, 1875, p. 174). The Gold

Hill *News* of February 11 reported that it had received copies. Issued also as No. 7 in AJSA, 1875.

Although the report covers the final two years of the term of S. N. Fisher, whose confusion in numbering his reports has been discussed under Nos. 525, 615, and 712, it was printed after he left office. His successor, S. P. Kelly, was probably responsible for putting a stop to the bewildering system used by Fisher; Kelly's own publications during subsequent years were consistently called simply "Report."

C. DHEW. M. NN. NjP. NvHi. NvU (microfilm).

NEVADA. *Secretary of State.*

[*Thick-thin rule*] | Exhibit | Showing Manner in Which | Appropriations have been Expended | by the | Secretary of State, | Appertaining to His Office, During the Ninth and | Tenth Fiscal Years. | [*thin-thick rule*] | [Carson City: John J. Hill, State Printer. 1875.]   [L805]

7 p. Description from half title in AJSA, 1875, No. 6.

Senate concurrent resolution to print 240 copies (SSN, 1875, p. 180). The report of the Assembly Committee on Printing shows the printing of 160 copies on February 12 (JA,1875, p. 310); the Reno *Crescent* reported receipt of a copy on February 17.

NEVADA. *State Controller's Office.*

Annual Report | of the | Controller of the State of Nevada. | [*short rule*] | W. W. Hobart, Controller. | [*short rule*] | Transmitted January 11th, 1875. | [*state seal*] | Carson City: | John J. Hill, State Printer. | 1875.   [806]

128 p. 23 x 15 cm. Wrapper title, in decorative rule border. Issued also in a cloth binding, with gold-stamped title: Annual Report of the State Controller of the State of Nevada. Transmitted January 11th, 1875. Cloth-bound reports have blind-stamped borders, front and back. Issued also as No. 3 in AJSA, 1875.

The Gold Hill *News* reported seeing advance sheets of the report in its issue of January 15; the *News* acknowledged receipt of the regular issue on January 27 and of the cloth-bound issue on February 10.

C (cloth). DLC (cloth). NN (wrapper). Nv-Ar (wrapper). NvU (wrapper).

NEVADA. *State Mineralogist.*

Biennial Report | of the | State Mineralogist | of the | State of Nevada, | for | The Years 1873 and 1874. | [*state seal*] | Carson City: | John J. Hill, State Printer. | 1875.   [807]

viii, 191 p. 23 x 15 cm. Wrapper title, in decorative rule border. Issued also in a cloth binding, with blind-stamped borders front and back and gold-stamped title: Biennial Report of State Mineralogist State of Nevada, 1873-74. Issued also as No. 15 in AJSA, 1875.

Senate concurrent resolution to print 3,000 copies, of which 500 were to be bound in cloth (SSN, 1875, p. 178). The Carson City *Appeal* reported on February 24 that the report "has just been issued and will be ready for distribution in a few days." On the 2nd of March, in noting receipt of a copy, the *Appeal* said that the "letter press of this pamphlet is creditable to the State Printer. The paper is the worst we have ever seen used in any State document."

C (cloth). MH-Z (wrapper). MWA (cloth). NvC (wrapper). NvHi (both issues). NvRW (cloth). NvU (cloth). PP (cloth). UPB (cloth).

NEVADA. *State Orphans' Home.*

[*Thick-thin rule*] | Report of the Directors | of the | State Orphans' Home, | for the | Ninth and Tenth Fiscal Years. | [*thin-thick rule*] | [Carson City: John J. Hill, State Printer. 1875.]   [L808]

14 p. Description from half title in AJSA, 1875, No. 22.

Senate concurrent resolution to print 1,000 copies (SSN, 1875, p. 175). The Gold Hill *News* acknowledged receipt of a copy on February 3.

NEVADA. *State Prison.*

Warden's Report. | [*double rule*] | Biennial Report | of the | Warden of the Nevada State Prison, | for the | Years 1873 and 1874. | [*short rule*] | Seventh Session of the Legislature of Nevada, 1875. | [*state seal*] | Carson City: | John J. Hill, State Printer. | 1875.   [809]

78 p. 23 x 14 cm. Wrapper title, in decorative rule border. Issued also as No. 12 in AJSA, 1875.

Senate concurrent resolution to print 750 copies (SSN, 1875, p. 176). The report of the Assembly Committee on Printing stated that 400 copies were printed on February 8 (JA, 1875, p. 310). The Gold Hill *News* reported receipt of a copy on February 10. CU-B. NvHi.

NEVADA. *Supreme Court.*

[Briefs. 1875.]

Barstow vs. Union Consolidated Mining Co. Brief of appellant, Union Consolidated Mining Co. 11 p. 25 x 18 cm. "In the Supreme Court of the State of California" appears on the wrapper, suggesting that the piece was printed by a California printer, but the text is clear that it is a document of the Nevada Supreme Court; also, handwritten on the recorded copy: "Filed Sept. 8, 1875 Chas. F. Bicknell, Clerk." Bicknell was Clerk of the Nevada Supreme Court. Nv-Ar.   [810]

Heydenfeldt vs. Daney Mining Co. Brief of appellant, Solomon Heydenfeldt. 51 p. 25 x 17 cm. Imprint on wrapper: Virginia, Nevada: Territorial Enterprise Book and Job Printing Office. 1875. Nv-Ar.   [811]

Heydenfeldt vs. Daney Silver Mining Co. Brief of respondent, Daney Silver Mining Co. 38 p. 23 x 15 cm. Imprint on wrapper: Virginia, Nev.: Brown & Mahanny, Book and Job Printers. 1875. CtY. Nv-Ar. NvU (microfilm).   [812]

Hunt et al. vs. Hunt et al. Brief of respondent, L. P. Drexler. 23 p. 24 x 18 cm. Imprint on wrapper: Virginia, Nevada: Printed at the Evening Chronicle Job Office. 1875.

Drexler was one of the respondents with Jane G. Hunt in a suit filed by Thomas D. Hunt et al. Nv-Ar. [813]

NEVADA. *Surveyor General*.

Report of the Surveyor General | and | State Land Register | of the | State of Nevada, | for | The Years 1873 and 1874. | [*state seal*] | Carson City: | John J. Hill, State Printer. | 1875. [814]

iv, [5]-50 p. 23 x 15 cm. Wrapper title, in decorative rule border. Issued also as No. 10 in AJSA, 1875.

Senate concurrent resolution to print 1,500 copies (SSN, 1875, p. 177); 700 copies were printed on February 15, according to the report of the Assembly Committee on Printing (JA, 1875, p. 310). The Gold Hill *News* acknowledged receipt of a copy on February 11.

NvU.

NEVADA. *Treasury Department*.

Report | of the | State Treasurer | of the | State of Nevada, | for | The Tenth Fiscal Year, Ending December 31, 1874. | [*short rule*] | Jerry Schooling, Treasurer. | [*state seal*] | Carson City: | John J. Hill, State Printer. | 1875. [815]

50 p. 23 x 15 cm. Wrapper title, in decorative rule border. Issued also as No. 5 in AJSA, 1875, and in SSN, 1875, p. [235]-284 from the same type.

A copy was reported received by the *Reese River Reveille* on February 11, 1875.

DLC.

NEVADA. *University. Board of Regents*.

[*Thick-thin rule*] | Majority and Minority Reports | of the | Board of Regents | of the | State University. | [*thin-thick rule*] | [Carson City: John J. Hill, State Printer. 1875.] [L816]

16 p. Description from half title in AJSA, 1875, No. 8.

Senate concurrent resolution to print 1,000 copies of the two reports and bind them together "in pamphlet form" (SSN, 1875, p. 179). The report of the Assembly Committee on Printing notes that 500 copies were printed on February 8 (JA, 1875, p. 310). The Gold Hill *News* of February 9 reported receipt of a copy "this morning."

NEVADA STATE AGRICULTURAL, MINING AND MECHANICAL SOCIETY. *Reno, Nevada*.

The Nevada State | Agricultural, Mining and Mechanical | Society. | [*thick-thin rule*] | Second Annual Fair, | At Reno, Nevada. | [*thin-thick rule*] | Speed Contests. | [*cut of race track, with horses prepared to start, grandstands, etc.*] | Opens October 4th; closes October 9th | Speed Premiums, $10,000. | [*filet*] | . . . | [*short rule*] | Eastman, print, 509 Clay St., S.F. | [1875.] [817]

Broadside. 61 x 23 cm. The same cut was used in the 1874 poster; see No. 757.
NvHi.

NEVADA STATE AGRICULTURAL, MINING AND MECHANICAL SOCIETY.
Reno, Nevada.

Second Annual Fair | of the | Nevada | State Agricultural, Min-
ing | and | Mechanical Society, | to be Held | October 4th to 9th,
inclusive, 1875, | at Reno. | [*filet*] | Please Circulate, and bring a
copy with you to the Fair. | [San Francisco:] Eastman, Printer.

[818]

38 p. 23 x 15 cm. Wrapper title, in decorative rule border; imprint below border.
Carson City *Appeal,* August 7, 1875: "We have received by mail a well-printed
pamphlet issued by 'The Nevada State Agricultural, Mining and Mechanical Society,'
the same containing the articles of incorporation, by-laws, Speed programme and list
of premiums offered by the said Society. The business seems well mapped out, and the
entire scheme indicates enterprise and progress. Here, in the list of premiums are
handsome prizes offered for race-horses, cattle, sheep, swine, poultry, and other live
stock; the agricultural products, and mineral products follow; and following these
come 'manufactures and mechanics,' under Group XXXIV of which we find premiums offered for 'best specimen of newspaper printing' and 'best specimen of job
printing.' Then come minerals, &c. *The pamphlet bears the imprint of Eastman, a job
printer of San Francisco.* This is not an encouraging beginning to the performances of
the 'Nevada State Agricultural, Mining and Mechanical Society.' The necessity of
going to San Francisco to get this pamphlet printed does not exist; for such work can
be done quite as well in this State as in California. State mechanical [unreadable word]
start out with the notion of helping the mechanics of the State; and in the certificate of
incorporation of this Society we find it declared that, 'We hereby certify that the
objects for which this corporation is formed, are to encourage improvements in
developing the agricultural and mineral resources of the State, and advancement in
mechanical science and mechanical and manufacturing skill amongst our people, and
general advancement in those arts which benefit mankind,' etc. As an earnest of their
motives the Society employ a San Francisco job printer to get up their pamphlet for
them. Perhaps this is an oversight and a blunder; but corporators and committees
whose self chosen business it is to 'encourage' the mechanics and artisans of their State
are unfit for the work they have taken on themselves if they have not their wits about
them constantly. This pamphlet is an 'encouragement' of the most fanciful type for
the printers who are not even offered an opportunity to bid upon the price of printing a
pamphlet, the first intimation of whose existence comes in the shape of the work itself,
with Mr. Eastman's imprint staring them in the face. A medal is a trinket; mechanics
receive substantial encouragement in profitable employment. When a combination of
our fellow citizens, whose association together is professedly for the encouragement
of the industries by which they are surrounded, start out toward the fulfillment of
their mission by ignoring one of the most important of those industries, there is more
of discouragement than anything else to be derived from their efforts." Other
newspapers took up the same theme, but none so wrathily nor so lengthily as the
editor of the *Appeal,* Henry R. Mighels, who as State Printer in 1869 and 1870
regularly sent all the state printing to San Francisco to be printed.
NvHi.

ODD FELLOWS, INDEPENDENT ORDER OF. *Nevada. Grand Lodge.*

Proceedings | of the | Ninth Annual Communication | of the | R. W. Grand Lodge, | of the | Independent Order of Odd Fellows, | of the | State of Nevada, | Held in Odd Fellows' Hall, Winnemucca, | June 8, 9, 10 and 11, 1875. | [*short rule*] | Virginia, Nev.: | Brown & Mahanny, Book and Job Printers. | 1875.   [L819]

[3], 912-1042, [1], ii-xiv p. Description from title page in bound volume for 1874-1879. Printed wrapper?

The Committee on Printing recommended setting aside $400 for printing (p. 1013). It also recommended (p. 975) that printing of the Proceedings be given again to the San Francisco firm of Joseph Winterburn & Company, which had had the contract for the previous two years. This latter recommendation was accepted (p. 976), but the decision was later rescinded and the Committee was instructed to award the printing contract to the lowest bidder (p. 992). The 1876 Proceedings (p. 1059) record payment of $380 to Brown & Mahanny.

PIPER'S OPERA HOUSE. *Virginia City, Nevada.* Program. Virginia City: Territorial Enterprise? March 2, 1875.   [L820]

Virginia City *Chronicle,* March 3, 1875: "We suggest to Mr. Piper that it would be well to have the programmes for his performances for use in the theater printed by printers who are sufficiently familiar with plays and possessed of enough general intelligence to spell the names of the characters and actors correctly. The bills which are now circulated in the audience are a disgrace to the art of typography. Last night, in giving the cast of Peg Woffington, Colly Cibber, with whose history everybody who knows how to read ought to be familiar, was given as 'Hilly Cibber.' Mr. Snarl was printed as Mr. 'Snod,' Sir Charles Pomander as 'Pomancher,' Lysimachus as 'Lysimactres,' Mr. Soap as Mr. 'Soaper,' Colander as 'Calondor.' The difficulty arose from intrusting the work to printers and proof-readers who are as innocent of any knowledge of Peg Woffington or the times in which she lived, as they are of any other idea above a lye-brush or a shooting stick." Whether or not the errors cited by the *Chronicle* actually occurred is problematical. Errors frequently did appear in playbills and programs because of the necessity for speed, but the number and silliness of the charges brought against the printer suggest, rather, an extension of the long-standing feud between the *Chronicle* and the *Territorial Enterprise,* which had the contract for Piper's printing during much of the period. But the *Chronicle* itself erred; Cibber's first name is spelled "Colley."

REESE RIVER MINING DISTRICT. *Ordinances, local laws, etc.*

Mining Laws | —of— | Reese River Mining District. | Adopted December 28, 1874. | [*filet*] | . . . | [Austin: Reese River Reveille. 1875?]   [821]

3 p. 22 x 15 cm. Caption title. Text printed in two columns, from the same type as in the *Reveille*'s issue of December 30, 1874.

Reveille, December 29, 1874: "The new district mining laws adopted by the miners' meeting held last evening, will be published in pamphlet form from this office. . . . The price will be 25 cents per copy; but a discount will be made on orders for a number of copies." It is not unreasonable to assume that the separate issue was run off before the end of the year. Yet the *Reveille* of March 13, 1875, contained a note saying that the pamphlet "has been neatly printed at the REVEILLE office," as if it had only recently been issued.

NvALR.

REESE RIVER REVEILLE. *Austin, Nevada*. Extra. August 28, 1875.

[L822]

Reveille, August 28, 1875: "When the news of the reported suicide of William C. Ralston was received, this morning, the REVEILLE at once issued an extra." On the failure of the Bank of California, which had been founded by Ralston, he reportedly swam out into San Francisco Bay and drowned himself. Many of the mines in Nevada were heavily indebted to the bank, and its closure brought about considerable financial discomfiture to some of them. See No. L780.

SHERMAN, EDWIN ALLEN.

"George Washington the Father of | American Freemasonry." | [*ornament*] | An Address: | Delivered by | Bro. Edwin A. Sherman, Before Carson Lodge of F.˙.& A.˙.M.˙. No. 1, | at its Celebration of Washington's Birthday, Monday | Evening, February 22, A.˙. L.˙. 5875. | [*ornament*] | Printed under the auspices of Carson Lodge F.˙. & A.˙. M.˙. No. 1, Carson City, Nev. | [*ornament*] | Committee of Publication: | Robert W. Bollen, M.˙.W.˙. Grand Master, | H. G. Parker. | Jacob L. Beam. | [*short double rule*] | Carson City: | Printed at the Office of the Carson Daily Appeal. | [*short rule*] | 1875. [823]

16 p. 22? x 14? cm. The recorded copy has been trimmed and bound with other pamphlets by Sherman. Wrapper title, in decorative border.
MBFM.

VIRGINIA SAVINGS BANK. *Virginia City, Nevada*.

By-Laws | of | Virginia Savings Bank, | of | Virginia, Nevada. | Incorporated April 12th, 1875. | [*filet*] | Office—No. 35 South C Street, | Opposite Bank of California. | [*filet*] | San Francisco: | Printed by Jos. Winterburn & Co., 417 Clay Street, | 1875.

[824]

16, [2] p. 17 x 11 cm. Printed wrapper. Title and text pages in single rule borders.
CU-B.

WASHOE TYPOGRAPHICAL UNION.

Constitution | and | By-Laws | of the | Washoe Typographical Union | No. 65; | Including | The Scale of Prices | and | List of Active Members. | [*short rule*] | Organized June 28th, 1863. | [*short rule*] | Virginia, Nev.: | Enterprise Book and Job Printing Office. | 1875.   [825]

31, [1] p. 14 x 9 cm. Printed wrapper. Title and text pages in single rule borders. On p. [2]: Revised and adopted March, 1875. The scale of prices is on p. [27], 29-31; see Appendix B.

The recorded copy, which belonged to an officer of the union, Wells Drury, has been interleaved with ruled paper.

CtY. NvU (microfilm).

~1876~

During 1876 a total of $4,773.30 was charged to the State Printing Fund, according to the report of the State Controller for 1878 (p. 30).

An article in the Gold Hill *News* on June 26 and entries in Alf Doten's Diaries and *Journals* from March 28 to October 20 chronicle the addition of new equipment to the office, including a "new Gordon press, Job type cabinet, etc." (Diaries, March 28). The steam presses were to be powered by a four-horsepower New York Safety Engine supplied by Berry & Place of San Francisco (*Journals*, May 27, June 29-July 2). By late June, Doten could write proudly that "for the first time the Gold Hill *News* was *run by steam*" (ibid., June 21), and four months later could say that he "had steam on *all* the presses in the *News* office for the first time today" (ibid., October 20).

The *News* of June 28 noted that Louise M. Wheeler had been admitted to membership in San Francisco's typographical union, the first woman admitted to that organization. The note continues, "Mrs. Wheeler is well known in Gold Hill, having worked for several weeks on the NEWS." No dates for her employment in Gold Hill are given, nor is it stated whether she set type only for the paper or also worked in the job operation; her name does not appear on the March, 1875 list of active members of the Washoe Typographical Union.

Carson City acquired a new paper for a short time in mid-summer; Silver City and Virginia City also had short-lived presses during the year. Pioche gained one newspaper, but lost two. Winnemucca lost one, but Reno and Ward each saw the establishment of a new one. All other presses that were active at the end of 1875 continued to publish throughout the year.

BARTLETT, MASON BROWN. Poster. September 16, 1876.   [L826]

Eureka *Sentinel*, September 17, 1876: "At an early hour yesterday morning, M. B. Bartlett withdrew from the [Democratic state] Senatorial contest in favor of Mr. Cassidy of this paper, the former causing posters to be displayed to that effect." George W. Cassidy, proprietor of the *Sentinel*, represented Eureka County in the state Legislature from 1873 to 1879.

CARSON CITY, NEVADA. *Funerals, etc.*

Funeral Notice. | [*filet*] | The friends and acquaint=|ances of the late | John V. Shrieves | Are invited to attend his Fu=|neral, which will take place | on Tuesday, October 31, 1876, | at 2 o'clock P.M., from the Methodist Church, in Carson   [827]

Broadside. 17 x 11 cm. Mostly script type. Funerary border.
NvMus.

COMSTOCK DAILY RECORD. *Virginia City, Nevada.* Prospectus. 1876.
[L828]

Territorial Enterprise, September 5, 1876: " 'THE COMSTOCK DAILY RECORD.'—We have received the prospectus of a new paper, to bear the above title, which is to be issued in this city on the 12th instant." The newspaper apparently lasted for a single week.

DEMOCRATIC PARTY. *Lyon County, Nevada.*

National Democratic Ticket. | [*filet*] | . . . | [*short rule*] | Lyon County People's Ticket. | . . . | [1876.]   [829]

Broadside. 25 x 10 cm. Same type faces and sizes as in No. 854.
The recorded copy has a handwritten note at the top: "Straight Democratic Ticket." E. G. Pendleton was the candidate for County Assessor. A variant in the same scrapbook in which the present copy is mounted has "Nash Democratic Ticket" handwritten at the top; it lists O. E. Nash for Assessor. See Nos. 744 and 854-855.
NvMus.

DOTEN, ALFRED. Sowing Hayes Seed. Gold Hill: Gold Hill Daily News Print. 1876.   [L830]

Doten *Journals*, August 23, 1876: "Gave my new song to the printer first thing this morning — Printed some slips of it for George Eells as will sing it tomorrow at the barbecue — Published it in the paper today." The song, containing five verses, had been written the previous night and was to be sung at the Republican state convention barbecue in Carson City.

DYER'S HALL. *Reno, Nevada.*

Dyer's Hall | [*thick-thin rule*] | Grand Carnival! | —of— | Mirth, Refined Wit and Humor | Engagement | For 2 Nights Only! | —of the— | Beautiful Queen of Comedy | Dickey | Lingard | Who will

appear in conjunction with | Ella F. Badger! | —and a— | Comedy
Company! | [*thick-thin rule*] | Opening Night, Monday, Oct.
9th | . . . | Second Love | . . . | [1876.]   [831]

Broadside. 55? x 22 cm. The recorded copy is wrinkled in a frame, affecting the long
dimension.

Reviewed in the Reno *Nevada State Journal,* October 10, 1876. The play originally
announced, *Second Love,* was not performed: *Naval Engagement* appeared instead.
NvRH.

GOLD HILL DAILY NEWS. *Gold Hill, Nevada.* Extra. June 28, 1876.
               [L832]

Doten Diaries, June 28, 1876: "Democratic Convention today at St Louis nominated
Gov [Samuel J.] Tilden of New York for President — Being too late for the paper I got
out an 'extra' this evening announcing it — sent some to Va as well as through Gold
Hill."

GOLD HILL DAILY NEWS. *Gold Hill, Nevada.* Extra. November 7, 1876.
               [L833]

News, November 7, 1876: "The NEWS this morning issued an Extra, which was
read eagerly by voters both in Gold Hill and Virginia. It contained Bob Ingersoll's last
magnificent speech, the latest telegrams and a variety of editorial small-shot crys-
talizing the issues of the contest. It was circulated through Gold Hill and Virginia,
and did some good work for the Republican cause. The demand was such that the
printing of a second edition was found to be a necessity." Doten *Journals,* November
7: "General election day — AM we got out a full page extra as a campaign document,
and sent it free to Va and through Gold Hill." The second edition is not listed as a
separate entry here because apparently it contained no new matter.

GOLD HILL DAILY NEWS. *Gold Hill, Nevada.*

[*Thick-thin rule*] | . . . | Gold Hill Daily News. | [*double rule*]
| Centennial Edition, July 4th, 1876. | . . . | [*double rule*].   [834]

Broadside. 30 x 19 cm. Text printed in three columns. Publication information,
subscription rates, etc., appear in compartments to the left and right of the text
transcribed above. The first two columns contain patriotic blurbs, while the third has
the program for the celebration on the Comstock. Reprinted in the *News,* from the
same type, on July 5.

The *News* of July 3 announced that no paper would be issued the next day. Doten
Journals, July 3, 1876: "Evening got up a little paper for tomorrows [*sic*] procession
— The Centennial Edition of the Gold Hill News." Ibid., July 4: "Grand celebration
of the 4th, joint celebration by Gold Hill & Virginia — Splendid — Among other
features, the 'trades' were represented — Had the *News* on wheels — Big platform 12
x 16, with red white & blue canopy over it — Chairs to sit in — Put our small eighth
medium Gordon press on it and printed a very nice little Centennial edition of the
Gold Hill Daily News — Printed and distributed them all through GH and Virginia —
About 3,500 of them — Great feature — I rode on the car with all the printers." Ibid.,
July 5: "Biggest & best Gold Hill News ever printed — Had the little centennial

edition of yesterday reprinted on the outside." *News,* July 5: "Although we printed and distributed several thousand copies of our little Centennial edition of the Gold Hill Daily News from our car in the procession yesterday, to the numerous spectators, it was impossible to come anywhere near supplying the demand. Hundreds of people came or sent to the office for them last evening, and we supplied them with all they asked. Having the form still standing, we will give everybody who wishes them plenty of copies free of charge. Come or send to the office for them. They are neat little souvenirs of the great occasion to send to friends abroad."
NvHi. NvU.

HUMBOLDT DISTRICT AGRICULTURAL, MINING AND MECHANICAL SO-CIETY. *Winnemucca, Nevada.* By-laws and announcement. 1876.

[L835]

Reese River Reveille, July 14, 1876: "We are indebted to J. H. Job, Secretary of the Society, for a copy of the by-laws and second annual announcement of the Humboldt District Agricultural, Mining and Mechanical Society fair to be held in Winnemucca, October 2d, 3d, 4th, 5th and 6th, 1876." The Gold Hill *News* acknowledged a copy "in pamphlet form" on July 15.

KNIGHTS OF PYTHIAS. *Austin, Nevada. Toiyabe Lodge No. 9.* Dance program. First annual grand uniform ball. November 9, 1876.

[L836]

Reese River Reveille, November 4, 1876: "The programme of dances for the coming ball of Toiyabe Lodge, No. 9, Knights of Pythias, of this city, is a splendid specimen of lithographic and letterpress printing, being far superior to anything of the kind ever seen in this part of the country." The ball, according to an advertisement in the same issue, was to be held at the Masonic and Odd Fellows Building in Austin. The use of lithography suggests out-of-state printing, probably in California, since there is no evidence of lithographic printing in Nevada at the time.

LYON COUNTY, NEVADA. *Board of Registration.*

List of | Registered Voters | —of— | Sutro Precinct, | Lyon County, Nev. | [*short rule*] | . . . | H. L. Foreman, | Registry Agent. | Sutro, Nev., October 19, 1876. [837]

Broadside. 18? x 5? cm. The recorded copy has been cropped on all sides. The names are printed in two columns.
NvMus.

LYON COUNTY TIMES. *Silver City, Nevada.*

Lyon County Times. | [*double rule*] | Friday [*dotted rule*] June 16, 1876. | [*thick-thin rule*] | Extra! | [*double rule*] | Ballots at the | Cincinnati Convention. | [*short rule*] | Governor Hayes Nominated. | [*short rule*] | [Special to The Lyon County Times.] | [*short rule*] | . . . [838]

Broadside. 20? x 5? cm. The recorded copy has been cropped on all sides. Line 7 printed in brackets.
NvMus.

METHODIST EPISCOPAL CHURCH. *Conferences. Nevada.*

Minutes | of the | Nevada Annual Conference | of the | [*ornament*] Methodist Episcopal Church, [*ornament*] | Twelfth Session, | Held in | Gold Hill, Nevada, | September 21st, A.D. 1876. | [*filet*] | San Francisco: | Bacon & Company, Printers, | Corner of Clay and Sansome Streets. | 1876.   [839]

16, [4] p. 21? x 13? cm. Both recorded copies have been trimmed and bound without wrappers.

The conference continued through September 23. The *Reese River Reveille* acknowledged receipt of a copy "in pamphlet form" on November 10, 1876.
CBPac. NcLjUM.

MINERS' UNION OF VIRGINIA CITY.

Constitution, | By-Laws, | Order of Business and Rules of Order | of the | Miners' Union, | of Virginia, Nevada. | [*short rule*] | Organized July 4th, 1867. | [*short rule*] | Virginia, Nevada: | Enterprise Steam Printing House. | [*short rule*] | 1876.   [840]

22 p. 14 x 9 cm. Printed wrapper.
NvHi.

NATIONAL GUARD HALL. *Virginia City, Nevada.*

National Guard Hall | [*thick-thin rule*] | Complete Success of the New Season! | [*thick-thin rule*] | To-Night | Friday, Sept. 22. | Complimentary Benefit! | —To— | Ella F. Badger! | [*thick-thin rule*] | Great Attraction and Double Bill | For This Occasion! | [*thick-thin rule*] | Rose Eytinge | Supported by the | California | Dramatic Comp'y | Will appear in her great character of Julia in Sheridan | Knowles' magnificent play, The | Hunchback | Ella F. Badger as Helen | [*thick-thin rule*] | Miss Badger will also appear, on this occasion only, as Margery, | in the Sparkling Comedietta, | The Rough Diamond | G. H. Badger as [*dotted rule*] Cousin Joe | [*thick-thin rule*] | . . . | [*rule*] | Evening Chronicle Steam Print, Virginia, Nevada. | [1876.]   [841]

Broadside. 71 x 22 cm. Facsimile following p. 314.

Reviewed in the *Territorial Enterprise*, September 23, 1876.
CHi.

NEVADA. *State Controller's Office.*

Annual Report | of the | Controller of the State of Nevada. | [*short rule*] | W. W. Hobart, Controller. | [*state seal*] | Carson City: | John J. Hill, State Printer. | 1876. [842]

107 p. 22 x 14 cm. Wrapper title in decorative rule border. Issued also as No. 2 in AJSA, 1877, vol. I.

The Gold Hill *News* of March 20, 1876, reported receipt of a copy.

C. DLC. NvHi.

NEVADA. *Supreme Court.*

[Briefs. 1876.]

Ruby Consolidated Mining Co. vs. Heynemann et al. Points, authorities and brief of appellant, Ruby Consolidated Mining Co. 32 p. 26 x 18 cm. Printed on wrapper: Filed [*dotted rule*] 1876. Nv-Ar. [843]

NEVADA. *Supreme Court.*

Reports of Cases | Determined in | The Supreme Court | of the | State of Nevada, | During the Year 1874-5. | Reported by | Chas. F. Bicknell, | Clerk of Supreme Court, | and | Hon. Thomas P. Hawley, | Chief Justice. | Volume X. | San Francisco: | A. L. Bancroft and Company, | Law Book Publishers, Booksellers and Stationers. | 1876. [844]

xv, [1], 17-501 p. 23 x 15 cm. Leather binding. Reissued, bound with volume 11, in a stereotype edition by Bancroft-Whitney in 1887.

The 1875 Legislature repealed the 1867 law regarding the printing of reports, then authorized the printing of 600 copies for the state and enough extra for the publisher to keep an eight-year supply on hand (SSN, 1875, p. 73). The Legislature appropriated $3,600, of which $1,200 was paid out (1876 Controller's report, p. 31) for the 600 copies that were purchased in June 1876 (1875-1876 report of the Secretary of State, p. 8). The binding may have been done in Ogden, Utah; there is a notation for a freight payment of $8.50 from Ogden in the Secretary's report, p. 12. In acknowledging receipt of a copy, "finely bound in calf, and stereotyped," on June 8, 1876, the Reno *Gazette* noted that previous volumes "have been held at from $5.00 to $10.00 per volume hitherto, and have for that reason been excluded from law libraries to a great extent. The present edition which can hardly be excelled, may be secured for $2.00, and the reduction together with the intrinsic worth of the volume will no doubt secure it a large sale."

Az. CU-B. DHEW. DLC. M. Nv. Nv-Ar. NvEuC. NvHi. NvLC. NvLN. NvPLC. NvRNC. NvRWL. NvSC (rebound). NvU. OrU-L. U-L.

NEVADA. *Treasury Department.*

Annual Report | of the | State Treasurer | of the | State of Nevada, | for | The Eleventh Fiscal Year, ending December 31, 1875. | [*short rule*] | Jerry Schooling, Treasurer. | [*state seal*] | Carson City: | John J. Hill, State Printer. | 1876. [845]

57 p. 22 x 15 cm. Wrapper title, in decorative rule border. Issued also as No. 4 in AJSA, 1877, vol. I, and in SSN, 1877, p. [232]-285 from the same type.

Carson City *Appeal,* February 6, 1876: "State Treasurer Schooling informs us that he has just completed his annual report and placed it in the hands of the State Printer." The *Appeal* acknowledged receipt of a copy on February 20.

CSmH.

NEVADA STATE AGRICULTURAL, MINING AND MECHANICAL SOCIETY. *Reno, Nevada.* Report of the proceedings of the Nevada State Agricultural, Mining and Mechanical Society at its second annual fair held at Reno October 4th and 9th (inclusive) 1875. San Francisco: Frank Eastman. 1876. [L846]

Carson City *Appeal,* February 2, 1876: "We have only read enough of it to see that it is the product, not of any Nevada mechanical institution, but that of the printing office of Mr. Frank Eastman of San Francisco. We do not care to go beyond this fact; for we are not particularly interested in what any job printer in San Francisco is doing." See No. 818.

NEVADA STATE AGRICULTURAL, MINING AND MECHANICAL SOCIETY. *Reno, Nevada.*

Third Annual Fair | of the | Nevada State | Agricultural, Mining & Mechanical Society | to be Held | September Eleventh to Sixteenth, Inclusive, 1876, | At Reno. | [*filet*] | No Entrance Fee Charged Except in Speed Contests. | [*filet*] | Please Circulate, and bring a copy with you to the Fair. | [*filet*] | San Francisco: | Frank Eastman, Printer, 509 Clay Street. | 1876. [847]

78 p. 23 x 14 cm. Wrapper title, in decorative rule border. An extra sheet, requesting suggestions for changes in the premium list for 1877, is tipped in after the front wrapper; it is printed on different stock and with different types, probably at a different time, and perhaps by another printer.

The Reno *Nevada State Journal* of June 9, 1876, reported only that the "work is now in the hands of a San Francisco printer for publication in pamphlet form," but the next day's Gold Hill *News* reported tartly that "being a Nevada institution for the encouragement of home industry, they have employed some San Francisco printers to print the list and programme in pamphlet form." Alf Doten, the proprietor of the *News,* apparently found it acceptable to send printing to San Francisco as long as it was returned with a local imprint; see No. 764. The June 28 issue of the Reno *Gazette* noted that the "speed programme, and premium list for our coming fair are now out in pamphlet form," but the *Reese River Reveille* took up the theme sounded by the *News* in its issue of June 30. "The document, which is issued by a society professing to encourage the industrial interests of Nevada, was printed in San Francisco. The same course has been followed with regard to printing in the two previous years of the existence of the Society. The excuse for this contradiction is the same as that offered by those who employ Chinese labor—it's cheaper."

NvHi.

Nevada State Sunday School Convention. Minutes. 1876. [L848]

Reno *Nevada State Journal,* August 20, 1876: "Several printed copies of the minutes of the State Sunday School Convention are left at this office for distribution." The convention had been held in Reno on May 1-2.

Odd Fellows, Independent Order of. *Nevada. Grand Lodge.*

History and Laws | of the | R.W. Grand Lodge | I.O.O.F. | of the State of Nevada, | to and | Including the Ninth Annual Communi-cation, | 1875. | [*filet*] | San Francisco: | Joseph Winterburn & Co., Printers and Electrotypers, | No. 417 Clay Street, between Sansome and Battery. | 1876.   [849]

63, [1], vii p. 23 x 15 cm. Printed wrapper.
CU-B.

Odd Fellows, Independent Order of. *Nevada. Grand Lodge.*

Proceedings | of the | Tenth Annual Communication | of the | R. W. Grand Lodge | of the | Independent Order of Odd Fellows | of the State of Nevada, | Held in Masonic Hall, Reno, Washoe County, Nevada, on | the 6th, 7th and 8th Days of June, 1876. | [*short rule*] | Virginia, Nevada: | Brown & Mahanny, Book and Job Printers. | 1876.   [850]

[3], 1046-1150, x p. 22 x 15 cm. Printed wrapper.

The printing committee recommended that $350 be set aside for printing the 1876 proceedings (p. 1123); $319.50 was paid to Brown & Mahanny for the job (1877 Proceedings, p. 1167).
CSmH.

Order of Union and Confederate Veterans. *Nevada.*

O.U. and C.V. | [*cut of clasped hands*] | . . . | [*dotted rule*] and Ladies. | You are respectfully invited to attend the | Reception of the Union and Confederate Vet-|erans, at Cooper's Hall, Virginia, Nev., on | Monday Evening, January 8th, 1877. | [*short rule*] | [Vir-ginia City:] Enterprise Print. | [1876.]   [851]

[4] p., printed on p. [1-3] only. In line 1 the word "and" is slanted upward. Printed in blue and red inks, partly in script type.

The day after the occasion the *Territorial Enterprise* devoted a considerable amount of space to what it called an event "of unusual interest." The hall had been hung with decorations representing both sides in the Civil War, including pictures of opposing commanding generals. The platform was hung with bunting and shields. The food served, however, was Spartan indeed, as a reminder of the hardships undergone by the participants: bacon and beans served on tin plates, and black coffee with brown sugar in tin cups. A number of letters expressing the regrets of Civil War generals, printed with the article, make it clear that invitations had been issued no later than

December 1876; it is less clear, however, whether printed invitations had been sent to them.

NvHi.

RENO OPERA HOUSE. *Reno, Nevada.*

Reno Opera House. | [*thick-thin rule*] | Friday Eve'g, Oct. 13, '76, | Grand Farewell Testimonial! | [*fist*] Tendered by the Citizens of Reno to the | Allen Sisters! | On Which Occasion will be Presented | A Mammoth Programme! | [*thick-thin rule*] | The Performance will commence with the Beautiful Musical Comedy, entitled: | Why Don't She Marry | . . .   [852]

Broadside. 43 x 18 cm.

NvRH.

REPUBLICAN PARTY. *Lyon County, Nevada.*

For Delegates | to the | Union Republican | County Convention. | [*filet*] | Dayton Precinct. | [*short rule*] | . . . | [1876?]   [853]

Broadside. 8? x 5? cm. The recorded copy has been cropped on all sides.

Tentatively dated in 1876 because surrounding items in the scrapbook in which the recorded copy is mounted are from 1876.

NvMus.

REPUBLICAN PARTY. *Lyon County, Nevada.*

National Republican Ticket. | [*filet*] | . . . | [*short rule*] | Lyon County People's Ticket. | . . . | [1876.]   [854]

Broadside. 26 x 10 cm.

Handwritten note at the top of the recorded copy: "Sorehead Ticket." The state and national offices are Republican, but the county ticket reprints the slate from the "Straight Democratic Ticket"; see No. 829.

NvMus.

REPUBLICAN PARTY. *Lyon County, Nevada.*

National | Republican Ticket. | [*short rule*] | . . . | [*filet*] | Lyon County Ticket. | [*short rule*] | . . . | [1876.]   [855]

Broadside. 25 x 10 cm.

Handwritten note at the top of the recorded copy: "Straight Repub Ticket." Three variants are pasted in the same scrapbook in which the present ticket is pasted. The first, headed by hand "Nash Repub Ticket," replaces Charles F. Brant with O. E. Nash for County Assessor. A second, headed by hand "Nov 7th 1876 Byrom Ticket," replaces J. D. Sims with W. W. Byrom for County Treasurer. A third, headed by hand "Bogus," replaces Republican candidates for state Senator, state Assemblymen, Sheriff, Assessor, Recorder, Clerk, Commissioners, Silver City Con-

stable, and Silver City Justice of the Peace with names from the "Straight Democratic Ticket." See Nos. 829 and 854.
NvMus.

REPUBLICAN PARTY. *Nevada. State Central Committee.* Circular letter. November 4, 1876. [L856]

Reno *Nevada State Journal*, November 5, 1876: "The following is a copy of the circular letter issued by the Republican State Central Committee to the members of the various organizations throughout the State." The circular contains a call not to split ballots and to challenge questionable voters.

REPUBLICAN PARTY. *Storey County, Nevada.*

National | Republican Ticket. | [*filet*] | Election, Tuesday, Nov. 7, 1876. | [*filet*] | . . . | [*short rule*] | State Ticket. | [*short rule*] | . . . | [*short rule*] | County Ticket. | [*short rule*] | . . . [857]

Broadside. 30 x 10 cm.
NvVSC.

REPUBLICAN PARTY. *Storey County, Nevada.*

National Republican Ticket. | [*filet*] | Election, Tuesday, Nov. 7, 1876. | [*filet*] | . . . | [*short rule*] | Storey County Republican Ticket | [*short rule*] | . . . [858]

Broadside. 24? x 10 cm. The recorded copy has been cropped.
NvHi.

SOCIETY OF HUMBOLDT PIONEERS.

Constitution, | By-Laws, | Order of Business and Standing Rules | of | The Society of Humboldt Pioneers, | of | Humboldt County, | State of Nevada. | [*short rule*] | Organized March 20th, 1874. | [*short rule*] | San Francisco: | A. L. Bancroft & Co., Printers. | 1876. [859]

18 p. 17 x 11 cm. Printed wrapper.

Membership in the society was open to all who were residents of Humboldt County prior to January 1, 1864.
CU-B.

VIRGINIA CITY, NEVADA. *Politics.* Handbill. 1876. [L860]

Reese River Reveille, April 29, 1876: "From a friend at Virginia City we have received a copy of a handbill which was posted on the streets of that city, the other day. It is addressed to 'all freedom-loving American citizens,' and consists of a denunciation of the Order of the American Union, or Crescents, which it says is mainly composed of 'ignorant foreigners, who love the American Union about as the Devil loves holy water,' and that they 'skulk to their meetings like Chinese chicken thieves.' The handbill is an electioneering document, but a curious one. It denounces J. C. Smith, the Republican candidate for mayor, A. V. Comstock, A. E. Pottle, James McKay and Thomas Moses, Republican candidates for Aldermen, as Crescents, and gives the date of their admission to that organization, and calls upon them, if innocent of the charge to subscribe to a form of iron-clad oath printed in the handbill. The Crescent organization, which exists principally in San Francisco and Virginia, is a secret organization having for its object the political proscription of Catholics.''

WASHOE CLUB. *Virginia City, Nevada.*

Constitution and By-Laws | of the | Washoe Club | of Virginia. | [*short rule*] | 1876. | [*short rule*] | Club House, | Douglass' Building, South C Street. | San Francisco: | Edward Bosqui & Co., | Printers.   [861]

50 p. 15 x 10 cm. Imprint from verso of title page. The recorded copy is a negative photostat, from which it appears that the original, whose location is now unknown, was bound in leather.

The organization, a club for the Comstock's socially prominent, was organized February 20, 1875.

NvHi (photostat).

WIEGAND, CONRAD AARON.

An Appeal | to the | Press and Legislatures | of the Civilized World, | Showing | Monetization of Silver | to be | A Need of Mankind; | Showing Also That | Legal Tender Silver Notes, | if Ordained Receivable for a Small Per Cent. of Customs, | Will Raise the Greenback to Par with Gold. | Being a Letter of | Conrad Wiegand, | Formerly Assayer U.S. Mint at San Francisco. | Reprinted from the Virginia City ''Enterprise,'' of April 23d, 1876.
                                                                        [862]

[8] p. 21 x 13 cm.
MH-BA. NvU (microfilm).

WIEGAND, CONRAD AARON. Circular. October 1, 1876.   [L863]

Territorial Enterprise, October 3, 1876: ''Conrad Wiegand, announced only by a small handbill, preached on Sunday evening last at the National Theater, on Hints of Immorality detectable in the Life and Death of Jesus Christ, apart from His alleged teachings.'' In the same issue Wiegand made a clarification: ''It seems to have been believed that I was to make a 'Silver' speech; yet the little circular announcing my *Theme* read '*Christ* and him *Crucified* as a light pointing to *Immorality*.' ''

WOODBURN, WILLIAM.

Tilden and his Friends. | [*double rule*] | . . . | [Virginia City: Territorial Enterprise. 1876.]   [864]

[4] p. 22 x 14 cm. Printed in two columns, from the same type as in the *Enterprise* of October 18, 1876.

Enterprise, October 18, 1876: "We gladly surrender a good deal of space to-day to the subjoined communication from Congressman Woodburn. It is a carefully compiled statement of the real opinions of the foremost Democratic journals and leaders of the character of Governor Tilden. These opinions were given when he was a prominent candidate for the Democratic nomination; they were the utterances of the best and wisest members of the Democratic party, made to save, if possible, the party from disaster. They were not sufficient to defeat the old Tammany chief, but they make the record of the estimation in which he is held by the best men of his party." The Reno *Nevada State Journal,* which distributed the pamphlet with its issue of October 22, 1876, had the following: "Tilden and His Friends.—Read the accompanying document, with the heading as above. It is a carefully compiled array of opinions of prominent Democrats of Samuel J. Tilden when he was spoken of as a candidate for the Democratic nomination for President, and expresses their real sentiments, no matter how well some of them have swallowed him since that nomination. The amount of gagging and belching that was required for this is beyond computation, and shows how little they exercise the 'liberty to think and vote' of which they boast. Read the pamphlet carefully and honestly answer the question, 'Can I trust such a man as this for President?' "

NvU.

~1877~

In an abbreviated Assembly session brought about by the approaching weekend, Speaker and former State Printer Henry R. Mighels introduced and saw through to passage on February 16 "An Act to Abolish the Office of State Printer, and Provide for the Public Printing." The vote was forty-seven for, none against, and three absent (JA, 1877, p. 217-218). The bill was amended before passage in the Senate, fourteen to eight, on February 27 (JS, 1877, p. 273); the Assembly concurred in the amendments, forty to nothing, with ten absent, later the same day (JA, p. 282), and sent the bill to be signed by the Governor the following evening (ibid., p. 317). Governor Lewis R. Bradley approved the bill on March 5 (SSN, 1877, p. 161). The journals of the Senate and Assembly record even less excitement than is elicited by a simple recitation of the bill's legislative history, but the reaction in the state's newspapers was nothing if not excited. Mighels himself led off with a lengthy editorial in the Carson City *Appeal* the day after he had introduced the bill and seen it passed by the Assembly. Parts of the editorial are quoted in the Introduction (p. 1). He published what was essentially a reprise three days later and then left the matter until passage in the Senate. But the pages of the *Appeal* were not devoid of the subject, for on February 22 a correspondent signing himself B. H. M. (probably B. H. Meder, a once and future state Senator and sometime Carson City printer) congratulated Mighels for his bill and the Assembly for acting on it with such dispatch. He went on to recall a similar bill passed by the Senate (of whose Printing Committee Meder had been a member) in 1867, only to be defeated in the Assembly; as a result, wrote B. H. M., the state had wastefully spent at least $60,000 in extra fees, "and nine-tenths of the work has been done in California." The writer continued by saying that "two years' experience as [state] printing expert satisfied your correspondent that the office of State Printer was a sinecure and an entirely needless one at that, and if rightly understood by the tax payers would be made a special mark of repeal by their representatives."

No other newspaper espoused the Mighels bill quite so enthusiastically as the one operated by its author, but the *Territorial Enterprise* on February 18 and the *Lyon County Times* of Silver City on February 21 both commented that the law would be a good one if it were first amended to require that anyone bidding for the state's contract to do the public printing must be a resident of Nevada. But other papers opposed it wrathily, most notably the *Nevada Tribune* in Carson City and the *Chronicle* in Virginia City. On February 17 the *Tribune* carried the article quoted in note 5 to the Introduction. The *Chronicle* went even farther. It suggested, also on February 17, that "this magnificent little scheme of Speaker Mighels at first glance appears as a gigantic stride in the path of retrenchment, but in reality amounts to just this: Should the bill become a law, all State printing, except the profitable current printing—bills, etc. of each legislative session would be done by a California contractor. As it is not likely that any one in Nevada would establish and maintain a printing office in Carson for the sole purpose of doing this bill and blank printing (which could not be done out of town), it is more than probable that the astute Mighels would secure this 'fat take' for his own office." Curiously, the Winnemucca *Silver State,* which was owned by John J. Hill, the incumbent State Printer, had no comment at all.

The law as passed established, in effect, two state printers—one to do the Legislature's incidental printing, to be executed in Carson City, and another to print larger works such as reports, laws, and journals, for which any printer in Nevada or California, but nowhere else, was eligible to bid (SSN, 1877, p. 161-164). Resident printers were to have preference when bids were equal. The act provided for a Board of

State Printing Commissioners, made up of the Secretary of State, the State Controller, and the State Treasurer, and the employment by the Board of a practical printer as an "expert." Two hundred and twenty-five copies was to be the "usual number" of legislative bills; the same number of journals of each house was to be printed, but 1,000 copies was the number of statutes to be printed. Two hundred and twenty-five extra copies of "any message, report, or other document in pamphlet form" ordered by the Legislature were to be printed for inclusion in an appendix. As with the original 1865 law relating to the State Printer the act was very specific with regard to style, but no mention was made of allowable rates.

The printing to be performed under this Act shall be as follows, to wit: The laws, journals, messages, and other documents in book form shall be printed "solid," in long primer type, on good white paper; each page, except the laws, shall be thirty-three "ems" wide and fifty-eight "ems" long, including title, blank line under it, and foot line; the laws to be of the same length as the journals, and twenty-nine "ems" wide, exclusive of marginal notes, which notes shall be printed in nonpareil type, and be seven "ems" wide. Figure work and rule and figure work, in messages, reports, and other documents in book form, shall be on pages corresponding in size with the journals, providing it can be brought in by using type not smaller than minion; and whenever such work cannot be brought into pages of the proper size by using type not smaller than minion, it shall be executed in a form to fold and bind with the volume it is intended to accompany. Bills and other work of a similar character shall be printed with long primer type, on white, plain, cap paper, commencing the heading one fourth of the length of the sheet from its top, and when said printing does not occupy more than two pages of such sheet, or less, the same shall be printed upon half sheets, and be forty-six "ems" wide and seventy-three "ems" long, including running head, blank line under it, and foot line, and between each printed line there shall be a white line corresponding with two lines of the body of the type, and each printed line shall be numbered. Blanks shall be printed in such form, and on such paper, and with such sized type as the officers ordering them may direct. The laws shall be printed without chapter headings, and with no blank lines, with the exception of one head line, one foot line, two lines between the last section of an Act and the title of the next Act; *provided,* that when there shall not be space enough between the last section of an Act to print the title and enacting clause and one line of the following Act upon the same page, such title may be printed on the following page. The journals shall be printed with no blank lines, with the exception of one head line, one foot line, and ten lines between the journal of one day and that of the following day. In printing the "yeas" and "nays" the word "yeas" shall be run in with the names, and the word "nays" shall be run in with the names.

Most of the law took effect on the first Monday in January 1879, and thus did not affect the incumbent State Printer's term of office, but sections establishing the Board and providing for the hiring of a printing expert were to be in force on approval of the act.

The Legislature busied itself with other printing matters as well. Another attempt was made in the Senate to authorize the printing of the territorial journals for the sessions of 1862 and 1864. The attempt failed, as usual, for the usual reason: the Committee on Printing estimated the cost at $4,500, more than it was willing to recommend (JS, p. 108, 166, 195). But while the Legislature was able to resist an appropriation for works that had never been printed, it could not as easily ignore the need for republication of the dwindling supply of Supreme Court Reports. Accordingly, a law was enacted that provided "for the republication and stereotyping of certain volumes of the Reports of the decisions of the Supreme Court" (SSN, 1877, p. 112-113). One of its sections stated that there should be published "by the publishers of the current volumes of Nevada Supreme Court Reports, from time to time, under the direction and by the approval of the Supreme Court, all volumes of the Reports . . . which shall be out of print, or so nearly so as to make the publication thereof, in the opinion of the Court, advisable"; it stated further that the price to be paid the publisher was $2.50 per copy for 400 copies of each volume.

In another development relating to Supreme Court Reports, the Reno *Nevada State Journal* reported on March 27 the receipt of a circular from A. L. Bancroft & Co. of San Francisco, which offered a complete set of eleven volumes of the Reports for $31.50.

The 1878 report of the State Controller (p. 30) shows that the entire $40,000 appropriation was expended in 1877 from the State Printing Fund.

The Gold Hill *News* of September 4 reported establishment of the Nevada Publishing Company in Virginia City. "Its object is to make known through books, pamphlets, maps and other special publications the resources of the State, its past, present, and probable future." But on September 28, the *News* noted that the Nevada Publishing Company had begun to issue a newspaper; it is not known whether the company published anything else.

Newspapers in Austin, Belmont, Carson City, Columbus, Elko, Eureka, Genoa, Gold Hill, Hamilton, Pioche, Reno, Silver City, Sutro, Virginia City, and Winnemucca that were active at the end of 1876 continued to publish throughout the year. Aurora, which had been without a press for nine years, acquired a paper in October; other towns with new papers were Battle Mountain (May), Belleville (three of them, one in October and the other two at undetermined times), Eureka (January), Tuscarora (two papers, neither of which saw the end of the year), Tybo (May), Virginia City (three, of which two survived), and Ward (April). Ward lost a newspaper in March; the plant, however, was used to print another paper there.

ADAMS, THOMAS M. To the Independent voters of Virginia City. May 6, 1877. [L865]

Territorial Enterprise, May 18, 1877: "We Retract. On Sunday morning it became our duty to say some pleasant things of Mr. T. M. Adams, late Independent candidate for Mayor. . . . Apparently not appreciating the disinterestedness of our motive in preparing such an article, Mr. Adams hastened, upon the appearance of the ENTER-PRISE on Sunday morning, to issue a reply to it in the form of a hand-bill, addressed 'to the Independent voters of Virginia City,' in which, referring to the article in the ENTERPRISE, he says: '*I pronounce the article wholly and willfully false.* '" Adams was said in the Sunday *Enterprise* article to have withdrawn as a candidate and the paper spoke highly of him for doing so; he apparently had not withdrawn, and it is this statement that he seems to be referring to in his handbill. Adams finished third in a field of three.

AU FAIT CLUB. *Carson City, Nevada.* Party invitation. November 23, 1877. [L866]

Reno *Gazette,* November 22, 1877: "We acknowledge the receipt of an invitation to attend to [*sic*] opening party of the Au Fait Club to be held to-morrow evening at Theater Hall, Carson."

BISHOP WHITAKER'S SCHOOL FOR GIRLS. *Reno, Nevada.*

Bishop Whitaker's | School for Girls, | Reno, Nevada. | [*fi-let*] | First Year. | Ending May 23, 1877. | [Virginia City: Territorial Enterprise. 1877.] [867]

19 p. 16 x 11 cm. Printed wrapper. Title and text pages in decorative single rule borders.

The format and types are identical to those used in the catalogue for the fourth and fifth years, printed in 1881, on which William Sutherland's imprint appears on the verso of the front wrapper. Until 1878 Sutherland was a printer for the *Enterprise;* it is likely that he simply adopted the style used in previous years by the paper's job office. NvHi.

CARSON CITY, NEVADA. *Mexican Veterans Ball.*

Thirty-First | Anniversary of the Battle of Buena Vista. | [*ornament*] | Mr. [*dotted rule*] and Ladies: | You are respectfully invited to at=|tend the Ball of the Mexican Vete=|rans, at the Arlington House, Carson, | On Thursday Evening, Feb. 22, 1877. | . . .
[868]

[4] p., printed on p. [1] only. 17 x 11 cm. Partly script type. Printed on gray paper, with the fold at the top.
NvHi.

CARSON CITY, NEVADA. *Miners' Union Picnic.* Miners' unions. Fourth annual picnic and excursion at Treadway's Ranch, Carson. Sept. 8, 1877. 4 p.   [L869]
Dawson 208:900.

DAILY NEVADA STATE JOURNAL. *Reno, Nevada.*

Convicted! | [*filet*] | Murder in the Second | Degree. | [*filet*] | "Better Than I Expected." | [*filet*] | To Be Sentenced Next | Saturday!! | [*filet*] | . . . | [We received this news after going | to press, and preferred this means of | announcing it to missing the mails.] | [*short thick-thin rule*] | [Reno: Daily Nevada State Journal. 1877.]   [870]

Broadside. 21 x 10 cm. Lines 7-9 printed in brackets.

Evidence in the regular issue of the *Journal* of January 28, 1877, indicates that the extra, or perhaps insert, was probably issued on that date. Reprinted from the same type in the issue of January 30. Thomas Kelly was hanged.
NvU.

EUREKA DAILY SENTINEL. *Eureka, Nevada.* Carrier's address. New Year's Day, 1878. 1877.   [L871]

Sentinel, December 30, 1877: "The SENTINEL carrier has prepared a very neat and tasty poetical address to his patrons, and will distribute the same on New Year's morning. It is an old custom that has obtained among the fraternity for years, and in these times of good cheer and liberal feelings, his faithful services are entitled to some consideration. In storm and sunshine, through rain and snow, he goes his rounds, and the paper is at their door long before the recipients have concluded their morning snooze. Remember these facts when he presents you with his compliments Tuesday morning." *Sentinel,* December 31, 1877: "Alf. Chartz, the carrier of the SENTINEL, will furnish his patrons with a New Year's address on Monday morning. He had engaged Bayard Taylor and Longfellow to write one for him, but they not coming up to the mark, Alf. discouraged them and secured the services of a local word-painter, the merits of which our readers will have an opportunity of judging when they receive it." January 1, 1878, was a Tuesday.

EUREKA DAILY SENTINEL. *Eureka, Nevada.* Extra. August 7, 1877.
                                                                    [L872]

Sentinel, August 8, 1877: "The SENTINEL's extra, chronicling the defeat of the Russian forces, was the subject of much comment among those who are interested in the Old World's affairs, and heated arguments relative to the status and merits of the combatants enlivened the clothing stores on Main street."

FREEMASONS. *Nevada. Grand Lodge.*

Proceedings | of the | M.˙.W.˙. Grand Lodge | of | Free and Ac-
cepted Masons | of the | State of Nevada, | at its | Special Grand
Communication, | Held at | Gold Hill, August 2, A.L. 5876;
| Also, at its | Twelfth Annual Grand Communication,
| Held at | Masonic Hall, in the City of Virginia, | November 21st,
22d, 23d, and 24th, A.L. 5876. | [*filet*] | San Francisco: |
Frank Eastman, Printer, 509 Clay Street. | 1877. [873]

[3], 408-634, iii p. 23 x 15 cm. Wrapper title, in decorative rule border.

$1,000 was set aside for printing the 1876 Proceedings (p. 432). The "usual number"
[i.e., 800], with the proceedings of the special communication at Gold Hill, were
printed, with 300 retained by the printer for future binding (13th Proceedings, p. 7);
the bill for "Printing," without specification, was $1,005.65 (ibid., p. 10).

The eleventh communication was never held because the building that was used by all
Masonic bodies in Virginia City was burned on May 19, 1875. Regular meetings were
held thereafter in the Odd Fellows' Hall, but it too burned on September 3. On
October 26 the big Virginia City fire destroyed most of the city, including all Masonic
belongings except the money and jewels that were in a bank. The annual communication was postponed to June, then November 1876, thereby skipping the eleventh
communication altogether (1876 Proceedings, p. 415-416).

NvHi. NvRFM.

FREEMASONS. *Nevada. Grand Lodge.*

Proceedings | of the | M.˙.W.˙. Grand Lodge | of | Free and Ac-
cepted Masons | of the | State of Nevada, | at its | Thirteenth An-
nual Grand Communication, | Held at | Masonic Hall, in the City of
Virginia, | June 12th, 13th, and 14th, A.L. 5877. | [*filet*] | San Fran-
cisco: | Frank Eastman, Printer, 509 Clay Street. | 1877. [874]

126, ii p. 23 x 15 cm. Printed wrapper.

$1,000 was set aside for printing the Proceedings (p. 9). The "usual number," i.e.,
800, were printed, with 300 retained by the printer for future binding (1878 Proceedings, p. 291), at a cost of $561.49 (ibid., p. 293).

NvHi. NvRFM. NvU.

FREEMASONS. *Nevada. Royal Arch Masons. Grand Chapter.*

Proceedings | of the | M.E. Grand Royal Arch Chapter | of the
| State of Nevada, | at its | Third Grand Convocation, | Held at |
Masonic Hall, in the City of Virginia, | November 23d and 24th,
A.D. 1876, A.I. 2406. | [*filet*] | San Francisco: | Frank Eastman,
Printer, 509 Clay Street. | 1877. [875]

[5], 54-71 p. 22 x 15 cm. Printed wrapper.

The Grand Secretary "had printed the usual number [350 were printed in 1878] of Proceedings of the Third Annual Grand Convocation . . . and one hundred copies remain in the hands of the printer, uncut, for future binding" (1877 Proceedings, p. 81). Costs for printing the 1876 and 1877 Proceedings were $284 (1878 Proceedings, p. 129).

No grand convocation was held in 1875 because of the series of fires in Virginia City that year (see No. 873); unlike the Grand Lodge, the Grand Chapter did not skip the numbering of its meetings.

IaCrM.

FREEMASONS. *Nevada. Royal Arch Masons. Grand Chapter.*

Proceedings | of the | M.E. Grand Royal Arch Chapter | of the | State of Nevada, | at its | Fourth Annual Grand Convocation, | Held at | Masonic Hall, in the City of Virginia, | June 14th and 15th, A.D. 1877, A.I. 2407. | [*filet*] | San Francisco: | Frank Eastman, Printer, 509 Clay Street. | 1877. [876]

[5], 78-117, [1] p. 23 x 15 cm. Printed wrapper. The Grand Chapter's Constitution, "as Amended and Revised June, A.I. 2407," covers p. [103]-116.

The "usual number" [350 in 1878] were printed, with 100 copies retained by the printer for future binding (1878 Proceedings, p. 128); see No. 875.

IaCrM. NvU.

GOLD HILL, NEVADA. *Ordinances, local laws, etc.*

Revised | Ordinances | of the | Town of Gold Hill, | County of Storey, State of Nevada. | [*short rule*] | With an Appendix, containing the Town Charter, and | the Rules of the Board of Trustees, and the | Names of the Town Officers. | [*short rule*] | Gold Hill: | Alf. Doten, Town Printer. | 1877. [877]

vi, 75, [1] p. 23 x 14 cm. Printed wrapper.

C. CU-B. NvU.

HUMBOLDT DISTRICT AGRICULTURAL, MINING AND MECHANICAL SOCIETY. *Winnemucca, Nevada.* Catalogue. 1877. [L878]

Reno *Gazette,* August 4, 1877: "We have received a catalogue of the Humbold't [*sic*] District A.M. & M. Society's affairs and premiums for the Fair of 1877. The exhibition will commence Oct. 1st and continue for six days." The Eureka *Sentinel* of August 7 referred to the catalogue as "published in pamphlet form."

KNIGHTS OF PYTHIAS. *Nevada. Grand Lodge.* Journal of proceedings. 1876. [L879]

Carson City *Nevada Tribune,* February 1, 1877: "The Grand Keeper of Records and Seals for Nevada . . . has our thanks for journals of proceedings . . . of the Grand Lodge, K. of P., of Nevada, held at Carson, August, 1876."

KNIGHTS OF PYTHIAS. *Reno, Nevada. Amity Lodge No. 8.* Invitation. April 10, 1877. [L880]

Reno *Gazette*, April 4, 1877: "We have received a complimentary invitation to be present at the third annual ball of Amity Lodge, K. of P. The Knights will all appear in full uniform, and Kimball's Hall will present a fine appearance upon the 10th inst." The issue of April 7 acknowledged receipt of a complimentary ticket to accompany the invitation.

METHODIST EPISCOPAL CHURCH. *Conferences. Nevada.*

Minutes | of the | Nevada Annual Conference | of the | [*ornament*] Methodist Episcopal Church, [*ornament*] | Thirteenth Session, | Held in | Susanville, California, | September 28th, A.D., 1877. | [*filet*] | San Francisco: | Methodist Book Depository, 1041 Market Street. | 1877. | [San Francisco: Bacon & Company, Printers, Corner of Clay and Sansome Streets.] [881]

[3], 4-15, [1] p. 22 x 14 cm. Printed wrapper. The type faces, ornamentation, and format are the same as on the 1876 Minutes (No. 839), which were printed by Bacon. The copies at CBPac and NcLjUM have been trimmed and bound without wrappers. The conference lasted to September 29th. CBPac. CU-B. NcLjUM.

MOTT, C. S. Address. December 27, 1876. 1877. [L882]

Carson City *Nevada Tribune*, January 27, 1877: "We received from one of our colored brethren a copy of C. S. Mott's address at the installation of the officers of St. John's Lodge No. 13, of Colored Masons, Dec. 27, 1876. The brethren had the address printed in pamphlet form at their own expense." The installation was at Turn Verein Hall in Carson City. Black Masons are generally ignored by white Masons, so the address by Mott, a white Mason in good standing, may have given the members of St. John's Lodge an added sense of brotherhood.

MOUNT ST. MARY'S ACADEMY. *Reno, Nevada.* Circular. September 1877. [L883]

Eureka *Sentinel*, September 13, 1877: "We are in receipt of the following brief note, and proceed to comply with the request therein contained: Mount St. Mary's Academy, Reno, Nev., September 7, 1877. Editors Sentinel: Please give us a local and oblige yours, etc., Sisters of St. Dominie [*sic*]. What is desired, of course, is that the SENTINEL call attention to the new school just opened by these Sisters at Reno. We do not know that we can fill the bill in any better manner than to give the main features of an accompanying circular."

NEVADA. *Adjutant General.*

[*Thick-thin rule*] | Biennial Report | of the | Adjutant General | of the | State of Nevada, | for | the Years 1875 and 1876. | [*thin-thick rule*] | [Carson City: John J. Hill, State Printer. 1877.] [L884]

24 p. Description from half title in AJSA, 1877, vol. I, No. 14.

Senate concurrent resolution to print 240 copies (SSN, 1877, p. 227). The Gold Hill *News* acknowledged receipt of a copy on March 14, 1877.

NEVADA. *Board of Capitol Commissioners.*

[*Thick-thin rule*] | Report | of the | Board of Capitol Commission-ers. | [*thin-thick rule*] | [Carson City: John J. Hill, State Print-er. 1877.]   [L885]

4 p. Description from half title in AJSA, 1877, vol. I, No. 20.

Senate concurrent resolution to print 240 copies (SSN, 1877, p. 227). The Reno *Gazette* reported receipt of a copy on February 3, 1877.

NEVADA. *Board of Commissioners for the Care of the Indigent Insane.*

[*Thick-thin rule*] | Report of the Commissioners | for | The Care of the Indigent Insane | of the | State of Nevada, | for | the Years 1875 and 1876. | [*thin-thick rule*] | [Carson City: John J. Hill, State Printer. 1877.]   [L886]

12 p. Description from half title in AJSA, 1877, vol. I, No. 11.

Senate concurrent resolution to print 1,000 copies in pamphlet form (SSN, 1877, p. 226). Carson City *Appeal,* February 9, 1877: "The report of the Commissioners for the care of the Indigent Insane has been published and was yesterday distributed in the Senate and House."

NEVADA. *Census, 1875.*

Census | of | the Inhabitants | of | The State of Nevada, | 1875. | [*short rule*] | Volume I. [II.] | [*short rule*] | [*state seal*] | Carson City: | John J. Hill, State Printer. | 1877.   [887]

848, 824 p. 23 x 15 cm. Wrapper title, in decorative rule border.

Volume I contains censuses for Churchill, Douglas, Esmeralda, Elko, Eureka, Hum-boldt, Lander, Lincoln, Lyon, Nye, and Ormsby counties; volume II contains cen-suses for Storey, Washoe, and White Pine counties. No copy of volume II of the wrappered issue has been located; the description here is from a copy bound as volume 3 of AJSA, 1877. See No. 893. The spine of the recorded copy of volume I has been repaired, obliterating any possible printing there. The volumes are entered separately in *Check List:* 212-213.

Senate concurrent resolution to print 1,000 copies, with 100 to be bound in the same style as AJSA, i.e., in half-leather, and the remaining 900 in pamphlet form (SSN, 1877, p. 223); $8,580.50 was paid out for volume I on May 11, 1877, and $8,429.79 for volume II on the same date (Controller's report, 1878, p. 226-227).

Eureka *Sentinel,* June 19, 1877: "We received yesterday from the Capital three books, printed at the State's expense. One of them contains the Statutes of 1877, and the others comprise volumes one and two of the Census Report of 1875—a work giving a list simply of the names of the inhabitants of the State of Nevada at that time, including Chinamen and 'Indians not taxed.' A sorry list it is, too. From a hurried glance at the names of this section, we found them so badly muddled that there is not a boy in the county who could identify his father. Typographically, the job is a disgrace to the craft. The publication of these volumes, at a cost of $25,000, was one of the grandest outrages ever perpetrated by a legislative body. The writer raised his feeble voice against the swindle, but it was not heeded." George W. Cassidy, owner of the *Sentinel* and author of this tirade, was a state Senator from Eureka County during the 1877 session.

NvMus (volume I only).

NEVADA. *Governor, 1871-1879 (Lewis Rice Bradley)*. Thanksgiving proclamation. Carson City: John J. Hill, State Printer. 1877. [L888]

The Reno *Nevada State Journal* of November 22, 1877, quotes the Carson City *Nevada Tribune*, noting that the proclamation had been "issued in circular form, and is a precise copy of the proclamation of last year." The next day's issue of the *Reese River Reveille* referred to the "sheet of yellow, aged-looking paper" that was posted on the bulletin board in front of the court house. A number of other newspapers commented on the Governor's failure to send it to newspapers for publication, the Gold Hill *News* saying that a few of the "small handbills" had been "distributed in some of the bar-rooms of Carson" (November 30). The *Territorial Enterprise* got in perhaps the best Republican licks at the Democratic Governor on December 12: "We will hold to personal accountability any gentleman who may be bold enough to hereafter declare, either as a statement of fact or an incentive to levity, that Governor L. R. Bradley failed to issue a Thanksgiving proclamation last month. True, the public journals received no notice of it, and the God-fearing people of Nevada knew nothing of its promulgation; but the pious ukase, irade, edict pronunciamento, bull, whatever it may be called, in deference to its rhetorical dignity and momentous import, was issued, nevertheless; not only issued, but printed in circular form; not only printed, but actually circulated to some extent by being handed around among a few of the personal and political friends of His Excellency in Carson. A copy, we understand, was forwarded to the State Prison, and another to the Executive cattle-ranch in Elko county. With the exception of a package of a half-dozen or more which we received, yesterday, the bulk of the remainder, we have reason to believe, still remain in the office of the Secretary of State. As a matter of economy, the date line might have been left in blank in the printed circulars, and then, by inserting the day of the month in pencil with each succeeding year, they would have lasted through the third term of His Excellency, or until he arrived at the conclusion that there was little on earth worth thanking God for." The Governor had issued his proclamation on November 16, setting November 29 as Thanksgiving.

NEVADA. *Governor, 1871-1879 (Lewis Rice Bradley)*.

Third Biennial Message | of | L. R. Bradley, Governor of Neva-da, | Delivered to the | Legislature, January 3, 1877. | [*state seal*] | Carson City: | John J. Hill, State Printer. | 1877. [889]

41 p. 23 x 15 cm. Wrapper title, in decorative rule border. Issued as No. 1 in AJSA, 1877, vol. I, from different type, on 28 p.

Assembly concurrent resolution to print 2,500 copies (SSN, 1877, p. 211). The Gold

Hill *News* of January 17 reported receipt of "a copy in pamphlet form."
CSmH. CtY. M. NN. NvU (microfilm).

NEVADA. *Homographic Charts*. Homographic chart of the Nevada state
government, A.D. 1877. Carson City: Carson Daily Appeal. 1877.
Broadside. 71 x 30 cm.   [L890]

In the early part of this study, when I was not yet convinced that transcriptions
recording lineation and ornamentation were altogether wise, I examined a copy of the
chart at NvMus. Following my visit parts of the collections were put into storage
during construction of an annex to the building. Later, when I wanted to check the
lineation, however, the chart could not be found. In this unique instance, then, a
"lost" imprint has a location symbol.

Carson City *Nevada Tribune*, January 2, 1877: "A. F. Tennant, one of the bulldozed
legislative candidates, has started in on a homographic chart, and will doubtless get up
a first class one, for he is a live young man. We beg leave to inform our Democratic
friends that there is no harm in it at all, as it is merely taking down their names, ages,
nativities and political proclivities, and in case any of the Democratic members are
bachelors of uncertain ages they can bulldoze Tennant and get him to put it away
down. A Democratic Senator from Churchill [county] refused, in 1867, to subscribe
to the damned thing because his mother had died in Missouri under the treatment of a
homeopathic physician. We assure our friends that the chart has nothing to do with
the practice of medicine." Carson City *Appeal*, January 26, 1877: "A homographic
chart of the government of the State of Nevada, for the present year, has been
prepared by Mr. A. F. Tennant, and printed at this office." The *Appeal* for January 21
published statistics about various state officers, so the copy had probably been
received by then. A Senate concurrent resolution to purchase copies was introduced
and tabled (JS, 1877, p. 174); it was taken up later and tabled again (ibid., p. 181).
NvMus.

NEVADA. *Laws, statutes, etc.*

Laws | Relating to | The Public School System | of the | State of
Nevada. | [*short rule*] | Compiled and Published by the Superinten-
dent of Public | Instruction, for the Use of School Officers. | [*state
seal*] | Carson City: | John J. Hill, State Printer. | 1877.   [891]

26, [1] p. 23 x 15 cm. Printed wrapper.
The Carson City *Nevada Tribune* acknowledged receipt of a copy on April 16, 1877.
M. MH. NjP (rebound; lacks wrapper). NvU (microfilm).

NEVADA. *Laws, statutes, etc.*

Statutes | of the | State of Nevada, | Passed at the | Eighth Session
of the Legislature, | 1877. | Begun on Monday, the First Day of
January, and Ended | on Thursday, the First Day of March. | [*state
seal*] | Carson City: | John J. Hill, State Printer. | 1877.   [892]

xvi, 382 p. 23 x 15 cm. Leather binding. On p. [231]-349: Reports of the State

Treasurer of the State of Nevada, for the Eleventh and Twelfth Fiscal Years, 1875 and 1876. Jerry Schooling, Treasurer.

A bill of $3,083.14 was paid on July 2, 1877, for printing and binding 600 copies (Controller's report, 1878, p. 226-227). The Reno *Nevada State Journal* acknowledged receipt of a copy on June 9.

Az. CU-B. CoD. CtY-L. DLC. IU. MBS. MH-L. NN. NjP. NvEC. NvEuC. NvGoEC. NvHi. NvLN. NvRNC. NvRWL. NvSC. NvU. NvYLR. OrU-L.

NEVADA. *Legislature.*

Appendix | to | Journals of Senate and Assembly, | of the | Eighth Session | of the | Legislature of the State of Nevada. ·| [*short rule*] | Volume 1. [2. 3.] | [*state seal*] | Carson City: | John J. Hill, State Printer. | 1877.   [893]

28, 107, 145, 57, 63, 13, 67, 51, 66, viii, 226, 12, 16, 8, 24, 26, 4, [5]-8, 4, 4, 4, 4; 848; 824 p. 23 x 16 cm. Half-leather binding. Numbering follows the table of contents. No. 1, Third Biennial Message of L. R. Bradley, Governor of Nevada, Delivered to the Legislature, January 3, 1877, 28 p.; No. 2, Annual Report of the Controller of the State of Nevada, for the Eleventh Fiscal Year, ending December 31, 1875. W. W. Hobart, Controller, 107 p.; No. 3, Annual Report of the Controller of the State of Nevada, For the Twelfth Fiscal Year, ending December 31, 1876. W. W. Hobart, Controller. Transmitted January 8th, 1877, 145 p.; No. 4, Annual Report of the State Treasurer of the State of Nevada, for the Eleventh Fiscal Year, Ending December 31, 1875. Jerry Schooling, Treasurer, 57 p.; No. 5, Annual Report of the State Treasurer of the State of Nevada, for the Twelfth Fiscal Year, Ending December 31, 1876. Jerry Schooling, Treasurer, 63 p.; No. 6, Biennial Report of the Secretary of State of the State of Nevada, for the Eleventh and Twelfth Fiscal Years, Ending December 31, 1876, 13 p.; No. 7, Report of the Superintendent of Public Instruction of the State of Nevada, for the Years 1875 and 1876, 67 p.; No. 8, Report of the Surveyor General and State Land Register of the State of Nevada, for the Years 1875 and 1876, 51 p.; No. 9, Biennial Report of the Warden of the Nevada State Prison, for the Years 1875 and 1876. Eighth Session of the Legislature of Nevada, 1877, 66 p.; No. 10, Biennial Report of the State Mineralogist of the State of Nevada, for the Years 1875 and 1876, viii, 226 p.; No. 11, Report of the Commissioners for The Care of the Indigent Insane of the State of Nevada, for the Years 1875 and 1876, 12 p.; No. 12, Report of Committee to Visit the Insane and Deaf and Dumb Asylums, 16 p.; No. 13, Report of the Attorney General of the State of Nevada, for the Years 1875 and 1876, 8 p.; No. 14, Biennial Report of the Adjutant General of the State of Nevada, for the Years 1875 and 1876, 24 p.; No. 15, Report of the Board of Directors of the State Orphans' Home, for the Eleventh and Twelfth Fiscal Years, 26 p.; No. 16, Report of Majority of [Senate] Ways and Means Committee to Visit New State Prison, 4 p.; No. 17, Report of Certain Members of the [Senate Ways and Means] Committee of State Prison Matters, p. [5]-8, continuing pagination of preceding report; No. 18, Report of The State Bond Commissioners, 4 p.; No. 19, Report of Clerk of Supreme Court, 4 p.; No. 20, Report of the Board of Capitol Commissioners, 4 p.; No. 21, Report of [Joint] Committee on Substitute Assembly Concurrent Resolution No. 3 in Relation to Visiting and Examining into the Condition of the State University at Elko, 4 p. Volumes 2 and 3 are the two volumes of the 1875 census, described in No. 887.

A bill for $875.48 was paid on July 2, 1877, for printing and binding 300 copies (Controller's report, 1878, p. 226-227); $1,412.24 was paid on August 6 for volumes 2 and 3 (ibid.). The Reno *Gazette* reported receipt of the three volumes on August 22. Az. DLC. M. MH. NN. Nv-Ar (vol. 2). NvHi. NvLC (vol. 2). NvLN (vol. 1-2). NvU. UU-L (vol. 1). WHi.

NEVADA. *Legislature.*

Rules | Governing the Legislature | of the | State of Nevada, | Together with | the Constitution of the State, | and | an Act Concerning the Number of Employés | in the Legislature, Etc. | [*state seal*] | Carson City: | John J. Hill, State Printer. | 1877.   [894]

xxxi, [1], 171 p. 17 x 11 cm. Gold-stamped cloth binding or printed wrappers. Assembly concurrent resolution to print 1,000 copies, with 100 to be bound in cloth, 100 in paper covers, and 800 stitched but not covered and leaves not cut, to be sent to the Secretary of State (SSN, 1877, p. 212). The estimated cost of printing, by the Senate Committee on Printing, was $400 (JS, 1877, p. 40-41). The Carson *Appeal* reported on January 25 that the rules had been distributed to members of the Legislature; the February 3 issue of the Reno *Gazette* acknowledged receipt of a copy. Nv (cloth).

NEVADA. *Legislature. Assembly.*

The | Journal of the Assembly | of the | Eighth Session | of the | Legislature of the State of Nevada, | 1877. | Begun on Monday, the First Day of January, and Ended | on Thursday, the First Day of March. | [*state seal*] | Carson City: | John J. Hill, State Printer. | 1877.   [895]

394 p. 23 x 15 cm. Half-leather binding. The Gold Hill *News* acknowledged receipt of a copy in its issue of August 20, 1877. CtY-L. DLC. M. MH. NN. Nv-Ar. NvHi. NvLC. NvLN. NvRW. NvRWL. NvSC. NvU. UU-L. WHi.

NEVADA. *Legislature. Joint Committee on Insane Asylum.*

[*Thick-thin rule*] | Report of Committee | to Visit the | Insane and Deaf and Dumb Asylums. | [*thin-thick rule*] | [Carson City: John J. Hill, State Printer. 1877.]   [L896]

16 p. Description from half title in AJSA, 1877, vol. I, No. 12. Assembly concurrent resolution to print 1,000 copies (SSN, 1877, p. 220). The Carson City *Appeal* reported on February 27 that the report "has been printed."

NEVADA. *Legislature. Joint Committee on University.*

[*Thick-thin rule*] | Report of Committee | on Substitute | Assembly Concurrent Resolution No. 3 | in Relation to | Visiting and Examining into the Condition of | the State University at Elko. | [*thin-thick rule*] | [Carson City: John J. Hill, State Printer. 1877.] [L897]

4 p. Description from half title in AJSA, 1877, vol. I, No. 21.

Assembly concurrent resolution to print, but with no stated number (JA, 1877, p. 238, 243). The Silver City *Lyon County Times* printed extracts from the report on February 28, 1877.

NEVADA. *Legislature. Senate.*

The | Journal of the Senate | of the | Eighth Session | of the | Legislature of the State of Nevada, | 1877. | Begun on Monday, the First Day of January, and Ended | on Thursday, the First Day of March. | [*state seal*] | Carson City: | John J. Hill, State Printer. | 1877. [898]

359 p. 23 x 15 cm. Half-leather binding.

The Gold Hill *News* acknowledged receipt of a copy on August 20, 1877.

CtY-L. DLC. M. MH. NN. Nv. Nv-Ar. NvHi. NvLC. NvLN. NvRWL. NvSC. NvU. UU-L. WHi.

NEVADA. *Office of Superintendent of Public Instruction.*

Report | of the | Superintendent of Public Instruction | of the | State of Nevada, | for | the Years 1875 and 1876. | [*state seal*] | Carson City: | John J. Hill, State Printer. | 1877. [899]

67 p. 23 x 15 cm. Wrapper title, in decorative rule border. Issued also as No. 7 in AJSA, 1877, vol. I.

Senate concurrent resolution to print 1,200 copies in pamphlet form (SSN, 1877, p. 225). The Carson City *Nevada Tribune* reported receipt of a copy on February 6, 1877.

DHEW. M. NN. NvU (microfilm).

NEVADA. *Secretary of State.*

[*Thick-thin rule*] | Biennial Report | of the | Secretary of State | of the | State of Nevada, | for the | Eleventh and Twelfth Fiscal Years, | Ending December 31, 1876. | [*thin-thick rule*] | [Carson City: John J. Hill, State Printer. 1877.] [L900]

13 p. Description from half title in AJSA, 1877, vol. I, No. 6.

Senate concurrent resolution to print 240 copies in pamphlet form (SSN, 1877, p. 227).

NEVADA. *State Board of Centennial Commissioners.*

Report | of the | State Board | of | Centennial Commissioners | of the | State of Nevada. | [*filet*] | Made in pursuance of Section Eight of an Act of the Legis-|lature of the State of Nevada, approved

March 5, 1875. | [*filet*] | Carson City: | Robinson & Mighels, Print-
ers. | 1877.   [901]

16 p. 22 x 15 cm. Wrapper title, in wavy-thin rule border. Errata slip bound in before
p. 1.

The Carson City *Appeal,* which was owned by Marshall Robinson and Henry R.
Mighels, reported receipt of a copy on April 8, 1877.

NN (rebound). NvU (microfilm). PHi.

NEVADA. *State Controller's Office.*

Annual Report | of the | Controller of the State of Nevada, | for
the | Twelfth Fiscal Year, Ending December 31st, 1876. | [*short
rule*] | W. W. Hobart, Controller. | [*short rule*] | Transmitted
January 8th, 1877. | [*state seal*] | Carson City: | John J. Hill, State
Printer. | 1877.   [902]

145 p. 23 x 14 cm. Wrapper title, in decorative rule border. Issued also as No. 3 in
AJSA, 1877, vol. I.

The Gold Hill *News* of January 27, 1877, reported receipt of a copy.

C. DLC. NvHi.

NEVADA. *State Controller's Office.* Circular. Carson City: John J. Hill,
State Printer. 1877.   [L903]

Silver City *Lyon County Times,* March 17, 1877: "State Controller [W. W.] Hobart
has issued a circular to Boards of County Commissioners informing them that 'the
rate of taxation for State purpose [*sic*] for the present fiscal year, commencing January
1, 1877, is ninety cents on each one hundred dollars valuation.' "

NEVADA. *State Mineralogist.*

[*Thick-thin rule*] | Biennial Report | of the | State Mineralogist | of
the | State of Nevada, | for | the Years 1875 and 1876. | [*thin-thick
rule*] | [Carson City:] John J. Hill [*dotted rule*] State Printer. | [*short
rule*] | [1877.]   [904]

viii, 226 p. 23 x 15 cm. Half title, with imprint from verso. Cloth binding, with
blind-stamped thick rule borders front and rear, and gold-stamped title: Biennial
Report of State Mineralogist State of Nevada, 1875-76. On p. [187]-226: Supplement.
Showing Proceeds of Mines in the State of Nevada During the Years 1871-72-73-74-
75, and 1st, 2d, and 3d Quarters of 1876. Compiled from County Assessors' Returns
in the State Controller's Office. Issued also as No. 10 in AJSA, 1877, vol. I.

Senate concurrent resolution to print 1,000 copies, with 500 to be bound in cloth
(SSN, 1877, p. 229); the remainder may have been issued in wrappers or sent unbound
to the Secretary of State (see No. 894). A bill for $1,650.04 was paid on June 4, 1877,
for printing 1,000 copies (Controller's report, 1878, p. 226-227).

C. MWA. Nv. NvHi. NvU.

Nevada. *State Orphans' Home.*

[*Thick-thin rule*] | Report of the Board of Directors | of the | State Orphans' Home, | for the | Eleventh and Twelfth Fiscal Years. | [*thin-thick rule*] | [Carson City: John J. Hill, State Printer.
[L905]

26 p. Description from half title in AJSA, 1877, vol. I, No. 15.

The Eureka *Sentinel* acknowledged receipt of a copy on January 26, 1877.

Nevada. *State Prison.*

Biennial Report | of the | Warden of the Nevada State Prison, | for the | Years 1875 and 1876. | [*short rule*] | Eighth Session of the Legislature of Nevada, 1877. | [*state seal*] | Carson City: | John J. Hill, State Printer. | 1877. [906]

66 p. 22 x 15 cm. Wrapper title, in decorative rule border. Issued also as No. 9 in AJSA, 1877, vol. I.

Senate concurrent resolution to print 1,000 copies (SSN, 1877, p. 226). The Gold Hill *News* reported receipt of a copy on February 1, 1877.

M. NvU (microfilm).

Nevada. *Supreme Court.*

[Briefs. 1877.]

McCausland vs. Ralston. Brief of respondent, A. J. Ralston. 43 p. 25 x 18 cm. Imprint on wrapper: Virginia, Nev.: Printed at the Evening Chronicle Job Office. 1877. Nv-Ar. [907]

Nevada vs. California Mining Co. et al. Brief of appellant, State of Nevada. 51, [1], xi p. 23 x 18 cm. Imprint on wrapper: Virginia, Nevada: Enterprise Steam Printing House. 1877. Nv-Ar. [908]

Ruby Consolidated Mining Co. vs. Heynemann et al. Appellant's petition for rehearing, Ruby Consolidated Mining Co. 31 p. 26 x 18 cm. Printed on wrapper: Filed [*dotted rule*] 1877. Nv-Ar. [909]

Ruby Consolidated Mining Co. vs. Heynemann et al. Points and authorities of respondents on rehearing, H. Heynemann et al. 19 p. 26 x 18 cm. Imprint on wrapper: C. A. Murdock & Co., Book and Job Printers, 532 Clay Street, San Francisco. Printed on wrapper: Filed [*dotted rule*] 1877. Nv-Ar. [910]

Solen vs. Virginia and Truckee Railroad Co. Brief of respondent, William Solen. 47 p. 25 x 18 cm. Imprint on wrapper: Virginia, Nev.: Brown & Mahanny, Book and Job Printers. 1877. Nv-Ar. [911]

Stevenson and Son vs. Mann et al. Brief of appellants, J. J. Mann et al. 23 p. 26 x 18 cm. Imprint on wrapper: San Francisco: C. H. Street, Printer, 522 California Street. (Building formerly occupied by W. U. Tel. Co.) 1877. Nv-Ar. [912]

Nevada. *Supreme Court.* Index to the Nevada reports, volumes I to XI, inclusive. By Benjamin Hunter, attorney at law, author of indexes to

Ohio, Iowa, Missouri and Tennessee reports. Published by the author. San Francisco, Oakland, Cal. Arcade Printing House. 1877. 140 p. [L913]

Check List: 480 described this piece by title only, stating that no copy had been located. In 1969 a card in the public catalog at DLC listed a copy there, and NUC 412, p. 38, locates a copy at Nv; neither copy can now be found. Because of the issuance in 1913 of a superseding index to the Reports, many libraries probably discarded their copies of the 1877 index.

NEVADA. *Supreme Court.*

Reports of Cases | Determined in | The Supreme Court | of the | State of Nevada. | During the Year 1876. | Reported by | Chas. F. Bicknell, | Clerk of Supreme Court, | and | Hon. Thomas P. Hawley, | Chief Justice. | Volume XI. | San Francisco: | A. L. Bancroft and Company, | Law Book Publishers, Booksellers and Stationers. | 1877. [914]

503 p. 23 x 15 cm. Leather binding.

Payment of $1,200 for 600 copies was made on May 17, 1877 (Controller's report, 1878, p. 220). Receipt of a copy was acknowledged by the Reno *Gazette* on May 24, 1877.

Az. CU-B. DHEW. DLC. In-SC (rebound). M. Nv. Nv-Ar. NvEuC. NvHi. NvLC. NvLN. NvRNC. NvRWL. NvU. OrU-L. U-L.

NEVADA. *Supreme Court.*

Reports of Decisions | of the | Supreme Court | of the | State of Nevada. | By | Hon. Thomas P. Hawley, | Chief Justice. | Publication Authorized by the Supreme Court of the | State of Nevada. | Volumes I. and II. | San Francisco: | A.L. Bancroft and Company, | Law Book Publishers, Booksellers and Stationers | 1877. [915]

xv, [2], 18-950 p. 23 x 15 cm. Leather binding.

A stereotype edition of 400 copies of the out-of-print Reports was authorized by SSN, 1877, p. 112; Bancroft, or the state, probably acquired the plates from the original printers for this edition. The Secretary of State had in his office on January 1, 1877, 90 copies of Volume I and 51 copies of Volume II of the original edition (Report, 1875-1876, p. 7-8)—too few, in the opinion of the Court; see 1877 Summary, p. 293. The Controller's report for 1878, p. 220, indicates that $2,000 was paid to Bancroft on May 9, 1877; the report of the Secretary of State for 1877-1878, p. 8-11, notes receipt of the 400 copies.

CU-B. Nv-Ar. NvEuC. NvHi. NvLN. NvRNC. NvRWL (rebound). NvU. OrU-L. U-L.

NEVADA. *Supreme Court.*

Reports of Decisions | of the | Supreme Court | of the | State of

Nevada. | Edited by | Hon. Thomas P. Hawley, | Chief Justice. | Publication Authorized by the Supreme Court. | Under Act approved March 2, 1877. (Stat. 1877, 112.) | Volumes III. and IV. | San Francisco: | A. L. Bancroft and Company, | Law Book Publishers, Booksellers and Stationers. | 1877.   [916]

xvi, [1], 18-1034 p. 23 x 16 cm. Leather binding.

400 stereotyped copies were authorized by SSN, 1877, p. 112; see No. 915. On January 1, 1877, the Secretary of State had available for distribution 63 and 192 copies respectively, of the original editions (Report, 1875-1876, p. 7-8); see 1877 Summary, p. 293. The Controller's report for 1878, p. 220, indicates that $2,000 was paid to Bancroft on September 1, 1877; the report of the Secretary of State for 1877-1878, p. 8-11, notes receipt of the 400 copies.

Az. CU-B. Nv. Nv-Ar. NvEuC. NvHi. NvLN. NvRNC. NvRWL. NvSC. NvU. OrU-L. U-L.

Nevada. *Surveyor General.*

Report | of the | Surveyor General | and | State Land Register | of | The State of Nevada, | for the | Years 1875 and 1876. | [*state seal*] | Carson City: | John J. Hill, State Printer. | 1877. [917]

51 p. 23 x 15 cm. Wrapper title, in decorative rule border. Issued also as No. 8 in AJSA, 1877, vol. I.

Senate concurrent resolution to print 1,500 copies (SSN, 1877, p. 225). The Carson City *Appeal* reported receipt of a copy on February 14, 1877.

CtY. NvU.

Nevada. *Treasury Department.*

Annual Report | of the | State Treasurer | of the | State of Nevada, | for | The Twelfth Fiscal Year, Ending December 31, 1876. | [*short rule*] | Jerry Schooling, Treasurer. | [*short rule*] | Transmitted January 8th, 1877. | [*state seal*] | Carson City: | John J. Hill, State Printer. | 1877.   [918]

63 p. 23 x 15 cm. Wrapper title, in decorative rule border. Issued also as No. 5 in AJSA, 1877, vol. I, and in SSN, 1877, p. [287]-349 from the same type. The printing of 1,200 copies was authorized by an 1873 law (SSN, 1873, p. 175). The Gold Hill *News* acknowledged receipt of a copy on January 30, 1877.

NvU.

Nevada State Agricultural, Mining and Mechanical Society. *Reno, Nevada.*

Fourth Annual Fair | of the | Nevada State | Agricultural, Mining and Mechanical Society | to be Held | October Fifteenth to Twentieth, Inclusive, 1877, | At Reno. | [*short rule*] | Competition Open to All the World. | [*short rule*] | No Entry Fee, except in Speed Contests. | [*short rule*] | Please Circulate, and bring a copy with you to the Fair. | [*short rule*] | Reno, Nevada: | Gazette Print. | 1877.   [919]

77, [3] p. 23 x 14 cm. Wrapper title, in decorative rule border. The word "and" in line 4 is nearly vertical.

The imprint in this case, as in so many others in Nevada printing history, is deceptive. The barbs thrown at the Society for sending its printing orders to San Francisco in previous years (see Nos. 818 and L846) apparently had their effect in 1877, and the printing contract was given to a local job office. But the July 26 comment of the *Gazette*'s local journalistic rival, the *Nevada State Journal,* is revealing: "The catalogue for our next Fair was received from below yesterday morning, and a number of copies distributed throughout the State." "Below," to a Nevadan, means California's Bay Area.

CSmH. CU-B (lacks [3] p. at end).

ODD FELLOWS, INDEPENDENT ORDER OF. *Cornucopia, Nevada. Cornucopia Lodge No. 29.*

Constitution, | By-Laws and Rules of Order | of | Cornucopia Lodge, No. 29, | of the | Independent Order of Odd Fellows | of the | State of Nevada. | [*filet*] | Instituted at Cornucopia May 31, 1877. | [*filet*] | San Francisco: | Jos. Winterburn & Co., Book & Job Printers, | 417 Clay street, between Sansome and Battery. | 1877.
[920]

80 p. 14? x 10? cm. The recorded copy has been trimmed and bound. Printed wrapper. Title and text pages in single rule borders. A membership certificate, not counted in the pagination, precedes the title page.

CU-B.

ODD FELLOWS, INDEPENDENT ORDER OF. *Nevada. Grand Encampment.*
Proceedings. Third annual session, 1877.   [L921]

Gold Hill *News*, July 18, 1877: "We have received the report of the proceedings of the third annual session of the R.W. Grand Encampment of the Independent Order of Odd Fellows of the State of Nevada, held in Odd Fellows' Hall, Carson, on the 4th and 7th of June, 1877."

ODD FELLOWS, INDEPENDENT ORDER OF. *Nevada. Grand Lodge.*

Proceedings | of the | R.W. Grand Lodge | of the | Independent Order of Odd Fellows | of the State of Nevada, | at its | Eleventh Annual Communication, | Held in the Senate Chamber of the Capitol Building at | Carson City, Ormsby County, Nevada, on the 5th, | 6th and 7th days of June, A.D. 1877. | [*short rule*] | Virginia, Nevada: | Brown & Mahanny, Book and Job Printers. | 1877.
[L921a]

[3], 1154-1237, [2], ii-viii p. Description from title page in bound volume for 1874-1879. Printed? wrapper; the index refers to material on the "third page of cover," but

it is not known whether the outside of the wrapper was also printed.

The Committee on Finance estimated that printing would cost $400 (p. 1198). The actual cost cannot be given because at the following communication the report of the Grand Treasurer indicated payments only by warrant number, with no identification of the payees.

ODD FELLOWS, INDEPENDENT ORDER OF. *Pioche, Nevada. Mount Vernon Encampment No. 8.*

Constitution, | By-laws and Rules of Order | of | Mount Vernon Encampment, | No. 8, | of the | Independent Order of Odd Fellows | of the | State of Nevada. | [*filet*] | Adopted, Pioche, Nevada, December 31, 1875. | [*filet*] | San Francisco: | Jos. Winterburn & Co., Book & Job Printers, 417 Clay street, between Sansome and Battery. | 1877. [922]

30, [2] p. 14 x 10 cm. Cloth binding, with gold-stamped title: Mount Vernon Encampment I.O.O.F. Title and text pages in single rule borders.
CU-B.

REESE RIVER REVEILLE. *Austin, Nevada.* Carrier's address. December 31, 1877. [L923]

Reveille, December 31, 1877: "It is usual for carriers of newspapers to deliver to subscribers on New Year's morning a paper called an address, in return for which his patrons present him a gratuity. The custom has never been followed here in Austin, because the address is usually composed in rhyme and hitherto there have been no poets connected with the REVEILLE. This year we have a devil who is a poet, and he prepared for the carrier an address which that functionary delivered to his patrons to-day. It was short and to the point, and was as follows: 'Monday morning I gets on my mettle / And calls on my customers to come and settle. / Put up or shut up my motto shall be; / If you don't ante up, no paper you'll see. / And to paying subscribers, from far and from near / I here wish a jolly and happy New Year.'"

RENO OPERA HOUSE. *Reno, Nevada.* Playbill. July 4, 1877. [L924]

"In addition to the programme announced on the printed bills of the entertainment at the Reno Opera House this evening, we are desired to put a clarionet solo by Valentine Gern." The main attraction at the performance was the McGinley Sisters: *Journal,* July 6.

RENO OPERA HOUSE COMPANY.

Reno Opera House Company. | McGinley Sisters. | [*triple rule*] | Dramatic Alliance!! | [*thick-thin rule*] | . . . | [*triple rule*] | At [*blank*] on [*blank*] | [*dotted rule*] | The performance will commence with the Beautiful Comedy of | Perfection; or the Maid of Munster! | . . . | [1877.] [925]

Broadside. 25? x 15 cm. The recorded copy has been cropped at head and foot. The

words "or the" in line 6 of the transcription are printed vertically. Red decorative border. The blanks on the recorded copy have been filled in to show that the performance was scheduled for Oroville, California, on Thursday, March 9. March 9 was a Friday in 1877, but clippings reviewing the performance, dated 1877, are in the scrapbook in which the playbill is mounted.
NvHi.

St. Peter's Church. *Carson City, Nevada.*

1877. Easter. 1877. | [*filet*] | St. Peter's Church, | Carson, Neva-da. | [*filet*] | . . .   [926]

Broadside. 28 x 19 cm. Chain border. Partly printed in two columns.
Words for hymns to be sung at Easter services.
NvHi.

Society of Pacific Coast Pioneers. *Nevada.*

Constitution, | By-Laws and Standing Rules | of the | Society of Pacific Coast Pioneers. | [*cut of bear on railroad track*] | State of Neva-da. | [*short rule*] | Organized at the City of Virginia, June 22nd, 1872. | [*short rule*] | Gold Hill "Daily News" Steam Print. | 1877.
[927]

31 p. 19 x 12 cm. Printed wrapper.

Alf Doten and George Paley were appointed as a committee to have the constitution and by-laws printed (NvU: Minute Book of the Society, 1872-1877) on October 12, 1876. Doten reported on February 22, 1877, that they had been printed, but that he was awaiting a list of the members from the Secretary, who announced that it would be ready and delivered to the committee "in a few days." The minutes of the meeting in Carson City on March 8 say that "Alf Doten, of the Committee on Publication of the Constitution and By-laws, reported the work completed and 100 copies present. The remaining 400 would be forwarded to the Society in a day or two."

The copy at NvHi has been taken apart and mounted in the manuscript constitution volume of the Society.
NvHi. NvU.

Society of Pacific Coast Pioneers. *Nevada.* Poster. Gold Hill: News. June 1877.   [L928]

Doten *Journals,* June 9, 1877: "PM rode to Va with Bill Gibson on Pioneer printing arrangements, as I have the posters and the advertisement in print — 100 3 sheet posters and 1 /2 column ad."

Tebbs, Moses. Circular. August 1877.   [L929]

Territorial Enterprise, August 5, 1877: "We have received a printed circular signed by M. Tebbs, in which he accuses our venerable friend of the Carson *Tribune* of prevari-cation, and says a good many things, the reverse of complimentary, of the deacon." The "deacon" was R. R. Parkinson, editor of the *Tribune.*

UNITED STATES. *Circuit Court. District of Nevada (Ninth Circuit).*

In the Circuit Court | of the United States | In and for the Ninth Circuit and District of Nevada. | [*filet*] | [*short rule*] | Eureka Consolidated Mining | Company, | vs. | Richmond Mining Company, | Of Nevada. | [*short rule*] | [*filet*] | Monday, July 23, 1877. | . . .   [930]

933 p. 27 x 21 cm. Lines 4-8, with preceding and following short rules, connected by brace. Half-leather binding. Binder's title: Eureka C. M. Co. vs. Richmond M. Co. Transcript of Testimony. Handwritten on the front board of the recorded copy: In Equity. Testimony & Exhibits. Filed Sept. 17, 1877.
CSbrFRC.

❧ 1878 ❧

The 1880 report of the State Controller (p. 28) showed that, because the entire 1877-1878 State Printing Fund appropriation had been spent in 1877, the State Board of Examiners had approved an additional expenditure for 1878 of $973.75.

On August 31, four months before the 1877 law abolishing the office of State Printer was to take effect, the first public rumblings about its inadequacy appeared in the Reno *Nevada State Journal,* which published the following: "The Legislature ought never to have abolished the office of State Printer. What should have been done was to reduce the fees about 40 per cent., and one of the first duties of the coming Legislature is to re-establish the office of State Printer, and fix the fees at such figures as will permit of a reasonable compensation. There is no question but what Crocker & Co., or Bacon, or Bancroft, or some other large firm of San Francisco, will secure the contract of doing the State work for the next few years. Our printing goes to California, our insane are kept there, and thus we are taking away from our own citizens $100,000 annually. If this is the policy we intend to pursue, if we are to continue to pay taxes for the benefit of other people, we might as well at once do away with a State Government and apply for annexation to California." The plaint was to be attended to by the 1879 Legislature, but in the meantime the Board of State Printing Commissioners was mandated to advertise for bids for printing during the 1879-1880 biennium. It began its newspaper advertising on October 7 in the required number of Nevada and California papers, stating that it would accept bids through November 7. The bids were opened on November 8 and, according to the Carson City *Appeal* of the following day,

> Bids were submitted by the following parties: B. H. Meder, of Carson; Brown & Mahanny, of Virginia City; Marshall Robinson, of Carson; Spaulding, Barto & Co., of San Francisco; Cottle & Wright, San Jose; Bacon & Co., of San Francisco; Oakland Tribune Publishing Co.; A. L. Bancroft & Co., of San Francisco; H. S. Crocker & Co., of Sacramento; H. R. Mighels, of Carson City; R. L. Tilden, of Carson City. The printing of the laws, journals, and pamphlet work was awarded to A. L. Bancroft & Co., of San Francisco. The prices were as follows: Plain composition 48 cents per 1,000 ems; rule and figure work, 60 cents per 1,000 ems; press work per token 40 cents; binding per volume, journals, 20 cents; binding per page for each 100 copies 3 cents. The contract for work to be done at the State Capital was awarded to Marshall Robinson at the following prices: Bill printing 1,000 ems 38 cents; press work per token 50 cents; folding and stitching per page one-sixteenth of a cent; blanks for Legislature and State officers $3 per thousand; proclamations $5 per thousand. All printing for State officers and the Legislature not properly coming under the above designation, composition plain, 74 cents per thousand ems; rule and figure work, $1.11; press work per token, actual work, 50 cents; advertising per square of 300 ems, 50 cents for first insertion and twenty-five cents for each subsequent insertion. For stationery for the State officers and Legislature the contract has not yet been awarded, but three bids are in, and the contract will not be awarded until samples are examined by the Board.

Entries in Alf Doten's *Journals* on December 9, 1877, and in his Diaries on January 8 and 15, 1878, show that he as proprietor of the Gold Hill *News* and Rollin M. Daggett of the *Territorial Enterprise* and Denis E. McCarthy of the Virginia City *Chronicle* had agreed on the earlier date to propose a reduction of printers' wages from seventy cents to sixty cents per thousand ems because San Francisco papers had reduced wages to fifty cents. Discussions continued through the early part of January, and on January 15 the three men and the Washoe Typographical Union agreed on a compromise reduction to sixty-five cents per thousand. Job rates were brought into line with this scale, as reflected in the Union's published scale; see No. L962 and Appendix B.

Part of the reason for the desire to lower printers' wages may have been a bill in Congress that would place what was considered to be a prohibitive tariff on type of foreign manufacture. The Reno *Gazette* had the following on February 1.

> A matter of great concern to all typos is now under agitation in Congress, and meets with sharp comment from the Western press. It is proposed under the new tariff bill to fix the duty on news and book type

at 15 cents per pound, which is 40 to 60 per cent. *ad valorem*. The rate on job and fancy type is 30 cents per pound, which is from 50 to 100 per cent. *ad valorem*. This means simply the exclusion of foreign made type from the American market, and the printer naturally takes much interest in a scheme which, if successful, will place him at the mercy of American type founders. It is urged by the fraternity that it has more claims for consideration than the founders, because it employs 70 men where the foundry employs one. Foreign type is now sold at American prices, and its makers claim for it superiority. It seems that this attempt at prohibition is a valid argument, both in favor of foreign type and against the new tariff. Men never attempt to exclude inferior articles from competition with them, and the following additional arguments against the proposed tariff seem to us entirely sufficient to prevent its passage: A tariff duty on type is a tax on education and intelligence, and, as such, works a positive wrong on the country. Cheap type means cheap books and newspapers; it means cheap and universal education. The tax on type protects twelve men at the expense of twenty thousand master printers. We hope the unjust tariff may be removed.

The new tariffs were not enacted.

Perhaps because of the reduced wages imposed upon them in January, the typographical union formally affiliated with the Mechanics' Union of Storey County on October 6. The *Enterprise* welcomed the action, editorializing two days later on the "wisdom and moderation" of the Mechanics' Union in the past and predicting "a satisfactory continuance of the same" because of "the well-known character of its component parts."

Belleville lost its paper in June; one of Eureka's papers ceased at about the same time, but its material was used immediately for another in the same town. The paper in Columbus stopped sometime in 1878. Cherry Creek gained a press as the year opened; at the same time Tuscarora's two papers merged to become one. Grantsville acquired a newspaper in October, as did Ruby Hill. Reno had two new papers for very brief periods. Virginia City saw the establishment of two new papers, one of which lasted for only a month in the fall. One of the previous year's entries did not live to see 1879. William Sutherland, a printer for the *Territorial Enterprise*, probably began his separate job operation in Virginia City during the year. All other newspapers in Aurora, Austin, Battle Mountain (although the paper there suspended for a month and a half in the summer), Belmont, Carson City, Elko, Eureka, Genoa, Gold Hill, Hamilton, Pioche, Reno, Silver City, Unionville, Tybo, Virginia City, Ward, and Winnemucca that had been active at the end of 1877 continued to publish throughout the year.

One Thousand Dollars
REWARD!!

TERRITORY OF NEVADA, EXECUTIVE DEPARTMENT,
CARSON CITY, February 19, 1863.

By the authority in me vested by law, as Governor of the Terrritory of Nevada, I hereby offer

$1,000 Reward

for the apprehension of

Edw'd W. Richardson,

charged with Murder and Robbery, and

Horace F. Swazey

charged with Murder ; both of whom escaped last night from the Ormsby County jail.

The above reward will be paid upon their delivery into the custody of the Sheriff of said county, at said jail ; or **FIVE HUNDRED DOLLARS** will be paid upon such apprehension and delivery of either of them, and also the expenses of his or their transmission to said jail.

Said *Richardson* is **22** years of age ; about **5** feet 8 inches high ; dark complexion ; black, bushy hair ; dark blue eyes, weighs about 155 or 160 pounds, large nose, has a wide scar on the right thigh, reaching from the groin to the knee ; an indelible ink ring on one or more fingers on one or both hands, and an indelible ink star on his right wrist.

Said *Swazey* is full six feet high ; strongly built, rather light complexion, awkward appearance, weighs two hundred pounds ; has powder marks on, and on each side of his nose ; scar on his chin ; two or three back teeth out, caused by pistol shot ; mouth not well yet ; light blue eyes ; about **28** years old.

ORION CLEMENS,
ACTING GOVERNOR.

"Washoe Times" Print, Washoe City.

162. NvHi

GOLD HILL NEWS

EXTRA!

THE LADY BRYAN FIRE

All the Miners Escape from the Shaft.

THE HOISTING WORKS DESTROYED.

The Loss Estimated at $200,000.

[From our Special Reporter.]

Early this morning fire was discovered near the boilers of the Lady Bryan works, and soon the whole building was in flames. The men in the works all fled, including the engineer, leaving the thirteen men in the mine to their fate. The first intimation given the miners of the fire was by a red-hot cage which fell to the bottom of the shaft. They rallied and climbed up the shaft, amid falling fire-brands, a distance of 280 feet, to the connection with the old works, and all made their escape. The loss is estimated at $200,000, which is said to be fully covered by insurance. The shaft is comparatively uninjured, only a few of the upper timbers being destroyed. The works will be rebuilt as soon as possible.

TERRITORIAL ENTERPRISE EXTRA.

CONTAINING

A FULL ACCOUNT

OF

"FRANK LESLIE" AND WIFE.

Found among the papers and effects of my uncle, E. G. Squier

Frank Squier

VIRGINIA CITY, NEVADA,

July 14, 1878.

National Guard Hall

Complete Success of the New Season!

TO-NIGHT

FRIDAY, SEPT. 22,

COMPLIMENTARY BENEFIT!

TO

ELLA F. BADGER!

GREAT ATTRACTION AND DOUBLE BILL
FOR THIS OCCASION!

ROSE EYTINGE

SUPPORTED BY THE

CALIFORNIA
DRAMATIC COMP'Y

Will appear in her great character of JULIA in Sheridan
Knowles' magnificent play, The

HUNCHBACK

ELLA F. BADGER as HELEN

Miss Badger will also appear, on this occasion only, as MARGERY,
in the Sparkling Comedietta,

The Rough Diamond

G. H. BADGER as ....COUSIN JOE

This evening the performance will commence with Sheridan Knowles' magnificent play,

THE HUNCHBACK!

JULIA			ROSE EYTINGE
HELEN	ELLA F. BADGER	FATHOM	
MASTER WALTER	J. B. ASHTON	WILFORD	R. TAYLOR
SIR THOMAS CLIFFORD	J. G. BARROWS	GAYLOVE	JOHN MAGUIRE
MASTER MODUS	GEO. OSBORNE	LORD TINSEL	J. WILLIAMS
			MRS. ROBINSON

The Evening's Performance will conclude with the Laughable Comedietta, The

ROUGH DIAMOND!

MARGERY			ELLA F. BADGER
LADY PLATO	MRS. J. B. ASHTON	SIR WILLIAM	J. B. ASHTON
COUSIN JOE	GEO H. BADGER	CAPT. BLENHEIM	J. MAGUIRE

SATURDAY AFTERNOON,
Last Grand Matinee of Rose Eytinge
WHEN WILL BE PRESENTED
ROSE MICHEL!

SATURDAY EVENING,
Farewell Benefit and POSITIVELY Last Appearance
OF
ROSE EYTINGE
WHEN SHE WILL APPEAR IN HER GREAT IMPERSONATION OF
CAMILLE!

PRICES OF ADMISSION.

Admission	$1 00	Reserved Chairs	$1 50
Gallery	50	Children under 12, Half Price	

Evening Chronicle Steam Print, Virginia, Nevada.

841. CHi

PIPER'S
OPERA HOUSE

PROPRIETOR...JOHN PIPER
Stage Manager..............W. Lloyd | Musical Director..............F. Schmidt
Scenic Artist.............B. McFarlane | Machinist..............O. N. Cronkite

Last Night but Three of the
Dramatic Season
1872

Engagement of Mr. Lawrence
BARRETT

SUPPORTED BY
Mr. HENRY EDWARDS,
And Mr. JOHN WILSON,
OF THE CALIFORNIA THEATRE, AND
Mrs. F. M. BATES!

THURSDAY Evening, July 4
THE BEAUTIFUL DRAMA, ENTITLED

ROSEDALE!
Or, THE RIFLE BALL!

ELLIOT GRAY,	Mr. LAWRENCE BARRETT
BUNBURY KOBB	Mr. HENRY EDWARDS
MILES McKENNA	Mr. JOHN WILSON
Col. May	C. Edmonds
Matthew Leigh	E. Plympton
Farmer Green	W. Lloyd
Romany	P. Thayer
Coporal Daw	J. Maguire
Docksey	E. Lipsis
ROSA LEIGH	Mrs. F. M. BATES
Lady Florence May	Miss Nelly Cummings
Lady Adela	Mrs. C. Edmonds
Tabitha Stork	Mrs. Edwin F. Stewart
Sarah	Miss Jennie Mandeville
Primrose	Miss Carrie Lipsis

Prices of Admission:

Dress Circle and Orchestra Chairs	One Dollar
Parquette	Fifty Cents
Private Boxes	Five Dollars

To-morrow Evening,
DIVORCE!

On Saturday Afternoon, at 2 o'clock,
Grand BARRETT MATINEE

"EVENING CHRONICLE" PRINT.

660. NjP

TO THE VOTERS OF STOREY COUNTY!

WHAT I KNOW ABOUT J. P. JONES.

It being on the eve of an important political election, I take the opportunity to say a few words as to the duty of voters on this occasion.

I have been prominently identified with the Union Republican party since its formation, but I consider it my duty to warn the people against casting their votes for the election of Legislative nominees who profess to be the friends of a certain individual who aspires to represent the State of Nevada in the United States Senate, called JOHN P. JONES. My reason for this warning is that his statements to individuals and the public cannot be relied on; that he will say anything that he considers will make him the most popular. Anti-subsidy is popular, and he tells the dear people that he is one of them, and would never vote an acre of land or a dollar of money to facilitate any private enterprise; that he is opposed to royalties and monopolies, and in fact that he is a bosom friend of the laboring man. This would all be very fine if carried out.

I speak from absolute knowledge when I say that no dependence can be placed on his statements, and this fact is well known by many also. He will say anything that he thinks will conduce to the accomplishment of his wishes. Such a man is not worthy of the position that he aspires to, but would disgrace the State by being sent to represent it in the councils of the nation, he is so notoriously unreliable. If so great a misfortune should happen as his being elected to the U. S. Senate at the next session of the Legislature, it will be found that it was the greatest mistake that was ever made, and that when too late, it will be regretted and repented of in sackcloth and ashes, except those perhaps who may be bought to vote for him.

I can prove that his word is not to be relied on, by written evidence, over his his own signature. Now, if he will write what he knows is not true and sign his name under it, what confidence can be placed in his verbal statements? I would ask the voters of Nevada to consider well before they cast their votes for legislators who will elect such a man to the position of U. S. Senator. Would you do so, knowing that he is a man of no integrity, and one on whom you could not rely to fulfill his promises to the people? It does not seem possible that such could be the case. I think that there is too much dignity and manhood in the voters of the State of Nevada to do so. We have had enough of that already, and it is time to reform; and above all to not allow ourselves to be deceived by an "Oily Gammon." Jones is the prince of Oily Gammons. If he is successful in obtaining his election, he will laugh at those who have been duped by his promises, and chuckle over the manner in which he has done it.

Voters of Nevada, will you place yourselves in a situation to be ashamed of what you have done? Will you be the dupes of a faithless politician, and be held up to ridicule by our sister States? God forbid! If you would not be thus ashamed and ridiculed, do not cast your votes where they will conduce to the elevation of JOHN P. JONES to the United States Senate.

JAMES DELAVAN.

FAT MEN'S BALL.

VIRGINIA, APRIL 28th, 1870.

Mr. *Sproston* and Ladies

You are respectfully invited to attend a

FAT MEN'S BALL,

(BURLESQUE ON NEW YORK.)

To be given on Thursday Evening, May Fifth,

········ AT ········

ATHLETIC HALL,

VIRGINIA.

You will be required to dress in such a manner as to personate a fat man, and give your weight at any figure from two hundred and fifty pounds to four hundred and eighty pounds—to be recorded at the door as you enter the Hall; the record of which will be sent to the New York papers, unless you wish your name withheld.

This invitation is issued by a Committee appointed by the FAT MEN of this city.

FATTY,

Chairman of said Committee.

FREEMEN of STOREY
AWAKE!

Worse than Highway Robbery is abroad!

The Officers of the LAW have become the Agents of Plunder ! Not alone the cheap thing by dreamers called LIBERTY is in danger, but your very precious COIN AND POCKETS are now in immediate Peril !

FRIENDLY WARNING TO TAX-PAYERS.

The Sheriff will surely, and if necessary, by main force, put his hand in the pocket of every man who owns anything and take out in U. S. gold coin, one half of one per cent. OF ALL HE OWNS, to be given, without consideration, and without " due course of law " to William Sharon and his Associates for filing a certificate of Incorporation under the Railroad Law, for the Virginia and Carson (miscalled Truckee) Railroad Co.

The only legal preventive of such physical force is voluntarily to pay the now assessed Tax to another officer of the Law. The intentions of this paper are to show to any one with a single flash of spirit in his blood or a grain only of manhood in his bones, (1) how he may cheaply get his money back. (2.) What the people should demand of the County Commissioners, and (3) how we should pray for those who despitefully use and persecute us.

1. How to Get Your Money Back.

Pay the Railroad Tax under protest, and when many have done so commence a joint suit for the recovery of the money, to be carried, if need be, to the Supreme Court of the United States, contesting the constitutionality of the most remarkable Railroad Bond Law ever passed in America.

A proper way to protest is as follows. Write out :

" I, [John Smith], of Storey County, Nevada, this [30th day of October, 1869], hereby protest against the levying and assessment of the Railroad Bond Tax upon property in my control, as having been done in accordance with an enactment of the Legislature, which I believe to be unconstitutional and inconsistent with the fundamental principles of Law.

" Furthermore, I protest against the payment, by me made, under the force of fear, of [thirteen dollars and seventeen cents] covered in the receipt of [A. L. Edwards] Deputy Tax Collector, for the larger sum of [ninety-three dollars and fifty-one cents] issued to me on [October 20th, 1869]. In witness whereof, I have hereunto affixed my signature on the date first herein mentioned, at Virginia City, Storey County, State of Nevada. (Signed) JOHN SMITH."

One copy of the above protest should be (if needful in the presence of a witness) served upon the Tax Collector or his Deputy, and on the face of a duplicate of the same, he should acknowledge service in terms following :

" VIRGINIA CITY, Storey County, Nev. [October 30th, 1869.]

" I hereby acknowledge the receipt and service upon me of a protest against the payment of the railroad bond tax, of " which the within is a duplicate copy. (Signed) A. L. EDWARDS, Deputy Collector."

Provided the money shall have been paid to Sharon & Co., though it may not be extracted from their pockets as now from ours, we will be able to get it again out of the County Treasury.

2. What We Should Demand.

We should mandatorily petition our County Commissioners not to issue one dollar in County Bonds to the Railroad Company, except in purchase of Railroad stock at par or at a less price ; which no doubt so just a man as William Sharon would consent to, as he only cares to see the railroad built and the mines prosper. At least he should have a chance to compel the people to believe he wishes to take an unfair advantage of their powerlessness in his hands, somewhat similar to that taken of men upon the Divide at night, by other gentlemen possessing a certain kind of power. At present the people, and perhaps unjustly, presume Mr. Sharon wishes to take such a cowardly advantage. He should have the opportunity to prove the injustice of their judgment. Then bid your Commissioners to give him a chance to do so without appearing in print, which in America is a crime !

THE MANDATES OF THE PEOPLE ARE HIGHER THAN THOSE OF THEIR ENTRAPPED OR BIASED OR CORRUPTED AGENTS. Therefore command your public servants, in language befitting Americans and Men, to regard Right and your own interests. It is not yet too late.

3. How We Should Pray for Those Who Despitefully Use and Persecute Us.

First.—We should charitably remember, that we are all of us trying to get " a good thing " for ourselves, and that is all Mr. Sharon is trying for.

Mr. Sharon, personally, should not be deemed a plunderer. In most of his private acts, he is a truly estimable man. If we were only able to know when he was about to slip into an exception to this happy general rule, all men could feel easier in trusting him ! But no one is perfect ; and on the whole, Mr. Sharon is a very good man. If his aim to get a good thing has led him a little too far, we should avoid a similar error ourselves and forgive his offence. When richer no doubt he will repent.

Second.—We should be careful to guard against any feeling of ENVY for Mr. Sharon's good things—ANY of them : houses or lands, man servants or maid servants. It is to be feared that a vast amount of the ill-will existing in the community towards this remarkable benefactor of Storey County and of mankind at large, if stripped to nudity, would be found to be no other than the fiend Envy itself. Envy is hateful in the sight of Heaven. Our prayers must be abortive if rooting in so unworthy a feeling.

Third.—We may properly remember that Mr. Sharon himself will liberally recognize our right to get our money back, especially as it will take nothing from him. I rather look to see the Bank of California pay the Railroad Bond-Tax under protest, and we should all of us be wise.

" LET US HAVE PEACE ! "

CONRAD WIEGAND.

P. S.—Very soon a fuller Address to the People will be issued, the patient perusal and study of which is respectfully solicited.

553. CSmH

WOMAN SUFFRAGE.

SPEECH

OF

HON. C. J. HILLYER.

DELIVERED IN THE ASSEMBLY OF THE STATE OF NEVADA,

TUESDAY, FEBRUARY 16, 1869.

CARSON CITY:

HENRY R. MIGHELS, STATE PRINTER.

1869.

Theater

MANAGER.................................Mr. L. F. BEATTY

PROMPTER.............Mr. W. T. CALDWELL | MACHINIST.................Mr. JOSEPH McKEE
SCENIC ARTISTE......Mr. J. W. HIRES | PROPERTIES, by Messrs. McCLURE and BATES
MUSICAL DIRECTOR.......................PROFESSOR JACOBSON.

First Night of the Great Sensation

AFTER DARK

NOTICE TO THE PUBLIC.—The manuscript of this truly great Play was obtained direct from the Author, DION BOURCICAULT, by Mr. D. C. Anderson while in London; also, the models of the scenery.

MISS SALLIE

HINCKLEY!

Has purchased the copy-right from Mr. Anderson and is the only person authorized to produce it on this Coast outside of San Francisco, where it has achieved the greatest success, at Maguire's Opera House, of any piece ever produced within its walls. This Drama will be presented here, as far as Stage capacity will allow, in the same style and grandeur as originally produced in London where it has passed its first hundred nights, and is still crowding the house. AN ENTIRE NEW SET OF SCENERY HAS BEEN PAINTED

BY MR. HIRES,

SCENIC ARTISTE, from PIPER'S OPERA HOUSE, with GRAND and NOVEL MECHANICAL EFFECTS by Mr. JOS. McKEE, assisted by Mr. GEO. HINCKLEY, who has supervised the entire production of this BEAUTIFUL PLAY.

Friday Evening, January 8th, 1869,

Will be presented the Great Sensation of

AFTER DARK!

Elisa Medhurst,	-	Miss Sallie Hinckley

Rose Edgerton,...Mrs. L. F. Beatty
Old Tom (a London Boardman)........................Mr. L. F. Beatty

GORDON CHUMLEY................Mr. GEORGE HINCKLEY	ARCA JACK....................Miss MINNIE PIXLEY
DICKY MORRIS....................Mr. S. J. DENNIS	POINTER BILL...............Miss LUCY PIXLEY
GEORGE MEDHURST (Bart.)......Mr. R. BENT FULFORD	TOMMY DODD (with original song)...Miss ANNIE PIXLEY
CHANDOS BELLINGHAM.............Mr. W. M. ROBINSON	BILLIARD MARKER..............Mr. W. T. CALDWELL
Mr. CRUMPET...................Mr. W. T. CALDWELL	Engineer of the underground Railway Tube....A. McCLURE
Mr. POINTER (a Police man).......Mr. W. H. BATES	ORANGE WOMAN..............Mrs. W. H. ROBINSON

Pretty waiter girls, railroad hands, newsboys, policemen, etc., by numerous auxiliaries.

N. B.—The Piece is so full of interest that any attempt at a synopsis would be futile. ☞ SEE AND JUDGE FOR YOURSELVES.

ADMISSION...ONE DOLLAR
Orchestra Chairs and Reserved Seats......One Dollar and Fifty Cents
PRIVATE BOXES..........(Six Seats), ...SIX DOLLARS

DOORS OPEN AT SEVEN O'CLOCK.

☞ The Curtain will rise precisely at eight o'clock in order to finish the performances each night before eleven. ☜

Daily Appeal Print, Carson City, Nevada.

DIALECT

OF

THE

SHO

SHONE

INDI

ANS.

Edited &

Published

—BY—

PAGE & BUTTERFIELD.

——:o:——

BELMONT:

G. L. C. FAIRCHILD & CO., PRINTERS, REPORTER OFFICE.

1868.

PETITION FOR LAND OFFICE.

To His Excellency the President, and to the Hon. Commissioner of the General Land Office of the United States:

Your Petitioners of *Esmeralda* county, State of *Nevada*, pray that a new Land District be organized, comprising the county of Esmeralda, State of Nevada, and also the counties of Mono and Inyo, State of California, and that the office of such district be established at Aurora, the County Seat of Esmeralda county; and respectfully state the following, among other reasons, why the same should be so established:--

Esmeralda County is one of the largest counties in the State of Nevada, containing an area of about Nine Thousand square miles, and including large tracts of valuable mineral and agricultural lands, and embracing the prosperous mining districts of Aurora, Esmeralda, Pine Grove, Washington, Silver Peak, Columbus, Palmetto, and other mining districts, and the Walker River and other valleys.

These lands are rapidly being settled upon and improved, and the business of Esmeralda County alone will require the establishment of such Land Office.

At present, Esmeralda County is included in the Carson Land District, the office of which is at Carson City, a point too remote for the convenience of the settlers of Esmeralda County, compelling them from the central and southern parts of such county, to travel a distance of about two hundred and fifty miles in order to reach Carson City.

The establishment of such district, and the office at Aurora, would also promote the convenience of the settlers upon the public lands of Mono and Inyo counties in the State of California. These counties are both situated east of the Sierra Nevada mountains, contiguous to Esmeralda county, Nevada, and contain a large area of rich mineral and agricultural lands. In Mono are the prosperous mining districts of Bodie, Cast'e Peak, Hot Springs, Montgomery, &c. Inyo county contains the rapidly improving mining districts of Kearsarge, Cerro Gordo, Fish Springs, Chrysopolis, &c. The Owens River valley, one of the finest bodies of agricultural land on the Pacific Coast, traverses both of these counties, and is being rapidly settled by an enterprising population.

The counties of Mono and Inyo are now attached to the Stockton and Visalia Land Districts, thereby compelling the citizens of such counties, at much expense, to cross the Sierra Nevada mountains (frequently impassable in the winter months) and to travel about three hundred miles in order to reach either the Stockton or Visalia land offices, when if a Land Office was established at Aurora, it would, at slight cost, be easily accessible from such counties. To a settler upon these lands the expenses of travel from such counties to either the Stockton or Visalia land offices, equals, if not exceeds, the cost of one hundred and sixty acres of land at the Government price.

Wherefore, your petitioners respectfully pray that a new Land District be organized, comprising the county of Esmeralda, State of Nevada, and the counties of Mono and Inyo, State of California, and that the office for such district be established at Aurora, in said Esmeralda county, and your petitioners will, as in duty bound ever pray, &c.

December, 1867.

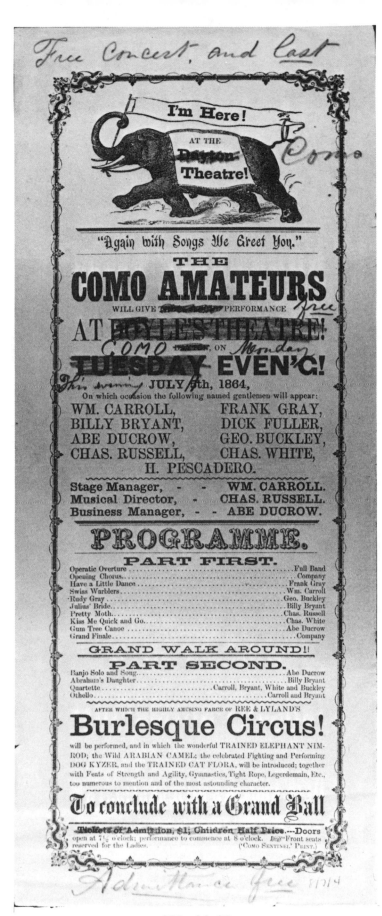

I'm Here!

AT THE

~~Dayton~~ Theatre!

Como

"Again with Songs We Greet You."

THE
COMO AMATEURS

WILL GIVE ~~THE SECOND~~ PERFORMANCE *free*

AT ~~BOYLE'S THEATRE!~~

COMO ~~DAYTON,~~ ON *Monday*

~~TUESDAY~~ EVEN'G!

This evening JULY 5th, 1864,

On which occasion the following named gentlemen will appear:

WM. CARROLL,	FRANK GRAY,
BILLY BRYANT,	DICK FULLER,
ABE DUCROW,	GEO. BUCKLEY,
CHAS. RUSSELL,	CHAS. WHITE,
H. PESCADERO.	

Stage Manager, - - WM. CARROLL.
Musical Director, - CHAS. RUSSELL.
Business Manager, - - ABE DUCROW.

PROGRAMME.

PART FIRST.

Operatic Overture	Full Band
Opening Chorus	Company
Have a Little Dance	Frank Gray
Swiss Warblers	Wm. Carroll
Rudy Gray	Geo. Buckley
Julius' Bride	Billy Bryant
Pretty Moth	Chas. Russell
Kiss Me Quick and Go	Chas. White
Gum Tree Canoe	Abe Ducrow
Grand Finale	Company

GRAND WALK AROUND!!

PART SECOND.

Banjo Solo and Song	Abe Ducrow
Abraham's Daughter	Billy Bryant
Quartette	Carroll, Bryant, White and Buckley
Othello	Carroll and Bryant

AFTER WHICH THE HIGHLY AMUSING FARCE OF REE & LYLAND'S

Burlesque Circus!

will be performed, and in which the wonderful TRAINED ELEPHANT NIM-
ROD; the Wild ARABIAN CAMEL; the celebrated Fighting and Performing
DOG KYZER, and the TRAINED CAT FLORA, will be introduced; together
with Feats of Strength and Agility, Gymnastics, Tight Rope, Legerdemain, Etc.,
too numerous to mention and of the most astounding character.

To conclude with a Grand Ball

Tickets of Admission, $1; Children Half Price.----Doors
open at 7½ o'clock; performance to commence at 8 o'clock. Front seats
reserved for the Ladies. ('COMO SENTINEL' PRINT.)

Thanksgiving Proclamation.

EXECUTIVE DEPARTMENT,
CARSON CITY, NEVADA TERRITORY,
November 17th, 1863.

THE rolling year has reached that point where harvest has succeeded seed time and the husbandman has filled his granaries with the rich products of the earth. Spring time and Summer have given place to Autumn. The reaper has gathered the promised reward and his heart is filled with thankfulness to the Giver of all good things. The Miner has gathered his rich harvest of the precious metals, his coffers are filled to overflowing and his heart is swelling with gratitude to a kind Providence for his goodness to him. The Mechanic, as the chill winds approach, looks around him with a grateful heart, and beholds as the result of his well rewarded labor, plenty and comfort surrounding himself and family. The Merchant, as he counts his gains can but be thankful that he has been prospered in his business. All of the honorable professions have been well rewarded and encouraged; plenty sits smiling before them. The unparalleled success of this Territory in all departments of its material interest demands a grateful acknowledgment at the hands of an appreciative people; especially ought this people to be thankful for their political progress. To-day they are casting off the garments of infancy and assuming the garb of maturity. Born as we were in Revolution, our progress is the more marked and providential. Notwithstanding our infancy has passed on the surging billows of Revolution, our frail bark has been so guided and directed as to anchor safely in the haven of the Union and Constitution, and clasp hands with our Sister States as an equal, clothed in the silver mantel of filial affection, thick inlaid with gold. Unbounded thankfulness from us to the Power that has so shaped our destinies by giving wisdom to our National Rulers, strength to our Armies, power to our Navy, skill to our Officers, courage to our Troops, love of country to our People, as to make them mighty against Treason, and irresistible in defense of the Republican Institutions; the choicest gift to man, earth's richest inheritance. How unspeakably thankful ought we to be that the power of the traitor is broken, that the wand of usurper is powerless against the eagle eye of Liberty. Thankful that the horrors of war are to give place to the beauties of peace; thankful that out of the fiery furnace of insurrection and rebellion comes unharmed the eternal principle of self-government; to establish which countless thousands have offered up their lives; thankful for the touch ing of this unnatural struggle, that a Nation that has once tasted the sweets of Civil Liberty, can not be enslaved or made to drink the bitter cup of servitude:

In order to uniformity and in accordance with the President's Proclamation, and that we may witness the sublime spectacle of a great and powerful Nation bowed in thankfulness before the God of the Universe, and in view of the innumerable reasons, for especial thankfulness, I, JAMES W. NYE, Governor of the Territory of Nevada, do hereby appoint

THURSDAY, THE 26th DAY OF NOVEMBER INSTANT,

As a day of PUBLIC THANKSGIVING TO ALMIGHTY GOD for his watchfulness and protection over us as a People and as a Nation through the year just passed.

IN WITNESS WHEREOF, I have hereunto set my hand, and caused the great seal of the Territory to be affixed, the day and year above written.

JAMES W. NYE.

ATTEST:

ORION CLEMENS,

Secretary of Nevada Territory.

(SEAL.)

160. NvMus

ANNUAL MESSAGE OF CAPTAIN JIM,

Chief of the Washoes, and Governor (de facto) of Nevada,

DELIVERED BEFORE THE THIRD HOUSE OF THE TERRITORIAL LEGISLATURE, FRIDAY, NOVEMBER FOURTEENTH, ONE THOUSAND EIGHT HUNDRED AND SIXTY-TWO.

On motion of MR. S. MYTH, of KING'S CANON, Five Hundred Thousand Million Copies of the Message were ordered to be printed and circulated throughout the fertile Realm of Sage Brush and Sand, for the better Enlightenment of the Benighted, Deluded and Heterogeneous Inhabitants thereof.

To the Officers and Members of the Third House of the Territorial Legislature of Nevada:

GENTLEMEN:—Again have you assembled, in your legislative capacity, to transact the legislative business so needful to the interest of your various constituency, as well as the favored Territory of Nevada. The time has now arrived when, under the provisions of the Organic Act of your Territory, it becomes my imperative duty to submit for your consideration such views, recommendations and suggestions, as in the judgment and discretion of your executive magistrate shall seem best adapted to the advancement of the prosperity and glory of our rich, fertile and beautiful young Territory, and such, too, as will have a decided tendency to secure to your constituents a more rapid and certain advance in all the arts and sciences, as well as to facilitate their onward progress in morality, enlightenment and civilization.

At this moment there exists, in a very considerable portion of our once happy and prosperous country, a slight exhibition of a determination to disobey the *ipse dixit* of those who, in accordance with the express provisions of the Magna Charta of American freemen, hold and control the reins of this great and glorious Government, and assume to dictate to their masters—the Sovereign People of this land—what shall and what shall not be done in the administration of the affairs of this powerful, gigantic and stupendous Government.

The disposition of disobedience manifested has, by some, been dubbed with the appellation of "a most monstrous rebellion;" while, in the judgment of your well-thinking and close-calculating Chief Magistrate, after the most earnest and profound deliberation, it amounts merely to "trifles light as air." That men born of an American ancestry, and sons of a blest and favored land, endowed by the God of Nature with that most precious and inestimable blessing which prevails to so limited an extent among our people, and which is so wholly and entirely neglected and unappreciated by your most ignorant and worthless constituency—good, common, hard, horse sense—can dignify the existing slight interruptions in our national policy, both foreign and domestic, by the title of a "monstrous, powerful and gigantic rebellion," is profoundly absurd in the veriest extreme, and deserves to be treated by men of your acknowledged wisdom, intelligence and reputed valor, as an emanation from the brain of some half-witted child of nature. Certainly the author of so palpable and self-evident an absurdity could never for a moment have reflected upon and duly calculated the mighty and inexhaustible resources of our great and glorious country. A proper conception of the colossal grandeur and sublime magnificence of this valorous and powerful people could never have found an abiding place within the confines of his demented pericranium! To insinuate that the present state of affairs constitutes serious interruptions in our foreign and domestic policy, or in the least retards our diplomatic relations, or has the slightest tendency to impede the progress and advancement of our national growth and greatness, can be viewed in no other light than an endeavor to cast upon our national character aspersions and imputations of the most foul and flagrant nature; and serves, most appropriately, to indelibly stamp the brow of their author with the glaring characteristics of a dotard and an imbecile.

Why, sirs, were these small difficulties within the reach of the militia of Nevada Territory, under the supreme command of your most excellent Chief Magistrate, assisted by his most accomplished and efficient military appointees, they would have long since been settled and adjusted, as irrevocably and completely as if adjudicated upon by your most worthy Chief Justice Stewart. Your Executive would without the least hesitation, evasion, or compunctions of conscience, have resorted to the last great war emergency, in the first place, by the immediate issuance of his proclamation, to take effect instanter, instead of *in futuro*, enslaving the millions of free born whites on this continent, and freeing the millions of enslaved blacks; rearing, in lieu of our present form of government, handed down to us by our revolutionary forefathers as a bequest to be transmitted to your and my posterity untarnished, a negro oligarchy, to become the supreme rulers of this benighted, ignorant and downcast people, who have neither the will or capacity to govern and control themselves, and thereby would have forever placed a quietus upon our existing difficulties. And now to-day, instead of wars and rumors of wars, and the martial tread of armed soldiery to the music of the stirring fife and martial drum, reverberating throughout the length and breadth of our distracted and unhappy country, all would have been peace and quiet, and every man, woman and child would be in the full enjoyment of all their innate and constitutional privileges, and permitted to worship their God under their own vine and fig-tree; then would peace, prosperity, plenty and happiness forever bless this now unfortunate land.

Your National Government has within the last two years, by legislative enactment, conferred upon you, under the management of the party in power, and of which your Executive has the honor of being one of its most officious members, great and incalculable benefits, the value and importance of which I am perfectly satisfied you, as the representatives of this people, with your very limited understandings, have not the intelligence to comprehend and appreciate; wherefore in this message I shall pass them over with a bare mention, and then proceed to the suggestion of such matters as your diminutive understandings, and my profound method of teaching, will enable you to comprehend.

The General Government has supplied you with a great transcontinental iron road, to be traveled by the mighty and majestic iron horse, with bated breath and eager for the race, with his distended fiery nostrils may be seen in the distance, as he moves with the ferocity of the untamed tiger, and the velocity of the wild antelope, from the snow-capped summits of the Rocky Mountains, through the dominions of Brighamdom, and into and over the great Basin of Nevada, and disappears across the great western slope of the majestic Cordilleras, finding a resting place only on the placid bosom of the Pacific.

Our National Congress, at its last session, without solicitation on our part, enlarged the borders of our Territory by an addition of one degree of land; not that we needed it, asked for or wanted it, but for the purpose of robbing one portion of her people to the aggrandizement of a more favored class, and thereby circumscribing the territorial limits of our already too insignificant neighbor and sister Territory; and I would here recommend to your most august body the imperative necessity of an immediate subdivision of the newly bestowed territory into as many counties as at present exist in Nevada, and the passage of an act of organization, conferring upon the Executive the right to appoint all officers for the same, thereby, as you will perceive, increasing the burden of taxation which is borne by your people, and increasing the patronage of your Executive, that he may be more completely surrounded by his servile tools under the name of Executive appointees; for, in my judgment, the common masses have no right to select their own officers and servants.

At your last session, you did me the honor of appointing me in conjunction with two of your honorable body, a commission to proceed to the State of California for the avowed purpose of bribing the Legislature of that State to wholly and entirely disregard their constitutional oaths and moral obligations, and sell to us a large portion of the patrimony secured to her people by their renowned and worthy relative, Uncle Samuel, by the admission of the State into the Union, with all her constitutional provisions. In this, your commission most signally failed, for the reason that your appropriation of $750,000,000 was wholly and entirely inadequate to the purposes for which it was intended. The expenses of the members of your commission was much greater than was anticipated, and the price of votes in the California Legislature far exceeded the most extravagant expectations of your commission. I would therefore recommend that your honorable body, for the purpose of securing our end, and placing beyond all question the consummation of this all important project, the reappointment of your Executive as a commission of one, and the early appropriation of the sum of $975,865,784, for the use of the commission, with the additional sum of $15,000,000 for the sole and express use and benefit of His Excellency, Governor Leland Stanford, with whom, since the adjournment of the Legislature of the State of California, I have had many interesting and important conversations upon this highly beneficial and important subject.

Another matter to which I desire to call your most especial attention, is the imperative necessity of fundamentally amending the Practice Act of this Territory. It is well known to you all that sometime since, one citizen of this Territory killed another; that the party killing was lawfully and rightfully indicted by the Grand Jury of the county in which the killing occurred; that the slayer was tried by a jury of his peers, and after hearing all the proofs in the case pro and con, and the able and eloquent argument of counsel for and against the prisoner at the bar, and the fair, impartial, able, logical and legal charge of the honorable court; and after fully considering and deliberating upon all matters and things proper and pertinent, and within their scope and province to consider and deliberate upon, the jury returned into court a verdict of murder in the first degree, whereupon the court, in accordance with the provisions of the law in such cases made and provided, proceeded to pronounce the sentence of death upon the criminal; and he would have been executed to a moral certainty, had he not, when least expected, have given our worthy penitentiary warden the slip, while that dignitary was engaged in playing a big hand at draw poker. Nor would he have escaped, had it not been for one of the judges of the Supreme Court of this Territory, who, in the exercise of his judicial functions, as the law provides he shall do, issued what is the right and privilege of every citizen, under our present judicial system, to have issued for the protection of life and liberty, and as a security against malfeasance in office, a writ of *supersedeas*, thereby hindering and preventing the immediate execution of this man, until his cause could be heard and adjudicated upon by the supreme judicial authority of the Territory of Nevada. Now, therefore, I would most earnestly recommend and seriously impress upon your deluded minds the paramount necessity of so amending the laws of this Territory, and disregarding the inalienable rights of your fellow-citizens, by expunging from your Statute Book, the wholesome and necessary writs of *Supersedeas* and *Habeas Corpus*, and all other legal proceedings now known to the law of the land, and esteemed and enjoyed by the people of your country as the mighty bulwarks of the blood-bought rights and privileges of American freemen, and confer upon your worthy Chief Executive the untrammeled right to hang whom he pleases, by the issuance simply of his proclamation to that effect. And henceforth care will be taken that such as incur his Excellency's displeasure will be hung first and tried in the Supreme Court six months or one year thereafter, as circumstances may direct. For, sirs, in the judgment of your Executive, it is far better that nine hundred and ninety-nine innocent parties should suffer the penalties and rigors of the laws, than that one criminal should escape.

It will be recollected by your most august body, that during your last session an appropriation of $5,000,000 per month was made to the Hon. Abraham Curry, for the safe keeping of our Territorial prisoners. The tax for that purpose, your Executive is fully satisfied, is too onerous to be borne by your poverty-stricken constituency, wherefore I would recommend to your honorable body the appropriation of $500,000,000 for the purchase of the Territorial prison. (Of course, your Executive does not intimate any interest whatever in the sublime and magnificent purchase; nor does he intend to insinuate that members upon the floor of this house will receive any share of the purchase money by way of inducement to the passage of this gigantic measure.) I would also recommend the convertion of a portion of the Territorial Penitentiary into a Lunatic Asylum, for the keeping and confinement of the members of the two lower branches of the Legislature; that their Governor be appointed warden of the institution, and the Secretary of the Territory door-keeper thereof.

The early, earnest and untiring consideration of your honorable body is most respectfully invited to the investigation and adoption by legislative enactment of the following recommendation of your Chief Executive. 'Tis true, beyond all controversy, that since the earliest ages of which we have any record, in accordance with the teachings of sacred and profane history, as also by precept, example and education, and all the rules of propriety, decency, morality and refinement, and the dictates of common sense, and a just and proper appreciation of the existing distinctions in the various classes of mankind, that there has heretofore, and at the present time, does, to a limited extent, exist among the enlightened, educated, refined and civilized nations of the earth, a marked and well defined distinction between our brother African and the Caucasian race, and that the difference has heretofore preponderated in favor of the white man. And by your present law, I discover that all persons having in their veins Nigger or Injun blood in certain quantities, are not permitted to to testify in your courts of justice. To this I am decidedly opposed. I hold that this usage of the barbarous ages should be forgotten, and this marked distinction between the races should be obliterated; and the black man, in every respect, should be entitled to fully enjoy all the rights, privileges and immunities, legal, social and political, of the white man; that the fountains of Justice should be opened to the reception of the testimony of all persons, without regard to sex, age, color or condition—wherefore, I most earnestly recommend the passage of a law permitting Niggers to swear in all cases, civil or criminal, in the Courts of Justice of this Territory, wherein white men or women are parties, whether the Nigger has any knowledge of the facts or not; and also, that Niggers, both male and female, be guaranteed by law the exclusive exercise of the elective franchise, and to hold and administer the various offices of this Territory, and to represent the people in the legislative halls and other deliberative assemblies, and that any and all persons failing to give a hearty and cordial support to the law, shall by common consent be adjudged guilty of a felony and hung like a dog, by the proclamation of your most worthy and philanthropic Chief Executive.

The subject of Common Schools is one that deserves your earnest consideration, and I would recommend the passage of an act abolishing and extinguishing both the public and private institutions of learning in our midst, for the reason that our people already know too much, and are too well versed in the management of our Territorial affairs.

I would also suggest for your consideration the passage of an Incorporation Law, with such barriers and obstacles thrown around it as to render it a perfect nullity, and as now, secure to the capitalist of California all they desire.

The financial condition of your Territory is firmly planted upon a solid basis. She is fully able to owe as much again as her present indebtedness, and no Territory is better calculated to refuse payment. Your Territorial Auditor and Treasurer have not as yet been able to raise one cent from the solid basis of your Territorial finance. However, those distinguished officers will report to your honorable body in due season, say two weeks subsequent to your adjournment.

Gentlemen of the Third House, your constituents are looking to you with eager eyes and palpitating hearts, for the passage of such laws as shall redound to the advancement of their best interest; and that by your united efforts, as the representatives of this great and glorious people, and the smiling providences of a great, good and beneficent Creator, they expect that our land of sage-brush and sand will continue to make her gigantic strides along the pathway of peace, prosperity and happiness, and that the day is not far distant when she, by her own effulgent rays, shall eclipse all other stars holding a place in the brilliant galaxy of the National Constellation.

BARNEY WOOLF, PRINTER TO THE THIRD HOUSE, CARSON CITY.

60. MH

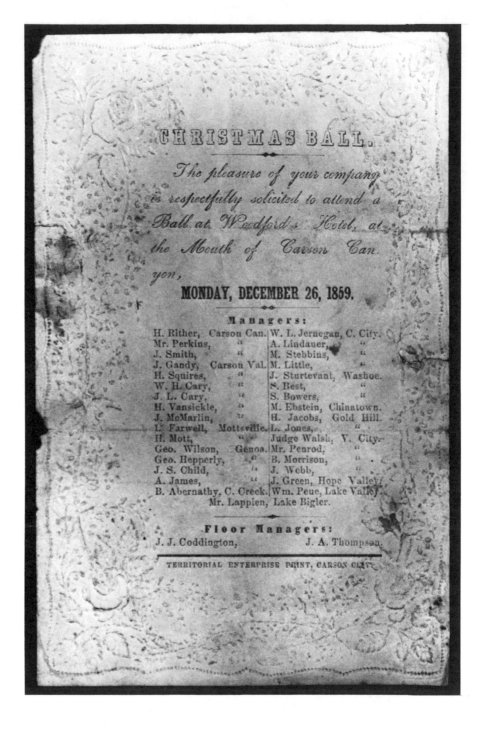

CHRISTMAS BALL.

The pleasure of your company is respectfully solicited to attend a Ball at Woodford's Hotel, at the Mouth of Carson Canyon,

MONDAY, DECEMBER 26, 1859.

Managers:

H. Rither, Carson Can.	W. L. Jernegan, C. City.
Mr. Perkins, "	A. Lindauer, "
J. Smith, "	M. Stebbins, "
J. Gandy, Carson Val.	M. Little, "
H. Squires, "	J. Sturtevant, Washoe.
W. H. Cary, "	S. Best, "
J. L. Cary, "	S. Bowers, "
H. Vansickle, "	M. Ebstein, Chinatown.
J. McMarlin, "	H. Jacobs, Gold Hill.
L. Farwell, Mottsville.	L. Jones, "
H. Mott, "	Judge Walsh, V. City.
Geo. Wilson, Genoa.	Mr. Penrod, "
Geo. Hepperly, "	B. Morrison, "
J. S. Child, "	J. Webb, "
A. James, "	J. Green, Hope Valley.
B. Abernathy, C. Creek.	Wm. Peue, Lake Valley.

Mr. Lappien, Lake Bigler.

Floor Managers:

J. J. Coddington,   J. A. Thompson.

TERRITORIAL ENTERPRISE PRINT, CARSON CITY.

4. NvMus

ALLENBACH, JACOB.

1879 | "Happy New Year!" | [*broken wavy rule*] | The Carrier of the | San Francisco Call, Post, Bulletin, Chronicle, Alta, | Examiner, Stock Exchange and Argonaut; | Sacramento Bee and Record-Union; | Virginia Enterprise and Evening Chronicle, | Makes his very best bow, and wishes to all his Patrons a | Happy New Year, | . . . | Jacob Allenbach, | Carrier. | Carson, Nevada, Jan. 1, 1879. | [Index Print, Carson, Nevada? 1878.]

[931]

Broadside. 34 x 17 cm. Decorative chain-link border. The border and some of the typefaces are the same as those used in No. 1010.

This example of the carrier's address does little honor to the genre. To call its verse doggerel would perhaps lend it more distinction than it deserves. It is written as if by the infant New Year, with all the attendant foolishness that often is a part of such writing. But out of this approach comes a rather softer plea for a gratuity than is found in the intimidating tone of No. L923: "Just buy the book of Allenbach / That mortals call an Almanac."

NvMus.

BENTON'S STAGE LINE. *Carson City, Nevada.*

Lake Tahoe, | —the— | Gem of the Sierra! | [*thick-thin rule*] | Tourists from the East, | Who wish to visit this beautiful lake in company with Hank Monk, will upon | atriving [*sic*] in Carson City. [*sic*] Nevada, take passage in | Benton's Stage Line | . . . | [*short rule*] | Morning Appeal Print, Carson City. | [1878?]   [932]

Broadside. 35 x 28 cm. Decorative border. Facsimile in Edward B. Scott, *Saga of Lake Tahoe* (Crystal Bay, Nevada: Sierra-Tahoe Publishing Co., [1957]), p. 401.

A copy at NvHi has a handwritten note saying that the poster was used in 1870, but Scott dates it in 1878, possibly because the newspaper whose job office printed it did not become the *Morning Appeal* until that year.

Hank Monk, who drove stages in Nevada for many years, gained enduring fame as the result of a hair-raising drive in 1859 from near Genoa to Placerville, California, with Horace Greeley as his passenger. The story has been retold and no doubt embellished by many writers, not the least of whom was Mark Twain in *Roughing It;* an attempt to sort out the truth from fancy is in Richard G. Lillard and Mary V. Hood, *Hank Monk and Horace Greeley; An Enduring Episode in Western History* (Georgetown, California: Wilmac Press, 1973).

NvHi. NvRH.

BISHOP, D. M., & COMPANY.

Bishop's Directory | —of— | Virginia City | Gold Hill, | Silver City, | Carson City | —and— | Reno. | [*short rule*] | Containing a | Business Directory | —Also— | City Governments, Public In-

stitutions, Churches, Societies, | Etc. Etc. | [*short rule*] | 1878-
9. | [*short rule*] | D. M. Bishop & Co., Compilers. | B. C. Vandall,
Publisher. | San Francisco: | B. C. Vandall, | 518 Clay St. | [1878.]
[933]

598, [6] p. 23 x 15 cm. Quarter-leather binding; printed boards. Thumb-indexed.
Title page on p. [13]. Line 1 in an arch over line 2. Pagination begins with p. [1] on the
front cover; p. 2 is the front paste-down. Advertisements throughout, some on
colored paper; those after the title page not counted in the pagination.

Canvassing took place at least between May 8 and June 17, 1878; the Gold Hill *News*
reported receipt of a copy on August 8, with a price of $4. The Carson City *Appeal*'s
local was fascinated by the thumb-indexing and wrote on August 17: "The publishers
have hit on a new dodge which is most gratifying. On the front of the leaves as you
look at the unopened book are finger holes gouged into the paper so as to enable one to
open the book instanter, at either of its several departments—each town being a
department in itself. It is fun to open such a book. We shall take pleasure in prospecting among its pages just for the pleasure of practicing on the new dodge."
C. CSmH. CU-B. CtY. DLC. NvHi (rebound). NvLN. NvVSR.

BISHOP WHITAKER'S SCHOOL FOR GIRLS. *Reno, Nevada.*

Bishop Whitaker's | School for Girls, | Reno, Nevada. | [*fi-
let*] | Second Year. | Ending May 29th, 1878. | [Virginia City: Ter-
ritorial Enterprise. 1878.] [934]

[20] p. 16 x 11 cm. Printed wrapper. Title and text pages in single rule borders. The
format and typefaces are identical to those that appear in the catalogue for the fourth
and fifth years, printed in 1881; see Nos. 867 and 1007.
NvHi.

BRADLEY, LEWIS RICE. Pamphlet. 1878. [L935]

Reno *Nevada State Journal,* March 16, 1878; reprinted from the Winnemucca *Silver
State,* which was unavailable for this study: "At the time of the discussion of the extra
session of the Legislature question last January, Governor Bradley's letter, in reply to
that of State Controller Hobart, was published in pamphlet form, and copies of it
distributed throughout the State. The Reno *Journal* charged that the work was done at
the expense of the State. . . . We are authorized by J. J. Hill, State Printer, to state
that the pamphlet was printed in his office at Carson and paid for by Governor
Bradley, without any expense whatever to the tax-payers of Nevada. Mr. Hobart,
who, as State Controller, audits all claims against the State, can substantiate the truth
of this statement." The January 20 *Journal* had reported receipt of a copy.

The *Territorial Enterprise* printed on January 4 a letter from State Controller W. W.
Hobart, a Republican, that called for a special session of the Legislature to reduce
property taxes and, to make up for the decrease in revenue, to transfer the idle building
fund to the general fund. He contended that these actions would provide more than
enough money to see the state through the end of the biennium. Six days later the
paper published a reply from Governor Bradley, with supporting figures from State
Treasurer Jerry Schooling, refuting at length both Hobart's idea and his figures. Both
Bradley and Schooling were Democrats. The Republican *Enterprise* strongly sup-

ported the Controller but, after printing his response to Bradley on January 13, gave up and no more was heard of it. The brief tempest was brought about, apparently, during the 1877 legislative session when Comstock mining interests unsuccessfully sought a reduction in bullion taxes that was opposed by Bradley.

CARSON CITY, NEVADA. *Turn Verein.*

Programme | ——of the—— | Virginia and Carson | Turn Verein Picnic! | Sunday, August 4th, 1878. | [*thick-thin rule*] | . . . | [*rule*] | ''Footlight Book and Job Printing House, Virginia. [936]

Broadside. 48 x 15 cm. Thick-thin rule border.
The picnic was held at Treadway's Park in Carson City.
NvMus.

CARSON CITY, NEVADA. *Virginia & Truckee Railroad Employes Ball.*

[*Cut of steam locomotive*] | Mr [*dotted rule*] and Ladies, | The Employes of the V. & T. R.R. | present their Compliments, | and solicit the pleasure of your company at their | Fifth Annual Ball, | to be given at | Theater Hall, Carson City, | Thursday Evening, March 14th, 1878. | . . . [937]

[4] p., printed on p. [1-3] only. 17 x 15 cm. Mostly script type. Facsimile on front of Talisman 13.
See No. L1012.
Pvt.

CARSON OPERA HOUSE? *Carson City, Nevada.*

. . . Opera House. | . . . | [*thick-thin rule*] | Grand Farewell Performance of | Mr. and Mrs. J. C. Williamson | [Miss Maggie Moore] | To commence at Half-past Eight O'Clock with the beautiful drama entitled | Clouds and Sunshine! | . . . | [1878.] [938]

Broadside. 27 x 18 cm. Line 4 of transcription printed in brackets.
The name of the opera house has been torn from the recorded copy; it has been tentatively identified as the Carson Opera House because others in the same collection are from there. The play was in Carson City on October 22, 1878, with a review in the Carson City *Appeal* the next day. It was also in Virginia City on October 20, however, and the bill may be for that performance.
CU-A.

CARSON OPERA HOUSE. *Carson City, Nevada.*

Carson Opera House. | [*thick-thin rule*] | . . . | [*thick-thin rule*] | Last Night! | [*thick-thin rule*] | This Tuesday Evening, Dec. 17th, 1878, | Rices [*sic*] Surprise Party, | After the most brilliant success ever known in San Francisco. | . . . | [*thick-thin rule*] | Byron's Fas-

cinating Musical Burlesque, | Babes in the Wood! | Or, Who Killed
Cock Robin? | . . .   [939]

Broadside. 27 x 12 cm.

CU-A.

CARSON THEATER. *Carson City, Nevada.*

Carson Theater. | [*thick-thin rule*] | First Concert | —of— | Mr. R.
A. Clark. | [*thick-thin rule*] | Tuesday and Wednesday Eve-
nings, | April 16 and 17, | Will be presented the beautiful little
Operata [*sic*], | Red Riding Hood! | [*short thick-thin rule*] |
. . . | [1878.]   [940]

Broadside. 52 x 17 cm.

The play was reviewed in the Carson City *Appeal* on April 17, 1878.

NvRH.

DAILY NEVADA TRIBUNE. *Carson City, Nevada.* Carrier's address. New
Year's Day, 1879. 1878.   [L941]

Tribune, December 30, 1878: "On New Year's Day Master Stanley Wright, carrier of
the NEVADA TRIBUNE, will be out with a New Year's welcome in verse, the like of
which has probably never been circulated on such an occasion."

DAILY TERRITORIAL ENTERPRISE. *Virginia City, Nevada.*

Territorial Enterprise Extra. | Containing | A Full Account |
of | "Frank Leslie" and Wife | [*filet*] | Virginia City, Nevada,
| July 14, 1878.   [942]

24 p. 19 x 13 cm. Printed wrapper. The text is reset from the original article in the
Enterprise on July 14, 1878. Facsimile following p. 314.

In the spring of 1877, New York publisher Frank Leslie undertook a transcontinental
railroad tour with his wife and a sizable entourage. One of the purposes of the trip was
to gather information for a travel book to be written by Mrs. Leslie. On reaching
California the party spent several days in and near San Francisco and Los Angeles
before beginning the return trip via Yosemite and Virginia City. After the splendors
of the Palace Hotel in San Francisco, William Sharon's estate at Belmont, and
"Lucky" Baldwin's ranch at Santa Anita, Miriam Leslie found Virginia City to be
squalid and "God-forsaken." Not only did she think it, she wrote it down in her
book, *California: A Pleasure Trip from Gotham to the Golden Gate,* which was published
later the same year in New York. She wrote of Virginia City's prostitutes, its
"forty-nine gambling saloons and one church," and its intensely hot mines, finding
space to laud only one thing, the new International Hotel. Her account was inaccurate
in several respects, but it was the condescension and disparagement, and particularly
her reference to "very few women except of the worst class," that aroused her readers
on the Comstock. Rollin M. Daggett, editor of the *Enterprise,* was especially annoyed,
and on July 14, 1878, he devoted most of the paper's front page to the material that was
later reprinted in the pamphlet described here. Daggett was well connected in New

York and knew how to get damning information about the woman who had written so disrespectfully about his city. In prefatory remarks he wrote that "in order to show the character of the authoress, we sent to New York and had the history of the Leslie family written out, together with the certified records of courts in which Mrs. Leslie figured in the past. It is one of the strangest stories of crime ever recorded." Although the unidentified author of the remainder of the work promised to "set down naught in malice," he wrote with considerable venom. He questioned Mrs. Leslie's legitimacy, mentioned that two people close to her—her first husband and her brother—had committed suicide, wrote of her brief stage career as the "sister" of Lola Montez and of a briefer affair with a former Tennessee Congressman, and went on feelingly and at length about her second marriage and the messy details of the subsequent divorce. He then turned to Frank Leslie, whom he claimed was born Henry Carter in England, and wrote of his "gaieties and extravagances," a business failure, his own divorce and immediate marriage to Miriam. The last part of the pamphlet is made up of court documents recording embarrassing facts about Mrs. Leslie's first divorce. For a fuller discussion of the episode, see *Purple Passage: The Life of Mrs. Frank Leslie* (Norman: University of Oklahoma Press, 1953) by Madeline B. Stern, especially her chapter, "*Extra* and Extravaganza."

Leslie was of course furious when he saw a copy of the extra. He even hired a detective to track down the author, but apparently never found out his name. Stern, however, speculates that it could have been no one but Ephraim George Squier, Mrs. Leslie's second husband, claiming that he was the only person who knew both parties well enough to write in such detail. Her evidence is plausible if not conclusive, but Squier did at least own a copy of the extra, the one that is now at NvHi. Stern also suggests the possibility that the book that was so offensive to Comstockers might not even have been written by Mrs. Leslie, but by her friend, Jane G. Austin.

NN. NvHi. NvU (microfilm).

DEMOCRATIC PARTY. *Nevada. State Central Committee.* Poster: Democratic State ticket. 1878.   [L943]

Reese River Reveille, October 22, 1878: "On the posters containing the Democratic State ticket, Governor Bradley appears as hailing from Lander county. This is an error." Bradley was a cattle rancher from Elko County.

DEMOCRATIC PARTY. *Storey County, Nevada.*

To the Public | [*short thick-thin rule*] | The following is a list of the Delegates to | the County Convention to be held in Virginia, | September 9th, 1878, who are favorable to the nomination of L. R. Bradley for Governor: | . . . | By order of the Executive Committee. | C. H. Belknap, | Chairman.   [944]

Broadside. 23 x 15 cm.

The poster, listing delegates from four Virginia City wards and two Gold Hill wards, may have been printed by Brown and Mahanny of the *Footlight;* John A. Mahanny is listed as a delegate from the second ward of Virginia City. Their print shop was in the same building as the law office of C. H. Belknap.

NvU.

DEMOCRATIC PARTY. *Washoe County, Nevada.*

Democratic State Ticket | [*short rule*] | . . . | [*short rule*] | For Senator, | John P. Richardson. | . . . | [1878.]   [945]

Broadside. 29 x 6 cm.

Richardson, a candidate from Washoe County, was defeated. The office of State printer is not listed because it had been abolished by the Legislature of 1877. NvHi.

EUREKA DAILY SENTINEL. *Eureka, Nevada.* Carrier's address. New Year's Day, 1879. 1878.   [L946]

Sentinel, January 1, 1879: "The SENTINEL's carrier, Mr. Ed. A. Skillman, and his assistant, will call on our subscribers to-day with the annual New Year's address."

FARRELL, MICHAEL J. Circular. November 2, 1878.   [L947]

Reese River Reveille, November 4, 1878: "On Saturday night last Hon. M. J. Farrell, [Republican] candidate for the State Senate [from Lander County], delivered an address at the Court-house on subjects pertaining to the present campaign, which was listened to by a large audience. The address related mainly a history of the bullion tax matters, and more particularly to the action taken by himself in the last Legislature, and the causes leading thereto, and a brief showing of the Silver bill, its workings, and the importance of sending a competent man to the United States Senate, who thoroughly understands the wants of further legislation in that direction. The address of Mr. Farrell has been printed in circular form for distribution. . . ."

FREEMASONS. *Nevada. Grand Lodge.*

Amendments to the Constitution, | Together with the | Standing Resolutions, | Adopted at the Several Annual Communications of | the Most Worshipful Grand Lodge of | F. & A.M. of Nevada, Since 1872, | Including the | Annual Communication of 1878; | To Which is Added a | Digest of the Decisions | Approved by the Grand Lodge during the same | period of time. | [*short rule*] | Published by Order of the Grand Lodge. | [*short rule*] | San Francisco: | Frank Eastman, [*sic*] & Co. Printers, 509 Clay Street. | 1878.   [948]

12 p. 18? x 11? cm. The recorded copy, which is in a private collection, has been trimmed and pasted on the rear endpaper of an 1872 constitution. On the verso of the title page, in an extract from the Grand Lodge minutes authorizing its printing, is the following statement: "Resolved, That such amendments be also printed on sheets of suitable size to be inserted in the Book of Constitutions."
NvU (microfilm).

FREEMASONS. *Nevada. Grand Lodge.*

Proceedings | of the | M.·. W.·. Grand Lodge | of | Free and Accepted Masons | of the | State of Nevada, | at its | Fourteenth Annual Grand Communication, | Held at | Masonic Hall, in the City of Virginia, | June 11th, 12th, and 13th, A.L. 5878. | [*filet*] | San Francisco: | Frank Eastman & Co, [*sic*] Printers, 509 Clay Street. | 1878.

[949]

[3], 130-342, iii p. 23 x 15 cm. Printed wrapper.

$600 was set aside for printing the proceedings (p. 293). 800 copies were printed, with 300 retained by the printer for future binding (1879 Proceedings, p. 523), at a cost of $844.10 (ibid., p. 525).

NvHi. NvRFM. NvU.

FREEMASONS. *Nevada. Royal Arch Masons. Grand Chapter.*

Proceedings | of the | M.E. Grand Royal Arch Chapter | of the | State of Nevada, | at its | Fifth Annual Grand Convocation, | Held at | Masonic Hall, in the City of Virginia, | June 10th, 11th, and 12th, A.D. 1878, A.I. 2408. | [*filet*] | San Francisco: | Frank Eastman & Co., Printers, No. 509 Clay Street. | 1878.   [950]

[5], 124-198 p. 23 x 15 cm. Printed wrapper.

350 copies were printed; 210 were distributed, 40 were put on file in the Grand Secretary's office, and 100 were left with the printer for future binding (1879 Proceedings, p. 208).

NvU.

GOLD HILL, NEVADA. *Fire Department.*

Constitution | and | By-Laws | of the | Fire Department | of | Gold Hill, Nevada. | [*filet*] | Organized May 22d, 1867. | [*short rule*] | Revised, May, 1878 | [*short rule*] | San Francisco: | H. S. Crocker & Co., Stationers and Printers. | 1878.   [951]

32 p. 14 x 10 cm. Printed wrapper.

C. CSmH. CtY. NvHi. NvU (microfilm).

GOLD HILL, NEVADA. *Republican Rally.* Poster. Gold Hill: News. October 28, 1878.   [L952]

Doten *Journals*, October 27, 1878: "Some of the printers busy in the office today . . . printing some Republican posters, 200 of them, about Ex Gov [George L.] Woods of Oregon going to speak tomorrow evening. . . ."

GOLD HILL DAILY NEWS. *Gold Hill, Nevada.*

Gold Hill News | Extra! | [*thick-thin rule*] | The Lady Bryan Fire | [*short rule*] | All the Miners Escape from | the Shaft. | [*short rule*] | The Hoisting Works | Destroyed. | [*short rule*] | The Loss Estimated at | $200,000. | [*short rule*] | [From our Special Reporter.] | [*short rule*] | [1878.]   [953]

Broadside. 22? x 6? cm. The recorded copy has been cropped on all sides. Line 10 printed in brackets. Facsimile following p. 314.

Doten *Journals*, October 13, 1878: "[H. B.] Loomis was on hand and reported the fire — We got it by telegraph and got out a Gold Hill News Extra . . . Subsidized little 'Black Dan' to distribute 300 throughout Gold Hill and Virginia *free*. . . ."

NvU.

GOLD HILL DAILY NEWS. *Gold Hill, Nevada.*

The Great Race. | [*filet*] | [Special to the Gold Hill Daily News.] | [*short rule*] | Gold Hill News Office, | July 4—4 P.M. | . . . | [1878.]   [954]

Broadside. 8 x 8 cm. Line 2 printed in brackets. Lines 3-4 connected by brace.

Doten *Journals*, July 4, 1878: "Big race at Louisville Kentucky today — Ten Broeck beat Molly McCarty — We printed an extra short couple of inches square — Gave them all away." Molly McCarty was named for the wife of a Virginia City businessman.

NvU.

GRANTSVILLE, NEVADA. *Independence Day Celebration.* Programme. Austin: Reese River Reveille. 1878.   [L955]

Reveille, June 8, 1878: "The REVEILLE job office has printed for Stub a lot of posters, containing the programme for the celebration of the Fourth of July at Grantsville . . . Concerning the ball the posters say: 'A general invitation to attend and take part in this shindig and its attendant festivities is extended to all the ladies and gents in the universe, particularly that portion of this mundane sphere comprised in the limits of Nye and Lander counties, and more particularly than all, the fair sex of that section, as aforesaid.' " "Stub" ran a stage line between Austin and Grantsville and other Nye County towns. Grantsville did not have a press until the following October.

METHODIST EPISCOPAL CHURCH. *Conferences. Nevada.*

Minutes | of the | Nevada Annual Conference | of the | Methodist Episcopal Church, | Fourteenth Session. | Held in Truckee, California, | September 19th-22d, A.D [*sic*] 1878. | [*filet*] | San Francisco: | Methodist Book Depository, 1041 Market Street. | 1878.

[956]

[3], 4-14, [4] p. 22 x 15 cm. Printed wrapper.

The Reno *Nevada State Journal* acknowledged receipt of a copy on November 27, 1878.

CBPac (lacks wrapper). CU-B. NcLjUM (lacks wrapper). NjMD.

MINERS' UNION OF GOLD HILL.

Constitution, | By-Laws, Order of Business, | and | Rules of Order | of | The Miners' Union, | of Gold Hill, Nev. | [*short rule*] | Organized December 8th, 1866. | [*short rule*] | Revised by a Special Committee, October 15th, 1877. | [*short rule*] | Gold Hill "Daily News," Print. | 1878.   [957]

20 p. 15 x 10 cm. Printed wrapper. Title and text pages in decorative single rule borders.
NvHi.

MORNING APPEAL. *Carson City, Nevada*. Extra. November 4, 1878.
[L958]

Gold Hill *News,* November 4, 1878: "The Carson *Appeal* issued an extra edition this morning, filled with rousing campaign editorials."

MORNING APPEAL. *Carson City, Nevada*. Prospectus. January 1878?
[L959]

Eureka *Sentinel,* January 4, 1878, quoting from the prospectus issued by Henry R. Mighels, who had become sole owner of the *Appeal* for the second time, on January 1: "The politics of the *Appeal* will be, as always, strictly Black Republican, or 'Radical,' and the editor anticipates with pleasure the probability that in supporting the next Republican candidate for the Presidency, he will support General Grant in 1880. Meantime, the *Appeal* will nail the Old Flag to the mast, and neither surrender to the adherents of the Lost Cause, nor give its support to a policy which demolished the Republican party of the South, and sought to handcuff it in the North. In short, the *Morning Appeal* will keep on an even keel and stand by the friends of Republican principles, Republican usage, and the Republican leaders of tried courage and ability." The prospectus may have been issued during the last days of 1877, with the issue of January 1, or, conceivably published only in the newspaper. Mighels was unable to give his paper's support to Grant in 1880; he died in May of 1879.

NEVADA. *District Court. First Judicial District (Storey County).*

In the District Court of the First Judicial District of the | State of Nevada, in and for the County of Storey. | [*filet*] | [*short rule*] | Murphy Virginia Mining Company, | Plaintiff, | vs. | Consolidated Virginia Mining | Company, | Defendant. | [*short rule*] [*filet*] | . . . | [1878.]   [960]

9 leaves. 35 x 22 cm. Caption title. Lines 1-6 at left of the page; connected by brace. Printed date on leaf 9: June 21, 1878.
Deposition of a witness, H. J. O'Reilly, taken at San Francisco.
NvU.

NEVADA. *District Court. Ninth Judicial District (Elko County).*

Rules | of the | District Court | of the | Ninth Judicial District | of the | State of Nevada, | in and for the | County of Elko. | [*short rule*] | Elko, Nev.: | Elko Independent Book and Job Print. | 1878.
[961]

13, [1], iii p. 22 x 13 cm. Printed wrapper.
MH-L. NvU (microfilm).

NEVADA. *Politics*. Circular. November 1878.   [L962]

Territorial Enterprise, November 3, 1878: "The last desperate fling of the desperate Democracy is to circulate a dirty circular about the part taken by Mr. [Rollin M.] Daggett in reducing the wages of printers. It was purely a business matter. The regular wages of the printers of San Francisco had been greatly reduced. At the prices here neither the Gold Hill *News* nor *Chronicle* of this city were making any money. [Since] it was necessary to reduce the price of the ENTERPRISE subscription one-half and to pay expenses and at the same time make a paper to compete with the San Francisco papers, a general reduction in prices was necessary. The San Francisco Typographical Union has always partially controlled the prices paid printers on this coast. At the time San Francisco was paying 60 cents the printers here received 70 cents per thousand, and when the San Francisco Union reduced the price to 50 cents the Virginia Union reduced to 65 cents—15 cents per thousand more than San Francisco. No *demand* for a reduction was made on the Virginia printers, but a request simply and the reduction was anticipated by the printers. On consultation the owners of the three principal papers of the county thought it right to ask for a reduction, and it was done. There never was a fairer or more business-like proposition made or accepted. The reduction was not confined to printers, but was general, and altogether necessary, and so well understood is this that every Republican printer in the city and many Democratic printers will vote for Mr. Daggett on Tuesday. At the old rates it was but a question of a short time, as business then was, when two at least of these offices here would have been closed and the compositors forced to find a new field. At present rates printers are better paid in Nevada than anywhere else on earth. When the ENTERPRISE was run by non-Union men under Mr. [Joseph T.] Goodman, Mr. Daggett was not in the office. A few weeks afterward, when Mr. Goodman sold the paper and Mr. Daggett took charge, his first act was to fire out the irregulars and to employ only Union men. Finally, the author of the circular against Daggett is to-day spending money to treat men to lubricate his arguments against Mr. Daggett which he ought to pay to the printers who worked for him and who have never received their pay for such services." Daggett won his election two days later over W. E. F. Deal for Nevada's seat in the U.S. House of Representatives.

NEVADA. *Politics*. Circular. Reno: Reno Evening Gazette. November 5, 1878.   [L963]

Gazette, November 5, 1878: "About 3 o'clock a circular was distributed by Mr. [C. C.] Powning's friends attacking H. H. Beck, accueing [*sic*] him of dishonesty, a crooked record and all sorts of political corruption, and calling upon everbody to vote for Powning. Mr. Beck, with the pamphlet in his hand, mounted a barrel and spoke to the crowd, ridiculing the attempts of his enemeies [*sic*] to cast any reflections upon his record. The circular was printed in the GAZETTE job office on the order of Mr. Pdwing's [*sic*] friends. It was then attempted to fpread [*sic*] the report that Beck had caused the pamphlet to be printed and more circulars were at once flying around. Powning for once dariug [*sic*] in a street dodger to vent his spite against the *Gazette* which had treated him with undeserved kindness during the campaign." Powning, owner of the rival *Nevada State Journal* in Reno, won his election to the state Senate.

Nevada. *Politics.* Flyer. October 1878.   [L964]

Gold Hill *News,* October 24, 1878: "Flyers are plentiful around the streets of Virginia on which are the following mystic words of some organization—probably a sell-out club: 'Unpledged. We meet October 24. You know where.—K. Z.' Candidates appeared more interested in the little slips than anybody else."

Nevada. *Politics.* The record of John Henry Kinkead. October 1878.
                                                             [L965]

Reno *Gazette,* October 30, 1878: "The Democrats are scattering pamphlets broadcast over the land. These efforts are very weak and the latest contains 'The Record of John Henry Kinkead.' The subject is certainly too deep for Democratic comprehension or discussion. Henry Kinkead's record is graven in the hearts of the thousands who knew and estemed [*sic*] him before Nevada was a state. As long as the Democrats confine themselves to Mr. Kinkead's record they will be engaged in a profitable study." Kinkead defeated Governor L. R. Bradley's bid for a third term in the November election.

Nevada. *State Controller's Office.*

Annual Report | of the | Controller of the State of Nevada, | [*short rule*] | W. W. Hobart, Controller. | [*state seal*] | Carson City: | John J. Hill, State Printer. | 1878.   [966]

101 p. 23 x 15 cm. Wrapper title, in decorative rule border. Issued also as No. 3 in AJSA, 1879.

The printing of 1,200 copies in pamphlet form was authorized by an 1873 act of the Legislature (SSN, 1873, p. 175). The Carson City *Appeal* acknowledged receipt of a copy on February 28, 1878, calling it "a very neat little pamphlet."
C. CU. Nv-Ar.

Nevada. *Supreme Court.*

[Briefs. 1878.]

Cohen vs. Eureka and Palisade Railroad Co. Brief and argument of respondent on appeal, A. M. Cohen. 46 p. 25 x 18 cm. Imprint on wrapper: [San Francisco:] Printed by Wallace & Hassett, Law Printers, 419 Sacramento Street, below Sansome. Printed on wrapper: Filed [*dotted rule*], 1878. Nv-Ar.   [967]

Cohen vs. Eureka and Palisade Railroad Co. Brief of appellant, Eureka and Palisade Railroad Co. 51 p. 25 x 18 cm. Imprint on wrapper: San Francisco: Printing Department of A. L. Bancroft & Company. 1878. Nv-Ar.   [968]

Cohen vs. Eureka and Palisade Railroad Co. Brief of appellant in reply, Eureka and Palisade Railroad Co. 24 p. 25 x 18 cm. Imprint on wrapper: San Francisco: Printing Department of A. L. Bancroft & Company. 1878. Nv-Ar.   [969]

Gleeson vs. Martin White Mining Co. Appellant's brief in reply, Kate Gleeson. 40 p. 25 x 18 cm. Imprint on wrapper: C. A. Murdock & Co., Book and Job Printers, 532 Clay Street, San Francisco. Printed on wrapper: Filed [*dotted rule*] 1878. Nv-Ar.
                                                             [970]

Gleeson vs. Martin White Mining Co. Argument of respondent, Martin White Mining Co. 61 p. 25 x 18 cm. Imprint on wrapper: San Francisco: Amanda M. Slocum, Steam Book and Job Printer, 534 Commercial-St. 1878. Nv-Ar. [971]

Gleeson vs. Martin White Mining Co. Brief of appellant, Kate Gleeson. 27 p. 25 x 18 cm. Imprint on wrapper: C. A. Murdock & Co., Book and Job Printers, 532 Clay Street, San Francisco. Printed on wrapper: Filed [broken rule] 1878. Nv-Ar.
[972]

Gleeson vs. Martin White Mining Co. Brief of appellant, Kate Gleeson. 30, 4 p. 25 x 18 cm. Imprint on wrapper: C. A. Murdock & Co., Book and Job Printers, 532 Clay Street, San Francisco. Printed on wrapper: Filed [broken rule] 1878. Nv-Ar.
[973]

Gleeson vs. Martin White Mining Co. Brief of respondent, Martin White Mining Co. 62 p. 25 x 18 cm. Hand-drawn and hand-colored tracing bound in. Imprint on wrapper: Women's Print, 424 Montg'y St., S.F. Printed on wrapper: Filed this [dotted rule] day of [dotted rule] 1878. Nv-Ar. [974]

Nevada vs. Yellow Jacket Mining Co. Brief of respondent, State of Nevada. 34 p. 23 x 18 cm. Imprint on wrapper: Virginia, Nev.: Printed at the Evening Chronicle Job Office. 1878. "Brief of Appellant" is printed in the wrapper and caption titles, but on the recorded copy "Appellant" is crossed off by hand and replaced with "Respondent" in both places. Nv-Ar. [975]

Nevada, ex rel Beck et al. vs. Board of Commissioners of Washoe County et al. Brief of relators. 45 p. 23 x 16 cm. Imprint on wrapper: Reno Gazette Book and Job Print. 1878. Nv-Ar. NvHi. [976]

Orr Ditch Co. vs. Larcomb et al. Brief of plaintiff, Orr Ditch Co. 10 p. 22 x 16 cm. Imprint on wrapper: Reno Gazette Book and Job Print. Handwritten on wrapper of recorded copy: Filed Sep 20, 1878 Chas F. Bicknell Clk. Nv-Ar. [977]

Solen vs. Virginia and Truckee Railroad Co. Points of appellant, Virginia and Truckee Railroad Co. 16 p. 25 x 18 cm. Imprint on wrapper: H. S. Crocker & Co., Printers, S.F. Handwritten on wrapper of recorded copy: Filed April 26, 1878, Chas. F. Bicknell Clerk. Nv-Ar. [978]

Stevenson and Son vs. Mann et al. Petition for rehearing by appellants, J. J. Mann et al. 22 p. 25 x 18 cm. Imprint on wrapper: San Francisco: C. H. Street, Printer, 522 California Street. (Building formerly occupied by W.U. Tel. Co.) 1878. Nv-Ar.
[979]

Stevenson and Son vs. Mann et al. Supplemental brief of appellants, J. J. Mann et al. 18 p. 25 x 18 cm. Imprint on wrapper: San Francisco: C. H. Street, Printer, 522 California Street. (Building formerly occupied by W.U. Tel. Co.) 1878. Nv-Ar.
[980]

NEVADA. *Supreme Court.*

Digest | of | Nevada Reports, | and | Sawyer's Circuit Court Reports, | Comprising | The Decisions of the Supreme Court of the State of Nevada, from Volume One to | Volume Twelve, Inclusive; and the Decisions of the Circuit and | District Courts of the United States for the Ninth | Circuit, from Volume One to Volume | Four,

Inclusive. | With a Table of Cases Cited, Criticised, Commented Upon, Affirmed | and Overruled. | By | Hon. Thomas P. Hawley, | Chief Justice of the State of Nevada. | San Francisco: | A. L. Bancroft and Company, | Law Book Publishers, Booksellers and Stationers. | 1878. [981]

444 p. 23 x 15 cm. Leather binding.

On the ninth of June, 1878, the Reno *Nevada State Journal* reported that H. A. Waldo and Thomas V. Julien, Reno attorneys, were engaged in preparing a digest of the Supreme Court Reports. Later in the month, however, on the 27th, the *Journal* announced that Bancroft had the Hawley volume "now in press," and nothing further was heard of the Waldo and Julien compilation. The Legislature of 1879 authorized the purchase of 400 copies (SSN, 1879, p. 59), for which $2,000 was paid out in 1879 (Treasurer's report, 1879, p. 31). The edition was reported received by the Secretary of State (Report, 1879-1880, p. 6).

CSmH. DLC. NjP. Nv. NvGoEC. NvHi. NvRNC. NvSC. NvU.

NEVADA. *Supreme Court.*

Reports of Cases | Determined in | The Supreme Court | of the | State of Nevada, | During the Year 1877. | Reported by | Chas. F. Bicknell, | Clerk of Supreme Court, | and | Hon. Thomas P. Hawley, | Chief Justice. | Volume XII. | San Francisco: | A. L. Bancroft and Company, | Law Book Publishers, Booksellers and Stationers. | 1878. [982]

509 p. 23 x 15 cm. Leather binding.

$600 was paid on March 15, 1878, for 600 copies (Controller's report, 1878, p. 220). The Gold Hill *News* acknowledged receipt of a copy on April 23. Reissued with volume 13 in 1887 by Bancroft-Whitney of San Francisco in a stereotype edition.

Az. CU-B. DHEW. DLC. In-SC (rebound). M. Nv. Nv-Ar. NvEC. NvEuC. NvHi. NvPLC. NvRNC. NvRWL. NvSC. NvU. OrU-L. U-L.

NEVADA. *Treasury Department.*

Annual Report | of the | State Treasurer | of the State of Nevada, | For the Thirteenth Fiscal Year, Ending December 31, 1877. | [*short rule*] | Jerry Schooling, Treasurer. | [*state seal*] | Carson City: | John J. Hill, State Printer. | 1878. [983]

83 p. 23 x 15 cm. Wrapper title, in decorative rule border. Issued also as No. 5 in AJSA, 1879, and in SSN, 1879, p. [169]-253 from the same type.

An 1873 act of the Legislature authorized the printing of 1,200 copies in pamphlet form (SSN, 1873, p. 175). The Gold Hill *News* acknowledged receipt of a copy "in pamphlet form" on March 21, 1878.

DLC. Nv-Ar.

NEVADA AGRICULTURAL, MINING AND MECHANICAL SOCIETY. *Carson City, Nevada.*

First Annual | Meeting and Fair | of the | Nevada Agricultural, Mining and | Mechanical Society, | to be Held | October 1st to 5th, inclusive, 1878, | at | Carson City. | [*filet*] | Read the Rules and Regulations. | [*short rule*] | Competition Open to All the World. | [*short rule*] | No Entry Fee, Except in Speed Contests. | [*short rule*] | Trials of Speed Conducted by the Society. | [*short rule*] | Please Circulate.   [984]

16 p. 15 x 10 cm. Printed wrapper.

The organization was not related to the Nevada State Agricultural, Mining and Mechanical Society in Reno.

NvMus.

NEVADA STATE AGRICULTURAL, MINING AND MECHANICAL SOCIETY. *Reno, Nevada*. Rules and list of premiums of the fifth annual fair. October 7-12, 1878.   [L985]

Territorial Enterprise, July 16, 1878: "We have received a neat pamphlet, embracing the rules, list of premiums, etc., of the Fifth Annual Fair of the Nevada State Agricultural, Mining and Mechanical Society, to be held in Reno on the 7th, 8th, 9th, 10th, 11th and 12th of October."

NEVADA STATE AGRICULTURAL, MINING AND MECHANICAL SOCIETY. *Reno, Nevada*. Speed programme. 1878.   [L986]

Reno *Nevada State Journal*, June 23, 1878: "The Agricultural Society is distributing the 3-sheet poster speed programme. Pamphlets will be sent around next week."

NEVADA STATE MEDICAL SOCIETY.

Proceedings | of the | Nevada State | Medical Society, | at its | First Regular Semi-Annual Meeting, | Held in | Virginia, July 1st, 1878, | Together With | A List of Officers, Members, Etc. | [*short rule*] | Virginia, Nev.: | Enterprise Book and Job Printing House. | 1878.   [987]

52 p. 21 x 14 cm. Printed wrapper.

The *Territorial Enterprise* reported receipt of a copy on October 20, 1878. Three days later, in acknowledging its copy, the Carson City *Appeal* referred to it as "an excellent specimen of typography," and said it "would be creditable to any printing office on this coast."

NvU.

NEVADA STATE TEACHERS' INSTITUTE. Circular. 1878.   [L988]

Carson City *Appeal,* April 4, 1878: "The following circular of information has been received at this office. . . ." The circular was issued from the "Office of State Superintendent" at Carson City, April 3, 1878; it listed the order of exercises for the meetings.

NEVADA STATE TEACHERS' INSTITUTE. Programme. 1878.   [L989]

Receipt of "the programmes" was noted in the April 4, 1878, issue of the Carson City *Appeal*. The usual practice in later years was to issue a separate program for each day of the institute, ordinarily a five-day affair.

ODD FELLOWS, INDEPENDENT ORDER OF. *Austin, Nevada. Austin Lodge No. 9.*

Constitution, | By-Laws and Rules of Order | —of— | Austin Lodge, No. 9, | of the | Independent Order of Odd Fellows | of the | State of Nevada. | [*short rule*] | Instituted at Austin, January 23d, 1864. | [*short rule*] | San Francisco: | Winterburn & Co., Printers and Electrotypers, | No. 417 Clay street, between Sansome and Battery. | 1878.   [990]

66 p. 14? x 10? cm. The recorded copy has been trimmed and bound. Printed wrapper. Title and text pages in single rule borders. A membership certificate, not counted in the pagination, precedes the title page; four blank, ruled leaves at the end. CU-B.

ODD FELLOWS, INDEPENDENT ORDER OF. *Nevada. Grand Lodge.*

Proceedings | of the | Twelfth Annual Communication | of the | R.W. Grand Lodge | of the | Independent Order of Odd Fellows | of the State of Nevada, | Held in Odd Fellows' Hall, Virginia City, Storey County, Nev., | on the 4th, 5th and 6th days of June, A.D. 1878. | [*short rule*] | Virginia, Nevada: | Footlight Book and Job Printing House. | 1878.   [L991]

[3], 1242-1353, [2], ii-vii p. Description from title page in bound volume for 1874-1879. Printed? wrapper; the index refers to material on the "third page of cover," but it is not known whether the outside of the wrapper was also printed.

The Committee on Finance estimated that printing would cost $450 (p. 1301). The actual cost cannot be given because at the following communication the report of the Grand Treasurer indicated payments only by warrant number, with no identification of the payees.

ODD FELLOWS, INDEPENDENT ORDER OF. *Pioche, Nevada. Pioche Lodge No. 23.*

Constitution, | By-Laws and Rules of Order | —of— | Pioche Lodge | No. 23, I.O.O.F., | of the | State of Nevada. | [*short rule*] | Instituted at Pioche, September 10, 1872. | [*short rule*] | San Francisco: | Jos. Winterburn & Co., Printers & Electrotypers, | No. 417 Clay Street, between Sansome and Battery. | 1878.   [992]

75, [1] p. 15 x 10 cm. Cloth binding, with blind-stamped border front and rear, and gold-stamped title: Pioche Lodge, No. 23, I.O.O.F. Title and text pages in single rule borders. A membership certificate, not counted in the pagination, precedes the title page.

The examined copy is in a private collection.

NvU (microfilm).

PIPER'S OPERA HOUSE. *Virginia City, Nevada.*

Piper's New Opera House | Virginia City, Nev. | . . . | [*thick-thin rule*] | Great Success | —of Mr.— | Chas. R. Thorne, Jr. | ——Miss—— | Fanny Morant | —and the— | Union Square Theater Co. | [*thick-thin rule*] | Grand Matinee this Afternoon at 2 | When will be Presented the Great Play of | The Danicheffs! | Prices of Admission as Usual. Children Under 12 Half Price. | [*thick-thin rule*] | This (Wednesday) Even'g, February 6, | Will be presented the Powerful Emotional Play, in Five Acts and Six Tableaux, entitled, | Led | Astray | Written by Dion Boucicault, Esq., expressly for the Union Square Theater Company. | . . . | [*thick-thin rule*] | Thursday Even'g, Feb. 7th | First time of the glorious Comedy, | Pink Dominoes | [*thick-thin rule*] | . . . | [*rule*] | [Virginia City:] Enterprise Steam Print. | [1878.]   [993]

Broadside. 51 x 22 cm. Thick-thin rule border.

Reviews of *The Danicheffs* and *Led Astray* appeared in the *Territorial Enterprise* of February 5 and 7, 1878, respectively.

NjP.

PIPER'S OPERA HOUSE. *Virginia City, Nevada.*

Piper's New Opera House | Virginia City, Nev. | . . . | [*thick-thin rule*] | Great Success | —of Mr.— | Chas. R. Thorne, Jr. | ——Miss—— | Fanny Morant | —and the— | Union Square Theater Co. | [*thick-thin rule*] | First Production in this City of the New Comedy, | Pink | Dominos | Now being played to crowded houses at the Criterion Theater, London, where it has already reached its Two | Hundredth Performance, and recently produced at the Union Square Theater, New York, | where for nearly 100 Nights it delighted the most critical and fashionable audiences. | [*thick-thin rule*] | This (Thursday) Even'g, February 7th, | Will be presented, the glorious Comedy of | Pink Dominos! | . . . | [*rule*] | [Virginia City:] Enterprise Steam Print. | [1878.]   [994]

Broadside. 51 x 23 cm. Thick-thin rule border.

The play was reviewed in the *Territorial Enterprise* of February 8, 1878, in which (as also in previous advertisements) the second word in the title is spelled "Dominoes." See also No. 993, in which it is spelled the same way. Contemporary criticism is no more clear, either, changing from one spelling to the other with no apparent concern

for the twentieth-century bibliographer.
NjP.

REPUBLICAN PARTY. *Ormsby County, Nevada.*

Republican State Ticket. | [*filet*] | . . . | [1878.] [995]

Broadside. 25 x 11 cm.
The ticket is headed by John H. Kinkead, who defeated Governor L. R. Bradley's bid for a third term. The Ormsby County Republican ticket follows the state recommendations.
NvU(NvMus).

REPUBLICAN PARTY. *Storey County, Nevada.* Straight Republican ticket. Gold Hill: News. 1878. [L996]

Doten *Journals,* November 4, 1878: "A blunder was discovered in printing the straight Republican ticket, in leaving out the name of E Nye, for County Commissioner out [*sic*] of one of the four forms in the chase — Went to work & printed 7500 to make up the deficiency — An error was made in printing another job of 5,000 mixed tickets so we had *that* job to do over — We thus lost 12,500 tickets." Nye was elected to a second term in Storey County.

REPUBLICAN PARTY. *Washoe County, Nevada.*

Republican State Ticket. | [*short rule*] | . . . | [*short rule*] | State Senator, | C. C. Powning. | . . . | [1878.] [997]

Broadside. 28 x 5 cm.
Powning won in the Washoe County state senatorial race. No candidate is listed for State Printer because the office had been abolished by the Legislature of 1877.
NvHi.

SOCIETY OF PACIFIC COAST PIONEERS. *Nevada.* Poster. July 20, 1878. [L998]

Carson City *Appeal,* July 17, 1878: "The great posters of the Pioneers' Picnic on next Saturday have already made their appearance on the walls and deadwalls of our houses, barns, saloons and fences."

UNITED STATES. *Circuit Court. District of Nevada (Ninth Circuit).*

[Briefs. 1878.]

Sierra Nevada S.M. Co. vs. Union Consolidated S.M. Co. Bill of complaint of Sierra Nevada S.M. Co. Certified copy. 19 p. 32 x 20 cm. Imprint on wrapper: Enterprise Printing House, Virginia, Nev. Date tentatively established from internal evidence. [999]
NvU.

UNITED STATES. *Circuit Court. District of Nevada (Ninth Circuit).*

Injunction. Jurisdiction After Dismissal of | Bill,—Nevada Statutory

Provisions. | [*filet*] | The Opinion | of | The Circuit Court of the United States, | for the District of Nevada, | in the Case of | The Eureka Consolidated Mining Company, | vs. | The Richmond Mining Company, of Nevada, | Delivered March 22, 1878, by | Mr. Justice Sawyer. | Concurred in by Mr. Jnstice [*sic*] Hillyer. [1000]

12 p. 24 x 16 cm. Printed wrapper.

Justices Lorenzo Sawyer and Edgar W. Hillyer were the judges involved in the case.
CU-B.

VIRGINIA CITY, NEVADA. *Ordinances, local laws, etc.*

Revised Ordinances | of the | City of Virginia | County of Storey, State of Nevada, | [*short rule*] | as | Revised, Compiled and Amended by | J. G. Graham | Assisted by A. F. Mackay, City Clerk. | [*short rule*] | With an Appendix | containing Rules of the Board of Aldermen; Rules and Regulations of | the Board of Fire Commissioners; and Rules and Regula-|tions of the Board of Police Commissioners. | [*short rule*] | Published by Authority of the Board of | Aldermen of Virginia City. | [*short rule*] | Virginia, Nevada: | Enterprise Steam Printing House. | 1878. [1001]

viii, 161 p. 22? x 14? cm. The recorded copy has been trimmed and bound. Printed wrapper.

Territorial Enterprise, June 8, 1878: "A copy of the revised ordinances of this city has been laid upon our table. The book is from the ENTERPRISE Steam Printing House. It contains 161 pages and is very handsomely printed."
CU-B.

WASHOE COUNTY, NEVADA. *Sheriff.*

Reno, Feb. [*blank*], 1878. | M[*broken rule*] | You are respectfully invited to | be present at the | Execution of J. W. Rover, | Which will take place on Tues-|day, the 19th day of February, | A.D. 1878, at 10 o'clock, A.M. | Yours Respectfully, | A. K. Lamb | Sheriff of Washoe Co., Nev. [1002]

Broadside. 22 x 13 cm. Mostly script type.

Accounts in the Reno *Nevada State Journal* for February 19 and 20, 1878, describe in grisly detail Rover's murder of I. N. Sharp, a miner, in Humboldt County nearly three years earlier, his two convictions there before the case was transferred to Washoe County where he was again convicted, his unsuccessful appeals, his hour-long plea of innocence on the scaffold, and his death by hanging.
NvHi.

WASHOE TYPOGRAPHICAL UNION.

Constitution | and | By-Laws | of | Washoe Typographical Union, | No. 65, | Together with the | Scale of Prices. | [*short rule*] | Organized June 28th, 1863. | [*short rule*] | Virginia, Nev.: | Enterprise Steam Book and Job Printing House. | 1878.   [1003]

32 p. 14? x 9? cm. The recorded copy has been trimmed and bound. Printed wrapper. The scale of prices covers p. [27]-32; see Appendix B.
CtY. NvU (microfilm).

WORKINGMEN'S PARTY. *Washoe County, Nevada.*

Delegates | —to the— | Workingmen's | County Convention: | [*filet*] | . . . | [1878.]   [1004]

Broadside. 23 x 9 cm. The top of the recorded copy has been torn on both sides, not affecting the text.

A list of twenty-five names of Washoe County residents, twelve of whom were to be chosen to attend the county convention on October 3, 1878. As with the better-known workingmen's movement in 1869, the animus was the Chinese workers who were willing to work for less than white workers and were thus more desirable to employers. The platform that was adopted at the meeting, reported in the Reno *Nevada State Journal* of October 4, demanded the cessation of Chinese immigration, a per capita tax of $100 per year on Chinese, the resulting fund to be used in anti-Chinese law suits, and the banning of Chinese on public works jobs. Since public works were defined to include railroads, canals, and mines, the last of which was the principal industry in the state, the exclusion would have put the Chinese out of nearly all paying jobs.
NvHi.

WRIGHT, WILLIAM.

The | Wonders of Nevada | Where They Are and How to Get to Them. | [*filet*] | A Guide for Tourists to the Great Silver Mines, | the Lakes, the Towns, and the | Mountains. | [*filet*] | Virginia, Nevada: | Enterprise Book and Job Printing House. | 1878. [1005]

32 p. 16 x 10 cm. Printed wrapper. Advertisements on wrappers and verso of a folded map. Reprinted in a facsimile edition in 1966 by La Siesta Press of Glendale, California.

The text was copyrighted by William Sutherland, a printer for the *Enterprise,* and on this evidence *Check List:* 237 entered its description of the pamphlet under his name. The libraries that are listed below as holding copies all enter it under Sutherland, and the La Siesta reprint attributed it to him as well. In announcing its publication on May 23, 1878, however, the *Enterprise* referred to Sutherland only as the publisher, and the reason was made clear several days later in notices appearing in other newspapers. Both the Gold Hill *News* of May 27 and the Carson City *Appeal* of May 29 identified the author as William Wright, the *Enterprise* local, who was better known by his pseudonym of Dan De Quille. The reasons for the mild subterfuge, or at least unwillingness to identify the author, are not clear, although they may be related to Sutherland's desire to put his name before the public and De Quille's lack of need for it. The latter was very well known on the Comstock, having been a regular on the *Enterprise* between bouts with delirium tremens since shortly after the paper's arrival in Virginia City. He had also written *History of the Big Bonanza* (Hartford: American

Publishing Company; San Francisco: A. L. Bancroft & Co.), with an "Introductory" by his former colleague, Mark Twain, just two years earlier, and had thus gained a measure of national exposure. Sutherland, on the other hand, was a young man of ambition who was shortly to leave the *Enterprise* to establish his own job office, and he may have chosen this publication to present himself favorably and to make his name familiar.

The *Enterprise* article of May 23 reported that "some 10,000 copies . . . will be issued in a few days," but its use of the past tense elsewhere in the description suggests that at least a few copies had already appeared.

An embarrassed *peccavi* is in order. While preparing for publication of his 1966 facsimile reprint, Walt Wheelock of La Siesta Press wrote to me to establish where copies of the original might be found. I knew then of the CSmH copy and no others, and my assurances of its uniqueness were cited in Wheelock's introduction. The relatively lengthy recitation of institutional holdings below is a rather damning indictment of the state of my knowledge at that time. In fact, NvHi has two copies. CSmH. CtY. DLC. ICN. NN. NjP. Nv. NvHi. NvU (microfilm).

~1879~

Between the eighth and twenty-second of November 1878, agreements were entered into between the Board of State Printing Commissioners and Marshall Robinson, who agreed to do the state's incidental printing in Carson City; A. L. Bancroft & Company, whose job it was to print the larger state works in San Francisco; and the firm of Cunningham, Curtis and Welch, San Francisco stationers, which contracted to furnish printing and binding papers to the state (Nv-Ar: Nevada Contracts, p. 33-38). Each of the contracts was for the two years ending on January 1, 1881. But within three weeks after the 1879 Legislature convened in January, bills began to appear that would amend or replace the 1877 law under which these agreements were made. The most significant of these bills was introduced in the Assembly by Josiah C. Harlow, a Virginia City printer. The bill's most salient feature was the creation of a salaried and elected office of Superintendent of State Printing, which was to be furnished by a State Board of Printing Commissioners with a plant in Carson City. The Superintendent was required to be a practical printer. Editorials in Nevada newspapers before introduction of Harlow's bill ran strongly in favor of such an action and support increased even more thereafter; there was even a favorable comment in the Bodie, California, *Standard*. Only the Carson City *Appeal,* which was owned by the author of the 1877 law that abolished the office of State Printer, suggested that to establish a new procedure without first giving the old one a fair trial was perhaps ill-advised. As support for the bill intensified among the state's printers and editors, however, the *Appeal* dropped its objections. The bill, which was to take effect in 1881, eventually passed both houses and was signed into law by the Governor on March 11 (SSN, 1879, p. 138-139).

Another attempt to aid printers and newspapermen was made when an amendment to the Civil Practice Act naming property that was exempt from taxation was introduced in the Assembly. The bill's author, William B. Taylor of the Tybo *Sun,* reasoned that if a physician or attorney or minister or surveyor could hold tax-free the "tools and implements of a mechanic or artisan necessary to carry on his trade," the printer should have the same privilege for his "printing presses, cases, type and other material," although the exemption should not "exceed the sum of $2,500" (*Territorial Enterprise*, January 28). The amendment made it through the Assembly on a close vote (JA, p. 172), but was defeated in the Senate (JS, p. 339). The bill's loss was an important one for the *Enterprise,* which commented on October 1 that "in the report of the doings of the [Storey County] Board of Equalization in last evening's *Chronicle,* it is stated: 'Incidentally it transpired that the presses, types, etc., of the ENTERPRISE Job Office, belonging to George Daly, have not been assessed at all for the last four years.' George Daly & Co., of the ENTERPRISE Job Office, wish to amend by saying that during all these years they have been paying taxes on a valuation of $1,200, and have the receipts to show to any one who may desire to examine them."

The 1880 report of the State Controller (p. 87) shows that $10,884.52 was expended from the State Printing Fund in 1879.

Acquisition of steam power for its newspaper and job operations brought forth the following from the Reno *Gazette* on March 13: "The office is . . . supplied with a nonpareil job press which for speed and good work is acknowledge [*sic*] to have no superior. It has a capacity of two thousand impression [*sic*] an hour. The job office is supplied with the finest and largest assortment of stationery, suitable for letter, bill and note heads, envelopes, cards, posters, society cards and notices, ever brought to Reno. Statements, tags, sign cards, blank book, [*sic*] work and pamphlet printing of all descriptions can be promptly turned out." The press "after next Saturday will be operated by steam, which will enable the office to turn out a finer class of work than ever, and with the shortest possible delay. One of the greatest drawbacks in a country printing office is the delays which are unavoidable, as men, turning a press by hand cannot be expected to keep up the labor without frequent interruptions. The work produced shows the effects of their fatigue also, and is much less uniform, neat and regular than where pressure is constant and steady. The proprietors particularly request that parties wanting first-class work, in any quantity, large or small, should come and see them before sending away for it." The office was further improved on December 30, when the paper reported that "the Gazette job office received today from Cincinnati, Ohio, a big font of pen script type, which the foundrymen say is the first order received from the Pacific Coast."

Presses that were active at the end of 1878 in Aurora, Austin, Battle Mountain, Belmont, Carson City, Elko, Eureka, Genoa, Gold Hill, Hamilton, Pioche, Reno, Silver City, Sutro, Tuscarora, Tybo, Ward, and Winnemucca continued to publish throughout the year, although Sutro's paper suspended for several months. Cherry Creek's only newspaper ceased operations during the year, as did the paper in Ruby Hill; one paper died in Virginia City. Grantsville's newspaper lasted until June. The state's only new paper began publication at Paradise in May.

AUSTIN SOCIAL TELEGRAPH LINE. *Austin, Nevada.*

Rules and Regulations | ——of the—— | Austin Social Telegraph Line. | [*filet*] | . . . | [*rule*] | J. E. Farrell, Proprietor. | [Austin:] Reveille Job Print. | [1879?] [1006]

Broadside. 31 x 20 cm. Light card stock. Decorative rule border. Facsimile in *Ghost Towns of the West* (Menlo Park, California: Lane Magazine & Book Co., 1971), p. 98.

Tentatively dated as an 1879 imprint on the basis of a brief article in the *Reveille* on March 27 of that year, describing the private telegraph lines in Austin and relating the playful artifices made possible by their use: "The art of telegraphing will soon be so common that everybody will be acquainted with its mysteries. Several private residences are connected in this city by telegraph. A young man has had a wire placed from his room to the residence of his sweetheaat [*sic*], and as no other member of the household understands the alphabet, he can carry on a conversation with her whenever he chooses, and the bystanders are in blissful ignorance of what is passing between the two." It was not an uncommon practice during the era for newspapers to include items related to recent productions of their job offices without specifically mentioning the products themselves. The code on the card is American Morse, used for land-line transmission in the United States and Canada. NvHi.

BISHOP WHITAKER'S SCHOOL FOR GIRLS. *Reno, Nevada.*

Bishop Whitaker's | School for Girls, | Reno, Nevada. | [*filet*] | Third Year. | Ending June 25th, 1879. | [Virginia City: Territorial Enterprise. 1879.]   [1007]

20 p. 16 x 11 cm. Printed wrapper. Title and text pages in decorative single rule borders. The format and types are identical to those that appear in the catalogue for the fourth and fifth years, printed in 1881; see Nos. 867 and 934.

NvHi.

CALIFORNIA. *District Court. Twenty-third Judicial District (San Francisco).*

[Briefs. 1879.]

Burke et al. vs. Flood et al. Argument for defendant on demurrer to complaint, James
    C. Flood et al. 116 p. 25 x 18 cm. Imprint on wrapper: Virginia, Nevada:
    Enterprise Steam Printing House. 1879. NvU.   [1008]

CARSON CITY, NEVADA. *Inaugural Ball.*

Grand Inaugural Ball. | M[*dotted rule*] | Yourself and Ladies are respectfully | invited to attend the Inaugural Ball, given | in honor of Gov. J. H. Kinkead, State | Officers, and Members of the Legislature, | At the Carson Opera House, | Wednesday Evening, January 15th, 1879. | . . .   [1009]

[4] p., printed on p. [1] only. 15 x 12 cm. Mostly script type.

The examined copy is in a private collection.

NvU (microfilm).

CARSON CITY, NEVADA. *Independence Day Celebration.*

1776! 1879! | [*cut of American flags*] | [*short broken wavy rule*] | Programme | of the | Fourth of July | Celebration | in Carson City, Nev. | [*broken wavy rule*] | . . . | Index Print, Carson, Nevada.
                                                                [1010]

Broadside. 57 x 15 cm. Chain-link border, with imprint below border. The recorded copy has been torn in two, not affecting the text.

The *Index* did not begin publication until Christmas Day, 1880, but a job office with the name in the imprint existed well before that time; see, for example, Nos. 1069-1072.

NvMus.

CARSON CITY, NEVADA. *Military Ball.*

[*Ornament*] Carson Guard [*ornament*] | [*Carson Guard emblem*] | [*ornament*] Company F, N.M. [*ornament*] | Mr. [*dotted rule*] Yourself and Ladies are respectfully | invited to attend | A Military Ball, | to be given by the Carson Guard, at their Armory, on New | Year's Eve, Wednesday, December 31st, 1879. | Tickets, $2.00. Dancing Commences Promptly at 9 o'clock.   [1011]

[4] p., printed on p. [1] only. 17 x 14 cm. Line 1 in an arch over the emblem; line 2 in a

reverse arch under the emblem; line 4 in a compartment. Printed in red and blue inks. The recorded copy is in an envelope, with the emblem of the Carson Guard. NvMus.

CARSON CITY, NEVADA. *Virginia and Truckee Employes Ball.* Invitation. March 20, 1879. [L1012]

Reno *Gazette,* March 14, 1879: "The *Gazette* acknowledges the receipt of an invitation to the sixth annual ball given by the employees of the V. & T. R.R. at the Opera House in Carson, on Thursday evening, March 20th."

CARSON OPERA HOUSE. *Carson City, Nevada.*

Carson | Opera House. | [*thick-thin rule*] | Friday Evening, June 27. | [*thick-thin rule*] | [*cut of steam locomotive and passenger cars*] | . . . | [*thick-thin rule*] | On this occasion the Carson Dramatic Club | will present to the public Augustin Daley's [*sic*] great | sensational drama entitled, | Under the | Gaslight! | [*thick-thin rule*] | . . . | [1879.] [1013]

Broadside. 52 x 18 cm. The author's name should be spelled "Daly."
The performance was reviewed in the Carson City *Appeal* on June 28, 1879. NvRH.

CARSON OPERA HOUSE. *Carson City, Nevada.*

Carson | Opera House. | . . . | [*thick-thin rule*] | Monday Evening, | March 31st, 1879. | [*thick-thin rule*] | Grand Complimentary Benefit tendered to | Curry Engine Co, [*sic*] No. 2, | To raise funds to pay deficiency on their new bell, on which | occasion will be presented with New Music, New Costumes, | and New Scenery by Mr. T. F. Laycock of Reno, the | Great Melo-drama entitled | Nick of the Woods! | . . . [1014]

Broadside 27? x 18 cm. The bottom portion of the recorded copy has been torn off. NvMus.

CARSON OPERA HOUSE. *Carson City, Nevada.*

Carson Opera House! | [*thick-thin rule*] | Positively for | Two Nights Only | [*thick-thin rule*] | Monday, April 28th | [*thick-thin rule*] | First Appearance in 5 Years | —of the— | Eminent Tragedian! | Lawrence | Barrett | In his masterly impersonation of Shakespeare's sublimest creation, | Hamlet | . . . | [*rule*] | Enterprise Steam Print, Virginia, Nev. | [1879.] [1015]

Broadside. 50 x 22 cm. Thick-thin rule border.
The performance was reviewed on April 29, 1879, in the Carson City *Appeal.* NvRH.

Carson Opera House. *Carson City, Nevada.*

Carson Opera House. | [*thick-thin rule*] | Saturday, April
12. | [*thick-thin rule*] | The Color Guard! | The Greatest Military
Drama ever produced; under the auspices of the Carson | Guards and
the Grand Army of the Republic. | [*thick-thin rule*] | Grand Tableaux!
Thrilling Situations! | [*thick-thin rule*] | Actual Camp Scenes during
the Rebellion, interspersed with the Comical and | Serious Incidents
in a | Soldier's Life. | [*thick-thin rule*] | The Color Guard | Under
the direction of W. H. Gunn, Proprietor and Manager. | [*thick-thin
rule*] | Mr. John H. Fay. | The Great Dutch Comedian, as Peter
Hygley, supported by the following | Cast of characters:
| . . . | [1879.]   [1016]

Broadside. 60 x 18 cm.

A review of the performance of the same play, produced the previous evening, is in
the Carson City *Appeal*, April 12, 1879. See also No. 1017.

CU-A. NvHi (damaged). NvMus.

Carson Opera House. *Carson City, Nevada.*

Special [*ornament*] | [*ornament*] Notice! | [*thick rule*] | Owing to the
inability | of numbers of prominent citizens fail-|ing to secure seats
last evening, the | Carson Guard have been requested to | perform
the | Color Guard | Again this evening, (Thursday, April | 11th.)
To-night the play will be re-|peated | Positively Last Perfor-
mance. | Box Sheet Now Open. | [1879.]   [1017]

Broadside. 26 x 14 cm. The peculiar wording in lines 3-5 defies placement of a [*sic*].

The day in line 9 is incorrect; April 11, 1879, was a Friday. The performance was
reviewed in the April 12 issue of the Carson City *Appeal*. See No. 1016.

NvMus.

Descovich, John. Circular. February 1879.   [L1018]

Reese River Reveille, March 24, 1879: "The Grantsville Sun, of Wednesday last [i.e.,
March 19], contains a lengthy article relative to an editorial in the Virginia Chronicle
of some days since, headed 'A Swindle in Nye county,' which was doubtless based on
a circular published and circulated by John Descovich, formerly an employe of the
Alexander Mining Company [in Grantsville]. As before stated in these columns the
Descovich circular was undoubtedly inspired for malicious purposes, to injure the
company, simply because the company saw fit to discharge him. The Chronicle was
hasty and short-sighted in stating that the property was a swindle, on information
from an individual alone, and in such shape, and at so great a distance from the mine."
The affair is described in the *Reveille* of February 24; an attack by Descovich on the
Alexander Mine is mentioned, as is a "publication" by him.

Freemasons. *Nevada. Grand Lodge.*

Proceedings | of the | M.˙. W.˙. Grand Lodge | of | Free and Accepted Masons | of the | State of Nevada, | at its | Fifteenth Annual Grand Communication, | Held at | Masonic Hall, in the City of Virginia, | June 10th, 11th and 12th, A.L. 5879. | [*filet*] | Virginia, Nevada: | Enterprise Steam Book and Job Printing House. | 1879. [1019]

[3], 346-573, [1], xiii p. 23 x 15 cm. Printed wrapper.

The report of the Finance Committee recommended printing the proceedings at home to save money, if "it can be done on as favorable terms, including incidental expenses connected therewith, at home as abroad, that it should be done *here*" (p. 530). A resolution was adopted to include the reports of the Committee on Foreign Correspondence in the printed proceedings, and "two hundred copies of each year's report printed and ready for distribution on the assembling of this Grand Lodge at each Communication" (p. 537). $650 was set aside for printing (p. 524). The "usual number" [i.e., 800] were printed (1880 Proceedings, p. 16); the cost of "Printing" was $1,029.75 (ibid., p. 19), but there is no breakdown to indicate how much of the expense was for printing the proceedings.

Territorial Enterprise, September 11, 1879: "A HANDSOME JOB.—There has just been printed at the ENTERPRISE Steam Book and Job Printing Office an edition of nearly 1,000 volumes of the 'Proceedings of the M.W. Grand Lodge, F. and A.M., of the State of Nevada.' The book contains 250 pages and is in every respect one of the best jobs of the kind ever done in Nevada." The boast, although honest, is rather empty, since all previous Masonic proceedings had been printed by Frank Eastman in San Francisco.

NvHi. NvRFM. NvU.

FREEMASONS. *Nevada. Grand Lodge.*

[*Thick-thin rule*] | Proceedings | of the | M.˙. W.˙. Grand Lodge | of | Free and Accepted Masons | of the | State of Nevada, | For the Years 1873, 1874, and 1876. | [*short rule*] | Volume III. | [*short rule*] | [*thin-thick rule*] | [San Francisco: Frank Eastman & Co., Printers, 509 Clay Street. 1879.] [1020]

[5], 4-243, [4], 248-405, [4], 408-634, [3], ii-iv p. 22 x 15 cm. Leather binding. On red leather patch at top of spine, in gold: [*thick-thin rule*] | Proceedings | of the | Grand Lodge | of Nevada. | [*thin-thick rule*]; on black leather patch at bottom: [*thick-thin rule*] | Vol. III. | 1873-1876. | [*thin-thick rule*]; stamped between the patches: F. & A.M.

150 copies, rather than the 300 that were customarily held by the printer for such purposes, were bound (1879 Proceedings, p. 524). It is not unlikely that some of the reserved copies were damaged in Eastman's shop during the years they were held there; see Nos. 684-685.

ICSR. MBFM (rebound). NvLN (binding upside down).

FREEMASONS. *Nevada. Grand Lodge.*

[*Thick-thin rule*] | Proceedings | of the | M.˙. W.˙. Grand

Lodge | of | Free and Accepted Masons | of the | State of Neva-
da, | For the Years 1877, 1878 and 1879. | [*short rule*] | Volume
IV. | [*short rule*] | [*thin-thick rule*] | [Virginia, Nevada: Enterprise
Steam Book and Job Printing House. 1879.]   [1021]

[5], 4-126, [5], 130-342, [3], 346-573, [2], ii-xiii p. 22 x 15 cm. Leather binding. On red
leather patch at top of spine, in gold: [*thick-thin rule*] | Proceedings | of the | Grand
Lodge | of Nevada. | [*thin-thick rule*]; on black leather patch at bottom: [*thick-thin
rule*] | Vol. IV. | 1877-1879. | [*thin-thick rule*]; stamped between patches: F. & A.M.
Extra binder's leaf after p. 126.

By the time this volume was bound the Grand Lodge had removed its business from
Frank Eastman's San Francisco establishment, perhaps because of his less than
adequate performance in retaining the full number of copies held for binding; see Nos.
684-685, 1020.

ICSR. MBFM (rebound). NvRFM. NvU (rebound).

FREEMASONS. *Nevada. Royal Arch Masons. Grand Chapter.*

Proceedings | of the | M.E. Grand Royal Arch Chapter | of
the | State of Nevada, | at its | Sixth Annual Grand Convoca-
tion, | Held at | Masonic Hall, in the City of Virginia, | June 9th,
10th, and 11th, A.D. 1879, A.I. 2409. | [*filet*] | San Francis-
co: | Frank Eastman & Co., Printers, 509 Clay Street. | 1879.
                                                            [1022]

[5], 204-304, [2], x p. 23 x 15 cm. Printed wrapper.

The "usual number" [350 were printed in 1878] of proceedings were printed (1880
Proceedings, p. 11) at a cost of $242, paid on October 2, 1879 (ibid., p. 13).

NvU.

FREEMASONS. *Nevada. Royal Arch Masons. Grand Chapter.*

Proceedings | of the | Most Excellent | Grand Chapter Royal Arch
Masons | of the | State of Nevada. | [*filet*] | Vol. I. | 1873-
1879. | [*filet*] | San Francisco: | Frank Eastman & Co., Print-
ers, No. 509 Clay Street. | 1879.   [1023]

[3], 4-48, [5], 54-71, [6], 78-117, [6], 124-139, [2], 144-198, [5], 204-304, [3], ii-x p. 22
x 15 cm. Red leather binding. The binder has inserted an extra leaf after p. 117.

An entry on p. 13 of the 1880 Proceedings shows payment of two warrants of $3.75
and $46.20 for "Book Binding."

IaCrM. MBFM. NNFM. Nv (lacks title page and p. [1-2]). NvU (microfilm).

FREEMASONS. *Reno, Nevada. Reno Lodge No. 13.*

By-Laws | of | Reno Lodge, | No. 13, | of | Free and Accepted
Masons, | Held at | Reno, Washoe County, | State of Neva-
da; | Being the Uniform Code | Recommended by the Grand
Lodge. | [*filet*] | San Francisco: | Frank Eastman & Co., Printers,

509 Clay St. | 1879. [1024]

23 p. 15 x 10 cm. Printed wrapper.
NvHi.

GOLD HILL, NEVADA. *Public Schools. Board of Trustees.*

Gold Hill | Public Schools. | [*short rule*] | First Annual Report | of
the | Board of Trustees | for the | School Year Ending August 31,
1879, | with | Rules and Regulations, Course of Study and | His-
tory from 1862. | [*short rule*] | Published by Order of the
Board. | Gold Hill, Nev. [1025]

61 p., including illustrations. 22 x 14 cm. Printed wrapper. Errata slip precedes title
page.

More than a month before the date indicated on the title page, on July 26, 1879, the
Gold Hill *News* had the following: "We find on the table of the NEWS a copy of the first
annual report of the Board of Trustees of the Gold Hill Public Schools for the year
ending August 31, 1879, with the rules and regulations, course of study and history of
the schools from 1862. The pamphlet contains sixty-odd pages, is neatly and plainly
printed, and contains besides the above a list of the officers of the Board, full school
statistics, including names of scholars and graduates, corps of teachers, etc., and is
valuable both for information and reference."
NvU.

INDEPENDENT ORDER OF GOOD TEMPLARS. *Nevada. Grand Lodge.*

Proceedings | of | The Inaugural Session | of the | Grand Lodge of
Nevada, | I.O.G.T., | Convened at Reno, February 25th, 1879.
| [*short rule*] | A. H. Wilbur, G.W.S. | [*short rule*] | [*state seal*] |
Sacramento: | H. S. Crocker & Co., Stationers and Printers.
| 1879. [1026]

8 p. 22 x 14 cm. Wrapper title, in decorative rule border. See also No. 1027.

The presence of the state seal on the publication of a private organization is a mystery;
perhaps the members thought it looked attractive.
NvHi.

INDEPENDENT ORDER OF GOOD TEMPLARS. *Nevada. Grand Lodge.*

Proceedings | of | The Inaugural Session, | of the | Grand Lodge
of Nevada, | I.O.G.T., | Convened at Reno, February 25th, 1879,
| A. H. Wilbur, G.W.S., | and of the | First Annual Session, | Held
in Odd Fellows' Hall, | Carson City Oct. 14th and 15th,
1879. | John F. Aitken, G.W.S. | [*filet*] | Reno: | Gazette Book and
Job Print. | 1879. [1027]

29, [3] p. 22 x 14 cm. Wrapper title, in decorative rule border. See also No. 1026.
Proceedings of the second session have not been located.

On p. 20, in the report of the Grand Worthy Secretary: "I would recommend that a

separate committee be appointed to attend to the whole matter of printing, and let the same to the lowest bidder—some complaint having been made that all our printing has heretofore been done in California, when we have members of our Order in this jurisdiction who will do the same at about the same price." On p. 26: "RESOLVED, That the Grand Worthy Secretary be, and is instructed, to have printed in one volume the corrected minutes of the inaugural session of this Grand Lodge, the minutes of the present session, and also to incorporate therein the Constitution of Subordinate Lodges, as provided by the R.W.G.L. and found in Chase's Digest, in sufficient numbers to supply each Lodge with two copies and each P.W.C.T. and P.W.V.T. with one copy. Carried."
NvHi.

MARYLAND TUNNEL AND MINING COMPANY.

Prospectus | of the | Maryland Tunnel | and | Mining Company, | and | Report on Same, | by a | Practical Mining Expert | of Twenty Years Experience. | [short rule] | Eureka, Nevada, | Daily Leader Print. | 1879.   [1028]

7 p. 21 x 14 cm. Wrapper title, in decorative rule border.

The report is signed by F. J. Mette, Ruby Hill, Eureka County, Nev., and is undoubtedly the same item partially described, but unlocated, in Check List: 239, entered under Mette's name. Gold Hill News, March 7, 1879: "We have received a small pamphlet prospectus of the Maryland Tunnel and Mining Company, Eureka, Nevada. The report upon the mine is by F. J. Mette, practical mining expert, as well as mill man."
CSmH. CtY. NvU (microfilm).

MECHANICS' UNION OF STOREY COUNTY.

[Dotted rule] and Ladies | The members of the Mechanics' Union | of Storey County present their compliments and | request your company at their | Second Grand Annual Ball, | At National Guard Hall, Wednesday Evening, | December 10, 1879. | Dancing to Commence at 9 o'clock.   [1029]

[4] p., printed on p. [1] only. 16 x 12 cm., folded to 8 x 12 cm. Printed in lavender ink on the bottom half of p. [1].
NvMus.

METHODIST EPISCOPAL CHURCH. Conferences. Nevada.

Minutes | of the | Nevada Annual Conference | of the | Methodist Episcopal Church. | Fifteenth Session. | Held in Winnemucca. | September 25th-29th, A.D. 1879. | [filet] | San Francisco: | Methodist Book Depository, 1041 Market Street. | 1879. [1030]

[3], 4-19, [1] p. 22 x 15 cm. Printed wrapper.

The Depository was the publisher, not the printer. There is an advertisement for Joseph Winterburn & Co. of San Francisco on the final page, the only ad for a printing establishment in the publication. Winterburn was the printer of the 1883 minutes and may have been for the 1879 minutes as well.

CBPac (lacks wrapper and final 2 p.). CU-B. NcLjUM (lacks wrapper). NjMD.

MINERS' UNION OF VIRGINIA CITY.

Constitution, | By-Laws, | Order of Business and Rules of Order | of the | Miners' Union, | of Virginia, Nevada. | [*short rule*] | Organized July 4, 1867. | [*short rule*] | Virginia, Nevada: | Brown & Mahanny, Book and Job Printers. | [*short rule*] | 1879. [1031]

20 p. 14 x 11 cm. Printed wrapper.

CU-B. NvHi. NvU(NvMus).

MOHAN, HUGH J.

Pen Pictures | of the | State Officers, Legislators, | Public Officials and Newspaper Men, | at the Capitol During the | Ninth Session Nevada Legislature | by | Hugh J. Mohan. | [*vignette with state seal*] | Virginia, Nevada: | Daily Stage Steam Printing House. | 1879.

[1032]

72 p. 23 x 14 cm. Wrapper title, in decorative border.

The Gold Hill *News* acknowledged receipt of a copy on March 4—only two days before adjournment of the Legislature.

C. CSmH. CU-B. CtY. NvHi. NvU.

NEVADA. *Adjutant General*.

Biennial Report | of the | Adjutant-General | of the | State of Nevada, | for the Years 1877 and 1878. | [*state seal*] | San Francisco: | A. L. Bancroft & Company, Printers, | 721 Market Street. | 1879. [1033]

29 p. 23 x 15 cm. Wrapper title, in decorative rule border. Issued also as No. 10 in AJSA, 1879.

Senate concurrent resolution to print 500 copies (JS, 1879, p. 91), although no action is reported for the Assembly in JA. An order for 400 copies was sent to Bancroft on January 30 (NvHi: PSPC, 1879, p. 18). The *Territorial Enterprise* merely reported receipt of a copy on February 26, but the Reno *Gazette*'s February 28 comment was more pithy: "We thought we had them all but we hadn't. The report of the adjutant general never reached our table until this morning. We cannot say where the blame for this delay lies but we demand a committee of investigation. See to it, senators, that the people are protected. The report before us is a very able one and will take rank in all military libraries. It contains a full report of the Duck Valley war including the flank movement in Shoo Fly creek. With great difficulty and danger the commander 'procured the bill for supplies and transportation,' amounting to $1,407.37. 'I take pleasure in saying that I believe them to be just and equitable and should be paid. Signed J. W. Adams, Adjutant Genl., N.M.' N.M. either means Nevada Mulligans

or Muldoons or else never mind." Jewett W. Adams, as Lieutenant Governor, was
the ex officio Adjutant General.

Nv-Ar.

NEVADA. *Board of Commissioners for the Care of the Indigent Insane.*

Report of the Commissioners | for the | Care of the Indigent In-
sane, | of the | State of Nevada, | for the Years 1877 and
1878. | [*state seal*] | San Francisco: | A. L. Bancroft & Company,
Printers, | 721 Market Street. | 1879.   [1034]

31 p. 23 x 15 cm. Wrapper title, in decorative rule border. Issued also as No. 17 in
AJSA, 1879.

Assembly concurrent resolution to print 1,000 copies in pamphlet form (SSN, 1879,
p. 151). The text was sent to Bancroft on February 6 (NvHi: PSPC, 1879, p. 20).

Nv-Ar.

NEVADA. *District Court. Second Judicial District (Washoe County).*

[Briefs. 1879.]

Marshall et al. vs. Golden Fleece G. & S.M. Co. et al. Points and authorities of
defendants, Golden Fleece G. & S.M. Co., and testimony. 53 p. 25 x 18 cm.
Imprint on wrapper: Sacramento: H. S. Crocker & Co., Printers and Stationers.
1879. NvHi.   [1035]

NEVADA. *Fish Commissioner.*

First | Biennial Report | of the | Fish Commissioner | of the |
State of Nevada, | for the Years 1877 and 1878. | [*state seal*] | San
Francisco: | A.L. Bancroft & Company, Printers, | 721 Market
Street. | 1879.   [1036]

7 p. 23 x 15 cm. Wrapper title, in decorative rule border. Half title: [*thick-thin
rule*] | First Biennial Report | oe [*sic*] thf [*sic*] | Fish Commissioner | of the | State
of Nevada. | [*short rule*] | H. G. Parker, Fish Commissioner. | [*short rule*] | Trans-
mitted to the Governor January 2, 1879. | [*thin-thick rule*]. The error in line 2 has been
corrected in the copy at NvU. Issued also as No. 15 in AJSA, 1879.

Senate concurrent resolution to print 2,000 copies (SSN, 1879, p. 158). The text was
sent to Bancroft on January 22 (NvHi: PSPC, 1879, p. 15). The Carson City *Tribune*
reported receipt of a copy on February 28.

CU-B. NvU.

NEVADA. *Governor, 1871-1879 (Lewis Rice Bradley).*

Fourth Biennial Message | of | Gov. L. R. Bradley, | State of
Nevada. | Ninth Session of the Nevada Legislature, 1879. | [*state
seal*] | San Francisco: | A. L. Bancroft & Company, Printers, | 721
Market Street. | 1879.   [1037]

16 p. 23 x 14 cm. Wrapper title, in decorative rule border. Issued also as No. 1 in AJSA, 1879.

Senate concurrent resolution to print 2,500 copies (SSN, 1879, p. 155). The text was sent to Bancroft on February 1 (NvHi: PSPC, 1879, p. 19).

CtY. M. NN. NvU (microfilm).

NEVADA. *Governor, 1879-1883 (John Henry Kinkead).*

Inaugural Address | of | His Excellency | John H. Kinkead, | Governor of Nevada. | Delivered Before a Joint Convention of Both Houses | of the Legislature, January 7, 1879. | [*short rule*] | San Francisco: | A. L. Bancroft & Company, Printers. | 1879. [1038]

7 p. 22 x 14 cm. Printed wrapper. Issued also as No. 2 in AJSA, 1879.

Assembly concurrent resolution to print 2,500 copies (SSN, 1879, p. 147). The text was sent to Bancroft on January 21 (NvHi: PSPC, 1879, p. 14). The Carson City *Tribune* of January 30 reported receipt of a copy "yesterday," commenting that it was "the first State report that has yet emanated from the hands of the State printer." Two days later the Virginia City *Chronicle* had the following: "A printed copy of Governor Kincaid's [*sic*] inaugural address, delivered twenty-five days ago has just come to hand. It should have been printed and circulated within twenty-four hours after its delivery, and would have been but for the absurd law which allows San Francisco drummers to outbid the printers of Nevada. The pamphlet was printed in San Francisco. We trust the Legislature will lose no time in repealing the present Cheap John law that deprives citizens of Nevada from doing the State's work, and sends thousands of dollars annually out of the State, never to return."

C. M. NN. NvU (microfilm).

NEVADA. *Governor, 1879-1883 (John Henry Kinkead).*

State of Nevada. | By the [*state seal*] Governor. | Thanksgiving Proclamation. | [*filet*] | . . . | . . .I hereby designate | Thursday, the 27th day of November, | A.D., 1879, as a day of thanksgiving and prayer; and I | do earnestly recommend to my fellow=citizens that, with heartfelt | and cordial unity, on that day, we render homage and thanks | to the Almighty Ruler for His many mercies. | . . . | . . . Done at Carson City, | Nevada, this 8th day of November, A.D. 1879 | . . . | [Carson City: Marshall Robinson, State Printer. 1879.] [1039]

Broadside. 27 x 21 cm. Line 1 in an arch over line 2. Mostly script type.

A joint committee of the 1881 Legislature was appointed to investigate alleged frauds during Marshall Robinson's two-year term, 1879-1880, as the local printer who executed smaller and more urgently needed jobs than those sent to Bancroft in San Francisco. When bidding for the position, Robinson set his price for proclamations at $5, but was alleged to have charged $10, a price that was approved by State Printing Expert C. A. V. Putnam, for this one. Governor Kinkead was displeased with Robinson's first effort and insisted that it be done over (JS, 1881, p. 293); Robinson and Putnam apparently felt justified in charging twice for doing the work twice, even though the first attempt was unsatisfactory.

M. NvU (microfilm).

NEVADA. *Homographic Charts.*

1879. 1879. | Homographic Chart | Ninth [*state seal*] Session | Nevada State Government | [*thin-thick-thin rule*] | . . . | Chronicle Steam Print, Virginia City, Nevada.   [1040]

Broadside. 63 x 54 cm. Ornamentation under line 1 and around the words in line 3. Line 2 in an arch over line 3. Printed in two columns, separated by a vertical thick-thin-thick rule. Decorative border, with imprint below the border.

The Gold Hill *News* acknowledged receipt of a copy from the compiler, Ben Stern of Gold Hill, on January 23; the *Territorial Enterprise* had commented on January 15 that Stern was preparing the chart. An attempt in the Assembly to purchase 300 copies for the state was defeated (JA, 1879, p. 220, 231, and 274). See No. L1041.

NvHi. NvU.

NEVADA. *Homographic Charts.* Homographic chart of the state government and legislature. 1879.   [L1041]

Carson City *Appeal,* January 14, 1879: "We are indebted to Mr. H. B. Maxon for a copy of his Homographic Chart of the present State Government and Legislature. It is neatly done. How correct it is we have not had time to ascertain." Inaccuracies may have been the cause of the preparation of another chart by Ben Stern; see No. 1040.

NEVADA. *Laws, statutes, etc.*

Certified Copy of | An Act | To Restrict Gaming and to Repeal all Other Acts in Relation Thereto. | [*short rule*] | . . . | [Carson City: Marshall Robinson, State Printer? 1879.]   [1042]

[4] p., printed on p. [1-3] only. 28 x 21 cm. Dated on p. [3]: March 12, 1879.

NvMiD.

NEVADA. *Laws, statutes, etc.*

Laws | Relating to | The Public School System | of the | State of Nevada. | [*short rule*] | Compiled and Published by the Superintendent of Public In-|struction, for the Use of School Officers. | [*state seal*] | San Francisco: | A. L. Bancroft & Company, Printers, | 721 Market Street. | 1879.   [1043]

[7], 8-28, [1] p. 23 x 15 cm. Printed wrapper.

Gold Hill *News,* July 17, 1879: "[Storey County] Superintendent [of Schools, T. B.] Janes has placed the NEWS under obligations by placing in its sanctum a copy of the laws relating to the public school system of the State of Nevada. These laws are in pamphlet form and published for the use of school officers, and contain the amendments of the Ninth Legislature, as well as a list of School officers of the State of Nevada, the Compulsory Law, the law establishing the State University, the law providing for the education of the deaf and dumb, and a list of the State series of text books.''

M. NvU (microfilm).

NEVADA. *Laws, statutes, etc.*

Statutes | of the | State of Nevada, | Passed at the | Ninth Session of the Legislature, | 1879, | Begun on Monday, the Sixth Day of January, and Ended on | Thursday, the Sixth Day of March. | [*state seal*] | San Francisco: | A. L. Bancroft & Company, Printers, | 721 Market Street. | 1879.   [1044]

xvi, 375 p. 23 x 15 cm. Leather binding. On p. [169]-362, printed from the same type as the separate and AJSA issues: Reports of the Treasurer of the State of Nevada For the Thirteenth and Fourteenth Fiscal Years, 1877 and 1878. Jerry Schooling, Treasurer.

1,000 copies in ''calf,'' to contain the laws, resolutions, and memorials, the report of the Treasurer, ''and such other matters as may at each session be enacted; but not any other matter, Act, report, or thing, shall be bound therewith,'' were authorized by SSN, 1877, p. 162. 1,000 copies were received of the printer by the Secretary of State (Report, 1879-1880, p. 405). Carson City *Appeal*, July 24, 1879: ''Secretary of State [Jasper] Babcock writes from San Francisco that the remainder of the edition of the laws enacted by the late Legislature will be up in a day or or two, when the books will be distributed to all who are entitled to them.'' The *Reese River Reveille* reported on July 28 that the Lander County Clerk had received copies ''for distribution among the several county officers.''

Az. CU-B. CoD. CtY-L. DLC. MBS. MH-L. NN. Nv-Ar. NvEC. NvEuC. NvGoEC. NvHi. NvLC. NvLN. NvPLC. NvRNC. NvRWL (rebound). NvSC. NvU. NvYLR. OrU-L.

NEVADA. *Legislature.*

Appendix | to | Journals of Senate and Assembly, | of the | Ninth Session | of the | Legislature of the State of Nevada. | [*state seal*] | San Francisco: | A. L. Bancroft & Company, Printers, | 721 Market Street. | 1879.   [1045]

16, 4, 101, 333, 83, 108, 23, 68, 54, 29, 90, 60, 33, 19, 7, 212, 31, 4 p. 23 x 15 cm. Half-leather binding. Numbering follows the table of contents. No. 1, Fourth Biennial Message of Governor L. R. Bradley of the State of Nevada, 16 p.; No. 2, Inaugural Address of His Excellency, John H. Kinkead, Governor of Nevada. Delivered Before a Joint Convention of Both Houses of the Legislature, January 7, 1879, 4 p.; No. 3, Annual Report of the Controller of the State of Nevada, For the Thirteenth Fiscal Year, ending December 31, 1877. W. W. Hobart, Controller. Transmitted January 22, 1878, 101 p.; No. 4, Annual Report of the Controller of the State of Nevada For the Fourteenth Fiscal Year, ending December 31, 1878. W. W. Hobart, Controller. Transmitted January 22, 1879, 333 p., including a folding table; No. 5, Annual Report of the Treasurer of the State of Nevada, for the Thirteenth Fiscal Year, Ending December 31st, 1877. Jerry Schooling, Treasurer. Transmitted

January 10th, 1878, 83 p.; No. 6, Annual Report of the Treasurer of the State of Nevada For the Fourteenth Fiscal Year, ending December 31, 1878. Jerry Schooling, Treasurer. Transmitted January 22, 1879, 108 p.; No. 7, Biennial Report of the Secretary of State of the State of Nevada for the Thirteenth and Fourteenth Fiscal Years, ending December 31, 1878, 23 p.; No. 8, Report of the Superintendent of Public Instruction of the State of Nevada For the Years 1877 and 1878, 68 p.; No. 9, Report of the Surveyor-General and State Land Register of the State of Nevada For the Years 1877 and 1878, 54 p.; No. 10, Biennial Report of the Adjutant-General of the State of Nevada For the Years 1877 and 1878, 29 p.; No. 11, Biennial Report of the Warden of Nevada State Prison for the Years 1877 and 1878. Ninth Session of the Nevada Legislature, 1879, 90 p.; No. 12, Biennial Report of the Board of Directors of the Nevada State Library for the Thirteenth and Fourteenth Fiscal Years, 60 p.; No. 13, Biennial Report of the Board of Directors of the State Orphans' Home of the State of Nevada for the Thirteenth and Fourteenth Fiscal Years, 33 p.; No. 14, Report of the Board of Regents of the State University of the State of Nevada For the Years 1877 and 1878, 19 p.; No. 15, First Biennial Report oe [sic] thf [sic] Fish Commissioner of the State of Nevada. H. G. Parker, Fish Commissioner. Transmitted to the Governor January 2, 1879, 7 p.; No. 16, Biennial Report of the State Mineralogist of the State of Nevada For the Years 1877 and 1878, 212 p.; No. 17, Report of the Commissioners for the Care of the Indigent Insane of the State of Nevada For the Years 1877 and 1878, 31 p.; No. 18, Report of the Clerk of the Supreme Court of the State of Nevada, For the Years 1877 and 1878, 4 p. Nos. 3 and 5, the annual reports of the Controller and Treasurer, were printed in 1878 during the administration of State Printer John J. Hill.

In addition to messages, reports, and other documents issued in pamphlet form, 225 extra copies were to be printed for inclusion in the appendix (SSN, 1877, p. 163).

DLC. M. MH. NN. Nv-Ar. NvHi. NvLN. NvRW. NvU. WHi.

NEVADA. *Legislature. Assembly.*

The | Journal of the Assembly | of the | Ninth Session | of the | Legislature of the State of Nevada. | 1879. | Begun on Monday, the Sixth Day of January, and Ended on | Thursday, the Sixth Day of March. | [*state seal*] | San Francisco: | A. L. Bancroft & Company, Printers, | 721 Market Street. | 1879.   [1046]

396 p. 23 x 15 cm. Half-leather binding.

225 copies were to be printed and bound separately from the Senate journal (SSN, 1879, p. 117). The Reno *Nevada State Journal* reported receipt of a copy on August 7, 1879.

CtY-L. DLC. M. MH. NN. Nv-Ar. NvHi. NvLC. NvLN. NvRWL. NvSC. NvU. UU-L. WHi.

NEVADA. *Legislature. Joint Committee on Insane Asylum.* Report. 1879.
[L1047]

Territorial Enterprise, February 6, 1879: "We have received the report of the Joint Committee of the Legislature appointed to visit and report upon the condition of the Nevada Insane Asylum at Stockton, California. The committee also visited the Deaf and Dumb Asylum at Berkeley, where our State has four patients."

NEVADA. *Legislature. Joint Committee on Railroads.* Majority report. Carson City: Marshall Robinson, State Printer. 1879.   [L1048]

Robinson charged the state $13.06 for printing 450 copies on February 24: $9.94 for 13,432 ems at 74¢ per thousand, $2 for four tokens of press work, and $1.12 for folding and stitching (NvHi: PSPC, 1879, unpaged). See No. L1049.

NEVADA. *Legislature. Joint Committee on Railroads.* Minority report. Carson City: Marshall Robinson, State Printer. 1879.   [L1049]

Robinson's charges were the same as for the committee's majority report; see No. L1048. The two reports may have been issued together.

NEVADA. *Legislature. Senate.*

The | Journal of the Senate | of the Ninth Session | of the | Legislature of the State of Nevada. | 1879. | Begun on Monday, the Sixth Day of January, and Ended on | Thursday, the Sixth Day of March. | [*state seal*] | San Francisco: | A. L. Bancroft & Company, Printers, | 721 Market Street. | 1879.   [1050]

393 p. 23 x 15 cm. Half-leather binding.

225 copies were to be printed and bound separately from the Assembly journal (SSN, 1879, p. 117). The Reno *Nevada State Journal* reported receipt of a copy on August 7, 1879.

CtY-L. DLC. M. MH. NN. Nv-Ar. NvHi. NvLN. NvRWL. NvSC. NvU. UU-L. WHi.

NEVADA. *Militia. First Brigade, Company F (Carson Guard).*

Rules and Regulations | of the | Carson Guard, | [*ornament*] | Company F, First Brigade, | Nevada Militia. | [*short rule*] | Organized, Carson City, September 17, 1875. | [*short rule*] | Carson City: | Morning Appeal Print. | 1879.   [1051]

17 p. 14 x 11 cm. Printed wrapper. Title and text pages in single rule borders. NvHi. NvMus.

NEVADA. *Office of Superintendent of Public Instruction.*

Report | of the | Superintendent | of | Public Instruction, | of the | State of Nevada, | for the Years 1877 and 1878. | [*state seal*] | San Francisco: | A. L. Bancroft & Company, Printers, | 721 Market Street. | 1879.   [1052]

68 p. 23 x 15 cm. Wrapper title, in decorative rule border. Issued also as No. 8 in AJSA, 1879.

Senate concurrent resolution to print 2,000 copies (SSN, 1879, p. 159-160). The text was sent to Bancroft on January 22 (NvHi: PSPC, 1879, p. 15). The *Territorial Enterprise* reported receipt of a copy on February 18, 1879. DHEW. M. NN. Nv-Ar.

NEVADA. *Secretary of State.*

Biennial Report | of the | Secretary of State, | of the | State of
Nevada, | for the | Thirteenth and Fourteenth Fiscal Years, | End-
ing December 31st, 1878. | [*state seal*] | San Francisco: | A. L. Ban-
croft & Company, Printers, | 721 Market Street. | 1879.   [1053]

23 p. 23 x 15 cm. Wrapper title, in decorative rule border. Issued also as No. 7 in
AJSA, 1879.

Senate concurrent resolution to print 2,000 copies (SSN, 1879, p. 158). The text was
sent to Bancroft on January 21 (NvHi: PSPC, 1879, p. 14). Receipt of a copy was
reported in the Virginia City *Chronicle* of February 15, 1879. The Reno *Gazette* of
February 21, in a skittish manner that perhaps reflected its opinion of many state
reports, had the following: "Public documents, such as biennial reports, messages,
etc., fly out of the state-house in flocks these times. The last to light on our table is that
of J. D. Minor, secretary of state. It gives an account of the books distributed, such as
state reports, statutes, etc., and lists incorporations of commissioners of deeds, and
notaries public, statements of moneys received and paid and all that racket. We
skipped some. It is poor entertainment. There is no hero."
CtY. Nv-Ar.

NEVADA. *State Controller's Office.*

Annual Report | of the | Controller | of the | State of Neva-
da, | For the Fourteenth Fiscal Year, ending | December 31,
1878. | W. W. Hobart, Controller, | [*state seal*] | San Francis-
co: | A. L. Bancroft & Company, Printers, | 721 Market
Street. | 1879.   [1054]

333 p., including a folding table. 23 x 14 cm. Wrapper title, in decorative rule border.
Issued also as No. 4 in AJSA, 1879.

The Carson City *Tribune* acknowledged receipt of a copy on February 5, 1879.
C. DLC. NN. NvHi.

NEVADA. *State Library.*

Biennial Report | of the | Board of Directors | of the | Nevada
State Library, | For the Thirteenth and Fourteenth Fiscal Years.
| [*state seal*] | San Francisco: | A. L. Bancroft & Company, Printers,
| 721 Market Street. | 1879.   [1055]

60 p. 23 x 14 cm. Wrapper title, in decorative rule border. Issued also as No. 12 in
AJSA, 1879.

Senate concurrent resolution to print 1,000 copies (SSN, 1879, p. 158). The text was
sent to Bancroft on January 21 (NvHi: PSPC, 1879, p. 14). The *Territorial Enterprise*
published extracts from the report on February 22, possibly indicating receipt of a
printed copy.
M. Nv-Ar.

NEVADA. *State Mineralogist.*

Biennial Report | of the | State Mineralogist | of the | State of Nevada, | for the Years 1877 and 1878. | [*state seal*] | San Francisco: | A. L. Bancroft & Company, Printers, | 721 Market Street. | 1879. [1056]

212 p. 22 x 14 cm. Wrapper title, in decorative rule border. On p. [177]-207: Supplement. Showing the Proceeds of Mines in the State of Nevada, During the Years 1871-72-73-74-75-76-77, and 1st, 2d, and 3d Quarters of 1878. Compiled from County Assessors returns in State Controller's Office. Issued also as No. 16 in AJSA, 1879.

Senate concurrent resolution to print 2,000 copies (SSN, 1879, p. 158). The text was sent to Bancroft on January 25 (NvHi: PSPC, 1879, p.17). This is the last report issued by the State Mineralogist; the Legislature of 1877 abolished the office, effective at the end of 1878 (SSN, 1877, p. 59-60).

NvHi. NvU. UU.

NEVADA. *State Orphans' Home.*

Biennial Report | of the | Board of Directors | of the | State Orphans' Home, | of the | State of Nevada, | for the Thirteenth and Fourteenth Fiscal Years, | Ending December 31st, 1878. | [*state seal*] | San Francisco: | A. L. Bancroft & Company, Printers, | 721 Market Street. | 1879. [1057]

33 p. 23 x 15 cm. Wrapper title, in decorative rule border. Issued also as No. 13 in AJSA, 1879.

Senate concurrent resolution to print 2,000 copies (SSN, 1879, p. 158). The text was sent to Bancroft on January 21 (NvHi: PSPC, 1879, p. 14).

Nv-Ar.

NEVADA. *State Prison.*

Biennial Report | of the | Warden | of the | Nevada State Prison | For the Years 1877 and 1878. | Ninth Session of the Nevada Legislature, 1879. | [*state seal*] | San Francisco: | A. L. Bancroft & Company, Printers, | 721 Market Street. | 1879. [1058]

90 p. 23 x 14 cm. Wrapper title, in decorative rule border. Issued also as No. 11 in AJSA, 1879.

Senate concurrent resolution to print 1,000 copies (SSN, 1879, p. 159-160). The text was sent to Bancroft on January 22 (NvHi: PSPC, 1879, p. 15). The Reno *Nevada State Journal* reported receipt of a copy on February 19, 1879, while the *Territorial Enterprise* published extracts from the report in its issue of the previous day, possibly indicating receipt of a printed copy.

CU-B. CtY. NvU (microfilm).

NEVADA. *Supreme Court.*

[Briefs. 1879.] In September the Supreme Court amended its rules to require all briefs in civil cases to be printed (Report of the Clerk of the Supreme Court, 1879-1880, p. 2).

Brophy Mining Co. vs. Brophy and Dale Gold and Silver Mining Co. et al. Brief of appellant, Brophy and Dale Gold and Silver Mining Co. 30 p. 25 x 18 cm. Imprint on wrapper: Virginia, Nev.: Printed at the Evening Chronicle Job Office. 1879. Nv-Ar. [1059]

Brophy Mining Co. vs. Brophy and Dale Gold and Silver Mining Co. et al. Brief of respondent, Brophy Mining Co. 8 p. 25 x 18 cm. Imprint on wrapper: Virginia, Nev.: Printed at the Evening Chronicle Job Office. 1879. Nv-Ar. [1060]

Brophy Mining Co. vs. Brophy and Dale Gold and Silver Mining Co. et al. Transcript on appeal. 65 p. 25 x 18 cm. Imprint on wrapper: Virginia Evening Chronicle Print. Printed on wrapper: Filed [broken rule] 1879. Nv-Ar. [1061]

Bunting vs. Central Pacific Railroad Co. Harrison vs. Central Pacific Railroad Co.: case no. 964. Points and authorites of respondent, Central Pacific Railroad Co. 21 p. 23 x 18 cm. Printed on wrapper: Filed [dotted rule] 1879. See No. 1153. Nv-Ar. [1062]

Drexler vs. Tyrrell et al. Brief of respondent, L. P. Drexler. 40 p. 25 x 18 cm. Imprint on wrapper: Printed at Enterprise Job Office, Virginia City, Nev. Printed on wrapper: Filed [dotted rule] 1879. Nv-Ar. [1063]

Drexler vs. Tyrrell et al. Points and authorities of appellants, A. J. Tyrrell et al. 4 p. 25 x 18 cm. Imprint on wrapper: Printed at Enterprise Job Office, Virginia City, Nev. Printed on wrapper: Filed [dotted rule] 1879. Nv-Ar. [1064]

Drexler vs. Tyrrell et al. Points and authorities of respondent, L. P. Drexler. 6 p. 25 x 18 cm. Imprint on wrapper: Printed at Enterprise Job Office, Virginia, Nev. Printed on wrapper: Filed [dotted rule] 1879. Nv-Ar. [1065]

Drexler vs. Tyrrell et al. Transcript on appeal. 161 p. 25 x 18 cm. Imprint on wrapper: Virginia, Nevada: Enterprise Steam Printing House. 1879. Nv-Ar. [1066]

Fishback vs. Miller. Brief of appellant, Jeremiah Miller. 49 p. 24 x 18 cm. Imprint on wrapper: San Francisco: Spaulding, Barto & Co., Book and Job Printers, "Scientific Press," 414 Clay Street, below Sansome. 1879. Nv-Ar. [1067]

Fishback vs. Miller. Brief of respondent, Henry Fishback. 42 p. 25 x 18 cm. Imprint on wrapper: San Francisco: Printing Department of A. L. Bancroft & Company. 1879. In the caption title on p. [1], "State of California" is printed in error; a printed slip correcting it to "State of Nevada" has been pasted over it in the recorded copy. Nv-Ar. [1068]

Floral Springs Water Co. vs. Rives. Brief of petitioner, Floral Springs Water Co. 7 p. 25 x 18 cm. Imprint on wrapper: Index Print, Carson, Nevada. 1879. See No. 1010. Nv-Ar. [1069]

Floral Springs Water Co. vs. Rives. Demurrer of respondent, Henry Rives. 4 p. 25 x 18 cm. Imprint on wrapper: Index Print, Carson, Nevada. 1879. See No. 1010. Nv-Ar. [1070]

Floral Springs Water Co. vs. Rives. Petition for writ of mandamus. 4 p. 25 x 18 cm. Imprint on wrapper: Index Print, Carson, Nevada. 1879. See No. 1010. Nv-Ar. [1071]

Floral Springs Water Co. vs. Rives. Points and authorities of respondent, Henry Rives. 8 p. 25 x 18 cm. Imprint on wrapper: Index Print, Carson, Nevada. 1879. See No. 1010. Nv-Ar. [1072]

Lachman et al. vs. Walker. Points and authorities of appellant, W. A. Walker. 4 p. 23 x 15 cm. Imprint on wrapper: Reno Gazette Steam Book and Job Print. Printed on wrapper: Filed [*broken rule*] 1879. Nv-Ar. [1073]

Lee et al. vs. McLeod. Brief of appellant, W. R. Lee et al. 20 p. 22 x 18 cm. Imprint on wrapper: Index Print, Carson, Nevada. A handwritten note on the wrapper of the recorded copy indicates that the brief was filed on October 9, 1879. See No. 1010. [1074]

Lonkey et al. vs. Cook et al. Transcript on appeal. 34 p. 25 x 18 cm. Imprint on wrapper: Virginia Evening Chronicle Print. According to a handwritten notation on the recorded copy, the transcript was filed on January 3, 1880. Because it was so early in the year, however, it is likely that the pamphlet was printed late in 1879. Nv-Ar. [1075]

Mackay vs. Western Union Telegraph Co. Brief of respondent, Duncan C. Mackay. 11 p. 25 x 18 cm. Imprint on wrapper: Virginia, Nevada: Enterprise Steam Printing House. 1879. Nv-Ar. [1076]

Mackay vs. Western Union Telegraph Co. Points and authorities of appellant, Western Union Telegraph Co. 11 p. 26 x 18 cm. Imprint on wrapper: San Francisco: Bacon & Company, Book and Job Printers, Corner Clay and Sansome Streets. Printed on wrapper: Filed [*rule*] 1879. Nv-Ar. [1077]

Marshall et al. vs. Golden Fleece Gold and Silver Mining Co. et al. Transcript on appeal. ii, 659 p. 25 x 18 cm. Imprint on wrapper: Crocker & Co., Stationers and Printers, 401 and 403 Sansome St., S.F. Printed on wrapper: Filed [*dotted rule*] 1879. A handwritten notation on the recorded copy indicates, however, that it was filed on January 5, 1880. Nv-Ar. [1078]

Merrill vs. Dixon et al. Appellant's reply to respondents' brief, N. A. Merrill. 3 p. 26 x 18 cm. The reply was filed on September 30, 1879, according to a handwritten notation on the recorded copy. Nv-Ar. [1079]

Merrill vs. Dixon et al. Points and authorities of plaintiff, N. A. Merrill. 3 p. 24 x 18 cm. The case was heard during the 1879 term; see Nos. 1081 and 1082. Nv-Ar. [1080]

Merrill vs. Dixon et al. Points and authorities of respondents, John Dixon et al. [2] p. 24 x 18 cm. Imprint on wrapper: Reno: Nevada State Journal, 1879. Nv-Ar. [1081]

Merrill vs. Dixon et al. Transcript on appeal. 21 p. 25 x 18 cm. Imprint on wrapper: Sacramento: H. S. Crocker & Co., Printers and Stationers. 1879. Nv-Ar. [1082]

Nevada vs. Hymer. Transcript on appeal. 71 p. 25 x 17 cm. Imprint on wrapper: Silver State Print, Winnemucca, Nevada. Printed on wrapper: Filed [*dotted rule*] 1879. Nv-Ar. [1083]

Nevada vs. Soule. Brief of appellant, William Soule. 12 p. 25 x 17 cm. Imprint on wrapper: Sacramento: H. S. Crocker & Co., Printers and Stationers. 1879. Nv-Ar. [1084]

Overman Silver Mining Co. vs. Corcoran et al. Brief of appellants, Philip Corcoran et al. 29 p. 24 x 18 cm. Printed on wrapper: Filed July [*broken rule*] 1879. Nv-Ar.
[1085]

Overman Silver Mining Co. vs. Corcoran et al. Brief of respondent, Overman Silver Mining Co. 88 p. 24 x 17 cm. Imprint on wrapper: Virginia, Nevada: Enterprise Steam Printing House. 1879. Nv-Ar. [1086]

Reese Gold and Silver Mining Co. vs. Rye Patch Consolidated Mill and Mining Co. et al. Transcript on appeal. 48 p. 24 x 18 cm. Imprint on wrapper: San Francisco: Daily Exchange Publishing Co., 306 Montgomery Street. 1879. Nv-Ar. [1087]

Ricord et al. vs. Central Pacific Railroad Co. Appellant's reply to respondent's brief, Central Pacific Railroad Co. 27 p. 25 x 18 cm. Printed on wrapper: Filed, [*dotted rule*] 1879. Nv-Ar. [1088]

Ricord et al. vs. Central Pacific Railroad Co. Points of appellant, Central Pacific Railroad Co. 34 p. 26 x 17 cm. Printed on wrapper: Filed [*dotted rule*] 1879. Nv-Ar.
[1089]

Tognini and Co. and Vanina vs. Kyle. Transcript on appeal. 59 p. 25 x 17 cm. Imprint on wrapper: Index Print, Carson, Nevada. Printed on wrapper: Filed December 10, 1879. See No. 1010. Nv-Ar. [1090]

Toombs vs. Consolidated Poe Mining Co. et al. Argument of appellant, Henry C. Toombs. 9 p. 25 x 18 cm. Imprint on wrapper: Reno: Nevada State Journal, 1879. Nv-Ar. [1091]

Toombs vs. Consolidated Poe Mining Co. et al. Argument of respondent, Consolidated Poe Mining Co. et al. 7 p. 25 x 18 cm. Imprint on wrapper: Reno: Nevada State Journal, 1879. Nv-Ar. [1092]

Toombs vs. Consolidated Poe Mining Co. et al. Points and authorities of appellant, Henry C. Toombs. [4] p. 24 x 18 cm. Imprint on wrapper: Reno: Nevada State Journal, 1879. Nv-Ar. [1093]

NEVADA. *Supreme Court.*

Reports of Cases | Determined in | The Supreme Court | of the | State of Nevada, | During the Year 1878. | Reported by | Chas. F. Bicknell, | Clerk of Supreme Court, | and | Hon. Thomas P. Hawley, | Chief Justice. | Volume XIII. | San Francisco: | A. L. Bancroft and Company, | Law Book Publishers, Booksellers and Stationers. | 1879. [1094]

572 p. 23 x 15 cm. Leather binding.

$1,200 was paid in 1879 (Treasurer's report, 1879, p. 31) for 600 copies (report of the Secretary of State, 1879-1880, p. 7-9). Reissued with Volume 12 in 1887 by Bancroft-Whitney of San Francisco in a stereotype edition.

Az. CU-B. DHEW. DLC. In-SC (rebound). M. Nv. Nv-Ar. NvEuC. NvHi. NvLC. NvLN. NvRNC. NvRWL. NvSC. NvU. OrU-L. U-L.

NEVADA. *Supreme Court.*

Reports of Decisions | of the | Supreme Court | of the | State of Nevada, | During the Years 1869, 1870, 1871 and 1872. | Edited by | Hon. Thomas P. Hawley, | Associate Justice. | Publication Authorized by the Supreme Court. | Under Act approved March 2, 1877. (Stat. 1877, 112.) | Volumes V., VI. and VII. | San Francisco: | A. L. Bancroft and Company, | Law Book Publishers, Booksellers and Stationers. | 1879.   [1095]

xvi, [1], 18-1182 p. 23 x 16 cm. Leather binding.

A stereotype edition of 400 copies of the out-of-print reports was authorized by SSN, 1877, p. 112. On January 1, 1879, the Secretary of State had available for distribution 94, 96, and 106 copies, respectively, of the original editions (Report, 1877-1878, p. 8-11); see 1877 Summary, p. 293. The Treasurer's report for 1879, p. 31, indicates the issuance of $3,000 in 1879 warrants. The Secretary of State's report for 1879-1880, p. 7-9, notes the receipt of the 400 copies.

CU-B. Nv. Nv-Ar. NvHi. NvLN. NvRNC. NvRWL. NvSC. NvU. OrU-L.

NEVADA. *Supreme Court.*

[*Double rule*] | Rules | of the | Supreme Court | of the | State of Nevada. | [*double rule*] | [San Francisco: A. L. Bancroft & Company, Printers, 721 Market Street. 1879.]   [1096]

[9]-16 p. 23 x 14 cm. Wrapper title.

A separate printing from the same type used in Volume 13 of the Supreme Court Reports, printed by Bancroft in 1879; see No. 1094. Page [9] of that volume includes part of the Rules of the State Board of Pardons; here it is a half title.

The *Territorial Enterprise* acknowledged receipt of a copy on September 19, 1879. NvU.

NEVADA. *Surveyor General.*

Report | of the | Surveyor-General | and | State Land Register, | of the | State of Nevada, | For the Years 1877 and 1878. | [*state seal*] | San Francisco: | A. L. Bancroft & Company, Printers, | 721 Market Street. | 1879.   [1097]

54 p. 23 x 15 cm. Wrapper title, in decorative rule border. Issued also as No. 9 in AJSA, 1879.

Senate concurrent resolution to print 2,000 copies (SSN, 1879, p. 158). The text was sent to Bancroft on January 21 (NvHi: PSPC, 1879, p. 14). The *Territorial Enterprise* of February 22, 1879, noted that the report had been published, but the Gold Hill *News* was the first newspaper to report receipt of a copy, on March 22. NvHi.

NEVADA. *Treasury Department.*

Annual Report | of the | Treasurer | of the | State of Nevada, | For the Fourteenth Fiscal Year, ending | December 31,

1878. | Jerry Schooling, Treasurer. | [*state seal*] | San Francis-
co: | A. L. Bancroft & Company, Printers, | 721 Market Street.
| 1879. [1098]

108 p. 23 x 14 cm. Wrapper title, in decorative rule border. Issued also as No. 6 in
AJSA, 1879, and in SSN, 1879, p. [255]-362 from the same type.

1,200 copies in pamphlet form were authorized (SSN, 1873, p. 175). A request was
made to Bancroft on February 7 to send 300 to 400 copies by express, with the
remainder to follow by regular freight (NvHi: PSPC, 1879, p. 20). The Reno *Gazette*
acknowledged receipt of a copy of the pamphlet on February 12, 1879.
CU-B. Nv-Ar.

NEVADA. *University. Board of Regents.*

Report | of the | Board of Regents | of the | State University | of
Nevada, | for the Years 1877 and 1878. | [*state seal*] | San Francis-
co: | A. L. Bancroft & Company, Printers, | 721 Market
Street. | 1879. [1099]

19 p. 23 x 15 cm. Wrapper title, in decorative rule border. Issued also as No. 14 in
AJSA, 1879.

Senate concurrent resolution to print 500 copies (SSN, 1879, p. 162). The text was
sent to Bancroft on February 1 (NvHi: PSPC, 1879, p. 19). The Reno *Gazette*
summarized the report on March 12, 1879, possibly indicating the receipt of a printed
copy.

The 1875 1876 report had been submitted to the Legislature, but "through some
oversight, was not printed or put in an available form as a source of information. It
will be necessary to reproduce the main part of this report, in order that you may have
a history of the institution under our charge during the first two years of our
administration," p. [3].
Nv-Ar.

NEVADA MONTHLY. *Virginia City, Nevada.* Prospectus. 1879.[L1100]

Gold Hill *News,* January 2, 1880: "A prospectus circular announces that a journal, to
be called the Nevada Monthly, is shortly to make its appearance at Virginia City."

NEVADA STATE AGRICULTURAL, MINING AND MECHANICAL SOCIETY.
Reno, Nevada. Catalogue. 1879. [L1101]

Reno *Nevada State Journal,* July 24, 1879: "The catalogues for the coming State Fair
have been received and are ready for distribution."

NEVADA THEATRE. *Reno, Nevada.*

Nevada Theatre! | [*thick-thin rule*] | John Piper, [*broken rule*]
Lessee. | [*thick-thin rule*] | Grand Success | ——of—— | Piper's
Dramatic | Combination | [*thick-thin rule*] | This Evening! |
Friday, October 10th | [*thick-thin rule*] | Only Performance of |

Shaughraun | . . . | [rule] | Reno Gazette Steam Book & Job Print.
| [1879.]   [1102]

Broadside. 41 x 22 cm.

The play, by Dion Boucicault, was reviewed in the *Gazette* on October 11, 1879.
Piper, who had run Piper's Opera House in Virginia City for many years, began about
this time to lease theaters in Reno and Carson City; throughout the eighties he booked
troupes into the three theaters in a regular circuit.

NvRH.

ODD FELLOWS, INDEPENDENT ORDER OF. *Nevada. Grand Lodge.*

Proceedings | of the | Thirteenth Annual Communication | of the
| R.W. Grand Lodge | of the | Independent Order of Odd Fellows
| of the State of Nevada, | Held in Odd Fellows' Hall, Virginia City,
Storey County, Nev., | on the 3d, 4th, 5th and 6th Days of June,
A.D. 1879. | [*short rule*] | Virginia, Nevada: | Enterprise Steam
Book and Job Printing House. | 1879.   [1103]

[3], 1358-1450, x p. 22? x 14? cm. The recorded copy has been trimmed and bound.

The 1879 communication resolved to have 200 copies of the 1874 and 1875 proceedings reprinted by the *Enterprise* at $1.80 per page, apparently in order to have enough
copies to bind with the proceedings of previous years; also to have 200 copies of the
unbound reports, including those of the present session, bound by Crocker at 60¢ per
volume; also to have printed by the *Enterprise* 820 copies of the proceedings of the
present session at $2.30 per page (p. 1411). However, the resolution was amended to
eliminate all but the last provision (p. 1412). The 1879 proceedings were printed at a
cost of $253, plus $8.50 for freight (1880 Proceedings, p. 23).

CU-B.

ODD FELLOWS, INDEPENDENT ORDER OF. *Nevada. Grand Lodge.* Report
of Grand Representatives. Virginia, Nevada: Enterprise Steam Book
and Job Printing House. 1879.   [L1104]

An entry on p. 23 of the 1880 Proceedings shows a payment of $15 to the *Enterprise* for
printing the report.

ODD FELLOWS, INDEPENDENT ORDER OF. *Tuscarora, Nevada. Tuscarora
Lodge No. 30.*

Constitution, | By-Laws and Rules of Order | of | Tuscarora
Lodge, No. 30, | of the | Independent Order of Odd Fellows | of
the | State of Nevada. | [*short rule*] | Instituted at Tuscarora, January
7th, 1878. | [*short rule*] | San Francisco: | Jos. Winterburn & Co.,
Printers and Electrotypers, | No. 417 Clay Street, bet. Sansome and
Battery. | 1879.   [1105]

62 p. 14? x 10? cm. The recorded copy has been trimmed and bound. Title and text

pages in single rule borders. A membership certificate, not counted in the pagination, precedes the title page.

CU-B.

RENO, NEVADA. *Reno Engine Company No. 1.*

By-Laws | of | Reno Engine Co. No. 1. | [*cut of fire wagon*] | Organized November 10th, 1875. | [*filet*] | Reno, Nevada: | Evening Gazette Book and Job Print. | [1879.]   [1106]

15 p. 13 x 10 cm. Printed wrapper. Title in thick-thin rule border.

The officers for 1879 are listed on p. 13; a certificate of incorporation, dated February 10, 1879, is on p. 14.

NvHi.

STEWART, WILLIAM FRANK.

Geological Report | upon the | "Golden Fleece" | Gold and Silver Mine, | Peavine Mining District, | Washoe County, Nevada. | [*filet*] | By | W. F. Stewart, | (Geologist.) | [*filet*] | Reno, Nevada. | Gazette Steam Book and Job Printing Establishment. | 1879.
                                                            [1107]

12 p. and folding map. 21 x 14 cm. Wrapper title, in thick-thin rule border.

The *Gazette* announced on April 11, 1879, that Stewart was engaged in writing a report on the mine, and that it would "shortly appear in pamphlet form." Extracts, including the map, appeared in the issues of April 15 and 16, so it is likely that the *Gazette* at least had the copy for the pamphlet at the time, and perhaps had already printed it.

CSt. CtY. NvU (microfilm).

STONE, M. N. Essay on the birth of Thomas Paine. 1879. [L1108]

Gold Hill *News*, February 18, 1879: "The essay read by Colonel M. N. Stone at National Guard Hall on the anniversary of the birth of Thomas Paine has been printed. It is a masterly effort, and is worthy of being read by every intelligent person in the State."

UNITED STATES. *Circuit Court. District of Nevada (Ninth Circuit).*

[Briefs. 1879.]

Monte Diabolo Mill and Mining Company vs. Callison et als. Opening brief for plaintiff, Monte Diabolo Mill and Mining Company. 87 p. and 4 leaves with pictures of ore specimens. 26 x 18 cm. Imprint on wrapper: San Francisco: Bacon & Company, Book and Job Printers, Corner Clay and Sansome Streets. Printed on wrapper: Due service acknowledged this 8th day of January, A.D. 1879. The mining company is referred to as the Mount Diablo Mill and Mining Company in other briefs for the same case; see Nos. 1110-1112. CSbrFRC.   [1109]

Mount Diablo Mill and Mining Company vs. Callison et al. Brief for plaintiff, Mount

Diablo Mill and Mining Company. 28 p. 25 x 18 cm. Imprint on wrapper: San Francisco: Spaulding, Barto & Co., Book and Job Printers, "Scientific Press," 414 Clay Street, below Sansome. 1879. See Nos. 1109, 1111, and 1112. CSbrFRC.

[1110]

Mount Diablo Mill and Mining Company vs. Callison et als. Plaintiff's reply to defendant's brief, Mount Diablo Mill and Mining Company. 66 p. 25 x 18 cm. Imprint on wrapper: San Francisco: Spaulding, Barto & Co., Book and Job Printers, "Scientific Press," 414 Clay Street, below Sansome. 1879. See Nos. 1109, 1110, and 1112. CSbrFRC.

[1111]

UNITED STATES. *Circuit Court. District of Nevada (Ninth Circuit).*

[*Thick-thin rule*] | Opinion | of the | Circuit Court of the United States | In and for the Ninth Circuit, and District of Nevada. | Mount Diablo Mill and Mining Company, | Plaintiff, | vs. | J. L. Callison et al., | Defendants. | [*short rule*] | At March Term, 1879. | [*thin-thick rule*].

[1112]

31 p. 26 x 18 cm. Wrapper title. The words "of the" in line 3 are slanted. Handwritten on wrapper of the recorded copy: Filed May 5, 1879. See Nos. 1109-1111. CSbrFRC.

VIRGINIA CITY, NEVADA. *Journalistic and Typographical Banquet.* Invitation. March 23, 1879.

[L1113]

See No. 1114.

VIRGINIA CITY, NEVADA. *Journalistic and Typographical Banquet.*

Journalistic and Typographical | [*ornament*] | Banquet, | at the French Rotisserie, | Virginia City, Nevada, March 23, 1879. | [*short broken-thin-thin rule*] | Bill of Fare. | [*filet*] | . . . | [*short rule*] | Songs, Speechees [*sic*], Stories, Toasts, Lies, Etc. | Footlight Job Print, Virginia, Nevada.

[1114]

[4] p., printed on p. [1] only? 20? x 13? cm. Description from facsimile in Book Club of California Keepsake Series, 1950, No. 5; possibly reduced. Line 1 in an arch over line 2; conjunction in line 1 in an oval compartment. Imprint below decorative rule border.

Gold Hill *News,* March 24, 1879: "The journalistic and typographic banquet at the Virginia French rotisserie last evening in honor of Messrs. [Josiah C.] Harlow, [Dan] Lyons and [William Frank] Stewart, was attended by nearly all the newspaper men on the Comstock. As indicated by the invitations, the especial object was to honor those members of the press fraternity who had proved true to their pledges as members of the legislature. In addition to the three gentlemen above mentioned, the other members of the Storey county delegation who did not 'fall down,' were invited as guests. This list included Senators [William D. C.] Gibson and [E. A.] Schultz and Assemblymen [John L.] Hanna and [Owen] Fraser [the name is also spelled Frazer]. More formal gatherings have doubtless been seen in Nevada, but it would be difficult to bring together a more genial company than the one at the French rotisserie last

evening. The very soul of sociability seemed to pervade the hearts of all present, and a most enjoyable occasion was the result. E. L. Colnon, of the Virginia *Chronicle,* presided in an acceptable manner. Toasts were responded to right heartily and appropriately by the representatives of the different papers and by the invited guests. The list of toasts included 'The Press,' 'Our Guests,' 'The Sack,' 'The Mechanics' Union,' and other sentiments of a grave and humorous character. After songs, anecdotes, etc., the meeting at 12 o'clock adjourned with three rousing cheers for the members of the Storey county delegation who did not 'fall down.' "
Pvt.

VIRGINIA CITY, NEVADA. *National Guard Social.* Programme. Virginia, Nevada: Enterprise Steam Book and Job Printing House. December 31, 1879. [L1115]

Enterprise, December 31, 1879: "The programmes for the National Guard Social, printed at the ENTERPRISE job office, are exceedingly neat affairs. One back shows a handsomely engraved marine view and the other a view of the wild regions of Labrador. The social will take place to-night at the hall of the company."

YELLOW JACKET SILVER MINING COMPANY.

Annual Report | of the | Yellow Jacket Silver Mining Co. | For the Year Ending | June 30th, 1879. | [*short rule*] | Daily Exchange Publishing Co., 306 Montgomery St., S.F. [1116]

16 p. and a colored folding chart. 22 x 15 cm. Wrapper title. Line 1 in an arch over line 2.

The *Territorial Enterprise* acknowledged receipt of a copy on August 16, 1879. The mining company, whose headquarters were in San Francisco, may have decided it was less expensive to have the printing done there than to contract with a Nevada printer who would send it to San Francisco for printing anyway; see No. L456.
C. CHi. CSmH. CU-B. NvU.

❧1880☙

The 1880 State Controller's report (p. 87) shows that $4,115.39 was spent from the State Printing Fund in 1880, and that the total expenditures since statehood amounted to $229,104.98.

When the Board of State Printing Commissioners met on November 22, 1878, two weeks after awarding Nevada's incidental printing for the 1879-1880 biennium to Marshall Robinson, it was presented with a communication from Nellie V. Mighels purporting to show that the bid of Henry R. Mighels was more favorable to the state than Robinson's. The State Printing Expert, Charles A. V.

Putnam, submitted a rebuttal to the charges of Mrs. Mighels, who claimed to be the real party in interest in her husband's bid. Putnam's arguments convinced the Board that it had acted properly, and it formally reaffirmed its decision in favor of Robinson (NvHi: PSPC, 1878, p. 12-13). Henry Mighels died in the spring of the following year after a long illness, leaving the editorship of his newspaper, the Carson City *Appeal,* to his widow. Family matters soon caused Mrs. Mighels to turn over the chair to another journalist, who was replaced in November by Samuel P. Davis. In July of 1880 Davis and Nellie Mighels were married; three months later a long series of strident attacks on Robinson and Putnam began to appear in the *Appeal.* Throughout October and November and much of December, Davis accused Robinson of fraudulently obtaining his position through Putnam's intervention and of performing his duties in a slipshod and dishonest manner, again with Putnam's connivance. For a month Davis's crusade was carried out alone, but early in November other papers began to cite his charges and to ask why neither of the accused had responded to them. Putnam finally did reply in the *Territorial Enterprise* on November 9 and 11, denying any wrongdoing on Robinson's part or his own. Davis was not mollified, however, and called for a legislative investigation. A joint committee of the 1881 Legislature exonerated both Putnam and Robinson, noting that the latter had charged a total of $15 more than he should have in printing four legislative bills in 1879 instead of the several hundred dollars claimed by Davis (JS, 1881, p. 292-294). Editorial comment quickly switched away from Davis, not only because of the findings but because his testimony at the hearings tended to differ from what he had published in the *Appeal.* Several papers published the committee's report in full; the *Appeal* did not.

While this tempest was going on another furor erupted over the appointment of John W. Maddrill as Superintendent of State Printing for 1881 and 1882. Joseph E. Eckley, foreman of the *Enterprise* office and a former State Printer, had been expected by some to get the job, and when he did not there were immediate accusations in the *Enterprise* of political chicanery on the part of Maddrill's employer, state Senator C. C. Powning of the Reno *Nevada State Journal,* and incompetence on the part of the new Superintendent. Most other newspapers saw the charges as sour grapes, and after Maddrill acquired presses and material for the state at astonishingly low prices the flurry ceased. According to the *Journal* of November 16, "the purchases, which include a No. 4 Hoe press, Baxter engine, half-medium Gordon, Gem cutter, and type, cases, etc., aggregate the sum of $5,863.23." The paper resumed its commentary on November 28: "The large Hoe press comes from New York and cannot arrive here before the first of February. In the meantime a Campbell press will be used, the loan of the same having been offered by the agents [Painter & Co. of San Francisco] from whom the Hoe press was contracted for." Maddrill engaged Josiah C. Harlow as foreman and, although Marshall Robinson and A. L. Bancroft & Company had contracts to do the public printing until January 1, Maddrill and Harlow began to print some of the state's work before the end of December (see Nos. 1131 and L1133).

An article and an advertisement in the Reno *Gazette* on February 4 indicated that F. Anthony had opened the Nevada Book Bindery in Virginia City.

Candelaria acquired a newspaper in June, and Carson City gained two new ones in March and December. A paper was started in Dayton in December with press and material from a paper that had died in Silver City. One of Genoa's newspapers ceased publication in July, its material going immediately to found another one there; one other paper began to publish in Genoa as well. Grantsville got a press in December, as did Ruby Hill in April, but papers were lost to Hamilton in December, to Paradise, Sutro, and Virginia City in November, and to Tybo in March. All other presses that had been active at the end of 1879 in Aurora, Austin, Battle Mountain, Belmont, Carson City, Elko, Eureka, Gold Hill, Pioche, Reno, Tuscarora, Virginia City, Ward, and Winnemucca continued to publish throughout the year.

AMITIE CLUB. *Reno, Nevada.* Invitation to a dance. February 26, 1880.
[L1117]
Reno *Gazette*, February 21, 1880: "The invitations to the Amitie Club dance were printed in the GAZETTE office. It is a mighty nice piece of work." The same issue contains a notice that the dance would be "in Kimball's hall next Thursday evening, instead of in the Pavilion as announced [on the invitation?]."

ANCIENT ORDER OF UNITED WORKMEN. *Virginia City, Nevada. Storey Lodge No. 3.*

By-Laws | —of— | Storey Lodge No. 3, | A.O.U.W. | [*filet*] | Organized August 7, 1879. | [*filet*] | Virginia, Nev.: | Chronicle Book and Job Printing Office. | 1880. [1118]
3, [1] p. 14 x 9 cm. Wrapper title, in wavy-thin rule border.
CU-B. NvU(NvMus).

AUSTIN, NEVADA. *Charters.* Charter of the City of Austin, Lander County, Nevada. Austin: John Booth Print. 1880. 25 p. [L1119]

Eberstadt 134:470. John Booth was the proprietor of the *Reese River Reveille.*

BISHOP WHITAKER'S SCHOOL FOR GIRLS. *Reno, Nevada.*

Thirteenth Rehearsal | of the | Department of Music, | School for Girls, | Reno, Nevada, | Wednesday Evening, December 15, 1880.

[1120]

[4] p., printed on p. [1-3] only. 9 x 12 cm. Decorative rule border. NvHi.

CARSON OPERA HOUSE. *Carson City, Nevada.*

Carson Opera House. | [*broken wavy rule*] | Benefit of the | Ladies' Library | Saturday Evening, | June 19, 1880 | [*filet*] | Programme | . . . | [Carson City:] Index.

[1121]

Broadside. 23? x 11? cm. The recorded copy has been trimmed and mounted in a scrapbook. Decorative rule border, with imprint imbedded in bottom border. See No. 1010. NvMus.

CARSON OPERA HOUSE. *Carson City, Nevada.*

Carson Opera House. | [*double rule*] | . . . | [*thick-thin rule*] | Saturday Evening, April 3d. | [*thick-thin rule*] | Benfit [*sic*] of Relief Fund of | Custer Post No. 5, G.A.R. | [*thick-thin rule*] | The following Ladies and Gentlemen have kindly volunteered and will appear: | . . . | [*thick-thin rule*] | To Conclude with the Beautiful Drama in Three Acts of | Dora | With the Original Music Incidental to the Piece. | [*thick-thin rule*] | . . . | [*double rule*] | [Carson City:] Morning Appeal Steam Print | [1880.]

[1122]

Broadside. 33 x 17 cm. Printed in blue ink.

The performance was reviewed in the *Appeal* of April 4, 1880. NvMus.

CARSON OPERA HOUSE. *Carson City, Nevada.*

"The Play!" | . . . | [*broken wavy rule*] | Carson Opera House | [*broken wavy rule*] | . . . | [*ornamental double rule*] | Second Performance and Complimentary Benefit of the | Rosedale Dramatic Club | Tendered by the Citizens of Carson. | [*ornamental double rule*] | Tuesday Even'g, July 20, 1880 | Tom Taylor's very Popular Play of | Still Waters Run Deep | . . . | [Carson City:] Index-Print.

[1123]

Broadside. 21 x 13 cm. Decorative rule border, with imprint imbedded in bottom border. Printed in blue ink. See No. 1010.
NvMus.

DEMOCRATIC PARTY. *Lyon County, Nevada.*

Regular | DemocratiC [*sic*] | Ticket. | [*filet*] | . . . | [*filet*] | Lyon County Ticket. | . . . | [*filet*] | Township Officers— Dayton. | . . . | [1880.]   [1124]

Broadside. 25 x 10 cm.

The ticket is headed by Winfield S. Hancock, Democratic presidential candidate in 1880.
NvMus.

EUREKA AND PALISADE RAILROAD COMPANY.

Eureka and Palisade Railroad Company. | Local Freight Tariff, | To take effect June the 10th, 1880. | [*double rule*] | . . .   [1125]

Broadside. 43 x 35 cm. Thick-thin rule border.

Rates are given for twenty-two stations along the line that connected the mining town of Eureka with the Central Pacific Railroad at Palisade.
CU-B.

FREEMASONS. *Nevada. Grand Lodge.*

Proceedings | of the | M.˙. W.˙. Grand Lodge | of | Free and Accepted Masons | of the | State of Nevada. | [*filet*] | [*ornament*] 1880. [*ornament*] | [*filet*] | Virginia, Nevada: | Enterprise Steam Book and Job Printing House. | 1880.   [1126]

191, viii p. 23 x 15 cm. Wrapper title, in decorative rule border. Proceedings of a special grand communication at Reno on October 4, 1879, cover p. [1]-5; the proceedings of the sixteenth annual grand communication at Virginia City, June 8-10, 1880, are on p. [7]-191, although a title page for the meeting indicates that the communication was held on June 18-20.

$650 was set aside for printing the proceedings (p. 18). They were printed and distributed "in accordance with custom," i.e., 800 were printed, with 300 retained by the printer for future binding (1881 Proceedings, p. 202); the cost of "Printing" was $551.35 (ibid., p. 214).
NvHi. NvRFM.

FREEMASONS. *Nevada. Royal Arch Masons. Grand Chapter.*

Proceedings | of the | M.E. Grand Royal Arch Chapter | of the | State of Nevada, | at its | Seventh Annual Grand Convocation, | Held at | Masonic Hall, in the City of Virginia, | June 7th, 8th, 9th, and 10th, A.D. 1880, A.I. 2410. | [*filet*] | San Francisco: |

Frank Eastman & Co., Printers, 509 Clay Street. | 1880.   [1127]
[5], 6-95, [1], iii p. 23 x 14 cm. Printed wrapper.
The cost of printing was $236.50 (1881 Proceedings, p. 107).
NvU.

INDEPENDENT ORDER OF GOOD TEMPLARS. *Nevada. Grand Lodge.*

Constitution | of the | Grand Lodge of Nevada, | I.O.G.T. | Organized February 25, 1879. | [*filet*] | Also, | Constitution for Subordinate Lodges | Working under the Grand Lodge of Nevada, | together with all Standing | Resolutions. | [*short rule*] | Virginia, Nevada: | Enterprise Book and Job Printing House. | 1880. [1128]
36 p. 15 x 10 cm. Printed wrapper. Title and text pages in thick-thin rule borders.
NvHi.

LASSEN COUNTY, CALIFORNIA. *County Clerk.*

Great Register | of the | County of Lassen, | State of California, | For the General Election, | [*ornament*] 1880. [*ornament*] | [*filet*] | Reno: | Evening Gazette Job Print. | 1880.   [1129]
17 p. 28 x 22 cm. Wrapper title, in thick-thin rule border.
Great Registers, listing names of eligible voters, were issued in each California county from 1866. A search of available Great Registers for counties bordering on Nevada has turned up no others that were printed outside of California.
CSmH. CU-B.

METHODIST EPISCOPAL CHURCH. *Conferences. Nevada.*

Minutes | of the | Nevada Annual Conference | of the | Methodist Episcopal Church. | [*filet*] | Sixteenth Session. | Held in Virginia City, Nevada, | September 23d-26th, 1880. | [*filet*] | San Francisco. | Methodist Book Depository, 1041 Market Street, | 1880.

[1130]

16, [3] p. 21 x 15 cm. Printed wrapper. See No. 1030.
CBPac (lacks wrapper). NcLjUM (lacks wrapper). NjMD.

NEVADA. *Attorney General's Office.*

First and Second Annual Reports | of the | Attorney-General | for | the Years 1879 and 1880. | [*state seal*] | Carson City: | State Office : : : J. W. Maddrill, Supt. State Printing. | 1881.

[1131]

19 p. 23 x 15 cm. Wrapper title, in decorative rule border. Issued also as No. 13 in AJSA, 1881.
Carson City *Times,* December 29, 1880: "The Attorney General's report, which will

make twenty-five pages, is now being printed, and other reports of State officers will soon be under way." It is not known how much of the report was printed in 1880; the Carson City *Index* reported receipt of a copy on January 8, 1881.

Nv-Ar.

NEVADA. *Board of State Printing Commissioners.*

Bids for | Printing Stationery | —for the— | State of Neva-da. | [*short rule*] | Bids will be received by | the Board of State Print-ing Commis-|sioners of the State of Nevada, up to and | includ-ing | December 11th, 1880, | . . . | Carson City, Nevada, Nov. 18, 1880. | no19-20d. | [*rule*]. [1132]

Broadside. 18 x 13 cm. A proof for use in newspaper advertising, as indicated by the code preceding the rule.

San Francisco prices were requested for the following: 200 reams book paper, 24" x 38", 56 lbs.; 50 reams book paper, 24" x 28", 44 lbs.; 100 reams flat cap, from 14 lbs. to 20 lbs.; 50 reams flat letter, plain, 10 lbs.; 50 reams flat (Carew), 12 lbs., ruled for letter heads; 5 reams flat note letter (Carew), 6 lbs., ruled; 10 reams 22 lb. folio post; 10 reams 24 lb. folio post; 20 reams check cap (best quality); 500 sheets Bristol board; 20 reams 16 lb. bill head paper (halves, ruled on one side); and 10 reams pamphlet cover paper, 50 lbs. (assorted colors).

NvHi.

NEVADA. *Governor, 1879-1883 (John Henry Kinkead).* Proclamation. Carson City: State Office, J. W. Maddrill, Supt. State Printing. 1880.

[L1133]

Carson City *Times,* December 29, 1880, in an article describing the new State Printing Office: "The office has just issued the Governor's proclamation to the effect that [Supreme Court Justice Charles H.] Belknap and [U. S. Representative George W.] Cassidy were duly elected, and that all of the proposed amendments to the State Constitution have been duly adopted and ratified . . ."

NEVADA. *Governor, 1879-1883 (John Henry Kinkead).*

State of Nevada, | Executive Department. | Carson City, Nev., 1880 | December 23, 1880. | . . . | Sir: | The Legislature of this State, desiring to afford the people of the State an oppor-|tunity of expressing their wishes upon the subject of Chinese immigration, passed | an Act, approved February 11th, 1879, entitled "An Act to ascertain and express | the will of the people of the State of Nevada upon the subject of Chinese immigra-|tion." | . . . | [Carson City: Marshall Robinson, State Printer? 1880.] [1134]

[4] p., printed on p. [1, 3] only. 23? x 20? cm. The recorded copy has been trimmed and bound. Mostly script type. The piece may have been printed by John W. Maddrill, the newly appointed Superintendent of State Printing, who by December 29 had begun to execute some of the state's work; see Nos. 1131 and L1133.

The election was held on November 2, 1880, with 183 for immigration, 17,259 against it, and 955 not voting. The document transmits the results to the President, Vice President, the Cabinet, Senators, Representatives, and all Governors of states and territories.

CU-B.

NEVADA. *Governor, 1879-1883 (John Henry Kinkead).*

State of Nevada. | [*filet*] | Proclamation | for a Day of | [*ornament*] Thanksgiving and [*ornament*] Praise, | —by— | John H. Kin-kead, | Governor. | [Carson City: Marshall Robinson, State Printer. 1880.] [1135]

[4] p., printed on p. [1, 3] only. 25 x 20 cm.

The date set for Thanksgiving was November 25, 1880.

CSmH. M. NvU (microfilm).

NEVADA. *Laws, statutes, etc.*

Laws | Relating to | The Public School System | of the | State of Nevada. | [*short rule*] | Compiled and Published by the Superinten-dent of Public In-|struction, for the Use of School Officers. | [*state seal*] | San Francisco: | A. L. Bancroft & Company, Printers, | 721 Market Street. | 1880. [1136]

28, [1] p. 23 x 14 cm. Printed wrapper.

CU-B.

NEVADA. *Politics.* Pamphlet. November 1880. [L1137]

Carson City *Appeal,* November 4, 1880: "A defamatory pamphlet circulated on the eve of election beat [Supreme Court] Justice [William H.] Beatty in the State, but White Pine and Ormsby [counties], where he was known, gave him handsome majorities. We will allude to this dastardly piece of work hereafter." In the next day's issue, after fuming at some length at the loss of the Republican judge, the Republican *Appeal* had the following to say: "We have before us a pamphlet charging Judge Beatty—by insinuation—with an impeachable offense . . . This pamphlet was not the only one circulated against candidates, and we hope that the next Legislature will pass a law making it a felony for any man to write, circulate or print a pamphlet derogatory to any candidate within thirty days prior to election."

NEVADA. *State Controller's Office.*

Annual Report | of the | Controller | of the | State of Neva-da, | For the Fifteenth Fiscal Year, Ending | December 31, 1879. | Transmitted January 15, 1880. | J. F. Hallock, State Control-ler. | [*state seal*] | San Francisco: | A.L. Bancroft & Company, Print-ers, | 721 Market Street. | 1880. [1138]

90 p., including a folding table. 23 x 14 cm. Wrapper title, in decorative rule border. Issued also as No. 3 in AJSA, 1881.

The Carson City *Appeal* acknowledged receipt of a copy on February 6, 1880.
C.

NEVADA. *Supreme Court.*

[Briefs. 1880.]

Abernathie vs. Consolidated Virginia Mining Co. Brief of respondent, Consolidated Virginia Mining Co. 31 p. 24 x 18 cm. Imprint on wrapper: Virginia, Nev.: Printed at the Evening Chronicle Job Office. 1880. Nv-Ar. NvU.   [1139]

Alderson vs. Mendes et al. Transcript on appeal. 49 p. 25 x 18 cm. Imprint on wrapper: [Carson City:] Daily Index. Printed on wrapper: Filed December 29th, 1880. The first issue of the *Index* appeared only four days previously. Nv-Ar.
[1140]

Baum et al. vs. Meyer at al. Statement on appeal. [2], 59 p. 25 x 18 cm. Imprint on wrapper: Printed at Enterprise Job Office, Virginia City, Nev. Printed on wrapper: Filed [*broken rule*] 1880. Nv-Ar.   [1141]

Borden vs. Sellers and Bender. Brief of appellant, C. T. Bender. 17 p. 25 x 18 cm. Imprint on wrapper: Reno Journal Book and Job Print. Printed on wrapper: Filed [*broken rule*] 1880. Nv-Ar.   [1142]

Borden vs. Sellers and Bender. Points and authorities of appellant, C. T. Bender. 2 p. 25 x 18 cm. Imprint on wrapper: Reno Journal Book and Job Print. Printed on wrapper: Filed [*broken rule*] 1880. Nv-Ar.   [1143]

Borden vs. Sellers and Bender. Points and authorities of respondent, R. V. Borden. 4 p. 25 x 18 cm. Imprint on wrapper: Reno Journal Book and Job Print. Printed on wrapper: Filed [*broken rule*] 1880. Nv-Ar.   [1144]

Borden vs. Sellers and Bender. Transcript on appeal. [2], 29 p. 26 x 18 cm. Imprint on wrapper: Reno: Gazette Book and Job Print. 1880. Nv-Ar.   [1145]

Brown vs. Warren et al. Brief of appellant in reply, Samuel Brown. 9 p. 25 x 18 cm. Imprint on wrapper: Virginia Evening Chronicle Book Print. Printed on wrapper: Filed [*broken rule*] 1880. Nv-Ar.   [1146]

Brown vs. Warren et al. Engrossed statement on appeal. [2], 31 p. 25 x 17 cm. Imprint on wrapper: Reno Journal Book and Job Print. Printed on wrapper: Filed [*broken rule*] 1880. Nv-Ar.   [1147]

Brown vs. Warren et al. Points and authorities of appellant, Samuel Brown. 3 p. 25 x 18 cm. Imprint on wrapper: Virginia Evening Chronicle Book Print. Printed on wrapper: Filed [*broken rule*] 1880. Nv-Ar.   [1148]

Brown vs. Warren et al. Points and authorities of respondents, R. W. Warren et al. 11 p. 25 x 18 cm. Imprint on wrapper: Carson City: Index Print. 1880. Nv-Ar.
[1149]

Buckley vs. Buckley. Points and authorities of appellant, S. Buckley. 3 p. 25 x 18 cm. Imprint on wrapper: Reno Journal Book and Job Print. Printed on wrapper: Filed [*broken rule*] 1880. Nv-Ar.   [1150]

Buckley vs. Buckley. Points and authorities of respondent, Armina Buckley. 4 p. 25 x 18 cm. Imprint on wrapper: Reno Journal Book and Job Print. Printed on wrapper: Filed [*broken rule*] 1880. Nv-Ar.   [1151]

Buckley vs. Buckley. Transcript on appeal. 36 p. 25 x 18 cm. Imprint on wrapper: Reno Journal Book and Job Print. Printed on wrapper: Filed [*broken rule*] 1880. Nv-Ar. [1152]

Bunting vs. Central Pacific Railroad Co. Harrison vs. Central Pacific Railroad Co.: case no. 964. Points and authorities of respondent, Central Pacific Railroad Co. 21 p. 25 x 18 cm. Printed on wrapper: Filed [*broken rule*] 1880. See No. 1062. NvHi. [1153]

Bunting vs. Central Pacific Railroad Co. Harrison vs. Central Pacific Railroad Co.: case No. 1041. Brief of appellant, Central Pacific Railroad Co. 44 p. 25 x 16 cm. Imprint on wrapper: Crocker & Co., Stationers and Printers, 401 and 403 Sansome St., S.F. Printed on wrapper: Filed this [*broken rule*] day of November, A.D. 1880. Nv-Ar. [1154]

Bunting vs. Central Pacific Railroad Co. Harrison vs. Central Pacific Railroad Co.: case no. 1041. Transcript on appeal. iii, 400; iii, 401-845 p. 25 x 18 cm. Imprint on wrappers: Crocker & Co., Stationers and Printers, 401 and 403 Sansome St., S.F. Printed on wrappers: Filed this [*broken rule*] day of [*broken rule*] A.D. 1880. NvAr. [1155]

Burns et al. vs. Rodefer et al. Points and authorities of appellants, W. T. Burns et al. 14 p. 25 x 17 cm. Imprint on wrapper: Silver State Print, Winnemucca, Nevada. Printed on wrapper: Filed [*dotted rule*] 1880. Nv-Ar. [1156]

Burns et al vs. Rodefer et al. Transcript on appeal. 59 p. and a folding map. 25 x 18 cm. Imprint on wrapper: Silver State Print, Winnemucca, Nevada. Printed on wrapper: Filed [*dotted rule*] 1880. Nv-Ar. [1157]

Cedar Hill Consolidated Gold and Silver Mining and Milling Co. vs. Jacob Little Consolidated Mining Co. Points and authorities of appellant, Cedar Hill Consolidated Gold and Silver Mining and Milling Co. 2 p. 25 x 18 cm. Imprint on wrapper: Virginia, Nevada: Footlight Book and Job Printing House. 1880. Nv-Ar. [1158]

Cedar Hill Consolidated Gold and Silver Mining and Milling Co. vs. Jacob Little Consolidated Mining Co. Points and authorities of respondent, Jacob Little Consolidated Mining Co. 3 p. 26 x 18 cm. Imprint on wrapper: Virginia Evening Chronicle Book Print. Printed on wrapper: Filed [*broken rule*] 1880. Nv-Ar. [1159]

Cedar Hill Consolidated Gold and Silver Mining and Milling Co. vs. Jacob Little Consolidated Mining Co. Transcript on appeal. [2], 16 p. 25 x 18 cm. Imprint on wrapper: Virginia, Nevada: Footlight Book and Job Printing House. 1880. Nv-Ar. [1160]

Chase vs. Chase. Brief of plaintiff, Edward R. Chase. 14 p. 25 x 18 cm. Imprint on wrapper: Independent Print, Elko. Printed on wrapper: Filed [*broken rule*] 1880. Nv-Ar. [1161]

Chase vs. Chase. Brief of respondent, Henry H. Chase. 8 p. 25 x 18 cm. Imprint on wrapper: Independent Print, Elko. Printed on wrapper: Filed [*broken rule*] 1880. Nv-Ar. [1162]

Chase vs. Chase. Transcript on appeal. 14 p. 25 x 18 cm. Imprint on wrapper: Index Print, Carson. Printed on wrapper: Filed [*rule*] 1880. Nv-Ar. [1163]

Ewing vs. Jennings: case no. 1016. Brief of appellant, Isaac Jennings. 6 p. 25 x 18 cm. Imprint on wrapper: Index Print, Carson, Nevada. Printed on wrapper: Filed April 19, 1880. Nv-Ar. [1164]

Ewing vs. Jennings: case no. 1016. Points and authorities of respondent, Thomas Ewing. 10 p. 26 x 18 cm. Imprint on wrapper: Index Print, Carson, Nevada. Printed on wrapper: Filed April 26, 1880. Nv-Ar. [1165]

Ewing vs. Jennings: case no. 1016. Transcript on appeal. 46 p. 24 x 17 cm. Imprint on wrapper: Index Print, Carson, Nevada. Printed on wrapper: Filed March 16, 1880. Nv-Ar. [1166]

Ewing vs. Jennings: case no. 1017. Brief of appellant, Isaac Jennings. 10 p. 25 x 18 cm. Imprint on wrapper: Index Print, Carson, Nevada. Printed on wrapper: Filed April 19, 1880. Nv-Ar. [1167]

Ewing vs. Jennings: case no. 1017. Points and authorities of respondent, Thomas Ewing. 7 p. 25 x 18 cm. Imprint on wrapper: Index Print, Carson, Nevada. Printed on wrapper: Filed April 26, 1880. Nv-Ar. [1168]

Ewing vs. Jennings: case no. 1017. Transcript on appeal. 32 p. 25 x 17 cm. Imprint on wrapper: Index Print, Carson, Nevada. Printed on wrapper: Filed March 16, 1880. Nv-Ar. [1169]

Ferris vs. Carson Water Co. Brief of appellant, G. W. G. Ferris. 12 p. 25 x 17 cm. Imprint on wrapper: Index Print, Carson, Nevada. Printed on wrapper: Filed [rule] 1880. Nv-Ar. [1170]

Ferris vs. Carson Water Co. Statement of the case; points and authorities of respondent, Carson Water Co. 8 p. 26 x 18 cm. Imprint on wrapper: [Carson City:] Index Print. Printed on wrapper: Filed [rule] 1880. Nv-Ar. [1171]

Ferris vs. Carson Water Co. Transcript on appeal. 26 p. 25 x 17 cm. Imprint on wrapper: Index Print, Carson, Nevada. The case was litigated in the 1880 term; see Nos. 1170-1171. Nv-Ar. [1172]

Fishback vs. Miller. Brief of appellant, Jeremiah Miller. 105 p. 25 x 18 cm. Printed on wrapper: Filed February [broken rule] 1880. Nv-Ar. [1173]

Gass vs. Hampton. Brief of appellant, W. C. Gass. 76 p. 25 x 18 cm. Imprint on wrapper: Printed at Enterprise Job Office, Virginia City, Nev. Printed on wrapper: Filed [broken rule] 1880. Nv-Ar. [1174]

Gass vs. Hampton. Brief of respondent, J. C. Hampton. 8 p. 25 x 18 cm. Imprint on wrapper: Printed at Enterprise Job Office, Virginia City, Nev. Printed on wrapper: Filed [broken rule] 1880. Nv-Ar. [1175]

Gass vs. Hampton. Points and authorities of plaintiff, W. C. Gass. 8 p. 25 x 18 cm. Imprint on wrapper: Printed at Enterprise Job Office, Virginia City, Nev. Printed on wrapper: Filed [broken rule] 1880. Nv-Ar. [1176]

Gass vs. Hampton. Points and authorities of respondent, J. C. Hampton. 2 p. 25 x 18 cm. Imprint on wrapper: Printed at Enterprise Job Office, Virginia City, Nev. Printed on wrapper: Filed [broken rule] 1880. Nv-Ar. [1177]

Gass vs. Hampton. Transcript on appeal. [2], 80 p. 26 x 18 cm. Imprint on wrapper: Printed at Enterprise Job Office, Virginia City, Nev. Printed on wrapper: Filed [broken rule] 1880. Nv-Ar. [1178]

Goodale vs. Goodale. Transcript on appeal. 31 p. 25 x 18 cm. Imprint on wrapper: Index Print, Carson. Printed on wrapper: Filed [rule] 1880. Nv-Ar.   [1179]

Hixon vs. Pixley et al. Points and authorities of appellant, Robert F. Pixley. 11 p. 25 x 17 cm. The name of the respondent is printed as Ellen E. Pixley; corrected by hand on the recorded copy to read Ellen E. Hixon. Imprint on wrapper: Virginia Evening Chronicle Book Print. Printed on wrapper: Filed, [broken rule] 1880. Nv-Ar.   [1180]

Hixon vs. Pixley et al. Points and authorities of respondent, Ellen E. Hixon. 9 p. 25 x 18 cm. Imprint on wrapper: Carson City: Index Print. 1880. Nv-Ar.   [1181]

Hixon vs. Pixley et al. Transcript on appeal. 183 p. 25 x 18 cm. Imprint on wrapper: [Carson City:] Index-Print. Printed on wrapper: Filed [rule] A.D. 1880. Nv-Ar.
     [1182]

Iowa Mining Co. vs. Bonanza Mining Co. Points and authorities of appellant, Iowa Mining Co. 11 p. 25 x 18 cm. Imprint on wrapper: Printed at Enterprise Job Office, Virginia City, Nev. Printed on wrapper: Filed [dotted rule] 1880. Nv-Ar. [1183]

Iowa Mining Co. vs. Bonanza Mining Co. Points and authorities of respondent, Bonanza Mining Co. 11 p. 25 x 18 cm. Imprint on wrapper: Printed at Enterprise Job Office, Virginia City, Nev. Printed on wrapper: Filed [dotted rule] 1880. Nv-Ar.   [1184]

Iowa Mining Co. vs. Bonanza Mining Co. Reply of appellant to points and authorities of respondent, Iowa Mining Co. 10 p. 25 x 18 cm. Imprint on wrapper: Printed at Enterprise Job Office, Virginia City, Nev. Printed on wrapper: Filed [dotted rule] 1880. Nv-Ar.   [1185]

Iowa Mining Co. vs. Bonanza Mining Co. Transcript on appeal. 63, [2] p. 25 x 18 cm. Imprint on wrapper: Printed at Enterprise Job Office, Virginia City, Nev. Printed on wrapper: Filed [dotted rule] 1880. Nv-Ar.   [1186]

Lachman et al. vs. Barnett et al. Points and authorities of appellants, D. and B. Lachman. 2 p. 25 x 18 cm. Imprint on wrapper: Reno: Gazette Book and Job Print. 1880. Nv-Ar.   [1187]

Lachman et al. vs. Barnett et al. Transcript on appeal. [2], 72 p. 25 x 17 cm. Imprint on wrapper: Reno: Gazette Book and Job Print. 1880. Nv-Ar.   [1188]

Lake vs. Lewis. Engrossed statement on appeal. [1], 25 p. 25 x 17 cm. Imprint on wrapper: Reno Journal Book and Job Print. Printed on wrapper: Filed [broken rule] 1880. Nv-Ar.   [1189]

Lonkey et al. vs. Wells. Transcript on appeal. 50 p. 26 x 18 cm. Imprint on wrapper: [Carson City:] Daily Index. Printed on wrapper: Filed December 29th, 1880. See No. 1140. Nv-Ar.   [1190]

Manning vs. Smith. Points and authorities of appellant, A. H. Manning. 3 p. 25 x 17 cm. Imprint on wrapper: Reno Journal Book and Job Print. Printed on wrapper: Filed [broken rule] 1880. Nv-Ar.   [1191]

Manning vs. Smith. Points and authorities of respondent, M. J. Smith. 4 p. 26 x 18 cm. Imprint on wrapper: Reno Gazette Steam Book & Job Print. Printed on wrapper: Filed [broken rule] 1880. Nv-Ar.   [1192]

Manning vs. Smith. Transcript on appeal. [2], 14 p. 25 x 17 cm. Imprint on wrapper: Reno Journal Book and Job Print. Printed on wrapper: Filed [broken rule] 1880.

Nv-Ar.   [1193]

Marshall et al. vs. Golden Fleece Gold and Silver Mining Co. et al. Brief of appellants in reply to respondents' brief, I. B. Marshall et al. 8 p. 25 x 18 cm. Imprint on wrapper: Crocker & Co., Stationer and Printer, 401 and 403 Sansome St., S. F. Printed on wrapper: Filed this [dotted rule] day of [dotted rule] A.D. 1880. Nv-Ar.
[1194]

Marshall et al. vs. Golden Fleece Gold and Silver Mining Co. et al. Brief of respondents in reply, Golden Fleece Gold and Silver Mining Co. et al. 8 p. 26 x 18 cm. Imprint on wrapper: Index Print, Carson, Nevada. Printed on wrapper: Filed [rule] 1880. Nv-Ar.   [1195]

Marshall et al. vs. Golden Fleece Gold and Silver Mining Co. et al. Points and authorities of defendants, Golden Fleece Gold and Silver Mining Co. et al. 16 p. 26 x 18 cm. Imprint on wrapper: Sacramento: H. S. Crocker & Co., Printers and Stationers. 1880. Nv-Ar.   [1196]

Marshall et al. vs. Golden Fleece Gold and Silver Mining Co. et al. Statement of case and brief of appellants, I. B. Marshall et al. 80 p. 26 x 18 cm. Imprint on wrapper: Crocker & Co., Stationers and Printers, 401 and 403 Sansome St., S.F. Printed on wrapper: Filed [dotted rule] 1880. Nv-Ar.   [1197]

Meyer vs. Virginia and Truckee Railroad Co. Transcript on appeal. [2], 38 p. 25 x 18 cm. Imprint on wrapper: Virginia Evening Chronicle Book Print. Printed on wrapper: Filed [broken rule] 1880. Nv-Ar.   [1198]

Nesbitt et al. vs. Chisholm et al. Brief of appellants, John Chisholm et al. 9 p. 25 x 18 cm. Imprint on wrapper: [Carson City:] Index Print. Printed on wrapper: Filed September 11, 1880. Nv-Ar.   [1199]

Nesbitt et al. vs. Chisholm et al. Transcript on appeal. 60 p. 25 x 18 cm. Imprint on wrapper: Index Print, Carson, Nevada. Printed on wrapper: Filed April 3, 1880. Nv-Ar.   [1200]

Nevada vs. California Mining Co. et al. Transcript on appeal. [2], 32 p. 25 x 18 cm. Imprint on wrapper: Virginia Evening Chronicle Book Print. Printed on wrapper: Filed, [broken rule] 1880. Nv-Ar. NvU.   [1201]

Nevada vs. Consolidated Virginia Mining Co. et al. Transcript on appeal. [2], 40 p. 26 x 18 cm. Imprint on wrapper: Virginia Evening Chronicle Book Print. Printed on wrapper: Filed, [broken rule] 1880. Nv-Ar. NvU.   [1202]

Reese Gold and Silver Mining Co. vs. Rye Patch Consolidated Mill and Mining Co. et al.: case no 1004. Brief of respondent, Reese Gold and Silver Mining Co. 8 p. 25 x 18 cm. Imprint on wrapper: [Virginia City:] Evening Chronicle Book Print. Printed on wrapper: Filed, [broken rule] 1880. Nv-Ar.   [1203]

Reese Gold and Silver Mining Co. vs. Rye Patch Consolidated Mill and Mining Co. et al.: case no. 1004. Points and authorities of appellants, Rye Patch Consolidated Mill and Mining Co. et al. 8 p. 26 x 18 cm. Imprint on wrapper: H. A. Weaver's Law Printing Office, No. 327 J Street, between Third and Fourth, Sacramento. Printed on wrapper: Filed [broken rule] 1880. Nv-Ar.   [1204]

Reese Gold and Silver Mining Co. vs. Rye Patch Consolidated Mill and Mining Co. et al.: case no. 1018. Brief of appellant on motion to reinstate appeal, Rye Patch Consolidated Mill and Mining Co. et al. 27 p. 26 x 18 cm. Imprint on wrapper: San

Francisco: Bacon & Company, Book and Job Printers, Corner Clay and Sansome Streets. Printed on wrapper: Filed [*rule*] 1880. Nv-Ar. [1205]

Reese Gold and Silver Mining Co. vs. Rye Patch Consolidated Mill and Mining Co. et al.: case no. 1018. Transcript on appeal. 106 p. 25 x 18 cm. Imprint on wrapper: Silver State Print, Winnemucca, Nevada. Printed on wrapper: Filed [*dotted rule*] 1880. Nv-Ar. [1206]

Royce vs. Hampton et al. Appellant's brief in reply, Thaddeus B. Royce. 7 p. 25 x 18 cm. Imprint on wrapper: Printed at Enterprise Job Office, Virginia City, Nev. Printed on wrapper: Filed [*broken rule*] 1880. Nv-Ar. [1207]

Royce vs. Hampton et al. Brief of appellant, Thaddeus B. Royce. 27 p. 26 x 18 cm. Imprint on wrapper: Virginia Evening Chronicle Book Print. Printed on wrapper: Filed, [*broken rule*] 1880. Nv-Ar. [1208]

Royce vs. Hampton et al. Brief of respondent, J. C. Hampton et al. 25 p. 25 x 18 cm. Imprint on wrapper: Printed at Enterprise Job Office, Virginia City, Nev. Printed on wrapper: Filed [*broken rule*] 1880. Nv-Ar. [1209]

Royce vs. Hampton et al. Transcript on appeal. [2], 86 p. 25 x 18 cm. Imprint on wrapper: Virginia Evening Chronicle Book Print. Printed on wrapper: Filed, [*broken rule*] 1880. Nv-Ar. [1210]

Solen et al. vs. Virginia and Truckee Railroad Co. Brief of appellants, William Solen et al. 6 p. 26 x 18 cm. Imprint on wrapper: Virginia, Nev.: Printed at the Evening Chronicle Job Office. 1880. Nv-Ar. [1211]

Solen et al. vs. Virginia and Truckee Railroad Co. Brief of respondent, Virginia and Truckee Railroad Co. 14 p. 25 x 18 cm. Imprint on wrapper: Printed at Enterprise Job Office, Virginia City, Nev. Printed on wrapper: Filed [*broken rule*] 1880. Nv-Ar. [1212]

Solen et al. vs. Virginia and Truckee Railroad Co. Transcript on appeal. 29 p. 26 x 18 cm. Imprint on wrapper: Virginia, Nev.: Printed at the Evening Chronicle Job Office. 1880. Nv-Ar. [1213]

Steel et al. vs. Gold Lead Gold and Silver Mining Co. Brief of appellants, John Steel et al. 6 p. 25 x 18 cm. Imprint on wrapper: Virginia Evening Chronicle Book Print. Printed on wrapper: Filed [*broken rule*] 1880. Nv-Ar. [1214]

Steel et al. vs. Gold Lead Gold and Silver Mining Co. Brief of appellants, John Steel et al. 31 p. 25 x 18 cm. Imprint on wrapper: Virginia Evening Chronicle Book Print. Printed on wrapper: Filed [*broken rule*] 1880. Nv-Ar. [1215]

Steel et al. vs. Gold Lead Gold and Silver Mining Co. Brief of respondent, Gold Lead Gold and Silver Mining Co. 9 p. 25 x 18 cm. Imprint on wrapper: Virginia Evening Chronicle Book Print. Printed on wrapper: Filed [*broken rule*] 1880. Nv-Ar.

[1216]

Steel et al. vs. Gold Lead Gold and Silver Mining Co. Reply to brief of appellants by respondent, Gold Lead Gold and Silver Mining Co. 17 p. 25 x 18 cm. Imprint on wrapper: Virginia Evening Chronicle Book Print. Printed on wrapper: Filed [*broken rule*] 1880. Nv-Ar. [1217]

Steel et al. vs. Gold Lead Gold and Silver Mining Co. Transcript on appeal. 30 p. 25 x 18 cm. Imprint on wrapper: Virginia Evening Chronicle Book Print. Printed on wrapper: Filed [*broken rule*] 1880. Nv-Ar. [1218]

Tognini and Co. and Vanina vs. Kyle. Brief and reply of appellants, Tognini and Co. and Vanina. 11 p. 25 x 18 cm. Imprint on wrapper: Index Print, Carson, Nevada. Printed on wrapper: Filed March 17, 1880. Nv-Ar.   [1219]

Tognini and Co. and Vanina vs. Kyle. Brief of respondent, Matthew Kyle. 31 p. 25 x 18 cm. Imprint on wrapper: Index Print, Carson, Nevada. Printed on wrapper: Filed March 1, 1880. Nv-Ar.   [1220]

Wall et al. vs. Trainor et al. Statement on appeal. [2], 44 p. 26 x 17 cm. Imprint on wrapper: Reno Journal Book and Job Print. Printed on wrapper: Filed [broken rule] 1880. Nv-Ar. NvHi.   [1221]

Wilder vs. Treadway. Transcript on appeal. 38 p. 25 x 18 cm. Imprint on wrapper: [Carson City:] Index Print. Printed on wrapper: Filed [rule] 1880. Nv-Ar.   [1222]

NEVADA. *Supreme Court.*

Reports of Cases | Determined in | The Supreme Court | of the | State of Nevada, | During 1879 and 1880. | Reported by | Chas. F. Bicknell, | Clerk of Supreme Court, | and | Hon. Thomas P. Hawley, | Associate Justice. | Volume XIV. | San Francisco: | A. L. Bancroft and Company, | Law Book Publishers, Booksellers and Stationers. | 1880.   [1223]

500 p. 23 x 15 cm. Leather binding.

600 copies were received of the printer (report of the Secretary of State, 1879-1880, p. 7-9); $1,200 was paid out in 1880 warrants (Treasurer's report, 1880, p. 27). Reissued in 1887 in a stereotype edition by Bancroft-Whitney, bound with volume 15.

Territorial Enterprise, July 25, 1880: "We are in receipt from the publishers, A. L. Bancroft & Co., San Francisco, of the 'Fourteenth Nevada Reports.' The author of this work is Charles F. Bicknell, the well-known literary gentleman who occupies the position of Clerk of the Supreme Court of Nevada. The volume is a novel of surpassing interest, and a romance of such intense excitement as to render it an absolutely necessary adjunct to the library of every lawyer in the State. It is bound in calf, which must not be construed as a reflection on its author . . ."

Az. CU-B. DHEW. DLC. In-SC (rebound). M. Nv. Nv-Ar. NvEuC. NvHi. NvLC. NvLN. NvRNC. NvRWL. NvSC. NvU. OrU-L. U-L.

NEVADA. *Treasury Department.*

Annual Report | of the | Treasurer | of the | State of Nevada, | For the Fifteenth Fiscal Year, ending | December 31, 1879. | L. L. Crockett, Treasurer. | Transmitted January 20, 1880. | [*state seal*] | San Francisco: | A. L. Bancroft & Company, Printers, | 721 Market Street. | 1880.   [1224]

81 p. 23 x 14 cm. Wrapper title, in decorative rule border. The half title notes that the report was transmitted on January 15. Issued also as No. 3 in AJSA, 1881.

1,200 copies in pamphlet form were authorized by an 1873 act of the Legislature (SSN,

1873, p. 175). The *Territorial Enterprise* reported receipt of a copy on March 4, 1880.
CU-B. CtY. Nv-Ar. NvHi.

NEVADA AND OREGON RAILROAD.

Prospectus | of the | Nevada and Oregon | Railroad. | (Narrow Gauge.) | [*filet*] | Reno Division: | Extending from Reno, Nevada, Northward through | Nevada and California to the Oregon Line. | [*filet*] | Reno: | Evening Gazette Job Print. | 1880. [1225]
[2], 4 p. 23 x 15 cm. Wrapper title, in thick-thin rule border.
CU-B.

NEVADA STATE AGRICULTURAL, MINING AND MECHANICAL SOCIETY.
Reno, Nevada. Catalogue. 1880. [L1226]
Reno *Nevada State Journal*, August 20, 1880: "The State Fair catalogues are now ready for distribution."

O. H. C. CLUB. *Austin, Nevada*. Invitation to a dance. November 25, 1880. [L1227]
Reese River Reveille, November 20, 1880: "Invitation Acknowledged.—The editor and printers of the REVEILLE hereby acknowledge the receipt of handsomely printed *vieuvenues* to the social dance, to be given by O.H.C.'s, at Irish-American Hall, on Thanksgiving evening, November 25." The O.H.C. Club was a secret organization.

ODD FELLOWS, INDEPENDENT ORDER OF. *Nevada. Grand Lodge.*

Proceedings | of the | 14th Annual Communication | of the | R.W. Grand Lodge | of the | Independent Order of Odd Fellows | of the State of Nevada, | Held in Odd Fellows' Hall, Virginia City, Storey County, Nev., | on the 8th, 9th, 10th and 11th Days of June, A.D. 1880. | [*short rule*] | Virginia, Nevada: | Enterprise Steam Book and Job Printing House. | 1880. [1228]
[3], 4-108, v p. 23 x 15 cm. Printed wrapper.
The Finance Committee recommended (p. 51) that "the R.W. Grand Secretary be instructed to have printed at the *Enterprise* Job Office, at a cost of $2 45 per page (less $20 allowance on Grand Representatives' Report, already in type) eight hundred and twenty (820) copies of the proceedings of this session of the R.W. Grand Lodge." For this job the committee further recommended (p. 71) an appropriation of $300.
CSmH.

ORMSBY COUNTY, NEVADA. *Board of Registration.*

[*Thick-thin rule*] | List of | Registered Voters | For Carson Township, Ormsby | County, Nevada, for the Year | 1880. | [*short rule*] | . . . [1229]

Broadside. 61? x 54? cm. The recorded copy has been cut into thirty-six pieces and mounted in a scrapbook. At the bottom of the last column of, apparently, seven columns: Given under my hand this 21st day of October, A.D. 1880. W. M. Cary, Register Agent, Carson Precinct, Ormsby County, Nevada.

The scrapbook in which the recorded copy is mounted was owned by Trenmor Coffin, an official of the Ormsby County Republican Party; the list was used to check official registration records against those of the party. Two of the thirty-six segments are printed on a different paper, are printed on the verso, and appear to have been clipped from a newspaper. The broadside is printed in a mishmash of type faces and sizes and may be a proof.

NvU(NvMus).

REPUBLICAN PARTY. *Ormsby County, Nevada.*

Republican | [*short rule*] | Election: Tuesday, November 2, 1880. | [*short rule*] | . . . | Ormsby County Republican Ticket. | . . . | Carson Township Republican Ticket. | . . . [1230]

Broadside. 25 x 11 cm.

NvU(NvMus).

REPUBLICAN PARTY. *Ormsby County, Nevada.*

[*Cut of eagle and U.S. flag*] | Straight Republican | Ticket. | And a New Deal. | [*filet*] | Primary Election, Tuesday, October 5th, 1880. | [*filet*] | Delegates to Ormsby County Republi-|can Convention. | [*short rule*] | . . . [1231]

Broadside. 23 x 10 cm.

NvHi.

RETAILERS PROTECTIVE ASSOCIATION.

No [*broken rule*] | Confidential. | [*filet*] | Delinquent List | —of— | Virginia City, Gold Hill, Carson | and Reno [*sic*] Nevada, and | Bodie, California. [*filet*] | Complied [*sic*] from Reports Received from the Retailers. | Virginia City, Nevada. | October 1880. | [over.] | [Oakland, California?] [1232]

21 p. 26 x 16 cm. Line 11 printed in brackets. Printed wrapper. The list is printed in two columns on p. [3]-21. On verso of front wrapper: "It is hereby understood that each party subscribing to this 'Delinquent List' thereby become [*sic*] a member of the Retailers Protective Association, of which C. W. Palm & Co., are managers. The object of this Association, [*sic*] is not the collection of uncollectable Bills, but to prevent in a measure, the contraction of such credits in the future."

C. W. Palm, a young California entrepreneur, distributed copies of the list throughout Virginia City on October 12, 1880. Its nineteen pages of closely-set type included the names of thousands of people whose willingness to pay obligations was put into question. Palm claimed to have interviewed 355 merchants and businessmen to obtain the names. Issuance of the pamphlet caused an immediate sensation, indignation aplenty, and not a few fist fights among those accused of being deadbeats and those accused of accusing them to Palm. The young man himself was able to avoid a severe beating only by his quick wit and even quicker feet. Virginia City newspapers devoted considerable space to a defense of local residents and to repeated attacks on Palm's attempts to blackmail the community's citizenry. The following partial account from the *Territorial Enterprise* of October 13 is fairly typical. "An individual from abroad came here to trade upon our people's necessities and misfortunes. He is only a young fellow, but, this morning, while pursuing his weary footing towards the railroad, he probably wished that he had thought up some other means of obtaining a livelihood than the levying of blackmail and the parading of men's misfortunes to disgrace them in the eyes of their wives and children. Not content with attacking the credit of men, this ghoulish young man gathered in his hellish Black List the names of some of the most respectable young ladies on the Comstock—good, virtuous girls, who strive and work and struggle to support themselves and to aid mothers and sisters to live. The names of these girls, when they came in alphabetical order in the devilish contrivance, were put in the same column with the names of the vilest prostitutes in the town. No mercy was shown to any one—the widows or the orphans who happened to owe a small store bill being gazetted as frauds and thieves. The young scalawag who thus attempted to make a trade out of the troubles of our young people did not get his just deserts. He was only whipped three times; it ought to have been twenty." The papers were for a time full of accusations and counter-accusations by those named and those who had presumed to name them. Then, after four days of near-hysteria, it was over, at least as far as the newspapers were concerned; it was, after all, a presidential election year and there were other things to write about. The excitement was even shorter-lived in Carson City, perhaps because fewer of its citizens had been named—and perhaps also because the furor on the Comstock made it impossible for Palm to distribute his list there. Not a word is to be found in Reno's papers, possibly for the same reason.

The pamphlet could have been printed locally, but it seems unlikely because a goodly number of printers are named as miscreants. Unless one of the local printing houses saw it as a grand joke to be played on members of the trade—and it would have been an expensive joke in terms of lost business if others had found out—it seems more probable that Palm had it printed where the printers included in it were less well known. Palm was said to have been from Oakland, California; that is probably as good a guess as any for the printing site.

CtY. NvHi. NvU (microfilm).

UNITED STATES. *Circuit Court. District of Nevada (Ninth Circuit).*

[Briefs. 1880.]

Marye et al. vs. Strouse. Brief for plaintiffs, George T. Marye et al. 18 p. 25 x 18 cm. Handwritten on wrapper of recorded copy: "May 7, 1880." CSbrFRC. [1233]

Parkinson vs. United States. Brief for defendant in error, United States. 57 p. 25 x 18 cm. Imprint on wrapper: Sacramento: H. S. Crocker & Co., Printers and Stationers. 1880. NvHi. [1234]

Van Bokkelen et al. vs. Cook and Derby. Argument, Thursday, November 18, 1880. 261 p. 25 x 19 cm. The recorded copy is followed in the bound volume by a 31 p. decision dated March 21, 1881. CSbrFRC. [1235]

Van Bokkelen et al. vs. Cook and Derby. In equity. Brief for complainants, Deborah Van Bokkelen et al. 106 p. 25 x 18 cm. Imprint on wrapper: [San Francisco:] M. D. Carr, Printer, with Wm. M. Hinton & Co., 536 Clay Street. The year 1880 is printed on the wrapper with a blank preceding it for recording the actual date of filing; on the recorded copy the date is changed by hand to read 1881, with the date "Jany 8th" handwritten before it. CSbrFRC. [1236]

Van Bokkelen et als. vs. Cook et als. In equity. Pleadings, decisions and testimony. viii, 803; viii, 805-1342 p. 26 x 19 cm. Imprint on title pages of both volumes: San Francisco: M. D. Carr, Printer, with Wm. M. Hinton & Co., 536 Clay Street. 1880. CSbrFRC (half-leather binding). CSmH (leather binding). [1237]

VIRGINIA AND TRUCKEE RAILROAD COMPANY.

Virginia & Truckee Railroad. | [short rule] | Annual Report— 1880. | [short rule] | Hon. Jasper Babcock, Secretary of State— Sir: | . . . [1238]

Broadside. 22 x 8 cm. Card stock.

The date in the title is the date of issuance rather than the year covered. CSmH.

VIRGINIA CITY, NEVADA. *Virginia Exempt Fire Association.*

Constitution, By-Laws | —and— | Rules of Order | —of the— | [ornament] Virginia [ornament] | Exempt Fire Association | Together with | A List of Officers and Members. | [filet] | Organized November 26, 1876 | [filet] | Virginia, Nev.: | Chronicle Book and Job Printing House. | 1880. [1239]

24 p. 14 x 10 cm. Printed wrapper. Cut of horse-drawn fire wagon on rear wrapper. Title and text pages in single rule borders.

The records of the association for 1876-1891 at NvHi indicate that on August 8, 1880, authorization was given to print 250 copies (p. 154); a warrant for $50 was ordered drawn to the *Chronicle* for "Printing By Laws" on September 12 (p. 156). CU-B. NvHi.

WASHOE COUNTY, NEVADA. *Board of Registration.*

Poll Lists | —of— | The Election | Held in the Precinct of | [broken rule] | —in the— | County of Washoe, State of Nevada, | —on the— | Second Day of November, | A.D. 1880. | [filet] | Reno: Evening Gazette Print. | 1880. [1240]

16 p. 32 x 20 cm. Wrapper title, in thick-thin rule border.

Includes ruled leaves to be filled in with names of voters and printed tally sheets. NvHi (lacks rear wrapper).

WASHOE TYPOGRAPHICAL UNION. Circular. May 1880. [L1241]

Gold Hill *News,* May 8, 1880: "The Washoe Typographical Union and the

Mechanics' Union of Storey County have issued a circular giving a history of the attempt made by the San Francisco *Chronicle* to reduce compositors' wages, and urging all miners and mechanics to discontinue their patronage of that paper."

WHITAKER, OZI WILLIAM.

(1.) | Domestic Missions, | Protestant Episcopal Church in the United States of America. | [*short rule*] | The Missionary Jurisdiction of Nevada. | By the Rt. Rev. O. W. Whitaker, D.D. | [*short rule*] | [1880?]   [1242]

8 p. 24 x 16 cm. Caption title. Printed in two columns. Contains illustrations. Tentatively dated in 1880 because the last date mentioned in the text is in 1879. CSmH.

APPENDIX A

U.S. TREASURY DEPARTMENT CIRCULAR, 1855

SECRETARIES of United States territories were accountable to the Treasury Department for all expenditures that were to be paid for by the federal government in their jurisdictions, from the salary of the governor to inkwells and spittoons for the legislative halls. In no area was the government in Washington more exacting than in the matter of the public printing. A considerable share of the correspondence between Nevada Territory's secretary and the Department is taken up with his difficulties in obtaining and keeping a territorial printer. Part of his problems were caused by the government's unrealistic rates for printing, but equally as important were the requirements set out in the following circular issued in 1855 and still in effect throughout Nevada's territorial period.

CIRCULAR

TREASURY DEPARTMENT,
COMPTROLLER'S OFFICE, *October 10th, 1855.*

To the Secretaries of the
Territories of the United States.

That uniformity may obtain as far as possible in all the Territories in regard to the execution of the public printing, both of an incidental and permanent character, the expense of which is liable to be paid by the United States: it becomes my duty to state a few general principles for your guidance hereafter 'in making payments, and I have to request you will be pleased to furnish the Public Printers, by letter to be duly recorded, with a certified copy of this circular.

1st. It appears that heretofore, if the practice has not been general, in some instances, at least in the journals and incidental printing, entire lines have been occupied by single words, and names of members so printed as greatly to increase the profits of the Printers.

2d. It has been observed in some cases that when the journal runs a single line over the first page, the whole of the second page has been charged for as if it contained printed matter.

3d. That memorials, petitions, and documents having no necessary connection with the duties of legislation or the dissemination of useful information among the people, should be excluded, and not printed at the expense of the United States.

4th. That it may be understood what is properly chargeable to the Treasury and what is not, specimens of all the incidental printing charged for, upon which to base a calculation by the accounting officers, will hereafter be required to be sent with the accounts of each Secretary of a Territory, the same as the laws and journals have been heretofore.

5th. It has been decided that the daily journal or proceedings should be printed in book form, and only one composition is hereafter to be paid for by the United States on account thereof, which is the practice pursued by both houses of Congress, and the State Legislatures. The facilities now afforded in the Territories for printing, which did not probably exist when organized, it is believed will enable this to be done daily, without detriment to the due course of legislation. The requisite number of copies for distribution will be retained, to be indexed as heretofore, and bound under your supervision. Specimens of the daily journals of the Senate and House are herewith transmitted, which you will please exhibit to the public printers. A copy may be filed with them.

That the vouchers of the public printers to be filed with the accounts of the various Secretaries may be examined by the accounting officers in detail in connection with the laws, journals, and full specimens of all the incidental printing, before final payment shall be made, you are advised and requested to continue to advance say one-half or two-thirds, on each proper voucher, respectively, which should be receipted thereon. If, however, the rendition of the account of the Secretary should be delayed, and the public printer is desirous that speedier action may be had, you are authorized to make the advance per receipt on the voucher as above, and in addition thereto to take a separate receipt specifying the particular work performed as charged in the voucher, and the date of the same. This receipt may be numbered, and charged in the next rendition of account in the proper abstract. The voucher can then be transmitted to this office, with the laws, journals, or specimens of incidental printing as the case may be, and when examined the same will be returned with the finding, when the balance can be paid, receipted, and charged to the United States, in the next succeeding rendition of account, and the voucher filed therewith.

If it is thought best, duplicates of the same voucher can be made, the first payment receipted as above upon each—one of which can be filed in the first rendition of account, and the other transmitted as aforesaid for examination. When returned the balance due is payable under the finding, and chargeable to the United States in the same manner as specified, in case a receipt is taken.

Vouchers for the printing of the Laws and Journals should not include incidental printing; and vouchers for printing should not include charges for personal services or supplies.

Most sincerely, yours,

Comptroller.

To

Secretary of

APPENDIX B

WASHOE TYPOGRAPHICAL UNION
CONSTITUTION, BY-LAWS, AND SCALES OF PRICES

THE Washoe Typographical Union was organized on June 28, 1863, as an organization of the printers in Storey County, Nevada Territory. It soon became a part of the National Typographical Union as its Local No. 65, and retained that number when the name of the parent body was changed in 1869 to the International Typographical Union. In 1878 the Washoe union affiliated with the Mechanics' Union of Storey County, which had been made up largely of mechanics employed in Comstock mines and mills. Between 1863 and 1878 the Washoe Typographical Union issued four constitutions, by-laws, and scales of prices. The 1863 constitution and by-laws are given below, as are the job scales for 1863, 1867, and 1878. Only newspaper rates were provided in the 1875 volume.

1863 CONSTITUTION

Declaration.

For the better protection of the interests of the trade in Storey County, Nevada Territory, the Printers of Virginia, in convention assembled, have resolved to establish a Union of all the journeymen printers who are now or may hereafter be employed at the printing business in this county; and believing, as we do, that union of action in all things appertaining to our profession is indispensable to our protection, we have enacted and do declare the following as the Constitution and By-Laws of the "WASHOE TYPOGRAPHICAL UNION," No.——.

Constitution.

Article I.

NAME.

SECTION 1. The name of this Association shall be the "WASHOE TYPOGRAPHICAL UNION," No. ——.

SEC. 2. The jurisdiction of this Union shall embrace the County of Storey, Nevada Territory.

SEC. 3. The objects of this Union shall be the maintenance of a fair rate of wages, the encouragement of good workmen, the prompt payment of their earnings, and the exposition and prevention of all subterfuges whatever by persons employed at the printing business, as journeymen or joint-stock proprietors, in working under any arrangement whereby less than the established rates are paid.

Article II.

OFFICERS.

SECTION 1. The officers of this Union shall be a President, a Vice-President, a Secretary, a Treasurer, a Sergeant-at-Arms, and a Board of Directors, to be composed of three members of the Union, who shall be intrusted with the management of affairs not included in the duties of other officers of this Union.

Article III.

MANNER OF HOLDING ELECTIONS.

SECTION 1. The officers shall be elected semi-annually, by ballot, and shall serve until the election and installation of their successors.

SEC. 2. The presiding officer shall appoint three members to act as Judges at each election held for officers of this Union. The polls shall remain open for three hours, from six to nine P.M., when the balloting shall cease, and the votes be counted by the Judges. Said Judges shall make out an exact and true return of the number of voters, and the number of votes cast for each candidate, and deliver such return to the presiding officer, who shall thereupon declare the result, a plurality being sufficient to elect.

SEC. 3. All elections for membership shall be had by the use of white and black balls, and two or more ballot boxes, according to the direction of the presiding officer. A majority of black balls shall reject an applicant; but by a majority *viva voce* vote, the Secretary may be directed to cast the vote of the Union upon the admission of applicants for membership.

SEC. 4. It shall be the duty of the Secretary to furnish the aforesaid Judges of Election with a complete list of active members previous to the semi-annual election of officers, and the persons named therein shall be entitled to vote.

Article IV.

DUTIES OF OFFICERS.

SECTION 1. It shall be the duty of the President, or, in his absence, the Vice-President, to preside at all meetings of the Union, keep order therein, direct the enforcement of fines and penalties, and generally to perform all duties usually pertaining to such office. He shall have the casting vote in all cases where the Union is equally divided on any question, and shall act generally for the good and welfare of the Union.

SEC. 2. The Secretary shall keep a correct record of all the proceedings of the Union; a list of the members thereof; issue calls for regular or special meetings, by direction of the President; notify candidates of their election; make out certificates, and attest all appropriations made by the Union; together with such other duties in connection with his office as he may be requested by the Board of Directors, or a regular or special meeting of the Union to perform. He shall receive for his services such compensation as the By-Laws shall direct.

SEC. 3. The Treasurer shall receive all moneys due the Union, notify members when they are in arrears, and pay all drafts upon the Treasury signed by the Board of Directors. He shall keep a correct record of all moneys received by him on behalf of the Union, in a book provided for that purpose.

SEC. 4. The Board of Directors shall investigate all matters touching the interests of the Union; act in concert with any other officers for the promotion of its interests; examine and audit all accounts against the Union; examine the books of the Secretary and Treasurer, and investigate the conditions upon which all printers are employed in each and every office within the jurisdiction of this Union. They shall also perform such other duties for the benefit and welfare of the Union as the members thereof at a regular or special meeting, may direct. If they shall have reason to believe that, under any pretext whatever, the Scale of Prices as established by this Union is being evaded, they shall notify the parties to such evasions to be and appear before a meeting of this Union to answer to such charges as may be preferred against them. A copy of said charges shall in all cases be furnished to the accused at the time of notification. Should the accused refuse or neglect to appear, or furnish, in writing, a valid excuse, such as sickness or unavoidable absence from the city, he or they shall be proceeded against in the same manner as if present.

Article V.

OF CHAPELS AND THEIR CHAIRMEN.

SECTION 1. In each and every office under the jurisdiction of this Union, a Chapel shall be constituted, which shall consist of the members of this Union therein employed. The members of the Chapel shall elect, immediately after the adoption of this Constitution, and thereafter at the time of the regular election for officers of the Union, one of their members, to be styled "Chairman of the Chapel," (who shall report himself immediately to the Secretary of the Union,) who shall preside at all meetings of his Chapel, collect all dues from the members thereof, and pay in the same to the Treasurer of the Union, taking his receipt therefor. He shall in all cases govern the office under the Constitution and By-Laws of this Union, and fix upon a day in each week for the payment of the weekly bills due the members of this Union employed therein. He shall in no case allow over two weeks pay to be due to any member; nor shall he permit a printer not a member of this

Union to work in the office, unless he is a stranger in the city, and signifies his intention of joining the Union at the first opportunity offered for his so doing.

Sec. 2. This Union shall adopt a Scale of Prices for the government of the trade in Virginia and vicinity, over which its jurisdiction extends, and any printer working for less than such Scale shall not be considered a proper person to become a member of this Union, and shall not be deemed an honorable man, nor one fit to be associated with printers in good standing.

Sec. 3. Any practical printer who has attained the age of twenty-one years, and who has a knowledge of at least one branch of the business, may become a member of this Union by complying with the requirements of this Constitution; *provided,* he is not at the time of application working for less prices than those established by this Union, or working in any office under its ban.

Article VI.

ADMISSION OF MEMBERS.

Section 1. The initiation fee for membership in this Union shall not be less than one dollar.

Sec. 2. All propositions for membership must be made at a regular meeting, and in writing, accompanied by the initiation fee, stating the name, age, and where employed, and the applicant must be recommended by three members of this Union. The candidate shall then be balloted for in accordance with Section Four of Article Three, and if he receive a majority of all the ballots cast, shall be entitled to admission; when, having taken the obligation and signed the Constitution, he shall be considered a member. Candidates who fail to come forward within one month after being elected, (unless sickness or absence from the city prevent,) shall forfeit their initiation fee, and shall not be admitted unless proposed and balloted for again.

Sec. 3. Any person applying for membership by deposit of card from any Union subordinate to the National Union, shall be admitted a member of this Union by signing the Constitution and taking the usual obligation.

Sec. 4. In case any applicant is rejected, his initiation fee shall be refunded.

Article VII.

INITIATION.

Section 1. The members of the Union shall rise and remain standing while members elect are taking the obligation.

Sec. 2. Every candidate, after being elected, shall give assent to the following pledge, to be administered by the presiding officer:

"You do solemnly pledge your word and honor, that you will conform to all the rules and regulations of the Washoe Typographical Union, without evasion or equivocation; and that you will on no occasion reveal the proceedings of this Union to persons not members of the same; and that you will always procure employment for members of this Union in preference to all others; and that you will not at any time, under any pretext whatever, by contract or simulated proprietorship, work for less than the regular rates of wages."

SEC. 3. After the member elect shall have signed the Constitution and By-Laws, the President shall announce the name of the person admitted, and proclaim him an elected, obligated, and committed member of the Washoe Typographical Union.

SEC. 4. The President shall then deliver the following charge to newly elected members, before taking their seats:

"You have been duly proposed and elected by the good will and votes of those whose truest wish is the success of our system of unity and protection. We are banded together for a laudable purpose, morally and legally; and you are obligated by your word of honor, before all present, to adhere to the principles of this organization; and you are committed by your own free will and handwriting, to abide by the Constitution and By-Laws. I therefore proclaim you, by virtue of the authority vested in me, a fully recognized and accepted member of this body; and may your conscience lead you to act in the truest sense for the good and welfare of this Union."

Article VIII.

INSTALLATION AND PLEDGE OF OFFICERS.

SECTION 1. All newly elected officers, before taking their seats, shall range themselves in front of the presiding officer, and subscribe to the following pledge:

"I, ———— ————, pledge my honor that I will, to the best of my ability, fulfill the duties devolving on me as an officer of this Union; and that I will act in my assigned capacity for the general benefit of the members hereof, when opportunity offers, or occasion requires. [Signature.]

Article IX.

STRIKES.

SECTION 1. In every office within the jurisdiction of this Union there shall be a regular weekly pay day, when all work done during the previous week shall be deemed due and payable; and failure to meet payments in full for two successive weeks, shall debar Union members from working in such office until all arrearages are paid; *provided,* if the Chapel of an office deem it necessary to "strike" for the payment of a previous week's bills, without waiting until the second week, they may do so, and their action shall govern all members equally with the "strike" required in the first clause of this section.

SEC. 2. When an office within the jurisdiction of this Union shall fail or refuse to comply with the requirements of this Constitution or the Scale of Prices, it shall be the duty of the members employed therein to cease work until such time as said office shall signify an intention to be governed by the regulations of this Union.

Article X.

RELIEF.

SECTION 1. This Union may, at any time, by a majority vote, afford pecuniary relief to any of its members in distress.

SEC. 2. In case of the death of an indigent member, the Board of Directors shall have power to draw from the Treasury a sum sufficient for his funeral expenses.

Article XI.

CONTRIBUTIONS AND ASSESSMENTS.

SECTION 1. In addition to his initiation fee, each member shall pay into the hands of the Treasurer, or the Chairman of a Chapel, the sum of one dollar per calendar month.

SEC. 2. If at any time the funds in the Treasury shall not be sufficient to meet all drafts upon it for contingent expenses made in accordance with this Constitution, an assessment to cover the amount necessary may be levied upon the members at any regular meeting, a majority of those present voting in favor of such an assessment.

Article XII.

APPRENTICES.

SECTION 1. Apprentices shall be considered to be boys who are put to work at case, and they shall be allowed in offices only according to the following apportionment: Each office (except morning paper offices) employing, permanently, five journeymen or less, shall be allowed one apprentice; offices employing ten journeymen, permanently, shall be allowed two apprentices; and one apprentice for each additional five journeymen.

SEC. 2. No apprentice shall work by the piece, unless he receives the Scale price; and no apprentices shall be employed upon morning papers from and after the adoption of this Constitution; *provided,* that nothing in this Constitution shall interfere with engagements existing at the present time.

Article XIII.

PENALTIES AND TRIALS.

SECTION 1. Any officer charged (by not less than five members) with neglect of duty, abuse of power, or breach of trust, shall be liable therefor to impeachment before the Union, and may be fined, removed from office, or expelled—two thirds of the members present at a regular meeting voting in favor thereof.

SEC. 2. The five prosecuting members so impeaching an officer of the Union, shall furnish the Secretary (or should he be the officer impeached, then the Treasurer,) with a copy of the charges, who shall forthwith furnish the accused with a copy of the same, and also notify him to attend the next regular meeting of the Union to answer the charges and make his defence. Should he neglect or refuse to appear, he shall be proceeded against in the same manner as though he were present.

SEC. 3. Members shall be expelled for the following causes, and no other:

First—Working for less than the prices established by this Union.

Second—Working in an office where Union members have quit work because their bills of the previous week have not been paid as prescribed by this Constitution.

Third—Working in an office where Union members have been discharged, for the purpose of subverting the Constitution or the Scale of prices, either in whole or in part; or where "Rats" are employed.

Fourth—For refusing or neglecting to pay dues or fines for the period of three months (unless the Union remit the same,) and after being duly notified by the Secretary of delinquency and liability to expulsion. Should this Union, by a two thirds vote, after giving a member a fair trial, declare him guilty of either of the above offences, he shall not be permitted to work in any office recognizing this Union, or where Union members are employed within the jurisdiction of this Union; *provided,* that nothing in this Article shall be so construed as to prevent a member expelled under the provisions of the fourth clause of Section Three of this Article from being reinstated to full membership upon the payment of his dues and fines.

SEC. 5. In the trial of members, the following rules shall be observed, viz.:

First—The accusing party shall name one member as prosecutor.

Second—The accused shall defend himself, or obtain counsel from among the members of the Union.

Third—The members of the Union shall sit as a jury, and shall not be permitted to discuss the merits of the question during the progress of the trial.

Fourth—A member may rise and call for information from a witness, when his testimony is not clear and to the point; but shall not ask a leading question, nor in any manner show bias for or against the accused.

Fifth—The Chair, on appeal from either of the counsel, shall rule out irrelevant testimony.

Sixth—When the testimony is closed and the case submitted, the regular standing rules of order shall govern the further disposition of the case.

Article XIV.

MISCELLANEOUS.

SECTION 1. Cards shall remain in the hands of the Secretary; nor shall they be issued or indorsed by him until the applicant shall have paid all dues or other arrearages—when they shall receive the signatures of the President and

Secretary, together with that of the member applying for the same, when the card shall be full and valid.

SEC. 2. The Scale of prices attached to this Constitution shall be regarded as part of the same, and shall only be subject to alteration or amendment as provided for in Section Three of this Article.

SEC. 3. No amendment shall be made in this Constitution, unless by a vote of two thirds of all the active members of this Union, and all motions for amendment or alteration shall lay on the table, in writing, at least one month previous to the same being debated; *provided,* that ten members of this Union may constitute a quorum at any regular meeting, when no propositions for alteration of the Constitution are to be acted upon.

SEC. 4. This Union shall not have power to dissolve itself while there are five dissenting members.

SEC. 5. All regulations adopted by the National Typographical Union for the government of subordinate Unions, shall be considered as a part of this Constitution; and anything contained in this Constitution in conflict with the Laws of the National Typographical Union, shall be considered void and of no effect.

BY-LAWS.

Article I.

REGULAR MEETINGS.

SECTION 1. The regular meetings of the Union shall be held on the first Sunday in each month. The hour of meeting shall be at seven o'clock, P.M.

SEC. 2. The meeting shall be called to order at the time appointed. Ten members shall constitute a quorum.

SPECIAL MEETINGS.

SEC. 3. Special meetings may, at any time, be called by the President when he deems the welfare of the trade demands it. On the application of five members, in writing, to the President, for a special meeting, he shall proceed to investigate the purposes for which such meeting is desired. If, in his judgment, the matter involved in the application can be disposed of satisfactorily by its reference to the Board of Directors, he shall call that body together, and submit it to them for their consideration. If the Board of Directors deem the subject of sufficient general importance to warrant them in calling a meeting of the Union, it shall then be the duty of the Secretary to post notices in the several regular offices of the city, calling such special meeting, and specifying in the notices that "business of importance" will transpire.

Article II.

ELECTION OF OFFICERS.

SECTION 1. The election of officers shall be held at the first regular meetings in June and December, in the manner prescribed by Article Three of the Constitution.

Article III.

COMMITTEES.

SECTION 1. The President shall appoint all committees, fill all vacancies occasioned by sickness, death, or absence from the city, etc., unless otherwise ordered.

SEC. 2. All special committees shall report, in writing, at the next regular meeting after their appointment, unless otherwise instructed.

SEC. 3. No members shall be appointed on a special committee unless present at the time of appointment.

Article IV.

FUNERALS.

SECTION 1. Upon the decease of a member, the Secretary shall cause the event to be published in at least one of the daily papers in this city. Attached to said notice shall be an invitation to the members to attend the funeral of the deceased.

Article V.

FINES.

SECTION 1. Any officer absent at a regular meeting shall be fined one dollar, and absent active members, fifty cents, unless excused on account of being at work, absence from the city, or from actual sickness.

SEC. 2. In case the President or Vice-President refuse or neglect to perform any duties pertaining to them, they shall be fined one dollar.

SEC. 3. Any officer having charge of the books of the Union, failing to have them in the meeting at roll-call, shall be fined five dollars.

SEC. 4. If any member appointed on a comittee shall refuse or neglect to perform his duty, he shall be fined one dollar for each neglect or refusal.

SEC. 5. The Secretary shall be subject to a fine of one dollar for neglect of any duty required of him by the Union, or the Constitution and By-Laws.

SEC. 6. The Treasurer shall be subject to the following fines: For neglecting to make a quarterly report, two dollars; for neglecting to perform any other duty which may be required of him by the Constitution and By-Laws, one dollar.

Sec. 7. The Sergeant-at-Arms shall be subject to a fine of fifty cents for neglect of any of the duties required of him.

Sec. 8. Any member coming into the meeting intoxicated, or making use of profane language in the meeting, or refusing to obey the President when called to order, or using disrespectful language toward the officers or members of the Union, shall be fined five dollars.

Sec. 9. If any member shall absent himself, without sufficient reason, from the semi-annual meetings at which the officers are elected, he shall be fined one dollar.

Sec. 10. Any member of this Union who is unemployed, may, if in arrears, be granted such further time for the payment of the same as the Union may direct.

Sec. 11. No member shall leave the room during a session of the Union, without permission of the Chair.

Article VI.

MISCELLANEOUS.

Section 1. Every member proposing a candidate for admission, shall do so in writing, with the name of the candidate, his age and address, stating the length of time he has been at the business, in what place he last worked, and the office, and whether a Union existed there or not; and the application must, in all cases, be accompanied by the initiation fee.

Sec. 2. All bills against the Union must be presented at a regular meeting before payment.

Sec. 3. It shall be the duty of every member, when he can procure work for a printer, to give preference to a member of this Union, or one who has a card from a sister Union.

Sec. 4. No person shall be admitted to membership in this Union who comes from any city or town in the United States where a Union is in existence, unless he has a card testifying to his good standing in the craft.—
[See "Extracts from General Laws of the National Typographical Union, (*sic*) p. 47.]

Sec. 5. Publishers, employers, (being practical printers,) or printers retired from the business, may be elected honorary members, by a majority vote, at any regular meeting; but no such member shall be allowed to vote, or be subject to dues or fines.

Sec. 6. The Secretary shall receive three dollars per meeting for his services; *provided,* that this shall not prevent the Union, at the expiration of his term of office, allowing him two dollars additional for each meeting.

Sec. 7. The ayes and noes upon any question shall be recorded at the request of five members.

Sec. 8. No proposition to alter, amend, or annul these By-Laws, shall be acted upon until it shall have been submitted, in writing, to a previous regular meeting of the Union; nor then, without the concurrence of two thirds of all the active members of this Union. But a By-Law may be suspended for one meeting by a two thirds vote of the members present.

SEC. 9. It shall be considered a breach of decorum for any member to smoke a cigar or pipe at any meeting of the Union, and the offender shall be liable to a fine of twenty-five cents for the first offence, and fifty cents for the second.

SEC. 10. This Constitution, By-Laws, and Scale of Prices, shall take effect on and after the first Sunday in July, A.D. 1863.

SCALE OF PRICES

BOOK AND JOB WORK

Except for the actual prices to be charged, the scales for 1863 and 1867 are identical. I have therefore given below the text of the 1863 scale, with prices in brackets representing the 1867 rates. The 1878 scale is much shorter and is given in its entirety.

1863 and 1867 Scales

1.—Works done in the English language, common matter, from Pica to Pearl, shall be paid at the rate of $1 [80 cents] per 1000 ems.

2.—Works done in Pica, or any larger type, to be counted as Pica.

3.—Works done in languages foreign to the English language, shall be paid for at the rate of $1 33 1/3 [$1.07] per 1000 ems; *provided,* a compositor shall not be required to make an extra charge for work done in his native language.

4.—Works in which superiors frequently occur, where they have to be made up in a letter smaller than that in which the work is being done, (as Agate in Small Pica,) shall be charged 20 cents [16 cents] per 1000 ems extra.

5.—Side notes to be counted the full length of the page, reckoning the lead or rule, which shall count at least one em, according to the type in which they are set; and when cut into the text, 20 cents [16 cents] extra for each note.

6.—Quotations, mottoes, contents of chapters and bottom notes, in smaller type than the body, shall be paid for according to the size of the type in which they are set.

7.—The head line, with the blank line after it, and the foot line, to be charged by the compositor, and counted not less than three lines; *provided,* it is customary in the office for the compositor to make up his work.

8.—All blank pages, chapter heads, etc., etc., shall be charged by the compositor according to the size of the type used for the work to which they belong; *provided,* it is customary in the office for the compositor to make up his work.

9.—Time occupied by alterations from copy, by casing or distributing letter not used by the compositor, etc., to be paid for at the rate of 80 cents [64 cents] per hour; *provided,* such labor does not amount to ten hours in the aggregate in any one week. When compositors are required to work beyond regular hours, they shall be paid at the rate of $1 [80 cents] per hour.

10.—All letter cast on a body larger than the face, (as Bourgeois on Long Primer,) to be counted according to the FACE; or on a body smaller than the face, (as Minion on Nonpareil,) to be counted according to the BODY. All fonts, the alphabets of which measure less than 12 1/2 ems, to be counted in width according to the next smaller size. [See Sec. 16, "Morning Paper Scale": All fonts, the alphabets of which do not measure according to the following rules, shall be counted in width according to the next smaller size: Pearl and Agate, fifteen ems to the alphabet; Nonpareil, fourteen ems; Minion and Brevier, thirteen ems; Bourgeois to Pica, inclusive, twelve ems.]

11.—Compositors employed transiently, (for one week or less,) shall in all cases be exempt from clearing away, tying up, or in any manner taking charge of matter which they have not set; *provided,* such clearing is not required in the course of the work.

12.—Bad manuscript, works of an intricate nature, etc., not governed by these articles, to be arranged between the employer and Chapel.

13.—Compositors shall receive not less than $40 [$32] per week of six days; ten hours to constitute a day's work. Over-work, $1 [80 cents] per hour. When a compositor is required to work less than thirty hours during a week, 80 cents [64 cents] per hour shall be charged.

14.—When compositors are required to remain in the office unemployed, awaiting orders from the employer, etc., they shall be paid at the rate of 66 2/3 cents [53 cents] per hour during the day, and $1 [80 cents] per hour at night.

15.—No member of this Union shall be held pecuniarily responsible to his employer on account of any alleged imperfections or errors in his workmanship; *provided,* that such moderate fines or penalties as the Chapel may acquiesce in, may be levied in such cases, subject to appeal to this Union.

COLUMN MATTER.

Column matter, as distinguished from table and tabular, is matter made up continuously, in two or more columns, not dependent upon each other for their arrangement, (as in list of letters,) and shall be paid for according to the following Articles:

1.—Two column matter, sixteen ems or under, of whatever type a work may be composed in, 13 1/3 cents [11 cents] extra per 1000 ems.

2.—Three columns, in pages twenty-one ems Pica wide or less, one fourth more than common matter.

3.—Four columns, octavo and smaller sizes, in pages twenty-eight ems Pica wide and less, one half more than common matter; in pages of greater width, one fourth more than common matter.

4.—Five columns, in folio and quarto, one half more than common matter; in octavo and smaller sizes, double the price of common matter.

TABULAR MATTER.

Tabular work is work set up in three or more columns, depending upon each other, and reading across the page. To be paid for in accordance with the following Articles:

1.—Three columns, with or without headings, one half extra.

2.—Four columns, with headings, and five or more with or without, double the price of common matter.

3.—Title headings to tabular matter shall be considered as part of such matter, and shall be paid for accordingly.

4.—Headings to tabular matter or column work, in smaller type than the body of the table, shall be paid extra according to their value.

5.—Short pages, in a series of tables, are charged as full pages table.

6.—Pages consisting of four or five blank columns, to be charged a price and a half; but when the columns are six or more, to be charged as table, cast up to the size of the type to be used in the work in which they occur.

7.—In casting up table pages, their headings and foot notes are to be reckoned in the square of the page; but if the note or notes extend beyond the page, the remainder of the notes to be charged as common matter.

8.—Compositors employed by the piece shall make up and impose all pages necessary to complete the work on which they are employed; *provided,* it is customary in the office for the compositor to make up his work; and shall correct one proof and one revise only. If other proofs of a form are required, they shall be taken by the office, and the compositor will thereby be exempted from locking up such form.

Compositors on Catalogue work, at night and on Sunday, shall receive not less that $1 33 1/3 [$1.07] per hour from the time of commencing such work until it is finished. The same kind of composition done during day-time, shall be governed by the scale for other time work; *provided,* no compositor shall do such work by contract (by the page) on terms which will contravene this rule.

FOREMEN.

Foremen of Job Offices shall receive not less than $48 [$38.40] per week of six days. When required to work seven days, the price shall be agreed on between the employer and foreman.

1878 Scale

CLAUSE 1. Composition in Book and Job offices, 65 cents per 1,000 ems, or $28 per week. Six days of ten hours each to constitute a week's work.

CLAUSE 2. All over-work shall be at the rate of 65 cents per hour.

CLAUSE 3. All work on time, except week or day work, at 1,000 ems per hour.

CLAUSE 4. When works, or portions of works are required to be leaded, and the leads are not furnished at the time of composition, such matter shall be afterwards leaded at the expense of the employer, and the compositor shall charge such matter the same as if he had originally put in the leads.

CLAUSE 5. In case the compositor is required to make up his matter, he shall be entitled to the head and foot lines, and all the blank pages that may occur in the work upon which he may be engaged.

CLAUSE 6. No work to be measured in a type larger than Pica.

STANDARD OF TYPE.

The following scale of measurement is adopted by this Union: Pica, 12 ems to the alphabet; Small Pica, 12; Long Primer, 12; Bourgeois, 12; Brevier, 13; Minion, 13; Nonpareil, 14; Agate, 15; Pearl, 16; Diamond, 17. Fonts of type falling below this scale, shall be cast up according to the width of type, by the rule of three, thus: If the alphabet measures 10 ems in width, as 10 is to 12, so is 1,000 to 1,200; and the font shall always be counted thus: Every 1,000 ems as 1,200; if the alphabet of a font of type shall measure 11 ems in width, as 11 is to 12, so is 1,100 to 1,200; the font counting every 1,000 ems as 1,100.

INDEX OF PRINTERS
AND PUBLISHERS

Agnew & Deffebach (San Francisco, California), 182

Alpine Miner (Monitor, California), 426a

Alta California (San Francisco, California), 344, 400

Anthony, James, & Company (Sacramento, California), 403

Appeal (Carson City), 432, 460, L498-506, 556-557, 582, 585, 691, 772a, 775, 823, L890, 932, L958-L959, 1051, 1122

Arcade Printing House (San Francisco, California), L913

Austin: *see* Reese River Reveille

Bacon & Company (San Francisco, California), 533, 565a, 570, 625, 655, 700, 839, 881, 1077, 1109, 1205; *see also* Towne & Bacon

Bancroft, A. L., & Company (San Francisco, California), 764, 781, 844, 859, 914-916, 968-969, 981-982, 1033-1034, 1036-1038, 1043-1046, 1050, 1052-1058, 1068, 1094-1099, 1136, 1138, 1223-1224

Bancroft, H. H., & Company (San Francisco, California), 507, 550

Batters & Waters (Virginia City), 19

Battle Mountain: *see* Measure for Measure

Belmont: *see* Silver Bend Reporter

Bethel, John D., & Company (Virginia City), 721, 772

Booth, John: *see* Reese River Reveille

Bosqui, Edward, & Company (San Francisco, California), 861

Boston, Massachusetts: *see* Radical

Brown & Mahanny (Virginia City), 740, L783-784, 812, L819, 850, 911, L921a, 944, 1031

Carl & Flint (San Francisco, California), 30

Carr, M. D., & Company (San Francisco, California), 469; *with* Wm. M. Hinton & Company, 1236-1237

Carr, Dunn & Newhoff (San Francisco, California), 652

Carson City: *see* Appeal; Church, John; Crawford, Israel; Drury, Wells, & Company; Eckley, Joseph E.; Fleishhacker, A., & Company; Goodman, J. T., & Company; Herald; Hill, John J.; Independent; Index; Lewis & McElwain; Lewis & Sewall; Maddrill, J. W.; Mighels, Henry R.; Nevada Tribune; Perkins, Charles L.; Post; Putnam, Charles A. V.; Robinson, Marshall; Robinson & Mighels; Silver Age; State Register; Territorial Enterprise; Woolf, Barney

Chicago, Illinois: *see* Middleton, J. W.

Chronicle (Virginia City), 660, 717, 813, 841, 907, 975, 1040, 1059-1061, 1075, 1118, 1139, 1146, 1148, 1159, 1180, 1198, 1201-1203, 1208, 1210-1211, 1213-1218, 1239

Church, John, State Printer (Carson City), 335-339, 343, 345, 347-350, 352-353, 357, 378, 382-383, 386-L397, 405-406

Church, John, & Company (Virginia City), 166, 302

Church, John, & Company, Territorial Printers (Virginia City), 208

Como: *see* Sentinel; Tri-Weekly Delta

Comstock Record (Virginia City), L828

Cooke, Wm. B., & Company (San Francisco, California), 8-9, 11, 23-24, 28-29

Crawford, Israel, Territorial Printer (Carson City), 197-201, 206, L209-

SUBJECT INDEX

NUMERALS GENERALLY REFER TO ITEM NUMBERS IN THE BIBLIOGRAPHY, BUT FIGURES IN ITALICS REFER TO PAGE NUMBERS IN THE INTRODUCTION OR ANNUAL SUMMARIES